CONRAD'S EYE

Stuart Slade

LION BY LION
PUBLISHING

Dedication

This book is respectfully dedicated to the memory of Dashiell Hammett and Raymond Chandler

Acknowledgements

Conrad's Eye could not have been written without the very generous help of a large number of people who contributed their time, input and efforts into confirming the technical details of the story. Some of these generous souls I know personally. Others I know only via the internet as the collective membership of "The Board" yet their communal wisdom and vast store of knowledge, freely contributed, has been truly irreplaceable.

I must also express a particular debt of gratitude to my wife Josefa for without her kind forbearance, patient support and unstintingly generous assistance, this novel would have remained nothing more than a vague idea floating in the back of my mind.

Caveat

Conrad's Eye is a work of fiction set in The Big One alternate universe. All the characters appearing in this book are fictional and any resemblance to any person, living or dead is purely coincidental. Although some names of historical characters appear, they do not necessarily represent the same people we know in our reality.

Copyright Notice

Contents

Books In This Series
Available From

LION BY LION
PUBLISHING

PREFACE
Medina del Campo, Castile, 1506

*Town Square, **Medina del Campo, Castile, 1506***

The sun beat down, hurting the eyes of the crowd gathered in the square of a small Spanish town. Standing in the mob, Conrad Antonio de Llorente felt its emotions swirl around him. Excitement. Relief. Some fear, for who knew whom the Devil had possessed? A man, or woman, for so often it was the women who were afflicted, might be possessed by the Devil and lured into the path of heresy. Truly, it needed the cunning expertise of the Inquisition to detect those who had fallen into the Devil's snares and return them into the arms of Divine Grace.

Conrad felt the excitement surge in the crowd around him. It was nearly noon and the doors of the town church were opening. Soon the Inquisitors would be coming out. They'd spent the morning praying for the souls of those who had been tricked, deceived by the Devil into forsaking the way of the True Faith. The stakes were waiting, the fires ready to be set; for, only by sending the heretics out of this world in fire, could they be protected from the eternal fires of Hell. Then, the procession started. The Inquisition lead out those whom it had detected in heretical practices.

Conrad Antonio de Llorente, a lieutenant of the famous Tomás de Torquemada, Inquisidor General of Aragón, Valencia and Catalonia, flung open the doors of the church to let the harsh sunlight fall within. The prisoners flinched at the sudden glare and at the sight it revealed. Eight stakes set in the town square, already surrounded by brushwood. Conrad looked at the prisoners. An old *conversos* couple; Jews who had converted to Christianity in order to gain riches and access to official positions denied to Jews. They had been accused of secretly practicing Judaism and engaging in uspeakable rites. The old man tried to put a comforting arm around his wife; she flinched as he touched her misshapen shoulders. The Inquisitors had tied her hands behind her back and then hung her by her wrists. She'd screamed as her shoulders dislocated and begged to know of the accusations made against her so she could confess to them. That wasn't the way things worked, of course.

Behind them shambled four young men. Two were more *conversos*. Another was a *morisco*, a Moor pretending to be a Christian so he could infiltrate and corrupt those who followed the True Faith. The last was a heretic who questioned Holy teaching. The Morisco was coughing, as he had been for days; a legacy of the water poured down his throat, holding him at the point of drowning for hours on end until he was persuaded that confession was the only option. The heretic had held out longest. His feet were torn and bleeding from the bastinado but it was the threats to his family that had finally made him confess.

His confession hadn't saved his sister, though. She was standing behind him, her mouth swollen and broken where she had been struck after spitting defiance at the Inquisitors and cursing their name. One morning she had been found with blood on her legs. She had screamed that "they" had raped her. And so it was that her confession to having had intercourse with the emissaries of the devil was noted; whom else could have gained access to her, in the very tribunal of the Inquisition?

With her stood another young woman. It was whispered that she had turned down a suitor; denouncing her for witchcraft and heresy had been his revenge. Perhaps she was the cleverest of them all. She had immediately made a very full and detailed confession and sincerely repented her sins. Her reward was around her neck; a rope. Of all the eight, she was the only one who would be strangled before the fires were set.

Conrad raised his cross and led the way out of the church. The sound of Psalms being sung drifted out across the square. His eyes scanned the crowd, seeking out those who were too enthusiastic in their condemnation of the accused. He looked especially for those who showed too much delight in those being taken to their fate. Every Inquisitor knew how devious and crafty were the ways of the Devil; a mere appearance of piety was no guarantee that even the greatest show was sincere. Indeed, too much piety was suspect. It was excess and a form of gluttony; gluttony was a mortal sin. Too much delight in the fate of the accused here today was a sign of an even worse sin.

As Conrad lead the procession out, the words of the Psalm passed his lips, measuring the slow beat of his steps across the town square. Behind him, other members of the Inquisition herded the accused forward, pushing them and ignoring their staggering and cries. There was an appointment to be kept at the stakes ahead.

Preface

Looking down from the Church balcony, high above the square, Conrad Antonio de Llorente saw the doors of the Church fly open and the Inqusitorial party stride forth; penitents in their robes in the middle, Inquisitors surrounding them. The crowd fell back in awe of the majesty and piety of the Inquisitors, those who took this burden on themselves in order to defend the Church against the attacks launched against it from without and within. Few were more aware of the vital importance of the Inquisition than Conrad. He was named after an earlier Inquisitor, Konrad von Marburg, who had taken part in the suppression of heresy, as part of the Albigensian Crusade in southern France. Then, Konrad von Marburg had become a hammer against the heretics and blasphemers of Germany. He was a mighty weapon against them, so much so the Devil himself had planned his assassination. Conrad Antonio de Llorente was determined to live up to his namesake's achievements.

If his meeting with Tomás de Torquemada was any guide, he would have plenty of chances to do so. It had been explained that King Ferdinand and Queen Isabella had brought the Inquisition into Spain in order to establish a sense of political and religious unity sorely needed after the centuries of occupation by Moors and division by Christians. *A centralized religion meant a centralized state and Spain needed both. It did not need the moriscos and the conversos. They could be used as scapegoats; sacrifices to bring about a sense of unity under the Holy Mother Church and its Catholic monarchs. They couldn't be trusted; everybody knew that. The campaign against them would kill two problems with one set of trials. And, if both the Church and Monarchy profited from confiscated estates, was that not just a sign of God's approval?*

To his annoyance, Conrad realized he had missed the doors of the church being thrown open and the penitents being dragged across the square while he had been musing on the politics of what was happening, *That will not do; will not do at all.* He went back to the beginning and made a point of watching the scene played out with added intensity. The penitents, five men and three women, were being dragged up onto the platform where the town priest was waiting for them.

In front of the stakes, Conrad Antonio de Llorente looked sadly at the accused being brought before him. He had been the town priest for many years, long enough to remember some of them when they had been children. The young man, the one accused of heresy, Conrad had once hoped that he might become a priest. Even when very young, he had shown a bright and inquisitive mind. But the Devil had taken advantage of those gifts and caused the young man to ask things that should not be asked, questions that threw doubt upon the Holy Scriptures and the teachings of the Church. *His sister, how had she come to this? She had been wild, no doubt of that. When the boys pulled a girl's hair to make her run so they could chase her, she was the one who turned on them*

5

with fingernails bared. Now, he could hardly recognize her after the beatings she had taken from the gaolers.

Conrad started reading the Office while the Inquistors lashed the accused to the stakes. They were true to their promise. When they got to the girl with the rope around her neck, one of them grabbed the loop and twisted quickly. The knot in front crushed her throat. She threshed against the stake for a few seconds and then died almost without pain, at least compared with what awaited the others. He stepped up to the others, asking each to repent. They were too gone in terror to listen. Except the sister, to Conrad's horror. When he stood in front of her, she spoke to him with words blurred by being spoken through lips and teeth crushed by a mailed fist.

"Go to hell, priest. You have shown me where the Devil truly lies. I curse you, I wish you agony and grief every day you remain alive."

She spat on him and his cross, the saliva mixed with blood trickling down his face.

Conrad staggered back, appalled by the blasphemy and the hatred that had caused it. Never, never had he seen or heard of such a thing. The crowd had been struck silent by the act, stunned by it. Even the Inquisitors were frozen for a brief second. Then they lit the fires. Conrad felt the heat of the blaze. Smelled the awful small of roasting flesh. Heard the screams from inside the flames. Then, horror and shock turned to something else. Suddenly, Conrad knew the girl had been right. He turned to the crowd, his mind begging the screams from behind him to stop, and held his cross on high.

"They are innocent, I tell you! Innocent!"

His voice gained strength, dominating the sounds of the fires behind him.

"THEY ARE INNOCENT! THEY ARE INNOCENT!"

Conrad Lorentz shot erect as he woke. His anguished shout still echoed around the room. That was why he lived here. The hotel had once been a palace-like hacienda; its walls were thick and soundproof. He was gasping. He knew his eyes were bulging, veins standing out on his forehead. He knew because sometimes he had seen himself in a mirror on waking. Once he had hoped they were the signs of an impending stroke or a heart attack, but he had long ago learned that he would not be so lucky.

Conrad rose from his bed. The sheets beneath him were so soaked with his sweat that they oozed moisture; a cold wetness that made his bed feel as clammy and unwelcoming as a deserted graveyard on a foggy night. He staggered slightly as he got to his feet and threw the covers back so the sheets would dry before he returned. Then, he made his way to the foot of his bed, dropped to his knees and started to pray, as he did every night.

"Dear Lord, I am not worthy of your mercy and have long ago forfeited any right to call upon you. My sins are so great that I cannot ask and do not expect to receive your divine Grace. I just beg that this burden be lifted from me, that I be allowed to die like other men die and my soul be sent to eternal punishment. I do not ask to be saved, for none deserve salvation less than I, who have committed horrible crimes and, worst of all, did so in Your Name."

Conrad stopped speaking. Instead, he started praying quietly to himself. A mixture of memories and feelings, Conrad relived his life from the moment that he had experienced the terrible realization of the depth and severity of his sins. He had long, long ago quietly assumed that he was damned for all eternity; that his crimes were so great that there could be no salvation for him. After his epiphany, he had gone down the route of penitence, of self-abnegation and flagellation. All too soon he had realized that there too lay sin. Ascetism and mortification could cease to become acts of contrition and become indulgences; their excesses the deadly sin of inverted pride.

In the clarity of vision he had gained, Conrad learned much. He understood that the man who had once been his hero, the Konrad von Marburg for whom he had been named, was no heroic defender of the Church. He had been a murdering, sadistic brute, a monster; the men who had killed him, heroes. Later, much later, Conrad had met the man who had planned that killing and could not condemn him.

For years, Conrad had wandered in the countryside. He lived the life of a hermit, avoiding contact with others. He slowly realized he was very different from those who were around him. Little bit by little bit, Conrad understood that he was not getting older.

At first, he had thought he was in Hell. Theologians defined Hell as a place where the ultimate agony was to spend eternity deprived of the Grace of God's presence. Conrad had no doubt that he was denied God's grace, that he was damned beyond any redemption. The discovery that he might very well live forever seemed to confirm that he was indeed in the Hell the theologians had imagined. Conrad had actually felt relief at that. He had slaughtered innocents; murdered them under the guise of law. His knowledge of that had destroyed his faith in Divine Justice. Yet, if he, Conrad, was condemned to Hell, then there was still justice. In a strange way, the knowledge he was receiving the punishment he deserved was a restoration, an affirmation of rightness and good.

One day, a few years later, he'd been walking through a wood when he had come upon a village. The path had turned sharply and the village was so compact he'd been in it before he realized it was there. The villagers hadn't seen him, not at first. The men were hustling a young man towards a tree. The women watched and wailed; a sound of grief, but also triumph. The tree had a noose hanging from it. The young man was about to be hanged.

Conrad's Eye

Conrad had run forward, shouting at the men to stop. In his robes, his air of authority as an Inquisitor hadn't left him; they did as he had told them. They faced him, still holding the young man secure; his hanging no longer imminent. Conrad had asked them what they were doing and why. There had been a young woman in the village, they explained. A good girl, now dead. Raped and murdered by this young man. Conrad had looked at the man who they had accused. *Young, weak-looking.* Seeing him, Conrad had seen what the village men would have, had they not been so steeped in rage and grief. The young man was one of those who preferred to love other men. *A sin, certainly, but not one that compared with rape and murder. Not that his way proved him innocent; he might have tried with the girl and failed. Then she'd laughed at him and in rage he'd killed her. It could be that way.*

So, he'd asked to see the body.

He'd been led to the hut where she lay at rest. Looking at her body, he knew the young man was innocent. The girl's hands were bloody, her nails torn and broken. She had fought hard for her honor and her life. The man who had taken them from her would bear the marks of the struggle. The young man outside was unmarked, except for the bruises he had suffered when being dragged to the tree. Conrad had him brought in and stripped. That convinced the villagers, for he had not a scratch on him. Conrad had also looked at the girl's neck. The bruises where the killer's hands had squeezed the life out of her were clear. They were from a man with big, strong hands. The youngster's grip was weak and small. No, the young man had not killed the girl and everybody knew it. Rage and hatred were replaced by guilt and shame.

The villagers had let the young man go. Conrad had left also, never letting them know his name or who he was. He never knew if the man who had killed the girl had been caught or not; to be honest about it, he didn't care. What mattered to him was that he had saved the life of an innocent wrongly accused. Walking through the woods that day, he'd had a second epiphany; one that controlled the course of his life ever since.

Conrad realized that he wasn't in Hell, doomed to an eternity cast out from God's Grace. He was in Purgatory, the place where those who had sinned were sent to expiate those crimes. God's Grace hadn't been withdrawn from him. It was never finally withdrawn, no matter how grave the sin. It was being withheld until Conrad deserved it once more. That was why he had been given his life without apparent end. For it was his fate to wander the Earth, finding those who had been falsely accused and proving their innocence. As he walked, his steps became lighter. He now had hope. That night his nightmares were slightly, very slightly, less terrible. One day, when he had saved enough innocents to expiate his guilt, he would be free. God's Grace would be returned to him and he would be allowed to die.

A few days later, Conrad had arrived at a small town. There he had saved another innocent, a young wife, falsely accused of infidelity by jealous rivals. In fact, he had saved two innocents there. The husband had stood by his wife, defended her honor and been ridiculed for it. But Conrad had used all the wiles of an Inquisitor; he'd laid a trap and caught her accusers in a lie. They claimed she had met her lover on a night when she and her husband were at a local church, praying together in the presence of five priests, five monks, three nuns and a bishop. In retrospect, Conrad realized the bishop had been over-egging the pudding, but it made no difference. The town was convulsed with laughter at the way the malicious tongues had been fooled into betraying themselves. Once again, after the innocents were saved, Conrad slipped away without telling anybody who he was or why he was doing what he did.

And that had been the pattern from then on. Conrad was convinced that God guided his footsteps from one town to the next, sending him to places where an innocent needed rescue. The alternative explanation, that there was so much injustice in the world that he would find it wherever he went, was one Conrad didn't want to think about. So, he went from town to town, finding the innocent and freeing them, never staying after the deed was done, never leaving his name. In time, the legend started to grow of the nameless stranger who arrived unannounced, righted wrongs, protected the innocent and then vanished again without a word. Also, in time, Conrad forgot that he was saving the falsely accused in order to expiate his sins and his mission became an end in itself.

One day he had been in Northern Italy, in the market of Florence. A wealthy noblewoman had been carried past, a beauty with a flowing mane of black hair. Conrad had felt a weird sensation in the back of his head; as if a candle had been lit there and was flickering inside his skull. Almost that instant, the woman had looked around and stared straight at him. Later, manservants came to his inn with a carriage. The noblewoman wanted to see him; in Florence the wishes of the nobility were not to be denied. He had been taken away in the carriage and had met her "family."

That was when Conrad had finally understood that he was not alone, that there were others like him. This group, an extended family in Florence, was one and they welcomed Conrad into their number. They had told him of his heritage, warned him that he was not immortal, that he could die. In turn, he had told them the truth. The truth of who and what he was. The truth of his mission and what he intended to do with his extended life. They treated him well; when he had left, they had told him that he would be welcomed back whenever he chose to return. They had also told him where to find another group of their kind, in a town over the Alps called Geneva. There, Conrad had met Loki, the man who had planned the execution of Konrad von Marburg.

Conrad's Eye

Ever since then, Conrad had continued to wander. First, heading north into Europe and, when the time came, he had crossed the Atlantic and visited the New World. He had wandered there too, always finding those who had been wrongly accused, who needed a champion to stand up for them. Once again, the legend of the nameless stranger who arrived in town to right wrongs and then leave started to spread. The work never ended. The times had changed. The crimes had changed, sometimes, but the old motives and sins remained constant. The law had changed as well. Mob violence had been replaced, sometimes, by colder and more sinister forces of public relations and corruption. Whispering tongues loaded with malice had been supplemented by newspapers desperate to sell more copies than their rivals. Sometimes, Conrad found it hard to believe that times had changed for the better.

One thing had changed. It was becoming harder and harder for him to maintain his anonymity. He had a feeling that the walls were closing in and the days of a nameless stranger who could enter town, right wrongs and leave were coming to an end. What he would do when that time came worried him.

Conrad stood quietly. His bed had dried and he remade it, straightening the sheets and the pillowcases. Then he laid down once more and closed his eyes. Soon, Conrad slipped back into sleep, where the sun beat down, hurting the eyes of the crowd gathered in the square of a small Spanish town . . .

EYE OF THE BEHOLDER
San Francisco, California, 1951

Conrad's Eye

CHAPTER ONE

Hotel California, San Francisco, California, USA, 1951

Conrad Lorenz looked in the mirror and patted his hair. It was thinning slightly. That might have worried most men, but his had been that way for 450 years now. Obviously, there was no need to worry about further loss. He glanced quickly around his suite to make sure it was tidy. He knew some people who were staying in hotels didn't bother; sometimes they even opened the door to the hotel staff unshaven or undressed. Conrad never did that. It was neither pride nor modesty; it was simply that he believed those who worked in hotels had a hard enough job without inconsiderate guests making their lives uncomfortable. As he finished his check, there was a light tap on the door. Room service.

Outside his room, Graciella smiled to herself as the door opened. *He is such a nice man, Mr Conrad is. So friendly and considerate.* All the staff at the Hotel California liked him. The kitchen took special care to make sure his breakfast was just so. The eggs the way he liked them. His bacon cooked crisp, not dried out or soggy. Graciella herself made a point of bringing it straight up to him so it would still be fresh.

"Good morning, Mister Conrad. Here is your breakfast."

"Thank you very much, Graciella. That looks very good."

She gave him a beaming smile and stepped back as he sat down at the table. *He really is such a nice man; such sad eyes though. And to think he has such horrible nightmares.*

When he had first come, one of the maids had thought he was possessed, but that couldn't be so. Then, one of the men had whispered that he thought Mister Conrad had served with the OSS on the Russian Front, fighting with the Partisans. The nightmares were his memories of what he had seen the Germans do there. That made sense. Graciella's family had been spared the horror of the Russian front. Her brother, a cousin and her boyfriend had all received their draft papers in 1947, but between the time they had been sent and the time they reported to the induction center, the B-36s had destroyed Germany. They had simply been told the war was over and they could go straight home. So they hadn't had to join the Army and now her brother and cousin were back in civilian life. Her boyfriend was now her husband and the father of her baby. Every Sunday, Graciella went to church and lit a candle to thank God for the B-36s that had saved the men of her family from the Russian Front. Nor was she the only one who did so.

"Anything else, Mister Conrad?"

"No thank you, Graciella. And please thank the cooks for me. This is very good."

The girl closed the door behind her. Conrad picked up his newspaper to read what was going on. He had the feeling that his services were going to be needed. He didn't need to look far to guess where. The front-page headline was just three words.

Black Dahlia Arrest.

Conrad scanned the story quickly. The police had detained, *not arrested*, Conrad noted, a man in connection with the notorious Black Dahlia murder down in Los Angeles some four years earlier. He read the details in the story. The body of Elizabeth Short had been found on January 15th, 1947, some six months before the end of the war. She had been mutilated and cut in half. Apparently the pictures were so gruesome, the police had never released them. What caught Conrad's attention was that the story was written as if the man who was detained by the police was guilty. There lay an injustice. Many men had been detained in connection with the murder. All had been released without being arrested, let alone charged. On the basis of the story as reported here, there was no reason to believe that this case was any different. Yet the whole weight of the newspaper report implied the latest suspect was guilty.

Was he even a suspect? The report didn't make even that point clear. It could simply be that he had been in the area at the time and might be a witness. He was, as the police liked to say, being eliminated from their inquiries. There was another factor to bear in mind. The San Francisco and Los Angeles police departments did not get on well. They were bitter rivals; if the SFPD caught Elizabeth Short's killer, they would have scored a mighty blow against their competitors.

That temptation could lead them to rush the case, to charge an innocent man. Conrad realized that all the crime reporters had good contacts with the police; if the paper was reporting as if this man was guilty, it was likely that the police thought the same way. Conrad read the rest of the story and folded the newspaper carefully. *The man might well be guilty, but perhaps an independent investigation might not be amiss. It wouldn't do any harm anyway.*

One thing to do before starting. Conrad left his room and stopped at the hotel registration desk. "I'd like to settle my account please."

"You're not leaving us, are you, sir?"

"No. But I'll be working away for the next few days and I don't know how much I'll be around. So I'd like to make sure my account with you paid up to date."

"Very well, sir." The clerk punched a stream of figures into an adding machine and cranked the handle. "There you are."

Conrad paid his bill, then pealed another bill out of his fold. "Please divide this between the staff. And don't forget the people in the kitchen.

City Prison, San Francisco Police Department

"Good afternoon, Sergeant. I am here to meet with Richard Soames. I have a letter of introduction from his attorney."

The desk sergeant took the letter and skimmed its contents. It had taken Conrad most of the morning to get this side of things organized. The newspaper article had simply given him the name of the man who had been detained, Richard Soames, age 28, unemployed, no other details. *Not much to start with.*

It had taken a few telephone calls to find out whether Soames was being represented by an attorney and who that attorney was. Somewhat to Conrad's surprise and relief, he'd found that Soames actually had his own lawyer. Unlike most criminals of his class, he wasn't relying on a public defender. That made things a little easier. He'd gone to the attorney and presented himself as a private investigator specializing in working for the defense. He had a cover story to explain why he never charged any fees. According to that story, a millionaire who had once been wrongly accused of murder had founded a charitable trust to defend falsely-accused innocents. It wasn't actually very far from the truth. As it turned out, he hadn't needed it, Soames may have had a defense lawyer of his own, but the man was as run-down and impoverished as his client. He was glad for some free assistance and hadn't asked any questions.

"That seems in order. If you will go down the corridor, third door on the left is a waiting room. An officer will meet you there and take you to the visiting room."

The visiting room and the waiting room were almost identical; both painted in a seedy institutional yellow with battered, official issue furniture. The only difference was the visiting room had two chairs and a desk while the waiting room had more chairs, no desk. Both smelled bad. *Cheap disinfectant, not used often enough.*

"Mister Soames? I'm an investigator, working with your lawyer. I'd like to hear your side of this."

"How do I know you're not stooling for the cops? Or that they're not listening in on this?"

"Mister Soames. I am an ordained priest." *Which is quite true,* Conrad thought, *although the date of my ordination would cause theologians worldwide to have paroxysms of palpitations and probably take to strong drink.* "Anything you say to me here is covered by the sanctity of the Confessional and cannot be used in a court of law. I understand the reason why you are being questioned in the murder of Elizabeth Short is that some of her property, jewelry to be precise, was found in your possession. Can you explain that?"

Conrad looked carefully at Soames as the man made his decisions. *It is a myth that the Inquisition always tortured its victims,* Conrad never even hesitated over the description victim, *the Officers of the Inquisition used their knowledge of human nature and understanding of the human condition much more than physical torture. Unfortunately, they had also supplied an environment where those of a more depraved and degraded nature could flourish.* Conrad could watch Soames making his decision and he would know before Soames did whether the man would tell the truth or not.

That wasn't why Conrad was so intent on watching the man. It wasn't that there was anything strange about him. He was normal, a bit bigger than most perhaps, but in a crowd he would pass unnoticed and be just one more person passing by. There was a problem; he wasn't just one more person. The weird sensation, the feeling that a candle was flickering in the back of Conrad's mind, was there. It had been ever since Soames had entered the room. *Soames is a long-lifer; a Daimones, as we call ourselves.*

Despite this discovery, Conrad listened carefully as Soames told his story. All Conrad's senses drunk in the body language and eye movements; Conrad listened to not only the words he heard, but the pauses between the words. Adding all that together, Conrad asked himself, *is this man telling the truth?* And his answer was, *I don't know.* His story was that he had robbed a bank, cracked the vault and the safety deposit boxes and the jewelry must have been in one of them.

"Do you know which one?" Conrad asked. He desperately wanted to ask 'how old are you really?' and knew he could not. But he had to know that, had to.

"Nah, no way. Look, mister, I'm in a vault, OK? Don't know how long I've got. I'm just cracking the boxes and throwing the contents into a bag. Ain't got time to note down what came from which box. So I gets back to my crash and starts to sort it out. See, I've got some jewelry, right? Women's stuff. Did it come from one box or several? Don't ask me. I don't know. I'd slung the lot into a box and was going to take it down to the shylock when the cops kick the door in. They bring me in for doing the bank, then they start all this thing about the Blue Dahlia."

"Black Dahlia." Conrad's voice was neutral. He was fairly convinced Soames was telling the truth. *A liar wouldn't have admitted ignorance so casually. Put bluntly, he'd have invented a better story.* Long-livers had a lot of practice in making up convincing stories. "Did you tell the police this?"

"Sure. They don't take any notice. Them that's got those boxes, they're the rich guys right? The one's with pull. The cops'll protect them and dump the blame on me. You watch."

Conrad made his decision. This man was innocent of the Black Dahlia murder, he was reasonably sure of it. *A thief, certainly; probably worse. But he hadn't murdered. Or, at least, he hadn't committed that murder.* "Mister Soames, if it's of any comfort to you, I believe your story. I am a skilled investigator, I will dig into this. I do warn you though, that I will inform the police, as well as your defense, of everything I find. My role is to make sure that an innocent man is not punished for a crime he did not commit, not to help a guilty man go free."

Soames nodded. "I can live with that."

Office of the Captain of Inspectors, Bureau of Inspectors, San Francisco Police Department, Hall of Justice

"Richard Soames? Oh, the Black Dahlia killer. That'll be Inspectors Malone and Carmady. You want to speak with them?"

"If I may, Captain. I know how busy your men are . . . "

"Too busy to try and get a killer off."

"Captain, my job is to protect the innocent, not the guilty. Whatever I find, you'll know about. And I won't find anything a competent defense attorney wouldn't get to, so isn't it better you find out any holes in your case now, not in court?"

Conrad's Eye

The Captain nodded; slowly, but in agreement. "Malone, Carmady, talk to this guy will'ya." The door shock slightly with the force of the shout. "He ain't on our side but he ain't agin' us either."

The two inspectors were wary. They'd made a prize catch and didn't want to lose him, but they didn't want to be made to look foolish either. This case was countrywide news; if they'd made a mistake, they'd be lampooned to the same extent.

"So, what do you know about Mister Soames?"

It was Malone who answered. *Obviously, the senior man of the pair.*

"His Army records show him being born in Philly back in 1923. Inducted into the Army 1942; went to Russia 1943. Served there until 1946, was badly wounded and evacuated that year. Given an honorable discharge late '46 but never settled down. Number of charges, all minor; mostly drunkeness. Was in LA from December '46 to June '48, then came up here. We've nailed him a few times: drunkeness, fighting, couple of domestic violences. Been suspected of doing a few bank jobs. He was a combat engineer in Russia, by the way; this is the first one we caught him on. Then, we found the jewelry and the black stuff caught Deke here's eye. He thought of checking it against the Black Dahlia file. We couldn't believe it, but it came back identified."

"Soames says it must have been in the boxes he cracked. He says you won't investigate that because the people who own those boxes have pull."

Carmady started to rise angrily, but Malone waved him back.

"I can see how he might think that. Look, Soames is a vet; a Russian Front vet. Deke and I both served there as well. I was in tanks, Deke was a mudfoot. We are not going to railroad a fellow vet; believe me on that. We know what Soames said, and we're doing our best, but do you know how hard it is to trace the owners of those boxes? He cracked fifty boxes; of those, at least 30 have addresses that are vacant lots and about as many have false names. Some modern banks have pictures of the guys who rent those safety deposit boxes, but this bank wasn't one of them. They just took the renter's word for who he was and where he lived. We're checking fingerprints now, but don't hold your breath."

"I'm sorry, I didn't mean to offend. But I do have to check my client's story out."

"Understood. Look, there's something you should know. It isn't just the fact that he had the jewelry. Hell, he could have got it from a pawnshop. That would have made a better story as well. He's not a nice man, your Soames. Some of his blotter? It's domestic violence calls. Likes to beat on his girlfriends. One left him and he went after her with a razor. Would have slashed her up good, only a couple of good citizens stopped him before she got hurt. Your Soames likes to cut on women, that's why we're holding him."

Malone took a deep breath. While he did so, Deke Carmady cut in.

"I see where you're coming from on this. You think this guy is innocent and you want to prove it. Well, fair enough. Think on this, though. You get him off and he *is* the Black Dahlia killer, he's going to do it again. You know how Elizabeth Short died. Ed, you've got our copy of her file; show our friend here what happened to that girl. Just show our friend here."

"I'd be grateful for a look at that file; I only know what's been published. But, something I can throw into the pot right now. You said whoever killed Elizabeth Short would do it again if he went free. Well, I'll say it differently. Elizabeth Short wasn't the first victim of this killer." Conrad winced slightly with memories. "These killers escalate. There will have been more before her and there should have been some after; worse ones."

Malone nodded. "We'd thought of that. There were a string of killings in Philadelphia from '38 to around '42, a bit similar. Or so we think; the Philly police aren't being what one might call forthcoming. You get the importance of the place and dates, of course."

"Of course, I might be able to help with those files. I've got some strings I can pull. Can you dig around the cold case files? See if there are any that might fit. Throw the disappearances in as well; it might be our killer has got good at disposing of corpses. One thought; did you check the other jewelry found with Soames against the property missing from other dead girls? They might all be trophies."

Malone and Carmady exchanged glances.

"No; that we did not. We checked them against stolen property, that's all. We'll get to that. Now, you want to see the Elizabeth Short file?"

Telephone Room, St. Francis Hotel

Conrad reached into his wallet and took out the telephone number. It was a new development; something that had been passed around, from hand to hand, by those who lived in the shadows because their extended lifespans made it hazardous to do anything else. A number that could be called if help was needed. What Conrad had learned this day meant he needed help.

"You're though, sir." The operator spoke respectfully when she had realized just what the number was.

"National Security Council. Good evening?"

"Could I have extension 13-666 please?"

"Certainly, sir."

There were some clicks and bangs on the line.

"Alexander was an idiot."

There was a brief chuckle on the line. "Right. Anne here. Who is this?"

Conrad smiled. He'd rescued Anne Bonney from prison, but not because she was innocent. He'd checked her record and found nothing that she was innocent of. But the baby she was carrying was innocent of everything, so he'd rescued the baby and Anne had no choice but to come along for the ride. "Conrad here. Is Naamah or Nell in, please? It's very urgent."

"Naamah's here. Hold on a minute. I'll transfer you."

"Naamah? Good. Look, we have a real problem here in California. You heard somebody's been arrested in the Black Dahlia case? Well, we share something with him."

"Damn." Naamah's voice was suddenly worried.

"There's more. I've seen the Black Dahlia file and a lot of it is pretty familiar stuff. You and Nell will recognize it. That can wait, though. The fact that one of us will be going down for a long stretch in maximum security is the real problem. That happens, and . . . "

"We're dead meat."

Naamah's concerned deepened. Privately, she regarded Conrad's obsession with rescuing the innocent as rather naïve, but the prospect of a long-lifer being in jail where his lack of aging would be immediately obvious was grim.

"I'll tell The Seer and we'll get out there."

"You and Nell come, please. You're needed for this one. And can you get some police files from Philly?" Conrad read over the names of the file and the dates of the killings. "And also every bit of information you can get on Richard Soames, Army Serial number . . . "

A few minutes later, Conrad hung up. What had started off as a simple exercise to make sure that an innocent person wasn't railroaded into prison or death row had suddenly become a lot more serious.

CHAPTER TWO

VC-121 Queen of Detroit, *En Route to San Francisco Municipal Airport*

"Are you sure this is legal?"

Naamah sipped delicately at a glass of champagne, wanting to finish it before the aircraft unloaded, or she woke up from the dream; whichever came first.

"Perfectly legal. Now, if we were government employees and were using an Air Force VIP transport for our personal benefit, we would all end up doing time. But, we're not. The United States Government pays the Hudson River Institute a flat annual fee for running the National Security Council. On its part, the HRI bears all the costs of operating the NSC. NSC employees, that's us, are actually hired and paid by the HRI. Any government facilities we use are also billed to the HRI. So, technically, HRI hired this aircraft to bring us over to California. All quite legal. The shareholders of HRI might have cause to complain about us using this aircraft, but the government doesn't."

"And who are the shareholders of the HRI?" Nell Gwynne was also taking advantage of the Italian champagne carried on board the Constellation.

"I'd have to ask Lillith for the exact breakdown, but I rather think the majority shareholder is me."

Naamah and Nell made 'We should have known' faces at each other.

"We got a good deal on this bird; she was coming out this way anyway. She'll be picking up a Congressional delegation and flying them up to Alaska, so we just thumbed a ride. HRI will get billed for our airfare, that's all. Much less than TWA would have charged."

The Seer waved out the window. A few dozen yards away, a red-and-silver TWA Constellation was unloading. Both Lockheeds were dwarfed by the Cloudliner parked the other side of the VC-121.

Conrad's Eye

"How about Pan Am? I hear their Cloudliners are really something." Nell's voice was curious.

"The Super Clippers? All low-density. Pretty much just first-class seating, sleeping compartments, a couple of spacious passenger lounges and large galley for cooking food, not just reheating it. A load of 250 passengers and Juan Trippe is losing his shirt every time one of them takes off. They're 80 miles per hour slower than the Connie and even with the ticket prices he's charging, he still has to fill the bird up before he makes money. The Air Force may have given the C-99s away, more or less, but they cost more to run than a Connie.

"Hughes has got the right idea. He's using the Connies for top-end travel and has sent his Cloudliner's to be redesigned inside. High-density seating; no lounges, no beds, small galleys, same as other airliners. He's aiming for 400 passengers. And he's talking to Convair and Boeing about ordering a stretched Cloudliner capable of carrying 450."

"But if Pan Am can't fill a 250-seater?"

"Trippe's charging 1,890 dollars for a ticket from California to Hawaii. Hughes is going to ask for 550 dollars, from anywhere in the USA. Without all those luxuries on board, his operating costs are lower as well. Hughes is gambling that flying the birds as max-capacity people-haulers will put the ticket price within reach of many, many more potential customers. Trippe believes that air travel will be what it always was, something only for the rich. Hughes sees air travel as something that'll be so commonplace, nobody will think anything of it. He's got a point too. How many guys out there do you think would grab a chance to go to Hawaii for vacation?

"I'll tell you this. If Hughes pulls it off, he'll change the whole face of civil aviation in this country. And then there's foreign travel. If its as cheap to fly to Italy or South Africa as it is to go to Coney Island, people are going to jump at the chance."

"Can anybody just fly aircraft to another country? What about national airspace?" Achillea had been hitting the champagne as well.

"I'll let you into a dirty little secret, one everybody is trying not to mention. There is no such thing as national airspace; not by international agreement, anyway. When we went in for 'Open Skies,' we more or less said to the world 'this is how it's going to be and if you don't like it, tough;' but that was straightforward 'might is right.' You see, back before the war, everybody had agreed that national airspace started at national borders or at the limits of territorial waters, but nobody ever defined how *high* that airspace went. Everybody had different ideas. Some wanted it to go three miles up, just as territorial waters went out. Some wanted it to go as high as the highest piece of land in that country; I guess Nepal liked that one."

"Huh?" Achillea was confused. Geography wasn't her strong point.

"Mount Everest, 29,000 feet. Some countries wanted it to go as high as anti-aircraft guns could fire; that would be about 36,000 feet. Some even wanted national airspace to go upwards to infinity. Then, where is it measured from? From sea level? From the highest piece of land? And what about the right of innocent passage? A warship can sail through even territorial waters as long as it's intent towards the country in question is peaceful. Could an aircraft fly through national airspace on innocent passage? Everybody was still arguing about that when the war broke out.

"Naamah, you probably remember my, hm, 'uncle' being involved in those negotiations. Of course, when the war started, nobody gave a damn about it anymore and no agreement was ever reached. So we've imposed one. We've stated, quite bluntly, that national airspace runs from low tide sea level up to 40,000 feet. Because *we* say it does. Anything above that is international airspace, just as anything outside the three-mile limit is international waters; because *we* say it is. Under 40,000 feet, the right of innocent passage applies, but the nation in question has the right to control routes and so on for safety reasons, because *we* say they do. As we have said, so shall it be.

"Anyway, Juan Trippe tried to screw Hughes over on this. He wanted to have a law instituted that restricted innocent passage to national flag carriers and have Pan Am designated as America's national flag carrier. Might have got away with it, as well; only Hughes put on a bravura performance and turned the hearings into a circus. Good for him, too. If Trippe had got his way, air travel would have been set back decades."

The Captain of the VC-121 coughed delicately before interrupting. "Ladies, gentlemen, we'll be unloading in just a few minutes. The crew will be taking your bags outside. I hope you had a pleasant flight?"

"Very pleasant, indeed; thank you, Captain."

Naamah smiled at him. Privately, she was relieved that the war had seen sunglasses come into fashion as routine wear. With her eyes hidden, she could be a lot more casual in how she spoke to people.

Conrad and Gusoyn were waiting behind the fence, along with the other people who had come to meet friends or just watch the aircraft. They had a limousine waiting in the car park just behind the grass meeting area. Gusoyn had flown out ahead to make those arrangements. Naamah was amused to see that the car had Federal Government plates; another thing that was being billed to HRI, she supposed. Achillea slid into the front seat alongside Gusoyn, while The Seer, Conrad, Naamah and Nell slipped into the back.

"Hi, Conrad. Long time, no see."

Naamah's voice had a slightly catchy quality to it, as if she was suppressing her amusement. Nell's mouth twitched as well.

"Naamah, Nell." Conrad acknowledged them politely but coldly. "Seer, we have a problem; a very serious one."

"One of us, about to spend a long time in jail. I know; Naamah's briefed me. We've got to get him out of there; that's why I brought Achillea along."

"It's not as easy as that, Seer. The situation has developed a lot over the last two days. I'm working with two SFPD inspectors, Jack Malone and Deke Carmady. They're good guys; once they understood I'm not here to show them up or get a guilty man off, they've been very cooperative."

Naamah snorted. "I wonder what the San Francisco Police Department would think if they knew they were working with the Spanish Inquisition?"

Conrad smiled sadly. "My dear, nobody expects the Spanish Inquisition. Jack and Deke have done a good job, though. Naamah, read this; what do you think?"

She took the paper handed to her.

The body was lying naked in the middle of the bed, the shoulders flat but the axis of the body inclined to the left side of the bed. The whole of the surface of the abdomen and thighs was removed and the abdominal cavity emptied of its viscera. The breasts were cut off, the arms mutilated by several jagged wounds. The face was gashed in all directions, the nose, cheeks, eyebrows, and ears being partly removed. The lips were blanched and cut by several incisions running obliquely from the corners of the mouth towards the ears. There were also numerous cuts extending irregularly across all the features. The various parts of the body were found scattered around the room. The chest was open below and the heart absent. In the abdominal cavity there was a partly digested meal of meat and potatoes, and similar food was found in the remains of the stomach attached to the intestines.

The neck was cut through the skin and other tissues right down to the vertebrae, the fifth and sixth being deeply notched. Both breasts were more or less removed by circular incisions, the muscle down to the ribs being attached to the breasts. The skin and tissues of the abdomen were removed in three large flaps. The right thigh was denuded in front to the bone, the flap of skin, including the external organs of generation, and part of the right buttock. The left thigh was stripped of skin and muscles as far as the knee. The right thumb showed a small superficial incision about one inch long, with traces of blood in the skin, and there were several abrasions on the back of the hand showing the same condition.

She frowned. "This is the autopsy report on Mary Jane Kelly, one of Jack the Ripper's victims. Well, not quite; it looks like a report based on those autopsy findings. How did it get here?"

Conrad leaned back in his seat. "It isn't Mary Jane Kelly. It's Crystal Mae Tarrant, aged 19; a black prostitute found dead in Los Angeles in November 1946. Are you beginning to think what I'm thinking?"

"Impossible. OK, Jack the Ripper was Daimones like us, but he's dead."

"Are you sure?"

"Of course I'm sure. I killed him. Very thoroughly."

"And I laughed in his face while he was dying." Nell's voice had a vicious cut to it; a viciousness that jarred those who were familiar with her normal friendly good nature. "And we were around when Montague John Druitt was fished out of the Thames. Recognized the body. No doubt about it. He's dead."

"Mary Jane Kelly was Druitt's last victim. Now read this." Conrad handed Naamah another sheet of paper. She stared to read, looked up at him, startled, then continued reading.

"We all know that serial killers are progressive. Each killing is slightly more elaborate than the last. What you have there is the autopsy on Elizabeth Short. It shows a clear progression from Crystal Mae Tarrant and Tarrant was so nearly identical to Mary Jane Kelly that you, of all people, couldn't spot the difference. I think we have to recognize the possibility that the Black Dahlia killer and Jack the Ripper are the same person. One of us."

"He's dead."

"Then there are two possibilities. Either he survived whatever you did to him . . . "

"Impossible. When I kill somebody, they stay dead. None of them have ever come back from the grave. Anyway, Nell and I both recognized the body the police fished out of the Thames. Montague John Druitt is dead."

"Then you killed the wrong person. You killed an innocent man." Conrad's voice nearly cracked on the last two words. "You not only killed an innocent man, you killed one of us."

For a moment, Conrad looked as if he was going to lose his composure. "Damn it, I TOLD you not to take the law into your own hands. I told you to hand him and the evidence over to the police and let them handle it. Oh no, you're so used to being the infallible autocrat. You so wanted to be back in the role of Queen, Judge, Jury and Executioner, you had to take the law into your own hands."

25

Naamah's temper flared. She squashed it down ruthlessly.

"And if I had done what you had said, what would have happened? They'd have put Druitt away; the one thing we *couldn't* afford. Sorry, Conrad; there was no doubt Druitt did it, Nell here nearly got herself killed proving it. Once we had him, he had to be killed, quickly and quietly. Otherwise, he'd have ended up in prison and we all know the consequences of *that*."

"That's ridiculous." Conrad was beginning to lose his temper. "This was Victorian England, remember? They hanged people like flies back then. Somebody could be hanged for stealing a few pennies. If you'd handed Druitt over, they'd have tried him; and, if the evidence was that good, they'd have hanged him. Problem solved."

Nell burst out into laughter; not amused, but vicious and cynical.

"Hell, Conrad, what world have you been living in? Not this one, that's for sure. Look, ducks, you might be the Inquisitor, the great investigator, *but I'm a whore*. Remember that?

"Druitt was the son of a pretty famous doctor; he was a University of Oxford graduate and a lawyer at a time when the name still meant something. Just to add juice, he was also a schoolmaster. That made him a pillar of the community. He was a man of respect, somebody who was a part of the establishment. A little part, but still part. In case you didn't hear me, I'm a whore. Somebody like Druitt could beat me into a pulp in the squad room of a police station, carve me up and all anybody would do is step over my body."

"That's a bit overstated, Nell."

Naamah's voice was slightly awed. It took a lot to make Gentle Nell lose her temper so comprehensively. She blinked as Nell Gwynne stabbed her finger within a quarter of an inch of Naamah's nose.

"Nammie, *you* spend a year selling what you're sitting on, to put food on the table for *your kids*, and then we'll talk. I might not have turned a trick for three hundred years and been a Duchess in between, but *I still know how things work* and they don't *ever* change. *Nobody*, not *then*, not *now*, is going to put a man like Druitt away for carving up a whore.

"You want proof? Look at the differences in the way Crystal Mae Tarrant and Elizabeth Short are being treated. Both carved up, mutilated, tortured to death. One's a celebrity murder case; the other is forgotten in the cold case files. Only difference is Crystal *was* a whore and Elizabeth *wasn't*.

"So, Conrad, forget the justice of this. There isn't any. If we'd handed Druitt over to the cops, they'd have either let him go and he'd have gone on killing or they'd have put him in a looney bin and watched him very carefully.

Which was the one thing we can't afford. So drop the sanctimonious posing and look at things the way they are. Nammie and I did what we had to do, for the good of everybody. Not just us, but the trollops out on the street as well."

Nell settled back in her seat, her anger spent. Silence filled in the car. Gusoyn concentrated on trying to drive through the traffic. Achillea and The Seer tried not to laugh. Naamah and Conrad were shocked into silence by the violence of Nell's outburst.

Eventually, The Seer casually spoke. "You know, I've never had a chance to ride on one of the trolley cars here. Remind me to fix that this trip."

His reward was a stony silence from the back of the car.

After the pause got to be painful, Conrad spoke carefully, not wishing to provoke another tirade.

"Very well, Nell, you've made your point. Perhaps you and Naamah did do what you had to."

"*Perhaps* . . ." Nell started to boil up again.

"I mean to say, I agree that you faced an impossible situation and you handled it as well as anybody could under the circumstances then and there. I was wrong to criticize that.

"But, the fact remains, we have a string of murders here in San Francisco and Los Angeles that bear a chilling resemblance to the Jack the Ripper murders. It's not just the Crystal Mae Tarrant case. We've found four others, all of which are so close to the comparable Jack the Ripper killings that it's hard to treat it as being coincidence. Look, we even have a double event. Two victims killed on the same night. There are differences. The time span is longer. In these new cases, the victims were tied down and their deaths were prolonged. The coroner says Elizabeth Short lived for two days while he was cutting on her. But the similarities are so marked.

"And we have a long-lifer in jail; one who is the primary suspect for these killings. A man, by the way, with a long history of violence against women and a known fondness for sharp objects.

"Did you bring those Philly cases we asked for?"

The Seer nodded.

"In the briefcase. The Philly Police were a bit reluctant to hand them over. They take it personally that the cases were never solved. We had to pressure them a bit; we linked it to an investigation of German attempts to land spies and saboteurs in the US and the sabotage at the Brewster Aviation plant. It was a bit thin, but it held. And who is 'we?' "

"Jack and Deke. I said, they're good people. Look, if those cases fit the developing pattern we have a real problem here." Conrad thought for a second. "1938 to '42 and '46 to '47. Soames was in Russia from '42 to '46. I don't suppose we can find out if there were any similar cases there?"

"Not a chance. No way anybody would know. If a body was found in that sort of condition, rightly or wrongly, people would just assume the Germans had done it. By '45, there was nothing anybody would say was beyond the Germans. But what about '48 to the present? Serial killers don't just stop."

"Jack and Deke are looking; so far, they haven't found any. Our working hypothesis is that the killer has got to disposing of the bodies so they can't be found.

"Look, Nell, Naamah, I don't mean any offense, but we haven't got many possibilities here. Either this is an eerily similar but unconnected case, or Soames is Jack the Ripper. I can't think of any other possibilities, can you? If the two cases are unconnected, that leaves us with the problem of Soames. If he is the Ripper, it means that either you didn't kill him when you thought you did or you got the wrong person. Again, I can't think of any other alternatives.

"But you do realize what that means? We can't just bust Soames out of jail . . ."

"Please, don't be so crude." Achillea was remonstrative. "We don't bust people out. We arrange for their release, sometimes a little unconventionally."

"OK, I stand corrected. But, if Soames is the Ripper, we can't arrange an unconventional release from jail and leave him loose to carry on his slaughter."

"That's not a problem." Achillea was confident. "We arrange his release."

"And I finish him off," added Naamah, equally confident. "Escaped and died of natural causes."

Conference Room adjoining Suite 503, St. Francis Hotel

"It's pretty compelling, isn't it? Naamah, Nell, you must have missed him. I don't know how, but you must have."

The Seer looked at the case files and notes. Some were very new, typed on crisp, white paper; others very old, hand-written and yellowed with age. They told the same story. Horrifying murders carried out with brutal violence; murders that were sixty years apart, yet were so nearly identical they might have been committed by the same hands. Which was precisely what The Seer was beginning to believe. The implications worried him deeply.

"We can't have done. Look, Seer, Druitt was about to do for Nell with that butchers knife of his and he had enough surgical equipment with him for the slicing and dicing. We as good as caught him in the act; a few seconds more, and he would have been caught in the act and Nell would have been gone. It *was* him."

Naamah's voice echoed her frustration. She knew she had killed the murderer, yet the case files in front of her pointed her in the same direction as the Seer was already heading. Two sets of murders so nearly identical, sixty years apart, pointed to one murderer with an inordinately long lifespan.

"Is it possible that he wasn't dead? Suspended animation, catatonia, something like that?"

Naamah shook her head. "I used a standard concoction, one potent enough to kill a horse. Nothing stylish or flashy; just a good, old-fashioned potion of instant death. Well, not instant; he threshed around for a few minutes while Nell taunted him, then expired. We kept him for 24 hours to make sure; then we weighted him with stones and dropped him in the Thames. Ten days later, he popped up, was brought in by the River Police and signed off as a suicide. Neat job, although I say it myself; one that was very final. He was still recognizable when he was brought in to the river bank. There's no doubt about it."

"Frustrating, isn't it? There's no other way around it, you must have got the wrong person. And now we've got a long-lifer sitting in Central Booking who looks like a very good candidate for the real killer. This is a mess."

The Seer was interrupted by the telephone ringing. He picked it up and listened for a few seconds. "Conrad's here, with his detective friends. They're on their way up."

"Mister Phillip Stuyvesant, I would like you to meet Inspector Jack Malone and Inspector Deke Carmady. They're the leads on the Soames Case."

The Seer looked at the two inspectors while they shook hands. They'd obviously put on their Sunday Best suits for this meeting.

"Pleased to meet you, Mister Stuyvesant. We're a bit curious though, how come the National Security Council has got involved in a murder case?"

Malone was genuinely curious about the sudden arrival of a group from Washington. There were already rumors starting to swirl about the reasons for the trip and they had little to do with a sordid murder.

"When Conrad turned up at the station, we put a tail on him." Carmady explained with more than a slight element of conceit. "Sometimes, when somebody tries to insert themselves into an investigation, it's because they did the crime. So we followed Mister Conrad about a bit, especially when he met you all at the airport yesterday. Then, we looked you up."

"That saves introducing myself, I suppose. May I present four of my associates, Miss Naamah Sammale, Miss Nell Gwynne, Miss Achillea Foyle, and Mister Gusoyn Rivers?"

"Blue Ford?" Gusoyn asked with professional interest.

"That's right."

"Thought so. Wasn't trying to evade though."

"Didn't think so. You still handled that big limo well; our driver had a job staying with you."

"Gentlemen, if you'd like to take a seat? It's our normal custom at these meetings to be on first name terms, if that's OK with you?.

"In answer to your question, the NSC is tasked with analyzing and reporting on threats to America and its citizens. That's a pretty wide remit, and it's more or less up to us to define it as we want. This case is developing some pretty nasty ramifications and if there's somebody around who's responsible for dozens, perhaps more, of these brutal murders, then that's a threat we should look at. Having said that, Jack, Deke, this is your case. Whatever credit is to be had for it, is yours. We'll stay in the background. After all, neither of us wants J. Edgar diving in to grab the headlines."

A laugh ran around the room.

Naamah picked up the files. "You've read these files we've had sent over from London, of course?"

"We have. At first, we thought you were insane, digging up murders that took place sixty years ago. But, when we read the details, we saw why. How did you get these, by the way? They're the Brit Home Office files, not the public ones."

"Back in the war, one of the things we handled was some liaison work with the British Resistance, especially with one of their team leaders, a guy called Newton. He's Deputy Home Secretary now, so we just called in a few markers."

The Seer paused for a second.

"This is what we call a Red Team meeting. Our experience has been that once an investigation or planning session starts, people get one idea, run with it and forget everything else."

Malone and Carmady nodded. They'd seen that happen; inspectors getting fixated on one suspect and missing other, vital, elements of the case.

"So the purpose of this meeting is to throw up objections to everything and put up alternative theories. Doesn't matter how weird or illogical they are. By knocking a dumb idea on the head, we might get an idea that leads somewhere valuable. As is traditional, I'll kick off.

"Are we even sure this girl Short was murdered? Could she have committed suicide?"

"No way. Not the way she was hacked up." Malone was quick to jump in, then thought for a second. "Is it possible she committed suicide, then somebody found the body and mutilated it? Perhaps they were drunk, or on drugs, or something?"

Carmady shook his head. "Coroner says she was alive when most of those cuts were made. Especially the ones to her mouth. What's up with those anyway? Some sort of ritual?"

"Psychological torture as well as physical. Any woman knows, she gets cut like that, she's ruined for life." Nell's voice was quiet. "Even the best surgeons can't fix that sort of damage. When the scars stretch and set, they twist the whole face up. Even if she'd lived, she'd never be able to go out in public again. Whoever did this really hated women."

Around the table, heads nodded.

Malone broke the brief silence. "Could this be consensual? I don't mean the whole thing but perhaps when it started? Some out there like to be threatened with knives. Perhaps that's how this started and it went out of control?"

"Jack, you don't sound like you think the Short case is linked to the rest." Conrad was surprised; he'd assumed everybody had accepted the cases were linked.

"It's a possibility. Have you heard of victimology?"

Heads shook, so Malone continued.

"Well, it's a study of the sort of person the victim was. By defining that, we can define the circle she moved in and see who entered that circle. Two victims, two circles, and the suspects are defined by where those circles overlap. The more victims, the tighter the net gets. Eventually, we get down to just one person.

"Well, Deke and I were talking this over last night, and the Short woman, her victimology isn't the same as the others. All the other victims, the London killings, the ones in Philly and all but one of the ones here, they were all street prostitutes. Elizabeth Short wasn't a prostitute; not yet, at any rate. Given a few more years she'd probably have made it, but not yet. But she's still in the list. So the victimology doesn't match."

Conrad had been listening carefully. "We started off by bringing in the Ripper files. Could it be the same person?"

That is the key issue that had to be raised and discounted. Nevertheless, Conrad felt Naamah's eyes staring at him. *Drink only from sealed bottles I have opened for a while.*

"The Ripper murders were in 1888. Assuming that the Ripper was twenty or so, that would put him at 80 years old in 1948. He could still be alive, but I can hardly see him killing a young woman, one who might fight back." Carmady couldn't get over the eerie sensation of reading almost identical files separated by so many years.

Conrad leaned back in his chair, a doubtful look on his face. *Time to start the discounting process.* "Of course, it might be his brain but somebody else's hands."

"What do you mean?"

"If the London Ripper is still alive, Deke, he's too old to do this. But suppose he's the master and he's got one or more disciples. People he's been teaching to go forth and slaughter. That would explain the similarities between the killings, the teacher's doctrine, and the differences, the disciple's interpretation. I've seen it before."

"Or a copycat." Malone let his chair ride forward. "Do you know we've had over 30 confessions to the Black Dahlia murder? Get a well-publicized crime and somebody thinks, 'gee that was a good idea' and they copy it. Perhaps somebody else read the Ripper files and thought the same, copied them and then added a few ideas of their own?"

"So where does Soames fit into all this." That was, after all, what Conrad really cared about.

"I'm liking him less and less as a suspect for all this. He doesn't fit into the victimology. He's a low-life; Elizabeth Short was a society hanger-on. He'd fit the prostitutes, no problem there, but Short? She was broke, so she hung out with people who had money and cadged off them. Promised them a good time then never delivered. That could have gotten her killed quite easily."

"Let's take that idea of a teacher a bit further." Achillea knotted her fingers in front of her. "We've got a group of six killings, assuming Short was one, here and five back in 1888. There's a set in Philly, but they're the ones that don't fit."

"Why not? It's the same m/o. Prostitutes knifed and cut up. If anything, it's more of a fit to the London killings than this latest group. The Philly women were dead when they were sliced."

"Knife wounds. Believe me Deke, I know knives. The London and the LA/SF killings all showed a lot of skill with a knife. Not surgeon standard, I admit, but above average. People think a knife is easy to use. It isn't."

Out of the corner of her eye, Achillea saw the two inspectors nodding.

"The Philly killings are just crude slashes. Not the same style at all."

"Could be Soames did the first killings without learning, went to Russia where he learned how to do it properly and then came back to carry on." *Which would mean Soames and the Ripper were not the same person.* Conrad could see Naamah had already fastened onto that.

"The army teaches people to use knives . . ."

"Bayonets!" Malone, Carmady and Achillea all spoke in unison. They deferred to each other until the Seer pointed at Malone.

"The Army teaches soldiers to use a bayonet; different thing entirely. This work? Achillea's quite right, it's a skilled job."

"Another thing." Gusoyn cut in diffidently. "Was it not a big thing against Soames that he tried to carve up a girlfriend, used a razor and got stopped cold by two citizens? It would appear to me that somebody who is good with a knife would be able to inflict serious hurts on unarmed civilians who got in his way. I seem to remember he did not do so well."

"They knocked him down, took his razor, then kicked the snot out of him." Malone recited the details with relish. He didn't like men who waved razors around. "Nobody got as much as a scratch. Soames got badly roughed up. Emergency ward job."

"Doesn't sound like a skilled knifeman to me. Looking less like Soames all the time." Conrad spoke with satisfaction.

"You're right there. More we look at this, the less fits. Been the same with every time a Black Dahlia suspect had been brought in. Looks good at first, but the devil is in the details."

Malone sounded gloomy; after all, he was watching a probable promotion evaporate.

"You should hear Finis Brown on the subject. The poor guy can't go to a party without somebody telling him their own pet theory of what happened to the Short woman and twice a year he gets a full confession from somebody."

"Back to teachers. We're talking about sets of six. Is there any indication that the London killings might have included a sixth?" Achillea shifted around a bit in her seat. Her stocky, over-muscled body got uncomfortable if she was sitting down for too long.

"Could be; people were dying all the time back in those days. Crime rate was appalling. The only reason why the Jack the Ripper case made the headlines was that it suited some political interests. There could easily have been a sixth nobody knew about. *Nobody would care.*" Nell finished by looking defiantly at Conrad, who flinched slightly. The significance of the exchange was not missed by the two inspectors.

Carmady took a swing at answering. "OK, then suppose this isn't a progression; suppose it's a cycle. The killer lives normally for a while, slowly building up frustration, then it gets too much and he kills his first victim. That kicks off the cycle, he escalates from one to six and the sixth leaves him drained."

"Which raises an interesting question. Why did he move to San Francisco? Los Angeles was perfect for him. Young girls coming in to make it big in the movie studios, fail and go to the streets. Then vanish. Who'll miss them when nobody knew they were there?"

Nell looked around the meeting. She'd made a telling point and everybody recognized it.

"He might feel he has to escape; 'the guilty flee where no man pursueth,' and all that. He could even be appalled by what he has done and wants to get away from the scene as soon as possible. So he moves to a new town and starts again, convinced that this time it will be different, this time he won't do it again." Malone sounded suddenly weary and depressed.

"That would explain why there were no more killings in LA and they haven't started here yet." Conrad spoke slowly, trying to marshal his thoughts. "He lived in LA, something kicked his cycle off and he killed his six victims, ending with Elizabeth Short. According to his routine, the moment he killed number six, he moved out and came up here. Nothing's kicked this cycle off yet."

"Something for you. Deke and I did a check on the safety deposit boxes. Found out how many had been rented since Elizabeth Short's body was found back in January '47. Of the fifty Soames admits he broke open, twenty-three were rented since then. Of those, twenty have fake names and addresses. Those twenty sound as if they might be worth looking at. We'll book Soames on the bank robbery charge; that'll hold him where he can't do any harm. I reckon he's still a candidate for the Philly killings."

"Something else." Nell's voice cut through the murmur of agreement. "If this killer is cyclic like Deke says, he's working up to a new series of six right now. I bet he does some non-deadly stuff first. Probably doesn't get reported."

"We'll ask around; see if the girls on the street know anything."

Nell snorted with laughter. "They won't talk to you. You're Bulls. They'll never talk to you about anything."

"We could send a police woman . . . "

"*Riiight,* ducks; I've seen the police women here. Heard some of them served in Russia; could turn a charging Tiger tank into stone just by glaring at it. Anyway, don't matter; man or woman, the street girls won't talk to the cops. You're the enemy. We'll have to think of something else."

The Seer knew very well what Nell had in mind and guessed it was probably better the police knew nothing about it. *Time to move on.*

"OK, so we're looking for somebody who roughs up street girls and who fits one of the twenty unknowns with boxes. Jack, Deke, if you have no objections, I'll contact your Captain and ask him for your assistance 'in a matter of national security.' Provided your department has no rules against moonlighting, I'll put you on the NSC books as temporary consultants. If nothing else, it'll give you an excuse to duck unwanted paperwork."

"Sounds good to us, eh, Deke?"

After the two inspectors left, The Seer leaned back in his seat.

"Right people, we're not out of the woods yet. We have several things we must do. One is, we have to find out how old this Soames guy really is. It's not impossible he is our killer or the Philly Killer. Secondly, we might have an explanation for what we're seeing, but we don't know if it's right or whether the killer is one of us or not. Allied to that, we still haven't proved whether he's the London killer or not.

"Naamah, I had a thought on that when the copycat thing came up. Is it possible that Druitt was a copycat? That he read about the Ripper, thought 'that sounds fun,' went out to try it and walked into the ambush you and Nell set up?"

Naamah thought for a second, glanced at Nell, and then thought again. "Yes, it is possible. Not likely, but possible. It's a hellish coincidence that we should get a copycat who is also a Daimones."

"OK, that means you two didn't kill the wrong guy, you just whacked the wrong killer. Quite a different thing."

"Thank you." Nell sounded bitter at the comment. Conrad's readiness to condemn her for killing an innocent person still infuriated her. She had risked her life to avoid that possibility and come close to losing it. *Conrad is all too willing to blame everybody except the person who had actually been accused. But, then again, he blames himself more than any of them.*

"It does leave open the question of whether Jack the Ripper and the Black Dahlia killer are the same person. If they are, he has to be a Daimones and that means we had two Daimones serial killers on our hands. That's not good. And we can't leave Soames in jail, even on a bank robber charge. That'll see him in for ten or 15 years, enough to blow everything open."

"Seer, this just sounds all wrong. I'm sorry, but it does. We've got at least three Daimones now. Druitt, the real Ripper and Soames. Possibly more. None of whom we've heard of before. I'm sorry, I just don't buy it. Too many."

Nell's voice was quiet and reflective, giving the impression that she was carefully thinking over the results of the meeting. In fact, she was reviewing the clothes she'd brought out; what would happen next required a specialized wardrobe.

"What do you think, Nell?"

"I think Druitt was the real Ripper. The guy who's doing the killing now is a copycat or disciple, whatever. Soames, no matter whether he is new or established, is just a bystander in this."

"Which is as viable a viewpoint as any other. People, I have to get back to Washington. Gusoyn, I'm leaving you in charge here. Nell's going to be risking her neck on this. I'm making you personally responsible for her safety. Understood?"

CHAPTER THREE

The Tenderloin

"You are not really going to go out there like that, are you?"

Gusoyn's voice was decidedly wary. Nell was sitting in the back of the limousine wearing high heels, a tight black skirt and a skimpy, semi-transparent top. As Gusoyn could see from where he was sitting, that was *all* she was wearing.

"It's all right, ducks; it's a warm San Franciscan night out there. It's not going to get frostbite."

"That is not what worries me. Suppose somebody tries to pick you up?"

"Then you pull up alongside and, like any good whore, I'll make for the most expensive car. Now, how do I look?"

"Honestly?"

"Honestly, ducks."

"You look like a cheap slut."

"Great. I had to buy these clothes for this job, I was afraid they'd look too new."

"I hate them."

"You'll hate them more soon. *You're* in charge; *you're* signing the expenses voucher for them."

Nell checked her bag. Inside was a new Czech Model 50 pistol, loaded with 7.62x25mm hollow points.

"Right, here we go. Watch my back."

She stepped out the car and started to cruise the pavement, bag over her shoulder, hips swinging in the traditional streetwalker's shimmy. *The body remembers,* she thought. *Once there, it's always there.* She rounded the corner, being careful to make sure she was still visible to Gusoyn sitting in the shadowed car the other side of the road, to where two street girls were standing, *One black, the other white or Latina.* Nell couldn't tell.

The black girl noticed her and prodded her friend. They left their work station and advanced on Nell, hostile, aggressive and threatening.

"Find yourself somewhere else, bitch. This corner's taken."

Nell lifted her arms slightly so her hands were visible. The black girl had her hands in her bag. *What was in there?* Nell wondered. *A knife? A bottle of acid?* She could feel her stomach clench slightly. Then she relaxed and shook herself. *This is America, not Cheapside. If there is a weapon in there, it would be a Saturday Night Special. Probably a .25 or a .32.*

"I'm not competing, ducks. I just want to talk, that's all."

A slight lessening of hostility, but now a healthy dose of suspicion.

"Who are you? A cop?"

"Lord love you, no. Look, the people I'm here for have an interest in us working girls. They've heard a slasher may be moving in here and they want him stopped before he starts."

The two girls looked at each other, comprehension dawning. Nell could almost read their minds. *The people who have an 'interest' in these streets are organized crime. If there was a slasher around, their income from vice would drop drastically. The girls think I've been sent to find out what they know. They probably think I hooked up with one of the crime bosses, met him when he was on the bottom, perhaps and he'd kept me on as he'd worked his way up the mob chain of command. Certainly his comare; just possibly his wife.*

The girls would spread word about her and that was a better protection than a gun or a bodyguard. It was a great story. Nell wished she'd thought of it first.

"Why you here honey?" It was the black girl speaking. "These ain't your streets; why should you care?"

"Look duck, I've been here, just not *here,* right?" Nell had once served strong drink in her mother's brothel and she knew the risks these girls were running. "Let me help you."

"What you want to know, Sugar?" *White girl speaking.* Nell decided to call her Sugar, and that made her companion Honey.

"Slashers start off soft and work themselves up to it. So, know any clients who get rough? Nasty ones?"

"That's all of them, ain't it?" Sugar sounded bitter.

"That bad?" Nell was surprised. "My day, we had'em sure but some were nice enough. A few got a real kick out of treating a whore like a lady."

"Not on these streets, Sugar. Show him, Sal." The black girl opened her blouse. There was a raw cut between her breasts, now healed to an angry scar. *Probably a razor.* It was a clean slice.

"That's the sort of thing I mean. Who did that?"

"Just a john. Since when did they ever give a real name? Bastards all of them."

"They're not all bad, Sal. Hymie's all right?"

"Hymie?"

"Old guy runs the deli down the corner. Nice old man. When he shuts up shop, he gives us girls cups of soup. Says it's left over and he doesn't want to throw it away."

"Yeah, and if it's a cold night he puts extra on to make sure there's enough leftovers. Couple of the sisters wanted to pay him in kind, but he wouldn't. Said his wife would geld him if he did."

Nell noted the name and location down on a notepad in her bag, *A name worth checking; not all monsters look the part.* "The john who carved you, anything at all you can say about him?"

"Green car. Sedan. Back seat was clean. Car had a California plate, OYA something."

"Anybody else?"

"All of them, like I said. You say you've been here. You know then. Cuts and bruises go with the job." Honey's voice was sour and bitter, but also resigned.

"And the odd welt from johns who like that sort of thing. How about I describe the man we think is coming. You tell me if it fits anybody."

"We'll try." The girls were more confident now; if anything, they were slightly flattered that their help had been sought, and almost pathetically grateful somebody cared enough about them to ask.

"Right. This man is a gent, or at least he tries to be. Dresses like it. Not much to look at; nothing really special about him. Got money. He might smell bad. He likes to hurt a girl. I don't mean smack her around, like you say, that goes with the job. He likes to really hurt and he's good at it. Knows what to do and where. You won't go back to him from choice; you'd rather take a beating from somebody else than go through that again. But he wants you back because he gets off on your fear."

Sugar and Honey looked at each other. Sugar took the lead again. "Yeah, we know a couple like that. Got that pad of yours?"

Sugar and Honey started speaking, remembering the ones who had given them bad times. Nell took the notes quietly, letting them talk out their bitterness and fear. And also listened to the bleak hopelessness in their voices. As they talked, the conversation drifted away from the topic to comparing their businesses and clientele. They had the impression Nell had worked the streets back East, years before; something Nell didn't challenge. *It was true, after all; I just hadn't said how far east or how many years before.*

It was weird; she was becoming a role model to them, a girl from the street who'd made good. How good they couldn't possibly guess, but she'd showed them there was a way up and out. They couldn't know it was closed to them by a freak of genetics.

"You girls carry protection?" she asked at last.

"Nah, johns pay better to ride bareback."

"Didn't mean that. I mean protection for yourself. Against a slasher."

Honey reached into her bag and brought out a can of pepper spray.

"Lord, ducks, is that all?" Nell was amazed.

"We got advice, some do-gooder, he said this was best. If we had a gun, it could be taken from us. What you got then?"

Nell opened her bag and took the sleek Model 50 out. She kept her Federal concealed carry permit right out of sight; it just wouldn't fit the image.

"Lord love us, the fool tells you when a slasher's coming at you with a butcher knife, you spray him with pepper oil and he'll run away screaming, but put three Tokarev Magnums into his chest and he'll take the gun off you? Where did these people come from? Gun or knife, girl; in our business, knife is better."

Few minutes of conversation later, Nell switched the bag over to her other shoulder, the signal for Gusoyn to come and pick her up. As the black limousine pulled over, she went to it and opened the back door.

"You watch your steps, watch each other's backs now, y'hear?"

The car confirmed what the girls had already guessed; Nell was attached to organized crime. She was about to climb in, then a sudden thought struck her.

"That smart-ass, the one who said don't carry a gun. Need his name, where we can find him as well."

Door closed, Nell dropped the act, relaxed in the seat and sighed.

"You know, Gusoyn, I'd forgotten. I'd just forgotten. Those girls should be scared stiff, but they're not. They're so used to being treated like dirt that's how they see themselves. We never got treated this bad; not in the cribs, not in the theaters. Look, drive around a bit while I change. I brought a dress and so on with us. There's a deli I want to look at and I don't want to do it looking like this. After we've been there, I'll change back and we'll find some more girls to talk to. Word about me will have spread by then."

The deli was easy to find. Parking the car was something different.

It's never a problem in the movies; the good guys can pull up right outside anywhere they want to go. Never really happens that way.

Nell and Gusoyn had a half-block walk before they could get inside. It was quiet in there. A few customers were talking quietly; one read a paper at the bar.

No juke box, no radio blaring. The place has a nice smell to it, clean and friendly.

"Sir, Ma'am, can I get you anything?"

Gusoyn was reading the menu chalked up behind the bar. "Corned beef on rye, please. And a coffee."

"Just coffee for me, please."

The old man looked at her, a gentle smile under his thin mustache.

"Wouldn't you prefer tea?"

Nell hesitated. *I don't want to offend the old man, not after Sugar and Honey spoke well of him, but Americans can't make tea to save their lives.*

The old man smiled a bit more broadly.

"I'll make you a pot of tea. If you don't like it, you and your young man have your meal on me. But if you do, put a five-spot in the box." He waved his hand. There was a Red Cross collection box by the till.

"Done. Are you Hymie? Some friends of mine spoke of you."

"That's me. I'll just get your tea."

Hymie was away for five minutes, before coming back with a teapot and cup. He put it down, Nell poured her milk, added the tea and sipped. Hymie grinned broadly when he saw her expression of delight and he rattled the collection box. Nell smiled back and put a ten-dollar bill in the box.

"Five for our bet and five for the pleasure. First decent cuppa I've had in years."

"I knew you were English, soon as you spoke. Been over here long?"

"Good few years, yes; came over before the war."

"My wife too. She's the one who taught me to make tea. She got out when Hitler was starting his thing, guessed how it would go and left while there was still a chance. Most of her relatives went to the gas."

Two men entered, both in silk suits with their hair slicked back. It was unobtrusive, but when they sat at the bar, Gusoyn watched Hymie slip them an envelope from behind the till. *Protection money.* The wiseguys ordered hamburgers and, when they came out of the kitchen, they paid for them.

On reflection, Gusoyn thought, *I have never seen gangsters who are collecting protection payments pay for their food before. They take, never buy.*

When Gusoyn and Nell finally left, a gentle rain was falling.

"Still want to go on meeting, Nell? Not much good in this. The girls will have gone in, will they not?"

"Some will; others will get slapped around by their pimp if they aren't out earning. But, you're right; we're done for the night. You saw Hymie, what do you make of him?"

"Seemed a nice old man."

"Not so sure. Did you see the way he sliced that corned beef? Achillea might be able to handle a knife that well, but there wouldn't be much in it. And with English connections as well. That really was nice tea."

"Not one of us though; no sense. He is a short-lifer."

"Yaa. Apart from that, he fits a lot of what we expect. We'll have to Conrad to check into him."

"Something else. Notice those mobsters paying for their burgers? Never seen that before."

"Makes you wonder about Hymie, doesn't it? And he knows all the girls. They probably trust him."

"But he has been here for years, not just the last couple. He is a fixture, part of the neighborhood. I would guess he knows the name of every kid within ten blocks."

Nell nodded. "Think so. It might be he's just a nice guy with a good heart. Mebbe those wiseguys just like him; does happen sometimes.

"Gusoyn, have you ever thought that some of the people who really deserve to live on, just get the normal three score and ten? I mean, what did we ever do to deserve what we are? And Druitt, why did he have to get our gift and that old man be denied it?"

"Pure chance. That is what the brainiacs in our circle say. Just a chance thing. Ask Conrad he will tell you it is God's punishment for our crimes and we live until we have paid off our debt. I bet every one of us has something different."

Nell sighed, looking at Gusoyn from the corners of her eyes. Most Daimones were women, two to one or thereabouts. That made it great for the men who liked women, but it was particularly hard for those who did not. There were very, very, few gay Daimones. Nell was prepared to bet that Gusoyn hadn't been in a steady relationship since Phaeton Phoebus Apollo had stormed out of their circle. That had been hundreds of years before Nell had even been born.

Naamah had told her about that fight. From her story it had been an epic that had nearly torn the circle apart. Phaeton had never come back, although Nell knew that both Naamah and Lillith had kept a quiet eye on him. Until the war. He'd been in Germany until 1938, after that they had lost track of him in the chaos. She suddenly felt very sorry for the quiet, lonely, man driving her car. She was a gregarious person who thrived on company and couldn't imagine being alone like that.

"Hey, Gusoyn, see that theater there? It's a bit like the one I worked in back in London. Before I met Charlie." She giggled. "I used to do the Breeches Part. That was a standard thing back then. Leading lady playing a man's part. Audience loved it. Gusoyn, I play the man's part well. If you want me to."

Gusoyn looked back at her. She wasn't teasing or goading him. She was just being 'pretty, witty Nell,' whose earthy humor, kindness and basic *goodness* had captivated a King.

"That is kind, Nell, but some other time perhaps. We have to see Conrad when we get back. We have got some people he has to talk to, and the sooner we start, the better."

"And I suppose he has to oil his rack and heat up the branding irons. Right enough then. Home, James, and don't spare the horsepower."

Conrad's Eye

Conference Room adjoining Suite 503, St. Francis Hotel

Conrad was playing cards.

Not with a normal deck, but with a pack of 6 by 8 inch filing cards; one for each suspect. Written on the cards was all that he knew about that suspect. A few had one of Nell's hand-drawn pictures of the person in question. Nell was quite an accomplished cartoonist. *Her pictures, though caricatures, capture the key parts of a person's appearance far better than a photograph would.* Rather morbidly, Conrad wondered what her pictures of him looked like. He was under no illusions about his standing with the Washington Circle. His idealistic commitment did not blend well with the intense pragmatism of the Americans. He got on much better, and felt more comfortable with, Loki and his group in Geneva.

A card. This one had no name on it, no information. It was blank but labeled "Local Crime Boss".

Nell insisted I put that one in. 'Look ducks,' she had said. 'The local boss takes money from the girls to protect them right? So every so often he has one of them beaten into a pulp anyway, just to keep the rest scared. Way of keeping them under control. So put his card in there. Gusoyn and I'll find out who he is soon enough.' When Conrad thought about it, that comment had an ominous ring to it.

Conrad thought hard, then put the card into the top row, the leading suspects.

Another card, this one labeled "Hymie Lowenstein". *The deli owner.* This card was packed with information, all written in Conrad's tiny, cramped and excruciatingly neat handwriting. One of Nell's pictures that had enabled Conrad to recognize the man instantly. They'd spent a fair time talking; business at the deli had been slow, and Hymie had been glad to speak to somebody strange, someone from out of town. Conrad, after all, was an Inquisitor and knew how to extract information without seeming to do so. He'd built up a good picture of the old man and come to the conclusion he wasn't the killer. He'd been living in San Francisco all his life; he'd been too old for the draft that had sent the younger men to Russia. Conrad had checked his birth details and everything fitted. He was who he said he was.

Of course, documents and birth certificates can be faked; histories re-written for convenience. We do it all the time. But Conrad was an Inquisitor and knew all too well how to expose the holes in even the most convincing set of stories. Guilt cramped his mind for a second. *So good, I exposed holes even when there were no holes to expose.*

No, Lowenstein is innocent. Conrad had no doubt about it. *That will please Nell; she took an instant liking to the old man.* That weighed in Conrad's mind as well. *Nell is a good judge of character.* His card went into the fourth row, the definitely excluded.

More cards; those that the women on the streets had described as potential slashers. Some cards were sparse; some had more detail in them. All of them sickened Conrad. *Such senseless brutality.*

He'd have liked to put them all in the top row, but that wasn't the object of the 'game'. He sorted through them, trying to pick out the prime suspects from the rest. Conrad pulled one from the stack. *This one for example, the one that Nell christened 'Honey's Slasher.'.*

He looked like a prime candidate, but reading the description, Conrad doubted it. *He'd held the girl down and sliced the skin between her breasts with a razor, holding it at an angle to make sure the cut would leave her scarred. He'd wanted to mark her, perhaps in some strange way to stake a claim, but not to kill.* Like most of the cards representing people who had attacked the street women, this one had no real name, just a vague description and a fragment of a car registration plate. *Second row, a person who was interesting but probably not the target.*

Conrad drew one that wasn't one of the attackers; in fact, there was very little on him at all. *Nell christened him ' The Idiot' because he was the one who had gone around 'advising' the street women that they shouldn't carry guns or knives to defend themselves.* That was the only real reason he was in the pack at all. Conrad was about to put him into the fourth row, when he stopped and reconsidered. *Why had he taken it on himself to give such advice?*

Conrad thought about it, then moved him up to the third row.

And so he spent the night, waiting for Gusoyn and Nell to return from their nightly expeditions with more suspects, more descriptions, more cards to be filled out and carefully placed in the correct row. It was better than sleeping. For when Conrad slept, the nightmares came.

Anything was better than the nightmares.

The Tenderloin

Nell approached their car with caution. She'd given Gusoyn the signal to pick her up, but he hadn't moved in. *Something is wrong and I have a good idea what it was. Something I've been expecting ever since we started.*

Her hand was in her bag and her fingers were wrapped around the butt of her Model 50. The hammer was back and the safety catch was off. Her index finger rested on the frame, just above the trigger. *Never, never, on the trigger itself until I intend to fire.* Henry McCarty was a good teacher and drove his lessons home well.

She was right. Two men stood by the car. One leaned on the driver's door, his right hand inside his jacket pocket, obviously pointing a pistol at Gusoyn's head. The other was slouched against the front wing of the car, staring at Nell. Their faces clicked. She recognized them; the two gangsters from the deli a few nights earlier.

"Whad'ya think you're doing, doll? These streets are taken."

Meaning, don't work here without paying protection money to the boss, Nell thought. *The next bit will be the tricky one.*

"I'm not working them, ducks. Just want to talk to the girls."

"Well, the boss don't like that. Reckons you might be thinking of moving in on him."

"No way, ducks. Got no interest there at all. Look, I'm going to get something out my bag right? No need to panic."

"We don't panic, doll. Just move slow. And keep your hand off the gun you've got in there."

Nell reached in and found the leather booklet while she stepped forward, off the road. The men tensed a little, but that was all. She took the book out. *This is the hairy bit.* For to do, so her right hand would have to leave the comfort of the Model 50. Then she opened it and showed the badge within.

When The Seer had the NSC identification badge designed, he made sure it looked a lot like a law enforcement badge. Sometimes, that comes in useful. This isn't one of those times.

"I'm National Security Council. So's my driver."

"Feds."

The gangster's voice is loaded. What with is an interesting question.

"NSC? What the hell are they doing here, Joey? They're not cops, they're . . . ." The other gangster, Nell quickly christened him Notajoey, hesitated. He didn't quite know what the NSC was.

"Well, if they ain't cops . . . " Joey was more confident now.

"We're contractors hired by the Government. We're outside the normal run of things; we can do what we like, where we like and to whom."

It's a pack of lies, but it is the way the Mob worked. They'll believe it because that sort of 'outside the law' status was a familiar part of their lifestyle.

"Look ducks, let's stop trying to scare each other, OK? We're advisors to the government on National Security. In the course of some other investigations, we've made a discovery that worries us and our task is to find things that worry us and look into them."

Nell relaxed a little. *If this is going to get ugly, it would have done so by now.*

"Believe it or not, we're on the same side here. Or, at least, I think we are. Why don't we talk to your boss? Joey, you really want me to meet your boss looking like this? Won't win him much respect. I'll change on the way. We'll take our car. I've got some better clothes in there."

Joey held the back door of the car for Nell, then slid in beside her. In front, Notajoey sat next to Gusoyn. To Nell's amusement, Joey was careful not to stare at her while she changed. The drive took a few minutes and ended up beside an Italian restaurant in a much better part of town.

Wonder of wonders, there is a parking spot right in front of the place. Then, Nell realized it didn't matter. *In this company, we can double park in front of a fire hydrant and nobody would do anything about it.*

"We're going in. Not you, friend. You wait here with Frank. Just the doll here. And she leaves her bag in the car."

On home ground, Joey was much more at ease.

"It's OK, Gusoyn. I'll be fine. This'll just be a friendly chat. Their boss might even buy me dinner."

They went in. As expected, the 'boss' was in back booth. Joey went ahead to speak with him, then waved her over.

"This is my boss, Tony Lima, She's clean, ain't no way she has anything concealed."

Mentally, Nell raised an eyebrow. *Perhaps Joey had watched me changing more closely than I'd realized.*

"Good evening, Mister Lima. I'm Nell Gwynne, I work for the National Security Council. Your boy here was worried about us making some investigations. Wanted you to be clear, nothing for you to worry about."

"Feds asking questions, always something to be worried about. Nell, you say? Eaten tonight?"

"No, sir. Been busy. What do you recommend?"

"Sausage linguine is good. Now, what you asking about?"

The waiter took her order and arrived with the plate inside a few seconds. Privately, Nell guessed that another diner would be waiting longer than expected for their meal.

"It's like this, ducks. We were making some investigations into people coming into the country illegally. All tied up with those German saboteurs that landed back in the war. We're afraid some Japs might try the same trick. Lot of Chinese in the Japanese forces now, and there's Chinatown for cover. Anyway, we started to notice something. There's been a lot of connected killings over the years. Street girls found hacked up, mostly around big ports; that's how we cottoned to it. Same m/o. Looks like there's a small group of killers out there, each done for a lot of victims. Frankly, Mister Lima, we don't give a damn about your operations or what you do. That's a police business and we're not police. We're national security and you don't affect national security."

"We did a lot for the docks in the war. Kept them running real smooth for you. No security problems, no food stolen from liferafts when we were on watch. Anybody talking too much about what they saw got their mouths adjusted."

Nell nodded. It was true, organized crime had helped a lot on the docks, particularly on the East Coast bases for the Arctic convoys.

"Right. But your activities now don't worry us. But the idea that there might be a small group of killers wandering around with dozens or hundreds of bodies behind them does. Should worry you too.

"Say, this is good linguine. Thank you for the recommendation."

The atmosphere at the meeting was relaxing and Nell's thanks won her a quick nod.

"But why should that worry us? We don't do the slashing; most times, we only kill each other."

"We have reason to think that one of these killers is going to start up here soon. *Very* soon. If that happens, the girls won't go out; they'll run or hide. John's won't be out on the street, 'cos the cops will be all over. Like that killing back in LA a few years back? The Black Dahlia? Ask Jack Dragna what that did to his business."

"You saying the same guy did that is coming up here? And you're right, Jack was not happy."

"He ain't coming here, ducks; he *is* here. And we want him. So do you. Unless you're using him."

The atmosphere went dead cold very quickly.

"And just what do you mean by that?" Lima's voice dripped ice and acid.

"We all know the odd girl getting beat is a way of keeping the rest under control. We're being honest here. You know that, I know it. So it's an honest question. You say otherwise, I apologize; but I had to ask."

"Right. Well, some work that way, I don't."

Lima paused, then spoke very carefully. "Girls pay for protection, that's what they get. As much as we can, anyway. We find a john what roughed up one of our stable, we do to him what he did to her. And then some. That ain't us being nice; it's better for business that way. Way you describe, may work for the now, but it ain't good for tomorrow."

Still angry, Lima leaned back. "So you want the guy you think is a slasher. Why? We've established you ain't cops."

"You've never been to Washington, have you, ducks? We're a new agency and the established ones try and put us down all the time. We're poaching their territory, trampling their turf. Like another family moving in on yours. So we need a really big score to get us established. Bringing in the Black Dahlia killer will do that. Proving he's done for dozens of others, that'll set us right for years. And, if we're right about these killers, we need a way of identifying them and tracking them down. Before they kill more."

"I thought the cops had the guy they think done the Black Dahlia thing."

"They can't prove it and he was in Russia when some of the killings we've linked took place. We think they've got the wrong guy. Won't be the first time."

The company laughed, breaking the ice that had formed earlier. Nell paused. What she'd said was a fine blend of truth and lies and all she could do was wait to see whether Lima would swallow it. He was nodding, slowly.

"Understand. So you and your friend ask the questions. But keep on asking them after you've got this guy, and you'll have trouble. I like you, Nell; you've got guts. Don't want to hurt you. So don't give me cause. Understood?"

"Understood, Mister Lima. We restrict our questions to this one thing. When it's over, we get out. If we come back, it's just to eat here, 'cause this really is great food."

"Right, so we understand each other. Joey Pants will see you out."

They left the restaurant. As they stepped out, Nell felt compelled to ask. "Joey, we saw you a few days back at the Diner, Hymie's place. Why you pay for the burgers? Never seen that before."

"Hymie's a nice guy; the whole neighborhood likes him. Been there so long he's a fixture, you know? And he always pays up on time; never whines about a hard week or a sick mother. So we treat Hymie right; show people play ball with us, we pay ball with them. Couple of places give us lip and try to pull fast ones; there, we don't pay. Hey Frankie, everything's cool for now. Boss wants us inside. Bye, Nell."

"Bye ducks."

Nell slid into the back seat of the limousine, then sighed a deep, heartfelt sigh of relief as the door closed.

"I think we can mark Lima, his people and Hymie off the list. That makes this a good night's work. There ain't a bomb been wired to the car, had there?"

Gusoyn shook his head. "I have been watching carefully. We are clear. It is time to go home."

Conference Room adjoining Suite 503, St. Francis Hotel

Conrad was sitting back in his seat, staring at the rows of cards on the conference table, when there was a knock on the door.

Malone and Carmady entered, their expressions grim and forbidding. Malone looked at the cards on the table, with understanding.

"We do that too. Good system."

"Seen the new machines? They've got cards with punch holes for each question. Feed them cards in and the machine sorts them all out for us. Takes just a few minutes. Impressive thing to see. They're getting them at Motor Vehicles right now." Carmady was obviously a science follower.

Malone caught Conrad's eye and rolled his own discretely. Obviously Carmady's fascination with new equipment was long-standing. "Come up with anything?"

Conrad shook his head. "We're compiling an impressive list of people who might be involved but nobody really comes to the top yet. How about you?"

"We've got a couple of things, neither of them good. We got a reply back from San Diego. They had a string of killings. Six girls, all pros, sliced up in late '43."

"When Soames was in Russia."

"Right, and they're the same as the sets we've been looking at. That's not the important thing though. Something else has come up as of this morning. Take a read of this."

Malone handed over a sheet of paper.

The victim had been severely beaten. Five teeth were missing, with bruising along the lower part of the jaw on the right side of the face; probably caused by a blow from a fist. There was a circular bruise on the left side of the face, possibly from the assailant holding her face while she was struck.

On the left side of the neck, about 1 in. below the jaw, there was an incision about 4 inches in length, and ran from a point immediately below the ear. On the same side, but an inch below, and commencing about 1 inch in front of it, was a circular incision, which terminated at a point about 3 in. below the right jaw. That incision completely severed all the tissues down to the vertebrae.

The large vessels of the neck on both sides were severed. The incision was about 8 inches in length. The cuts must have been caused by a long-bladed knife, moderately sharp, and used with great violence.

On the left lower part of the abdomen was a wound running in a jagged manner. The wound was a very deep one, and the tissues were cut through. There were several incisions running across the abdomen.

There were three or four similar cuts running downwards, on the right side, all of which had been caused by a knife, which had been used violently and downwards. The injuries were from left to right and might have been done by a left-handed person. All the injuries had been caused by the same instrument.

"Doesn't this seem very familiar to you?" Malone looked grim and Carmady was visibly disturbed by the description of the victim's injuries.

"Same pattern as the first of the Los Angeles killings and very similar to Mary Ann Nichols, the first London killing." Conrad shook his head. "San Diego you said? And '43, that's exactly four years before the LA killings. If that's a pattern. . . ."

"That ain't the San Diego killing. We haven't had the full reports yet, still on they're way. We compared it with the report from London on Mary Ann Nichols and they could be the same person. Hell, sixty years later and the reports could have been written by the same man. I guess coroners use the same language the world over. Training I guess.

Malone stopped and steadied his voice. Inspectors were not supposed to become emotionally involved in the cases they handled but few of them managed to comply with that ideal all of the time. This case was proving one of the exceptions for him. "Only, it ain't Mary Ann Nichols or the San Diego victim. That's Delia Jane Graham, prostitute, found dead this morning. Here in San Francisco. The report is hot off the printer, the autopsy's only just been finished. We've kept it out the papers, but if everything we've got here is right and there ain't no reason why it shouldn't be . . . "

"He's starting again." Conrad's voice was infinitely sad.

CHAPTER FOUR

Late Evening, Suite 503, St. Francis Hotel

"We have to face it, Nellie. We got the wrong one."

Naamah spoke the words very carefully before getting up to refill her glass. She'd miscalculated slightly. The bottle of Italian champagne was too far away for her to reach without taking a few steps across the room. The problem was that the room wasn't quite steady and the floor persisted in trying to escape from under her feet. She took a deep breath, aimed carefully and took a determined series of steps. The bottle tried to elude her grip, but she seized it firmly by the neck and succeeded in dominating it by sheer force of willpower.

Filling her glass wasn't that easy either. *The hotel supplies proper fluted champagne glasses, not the wide, flat things that let all the bubbles escape.* Naamah frowned at that thought. *It is vitally important that the bubbles do not escape.* Then she slumped back on the couch, mission accomplished.

"I don't see how, ducks; honest, I don't. Druitt had a butcher's flensing knife. Vicious thing it was. I should know, he was about to stick it in me. It had to be him. It fitted; everything did and he was a Daimones, just like us."

Nell eyed Naamah carefully. She'd been hitting the champagne as well, but Nell was rubinesque compared with Naamah. The greater body mass meant she wasn't quite as drunk. *Not yet, a situation I mean to rectify.*

"At worst, he was a copycat, but I don't buy it. Three Daimones mixed up as the killers in this case? Too many."

"Three sets we've got, all so imentrifal . . . " Naamah hesitated and tried again, " . . . so alike, we can't tell them apart. Has to be the same man. Spread over 80 plus years, has to be one of us. We've got sets from '47 and '43 and now one starting here. Wanna bet there's a '39 set? And a '35? A '31? All the way back to 1888? How many does that make?"

Naamah tried counting on her fingers, lost count twice, then finally succeeded.

"*Seventeen* sets. That's a hundred and six girls carved up because we screwed up and got the wrong man." Naamah stared angrily at the wallpaper. *The contractors who built this hotel hadn't known their trade. Built walls that keep going out of focus.*

"Timing doesn't quite work. On that, the London set should have been '87, not '88."

"Right, so he messed up sometime. Did one set a year early or something. And how many before that? How long has this guy been around?"

"Nothing like that back in my time, ducks. Believe me, I'd have heard. London wasn't so big then, and we heard *everything* in my mum's place. Anyway, we've got no evidence of anything before 1943. Jack and Deke haven't turned anything up yet."

"Look at the map, Nellie. He's moving up the coast. First San Diego, then Los Angeles, now here. Wanna bet the next group will be in '55? Say, Portland? Or Seattle?. Now take it back, looks like the '39 set was down in Mexico. He could have been down there for years, nobody would ever know. Even now, villages hardly talk to each other. There could be hundreds of cases down there and we would never know about any of them."

Nell thought carefully about that.

"You know what really gets me about this, love? Conrad. Being right and all. Hate that."

"Yeah. Think's he's so clever. Walks around like he's got two hairs in his ass tied together. I'll slip him some cascara and castor oil before this mess is cleared up, you watch."

"Just like Moll Davis?"

Both women erupted laughing. Moll Davis had been Nell's rival for the affections of King Charles II; competition that had been eliminated when Naamah had slipped a powerful dose of laxatives and diuretics into her evening teacakes. The results had been explosive, in every sense of the phrase, and Moll Davis's campaign had crashed and burned on the spot.

"Just like that. You watch. In the meantime, pretty Nell, our bottle's empty. Call room service and have another sent up."

"*No.*"

Nell's voice was emphatic, startling Naamah slightly.

"I'll call down for *two* more instead."

Next Morning, St. Patrick's Shelter

"Mister Davidson?"

"That's me."

The man working on the broken table eased himself up from under it, laying his tools on the surface as he did so.

"James Davidson?"

"Aye, though most people call me Jimmy. And you are?"

"I'm an operative from the Continental Detective Company. Working for a family back east. No names, no pack drill; their daughter's a runaway. Got all sorts of crazy ideas about being a movie star, you know how it is."

"Shouldn't you be down in Los Angeles then? Hollywood's there, not here."

"Been there, got on the tail of young Nao . . . of the girl . . . but she'd moved on. Taken up with a guy, told her friends she was moving up here. Been asking around up here, nobody's heard of her. So I thought I'd ask the women on the street. They didn't know, but a couple of them said you might. Said your shelter helped runaways. Got a picture here, you recognize her?"

Conrad handed a picture over. It was one of a stock he kept for situations like this. Davidson took it and studied it carefully. Then he shook his head.

"I'm sorry, haven't seen her. I'll spread some word around; there's a good chance she'll turn up here. You're a Continental Op; you know how it goes. Girls like this, they meet a guy who sweet talks them, promises them everything. They go off with him and a few weeks later its 'darling, just this once, to pay the rent' and next thing, they're on the street with lumps if they argue.

"Eventually, if they're bright, they run and come here. I put them up. If they want, I'll contact their families and get them to collect her; if not, at least give them some idea on protecting themselves. Try to point them at a decent job, but want to guess how few of them are interested? I guess they cling to work where they get at least an idea somebody wants them."

"You say you teach them how to protect themselves. The girls say you give them pepper juice."

"That's right. I abhor violence, Mister Continental Op. It's wrong; it's evil. No matter where, no matter when, no matter why. You carry a gun, I guess; most of your kind do. Well, I don't. Never have, never will. Guns are instruments of violence and they're evil. I'll never tell anybody they should carry one. Pepper juice spray is as far as I'll go. You seen them? Pump them up and they spray out just like a water pistol. Gives the girl a chance to run away."

"Doesn't seem much to help a hundred pound girl fight a two-twenty pound man. More likely just to make him mad."

"Better than violence. Look violence is wrong, evil, and that applies to fighting it just as much as the original act itself. Every act of violence starts off other acts; a long chain that never ends until somebody stands their ground and says 'no, I won't do it.' Only then is the chain broken and the evil ended. Well, I'm standing my ground, and I won't do it."

"Not even to save somebody else?"

"No."

"Well, how about people like Hitler? Evil that had to be stopped before it destroyed us all."

"And didn't fighting him do that? Look where resisting him ended up. The Big One, an entire country destroyed. A whole people wiped out, just like he tried to do. Only Hitler only *tried* to wipe out his enemies, we *succeeded*. Is that what this country was created for? To wipe out whole peoples?

"No, by resisting him, we made ourselves just like him. If we hadn't, then the threads of evil he'd started would have died with him. Violence begets violence, Mister Continental Op, and it never ends until we say it ends by refusing to take part in it."

Davidson stopped himself suddenly, his middle-aged face covered with sweat and his eyes bright.

"I am so sorry, I didn't mean to get personal. It's just I feel so strongly about this and when I saw the pictures of what we did to Germany, I wept. Fanatics can be so depressingly . . . ohhh, fanatical, I suppose."

"I have suffered." Conrad's voice was ironically grave.

"I can see." Davidson's voice was equally grave. "If I can have that picture, you have copies, I guess? I'll hand it around, see if anybody knows of her. We'll get a lot of the women in tonight, because of that murder yesterday. I'll do what I can."

Conference Room adjoining Suite 503, St. Francis Hotel

"The Captain of Inspectors called us in today." Malone's voice was non-committal. "Wanted to know what we were doing. I told him everything we had;

showed him the links. Not the London ones, of course; that's too weird for him. But the San Diego and Los Angeles cases. Showed him how close they were."

"And?"

Naamah's voice was steady, which was surprising considering the marching band that was parading up and down inside her head. Nell was still in her room, sleeping it off.

"Like most Captains, he's a thick mick, until you get to realize just how smart he is. He spotted this right enough and guessed we've got five more gruesome murders coming down the pike. And he don't want them on his patch. That's the police captain speaking; the police officer in him says he don't want them on anybody's patch. I told him our deal. You get us Federal assistance without us going cap in hand to the FBI and we get the credit for the busts."

"And we get?" Gusoyn was curious.

"A San Francisco Police Department that owes you people and believes in paying its debts. In fact, we already owe you. If we'd charged Soames with the Black Dahlia murder the way we would have, we'd be the laughing stocks of the country by now. Anyway, our working with you is really official now. Full time; any resources we want and the PD has, we can get. We can even have a radio car if we need it."

"Captain came up with an interesting thought." Carmady stubbed his cigarette out. "Two sets of six murders in twelve years, with the third starting here. Eighteen women, seventeen of them prostitutes. They all went unnoticed. I hate to say it, but Nell's right; when one of them gets killed, it just never surfaces. Most times it never gets investigated; not properly, anyway. But the eighteenth was Elizabeth Short. Now, she wasn't on the game, but the way she dressed and acted, it's a mistake that could be made. A lot of people have; at least half the newspaper stories on her say she was working the streets. So, suppose the killer did the same? Thought she was on the streets and killed her. Then, when the story blew, realized his mistake. What's that going to do to him?"

Naamah sipped her coffee. "He's used to his murders, even the last, most gruesome ones in each set, going unnoticed. So all the attention will have scared him. Even if he enjoys the publicity, it'll scare him as well. So, he's going to take a lot of extra care to make sure that his next set of victims are street women. Not going to take any chances at all. That means he'll take them from the streets, not from clubs or bars. I guess he must have picked the Black Dahlia up from a bar."

"That's what we figure. And that means he'll be using a car, right?"

"That's what I think. Different reasons, but I think so." Conrad had entered the room while Carmady was talking. "I've been talking to our pepper juice friend, Davidson. Where's Nell?"

"Sleeping off a hangover. What's Davidson like?"

"So good and noble, talking with him for five minutes made me want to go out and stamp on a cat's tail. I gave him a dummy picture to show around, just to keep him happy."

"You say he'll use a car. What makes you say that?"

"Check back to the London killings. All the women except Mary Jane Kelly were killed in the open, where they were cruising for trade. Kelly was found in a room. Pattern there is they were killed where they worked, probably because London didn't have any real private transport in those days. Now look at San Diego and Los Angeles. Most of the bodies found in rooms. Where they worked, but *not* where they cruised for trade. Somehow, he had to get them to the rooms where they died. The Black Dahlia looks like an exception, but it isn't. She didn't die there. She was dumped."

Carmady was looking at him curiously. "You sound like you believe it's the same person who did the London killings who did these. Strange way to think."

"Can't be the same person. A copycat, perhaps? But it's a very, very detailed copycat. But everything points to him using a car. Something Jack the Ripper never had."

"We're agreed then. The killer uses a car. Deke and I used our new-found status to go to the Motor Vehicles Division, pulled some plate numbers. Deke was right; that new punch-card machine is really something. Took just twenty minutes to do each search. We tried the fragments we got from the girls first; none of them came up with anything useful. The first one Nell brought back gave us four-dozen hits, over twenty of them green. Lot of green cars out there. Must be the war or something."

Conrad sighed. *I've done my job, Richard Soames would not be railroaded for a crime he hadn't committed. The trouble is, the way this case had grown, I can't just walk out. I've been trapped into doing the one thing I swore I would never, ever do again. Try to find the guilty.*

"If the killer hadn't made that mistake, we would never have guessed he was out there."

"Yeah, and only the Good Lord knows how many people he would have killed before we'd got him. Be grateful for small mercies, is what I say. Anyway, Deke, you did the machine, you do the honors."

"Right. Starting at the top, Nell's friend Tony Lima drives a black Cadillac, what else, 2189 KHG. His hoods, Joe "Pants" Catalina drives a black Ford, 9823 WLS and his mate Frankie "Dogs" Castillo another black Ford, 6728 CBV. Incidentally, Dogs was in stir during the '43 killings, a minor dispute with the government over forged gas coupons.

"We got four hits on the safety deposit boxes. A Jenny Archer, blue Buick, 6671 ELK; Michael Burgoyne, red Packard, 1087 AQR; Jack Webb, white Lincoln, 9605 RKH. He was in Los Angeles; in fact, he's there most of the time but his alibi's solid for the San Diego and Los Angeles killings. Ronald Quilliam, red Chevrolet, 7728 EAN.

"Let's see. We also have your saintly friend, James Davidson, green Oldsmobile, 6780 YAB. Another full plate one of the girls reported cruising at the time Delia Jane Graham vanished, a blue Oldsmobile, 8905 GRK. Oh yes, and a black Ford, 4523 YLA, only that one turned out to be a Vice Squad radio car on official business."

"No mayors, city councilmen, prominent members of the community or local bishops?"

Naamah looked round. Nell had quietly slipped into the room, looking fresh and rested. *How did she do it?* Naamah found herself asking, deeply envious of the apparent ability.

"None, Nell."

"Really?" Nell's skepticism rang through the question.

"Really, promise. We ain't going to hide this one; not at this stage. If we have to, that'll come later. And the decision to call us off will come from much higher up."

"Fair enough."

In theory, Nell should have been angered by the idea of a cover up, but she knew it was inevitable if the killer was too prominent. And busting the chops of two street cops over it wouldn't do any good at all. In any case, the cover up could easily be a sudden heart attack or mysterious car crash.

She was still musing on that when the telephone rang.

"This is Sal. Could I speak to Nell please?"

The voice was tiny, terrified, scared almost witless.

"I'm here, ducks."

"It's Sal. Nell, you talked to us a couple of nights back. On the street, a salt-and-pepper pair? Please help us."

"Of course. What's happened, you been booked?"

"If only. Sandy got picked up tonight. He beat her up, beat her up real bad. Threw her out the car back here. She's busted up awful bad, Nell. Please help us. I got the plate number"

The girl sounded defeated, as if she expected to be turned away, the plate number held out as a feeble bribe.

"We're on our way, Where are you?"

Nell scribbled down an address and turned around.

"We've got an attack, sounds critical. Gusoyn, we need to get out there fast, can you drive Nammie and me please? Jack, Deke can you organize the official side of this? Police cruiser, an ambulance as fast as you can."

The Tenderloin

Gusoyn beat the ambulance by a clear five minutes. There was no mistaking which corner to go to. The streetlight formed a pool of yellowed brightness on the dimmed sidewalk, two women almost motionless in the middle. One was kneeling, holding the other. She jerked around as she heard the car jump the curb. There was raw terror on her face, a look that turned into relief as Nell jumped from the back seat and ran over to her. Naamah was only a few paces behind, quickly taking in the scene.

"Why you holding her face down like that?"

Naamah's voice was loaded with the authority of a Queen and a High Priestess. It was enough like that of a police officer to make Sal instinctively look for a way to run. In contrast, Nell's voice was warm and reassuring.

"It's fine, ducks. This is Naamah; she's a friend of mine. She's a . . . a nurse. She'll help Sandy 'til the ambulance gets here."

"She was choking; I turned her over so she wouldn't."

"You probably saved her life."

Naamah knelt by the injured woman. She didn't add *'and if her spine's damaged you probably crippled or killed her,'* but the thought was there. *First, clear the air passage.* She ran her fingers around inside the woman's mouth; wincing as she felt the sharp edges of broken teeth. She hooked the wreckage inside with her finger and cleared it out. When she did, the blood and broken teeth splattered on the pavement.

"I got the car's plate number, Nell."

"Worry about that later, ducks. When he stopped, did you see anything of him?"

"He didn't stop." Sal's voice was bitter. "He didn't even slow down. Just threw her out as he passed."

Naamah didn't let it register; there would be time to get angry later. Her fingers felt gently around the woman's skull, then down her neck and shoulders. To her relief, she couldn't feel the ugly signs of a broken skull or crushed back. The woman's ribs were bad. She could feel breaks and see bruising. Bruising so bad, it looked like she was wearing a blue-black corset.

"Coats; anything to keep her warm. She's in deep shock and bad concussion."

Gusoyn pulled of his jacket, covered the stricken woman with it, then ran back to the car. There was a blanket on the back seat. Naamah took the opportunity while he was away to look under the injured woman's dress. And winced again at what she saw there.

"How bad, Nammie?"

Nell's voice was quiet.

"Very. She's been raped, front and back. Lot of injuries down there, from the bleeding. No knife wounds, I'd say she was beaten with a heavy belt or something like that. Most of the bad stuff is the rape or when she was thrown from the car."

Naamah looked up as the sound of the ambulance swelled. The siren was much more effective than the bells that had been used until recently. A police cruiser was leading the white vehicle, lights on, siren howling. Sal turned to leave but Nell grabbed her.

"You stay here, ducks. We need you. Sandy needs you. And this time, the cops are on *your* side."

Sal didn't look as if she believed that, but she knelt back down again, holding her friend's hand. The ambulance men were already jumping down, unloading a gurney. Naamah went up to them.

"Severe concussion; deep shock. No sign of a depressed skull fracture; might be a hairline. Back and neck seem OK, but there might be hairlines there as well. She was thrown from a moving car; left arm's broken above the elbow, three ribs at least broken that side, fractures as well. I think the pelvis might be cracked and there's a very bad break below the left knee. Severe surface trauma from the beating she took . . . . well, pretty much everywhere. That's all I've got."

"You're a doctor?"

One of the ambulance men was suspicious. Rightly so, in Naamah's eyes. He had no idea who she was.

"A nurse, from back East."

The man relaxed. She was a fellow pro and knew what she was doing.

"OK, we'll get her to SF General."

"NO!" Nell's voice slashed like a whip. "Nearest emergency ward and best one. Which fits both?"

"St. Francis Memorial."

"Get her there."

"Nell, we can't afford to go there. And they won't let me in, I'm . . . "

"Don't worry about money, I'll pay the bills. You don't have a color bar, *do you.*" It wasn't a question.

The ambulance attendant shook his head anyway.

"No, we're deseg. Have been ever since we handled casualties brought back from Russia. Once they all started coming back, we looked at the wounds, not the skin around them. As long as somebody can pay the bills, it's the same now."

Which amounted to segregation, Nell thought, *but not this time.* By this time, the injured woman was already being lifted into the back of the ambulance.

"I'll ride with you, you'll need all the help you can get."

It wasn't a question or an offer and the ambulance man didn't argue with Naamah's order.

"Gusoyn, you take Nell and Sal, follow us. Deke, you join them, get Sal's statement, see if you can work some magic with the number plate she got."

As Deke scrambled into Gusoyn's car, he wondered why nobody had argued with the string of orders that Naamah had tossed out.

Emergency Ward, St. Francis Memorial Hospital

Sal was sitting quietly now. Carmady had been speaking to her, carefully extracting what she knew. Then Conrad had arrived. His skills, gently applied, had got more out of the near-hysterical woman. In doing so, he'd calmed her down and given her some hope. Naamah had brought some coffee for them and they'd just waited while the clock ticked onwards.

"Jack's over at Motor Vehicles. It's night shift there, but we've lucked out. One of the night-duty clerks knows how to work the card sorter, so we should have an ID to go with the plate number soon."

"Are any of you people her family?" A doctor had come out, at long last.

"I am as near as there is."

The doctor looked doubtfully at Sal. Obviously, the black girl wasn't related to the victim. Equally obviously, they were both street women and that meant her comment was quite right. She probably was the nearest thing to a family the poor scrap had. Which raised another question, but the doctor didn't want to bring that up right now.

"Your sister is stabilized, as near as we can. We've stopped the bleeding; set the broken bones. Given her a big blood transfusion to replace the losses. She nearly bled out. If your friends hadn't moved so fast, she wouldn't have got here. Who are you, by the way?"

"Just friends."

Nell spoke in a neutral voice that made her English accent more obvious. She'd jumped in first, to stop Naamah speaking. Naamah's anger at the vicious brutality was so obvious, Nell was actually afraid of what she might say and do.

"Wish I had friends like you. Look, we'll keep her here, stabilize her. Then, when she can be moved, we'll move her over to SF General."

"No. She stays here." Nell was quite determined on that point.

The doctor dropped his voice. "If I put down that she's to go to SF General as soon as possible, the Hospital eats the emergency care bill. But, if we take her in, the clock started running and the till ringing the moment she came through the door. Her chance of getting through the rest of the night and recovering enough to go to SF General? No more than fifty-fifty. A generous fifty-fifty."

"Doesn't matter, ducks. She stays here."

Nell reached into her bag, took out a checkbook and started writing.

"St. Francis Memorial Hospital?"

"That's right."

"Right. Enough zeros?"

The doctor looked at the check and his eyebrows moved in three separate directions.

"More than enough. We'll know more about your friend in an hour or so. Inspector, I have the injury report for you. My professional opinion is that you should treat this as attempted murder."

"Never intended to do differently, Doc. We'd better find somewhere quiet."

Carmady meant where the women won't here the full awfulness of what had happened. But, thinking about it, he got the impression that the redhead with the dead eyes could tell him more about horror than he ever wanted to know.

Sal was looking at Nell oddly. Especially at Nell's clothes. Expensive and in good taste. Not like the outfit Nell called her 'whore suit.'

"Nell, why you pretend to be one of us? You ain't, I see that now."

"Men out. Girl talk coming."

Nell watched Conrad and Gusoyn back off.

"I am a whore, ducks. Once you are, it never leaves you. I just made good that's all. I was lucky, I had friends I could count on. Naamah there for one; a very wonderful man called Charlie Stuart for another. But we're sisters, you and I. Just look on me as your older sister who got lucky."

"I saw how much that check was for, Nell. I can't repay you. No matter how hard I work."

"You don't have to, ducks. Just promise me that you won't turn your back on another sister of ours when she needs a helping hand. We've got nobody else, ducks; we've *got* to look out for each other. If we don't, if we turn on each other, that's when we end up like Sandy. And, if you make good as well, always remember where you came from."

The door banged open. Malone strode in, with Achillea at his heels.

"We got him. Motor Vehicles pulled the plate and gave us an address. May the Good Lord bless the International Business Machines Corporation. An unmarked unit's on the way there to seize the car now. We get there, we'll pull him in."

"Who is it?"

Naamah spoke tonelessly and that made her words all the more menacing. Malone had heard the same tones used by judges passing a death sentence.

"A kid, would you believe? The car's a jalopy; a pre-war Buick. Achillea, if you're coming, you'll need a gun."

"No, I won't. Don't need them."

"You don't like guns?" Malone found that surprising, completely out of character.

"I love them. I collect them. And knives. Come to Washington, I'll show them to you. But I don't need one. Show you. Draw yours."

Malone frowned, then drew his service .38. As he did so, he felt a smack on his wrist. When he looked down, his hand was empty. Achillea was holding his Smith and Wesson.

"Jack, within 15 feet I can take a gun or knife out of your hand before you can use it. So let's not waste any more time. Let's get this creep."

Location of Suspect, near San Francisco State College

"That the car?"

The uniformed officer nodded.

"We've sealed it, Inspector, for the Crime Laboratory, but we can see blood on the passenger door. The one you want's up there, where the music's coming from. Partying with a few friends, I guess. Lot of students live around here. Landlords make more money renting rooms singly than the whole house."

Malone nodded and led the way up the stairs. The music was coming from the other side of the door opposite the stairs. Malone turned to Achillea and gestured at the door.

"Want to try that?"

Having a gun taken out of his hand still rankled. It rankled even more because, without changing expression, Achillea bounced on one leg, then slammed a kick just beside the door handle. Malone didn't know it but he'd just seen a gladiator's kick that could cripple a joint protected by metal armor. The door didn't stand a chance. It shivered and shattered as it smashed open, the lock hanging useless from the door frame. The room went silent as the students inside registered the crash.

"Police. Don't move. Don't do *anything*. Is Samuel Kincaid here?"

Malone didn't need an answer; instinctively, everybody glanced at a young man standing by the record player.

"Samuel Kincaid, you are under arrest."

"Why? I haven't done anything. I've been here all evening, haven't I?"

He looked at the other students; some nodded.

Conrad's Eye

"That's right. He's been here all evening, with me." The girl spoke earnestly, hurriedly; too hurriedly.

"Your name, Miss?"

"Cathy, Cathy Hendricks."

"Cathy Hendricks, you are under arrest. Hook her up, Deke. Charge is obstruction of justice and accessory to murder."

"WHAT!?!?"

The girl was appalled as she was spun around and handcuffed. She looked confused and horrified as her eyes found Kincaid and she stared at him.

"Sorry, forgot to tell you that. Kincaid here is charged with murder in the first degree. So anybody here who gives him a false alibi is part of the conspiracy."

Malone made an ostentatious show of counting heads.

"Yup, the gas chamber's big enough to hold all of you; just don't all breathe in at once. Now, about that alibi?"

The other students started shaking their heads vigorously. Hendricks was crying.

"Sammy came in about an hour ago, said he'd picked up a hooker on the street but a cop car had seen him. Said he was afraid he'd be arrested for pandering and asked us to cover if the cops came. Never said anything about murder."

"He wouldn't, would he? Let her go, Deke. Bring along Kincaid."

They left, Malone looking sadly at the shattered door as they passed. The music in the room never restarted.

Interrogation Room, Bureau of Inspectors, San Francisco Police Department, Hall of Justice

"You ain't got nothing. I ain't telling you nothing."

"Don't tell them anything, Samuel."

The lawyer spoke, but it was hopeless. The man doing the interrogation always got the answers out. It had got to the point where the lawyer was afraid to say anything for fear of what he might find himself confessing to.

Sitting by the desk, Malone was awe-struck. He'd seen interrogations before, more than he could count. But, the way this strange investigator was

66

working, this he'd never seen before. Kincaid was trying not to answer, but the questions would flow around him and he'd end up speaking before he could stop himself. Malone had stopped trying to take part. Now he was just watching and learning, trying to remember the tricks and the verbal games that were making Kincaid talk his way into a prison cell.

"You don't have to. We've got you cold. The blood in your car matches that of your victim. We found bits of her teeth on the seat."

"Somebody took the car, borrowed it." Kincaid cursed with the realization he'd dug himself in ever deeper.

"See, now you're telling us things. Next stage is you'll start telling us the truth." Conrad smiled gently. "You made a mistake, Sammy; the woman you killed had a friend and she saw you. Gave us a good description. How do you think we walked straight to you? So that puts you in the car with the woman. And has you throwing her out. It's the injuries that you caused doing that, they're the ones that killed her."

"I ain't saying nothing."

"That's right, Samuel, don't say anything."

The lawyer still looked doubtful at the point of issuing advice that couldn't be followed. He'd just filed his tax returns and he devoutly hoped this interrogator didn't work for the IRS.

"That's right, Kincaid; don't say anything. Listen to your lawyer. Then, do as he says while you listen to me. We've got you. Sammy, you interfered with a Federal investigation. That makes this case Federal and you'll be doing time in a Federal Pen. Life, for murder, in a Federal Pen.

"You know what's going to happen when you go down there? A pretty young guy like you, with all the lifers there? Ever heard of a Sing Sing Scrub? It's when they get a floor brush and mix up some lye, really strong solution of lye. Makes your eyes run just to smell it. Then they hold you down and scrub that thing you're so proud of using tonight until there's nothing left. That's East Coast. Jack, they've got something similar on Alcatraz, I guess?"

"Sure have; they call it rubbin the rock."

"Right, so we won't have to transfer Sammy here East. Because then, Sammy, when they've turned you into a woman, that's how they'll use you. And you will never be getting out, Sammy, because every time you come up for parole, there'll be a letter from the Federal Government saying you're a threat to national security. The judgment on your parole won't be 'no;' it'll be 'hell, no.'. Now, tell us what we need to know, and we'll forget this is Federal. You'll do time in State. Lot safer in State, Sammy; the lye is kept under lock and key. Tell us, why you did it. What had she ever done to you?"

Under Conrad's gentle, unforgiving, merciless gaze, Sammy wilted and started to cry.

"I just wanted to see what it felt like. Beating a woman like that. And the other things. My old man said you had to show them who was boss. Why you making such a fuss about this? She was only a hooker."

Conrad mentally gave thanks that Naamah and Nell weren't around to hear that. Then he remembered Achillea was outside and for a very brief second he pitied Kincaid if she got her hands on him.

"How long you been here?"

"Four years." Conrad and Malone exchanged glances. That sort of fit, but Kincaid was 20 years old. That put him at 16 in the previous set of killings, twelve for the San Diego set. No matter who else he was, he wasn't the killer they were looking for.

"Where's your old man?"

"Don't know. Gone away. Used to be a carpenter, but he worked for some priest or something. Got fired, accused of stealing. Don't know what. Haven't seen him in weeks."

"Sammy, when you beat the hooker, how did you feel?" Conrad's voice was still calm, gentle.

Kincaid stared across at the man sitting opposite him. "Ooh, I liked it."

"Well, I got news for you, Sammy; she isn't dead. She's badly busted up but she's got a good chance of making it. Jack, what are the charges?"

"Attempted murder, aggravated rape, sodomy, aggravated battery, driving in a manner likely to endanger other road users. Quite a few more. The District Attorney is having a field day. You should hear the speech he's writing for the press. 'Let every woman in San Francisco know that, whatever her station in life, any crime against her will be pursued with every resource our police department can muster.' Sounded real good. I cheered him on and I know he's a jerk."

"Any chance of cutting a deal?"

The lawyer sounded hopeless. Despite being a public defender, he was a skilled man and knew his client had talked himself into a long, long prison term.

"Full confession, he gets the max and with luck he never gets out. Your client is one sick little bastard, so that's all he gets. He goes to jail and he's lucky. With the statement my partner here got out of him, we could burn him at the stake."

As the Kincaid was taken out, Malone looked at Conrad, shocked. For on hearing Malone's last words, Conrad had gone dead white and tears were trickling down his face.

Conference Room adjoining Suite 503, St. Francis Hotel

"As the Boss would say, the lodge is tyled. Jack and Deke are out, looking after the official side of this business. Is there any news on Sandy?"

Gusoyn looked around, half expecting bad news. Then he was honest with himself. *Much more than half expecting.*

"She's holding on. She's a fighter; she has to be, I guess. Sal's sitting with her, she slept there last night."

"Does she not have to be at work? I thought you said the pimps worked the girls hard."

"They do." Nell's face clouded for a second. "Not this time, though. I'll call our friend Mister Lima later in the day, ask him to ease off on her for a few days. If necessary, I'll make good the income. She'll have to find a new partner though; Sandy won't be working again."

As if on cue the telephone rang. Sitting by the door, Achillea picked it up.

"It's for you, Nell."

"Hi Doll. Hear there was a problem with one of our girls last night?"

"That's right, ducks. Picked up a bad John and got beaten into a pulp. Her partner called me and we got her to hospital. I've paid the bill, but tell the truth it ain't looking too good for her."

"Guess I owe you then, Doll." There was a pause, then Lima's voice sounded almost too casual. "Also hear you got the guy that did it."

"Cops did. We just helped."

"Good." The voice became even more casual. "What happened to him?"

"He confessed. I suppose he's in City Prison now. Look, Tony, your girl's partner, she wants to stay with her friend until we know whether she'll make it or not. Could you cut her some slack for a couple of days? I'll make good if you want."

Yet another pause.

"She's got two days, running from six tonight. Six o'clock, day after tomorrow, she's back at work, or you make good. Fair enough?'

"Fair enough, Tony. And thank you."

"Thank you, Doll. I'll be sending around something to show my appreciation."

Nell put the phone down and looked around. "Sal's got two days. We should know by then."

There was a grim silence for a second. Then Gusoyn picked up again.

"Well, where does that leave us?"

Naamah spoke carefully. "What happened to Sandy was nothing to do with the case that actually concerns us. The bastard that did her, he's a short-lifer, a kid. I suspect we've just got a case here of a brutal and stupid father who brought his kid up in his own image. We've all seen that before; a vicious and abusive father results in kids that follow the same ways.

"We're going to have to accept something. The man Nell and I killed back in '88 wasn't the Ripper."

She lifted a hand to forestall both Conrad and Nell.

"That's not the same as saying the man we killed was innocent; he wasn't. But he wasn't the Ripper. In fact, until now, we've had no real evidence that the genuine Jack the Ripper was a Daimones. We zeroed in on Druitt, realized he was one of us and jumped to the conclusion that the Ripper was a Daimones. So when we killed Druitt, who richly deserved killing by the way, we assumed we'd got a Daimones Ripper. In fact, we've had no evidence, other than that we've had in the last few days, to suggest the Ripper did share our peculiarity.

"But now we have. The correlation between the groups of murders is so close. It would be nice if we could find a correlation for the sixth murder in the London 1888 group, just to tie it down, and some signs of groups in between 1888 and 1943."

"There was one murder, a Carrie Brown in New York, 1891. Pretty much identical to the Annie Chapman murder in London and the Delores Hart killing in San Diego. So much so, a lot of Ripperologists include her in the list as evidence the Ripper went to America after the hue and cry over the London killings." Conrad was still shaken by the interview in the police station. His voice, normally firm and confident was tentative, uncertain.

"1891; the dates fit. It's a direct carry-though from then to our known 1943 and 1947 sets."

"Nammie, perhaps there never was a sixth London murder? Perhaps we stopped the killer before he could complete his set and forced him to leave London. And that's why there's only a three-year gap between the London and New York killing. We interrupted his ritual so pressure to do the next series built up faster."

There was a series of nods around the table. Gusoyn took the lead again. "Are we agreed then that we are facing a Daimones Ripper? One who escaped Nell and Nammie last time around? That is not saying you did the wrong thing in whacking Druitt, ladies. As you say, he needed killing."

Everybody but Nell nodded.

"Sorry, ducks, I still can't swallow it. We miss a Daimones ripper, we get a Daimones ripper wannabee and now we have a Daimones fall guy in the slammer. Too many. There just aren't that many of us."

"Have you got a better explanation, Nellie?"

She shook her head.

"Well, if we assume as a working hypothesis that the killer is a Daimones, then that does rule out any connection with the attack on Sandy. We do not have children after transition and the London Ripper would be way past transition by now. So that rat Kincaid can not be associated with us. It appears poor Sandy was just a street casualty."

"She is a person, ducks, not 'just a street casualty.' "

"I am sorry, Nell; I did not mean to imply otherwise."

"All right. But there is another way of looking at this. If we stipulate that our killer is a Daimones, then almost by definition he can't have kids. But he can adopt one, or steal one. He could bring a kid like that up in his own image; to act as a decoy, if you like. If the heat gets too strong, sends the kid out to do a few killings, get him caught and the kid takes the fall."

"It is possible." Gusoyn sounded doubtful. "I would make another point though. That does not really matter too much. The truth is that the real killer, whether we call him Jack the Ripper or the Black Dahlia killer or whatever other names he has had over the centuries, we do not know who he is or what he looks like. We are no closer to him than we were a week ago."

"In fact, the only thing we have achieved is that Richard Soames is off the hook on the Black Dahlia killing." Conrad was clinging to that; his consolation, the one achievement that he valued in this whole affair. "Which raises another problem, what do we do with him? He's a low-life, but he's still one of us. If he does time . . . "

"He can't." Naamah spoke decisively. "I suggest we let the Philadelphia police know he's implicated in the killings back there, so they'll ask for extradition, or at least for him to be sent over for questioning. He'll go over by rail and we can lift him off the train on the way. After that, we can tell him who and what he is and impress on him that he can never, ever take the chance of going to jail. He can be a crook if he wants, but he'd better be a very good one."

"Company coming."

Achillea was seated where she was to give precisely that warning. A few seconds later, Malone and Carmady entered.

"Well, that's over."

Malone's voice was rich with satisfaction.

"How did it go, ducks?"

"The defense always knows a hearing is going badly for their client when the members of the grand jury sit in their box making nooses out of bits of string and swinging them backwards and forwards. When I read out the statement we obtained, they actually started hissing. Especially that bit about enjoying it. Grand jury made the decision to indict in eleven minutes; they were hardly out of the box. ADA Norton reckons the case is a slam-dunk. Kincaid should be going down for 15 to 20, at least. If the woman dies, it'll be murder one and the gas chamber. Anyway, Kincaid's on his way to City Prison, or should be, about now. Anyway, any progress at this end?"

"Not really, Jack. We have spent the last half hour convincing ourselves just how little we know. Not that we needed much convincing; for all our efforts, we have made zero progress." Gusoyn made an irritated gesture with one hand. Malone and Carmady exchanged glances.

"So the maniac is still out there. Looks like the only place a woman's going to be safe for the next few days is down by North Beach."

"What do you mean, Jack?" Nell was curious.

"That's where the . . . "

Malone glanced at Carmady, trying to find an inoffensive word. They didn't want to offend Gusoyn, but language was having a hard time catching up with social changes.

". . . the homos spread out. There's a couple of blocks down there where they go to meet others of their kind. We, the police, we knew about it before the war, but turned a blind eye to it. We always reckoned that nobody could help what they are and everybody deserved a life. Once the war started, troops on leave from the Russian Front went there if they were so inclined, and that made the area sort of respectable. As far as anybody was concerned, if somebody was serving on the Russian Front, that was all that mattered. By the time the war was over, nobody really cared any more. But it's still their spread."

Mention of the Russian Front caused a brief silence to settle on the room. Conrad had noticed this happening before; just mentioning the nightmare of the Russian Front and the years of pages-long casualty lists would bring even the noisiest party to a stop. The chilled silence was broken by the telephone ringing. Again, Achillea answered.

"For you, Jack. Courthouse and happy they are not."

Malone took the phone and listened, just answering with a few monosyllables. Eventually, he sat down again.

"Well, that saves the City the expense of a trial. Samuel Kincaid was being put on the bus back to City Prison and another bus from the City Prison, prisoners being brought in for this and that, somehow got sent to the same dock. There was an altercation between a prisoner going out and a prisoner going in. Apparently some remarks were not appreciated and it turned into a riot. During said riot, Samuel Kincaid got stabbed and expired. Everybody denies it, of course. Homemade knife, of course; from a piece of bed-spring. That suggests it was a prisoner coming in, but nobody knows. Probably never will know. The CO, keeper and turnkeys will go through the motions, but these things usually never get solved. You didn't want to talk to the guy again, did you?"

Conrad started to shake his head but Achillea interrupted him.

"Visitors, bearing gifts."

She went outside, into the anteroom then called out.

"Nell, it's for you. And it smells good."

Nell joined her and opened the package. It was a giant-size bowl of fresh sausage linguine, still hot from the kitchens. With a card 'For My Doll.' Across the room, Naamah saw the package and ambled over to have a look.

"It's from Tony Lima. I told him how much I liked the sausage linguine he recommended, and he said he would be sending over a sign of his appreciation for helping out with Sandy."

"I wonder if it's poisoned?"

Naamah was thoughtful. Nell jerked; it was something that hadn't occurred to her.

"Why should he do that, ducks?"

"You agreed only to investigate the slasher. Sandy's case falls outside that. And, it could be argued, it was your questions that got her sent to the emergency ward."

Nell stared at the linguine curiously.

"No, I don't think so."

Then she thought again.

"Could be, though; might be he thinks he has to make a point. How do we know?"

"We can't. And if we chuck it out and it wasn't poisoned, he'll know and be offended. That would not be good."

Naamah sighed.

"There's only one way to find out. Where's the china around here?"

The two women searched until they found the right cupboard. Naamah took a china bowl and spooned a generous helping of the linguine into it. Then, she looked at it and sighed resignedly.

"Conrad!"

He appeared at the door and Naamah handed him the bowl. "We've had some food sent up and you haven't eaten all day. Wrap yourself around that while we get everything ready for the others."

"Why, thank you."

Conrad sat down and tucked into the bowl. It really was very good; the sauce was delicious and the pasta done just right. Meanwhile Naamah and Nell were fussing around, getting plates and napkins out, making sure the cutlery was clean. After a couple of minutes, Conrad begun to wonder whether they were making an unnecessary amount of work out of it.

"Do we really need to do all this?"

"The trouble with you, ducks," Nell spoke with asperity, "is that you are so used to other people waiting on you, you have no idea what goes on behind the scenes. You just tuck in and leave things to us. How is it, by the way?"

"Wonderful; excellent. Good pick."

"Sauce not too rich? Not making you feel sick or anything?"

Naamah's voice was filled with concern.

"No, just fine. Perfect."

The two women nodded at each other and carried the food in.

"Dive in, everybody, I'll join you in a minute. Just got to make a telephone call."

Nell looked up the number and called the restaurant.

"Could I speak with Mister Lima, please?"

There was a pause, then a voice on the phone.

"Yeah, who is this?"

"Nell, Tony. Just wanted to thank you for the linguine. Everybody's tucking in now. By the way, the guy who beat up Sandy, he's dead. Got killed in a prison riot a few minutes ago."

"You don't say. Guess there is some justice after all."

"Tony, odd question. How many redheads work the streets?"

"About thirty or so. About the same for Mike Abati."

"As many as that?"

"Sure. Lot of blondes dye their hair red. Ain't good for business to look like a German. Why you wanna know?"

"How difficult would it be to get them all off the street for a night or two?"

"Really wanted to, not too hard. Just tell the girls they're doing a red-head night for the boys. You ain't answered why, Doll."

"Because, ducks, the slasher we're hunting has a pattern. Second victim a redhead. And he's due."

Over the phone, Nell could hear Lima sucking his teeth as the implication sunk in.

"Nell, said it before, say it again. You've got guts, Doll."

Back in the room, Nell sat down again.

"We're running out of time, people. If our killer holds to his previous pattern, he'll be after his next victim in three days. Tell me what these second victims have in common. Annie Chapman, London, 1888; description says hair was either black or red depending on who gave that description. Delores Hart, San Diego, 1943; description, red hair. Sheryl Wright, Los Angeles, 1946; description, red hair."

Jack put his spoon into his bowl.

"So in each set, the second victim was always a redhead. I don't like where this is going."

"We've got no other choice, ducks. We can't get to the killer; we have to make him come to us. I've checked; we can clear every other redhead off the streets. He won't go to clubs or bars. He'll be scouring the street looking for a flame-top. So we make certain he finds one. Either me or Naamah."

"Can't be you, Nell; you're known on the street as somebody asking questions, either a local or a Fed. Has to be Nammie."

"Can't allow it. This is our town, we can supply a couple of policewomen."

"Jack, I appreciate the thought, but how many redheads the right age are policewomen? And can look the part? And we have to keep this tight. If word leaks out, it'll be a disaster. We're running close to the line with the other girls getting called-in as it is."

Malone sighed. Naamah was right. "OK, but you tell us everything you need; we'll get it."

Achillea cut across. "Radio cars, for certain; preferably four. And drivers who really know the streets. When the killer picks Nammie up, we need four cars for the tail."

"Can do that; as for drivers, Deke and I are two. You want me to find two more?"

"That's fine, Jack; I think I know two more who'll fit. Now, I've got three days to get Nammie ready so I can put her on the street."

Nell gave a wicked grin.

"You know, I've been wanting to do that for years."

CHAPTER FIVE

.

Suite 503, St. Francis Hotel

Naamah felt the hand grab her and she was bundled forward, slamming into the wall.

"Nammie, I'm going to get Achillea up here to do this. If she throws you into that wall so hard you bounce, you might remember. Never, ever turn your back on a john. In fact, never let him out of your sight. Watch all the time. Watch his hands; watch his *eyes*."

"But how?"

Naamah almost wailed. Nell had been showing her the tricks of the trade and she knew very well she needed to learn everything she could in the little time they had left. The trouble was there was so much to learn.

"Remember, if they're bent, they want to get behind you; gives them the advantage. So if they start to try something, you should get your guard up. Look, ducks, I know this isn't easy for you. I learned all this when I was ten years old, serving strong drink to the gentlemen in my mother's bawdy house. You've never had to. But, for pity's sake, love; try to learn, right?"

Naamah sighed. "I am trying; really I am, Nell."

"I know; let's try this again. You're with your john, coming up to the door of the room. He seems polite, opens the door for you. This time, the door opens towards you. What do you do?"

"Step through?"

"And he slams the door on you; you're now winded and off- balance. Hold the door for me. I'll show you how to do it."

Naamah pulled the door open. Nell stepped past her, doing a half turn as she did so. As she did she reached out and put one hand on the door, her side of it.

"Right ducks, now look where I am. If he tries to slam the door on me, I've got a hand on the door to break the momentum. Look down. See where my foot is? The door will hit that and bounce into his face. But, if he's just a gentleman who holds the door for a woman because he's wired that way, I give him a pretty smile, complete my turn and hold the door for him as he comes through. All nice and polite, no feelings hurt. You try it."

Naamah tried to copy the move.

"NO, ducks. Don't wrap your fingers around the door. If it slams, they'll be crushed. Enough people hurt themselves by closing doors on their own fingers as it is. Hand flat against the door, your side. Like that. That's it. Try again. There, that's better.

"Now we'll try with a door that opens away from you. Much easier, you don't have to worry about a slam. But, you'll pass close to your john as you go through. Remember to turn as you do so you face him all the time. Try it."

Naamah walked up to the door as Nell opened it. She smiled at Nell and passed through, half turning as she did, then stepped through and backwards, still facing her friend.

"Better?"

"Much better ducks. How d'you like your hair?"

"I don't like wearing it up like this. Much prefer to wear it down."

"Wearing your hair down is bad, ducks. Two reasons. One is somebody can grab it and use it as a handle, swing you round by it. Ever had that happen?"

Naamah shook her head.

"You don't want to either. It hurts more than you can imagine. The other thing is, hair piled up like that is protection. Somebody throws you into a wall with your hair down, you're stunned at best; got a fractured skull at worst. Your head padded like that? You get a bit dizzy, might be."

Naamah shook her head again, appalled at what she was learning.

"Is everything we do because we expect to get attacked?"

"Everything, ducks. Look, a whore with her john is about as vulnerable as a human gets in this world. Perhaps a new-borne babe is more, but there ain't much in it. You have to be ahead all the time. You have to anticipate, you have to expect the worst and be ready for it. Remember, your john is calling the shots. He's paying for that, after all; but *you* have to control him, make sure he only calls the shots you want. All the time. Try not to let him get on top of you; make him want you on top. If you can't help being under, keep one foot on the floor so you've got leverage to throw him off."

Naamah's face was appalled.

"I'm not going to go through with turning a trick. You can't expect me to do that?"

"If everything goes as we think, you won't have to. We'll have people all around you. Some of us'll be two minutes behind you, tops. Sal will be partnering you out there; when a john turns up, she'll cut you out of the game and take him. If he ignores her and goes for you, he's the one we want."

"How can you be so sure?"

"Because Sal is a whore and you're not. She can cut you out so smoothly, you won't stand a chance."

"Thank you." Naamah sounded bitter.

"Don't take it to heart, ducks. You've got looks and you've got brains, but they don't count out there. Sal does what she does to eat. It's her living. If she isn't good at cutting you out, she doesn't eat. And we've got back-ups for her, so you won't be alone out there. *Believe* me on this. If the john wants you, it's only because you're a flame-top. And that means we want him. We're playing odds Nammie, but they're stacked in our favor.

"But, if everything goes wrong and you're with a real john on your own and we can't get to you, you'll have a choice to make. Go through with it and carry on, or blow the cover and throw our chance to get this creep. That's your choice, Nammie; nobody'll think badly of you whichever way you jump. I know this is hard, love; really, I do and I wish I could be out there instead. But, we've got to play this hand the way it got dealt.

"Now, time to practice your sidewalk strut."

Conference Room adjoining Suite 503, St. Francis Hotel

The air was thick with tension. It wasn't coming from Conrad, sitting at one end of the table with an embarrassed look on his face. It was coming from the left hand side. Inspectors Malone and Carmady sat facing two gangsters, Joe Catalina and Frankie Castillo. Every so often, one of the four started to say something and then changed his mind. At the other end of the table, Gusoyn was intent on working with a sheet of paper from his pad. Eventually he'd finished, folded it into a paper dart and flipped it down the room. It glided perfectly.

"Nobody told us there'd be a couple of bulls involved." Castillo sounded resentful.

"Nobody told us we'd be working with a couple of hoods." Carmady was equally aggrieved.

"We need four drivers who know the streets intimately and who can fit in. We have got one strangeness already; the number of girls on the street will be down. We do not want more."

Gusoyn's voice was eminently reasonable.

"In a way, we lucked out that Sandy got hurt so badly, Sal is needing a new partner. Everybody knows who you two are, Frankie; nobody is going to be surprised at you dropping her off with a new girl. Everybody knows who you are, Jack. You show up too soon and the whole game is blown before we start. Believe me, people; we know this game. One day I will tell you about the fun and games we had in Geneva during the war."

Actually I can not, he smiled to himself. *I was not in Geneva, but Henry McCarty was and he tells the stories well. I have a lot of experience of my own to fall back on; though the dates would be rather difficult to explain.*

"We picked this team out carefully; we all have our parts to play here. Jack, Joey, we all need each other, or there will be hell to pay. We have all got a lot invested in this. Joey, your boss got the situation set up and loaned us the girls to make it work. Jack, your boss got us the equipment we need. And, if all of *that* does not matter, just remember that Nammie is putting her life on the line. She is trusting us, right?"

The men nodded. Gusoyn smiled to himself, *Appeals to gallantry always worked. It would be a sad world if it didn't.*

"When the ladies come down, Joey, you and Frankie drive them out to their street corner. I will follow you with Nell. Once you have dropped them off, we will swap partners. Nell can ride with you, Joey; Frankie, you ride with me. Conrad, you pair with Deke here and Jack, you and Achillea work together. That gives us four pairs in four cars, all with radios and somebody who knows the locality in each. Once Nammie has been picked up, we do a box tail on her car. Radio contact all the time."

"What happens if the car radios fail?"

Carmady sounded worried. Gusoyn liked that; he appreciated having people around who assumed things would go wrong.

"I went to an Army surplus place, bought four walkie-talkies. They are not so hot in built-up areas, but they are a good back-up. New batteries, everything. It is amazing what those places have, with the Army being downsized the way it is.

"Talking about armies, we're all carrying, I assume?" Malone eyed the two gangsters with a degree of reserve.

Opposite him, Catalina and Castillo grinned back.

"You bet." Castillo reached under his jacket. ".45 Colt auto."

Catalina's hand moved as well. He had a near-identical Colt; the only difference, it was longer.

"Long slide M1911A1. We've both got the new 8-round mags. What you got, Gus?"

"We have all got Czech Model 50s; they are loaded with hollow-point Tokarev Magnums. Model 50 is the only semi-auto pistol that can take them. The TT-33 and Canadian Browning all use standard seven-sixty two Tokarevs."

"Nice pieces. And you two?"

Malone and Carmady produced their .38 police Specials. Catalina stopped himself from sneering too openly.

"I thought so. You'll need something better than that. Here. We'd like them back when you're done. Don't look for serial numbers; they met with an accident."

He slid two standard M1911A1s over the table. Malone looked at Carmady and grinned sheepishly. It was notorious that the police were undergunned. Tonight would be different.

"Gentlemen, may I present the latest addition to San Francisco's entertainment industry? Sal and Nammie!"

Nell's voice was that of a saleswoman. For a brief second, Gusoyn could hear an echo down the centuries. *'Oranges, will you have any oranges?'*

It was interrupted by the sight Nell had brought in with her. Naamah did not look like the quietly dignified person he'd known for so long. Nell had done a good job of dressing her for the new part she had to play. For a brief second, Gusoyn hated her for making the change.

"Right, we are ready to move out. When will you be ready to start, Joey?"

"An hour, more or less. We start the ball rolling at six."

"Ten to five now. Time to move. Jack, Deke, Conrad, Achillea, we will meet you around Nammie's street corner at six."

The room seemed to empty all by itself. Malone leaned back in his seat.

"Well, I'd never expected to end up doing this. What do you think? Who are we going to trawl up?"

Carmady dropped the magazine from the Colt he'd been given and checked it. Loaded, also one of the eight-rounders.

"This whole thing, the way he does this, it's obsessive; the exact repetition of the way each crime is done. Like a cook following a recipe."

"Good cooks don't follow recipes. That's what makes them good." Conrad spoke almost absently. "But, you're right; this guy is obsessive. Good cooks use their imagination; they change things each time they do them, to exploit strengths or to hide weaknesses. It's the average cooks who take a recipe and stick to it blindly. This killer is an average man; he's got a winning recipe so he sticks to it without changing, without imagination. He can't see that circumstances make all the difference to how the recipe turns out. Obsessive, unchanging, makes no allowances. Just like that guy Jimmy Davidson at the shelter."

"Just like that guy Davidson." Carmady sounded thoughtful.

"He's so strongly anti-violence that he wouldn't even defend himself. Can't be him."

"Remember Nietzsche? 'Stare long enough into the abyss and eventually the abyss stares back.' Perhaps, somebody who stares too long at violence in abhorrence, one day violence stares back at him. What does your card say about him?"

"He's a pastor. Works at the St Patrick's Shelter; drives a green Oldsmobile, 6780 YAB. Takes the 'turn the other cheek' business very seriously. I got his telephone number, KL5-42-61."

Carmady looked up sharply.

"Give me that card a moment." He took out a pen and made two quick marks. "Now, the card you had for the man who cut Sal. Read it out please."

"Drives a green sedan; license plate has the letters OYA."

"Good, now read this card description the way I marked it."

"Green Oldsmobile, 678 - OYA - B. Oh my God. It was staring us in the face the whole time."

"I never saw it either, I didn't even think of it until you read the phone number with that odd spacing. Sal didn't see Oh-Y- A, she saw Zero-Y-A. I think we need to speak with Mister Davidson right now."

St Patrick's Shelter, San Francisco, California

"Mister Davidson? Malone and Carmady, Bureau of Inspectors. We'd like to ask you a few questions."

"What about, Inspectors?"

"Do you own a green Oldsmobile sedan, license plate 6780 YAB?"

"In a manner of speaking."

"In *any* manner of speaking, Mister Davidson."

"The car is here, yes. It isn't mine, though; it belongs to the shelter."

"Are you the only person who drives it?"

"Now, yes."

"What do you mean 'now?' "

"We had a handyman here, used to do odd repairs around the place. Sometimes he'd take the car to pick up supplies. Then, I found he'd been using the car for his own purposes. That made me look around a bit and I found he'd been stealing from the shelter. So I fired him. That was a few days ago."

"We need to see that car now."

"Very well; come this way."

Davidson lead the way out to a garage at the back of the site. He opened the doors and then stopped dead. The garage was empty.

"Mister Davidson, this is very important. When did you last see that car?"

"Why, this morning. I went down to the store to get the supplies for the week. We ran a bit short; the killing, you know. It made a lot of the women come in for help."

"And I assume this handyman of yours had keys?"

"Of course, but I got them back."

"And he probably made copies. My guess is he has a copy for every door in this place. Deke, get to the car; call the others. Tell them we've got a fix on the vehicle the killer will be using. Green Oldsmobile Sedan, plate 6780 YAB. Make sure Catalina and Castillo get the message."

Conrad looked at the empty garage. "Mister Davidson, what was the handyman's name?"

"Drewett. James Michael Drewett."

The Tenderloin

"Did you get your message?"

Fantasia spoke as if she couldn't believe what she was saying.

"Our man is driving a green Oldsmobile sedan, plate number 6780 YAB. Sal told me before she went off on a trick."

The switch had been smooth. The man had pulled up in a white convertible, Naamah had done her best, but Sal had moved in and hooked the man away from her without even trying. As soon as she'd gone off, Fantasia had appeared. Tony Lima had done his part of the operation perfectly.

"That's the man who slashed up Del?"

"The very same, and he cut Sal some time ago. That was when he was just getting worked up."

"And when he comes and asks you to go, you're just going to get into the car with him and drive off? Knowing what he plans to do to you?" Fantasia was stunned at the very concept. "Why?"

"Because we've got to get this creep before he slaughters any more women. This is the only way we can do it. At the moment, all we can get him for is stealing a car and robbing a shelter. He could be out in one to five years; then he'll be free to kill again. It might be years before we catch up with him. So we've got to be able to pull him in for these attacks. And that means we have to catch him more or less in the act."

"You'd do this? For us?"

Fantasia was bewildered. The idea that somebody cared enough about her to risk their life for her was something she'd never suspected.

"And why not?"

Naamah took her sunglasses off. For a second, her eyes gleamed red in the streetlight. Then there was the sound of a car and she turned around. Green sedan. She strained her eyes looking at the plate. It was the right green sedan.

Showtime.

"He's here. Try and hook him away from me. If he still wants me, we can be pretty sure we've got the right one. Don't worry. If he picks you, there'll be a car following you and we'll get you out."

The car pulled up, the two women cruised over to it.

"Hey, honey, you lookin' for a party?"

Naamah was doing her best, but she just didn't stand a chance. Fantasia swung in, across her simultaneously cutting Naamah off from the car driver while giving him a preview of coming attractions. The driver listened to her pitch; as Naamah had to admit, it was far better than anything she could manage.

Nevertheless, the driver was quite determined. He pushed the Mexican girl out of the way.

"Want a party, Red?"

"Got a twenty?"

"Yeah."

"Then we'll party."

Naamah slipped into the front seat of the car. Her nose wrinkled slightly. The man smelled bad, like pork that was starting to turn. As Naamah closed the car door behind her, she watched Fantasia fingering the small gold cross around her neck.

Her lips moved in silent prayer.

Car One. Gusoyn and Castillo

"She is in the car. Looks like we have got action. Call everybody; tell them we are moving."

Gusoyn slid out of the parking spot they'd been sitting in for more than an hour. He timed it perfectly. The green Oldsmobile was already moving and he slipped into position, two cars back but holding it in sight. A quote from one of Conan Doyle's novels ran through his mind,

'The game's afoot.'

Car Two. Catalina and Nell

"We're on the move, doll."

Catalina waited unto the green car was moving, then turned right onto the same road. Now, he was in position, three cars ahead of the suspect. He could see them clearly. He even saw a flash of Naamah's hair in the front seat and, behind them, Gusoyn in his unmarked radio car.

Car Three. Malone and Achillea

"Hail Caesar, we who are about to die salute you."

"What was that, Achillea?"

Malone didn't speak Latin; there was no reason why he should.

"It was a Latin motto, Jack. It means, let the hunt commence."

Malone nodded. He was running parallel to, and roughly level with, the suspect's car, one block to the right. He couldn't see them, but the messages coming in over the radio kept him advised of what was happening.

Car Four. Carmady and Conrad

"We've got the go message."

Carmady looked over at his passenger. Conrad's lips were moving as he prayed to the God he believed had turned his face from him, that the innocent would be protected this night. Carmady nodded gently.

"Good idea. I'd join you, but I've got to drive."

Carmady swung his car out and took off. He was running level with Gusoyn, one block to the left.

Car One. Gusoyn and Castillo

"Looks like he's going for The Meat Rack."

"What is that? Butcher's district?"

"Nah, it's a batch of cheap hotels. Mostly little better than flophouses. Johns take cheap whores there; sometimes, one'll take an expensive girl there. Thinks it will humiliate her, I guess. Bad area; even us wiseguys watch our backs round there. Good area for this creep. Even if the girl screams, nobody will pay too much attention."

Gusoyn watched the green Olds up ahead. Suddenly, it had started to slow.

"Frankie, he is slowing. He is going to turn any second. Spread the word; shuffle coming."

The Olds suddenly turned right without signaling.

"Shuffle right."

Gusoyn and Castillo drove straight on, past the sideroad down which Drewett was driving. Ahead of him, Malone and Achillea turned out of a sideroad to take position in front. Catalina and Nell made two quick rights and a left to take over from Gusoyn in the tail position Gusoyn himself followed Castillo's directions; making a right a block down and taking up position on Drewett's left. They couldn't see it, but the radio squawked out confirmation. Carmady and Conrad had swung right as well and accelerated up to fall into position on Drewett's right. Even if Drewett had been watching, there was no way he could have realized that four cars had just changed position around him and that every way he could take was blocked.

"He'll stay on this road for a few minutes nowl if he's heading for The Meat Rack, that is. Where did you learn to tail a car like this?"

"Geneva, during the war. Guy who thought this up plays the futures market for a living. Used to making patterns out of numbers. Saved our skins a lot of times."

And that is true enough, Gusoyn thought to himself. *Loki and his Red Orchestra ran rings around both the Gestapo and the NKVD.*

"Right, Frankie; it has been a couple of minutes. Radio up; right lateral shuffle.

Gusoyn stayed put for a moment. Meanwhile, Catalina and Nell got into the central lane and overtook the green Oldsmobile. There were two reasons for that. One was to keep the positions of the cars changing; the other was to let Naamah know they were still with her. Then, Catalina indicated left and they turned down a side street. As they did, they saw Gusoyn and Castillo turning left themselves, to take up position ahead of Drewett. Malone and Achillea were already indicating right, turning off so they would be paralleling their quarry. Carmady and Conrad turned out to take up the tail position. A brief radio check and the shuffle was complete.

Castillo shook his head in amazement. "National Security Council you say? Remind me never to get in youse guys way."

Gusoyn grinned at him. *It is nice to be appreciated.*

They did another lateral shuffle on the way, the cars switching and changing position in bewildering patterns. It was the driving techniques that had tailed the hardened professionals of the Gestapo, the NKVD and even the OSS on one occasion - but that was another story - in Geneva and which Henry and the rest of the team there had brought back with them. Even if Drewett had been on his guard, there was no way he could spot the constantly shifting tails that had him boxed it.

"Entering The Meat Rack now. My guess, he's heading for the Superior. That's the worst-named place in the area. It's an old building. Pre-quake, converted into a flophouse and been going downhill ever since. Got thick walls; ideal for your guy."

Castillo was right. The green Oldsmobile pulled up outside a run-down, sleezy hotel with a weather-eroded sign reading 'Superior.' They could see the driver getting out and taking Naamah up the steps to the door. He was holding her arm firmly; not quite dragging her up, but certainly not giving her the chance to argue. Then they vanished inside.

Gusoyn pulled in. He and Castillo left the car. Behind them, Malone and Achillea had stopped as well. As they crossed the street, Catalina and Nell arrived. Carmady and Conrad were just a few seconds behind them.

"Give them two minutes; not a second more. That is what we promised Naamah."

The group paused, literally counting seconds.

"Right. Go."

There was a clerk behind the counter, as seedy and sordid as the hotel he served. Malone flashed his badge.

"Redhead and a man, just came in. Which room?"

The clerk pursed his lips and said nothing. Malone was about to speak. Catalina and Castillo pushed past him. One grabbed the clerk and hauled him over the counter, spreading his hand on the top. The other produced a bowie knife and laid it across his fingers.

"Now, chump. Or which body part do you value least?"

The clerk looked panic-stricken. The two inspectors ostentatiously turned their backs to the scene. Catalina raised an eyebrow. He started to press the knife down.

"Room three-oh-six, third floor."

"Thank you."

Catalina glanced around. No phones, so he couldn't call ahead to warn the killer.

"Let's go."

Room 306, The Superior Hotel

Naamah was on her back, fighting for her life. She was grimly aware she wasn't doing a very good job of it. She'd done the entry to the room right. She'd turned as Nell had shown her, always facing Drewett, but it hadn't done her any good.

The man's charge had simply overwhelmed her. He threw her backwards. The edge of the bed caught her knees and forced her down. He'd hit her hard, in the face; it stunned her for a few, crucial, seconds. At first, only one hand had tried to grip her throat. The other tore at her clothes. Now the flimsy clothing she wore was gone. Both hands were around her neck, trying to work their thumbs down so he could start to strangle her. Once she was unconscious, the rest of the murderer's ritual would follow.

Naamah was keeping her chin pressed down, trying to deny his hands the purchase they sought. Her legs were tightly crossed. It had been almost instinctive on her part. She knew it was been a bad mistake. She'd forgotten Nell's instructions to keep one foot on the floor. Now she had no leverage to throw Drewett off her. Naamah thrashed on the bed, unable to get free of the weight that was holding her down. Her legs ached with the strain of holding them closed. His knee pushed against her thighs with the whole weight of his body on it, forcing her legs apart.

The room was filthy. The bed was worse, probably unchanged since its previous occupants. Naamah didn't want to die here; *not in this dirty room, on this disgusting bed.*

She forced her chin down further. The man's thumbs were working their way down. Pinned as she was, her arms were almost useless. She flailed at him, but he just ignored her efforts. His thumbs reached her throat. His weight finally forced her legs apart. He gave an obscene giggle, then spat in her face again. Naamah summoned her last strength for a last-ditch struggle. She felt his thumbs caress the rippled cartilage of her windpipe.

Then there was a crash. The weight pinning her was gone.

Outside Room 306, The Superior Hotel

Malone and Achillea lead the charge up the stairs. Malone actually reached the door of 306 first. He knew what was coming and simply got out of the way. Achillea didn't even break stride. She bounced on her left foot, kicking out with her right. The old wood of the door exploded under the impact. The hinged side still adhered to the frame, but the lock side just vanished into splinters. Despite the power of the kick, Achillea didn't break stride. She plowed through the wreckage into the room.

Ahead of her, Naamah was on the bed, naked. Her legs were spread; her face beginning to discolor from the grip of the man's hands strangling her. Achillea never consciously assessed the situation or decided what to do. Centuries of experience in fighting for her life meant that the combat part of her brain had assessed the situation, reviewed the options, come to a conclusion and acted on it long before her conscious mind formulated thoughts or questions.

Achillea crossed the room in two very fast paces. She grabbed the man around the waist. With all the speed and momentum she'd built up, she rolled sideways. The immense leverage she had gathered plucked Drewett off Naamah and dragged him away from the bed.

As Achillea hit the floor, she rolled. He was briefly on top of her. At that point, she let go, pushing hard with her legs. Drewett flew off her and crashed into the wall opposite.

Malone and Catalina were already in the room, guns drawn. They would have opened fire, but Achillea was directly in the way. Drewett rose, shaking his head slightly. Achillea watched him. Her body took an odd stance; half crouched, her legs slightly spread, her arms bent and hanging by her sides. Only the classically-educated Conrad recognized it immediately; the traditional gladiator's stance.

Drewett rose to his feet. Achillea bounced and kicked.

Malone had seen her kick before. Intellectually, he realized the force in one of those ferocious foot strikes, but he'd never projected the damage he'd seen done to doors onto a human body unprotected by armor. Drewett's leg bent backwards through almost 45 degrees. His bones gave up the unequal struggle and shattered. Their destruction was heard clean across the room. Drewett collapsed on the floor, screaming.

Within seconds, there were six guns pointed at him; four M1911s, two Model 50s. Drewett ignored them. He was cradling his crushed leg, as if his hands could heal the appalling damage Achillea's kick had inflicted. His agonized screams echoed around the room, causing physical pain in the ears of those around him. Catalina looked down at him with infinite disgust.

"Oh stop screaming, or I'll give you something to scream about."

Behind them, Nell rushed into the room. She'd hung back in the charge; partly not wanting to get in the way, partly because she was carrying a bag. It held her gun, but also other things. In her eyes, much more important ones. In front of her, Naamah was still on the bed, rolling. Her hands covering her face while she wailed. Nell went over and sat beside her.

"It's all over, ducks; we got him."

Naamah's eyes widened in shock and disbelief, unable to credit the fact that the attack was over and she was still alive.

"Nell?"

"Yeah, ducks, it's me. It's all overl you're safe. Told you, you would be. I know it seemed like an age longer, but he had you for two minutes, ten seconds by my count. So we owe you ten seconds. Let's get you cleaned up."

Malone came over. He took off his jacket and draped it around Naamah's shoulders. She smiled, weakly, in thanks.

"There's a wash basin and pot behind the curtain over there. Take her back there; we don't need any evidence from her."

Nell nodded. She carefully lifted Naamah up and took her behind the curtain that marked off a portion of the room. The people surrounding Drewett heard the sound of running water. A few seconds later, a woman vomiting. Nell's voice was clear.

"That's right ducks, throw it all up. I don't know why it helps, but it does."

Malone looked around. Next order of business. "Catalina, Castillo, you'd better get out of here. The place will be crawling with cops soon. Before you go, want you to have these."

He handed over two cards.

"They're get out of jail free cards. Good for one time only. Use them with common sense; you know what we can bury and what we can't."

The two gangsters grinned in response. Malone picked up a cloth and wiped his .45 down, then handed it back. His Smith and Wesson .38 felt feeble after the weight of the semi-automatic. Carmady did the same.

"Deke, get back to one of the cars, call for back-up and an ambulance. Tell them we've got the man suspected of the Delia Jane Graham killing."

As the two gangsters left, Gusoyn stopped them.

"Thank you, guys, and thank Tony for us. Add to what Jack and Deke said, we owe you. You need help one day, need it very badly, just call us."

The curtain in the corner rustled as Nell brought Naamah out. She was wearing the clothes the others normally associated with her and had some make-up on. They didn't hide the bruising to her neck and the left side of her face, or the beginning of what promised to be a vicious black eye. Her hair was wet and plastered flat. Conrad shook his head in amazement and spoke very quietly to Nell.

"You brought a change of clothing for her."

Nell was equally quiet.

"And I keep telling you, Conrad but you don't listen. I'm a whore, not a fighter or a brainiac. I leave the fighting to people like Henry and Achillea and the thinking to The Seer, Nammie and the rest. But dealing with people is my thing. This isn't the first time I've put a girl back together after something like this."

Naamah crossed the room and looked down at Drewett with eyes that were their usual dead expressionless self. Then, she stamped down, hard, on his shattered knee. Her foot twisted to grind the broken bones. Drewett couldn't help himself. He screamed again. Then his eyes rolled up and he passed out. Carmady looked at the ceiling.

"I didn't see a thing."

Malone nodded in agreement, then looked at Naamah.

"Assault, attempted murder, aggravated battery . . . "

His eyes were questioning.

"Rape? No, he didn't quite get to that. Not quite. Achillea got to him first. Attempted rape, certainly."

Outside the hotel, there was a wailing of sirens; three police cruisers and an ambulance. Nell took Achillea to one side.

"Go with Nammie, stay with her through the emergency ward, they won't keep her in, and then take her back to the hotel. Call the Seer; tell him what happened and why. Then call Henry and tell him. Get into his head that he's going to have to be very understanding for a while. Then, sleep with her tonight."

Achillea raised an eyebrow, a gesture that made Nell smile.

"No, ducks, not like that. Just hold her. She mustn't be alone tonight. She'll argue. She'll tell you she's all right but she isn't. Just ignore her and makes sure she's got a shoulder to cry on when this all hits home."

"I don't need to go to hospital."

Naamah's voice was firming up. All she wanted was to get away from the room and back to where the surroundings were familiar enough to be comfortable. Above all, she wanted to be somewhere she felt safe.

"Yes you do, ducks. Just in case there's more damage than we can see." *And there is. It's just inside your head where we can't see it.*

The ambulance attendants came in. Naamah and Achillea left with two of them. Two more started to look at the unconscious Drewett. They winced when they saw the shattered leg.

"That's gone. There's nothing left to save there."

"Wait a minute."

Malone went through Drewett's pockets, pulling out his wallet. "Well, whad'ya know. Driving license in the name of Amos Kincaid. And an address we can check out." Malone pocketed the documents.

"Another Kincaid?" Conrad had a terrible feeling as to where this investigation was leading. "Who here thinks that this man is Samuel Kincaid's father?"

"Fits the description, doesn't he? And was bringing his son up in the same image."

Malone looked at Kincaid with something close to horror. Even unconscious, the man seemed to ooze malevolence.

"Father, I've been a police officer ever since I got back from the Russian Front. This is the first time since then that I've seen true evil."

Conrad nodded in agreement.

"True evil exists, and we see it in little doses all the time. Once in a while, we get a big dose of the real thing and it overwhelms us. We react to it, and, unless we are very careful, we become evil ourselves. That Davidson man at the shelter had the right idea; only, he never thought it through properly. He forgot that all that is necessary for evil to triumph is for good men to do nothing. It's that easy, just do nothing and let the Devil have his way. "

"We did that, didn't we? When we ignored the killing of prostitutes because we thought we had better things to do."

Malone hesitated, realizing the implications of something he had taken for granted.

"No, that's not true. We didn't think we had better things to do, we didn't think the girls were important. And so, this grew right under our noses. Nell was quite right all the time wasn't she?"

Conrad nodded, understanding that the Inspector was having a crisis of faith of his own. "She was. And I never gave her credit for it."

"Father, I'll confess this. I feel like shooting Kincaid in the head, right now. I guess that's what you mean when you said that we had to be very careful."

"That's another thing about evil. It creeps up when we aren't looking and disguises itself very carefully."

Malone then cuffed the unconscious man to the gurney. Carmady did the same.

The ambulance attendant looked startled.

"Is that really necessary? I doubt if he can even crawl with that leg, let alone run. Even an attempt to move it will be agony."

"It's necessary. By the way, the road to the hospital is pretty bad. Filled with potholes.

"Don't miss any."

CHAPTER SIX

The Seer's Office. National Security Council Building, Washington, DC

"Sit!"

Nefertiti Adams pointed straight at the Seer.

"Stay!"

Her hand moved so that her palm was now facing him.

The Seer blinked in surprise, stared at her, then muttered "woof woof." Outside the door, Lillith snorted with laughter at the scene.

Her point made, Nefertiti sat down opposite his desk.

"You're not going to California again." Her voice was firm, yet agreeable.

"I've got to, Lord knows what those clowns out there will get up to next. Naamah's nearly been killed. Achillea's going around San Francisco wrecking more hotels than the great quake of '06. Gusoyn's staging the San Francisco 500 races all by himself and the whole gang are single-handedly master-minding an alliance between organized crime and the local police force. We all know that organized crime pays off elements of the police, but staging joint operations? Give me strength."

"You don't have to. You can't anyway; and, even if you could, you shouldn't. Look, your first trip out there caused some eyebrows to be raised. Why was the head of a Government department suddenly leaving Washington and heading for the West Coast? *Especially* you. Rightly or wrongly, people watch you as a guide to what's happening in the world. When you headed for California, rumors started to fly around the whole Washington scene. Those who were 'in the know' and 'privy to the secrets' were claiming everything from an attack by Japanese bombers was imminent to we were going to pre-empt it with a second Big One. You know everybody's been on edge since the Japanese started to put their Frank bomber into service. There's a guy called McCarthy who's using it to raise all kinds of hell. Wants investigations and so on. Your sudden trip just poured gasoline on to the fire."

"I know all that. For the first time, another country's got the ability to really hurt us and we can't do much about it. But, there aren't many Franks yet; and, by the time there are, we'll have some adequate fighter and missile defenses. That doesn't change the facts of this issue though."

"Yes it does, Seer. We've leaked out a rumor that you were in California to check on the progress of building up our defenses there, with special emphasis on the Frank. That defused the issue, but it still *happened.*

"Seer, you can't go running off handling everything yourself. You've got a staff to deal with the little things, they do already, more than you realize. Handling everything yourself worked fine when we were just a small group looking after our own interests but everything's changed now. We've become a whole section of the government; one you finessed into an important part of the government. You've got to learn to delegate."

"I'm not some sort of control freak."

Outside, Lillith started making choking noises. The Seer shot her an '*et tu Brute*' look.

"Hmmm. I can think of some people who would argue that." Nefertiti sipped her tea. "That brings us to what's going on in California. Sit back and think about it. Strip away all the irrelevant issues and look at it coldly. The way you would a strategic problem. In fact, Gusoyn has the situation under control there."

The Seer started to speak but Nefertiti raised a hand slightly.

"Think about it. For a while, it looked like we had a Daimones serial killer who has been running around for at least a hundred years, slaughtering women. Can you imagine what would happen if that got out? Instead, he has everything nicely contained.

"Naamah wasn't in serious danger; the boys were all around her all of the time. She got beaten; well, that's happened before. And she nearly got raped, which hasn't. And she's been badly shaken up.

"But, by taking that chance, the police have the guy who did it and we know he isn't one of us. He's a short-lifer, That controls the problem. Everything else that happened, did so with minimum resources and in a way that is self-limiting. And we've got a lot of prestige and respect out of it. Tell me, if you had been out there, what would you have done differently?"

"OK, point taken. But it's still quicker and easier for me to do it than to brief and train somebody else."

"Which is the feeble excuse made by every poor manager since the world began. Anyway, on to something else. What's going on with the CIA?"

"The Congressional Intelligence Agency? Nothing. But the President wants DCI, the Directorate of Central Intelligence, reorganized to run the same way as the NSC. Slight difference. In DCI, the Director of Central Intelligence himself will be a political appointment, but we would recruit, train and supply his staff. President Dewey is not well pleased with the material coming out of DCI at the moment. He thinks a lot of it comes via New Dealers who want back into the power loop and are manipulating intelligence summaries accordingly."

"You going to make all the decisions there as well?"

The Seer thought for a minute. "We won't be making any decisions. All we'll be doing is making sure that the people who do make them get information they can rely upon. This is getting away from the point though. All this about catching a serial killer is forgetting the main issue here. We have one of us, Richard Soames, sitting in jail, facing a long term inside which blows us just about as effectively as taking out a front page advertisement in the Washington Times."

"You mean the Post; nobody ever reads the Times."

"Details, details. The fact is the Richard Soames issue is the one that really concerns us and the gang out there are so busy running around playing detective that they haven't even started to address that."

"Well, actually, the details of our friend Mister Soames have been passed to the Philadelphia police, with his San Francisco records and the concordance between his time in Philadelphia and the killings there. By the way, the Philly police have checked his fingerprints and they have a record of him at sixteen, petty theft. So he is newly-emerging; quite a bit early for transition, but Russia and bad wounds might have brought that about. Anyway, Philly has asked San Francisco to send Soames over and he'll be on a train with a US Marshal in a couple of weeks time. Henry's been given a heads up and will be waiting to lift him off. Then, we can have a talk with Mister Soames."

"How did this all get fixed?"

"Your staff did it. You know, the ones it takes too much time to brief and train?"

Nefertiti's expression was that of a cat that has found herself the sole heir to a cream factory. She finished her tea and left The Seer in his office, dropping her cup and saucer off with Lillith as she left. Then, she returned to her own, to continue studying for the role of Executive Assistant to the Director of Central Intelligence.

97

Conrad's Eye

Outside Amos Kincaid's Home, San Francisco

"We're hot to trot, Jack. Judge Weatherbie signed off on the warrant a few minutes ago. He says we could have gone on exigent circumstances, but this way dots all the i's and crosses all the t's. By the way, word that we've got the Black Dahlia killer is already leaking out. The press are beginning to gather outside City Prison."

Carmady had pulled up outside the house just a few seconds before and come running up, waving the piece of paper. Malone read it with great satisfaction.

"Right, we're ready to go. By the way, what's the word on our friend?"

Malone had called to get the hospital report before they left. "Kincaid? They took his leg off overnight. Midway between the hip and knee. Achillea did a good job, there wasn't an intact bone below mid-thigh. Even the splinters were broken. Where in hell did she learn to do that?"

Conrad grinned at the thought of telling the two inspectors the truth; but, in the end, he stuck with something they would believe. "I think she went to school in a rough neighborhood. One where even the nuns wore brass knuckles."

"Has to be New Jersey. She still with Naamah?"

"Still. Nell said that Naamah had a bad night; woke up screaming twice. She's better now though. Achillea's taking her out for a tour of the stores. That'll help. Nothing quite like spending a lot of money shopping to soothe a woman's soul."

"Remind me never to introduce you to my wife. Pity Achillea's not here, though. We're going to have to do this the old-fashioned way."

Malone opened the trunk of his car and got out a 20-pound sledgehammer. Then, he took position beside the door, ready for the swing.

"Hadn't you better try the handle first? Just in case?"

Malone sighed, then tried the door handle. It was locked. Content with the knowledge that Conrad wasn't always right, he repositioned and swung. The lock shattered with the impact. Compared with Achillea's wholesale destruction of doors, it was anticlimactic.

Inside, the house was sleazy and disorganized. Papers were strewn all over the floor; dishes piled in the sink.

"I wonder how long he's lived here." Carmady's voice was weary rather than disgusted.

Conrad decided on an evidential approach. "Look around. Find the newspaper on the floor with the oldest date. That should tell us."

Carmady snorted. "Look, your help has much appreciated, but can you *please* leave the search to us? The last thing we want is some technicality getting whatever we find thrown out. Just stand and watch, OK?"

The two inspectors started methodically going through the main room, then moving around the house. The kitchen was even worse than the living room. There was a distinct smell of rot in the air. On the table, a cabbage had been cut in half; its decay had glued it firmly to the table top.

"Found something." Malone's voice wasn't triumphant; more matter of fact. "Picture of Amos and Samuel Kincaid. Father and son, just like we thought."

"Son was carrying on the tradition." Conrad's voice was taut. "Well, he's dead and his old man isn't going anywhere. So it ends here."

"I hope so, but unless we can find something to tie him to the other killings, we're stuck with the attack on Naamah. That'll put him away for 25 to life, but . . ."

The search continued. They found a few hints; items that confirmed the relationship between Amos and Samuel Kincaid, but nothing else. By the afternoon, they'd searched the house from top to bottom, finding nothing of substance.

"Any ideas, people?"

"How about a loft?"

"We've checked for access. Nothing."

"One thing I noticed."

"We'll take anything at this point."

"The floors are all bare wood, with those tattered rugs thrown around. But, the clothes cupboard, under the stairs? That was carpeted. I wonder why."

"I wonder indeed."

Malone looked at the carpet in the closet, then probed it with a penknife. After a few seconds, he found a corner and lifted it up. The center of the carpet had been carefully cut away and then stuck to a trap door in the floor. Carmady levered it up with a tire iron from the car. The hole in the floor looked threateningly black.

"Can't see anything. Wait, there's some steps. Lord, they're rickety; looks like a home-made step-ladder. Going down now."

Malone felt his way carefully down, then shone his flashlight around.

"Right, there's a string here attached to a switch."

He pulled it and a light came on. A feeble light. A single bulb hung from the joists of the floor above. "Looks like this is the crawlspace. There's a room been built down here; bet it isn't on the planning commission files. Looks home made. The door's . . . unlocked."

There was a pregnant pause. "You'd better come down and have a look at this."

When they gathered in the crawlspace room, they could see why Malone had called. The room was lined with books; every book on Jack the Ripper that had ever been published. Pictures from films lined the walls. Clippings from newspapers pinned up; some original, the older ones copies.

"A copycat, obsessed totally. He even used a pseudonym based on one of the Ripper suspects."

"Does anybody want to bet what that is?" Carmady broke the hushed silence, gesturing at a slender cabinet on the end wall. It was locked, but the doors were easily broken open. The back of the cabinet was lined with pictures.

"His trophy wall. Those are photographs of pictures showing the original Ripper killings at the top. Look at the sets underneath; he's posed the bodies so the pictures are identical." Malone pointed at the first picture of the fourth set. "Delia Jane Graham. I'll bet if we look around this crawlspace, we'll find out where he processes his pictures. He doesn't send those down to the drugstore."

"Elizabeth Short." Conrad pointed at the last photograph of the third set. "There's your link. You've got the Black Dahlia killer."

"And the San Diego killings. They're the second set. I wonder where the first set were taken. Any one of the big cities, I suppose. You know, if he hadn't made a mistake and killed Elizabeth Short, nobody might even have put this together."

"You're right there. Nell had the truth of it. Nobody gave a damn about a few whores being sliced. Only when one wasn't a whore, then it became the big mystery."

"I can't say anything, because Nell was right and we're all wrong. Somebody should have cared and nobody did. Us most of all, because we're cops and it was our job to care; only we didn't."

Malone spoke sadly. A sense of grievous sin weighed on his soul. This was something he would make a special trip to church over; a special confession dedicated to how he'd failed.

"Conrad, please tell Nell she has my word on this. Deke and I will find out who those first set of women were, even if we have to visit every police department in America. We'll find them, we'll give them back their names and there'll be an accounting for their deaths."

Conrad nodded. It was a start, at least; one that would put Nell's mind at ease. Then something occurred to him. "This is his trophy room right? Where he keeps souvenirs to remind him of his kills? Nine times out of ten, they're items of clothing or jewelry. Here, we can be sure it's the latter. So why did he put the jewelry in a safety deposit box?"

Manager's Office, Community Mutual Bank

"Do you recognize this man, sir? Is he one of your safety deposit box holders."

"The older man, this one, no. The young man, yes. He held one of the boxes that was robbed. Poor young man, I remember him well. He told us that he was going to college and wanted somewhere safe to keep his papers and some valuables. Didn't trust a college dorm. And to think we let him down."

There was a knock on the door. A secretary stuck her head through, "Sorry to disturb you gentlemen, but the Chief of Police is about to make a public statement on the radio."

"Do you mind?" The bank manager turned the radio on. He was just in time to catch a station ID, then the Irish brogue of the Chief of Police filled the room.

"My fellow citizens, I am pleased to announce that the Bureau of Inspectors have, with the assistance of a Federal Task Force, arrested a man in connection with a series of killings in California over the last twelve years. One of these killings is that of Elizabeth Short, better known as The Black Dahlia. This arrest follows an investigation into the killing of a local citizen, Delia Jane Graham. I feel humbled to note how every sector of San Francisco society pulled together in the effort to prevent further killings of this type in our city. I am even informed that members of the organized crime syndicates came forward to provide valuable assistance in the investigation. Surely nothing can confirm San Francisco's standing as the leading example of Californian virtues than the way we have all come together to put this vicious criminal out of business. On behalf of everybody I thank you all, especially our inspectors and the brave policewoman who acted as a decoy in springing the final trap."

"Well, that's one in the eye for the Los Angeles PD." Carmady's voice was smugly satisfied. He and Malone had flipped a coin to see who made the call to the Captain of Inspectors and then brief the Chief of Police, telling him the case had been tied to the Black Dahlia. Carmady had won and had the privilege of hearing his topmost superior actually dancing with glee.

"Who have you arrested?" The bank manager was curious.

Malone reached over and tapped the picture. "Him," pointing to the older man. Then to the younger man. "That was his son; started following in his father's footsteps, but he was sloppy, careless and we got him. Then he got shanked in prison."

"That nice young man . . . he killed a woman?"

"Not quite; his victim's still in a coma. Don't know when or if she'll come out. Anyway, sir, thank you for your assistance. We'll need to keep working on identifying all the owners of those boxes."

Outside, Malone turned to Conrad. "Well what do you make of that?"

"Young boy grew up in that atmosphere. He said how his father kept on about 'showing them who's boss.' I shudder to think how his mother died, but everything I know about cases like this tells me that he watched every minute of what happened to her. My guess is that he could see the next cycle starting again and, for some reason we can't guess at, decided to run away. He stole the jewels, put them in a safety box and wanted to use them to fund his way through college. But, brainwashing from childhood caught up with him I don't think he could help himself. Then he was killed. Being robbed and deserted by his son, then fired from his job, pushed his father over the edge. Then, when his son was arrested and killed, that really sent him wild."

Conrad stared thoughtfully at the sky. "Amos Kincaid killed the Black Dahlia - and a lot of other women. Samuel Kincaid was following in his father's footsteps. Have you ever wondered about Amos Kincaid's father? And whether the line of serial killers goes back to 1880s London?"

Malone stared at Conrad with dawning horror on his face. "A family with each successive generation devoted to butchering women? Serial killing a tradition being handed down from father to son? That's a thought worthy of Hell itself."

Conrad nodded slowly, the enormity of the picture sinking in on him as well. *Does the line go back just to 1880's London? Or does it go back further still? Is this the family that gave birth to the legend of Sawney Bean? Or Christie-Cleek? Dear God have mercy on us, for there is more than one way for something to be immortal. Last night we may have looked into the face of the Devil himself.*

CHAPTER SEVEN

Bureau of Inspectors, San Francisco Police Department, Hall of Justice, Three Months Later

"There's a speck of dust on the right hand corner."

Lieutenant Jack Malone looked at his new desk, then carefully reached out and moved the name label about a quarter of an inch to the left. That made it look a little more centered. Then he checked the right hand corner. He didn't think he could see any dust. Behind him, Lieutenant Deke Carmady snickered.

"So, is the verdict in?"

Malone could feel his gut tense up as he asked. The case had gone through on the fast track. The Assistant District Attorney had said it was a slam-dunk, and he was still tense. He and Carmady had got their promotions as a result of nailing the Black Dahlia Killer, and yet he was still worried about it. *What if something has gone wrong, if the Jury had somehow, for some reason defied common sense. What if they had ignored the slam-dunk case and let Amos Kincaid walk?*

"Yes. Few minutes ago. At the 14th Section of the Superior Court of San Francisco . . . "

"Oh, get on with it." Malone grunted.

"The jury found Amos Kincaid guilty in the charge of murder in the first degree of Delia Jane Graham and guilty in the charge of murder in the first degree of Elizabeth Short."

"YES!"

Malone couldn't restrain himself. Two convictions of murder in the first degree meant the gas chamber. And, if anything went wrong, if the conviction was tossed for any reason, they had six more slam-dunk murder charges to make sure it didn't happen again. Even more, whatever happened now, it was official. They'd got the Black Dahlia Killer

"Should we tell our friends from Washington?"

"They'll know. They probably knew before we did. Did that bunch strike you as a bit odd?"

"Yeah. They're Feds though. Probably explains it. You know, it's been kinda dull here since they left."

"Well, perhaps this will change things."

Malone picked up his desk sign again, looked fondly at the word 'Lieutenant' and positioned it carefully once more. Quietly, Carmady promised himself, he'd steal that sign as soon as he got the chance. "Remember that guy Richard Soames?"

"Sure, the one we picked up before we nailed Kincaid. The one, Conrad was so determined to prove didn't do it."

"Yeah, *that* Richard Soames. Philadelphia came through with an extradition warrant for him, connected with a string of prostitute killings there. Looks like Soames was good for them, so the Marshals took him back there to answer questions. Or tried to."

"Tried to?" Carmady felt a sense of growing unease. "I don't like the sound of that. What happened?"

"He was being escorted by two US Marshals. Anyway, it appears a confederate of his slipped something in their coffee and sent them both to sleep. When they woke up, he was gone. Train never stopped and he sure as hell wasn't on it. Both the US Marshal's office and Philly have got egg all over their faces. There's a warrant out for Soames now. It's possible he may come back here."

"Unlikely, but it doesn't matter, Jack. You know his kind; he's a low life, a dirtball. Six months, a year, he'll pull some stupid stunt, stick up a likker store or swipe an old lady's purse. Whatever he fondly thinks is the perfect crime. He'll be busted or killed in the act, they'll take his dabs and he's nailed."

"You don't think our friend helped him out? He was mighty determined to prove Soames didn't do the killings."

Carmady shook his head. "He wanted to prove him innocent, not get him out. Anyway, he isn't the kind. Whoever he really is, he's a good man. I mean real good, deep inside."

Carmady thought for a few seconds. "So Soames had a partner who busted him off a moving train? Just who the hell does he think he is, Billy the Kid or something?"

The Sunrise Diner

"So did you see the guy in the place about doing the thing with the person?"

Anthony Lima nodded carefully and held up five fingers. It had cost five thousand dollars to set up the killing of Amos Kincaid. One day, soon, he'd be taking a shower or in the exercise yard and there would be a scuffle. A quick stab with an improvised knife and he'd be dead. Nobody at this meeting was naive enough to believe it was being done to avenge the girls he'd killed. Not directly, anyway. It was being done to show what happened to people who crossed the mob. No matter what happened to them, no matter where they went, the mob would find them and exact a just, dispassionate revenge.

Behind the counter, Hymie Lowenstein nodded contentedly. San Francisco had to run smoothly and efficiently and the last thing the boss of the San Francisco Family wanted was to end up in jail himself. So he lived here, quietly, unobtrusively, the gentle, good-natured, old man who everybody liked and everybody trusted. The "public" faces of the Family bosses came and went. Tony Lima was just the most recent of many. He'd be gone soon enough; arrested by the cops, or whacked by a jealous subordinate. Another would take his place and the Family Consiglieri would take him to one side and tell him the startling truth. That the glamour and the authority were all his, but he would take his orders from the quiet old man who ran a deli in one of the worst parts of town.

"The Feds have gone?"

Lima nodded. "They left as soon as he was indicted. Just quietly pulled out in the night. Nell didn't even say goodbye."

"The British woman? She'll be back. She owes you for the help and she's the kind who'll remember. If she does, bring her here and I'll make her a pot of tea. She'll enjoy that."

The two men, the one who everybody thought was the Family boss and the one who really held the power, talked quietly for another hour, sorting out some family business. The Black Dahlia Killer was condemned to death by both the forces of the law and the underworld, but the business of running the city's crime carried on.

Conference Room, The White House, Washington DC.

"So how did the National Security Council get involved in the Black Dahlia killing?" President Dewey sounded curious more than disturbed.

Well, it had worked before, The Seer thought, *let's try it again*. "Sir, we were investigating the possibility that saboteurs may be landed by submarine to sabotage activities in our factories and ports. The Germans tried that several times during the War, with a signal lack of success. Due to the vigilance and efficiency of the Federal Bureau of Investigation . . . "

President Dewey saw J. Edgar Hoover drop his petulant air and suddenly start listening intently. *Odd,* he thought, *I never considered The Seer a politician. A brilliant strategist, yes, but never a politician. Perhaps one of his staff was the political brains.*

"... we nailed nearly all of the saboteurs before they could do any harm. In all of the War, there was only one case of industrial sabotage, at the Brewster Aviation plant."

A murmur ran around the table. The Brewster Aviation sabotage had been a carefully guarded secret at the time. A saboteur had infiltrated the plant and a batch of F3A Corsairs had been delivered with their arrester hooks three quarters sawn through. If they'd reached the fleet, they could have caused serious deck accidents. The case had caused an investigation of the whole company, as a result of which it had been peremptorily closed.

"However, another point concerned us. Nuclear weapons are getting smaller all the time. One day it may be possible to build one that can be carried by a man. Or we may see them smuggled into the country by ship. So we started to look into port security. In doing so, we were struck by the number of gruesome murders that took place around such places. By sheer coincidence, we were examining port security in San Francisco when the latest series started and we were able to provide the police with some small assistance. Mister Hoover, could I ask a favor of you? Could your organization take the credit for that aid? I do not wish our involvement in this whole affair to become too widely known. We have no official investigative authority, of course."

Hoover nodded, his face a picture of conflicting emotions.

The Seer carried on smoothly. "I think it is obvious though that there are more mass murderers around than this case can account for. The Black Dahlia killer escaped justice for so long because each set of killings was local and did not therefore involve the FBI. The local police forces had no means of sharing information, so the patterns were never seen. I would therefore like to propose that the Federal law enforcement agencies start a central file for the collection of information on murders; particularly those who have a specific sexual dimension. This file can use the new punch card systems being developed by IBM. Local police can feed details of a homicide they feel may be appropriate into the file, or they can consult it to identify similar homicides. I would suggest this file be administered by the FBI and their funding be adjusted to accommodate the added cost."

Dewey looked at Hoover. The Director of the FBI had an almost dreamy expression of delight on his face. He'd come into this meeting ready to repel an attack on his turf, only to find the expected attacker was a staunch ally. Hoover was a man who always paid his debts and liked to do so as quickly as possible so they wouldn't be hanging over him. His reply confirmed that impression.

"This affair has revealed something else. National security requires active investigation as well as passive analysis. I believe that the National Security Council should have an investigative arm of its own, a small one, of course, assigned to look into cases that do not fall under the remit of existing agencies. Following the death of Director Donovan, the NSC has already absorbed most of the OSS. Rather than disband what is left as we had planned, we should use it to form the core of that investigative arm."

Dewey looked around the conference table. "Our primary duty is to protect the citizens of the United States. I believe that this both these proposals should be instituted with immediate effect. Director Hoover, you will implement the National Security Council recommendation immediately, using funds from the Government's contingency reserve. Seer, your NSC will use the rump of the OSS as the basis of your own investigative group. But, I will have nothing that could grow into a political police in this country. Your group will, therefore, have no powers of arrest. In the event of one of your investigations leading to the necessity of making arrests, you will transfer the case to either local law enforcement or to the FBI, depending on circumstances. Now, moving to our next topic."

Nell Gwynne's Office, NSC Building, Washington DC

"Lord Charles de Vere Beauclerk, Thirteenth Duke of St Albans." The secretary's voice was awed. It always amused Nell how even the most republican of Americans were impressed with titles.

"Charles, it's good to see you again ducks. I just wish the circumstances could be happier."

St Albans smiled sadly. "Obby was getting on, Eleanor, and the war was a terrible strain for him. I think he hated seeing how low England has sunk. There's light at the end of the tunnel now and I think he hung on just long enough to see it. Still, he had a good innings; had his three score and ten plus a few extras."

"And he served England well, ducks; never forget it. As did you and don't forget that either." Despite his years, Osbourne de Vere Beauclerk, 12th Duke of

St Albans, had been the head of the British Resistance movement, running the network under the very noses of the Germans who could not believe such an aged and eccentric man could hold such a position. His cousin Charles had been a Colonel in British intelligence and responsible for coordination with the Americans and Russians. The strain had been telling on them both. The 12th Duke had gravely harmed his health and shortened the few years he had left; the present 13th Duke had been matured beyond his years.

"So, this is the National Security Council. You've settled in well, Eleanor." There was almost a note of reproof in St Alban's voice.

"America's my home now."

St Albans nodded. He could understand that. But, his duty was with England and to rebuild England, to make her more than she had been before. To put the past behind her and prepare her for the future.

"Anyway, Obby wanted you to have this."

'This' was a gold ring with a carnelian cameo portrait of Charles I, who had given it to his confessor just before his execution. It was a Beauclerk family heirloom.

Nell glanced at the door. It was closed and her office was secure.

"That was kind of Obby, and it was kind of you to bring it Charles."

"It was no trouble." St Alban's voice dropped. "Great-Grandmother."

Tenement House, San Antonio, Texas.

"So, where do we go from here?"

Conrad leaned back in his chair, looking at Richard Soames with dislike. Not all people who were innocent of the crimes they had been accused of were nice. Soames was definitely not.

Across the room, Naamah nestled comfortably in Henry McCarty's arm. She hadn't been away from him in the time since they had come back from San Francisco. Her recovery had been quick; physically, at least. Mentally, it was slower, although the nightmares and the fear had left her at last. Achillea sat between Soames and the door. That both of the Circle's heavies were in the room wasn't a coincidence.

The other occupant was Richard Soames. He was sitting at the table, his face gleaming with anticipation and glee. He'd been told of his heritage and what it implied. Also, that he had to keep in the shadows, keep out of sight, not draw attention to himself. Naamah looked at him and saw the gleam of calculation on his face. For a second, she had a flashback; Amos Kincaid spitting in her face. Nobody had ever done that to her before. It had shocked her more than any other part of the two minutes she'd spent pinned on that bed.

"Philly has a warrant out for you. San Francisco also. You'll have to see that you stay out of sight until they expire." McCarty spoke gently. "We all know the San Francisco warrant is good. It'll stick. Will the Philly warrant?"

Soames looked around, his eyes gleaming. Not red, the way the women's eyes shone when the light was right, but silver. It was a gleam of lust, greed and pure, undiluted evil.

"Yeah, I was fourteen. Big for my age. Wanted to try it, so I went to a hooker, one on the street. I'd done a store to get the money *and she laughed at me.* Told me to run home to my mother. So I waited in the shadows until she passed and I stuck her. Right in the liver. And I slashed her while she was down, so she'd know she was dying ugly. Couple of other times when they laughed at me, gave them the same. What of it?"

"It's a problem. No statute of limitations on murder. Only, being 14, they'll probably put you away."

"And you can't afford that can you?" Soames voice was triumphant. "You have to make sure I don't get caught. In fact, I can do whatever I like, can't I? You have to cover for me; because, if I get caught and go down, you all go down with me. So it isn't a problem, not for me. It's for you; you deal with it. And, for your sakes, you'd better deal with it damned well."

"Let's calm down and think about this."

Naamah got up and took a handful of beer bottles from a case and put them on the table.

"We've been talking for hours. Henry, want a beer?"

"Please, Nammie."

She picked out a bottle at random, used the bottle-opener to uncap it with the ease of long practice and handed it over. McCarty gulped it down. His mouth was dry; partly from talking but also from the knowledge that all of the talk had been futile. It was obvious to him that this conversation, this conference, whatever it was called, would only end one way. In his eyes, the only question left was whether he or Achillea would end it.

"Achillea?"

She nodded. Naamah opened another bottle with a quick flip of the opener and passed it over.

"Anybody else?"

"I'll have that one."

Soames pointed at a specific bottle. Naamah picked it up, unscrewed the cap with her hand and passed it over. Soames gulped it down.

"You can think about it. I'm going to go now. And you had better start looking after me. *Whatever* I might decide to do."

He stomped out the room, out of the building and made off down the street.

"Well, I don't think we can consider this to be one of our more successful inductions." The Seer sighed and shook his head. Transition was the most dangerous time for a Daimones, having to deal with a wrenching change in their whole outlook on life at a time when they were sick and ill. It had been worse before the stable groups had formed and were available to help with adapting to the changes.

"Shall I follow him?" Achillea had drawn a knife, her favorite Bowie. The message was obvious.

"You can't do that!" Conrad was horrified. "You can't kill a man for what he might do!"

"I already have, Conrad." Naamah's voice was icy. "It was in his beer."

EYE OF THE DECIEVER
Birmingham, England, 1956

Conrad's Eye

CHAPTER ONE

Site of the CBAF, Castle Bromwich, Birmingham, UK, 1956

The devastation was total. The car factories, the Castle Bromwich Aircraft Factory, the airfield; everything had been blasted into ruins. More than two-dozen B-36s had dropped over a thousand tons of bombs in a few seconds onto what had once been a thriving industrial area. It hadn't been the number of bombs, or even the total weight that had been devastating; it had been the fact that they had been delivered within a few seconds. A thousand tons of bombs delivered in less than a minute was a very different thing from the same weight dropped over a period of hours. Even now, more than a decade after the bombing, the area was still a hopeless ruin, quickly reverting to a pre-industrial wasteland.

That isn't strictly true, Constable George Skelton thought to himself. Pre-industrial wastelands didn't have brick ruins sticking out of them; didn't have masses of rusty iron on the ground, waiting to snare an unwary foot. Nor did they have unexploded bombs ready to kill unsuspecting victims. It wasn't as if the wreckage here was just industrial; there had been houses as well, nestling in between the great factories. The worker's homes had died with the factories; their owners were still buried down there, somewhere. The bombing had caved the air raid shelters in, sealing their occupants under hundreds of tons of dirt and rubble. There was talk, now, of going in and recovering the bodies; trying to give them decent burial. Britain was richer; it was recovering at last from the occupation and the long years of bleak recession that had followed. Now, there was money for gestures like trying to recover the bodies of those who had died on the last day of the war. Perhaps, once that was done, this desert of bomb craters could be returned to something useful.

Until that time came, Skelton would continue to patrol the area. After the war, it had been a sanctuary for criminals. During the day, children would ignore their parent's orders and play in the ruins and craters; but, at night, black marketers had worked out of the area. It was rumored they had even used the ruins to raise animals, better not to ask what kind, for meat. That racket had been prosperous enough for the black marketers to protect by killing, as some police had found out to their cost. The black marketers had faded away, to be replaced by a different sort of criminal, but one no less dangerous. Food rationing was still in place, nowhere near as strict or all encompassing as it had been, but it was still there and that meant a black market still existed. Where there was rationing, there were those who sought to find a way around it.

Here, in the Midlands, there was little sympathy for what had happened to German cities during The Big One. The destruction wrought by the conventionally armed B-36s had been too great for that. Yet, Skelton knew that the havoc here had been only a pale shadow of what had befallen Germany. The destruction there was total and universal; here, it was restricted to major military industries and bases. Even in those cases, there were pockets where the bombs had left some semblance of structures standing. Skelton was approaching one such patch now. By a freak of chance, perhaps a wind shift that had moved the stream of bombs a fraction to one side, a small group of houses had partially survived. Their roofs had gone, their windows and doors blown in, their walls scarred and ripped, but the shells were still standing.

In the past, these few standing houses had been the sites of some of the illegal activities the area had been infamous for. Even now, Skelton approached them with caution. He saw a hint of movement from there. *An animal, perhaps? Or a more than usually adventurous child?* He took a firmer grip on his truncheon and went inside.

Less than 30 second later, Skelton was out again, vomiting helplessly onto the ground.

Solihull, 36 hours later

There was a very distinctive sound to a mob that was bent on murder. A normal mob was a chaotic thing. It had no sense of direction or purpose; even if it acquired one, it would be short-lived and quickly forgotten. A lynch mob had unanimity of purpose; one that was evident in its sound and movement. Conrad Lorentz had heard lynch mobs before and he knew he was hearing one now. He knew something else about lynch mobs; the person they chased and killed was very rarely guilty of anything more than being in the wrong place at the wrong time. He knew now why he had found his footsteps being drawn here; once again, he was being lead to an innocent who needed saving. Almost without thinking, or making the decision, he broke into a run, heading for the sound of the mob closing in on its prey.

It was a small mob, no more than a dozen men. It was none the less dangerous for that. A dozen men can kill just as efficiently as a hundred; perhaps more so. This mob had gathered around a doorway, trapping two police officers. The abuse was verbal at this point; Conrad knew that bricks would soon follow, then boots, and the lynch mob would draw the blood it wanted.

Once, the presence of the police would have been a shield against such mobs. No longer. Quite unfairly, quite unreasonably, the British police had been tarred with the brush of collaboration. Sensible, intelligent people pointed out that the law had to be upheld. Murderers, rapists and robbers were all still murderers, rapists and robbers, whether Halifax or Churchill was Prime Minister, and it was the Police's duty to arrest those who committed such offenses. But prejudice and bigotry were never sensible or intelligent. The police had been seen as the tools of the Halifax government and their reputation had been stained. Some argued, irretrievably; others said that, given time, the old ways would return as the sting of occupation faded. That didn't matter. What mattered was the here-and-now.

Conrad broke out of his run, returning to a fast walk. *Running now conveys the wrong image.* He could see the situation better. The two police officers had a third man with them; one who was obviously under arrest. Equally obviously, it was that man the mob wanted. Conrad nodded to himself. His earlier guess was right. *Here is the man who needs saving; this was why I had felt my footsteps directed here.*

As he approached the scene, the first brick was thrown. *A brickbat; part of a brick, anyway. There are enough of those around. Nearly ten years after the war had ended, there are all too many bombed out houses left to provide ready ammunition.*

He would just be in time to do something.

Conrad stepped in front of the little group hiding in the doorway, putting himself between them and the mob. As he did so, another brick flew out of the men gathered there. Conrad could have ducked it, but he did not. He stood stock still as it hit him in the chest. The blow made him stagger slightly, but he maintained his position. Then, he held up his crucifix.

"Good people, I beg you, *stop this*. Let the law do its work here."

"Get out of the way, Father; this isn't your business."

The voice from the crowd was filled with hate, but Conrad relaxed anyway. *When people talk, they don't lynch.*

"Yeah, get out of the way. He killed our Jenny!" There was a murmur of agreement, of rage and hatred.

"Are you so sure of that? Has he been tried and found guilty? Has he even been *charged?*"

Conrad's voice was commanding; he threw all his talents as an Inquisitor into the fray. A slightly abashed mutter of negatives rewarded him.

"Then why are the police taking him away?" It was the same voice from the crowd that had shouted out before.

"Is the police taking a man away a sign of guilt then? How many innocent men were taken away during the Occupation, never to be seen again?"

Too many was the answer to that question, and everybody in the crowd knew it.

"How many innocent men died because of a false accusation made in the darkness?"

The answer, again, was *too many*. The unspoken question, *how many had made such accusations,* hung in the air. Still the answer was *too many*.

The crowd certainly knew the answers. It made them look at themselves in a way that none of them liked. Conrad breathed easier; *the mob mentality of the crowd is breaking up*. They were individuals again, looking into themselves. As individuals, they were good people. As such, what they had nearly done appalled them. It always did, when the mob broke up and people thought for themselves again.

"He's a German!" It was the same voice again, now desperate, seeing his domination of the crowd fading fast.

"So what?" It was another voice in the crowd, one that was still lacking in confidence. "We don't know he did for our Jenny. Like the Father said, let the law do its work."

The crowd was breaking up, people drifting away. Grudgingly, unhappily, but breaking up and going home none the less. One man was left. Conrad guessed he was the agitator; the one who'd started this and the one who'd been shouting from the safety of the crowd. He had a brick in his hand, but Conrad caught his eye and held it. The man dropped the brick and just stood there, his head hanging down. Throwing bricks from the safety of the crowd was one thing; to do something on his own was quite another. Conrad watched him deflating and went over to him.

"I don't want a lecture from you."

The man was hostile, probably with good cause; in his eyes, at least. That was perhaps the hardest lesson for people to absorb; few were guilty in their own eyes. They honestly believed they had right, if not the law, on their side.

"I have no right to give you one. I was merely going to suggest that it might be time to go home. Nothing more will happen here today."

The man's eyes were inflamed and red. The glare from them seeming to pierce the air around him. "They killed my boy. What have you to say to that?"

"What I say to all those who suffer loss. That every death is a tragedy and a cause for grief. Each death diminishes us all and to sorrow for those we have all lost is both right and proper. Your boy was in the Resistance?"

"*Hardly*. He was just a nipper, playing in the street. One of their big half-tracks ran over him. A half-track! By the time the driver stopped, there was nothing left of my kid. Just bits of flesh and bone. We didn't even have a real body to bury. The driver, he said he was sorry, that he hadn't seen the little one playing in the road but if he hadn't been here, it wouldn't have happened."

And when the Inquisition finished its murders, all that was left were ashes. The grieving relatives also didn't have the comfort of burying the body. God have mercy on me for my part is those atrocities.

"That is indeed a terrible thing. But, you still have your memories of him. If you had stirred the crowd to murder today, would that not have stained those memories of your boy and deprived your family of what little they have left? Would you or your family have ever been able to remember your boy again without also remembering this day?"

The man stared at Conrad, mixed feelings warring in his eyes. Confusion slowly conquered them all.

"I don't know. I just don't know."

"The two policemen over there. Do they condemn you for your acts today? Or the man they have with them?"

The man looked at them. They had heard what he said; he saw the pity in their eyes rather than hate. "No, Father, they do not."

"Neither do I condemn you. Go your way; from now on, sin no more."

The man turned and walked away, his head hanging down.

"Thank you, Father." The elder of the two policemen took off his helmet and wiped his forehead.

The younger man looked aggrieved, despite his relief. "Father, I was in the Resistance as well. A lot of us at the Station were. More than those who supported That Man."

"I know, Constable." Conrad spoke slowly. "It is the curse of our times that the many are judged by the acts of the few. What are your plans now?"

"We must take our prisoner to the Station. He's wanted for questioning in the matter of the murder of Jennifer Durham. Horrible murder it was; terrible. That's why feeling is running so high. She was a nice girl. Everybody liked her,

and to die the way she did, I dunno, Father, makes me question things, it does."
The older policeman shook his head.

"I didn't do it! I didn't do anything to her." The prisoner had remained silent, but now his denial rang across the street. Conrad looked at him. "Please believe me, I didn't hurt her."

"Tell that at the station, Cross. They'll take your statement there. You haven't been accused of anything, yet; we just want your statement. We're taking statements from everybody who knew Miss Durham."

Conrad knew it was a rock-solid bet that only Cross had been singled out for the attentions of the mob. Churchill had begged his people to forgive and forget, to accept the refugees from Germany as their guests; but that had been a big thing, an impossible thing, to ask. The Germans had stayed, they'd dispersed into the population, and they'd been accepted, on the surface. The doubts, the memories were still there and when they surfaced, they were ugly.

"Constable . . . "

"Skelton, Father. George Skelton."

"Constable Skelton, would you mind if I walked with you back to the station?"

"I'd appreciate that, Father." Skelton and Conrad both knew exactly what he meant by that. A mob that dispersed could reform, or an agitator could find more people to listen to him. Three escorts were better than two. "It's not so far."

Walking a prisoner back to the station. Conrad shook his head quietly to himself. He'd been living in America for many years and he was used to American ways. There, Cross would have been put in the back of a police cruiser and driven to the station.

Conrad had come to England on a whim, feeling the urge to travel again. The sight of the country had been a real blow to him. What was worse, he knew that what he was seeing now was the result of almost a decade of slow, painful recovery. In America, an America that had never known occupation, there were those who criticized the inability of the occupied countries to recover. Somehow, they expected Britain and the rest to magically return to their prewar condition, as if nothing had ever happened. Such people had never been to those countries and not appreciated what had happened there.

Even had the Germans been merciful and benevolent occupiers, the damage caused simply by the shock of occupation and foreign rule would have been profound. The German occupation had been neither merciful nor benevolent, although Conrad made the concession that they had been fair. *The half-track driver who ran that child down probably suffered greatly for his error.* But the occupied countries had been resources that were maintained only to feed the German war machine, not provinces of some greater whole. Britain had suffered less than most, but only because its industries were that much more valuable.

"The trams will be coming out this way soon." Skelton spoke companionably. "They're in the city center already and there's a spur line coming out to here. They'll be rebuilding the roads at the same time. Make traveling around a lot easier, I can say. Wife and I got a little Velo on order, should come in a few months."

"Trams? I like them; rode on the ones in San Francisco a lot."

"San Francisco? You a Yank then, Father?" Companionship faded, replaced by dislike and suspicion.

"No; I just lived there for a while. My calling means I travel a lot."

Skelton relaxed; the amiability returned to his voice.

"Spent the war there did you? I saw the bombing the day the war ended. One minute there was nothing wrong; we never even saw the bombers, they came in so high. Just heard the air raid sirens. Then there was the roar and the dust going up. The ground shook so much; them that was closest yet still lived were shaken from their feet and left to sprawl in the dirt. When it settled, everything over there had gone. Just ruins left. That's where we found poor Jenny's body. Never want to see a sight like that again, I can tell you. Here we are, Father; the old Blue Lamp."

They were outside the police station. Conrad looked around and made his decision.

"Constable, I need to make a long-distance call to London. Could I use your station telephone, please?"

Office of Sir Humphrey Appleday, Home Office, Whitehall, London

The telephone on Sir Humphrey's desk buzzed. The sound made him put the Times crossword down, albeit with a certain degree of resentment. He took an annoyed breath, and then picked up the receiver.

"Yes, Alice?"

"Sir Humphrey, there's a Mister Lawrence on the direct line telephone."

Sir Humphrey was seized with a sudden wild attack of panic. *Surely it couldn't be T. E. Lawrence come back from the grave to haunt him? It had been a blessed relief when that one had gone down with the godlike delusions and killed himself on a motorcycle.*

"Put him through please, Alice."

The fact that Sir Humphrey's direct line had been used meant this was either a major national emergency or one of the Piccadilly Circus wanted to speak with him.

"Sir Humphrey, it's Conrad Lorentz here. I was wondering if I might ask a favor of you?"

"Conrad, good to hear from you. Where are you calling from?" Sir Humphrey very carefully didn't commit himself to anything.

"Birmingham. I've got myse . . . "

"Birmingham. Depressing area; much worse since the bombing. It's taking a long time to work on the damage up there. The small towns along the south coast are much more pleasant."

At the other end of the line, Conrad carefully kept his reserves of patience in order.

"Sir Humphrey, I've got involved in what sounds like a very nasty murder up here and I could use some official authority. Is there anything you can do?"

"Birmingham? Oh yes, the Jennifer Durham murder; horrible affair. How did you get yourself involved in that?"

"The prime suspect is a German. I think he's being railroaded. There was nearly a riot up here while the police were bringing him in. I happened to be there and managed to defuse the situation. The police up here are doing their best but, well, they're local police. They don't know how to handle a case like this. Are there detectives on their way to help out?"

Railroaded indeed, thought Sir Humphrey. *Conrad has spent too long in America.*

But his question had been far too sharply pointed for Sir Humphrey to ignore. The Metropolitan Police had been virtually destroyed during the Occupation. Its key personnel had left, been killed, or deported and vanished. Their function had been taken over by the Gestapo. They had taken over the Scotland Yard building as well; turning it from a center of crime-fighting expertise into a house of screams, where the only heroes were those who died with sealed lips.

Would Scotland Yard ever lose that grim connection and become once more a synonym for dedicated and professional police work? Sir Humphrey didn't know; once again, he reflected on how severe the hidden costs of defeat and occupation really were.

Then, with the destruction of Germany, the Gestapo had also gone. Churchill's appeal for forgiveness hadn't extended to them and the other Germans in the country had been almost as enthusiastic about hunting down the Gestapo men as the British had been. *A shared purpose can work wonders in bringing people together.*

With nothing of the pre-war Metropolitan Police left, rebuilding the force, and more importantly, its expertise was taking a long, long time. It was desperately understaffed and had all too few skilled investigators. Its equipment was hand-me-downs from the American FBI, and that supply was something Sir Humphrey had only been able to get by using his non-professional contacts with the American Washington Circle.

No, the Metropolitan Police can't help much. It can't be everywhere it was needed and a single murder in the Midlands was well down on the priority list. Then one of Conrad's comments struck home.

"A near riot you say? How bad?"

"A dozen men or so, cornered two coppers and the suspect. It's the start of something bigger, though; I can smell it. I don't know why, not yet, but it's generating a lot of anti-German feeling."

That does it. Sir Humphrey knew that the long, hard recovery from the Occupation was taxing people's patience and they could easily end up looking for scapegoats. If it starts in one city, it could spread. That would mean a disturbance in order and tranquility, something Sir Humphrey feared more than almost anything else.

"Conrad, I'll speak to the Inspector for you. Can you transfer me?"

"He's right here, Sir Humphrey."

There was a click and rustling noises as a telephone receiver was passed from one person to another.

"Inspector Malcombe here."

"Inspector, Sir Humphrey Appleday here. Deputy Assistant Permanent Secretary for the Home Office. I am most terribly sorry to inform you that our police force here is unable to send any formal assistance to aid in that most unfortunate affair you've got up there. We have far too few trained investigators and those that we do have are inextricably involved with other cases. If there was any assistance we could offer, we would. When resources are available, I can assure you that your case will be the top of the list. However, as an interim measure, I understand that a Reverend Father, who is one of our criminal investigation advisors, is with you now?"

"Err, yes, bu . . . "

"Then you are most fortunate. The Father has a sterling reputation as an investigator, with many years of experience and a fund of knowledge that few others can match. He was a key part of many of the post-war criminal investigations, both here and on the mainland. You may remember that awful business in Belgium just after the war ended? He has also been a most valued part of the team helping to rebuild our police force. The Home Office is quite sure, Inspector, that he'll be of the greatest help to you."

"Why, um, thank you."

"Excellent. We're pleased to have been of assistance."

Sir Humphrey hung up the phone and then returned to his crossword. The clue stumping him was eleven across. *Gegs. Anagram, two words, nine and four letters.*

CHAPTER TWO

Solihull Police Station

Inspector Malcombe put the receiver down gingerly, as if it would suddenly develop fangs and bite him.

"The Home Office speaks highly of you, Father. Lord knows we need help with this case."

"I am pleased to be assistance. I must say one thing, though. My work is concerned with ensuring that an innocent person is not punished. If that means finding the guilty, well, that's fine, but it's not my primary aim. So, can I start with the man we brought in today? Who is he and why was he, in particular, singled out?"

"Who is quite simple. Currently, he lives under the name of Matthew Cross, a painter. Before that he was Matthias Krause, a private in the German Army. He was here in 1947 and stayed on. Like most of his kind, he had nowhere else to go.

"Why was he singled out? Partly because we are taking statements from everybody who had any contact with Jennifer Durham. As for the rest, well, take a look at the file. The photographs of the body are at the top. We've kept the details secret, but enough has leaked out to get the whole neighborhood out for blood."

Malcombe handed over the file. Conrad opened it and looked at the pictures. A spread-eagled body, charred black. The head twisted around. The mouth open with screams.

The sister spoke to him, with words blurred by being spoken through lips and teeth crushed by a mailed fist. "Go to hell priest. You have shown me where the Devil truly lies. I curse you. I wish you agony and grief every day you remain alive." And then she spat on him and his cross, the saliva mixed with blood trickling down his face. He staggered back, appalled by the blasphemy and the hatred that had caused it. Then the Inquisitors lit the fires. He felt the heat of the blaze, smelled the awful smell of roasting flesh, heard the screams

Conrad's Eye

from inside the flames with the young woman still cursing God, Christ, the Church and the Inquisition as she died.

Conrad was white, his lips moving in prayer for the soul of a young woman who had died centuries ago. According to doctrine, she should be consigned to hell for all eternity for those last acts and words. *Yet, how could anybody be blamed for words said in hatred and despair when they had been so appallingly wronged?* Watching him, Malcombe misinterpreted Conrad's expression.

"Everybody else who's seen those has been pretty sick as well. Nothing to be ashamed of. I went all through the Occupation and never saw anything like it."

"She was burned alive?"

Malcombe shook his head.

"She wasn't that lucky. Her body was found tied down to an old iron bedframe. Whatever bastard did for her, set the fire underneath. Roasted her alive."

Conrad shook his head. It was unpleasantly similar to some of the things the Inquisition had done. "Why does that point to a German?"

"Because the SS and partisan hunters in Ireland killed a lot of people that way. It's been in the papers a bit, the situation in Ireland being what it is."

"So, somebody could have just read the newspaper accounts and decided to try it out?" Conrad knew that wasn't it even as he spoke. It was a tenuous link though.

"It could be." Malcombe looked at the hideous pictures again. "Who would want to do something like that to a teenage girl?"

Conrad wrestled his mind back to the problem at hand. "I think we had better start with why, not who. If we can determine why the person did this, we'll know what sort of person he is. That will define our suspect list a bit more closely. There are four reasons why somebody would do this. Running from the hottest to the coldest they are lust, hate, revenge and information.

"Let's start with lust. The person got sexual pleasure out of watching this poor girl die. Any traces on the floor around where she died? Is it possible to tell if she was raped first? Was she dressed? If so, how?"

"Answer to the first two questions is no; not as far as we know. The body is too badly burned for any real evidence. There's traces of burned fabric around her hips and upper chest though."

"Undergarments. She was stripped of her dress but left in those. That was probably to ensure her dress did not catch fire and burn her too quickly. Have there been any other killings that are like this? Or finds of animals burned?"

"No, Father; this isn't America. This is the first killing we've had here in years. Had a few immediately post-war, mostly black market related. You know the sort of thing; fighting over supplies or market areas. We hanged a couple of spivs who took shots at police officers and that quieted everything down. Once they'd been ended, we've had nothing of the kind since. That was all guns and knives though; nothing like this. Father, this is going to sound foolish but the local Firm, they're not bad people by their own standards. Most of them were in the Resistance. If they knew something about this, that would be ringing right now."

Malcombe gestured at his telephone.

"As for animals, a few birds or other creatures were shot or snared for food, especially in the Great Famine. That wasn't a good time to be a dog or cat. But horrors like this? Nothing."

Conrad nodded. Eliminating that possibility was a great relief.

"So we can say this wasn't a lust killing, then. There would have been more of a history; people who do that build up to this sort of level. Also, if it had been one of those killings, the body would have been naked.

"That brings us to hate. Have you any idea if this girl had enemies? I don't mean minor jealousies. I mean real, cold-blooded hatred; deep enough to set this up and then execute it."

Malcombe shook is head. "It's hard to think of a girl that young being hated so much that somebody would want to do this. We're doing some checking of course, but it seems unlikely."

"I agree, but we can't eliminate it. Hatred can warp the mind. A minor thing can become something out of all proportion to its original cause. That's one reason why hate is a deadly sin. We should ask around at her school; perhaps her teachers might know. She was of an age where she might have taken somebody else's boyfriend; we don't know. There's another thing, she might not have been the subject of hatred, but she stands in for somebody else. Whoever did this, might have an intense hatred for a specific young girl, but be unable to harm her for some reason. Perhaps because she's already dead. So, he transfers that hatred to Jennifer Durham, perhaps because she resembles the real victim of his hate, and kills her instead. If we are dealing with that kind of case, we have a real problem finding the killer. In any case, if this is a hate killing, then we've got a killer who is, literally, murderously unstable. He, or she, will kill again."

Malcombe sucked his teeth. "Another killing like this? I hope to God not. Sorry, Father."

"If this is one such case, we'll need God's help. Your prayer to him is timely. The next category is revenge."

"Who'd want 'revenge' on a young girl by doing *that* to her?"

"The SS, remember? She may not have been the target, though; this might have been done to her to punish somebody else. Her parents, for example. That would fit the SS and the partisan hunters as well. They made a big thing out of 'punishing' whole families and communities this way. It's possible her parents were in the Resistance and a partisan-hunter came back for revenge."

That was all too true, Malcombe reflected. *The litany of entire communities wiped from the face of the earth in Ireland went on almost without end.* "Cross was German Army; panzergrenadier, not SS or partisan-hunter."

Conrad grimaced. "Doesn't make that much difference. The Russians say it doesn't make any. Both Army and SS have bloody hands; it's just a question of whose drip more. We might also be looking at somebody else though; If somebody went right off the deep end, they could have blown a minor irritation into a major event. The last one is interrogation. This is the coldest of the lot. This girl knew something that somebody wanted to find out and this was how they went about it."

Malcombe was openly skeptical. "Again, what could a young girl like this know that warrants such torture? And if she did, somebody could beat it out of her; they wouldn't need to do this. She'd tell him after he'd slapped her around a bit."

"Not if she didn't know what he thought she knew. That's every prisoner's nightmare." Conrad's voice was mild. "Although an intelligent interrogator would quickly realize that she genuinely didn't know. Have we got a display board we can use? I need to pin up some cards."

"Over there."

It was a corkboard. By its battered appearance, it looked prewar. Conrad pinned up four cards, one for each of the motivations he'd described. After a little thought, he put the lust card at the bottom, then punishment, then interrogation, then hate at the top.

"How does that look to you, Inspector? Most likely at the top."

Malcombe nodded. Conrad wrote the name of Matthew Cross on another card and looked at the board.

"Our first suspect. Where do you think we should put him?"

The police officer pursed his lips. "Based on that list, I wouldn't say any of them. Force me, I'd say lust, but he doesn't seem the type."

"They never do, Inspector. I agree, though. The fact that it is so hard to fit him into any category is something we must consider in his favor. Perhaps we had better talk to him."

Interview Room, Solihull Police Station

"So, you are now Matthew Cross?"

"That is so, yes. I was born Matthias Krause, in 1925. I am from Dusseldorf, I was from Dusseldorf. Now, I am from here. I have nowhere else to be."

"When did you join the Army?"

"I was conscripted in 1945 and sent to Panzergrenadier-Regiment 29. We served in Russia until January 1947. Then we were withdrawn from there and sent to England to rebuild. We were still here when the bombs fell on Germany. Most of us are still here."

"Where was your unit based, Matthew?" Conrad leaned back a little, trying to get a sense of how this man thought and behaved.

"Myself? We were stationed near Ipswich. But the division was split up and was all over England. Partly that was to avoid too much attention from the jabos. Towards the end of the war, they were all over us. Nobody could move without being strafed or bombed. Or both. So, we were split into small units. That way we would not draw them down. Being in small units helped in other ways as well. We were reforming, I said that, I think, and we were taking in recruits. Many of these were English. Often there would be perhaps one German unit who were training one English. Much of the unit was in Wales. They were there when the war ended."

Cross smiled sadly, "We heard from them up to the end of the war; they said it was still possible to get good beer in Wales. But after the end? From some units we heard, from others we did not. I think the Ami zehnmotoren or the jabos got them. My unit was unlucky. We had three platoons, but we never heard from the other two again. They were in Wales; a place called Angelsey."

"Zehnmotoren?"

"I am sorry, the B-36. We used to call the B-17 the viermotoren, the four-engine, and the B-29 the grossviermotoren, the big four-engine. So the B-36 we call the ten-engine."

"So what happened the day the war ended?"

Conrad's Eye

"I was in Dover, waiting to go on leave. There were several of us going. If the bombing had been a day later, we would all have been in Germany. The Amis never managed to stop the ferries crossing the Channel or the North Sea. Their *jabos* did not have the range to hit the ports on the east coast, so life went on there. It is strange, but crossing the North Sea was more dangerous when we were closer to Germany. The British and Canadian submarines saw to that. Sometimes they would torpedo ships right inside the Kattegat.

"That day, we were waiting for a ship when we heard the explosions over Germany. We knew then something terrible had happened. After a while, the port master told us that there had been a great disaster and we could not leave. We all stayed there in the port building, until we heard that Germany had surrendered and that the troops in England were doing so also. That was when we heard Churchill was coming back. Slowly, we learned the truth. Germany had gone. There was nothing left; just a few survivors scattered away from the big towns. We were told there was nothing to go home to. Some wanted to go anyway. They did; we never heard from them again. The rest of us we were put in a camp for displaced persons. We stayed there for a while and then we were dispersed into the population. I was told to come here and I did."

"How do you make a living, Matthew?"

"I am a painter. That is a good way to work now. Many houses are damaged and need repair. Many have not been painted since before the war. Even though people have a little money again, they cannot afford new houses, even if there were such things to buy. So they spend what money they have on painting the house they have."

"Do the people who employ you know you were German?"

"Of course."

"Have any problems with any of them?"

"I do not think so. None said anything to my face. What they say when I am gone, of course, I do not know."

"Did you know Jennifer Durham?"

"Some, yes. I repainted her parents house not so long ago. She was doing some research for her history class; a project on the Occupation. She asked me many questions about the German Army and what it was like to be in the Army here during those years. I told her what I knew; gave her some pictures I had for her to use. Not important ones, or ones I valued; just some of my unit, of our half-tracks and so on. The sort any old soldier has too many of."

"Did you ever see her alone?"

"Of course not. Her parents always made sure there was one of them with us. And I would not have it otherwise. That would cause talk behind my back and that would not be good for my business."

"And you have not seen her since?"

"I have not. For a man with his own business, it is . . . " For the first time, Cross hesitated; obviously searching for the right word. ". . . not prudent to have too close contact with young girls. Even innocent conversations can be misunderstood and harm my livelihood."

Conrad laughed; that, at least, was an honest reason for a man not to be alone with a young girl.

"Thank you, Mister Cross; you've been very helpful. Inspector Malcombe?"

"Mister Cross, I'd like to keep you in protective custody for a couple of days while we complete our inquiries. Let local feeling simmer down a little. Have you a lawyer to represent you?" Cross nodded. "Very well. You may call him and meet with him here. I emphasize, you are being detained as much for your protection as anything else. Frankly, in view of what happened this morning, we cannot guarantee your safety at this time."

Outside, Malcombe leaned up against the wall. "Well?"

"Not a very good suspect at all. He talked a lot; more than he had to. So he is either a superb liar or he has nothing to hide. Also, he doesn't fit any of our categories. And that bit about not being alone with the girl rang true. Of course, it's possible that she sneaked out, went to see him and then either tried to back out or threatened to tell people what had happened. But if that was the case, I'd expect a killing by strangulation or beating; not what happened to that poor girl. There was a coldness to that killing that does not speak of passion to me."

"My thoughts also. Look, Father, I can't spend more time on this case, much as I would like to. The whole police force is understaffed. I'm doing work now that would have been assigned to three people before the war. And I haven't any detectives trained enough for this sort of thing. I'll be honest with you, I resented being told to give you the facilities you needed. But, the truth is, we need you. I can offer you a uniformed officer to help with the leg work and if you need more, I'll see what I can find. But I can't promise much."

"A uniformed officer would be very helpful, Inspector. And thank you."

"Where are you going next?"

"Talk to the girl's parents. That can wait until tomorrow though. Too late now; I'm going to sleep on this problem."

Conrad's Eye

The Red Lion Inn, Solihull

Conrad started with surprise. He'd decided to treat himself to a glass of beer after the day's work and had expected a pint of the thin, watery "National Beer." The last time he'd had a beer in England, that's what he'd been served and he'd had to force it down. *'If this came from a horse, the poor thing would be unfit for work' had been Nell's comment.*

This beer was better, richer, more flavorful. A long way to go before it got back to the beer Conrad remembered, but it was a good start.

"Now that's a lot better."

The girl behind the bar smiled. "The National Beer went away start of this year, Father. The breweries can make their own beers again now. Big ones have gone, of course, so there's lots of little ones starting up. Been away from England long, Father?"

"Quite a few years. Last time I was here was just after the war. Things are picking up well."

"Excuse me, Father."

The voice came from behind him. Conrad turned around; there was a sallow-faced man behind him, holding a cloth cap in his hands. Conrad had a vague sense of familiarity with him, but couldn't place it.

"Can I help you?"

"Please Father, I was one of that crowd this morning, I don't know what came over us, really I don't. I wanted to apologize to you, ask your forgiveness. I'd go to the bobbies as well, but I'm scared they'd collar me."

"And you should also ask forgiveness of the man you hunted." Conrad's voice was stern; he was stressing it for the benefit of the man who, at least, had had the courage and decency to try and make amends. "You know the police only wanted a statement from him. His only crime appears to be to have sat with a young girl's parents, helping her with her homework." *That is pushing it a bit, but I want the word out as quickly as I can.*

"So I hear. I told 'er indoors about it and she's giving me a terrible time."

Conrad was bewildered at the "'er indoors" and glanced at the barmaid for help. She grinned and mouthed the word "wife" to him.

"And now you see why anger is one of the deadly sins, don't you? You didn't just threaten a good, honest man and two police officers doing their duty; but you ruined your own domestic harmony as well. Well, put it all behind you. Join me in a beer and then go home and make peace with 'er indoors."

"That's kind of you, Father. Let me buy the round, though; it's the least I can do."

"If you'll accept a small gift from me."

Conrad reached into his pocket and pulled out a small medallion he had there. It had no material or sentimental value to him. In fact, he wasn't quite certain why he had it in his pocket. But, to this man, it might well put the seal of acceptance on his act of contrition. It might also act as proof to his wife that he'd made the apologies she had demanded.

"This is Saint Justin, the patron saint of those who have the courage to make amends for their transgressions. Perhaps it might help restore peace to your home."

The man took it, kissed it lightly with the trace of a tear in his eye, and put it carefully into his pocket. By the time he had finished, their glasses had been refilled. In quiet peace and fellowship, they drank their beers. The man left after making another series of apologies.

That was when Conrad realized he had been much more deeply disturbed by this case than he had realized. He turned to the barmaid.

"Is the beer still rationed, or can I have another?"

"Beer's off the ration now, Father. I'm Alice; everybody calls me Allie. What you just said, are you the man what came up from London to help with the murder?"

"I was up here anyway, passing through, and I was asked to help, but yes."

Allie looked nervous and flustered. "Please don't get me wrong, Father, but I've got to ask. We hear poor Jenny was tortured; that's not true is it?"

Conrad sighed. *A question, to tell the truth or not?* In the end, he decided Allie deserved the truth. *Too many problems are caused by ill-advised attempts to shield people from it.*

"I'm afraid the stories are true, Allie; she was brutally treated before she died."

The girls went white and her lips started to move. Conrad read them and knew she was praying.

"I'm sorry, Father, but I have to walk home in the dark after work tonight. Could be me next."

"Allie, I don't think there will be a next. This has all the signs of an isolated crime. But, closing time is in a few minutes; would you like me to walk you home?"

Conrad's Eye

"Please, Father; you're a big man and a . . . and nobody will bother you. I'd be very grateful. My parents' house is only a few minutes away."

The street lighting was still very poor. Conrad could see why the girl had been so frightened. The lamps gave puddles of light, but the areas between were pitch black; all the more so from the contrast with the lighting. If somebody was going to be attacked, the environment was almost perfect for it. The attacker could lurk in the darkness and drag their victim off between the lights.

"Are the streets this dark in the morning as well, Allie?"

She nodded. "The Government says they'll bring back Daylight Saving Time next year. Until they do, this time of year, it's still dark when most people go to work. Good thing about being a bar maid; my job doesn't start until three and I get to walk to work in daylight."

They walked on, Conrad listening to the click of her heels on the broken pavement. Eventually they reached her house and the door opened.

"Allie, you never told us you were walking out with somebody. Who is this . . ."

The mother's voice, shrill with anger, broke when the light from the doorway fell on Conrad.

"Oh, I'm sorry, Father. I didn't realize."

"The Father walked me home because the murder frightened me. You apologize to him right now."

Allie's voice was equally shrill, equally indignant. For a moment, Conrad pitied the man who she would eventually marry. *I must not judge. Her anger might also be the result of fear and the relief of being home where she was safe. If she is safe, when there might be a maniac around.*

His thoughts had made him miss some of what Allie's mother had said. She was still speaking, though. "I'm sorry, Father; it's just with what happened, you know . . . Do you want to drop in for a cup of tea?"

"No need to apologize, ma'am. It's a mother's duty to watch over her children. For if she doesn't, who will? Some tea would be very nice, but another time perhaps? I have to get back to the inn before the landlord locks the doors for the night."

"Oh. Well, another time then. And thank you for walking Allie home."

The door closed and Conrad went back to the inn, carefully avoiding the potholes in the pavement. The care was automatic, though; his mind was chewing over the things he'd learned during the day.

CHAPTER THREE

Breakfast Room, Red Lion Inn, Solihull

"Your breakfast, Father."

The waitress beamed at him and unloaded her tray. *A plate with a fried egg, a rasher of bacon, a fried half-tomato and some fried potatoes. A cup, a pot of tea and one of the strange metal racks the British had designed to help toast get cold faster.* The eggs and bacon were still rationed, but bread and potatoes were off-ration now, as were tomatoes. The latter were just very expensive. Conrad had paid extra for his half-tomato, but he did like fried tomatoes and he felt like indulging himself.

He started into his meal, missing the breakfasts at the Hotel California, and determined to eat what he had before it got cold. The toast went quickly as well, Conrad using the last slice to wipe his breakfast plate clean. Something he'd noted everybody doing; things might be looking up in Britain, but wasting food had become a social crime. Settling back with his tea, he started to look through the morning paper.

Even though it was a London paper, the Jenny Durham murder was still on the front page. He glanced quickly down the column; there was nothing new, there although 'a police source' was quoted as saying a number of avenues were being investigated. That sounded like a newspaperman covering for the lack of any progress in the case. There was a strike at the shipyards, again, and some more relatively insignificant items.

The international news was equally mundane. The lead 'foreign' story was that the Russians had finished off another of the little German warlord states left over from the War. Conrad had lost count of how many such self-styled states had been mopped up in the aftermath of the war.

A bit further down the page was a 'Commonwealth' story. Australia and India were in the middle of a multi-sided dispute over some of the islands that had once formed part of the Netherlands East Indies. Indonesia was majority Moslem, but Bali was predominantly Hindu and Timor was mostly Christian.

133

So, India had appointed itself protector of Bali while Australia had done the same for Timor. Of course, Indonesia objected strongly to that arrangement. *I wonder if Sir John Hawkwood is back in that part of the world and, if so, whose side he is on this time.*

The only really interesting item was from Ireland. Of all the Northern European countries, Ireland had probably been the worst hurt by the Occupation. Whole swathes of the countryside had been depopulated and the administrative system had been totally destroyed. What was worse, the Germans had made a point of killing off all the natural community leaders. They intended to replace them with their own as a first step towards their final objective. The SS leaders had had a long-term plan for turning Ireland into a wholly SS state. It was to have been a retirement community for SS combat veterans, where only those who had met the standards of the SS would be allowed to reside. There was no place for the indigenous population in that vision and their days had been numbered. When Ireland had been liberated, the British and Australian troops had pretty much wiped out the SS and partisan hunters. First defeating them in the field, then hunting down and killing the remnants as they'd fled for safety. After what the Commonwealth troops had seen, they hadn't been inclined to grant the Germans any quarter.

The result had been utter chaos. The country had split down into small communities, each clinging to a local leader or authority. For a while, it had been an open question as to whether Ireland would remain independent or collapse back into the U.K. They'd stayed independent, just. For the last decade, the Dublin Government had been trying to bring everybody back under a semblance of central control. Of course, the fact that Dublin was dispersing food and economic aid had helped. The country was reforming as a very weakly centralized federation, with the individual counties largely autonomous. That had solved the religious problem, so the article said anyway. The Catholic and the Protestant counties were accepting the new arrangement. There was a lot of population movement, of course. Protestants were leaving Catholic dominated counties, Catholics leaving Protestant controlled areas. But, it looked as if Ireland was slowly sorting itself out. *That would be a first*, thought Conrad.

He was aware of the waitress speaking to a uniformed police officer and pointing to his table. Conrad folded his newspaper and rose and the man joined him.

"Constable Skelton, isn't it? Sit down; may I offer you a cup of tea?"

"That would be very kind, Father; thank you."

Conrad waved the waitress over and ordered a second pot of tea. He wasn't aware of it, but a few months ago, he wouldn't have been allowed to do, so unless the Constable had a spare tea coupon. Another small sign of normality slowly returning; the British had their tea unrationed again.

Skelton sipped his tea gratefully; Conrad noted he used milk very sparingly and sugar not at all. Both had been rationed much more strictly than tea ever had, and the habit of using them was broken.

"Inspector Malcombe has assigned me to assist you in the investigation of the Jenny Durham murder. How would you like to start?"

"We have three priorities. I'd like to look at the scene of the crime and the area around it. Then I would like to talk to her parents. Finally, we need to go to where Cross lived; have a look around there."

"He has a room in a boarding house, Father. We'd need a warrant to search there."

"How do we get that? Go to a judge?"

"The local magistrate. There'll be no problem in getting it, but it'll take a few hours to sort out the details. I'd suggest we get that going first, then do the others while we're waiting for the warrant to be signed. Then we can pick it up and go to his flat."

"Good idea, Constable. After we've applied for a search warrant, we'll go to where the body was found. I'm sorry to make you go back there."

"That's all right, Father, just as long as I don't have to look at that body again."

Site of the CBAF, Castle Bromwich

"You say this area will be cleared and rebuilt soon?"

Conrad looked around at the desolation. Nobody spoke much of the conventional bombing that had been part of The Big One; people just remembered the nuclear attack on Germany. The sight of what had once been a vast factory complex and its surrounding community drove home just how devastating the conventional attack had been. This wasteland went all the way back to Solihull.

"That's right, Father; the authorities say they'll start clearing it soon. Once the bomb disposal teams get here. I suppose they'll build new factories and homes here."

"I'll tell you this, Constable, I hope they make the site of this house a park or something. I wouldn't care to live on the site of what happened here."

Conrad's Eye

Skelton nodded. The whole area was silent, as if even the birds and animals had been driven away. He could sense the horror, driven into the shattered brick walls by the sheer force of what had happened. *No, I wouldn't want to live here either.* He looked over to where Conrad was staring at an old iron bedframe, blackened by the fire that had been lit underneath it.

"That's right, Father; that's where I found her." Skelton shuddered at the memory. The sickness returned to his stomach.

Conrad shook his head. *Back in America, the frame would have been taken away for examination. That is the trouble with trying to rebuild destroyed institutions from scratch; all the established expertise was lost.* He looked down and saw wire looped around the corners of the frame.

"She was tied down with wire, Father. I suppose the man who killed her didn't want the ties to burn through."

Conrad nodded. *That makes sense.*

The Marquis Leonardo de Salamanca had been only twelve when his father had died, leaving the Church as administrator of the estate. For nine years, the Church had enjoyed the proceeds of that estate. Then the young Marquis had come of age and wanted to take the estate back into his own hands. The accusation had been made: wizardry and consorting with the Devil. Charges that, if proved, meant his estate would become the property of the Church again. The local Inquisition had sat him over hot coals to make him confess, but the young man refused. Then I arrived, and, dear God forgive me, tricked the man into making his confession.

The haunting memory clouded Conrad's mind for a moment.

He looked closer at the frame. There were heavy, black, encrusted stains on the wire and frame. Blood; baked hard by the fire. Skelton saw what had caught his attention.

"Jenny tried to escape, Father; cut her wrists to the bone, she did."

Conrad sighed and shook his head.

"No, Constable. She wasn't trying to escape; not the way you think. She knew she couldn't. That she wouldn't be allowed to live. That the people who did this to her couldn't let her live, no matter what she said or did. She took the only way out left to her."

The memory of the Inquisition made Conrad drop to his knees. He prayed quietly for the girl who had died here. When he opened his eyes, Skelton was kneeling beside him.

"I hope you didn't mind, Father, me being Church of England and all. But what you were doing seemed right. Wanted to be part of it."

The rest of the building has the same forlorn aura of misery and suffering permeating every part of it. In one corner, there was a bank of rubble. *Probably where the roof had caved in.* The weeds there had been crushed. Mixed in with them was more of the thin wire, lying looped and tangled on the ground. Looking closely at some of the iron fragments, Conrad saw a tiny fragment of cheap white cloth hooked on a jagged edge. That made him reach down and touch the ground there. Even after the hours that had gone by, he could still smell the urine.

"Jenny was kept here, Constable; probably for several hours. She tried to escape, but couldn't. Then she was killed."

Conrad looked again at the desolate ruin, feeling the terror of the young girl who had been held there waiting for what she knew must have been certain death. *No, I would not like to live in a house built on the site of what happened here. Evil permeates everything around it; its echoes can last for longer than the cynical might wish to believe. This place will attract evil and the innocent would be well advised to keep clear of it. Especially young girls.*

Privately, he decided to reorder the motive cards on his display board. The fact that she had been kept waiting for her death suggested moving interrogation to the top of the list.

Durham Household, Castle Bromwich

The man looked slightly confused at the sight of Conrad and Skelton standing on his doorstep. He half-opened the door, hesitating; not quite sure what to do next.

"Mr. Durham?" Conrad spoke quietly, sympathetically.

"Aye." A very guarded, suspicious response, Conrad couldn't blame him.

"We must talk to you about Jenny. I'm truly sorry to disturb you at this terrible time, but the faster we move the more likely we are to catch the people who did this. May we come in?"

"Aye, very well. I do not know what more we can say, though."

"Who is it there, John?" A woman's voice, shaking and strained from crying, echoed through the house.

"A copper and . . . somebody else . . . investigating Jenny, Luv."

"Can you tell us what happened that last day?"

Conrad's Eye

"Aye. Jenny went off to school, same as always. She was going to her friend's house afterwards, so when she didn't come home at the usual time we thought nothing of it. But evening came and there was no sign. We were about to call the police when we heard of the body being found. We just knew then who it was. We went to the station, told the coppers that Jenny was missing and that was it. They'd found a young girl; there was nobody else it could be. They wouldn't let us see the body. Said it was being examined for evidence."

I wish that was true. Conrad was missing the police facilities in America. In dime store novels, the private detectives always solved the most baffling of cases with a combination of brilliance and muscle. Conrad was well aware of how fictional that presentation was. *The police have resources and expertise no private detective agency could ever match, let alone a lone-wolf private eye.* Conrad always worked with the police when he could, taking advantage of their resources and offering his knowledge of the human condition in exchange. Even here in England, where the police were desperately under-resourced and still suffering from the stigma of occupation, they were a center of expertise. The fact that they had not allowed the parents to see the tortured body of their daughter showed that they were also a center of basic human decency.

"Has anything unusual happened in the days before her death? People hanging round the house? Strangers who hurried away when it looked as if they might be approached?" Conrad asked the question quickly.

Durham thought carefully. "You know, it's an odd thing, but I did get a feeling that we were being watched. There's no reason for it; none at all. Just, sometimes, the hairs on the back of my neck felt strange. I suppose that's just superstition to you?"

Conrad shook his head. "There is a friend of mine who tells anybody who will listen that instincts are your senses picking up something below the threshold of awareness and frantically screaming a warning." *And, after five years of Occupation, those instincts were finely honed. If they were telling you somebody was watching, then somebody was. If I tell this man that, he will spend the rest of his life blaming himself.* "But, after the Occupation, everybody is on edge and wary. There was no way you could have known that the threat was real this time, where it was coming from or what form it would take."

There was a pause and a woman joined them, obviously Mrs Durham. "Can we see Jenny soon, please? Just one last time?"

"You don't want to do that." Conrad's voice was filled with sympathy for the woman's grief. "It's better you try to remember her as she was."

"It's that bad?" John Durham was trying to speak normally, to give strength to his wife. "We'd heard rumors, but we thought . . . we hoped . . . they weren't true."

"Mister Durham, could we speak in private please?"

Conrad stepped outside with the father of the victim. "I want you to know something. Your Jenny did a very brave, very courageous, thing as her last act on this earth. The person, or people, who killed her wanted something she knew or had. They wanted it very badly indeed. She knew that and knew that they were going to kill her anyway. So she decided that, whatever else happened, they wouldn't get what they wanted from her. She'd been bound with thin wire and she used that wire to cut her wrists open. That way, she bled out and died before they could make her tell them what they needed to know.

"She beat them, Mister Durham. She was alone, helpless and being attacked with unimaginable cruelty, and yet she found a way to beat them. When the day of judgment comes and the monsters who did this to her are cast down for all eternity, the men and women who are numbered as the bravest of the brave will come forward to take her by the hand and welcome her into their midst."

Durham straightened slightly; pride in what he'd been told just slightly eased the grief. Then he frowned.

"But, isn't that suicide? Our priest is set in his ways, old-fashioned. Won't he deny . . . "

"No. Your daughter was murdered. She died by the violence of others. All she did was soften the agony of her death. The Society of Jesus has considerable spiritual authority in such matters of doctrine. If your priest argues with that, refer him to me."

Conrad straightened. Energy seemed to crackle from him.

"I will speak with him and, truly, I will put the fear of God into him."

Matthew Cross's Rooms, Solihull

The warrant had been waiting for them when they had got back to the police station. They'd taken it and made their way to the rooming house where Cross lived. There were a lot of such houses in Birmingham and across the rest of the country. So many people had lost their homes while so many others had been short of enough money to live. Taking in lodgers had become a national pasttime. Some of the older, larger houses had been converted into shared residences; groups of rooms made into self-contained apartments called "flats." Cross had one of those.

Conrad's official status was still shaky, despite the telephone call vouching for him. So, as the officer of the law present, Skelton tried the door handle. To his surprise, the door was open. There had been a time when few people locked their doors in England. Those days had long gone. The owner of the building shrugged and went away, his master key not needed.

Inside, the flat had been almost completely destroyed. The main living room was a devastated mess. Drawers were opened and overturned; shelf contents dumped on the floor. Pictures had been taken off the wall, their glass smashed and the contents thrown down. The seats and other furniture had been broken and their upholstery slashed.

In the kitchen, the destruction was even worse. Cabinets had been ripped from the wall and their contents emptied on the floor. Even the sticky paper covering the shelves had been ripped off.

The bedroom was the same. The bedding had been ripped off the bed and torn up, although the bed itself was still in position by the wall. All the toiletries had been swept off the dressing table and lay in a jumbled mess on the floor. Conrad noted that none of the bottles had been broken. He shook his head at the sight.

Cross had been a soldier, a German soldier, and the habits were too deeply ingrained to be lost so easily. Conrad was prepared to bet that, when Cross had last left this room, it had been immaculate. The hair brush now lying broken on the floor would have been on the dressing table, its handle exactly 90 degrees to the edge. There had been a little case where Cross had kept his medals. Conrad guessed it wasn't on casual display, but that didn't mean that it wasn't treasured. Now it was broken also; the glass front shattered, the contents thrown down.

"Vandals." Skelton spoke with disgust. "They couldn't get to the man, so they came here and wrecked his things. Sniveling cowards. Makes my stomach turn, people like that."

"Perhaps not." Conrad spoke reflectively. His absentminded phrase made Skelton look at him in shock.

"Surely you don't approve . . . "

"No, no; of course not. I meant this might be vandalism; it might not. It's very thorough for vandalism. Look at the pictures. They've been taken out of the frames and the frames themselves broken. Wouldn't a vandal have just broken the whole thing against a chair or something? And wouldn't they have torn the pictures up? If they were really trying to hurt this man, they'd have destroyed his pictures, not just their frames."

"They were looking for something?" Skelton's voice was careful.

"They might have been. If so, they didn't find it. If they had, the wrecking would have stopped at some point. Whoever did this tore the whole place apart. So, if they were looking for something, they didn't find it."

"Or they did, but didn't want to give us a clue what it was they were looking for." Skelton looked at Conrad for approval and got it.

"That's right. Anyway, let's look around. See if they missed anything."

Conrad started looking through the debris in the living room. Cross had a radio; now it lay on the floor, the back torn out. Books, some German, some English, were thrown on the floor also; opened, then kicked out of the way. Just what might be expected if somebody of no great importance had their home wrecked. Conrad found a Luger P.08 on the floor, thrown away like everything else. The box that had held it was torn apart. The gun wasn't damaged. It appeared to be a nice specimen, although it looked odd to Conrad.

"Ever seen one of these before, Constable?"

"He isn't supposed to have that, I can tell you. Nobody should have a gun without a certificate."

Skelton spoke with what could only be described as amused despair. After the Occupation, the combination of American wartime deliveries of unknown numbers of weapons to the Resistance and the surrender of the German Army in the U.K. had meant there were huge numbers of unregistered weapons floating around. It was Skelton's professional guess that there were at least three greaseguns, an RPG-2 and Lord knew how many German rifles and handguns in this building. *Probably a lot more than that, if a Resistance cell had been based here. None of the weapons would have a 'certificate,' and all of them would be well hidden against searches.* The British had learned a lot during the Occupation.

"It's an artillery Luger, Father; same as a normal Luger, but with a longer barrel. They're pretty rare and worth a lot of money. Wonder how an infantry private had one?"

"We'll find out. Worth a lot of money, you say? That might rule out robbery, then. A valuable gun is something that a thief can convert into cash." Conrad laughed softly. "A friend of mine back in the States would like this; she collects other people's guns."

Skelton tried not to hear that last remark. He carried on searching through the flat, although the thoroughness of the previous searchers seemed to make it pointless. Yet, a couple of minutes later Conrad heard a strangled call from the bedroom.

"Father, you'd better come and see this."

Conrad entered the room. Skelton had pushed the bed to one side and was looking down at a twisted pile of gray cloth.

"It struck me as odd that the bed was still in place, so I moved it. Do you think this is what I think it is?"

"I'm afraid so." Conrad picked it up and put it on the bed. It was a cheap gray dress, button-through with square neckline. A girl's school uniform dress. Inside was a name tag, Jennifer Durham. There were stains on the front, up around the neck. Conrad couldn't prove it, not yet, but he was prepared to bet that they were bloodstains.

"Suddenly it looks very bad for Matthew Cross."

"We'd better call Inspector Malcombe, Father. We need to have this place sealed off for a while."

"I agree, and it's a good reason to keep Cross in a cell for a few days. By the way, we can't leave that gun here; we ought to have it locked up as evidence. We leave it here, it won't be here when we get back."

"You're right, Father. I'll put in the call. Then, once some Constables have got here and the place has been sealed off and guarded, where do we go next?"

"To Jenny Durham's school, I think."

Solihull Grammar School, Solihull

"Can I help you gentlemen?"

The teacher looked confused at the sight of a police constable and a priest in her office.

"I'm Constable George Skelton, investigating the murder of Jennifer Durham. The Father is an experienced investigator from London, here to help us. I understand Jenny Durham was in your class?"

"I thought detectives investigated crimes?"

"They do, ma'am; but we haven't got enough detectives who are skilled enough for this investigation. Well, to be honest, we haven't got any detectives specializing in murder investigations at all. Like everybody else, we're making do with what we've got. We're lucky to have the Father here to help us. The Home Office spoke very highly of him."

"An investigating priest? Sounds like something from the Spanish Inquisition."

"Ma'am, nobody expects the Spanish Inquisition." Conrad spoke gravely. "I'm just here to help."

"That's right, ma'am. We're just getting some advice from an expert." Skelton hesitated for a second. "Without him here to help us, we'd be in a real mess, I can tell you. Now, Jenny Durham was in your class?"

"That's right. I was the form teacher for her class and also the history teacher." Suddenly the old woman looked heartbroken. "Every teacher waits for that one pupil, the one who is something different. The one who has the spark. Jenny had it. She could use words to paint pictures. She could bring history to life with a few short phrases. I'll tell you how good she was at it. This year, there was a class project on the Occupation. You know, each child had the entire term to write an extended essay. Most of the children did the same thing, just a description of the events, almost copied from the textbook. They thought I wouldn't realize they'd left the whole thing until the night before it was supposed to be handed in and then just did the quickest job that they thought they'd get away with.

"Jenny was different. She worked hard at it, but she used her imagination as well. She used the time she had to find things that weren't in the official history. She went out; she talked to people from all over. People who'd been different things. A policeman. A local man who's been a black marketeer; another who'd been in the resistance. Others who had just kept their heads down. She got a German soldier to tell her about his experiences here, and even got some stories from one of those who supported That Man. She wrote all their stories down, wove them into a picture of what the city was like during the Occupation. It was brilliant, just brilliant. She even got some pictures to illustrate it.

"I sent it to Oxford University Press. They are just starting up again and are looking for authors. They saw the manuscript, the list of pictures to go with it; I didn't send them the originals, of course. They leapt at it; accepted it on the spot. At first, they thought I was the author and the publisher offered me the contract. They couldn't believe it when I told them the author was a 16-year-old girl. They thought I had written it and they took a lot of persuading otherwise. When they finally understood who the real author was, they were going to give her an advance. It wouldn't be that much but a little money goes a long way. Her parents had already made a lot of sacrifices to keep her in school."

Suddenly the teacher burst into tears. "She would have been set up for life, with a start like that; a university scholarship, a career as a historian. She could have been one of the great historians; one of the ones people like to read, not one whose books sit on shelves gathering dust. Now she's dead and it's my fault. If I hadn't sent that book to the Press, she'd be alive."

"Why do you think that, Miss . . . "

"Rosedale, Evelyn Rosedale, Father. Isn't it obvious? When word started to spread that Jenny's book was going to be published, everybody knew she had money coming in. And now, there's stories all over town about how she died. Somebody heard about her advance and tried to make her give it to them. They didn't know she hadn't got it yet, and anyway, it would have been given to her parents; she was far too young for money like that. It's all my fault, the poor lamb."

"No, Miss Rosedale. I don't think so. Anybody who went to this length would have known that. In any case, you were doing the girl a great kindness. Even if evil men did get involved, the blame lies with them, not you. Now, did Jenny have any enemies here?"

Miss Rosedale dabbed her eyes and tried to settle down. "No, I don't think so. Everybody liked her."

Conrad tried not to roll his eyes. *Every time there is a murder, those who knew the victim stressed that everybody liked the deceased, despite the blatantly obvious fact that* somebody *hadn't.*

"Think, Miss Rosedale. Everybody liked her? No jealousies? Or petty squabbles?"

"Well, there were the usual schoolgirl things. Jenny's class were just getting to the age when they started to find boys interesting, so there were squabbles over that. And one or two of the girls started spreading nasty rumors about the others. I think one of them was that Jenny had been walking out with a German, but that was all."

"Walking out with a German? Any truth to that?" Conrad watched the woman's face carefully.

"Dear me, no. I know what started it off. She interviewed one of the German soldiers, a housepainter, he is now, for her book. But it was all very decent and proper; the young man wouldn't see her unless her parents were present as well. But you know that; you're holding him, aren't you?"

"Yes we are, ma'am." Skelton was glad to be back in the conversation; he'd been feeling distinctly left out.

"Well, you can let him go. I've met him; he's such a nice young man."

Skelton and Conrad both had the sensation that they were expected to jump up and release the man immediately. Skelton put on his most serious 'move along, nothing to see here ' face.

"We can't do that, ma'am. There are issues we have to finalize and some explanations we need made. Anyway, with the strength of feeling in town, he's better off inside for a few days. We've nearly had one riot; nobody wants another."

And that summarized what Humpty is mostly concerned about. The thought crossed Conrad's mind and was quickly followed by another.

"Just one more question. The day Jenny's body was found, did she leave school at the usual time?"

Miss Rosedale frowned. "No; she wasn't here at all that day. She wasn't present for registration, didn't appear at all. I sent word to the school secretary to visit her parents to find out of she was ill, but there had been a break-in at the school office the night before and the police were here. You must remember that, Constable."

"Wasn't here myself, ma'am; I believe one of the other constables made the report. Nothing stolen, so I understand?'

"Nothing. The constable who came here said it was just some vandals throwing paper around. Didn't even break a window; just forced the catch. They really ruined the records office though; everything was taken out of the files and thrown on the floor. Some of those files went back years and years. It was a terrible job getting them all sorted and back in place again. Anyway, with all the efforts to get sorted out, the message to check with her parents got lost in the cracks."

Outside, Conrad and Skelton walked away from the school, both remembering their own school days. Eventually, Conrad broke the silence.

"What do you think, Constable?"

"Well, Father, I think we know how the rumor that Cross did it got started. Some stupid schoolgirls spreading tales and it blew up from there."

"I agree; that dress looks bad though." Conrad looked at Skelton curiously.

"I don't know about that, Father. It wasn't hard to find; in fact, it would be harder to miss than find. If his room was ripped up by vandals, wouldn't they have found the dress and got it to us? Or told us it was there if they didn't want to be collared for malicious damage? If the room was searched, why wasn't the bed moved? Or, if it was, why was it put back? Nothing else was. No, Father, I don't like that dress at all. In fact, if I was a conspiratorial sort of bloke, I'd say that somebody put it there for us to find."

Conrad nodded proudly. *This Constable will make a good detective.*

"I'm not a conspiratorial sort of bloke either and I'm fairly sure somebody put that dress there for us to find."

Interview Room, Solihull Police Station, Birmingham

"Not her, surely?"

145

Conrad's Eye

Constable Skelton looked surprised as Conrad wrote Miss Rosedale's name on a card and pinned it to the notice board.

"Can't ignore her, Constable. I have our suspects, such as they are, all on cards. Four rows on the board; most likely suspects at the top, pretty much excluded at the bottom. Other board has the suspects according to motivation.

"Anyway, Miss Rosedale. Knew the victim well. I don't know about you, but that outburst of hers, blaming herself, seemed a bit contrived to me. As if it was the sort of thing she knew she was expected to say."

"She's a schoolteacher, Father. Back in the first war, lot of men of her generation were killed. There just weren't enough husbands to go around. Being a schoolteacher was one of the few ways a single woman could earn a living, but that meant they had to fill the expectations of parents who knew the teacher was around their children all the time. Caesar's wife and all that. So she's been acting a part all her life. In that respect, acting the way that she's expected to act has become so much a part of her life that she can't stop. But why would she kill Jenny? Why so horribly?"

"Her most likely motivation would be hate, coming from jealousy. She's a history teacher. That means she's knowledgeable about history; probably is quite a good historian, but not quite good enough to make a career out of being a historian. Then she sees this young girl who's going to pole-vault into the top of the profession, probably be famous before she was twenty. She'll get everything Miss Rosedale wanted, with none of the costs she paid. To somebody who is obsessive, jealous, frustrated, that could be enough to send her over the edge. But, you're right; she's not a good suspect. Third rank, I think."

"And you've moved Cross to the second rank. Because of the dress I suppose?"

Skelton looked closer at the three cards pinned to the board.

"Her parents? You've got to be making a bad joke there."

"Not in the least. Any idea how many children hate their parents, often with good reason, and how many parents hate their children, often for reasons that are far from being good? Even the Bible says 'honor thy parents;' it says *nothing* about liking them. The idea that every family is happy is a romantic myth; it's a lot closer to say that in every family there's a good tradition of love and hate, all mixed up. That's just 'normal' families. There are a lot of families out there that don't even get close to being normal. Third rank as well. And that sums it up. We're just very short of suspects.

"We've got one valuable thing today, though; a timeline. Establishing that is one of the most important aspects of investigating a case. Once we have a timeline, we can focus the investigation on specifics instead of generalities. We can be reasonably sure that Jenny was picked up on the way to school. It would still be more or less dark then and her kidnapping would be less likely to draw attention. She was kept in that ruined building for several hours, I'd guess until mid-afternoon; then she was killed. You found her late afternoon and the word got out by early evening. That gives us a time to ask questions about."

Skelton thought for a minute. "Doesn't that exclude Miss Rosedale then? She would have been in school all that day?"

"She could have grabbed Jenny on her way to school. Nobody would think it amiss if a teacher and her protégé were seen walking together. Left her in the building all day and killed her after school. That would mean Jenny was left alone, though; that doesn't ring true to me.

"That's another importance of the timeline. It's beginning to tell us, quite strongly, that more than one person was involved in her killing. And that excludes a whole range of possibilities we had to consider before."

"I don't know about that, Father. Perhaps you'd better refocus on Cross." Inspector Malcombe's voice was stressed. "We found these in his room."

Conrad took the pile of pictures and flipped through them, grimacing as he did so. "This poor girl is Jenny Durham?"

"That she is. They're all of her undressed and tied up in the building where she was found. These must be Cross's souvenirs."

Conrad looked at the pictures again, then frowned. "Inspector, did you find Cross's camera?"

Malcombe looked confused. "No, why?"

"Take a look at these pictures. Notice how sharp they are? And look at the depth of field. Almost everything is in focus, from about 12 inches to some ruins 40 or 50 yards away. To get this quality of picture, they must have been taken with a very expensive camera using some high-quality film. Neither are easily available in Britain right now. You can be pretty sure that it's a pre-war German camera; probably a Leica. Nothing else has lenses good enough. Now, how many people in this town have a camera like this? I'd really be surprised if anybody has one. If they do, I'd say they have one because their work requires it. A journalist, perhaps? Some sort of professional photographer certainly."

"A pornographer?" Malcombe's voice was still strained with anger.

"Could be. If that's the case, and Jenny was just a random victim picked up and killed so these pictures could be taken and sold, then we have a very bad problem on our hands. Somehow, I don't think so though. There's no history of this; no evidence of any previous similar events. Nothing. I still think this is an isolated event.

"I'll ask something else. How did these pictures get processed? These pictures had to be processed privately, probably in somebody's own dark room. That points to this being an isolated incident as well. So, back to my original point, any sign of a camera?"

"No. He could have got rid of it."

"Got rid of a very expensive and irreplaceable camera yet kept the incriminating pictures. Doesn't sound very plausible, does it?"

"Could have been stolen, by whoever turned that room over."

"Yet the same people left a rare and valuable handgun in the room. Where were these pictures found?"

"Taped to the back of a drawer. Foolish really, that's the first place a detailed search would look . . . Oh."

"Inspector, does any of this smell right to you?"

"No, Father. It doesn't."

Interview Room, Solihull Police Station

Cross had a lawyer with him. He'd been cautioned and was aware that things had taken a turn for the worse, for him at least. His lawyer looked grave. He'd guessed that some evidence had been found that had changed the whole sense of the case.

"Mister Cross." Malcombe spoke in his dead-pan official voice. "You say that you only spoke with Jennifer Durham in the presence of her parents?"

"That is true. I insisted. I know how things can be made to look."

"You never saw her at any other time?"

"No, sir."

"She never tried to see you at any other time?"

"No, sir."

"Do you recognize this?" Malcombe put the dress on the interview table.

"It is a schoolgirl's dress. Jennifer's."

"How did you know that?"

"Why else would you show it to me?"

148

"Mister Cross, it was found in your flat. In your bedroom, beneath the bed."

Cross looked bewildered, frightened and confused, which was exactly what Malcombe was hoping for.

"We also found these pictures." Malcombe put them on the table, spreading them out so they were all visible. Cross went gray. His lawyer shook his head; it was a small community and he'd known Jennifer Durham since she was a small baby.

"They were found in your flat as well. Clumsily hidden."

"My God, I do not understand. These are terrible things. How could anybody want such things?"

"Inspector Malcombe, is my client being charged with this murder?"

"No, sir. These pieces of evidence are incriminating, certainly; but there are many questions we still wish to have answered. Mister Cross, where were you at the time of Jennifer Durham's murder?"

"I was painting the Haskins house. It was some way away, I was there all day, until late in the evening. I started early and finished late, I did not want to make such a long journey more than I had to. Mrs. Haskins was in and out of the rooms I was painting all day. She can confirm; you ask her."

"We will, Mister Cross. In the meantime, I must advise you that you are now being formally detained for further questioning in the case of the murder of Jennifer Durham."

The Saloon Bar, Red Lion Inn, Solihull

"My round, I think." Conrad waved for the barmaid and pointed to the empty glasses. She waved back and started to draw the pints.

"Where do we go from here, Father? We've got three suspects and I don't think any of them look good. The top space on your card display looks pretty empty to me."

"They are. That tells me we're missing something very important. We're seeing only a small part of the story here. I think, the part we're missing is linked to our friend Cross."

"You think he might have done it after all?"

Conrad thought for a second. "I don't know. We still have to count it as a possibility. But it seems to link to him rather than be about him. Searching his room like that planting the evidence against him. Somebody wants this case to begin and end with him. At the moment we have a discrete incident, one that is contained to a very small group of people. If our suspicions are right and there has been a concerted effort to frame Cross, then it all remains contained. If it looks like we don't buy the frame, the real criminals here will know that we're looking at other people involved and that might lead to them. They might well really do another random murder to divert us. They can't do that now as long as Cross is inside and stays inside. While he's in a police cell, he's got a perfect alibi and a repeat murder will prove him innocent. That will make sure we look elsewhere. In an odd way, by being inside for this, Cross is protecting every woman in the neighborhood."

"Here you are gentlemen. Two pints." The girl hesitated a second, then plowed on. "Father, I heard how you walked Allie home last night, could you do the same for me? I live only a couple of streets away."

"Of course. It would be my pleasure. Just let me know when you have finished up for the evening."

"Rose! Stop disturbing our guests. I'm sorry, Father, Constable, Rose has no call to put you out like this."

Conrad looked at the landlord, catching the tiredness in the man's eyes. "No trouble, and it's a pleasure to walk the ladies home, I like a walk before retiring." Conrad shook his head. "It's a hard life running an inn, isn't it?"

"That it is, Father. I have to clear up each night after closing time and be up again at seven to start taking deliveries and making sure the guests have their breakfast's done right. Fair wears me out, it does."

"You know, there are ten rooms here and only two occupied by guests. I'm sure if you allowed the barmaid to use one instead of walking home late at night, she'd help you clean up after closing time and you'd get to bed early for a change. Her parents would have to agree, of course, but I'm sure they wouldn't object."

"I'll mention it to my girls, Father; thank you for the idea."

Conrad took a pull of his beer. "George, I'm going down to London for a day tomorrow. Talk to some people I know about finding the people who knew Mister Cross the best; the men in his old unit. When does the first train leave?"

"Six-thirty Father. You'll have to get a local up to Birmingham Main Line and then get the Express from there to London. It'll take most of the day, I warn you of that, and it's not an easy ride. The track was repaired postwar, but the repair crews used salvaged rails and filled in the holes in the track bed rather than relaying it. The line works, but it's still rough. I'd get some sandwiches at the station as well; chances are, you won't find any on the train."

"Then I'd better get some sleep. After I've walked Rose home."

CHAPTER FOUR

Office of Sir Humphrey Appleby, Home Office, Whitehall, London

"Yes, Alice?"

Sir Humphrey answered the telephone with a certain degree of relief. He was reading a report from the Ministry of Aviation. His nose, honed by more decades of experience in the civil service than he could possibly admit, was detecting an unpleasant odor; an odor that reminded him of scandalous events that plagued governments in years past.

"There's a Mister Aurens here to see you, sir. A religious gentleman."

Sir Humphrey sighed. *That has to be Conrad Lorentz. I've been half expecting the meddlesome priest to come and see me. This whole Birmingham affair is a ghastly business and Conrad getting involved isn't going to make things any easier. He has such a definitive view of black and white, of guilt and innocence.*

"Conrad, my dear fellow. I'm pleased to see you. A glass of sherry?"

"That would be most acceptable, Humpy. I came down yesterday and I can still feel the bumps shaking my bones. I'm afraid your railway lines have a long way to go before they reach pre-war standards."

"Well, your American friends did go to great lengths to ensure we would have a long way to go. There are still some tunnels we haven't cleared out yet." Sir Humphrey poured out a class of sherry and passed it to his guest. "South African sherry, I'm afraid, but quite acceptable."

"We all have to make sacrifices in this post-war era Humpy. Spain not being in the Sovereign currency block must make things difficult."

"Not just for us, Conrad. The French vineyards were never the same after the Great Famine. They struggle to compete with the Spanish and Italians, but the French chateaus have a hard fight on their hands."

Conrad's Eye

Sir Humphrey sighed. The decline of his beloved French chateau wines was one of the great sadnesses of his life.

"Now, the Australian wines, Humpy, they're really coming up in the world."

"Bondi Bleach and Kanga Rouge? Surely you jest, Conrad."

"Those days are past. They're turning out a really quite acceptable range of wines now. And the South Americans are looking up as well."

"South American wines." Sir Humphrey could hear his voice shaking with outrage. *The days of the great French vintages may be a long time returning, but drinkable wine from South America? Unthinkable.*

Conrad heard the tremor and pressed his advantage home. "The Napa Valley in California has also started producing some very palatable vintages as well. Of course, the cheaper ones have 'added wine flavorings.' "

Sir Humphrey went white and started to shake from the blasphemy of 'added wine flavorings.' He dithered for a few seconds, quite at a loss for anything sufficiently emphatic to condemn the outrage, then decided he had better give up. *On reflection, I should have known better that to try verbal jousting with somebody who'd trained with the Jesuits.*

Once his voice was under control, he got down to business. "Anyway Conrad, what can I do for you?"

"It's this Birmingham affair. There's something missing in the whole picture; a big part of the case is missing."

"I thought the police had a good suspect."

"We do, but so much doesn't fit. He has a rock-solid alibi, and he just doesn't seem the type to take part in a beastly affair like this. If the girl had been beaten or strangled, yes, I might see it; but not this. I need to know a lot more about him. What happened here when Churchill returned?"

Sir Humphrey filled his own sherry glass and topped up Conrad's. "At first, everybody just stayed put. The Free British Army landed and started to take over the UK. The ANZAC units went to Ireland, of course. Frightful business there; what they found horrified everybody. Over here, most of the German units just kept order until a British unit reached them; then they surrendered. That took some time. The re-occupation forces seized the key areas of the country quickly enough. They called it Operation Leopard and they'd planned it well; but the more remote areas, that did take time."

"How long before you got there?"

"Really remote places? Six months or more. North of Scotland, parts of North Wales, they took the longest. We had to secure the cities first; remote, sparsely populated areas could wait."

"So what did you do with the Germans?"

"They were interned and their identities checked out. Then we gave them new identity cards and sent them to live around the country."

"You checked them out?"

"Yes, we contacted the German Paymaster General using a Ouija Board. One knock for he's genuine, two knocks for he isn't."

Sir Humphrey arched his eyebrows and smiled. Conrad lifted his glass in acknowledgement of the sally. His host returned the salute, a little mollified at having gained a measure of revenge for the frightful blasphemy of 'added wine flavorings,' and carried on.

"The Germans had their identity papers, of course; we did what checks we could and that was that. Here wasn't a problem really; everything was quite straightforward. Ireland, it was different. The ANZACs had a most difficult time working out who was who. I believe in the end they flipped a coin. Heads, they shot them; tails, they sent them to the Russians."

Sir Humphrey dipped his head and looked at Conrad under his eyebrows. The Ouija Board had been a joke, this wasn't. There had been no mercy for the SS and *partisanjäger*s in Ireland. It hadn't mattered that some of the worst were Irish. German or Irish, Protestant or Catholic, they'd been shot or given to the Russians who had then sent them to work in the gold and uranium mines.

"How did you organize things? I suppose it was easy enough for the formed units, but what about the rest? Troops in transit and all that?"

"We just did the same. We just put them into an internment camp, looked at their identity cards, gave them a new one and took them where they were to live."

"You never put them back with their units?'

"No, indeed; why should we? We were busy trying to split units up, not consolidate them. The last thing we wanted was German units getting back together as organized bodies of armed men."

"Can we still trace people from the German units?"

"Of course. The Civil Service has been trying to get the British to carry identity cards for two hundred years. Then the Germans brought it with them and enforced it in the Occupation by shooting anybody who didn't have one. So, we just kept the system, *without* the shooting bit, of course. We keep a check on where the Germans are and what they do; just a safety precaution, nothing obtrusive. Just like we watch certain people who supported That Man."

Sir Humphrey looked at his watch. "Why don't I walk you around to the Old War Office Building; that's where those records are kept. Then we can go to Paradiso e Inferno for lunch. Very acceptable little Italian restaurant; all its dishes are off the ration."

"That would be very kind of you, Humpy. Allow me to buy lunch, by way of appreciation."

That is, Sir Humphrey thought, *exactly what I had in mind.* The Civil Service had fallen from its days of glory as well; even the senior ranks found their salaries didn't go very far. He lead Conrad out, stopping only to tell Alice where he would be, then took Conrad down the main stairs onto the street outside. Outside, Whitehall was occupied by a thin stream of motorcycles passing up and down the street, impassively watched by the Guards in their sentry boxes opposite.

"Have you been to Paris recently, Conrad?" Sir Humphrey had to raise his voice over the sound of the motorcycle engines. It wasn't that there were that many of them, but they were noisy. And the noise was one that he found peculiarly irritating.

"I'm afraid not."

"They've finished repairing the Champs Elysee now. An unimaginative reproduction of the old buildings, I fear. I think they would have been better off building something modern, the way the Russians are rebuilding Moscow. They've even rebuilt the Arc de Triomphe, as garish and tasteless a structure as it ever was."

"I'm glad to hear that. I thought that bombing was a mistake, I think even the Americans are coming to the conclusion it might have been."

"Really, Conrad? What we can't work out is why they did it and why they chose Paris."

"The why was easy. They wanted to serve notice on the world that they wouldn't allow any more wars; that, if a country started one, American bombers would be coming for the heart of the government. So they wanted to take out the administrative center in a capital that everybody knew and would recognize. Rome, Geneva and Madrid were neutral, so they were off the target list. Nobody had ever heard of The Hague and even fewer had heard of Belgium let alone Brussels. That left London or Paris. So they took out the Champs Elysee."

"We've often wondered why they didn't do the same to us. Half the Civil Service think its because the Americans hated the French and just wanted an excuse to smack them around. The other half think it's because they still felt attached to us and wanted to spare the heart of London. Symbol of the mother country, and all that. A handful of us think the Americans laid off London because they didn't want to take the chance of alienating everybody here by flattening the Palace."

Conrad laughed rather cynically. "You've never worked with The Seer, have you?"

"We did work together a little, before the war. He was Peter Stuyvesant then, of course, and owned the Herreshoff Shipyard, although that was buried behind proxies. Mostly concerning building small craft for the Navy. Apart from that, we've spoken socially, at cocktail parties and so on. Odd, the room temperature always seemed to go down a bit when he and his, targeteers they called themselves, were around.

"Before that, I never met them when they were all down at Avebury. I joined our little circle just after they left. I was identified by the ones who stayed behind here in Britain and became the Piccadilly Circus. They've always been more associated with Loki's group in Geneva than the Washington Circle. And there's no love lost between Loki and The Seer, that much I do know. When Loki speaks of The Seer and his harem, you can almost hear him spitting."

"Not surprising. Loki lost a lot of his people in The Big One. The Seer never even hinted it was coming and they were in the cities when the bombers arrived. Even worse, from Loki's point of view, the Germans who'd been taking grave risks to keep information flowing to him and then to Washington throughout the War were pretty much wiped out. The Seer had no choice, of course; security had to be absolute. But Loki doesn't see it like that. He sees it as black treachery. Also, he doesn't understand that The Seer doesn't run the Washington Circle, Nefertiti does. Oh, it's an easy mistake to make. The Seer's the strategist, there's no doubt about that, but it's Nefertiti who calls the shots.

"Loki doesn't help himself, I'm afraid. Cheap cracks like that comment about the women over there being The Seer's harem cause a lot of ill-feeling. Look, things like hatred or affection don't even enter The Seer's decisions when it comes to what needs to be done or what people do where. He staffed the NSC purely on people's talents and their ability to get the job done. Everybody who works for him, either in the NSC or elsewhere, knows that. So Loki going around suggesting they get their position for any other reason rubs all of them up the wrong way.

"Then add in the fact that they're two totally different people. Loki's a humanist; he places trust in feelings and instincts. Ask him for advice and he'll tell you to 'look into your heart.' The Seer's cold. An ice-cold strategist, probably the best there's ever been, but he's emotionless; outwardly, anyway. What he keeps bottled up inside him, well, I'd guess there's only three or four people who know the truth there. Igrat, of course, Lillith and Naamah, certainly. Inanna and Nell, probably. Nefertiti and Messalina, perhaps.

"He made the decision to hit Paris personally, and it was based on one thing alone. Look behind you and you can see it from here. The Champs Elysee is straight; as dead straight as makes no difference. Whitehall has that big bend in it. A B-36 can't change course quickly enough to keep the stream of bombs on Whitehall around that turn. That's it; as simple a reason as that."

"Incredible."

Sir Humphrey shook his head. That his beloved Whitehall had been saved by as simple a thing as a bend in the road. "Here we are. The Central Records Office. We'll find everything you need in here."

The doors were rotating glass set in wood. As he passed through them, Sir Humphrey quickly reflected on the people who'd entered the building and what had happened to them. If those doors could talk, they had quite a history to tell. Since Sir Humphrey had been passing through them for more years than he could comfortably explain, he'd long ago decided that if the doors did decide to talk, he'd have them as the guest of honor at a bonfire.

"Now, what unit was it you were interested in?"

"The 29th Panzergrenadier Regiment."

"Ah, yes."

Sir Humphrey went through the files until he came to some cards. "That's right; one of the units from Russia, here to rebuild. When we picked up its personnel, there were eight of them in Ipswich, sixteen in Anglesey, North Wales and we collected one stray in Dover. He was going back to Germany, on leave, the day of The Big One. Must rank himself the luckiest man alive."

"I don't think so." Conrad was looking at the cards, appalled. "He's the one sitting in a jail cell. Matthew Cross now, was Matthias Kraus. There are only 25 of them, from a whole regiment."

"Not unusual, sir."

Conrad turned around to face the voice that had come from behind him. A British officer, complete with Sam Browne belt. Conrad felt the light flickering in the back of his mind. *Another member of the Piccadilly Circus?*

"A panzergrenadier 'regiment,' they were actually battalions, but by 1947 the Germans had shifted their nomenclature and called them regiments, had a total strength of 852 men of all ranks. More precisely, 24 officers and 828 other ranks. A unit coming out of Russia to be rebuilt could easily have as few as 25 men left. A lot of Allied units weren't much better. It was a happy thing that kept the Free British units off the Russian Front. Canadians don't see it like that, of course; they bled badly in Kola."

"Conrad, may I introduce Brigadier Strachan? He is in charge of the records here. Amongst other things."

"Please to meet you, sir. I cannot conceive of such casualties." Conrad frowned for a second. "Why did the unit not go back to Germany to regroup?"

"Not enough men there. By 1947, the Germans were taking men from wherever they could find them. That's why the 29th was split up; to find local recruits and train them. As far as we can tell, they hadn't started that when The Big One made it all irrelevant. We picked up the Ipswich group early; the Anglesey group some six months later. Your stray in Dover was the first out; we sent him off to civilian life before the rest."

Strachan looked at the list. "That's right; one officer, 24 men. Three SdKfw-251/17 half tracks. Good vehicles; we're still using them. My first command after the war was the reconstituted 14th/20th King's Hussars with SdKfw-251/17s and Panther IIs. You want to find these men?"

"Conrad is investigating that horrid murder up in Birmingham." Sir Humphrey was keen to get moving; he was looking forward to his lunch.

"Ah yes, I've been reading about that. Poor girl. We heard about that sort of thing going on in Ireland but never here. Oh, we had hostages shot and so on, but the German troops here weren't the worst sorts. They'd execute by the dozen if they had to, but they'd do it quickly. Never string things out the way the SS and partisanjägers did. Once the ANZACs had cleaned out the Germans in Ireland, we thought we'd seen the end of all of those filthy things. Never thought I'd hear of that sort of thing happening here."

Strachan looked grim for a second. He'd seen the results of partisan warfare and Lidice Rules in Russia and Ireland.

"Anyway, who would you want to talk to first?"

"The man who knew Cross best. His officer, I suppose."

"You're never a soldier, Conrad. Not the man's officer. His sergeant will know him best. Sergeant Gerhard Schmidt, now living as Graham Smith. He works at a printers up in Oxford."

"Thank you, Brigadier. Sir Humphrey and I were going for lunch at Paradiso e Inferno; would you care to join us?"

157

Conrad's Eye

"That's very kind of you Conrad. I'll have copies made of these ID cards; you can pick them up this afternoon. *Paradiso e Inferno*, you say? That's a very good place indeed. Stocks an excellent range of Hungarian wines."

As the party left the records office, Conrad and Brigadier Strachan were convinced that they had heard Sir Humphrey whimper slightly

The Academe Printing Company, Oxford

"Thank you for seeing me, Mister Smith. It was very kind of your company to allow me to speak with you during working hours. May I ask what you do around here?"

"I'm a linotype setter, Father. I type the copy into the machines and it sets the lines of type automatically. All the spacing is done automatically."

"It sounds a skilled job. Were you a printer before the war?"

"Yes, Father. And the machines here are German anyway; they were brought in during the war to print occupation orders and so on. They are not quite the same as the ones I used before the war, but they were made by the same company. It took a little time to get used to typing in English, and, of course, there are no uses for my ability to prepare documents using Fraktur, but my familiarity with the machines more than made up for that. Forgive me, Father, but surely you did not wish to speak about printing work with me?"

"No indeed. Tell me, do you remember one of your soldiers, a private called Matthias Krause?"

"Matthias Krause?" Smith hesitated for a second. "Yes, I remember him. Mattie, everybody called him. A good soldier; always did his duty, popular with the rest of the unit."

"Did you meet him post-war?"

"No. None of the old gang from the 29th met up after we surrendered and were dispersed. When we were sent here, we were re-organized as three infantry squads, each with a half-track. All that was left of a regiment. We went to Russia with a headquarters company, a heavy weapons company and three rifle companies. We came out with three rifle squads. One of the squads went to a town in Eastern England, to help keep security there. Our officer took the rest of us when we were sent to North Wales. There we were to absorb replacements and to retrain."

"When did you arrive in North Wales?"

"We arrived in mid-April 1947, about six weeks before The Big One."

158

Conrad frowned slightly. "I believe you left Russia in January 1947. What did you do between January and April?"

"We were first stationed in Poland along with the rest of the division. That was just an administrative pause, you know; to assemble the unit. Then we were sent across Europe to England. It was a long trip. The first part was very quick, but the last part took much time. The Amis had shot up all the railways, much worse than here. Once we were into France, we could only travel on the trains at night and the trains were very bad. Then we had to wait for a ferry across to England. Supplies for England took priority over us, and we had to wait for a cloudy night with bad weather so we could use a ferry without fear of the Ami *jabos*. When we could finally cross, the ferry took us to a small port in the east somewhere. I think it was a fishing port, but I do not remember its name. As soon as we had landed, the unit split up. It was a long trip across England to Wales. That also took much time. Once again, we were travelling mostly at night to avoid the jabos."

"Tell me, Mr. Smith. Have you ever wanted to go back to Germany?"

"Why? I have nothing there. The Amis killed my family with their Hellburners. This life here is all I have now. Anyway, to go back to Germany is death. Everybody knows that."

"And you have no contact with anybody from the 29th now?"

"None at all. We were dispersed all over the country and we never saw each other

Conrad looked as his notes. "You say Krause was popular with the unit?"

"That is so. He was always pleasant; he never failed to offer a helping hand to those who needed it. And he was very good to go on leave with. Always an exciting time with Mattie."

Smith chuckled nostalgically. "He was very much of a lady's man also. No matter where we were, he would always be able to find ladies to keep everybody company. Not just the usual sort who hang around Army rest areas either; he had a true talent for finding young girls who were still fresh. Some say he was a bit rough with them, but I think that was just jealousy from the other men. Why do you ask about him?"

"There was a murder in the town where he settled. A young girl. Her body was found in wasteland and he is the prime suspect. I am trying to find out more about his background."

"That is terrible. I knew nothing of this. To think that Mattie would have done such a thing. Do you really think that he did it?"

Conrad hesitated for a moment and looked at Smith carefully.

"To be honest, I have very few doubts in the matter now.

CHAPTER FIVE

Solihull Railway Station, Birmingham

"Congratulations. I suppose it's Detective Skelton now?"

"Detective-Constable (acting), yes, Father. Inspector Malcombe wants to see how I do as a detective. If I make a go of it, he'll send me on the right training courses. Big break for me, Father; 'er indoors is right pleased about it. And, to top it off, our Velo came thus morning. Took the morning off to collect it."

"That's one of those little motorcycles, isn't it?"

"That's right, Father; we got ourselves a Velocette KOV, complete with a sidecar for the Missus. Room for a nipper too, if we're blessed. Bit much for a policeman's pay, but our house is all paid for, thanks to my dad. Worth being tight on readies for a couple of years to be able to move around again. And if I make a go of it as a detective, well, we'll be just fine."

"Congratulations. What sort of engine does it have?"

"500cc overhead camshaft. Cost a little more than the 350 but, pulling a sidecar, thought the extra power would be useful."

"Well, I see you've had your share of good news. Anything else happen while I was away?"

"Yes, Father; something I'm sure is part of our case."

"I got a lot as well; some things are quite disturbing. What happened here?"

"Last night, Father. Somebody broke into the Durham's house. Really nasty-minded it was. They waited till the family was at Jenny's memorial service before turning the house over. Really made a mess, they did. Upset everybody, it has; the whole neighborhood has made a collection to give Jenny a nice memorial stone and then this has to happen."

Skelton thought for a second. Then he spoke, slowly, as the ideas formed and fitted together into his mind. "That's right, Father. I didn't think of it like that until I said it, but it's right. This did have to happen, didn't it. It's another piece of the pattern. It follows from everything that's gone before."

Conrad nodded. "I think you're right. We need to talk with John Durham again, but I think you've got it. It's a long way there, but we can probably fit a talk with him in before tonight."

"Don't doubt that, Father. I brought our new Velo down to give you a ride. Official business, see; so I even get the petrol off the ration. As long as you don't mind riding in the sidecar . . . "

Durham Household, Castle Bromwich, Birmingham

"I'm sorry, Father, Constable; I'd offer you some tea, but we're still trying to clear up the mess. They turned the place over right proper, I can tell you. Made a right old mess."

"Did they do any rooms in particular, sir, or did they just do the whole place?"

Skelton was looking at the wrecked house with a professional eye. It looked like the same job that had been done on Cross's flat. *Same peculiar mix of thoroughness and negligence.*

"They might have done the bedrooms a bit more than the others; I'd think they guessed that would be where the valuables were. Fat chance of that; we sold everything valuable we had to buy food down the corner during The Great Famine."

Durham eyed Skelton a little apprehensively while making that admission. Going to the Black Market, even during the Famine, was illegal.

"So did I, sir; so did everybody."

Skelton paused to explain. "That's why we have so little burglary these days, Father. Houses just don't have enough valuables in them to steal. Robberies? Well, a man might get knocked down and his pay packet taken if he's careless or has too many in the pub, but burgling houses just isn't worth the effort. Anyway, it's too dangerous." Skelton didn't need to say why; another result of most of the guns given to the Resistance never having been recovered

"Was anything taken, Mister Durham?" Conrad tried to make the question nonchalant, but he knew there was an eagerness for the answer in his voice than nothing could hide.

"No, Father; not as we can find. Oh, we've lost some stuff; our weekly sugar ration's been thrown on the floor and wasted." The bitterness in Durham's voice was evident; people never really missed sugar until they didn't have any. "Things like that. Spiteful things. But nothing's taken, no."

Conrad didn't reply, but looked around at the ruined rooms. The damage wasn't actually that bad, he guessed the things smashed were accidents more than anything else, but everything had been thrown around. Just as if the place was being searched rather than robbed. Almost as the idea formed in his mind, he saw the faces of the other two men change. He knew that thought had occurred to them as well. Durham got it out first and took it to its logical conclusion.

"They weren't out to steal anything, were they? They wanted to find something particular and were looking for it." His face darkened as he made the final link. "They must have been looking for the same thing they killed our poor Jenny for. Must be the same people. God must have been looking after us, Father, by getting us to the service. If we'd been here, they'd have given us what they gave Jenny."

"God always watches over us, even though even he cannot always save us, Mister Durham." Conrad's voice was gentle. "But I think it is more likely that the people who went over your home watched it until they were sure you were not there. They wanted time to search thoroughly. To their minds, what they did to Jenny was the easy way of finding what they were looking for. When she defeated them, they have been forced to take the harder and more dangerous route. Dangerous for them, that is. Every act like this carries its risk of exposure."

Skelton was thinking, slowly piecing the situation together. "Father, we got it wrong before. We said that everything in this case linked back to Cross, somehow. Well, it doesn't. Put everything together. We have Jenny's murder. The break-in at her school, which looks more like a search every time we get further into this case. We've got the break-in at Cross's flat that was a search as well as an effort to frame him. We've got the break-in and search here now. The constant factor is Jenny. Somehow, she was in the middle of all this. Everything seems to be happening round her."

"What are you saying?" There was aggression in Durham's voice, as if he detected an effort to shift the blame to his daughter.

"We're saying, sir, that, incredible as it seems, Jenny must have done something or learned something that kicked this whole affair off. Whoever murdered her thinks that, whatever it was that she found or learned, is a deadly threat to them."

"And there is only one thing Jenny has done in recent months that is out of the ordinary. She wrote that book on Birmingham during the Occupation that

163

would have made her famous. There must be something in there; it's the only possible explanation. At the end, Jenny knew what it was and understood that if she kept it out of their hands, it would eventually destroy the people who were killing her."

Skelton and Durham nodded in agreement with Conrad's words. At long last, a solid motive for Jennifer Durham's murder was emerging.

Conrad drummed his fingers. "Mister Durham, your daughter was a truly remarkable young lady. I must read that book of hers; perhaps I can spot what it is that turned out to be so important. Is there a copy here I might borrow?"

Durham shook his head. "Not here, no. Jenny wanted somewhere really safe for all her notes and the manuscript."

"Where did she put them?"

"A safe place, of course." For the first time, Durham almost grinned. "When she knew she was getting an advance and royalties and such things, she wanted to open a bank deposit account. You know, keep the money building, earn some interest and get herself a good start in life. She was too young to open one by herself, so we both went down to Swallows Bank. That way, I could sign it with her. She drew the money out of her post office account, princely sum it was. Less than a couple of quid, and the Missus and I gave her a bit more to get her new account started."

Then Durham really did laugh, the memory easing the pain of a lost child. "*Us* go along to look after *her*? After that meeting, I made up my mind; next time I went to the bank, she would come along to look after *me*. She ran rings around that poor manager. Talked him into giving her a package that was intended for much bigger accounts; a higher interest rate, low charges and all that. Then, when he was in shock, she made him throw in a free safe deposit box for all her notes, the papers, photographs, everything. That way, it would all be safe. Even if the bank burned down, the safe and the box would protect her precious notes. She said she had to protect her sources so that people would know where her information came from."

"Does anybody else know about that box?"

"Only the missus; we didn't tell anybody else. Least said, less to spread, you know that."

Skelton nodded; the reply confirmed what he had guessed.

There had been too many informers during the Occupation. The habit of confiding in neighbors had gone, probably never to return. Too many accusations made in the darkness from spite, envy and to avenge some real or imagined slight. Trust was a fragile thing indeed.

Was that what had happened to Jenny Durham? She'd innocently uncovered something, an informer who had paid off an old score by a whisper in the night and was now trying to cover his tracks from vengeful relatives?

It was possible; it fitted the motivation on one of Conrad's cards. It just didn't seem right somehow. If that had happened, Jenny would have been found with a broken neck or shattered skull. It was what had happened to her that had been the mystery. Now, that mystery was fading as the full light of day began to illuminate its darkest shadows.

"Mister Durham." Conrad's voice was urgent. "Can we get at that box? Whatever lies at the heart of this case is in there. I know it. Constable, can we get that information locked up in the police station? It's more than just evidence; I think it is the case itself."

"I can have the manager open the box, certainly. It's a double signature to open it; mine is one, Jenny's is the other. She was too young to have the box restricted to her access only. If we hurry up, we can get there before the bank closes."

"Constable, can you take Mister Durham on your motor cycle? I will follow on foot."

"No need for that, Father; you get in the sidecar and Mister Durham can ride on the back. Bit uncomfortable, but it's only a short hop." Skelton rubbed his hands in simulated glee. "Official duty again, more off the ration petrol."

Conrad and Durham exchanged glances; they knew very well that the policeman was relishing every chance to show off his new motorcycle. Ah well, at least it was a sign that the country was, at long last, getting back on its feet.

"That's settled then. I assume you can instruct the manager to keep the vault open once you're there?" Conrad wasn't sure whether a warrant would be needed for that as well.

"I can, Father. As I said before, everybody has had illegal dealings with the Black Market from time to time. If he argues, my memory of who and where might get a little clearer. Policeman's discretion, one might say."

Conrad's Room, The Red Lion Inn, Solihull

Conrad closed the last page of Jennifer Durham's manuscript and looked at his watch with shock. It was half past two. He'd been reading for more than three hours, without realizing how time was passing. He'd been lost in a world that hadn't existed for almost a decade; an occupied Birmingham in which people tried to carry on with their lives, surrounded by an environment they'd never expected could come to them. One in which black marketeers hid in the

165

shadows, while German Army halftracks stood on the cross-roads in the sun. A world where German military police directed traffic, while the British police tried their best to enforce the law while protecting the people of the city.

Miss Rosedale had described the book as a picture of Occupied Birmingham. That wasn't true. Jennifer Durham had taken the stories she had been told and woven them into a complex tapestry that was much more than just a picture; it was a flowing, living document. She'd shown the city living through the eyes of all its inhabitants; resistance fighters trying to hurt the enemy without bringing down a cataclysm on the city, homesick German soldiers who were mostly little more than boys, Halifax supporters, bewildered by how their excellent intentions and noble ideals had lead to this disaster. Above it all, she had written of the city itself; a city that was determined to survive regardless of what was happening within its boundaries.

Conrad had thought the descriptions of Jennifer Durham's achievement had been overstated, a kindness to her parents; but they had not been. The girl had been a genius. As Miss Rosedale had said, she had the spark; the ability to make the mundane and routine part of an inspiring whole. The book was a marvel; a classic history and one that would become a standard part of the social history of the war. Conrad was quietly determined to make sure that it would still be published and that Jennifer Durham's story would be told.

There were only two things wrong with her book. One was that it was written by a 16-year-old girl and the language and writing style sometimes betrayed that. A good editor would fix that. The other was that nowhere was there any indication what Jennifer had learned that had brought her to her death.

Conrad put the manuscript carefully to one side. There had been three copies in the safe deposit box, along with a pile of photographs and notebooks full of details from her discussions with people who had lived through the Occupation. One copy, plus the notes and pictures, was in the police station, in the evidence room under lock and key. The second was still in the safe deposit box, with a police seal on it and the keys in secure storage. The third was in Conrad's hands. He felt an intense desire to read it again, just to enjoy the pictures so skillfully brought to life.

He turned again to one passage that had caught his eye, describing how the journalists writing the stories in the newspapers had used all their skills to make sure the details would be understood by their readers but not by the German censors, who were unfamiliar with the Brum dialect. The whole section had a lightness of touch that made the antics of the journalists and editors seem amusing; yet the seriousness of the deadly game they were playing was still there and evident.

Outside the inn, the streets were dark; lights were sparse and dim. It wasn't like America, where a city night was a riot of neon signs and streetlights. Britain's power stations had been one of the earliest targets for the U.S. Navy's fighter-bombers. They had been shattered with the same ruthless efficiency that the Navy had applied to all its other targets. Even now, electrical power was in short supply and was rationed; essential uses only. The dim light in Conrad's room, all that the rationing system allowed, made his eyes ache. He knew he would have a headache tomorrow. Gas wasn't much better. The great gasworks and gasometers had been easy targets for the Corsairs and Skyraiders. Most of the cylindrical structures had been so shot up they were far beyond repair. Building new ones was an expensive undertaking.

That was the problem; not the whole problem, but a big part of it. Rebuilding industry needed energy supplies, but producing energy supplies couldn't be done until energy was supplied. In some cities, power was supplied by old warships tied up alongside and converted to floating power stations. Even a little power was a world better than none.

Conrad looked again at the manuscript in his hands. *Jennifer Durham was immensely talented; she'd had a gift from God that would have enriched everybody. Yet she'd been brutally murdered and the world deprived of that gift. In the end, all she'd been able to do with it was to cheat the men who were killing her of the things they had sought. How many more like her had died? Of the more than 160 million people who had perished in the Second World War, how many had been Jennifer Durhams?* As he looked over the darkened city, Conrad felt tears trickling down his face with despair at the loss.

Then, he sighed and went to bed. The dimmed light turned off, he felt sleep coming quickly to him, *where the sun beat down, hurting the eyes of the crowd gathered in the square of a small Spanish town. Standing in the mob, Conrad Antonio de Llorente felt its emotions swirl around him. Excitement, relief, some fear, for who knew whom the Devil had possessed?*

Breakfast Room, The Red Lion Inn, Solihull

"Will you have white bread or brown for your toast, Father?"

Conrad jumped slightly at the unexpected question. "I'm sorry?"

"White bread or brown, Father?" Allie smiled at her favorite guest. "The National Bread was ended at the beginning of the week. No more grey standard bread; a local bakery has started its own bakes again. They're doing white or brown bread and next week we'll have bread rolls with dinner. And we've just had word from the local rations office; butter will be off the ration next month."

"That's wonderful. I'll have white toast, if I may. And my usual breakfast, with a fried tomato. I didn't know you did breakfasts, Allie?"

"While you were away, the landlord said girls who were working late could stay overnight, provided they helped with the breakfasts. I asked my mum and she said it was all right. Made me promise to wedge a chair under the door handle every night, though. Rose tells me it was you we should thank for the idea. Saves all of us from a bad fright, it does. Breakfast will be right up, Father."

Allie went off to the kitchen where the cooks were making the breakfasts. Conrad would never know it, but the girls had put aside slices of both types of bread to make sure he could have whichever one he wanted. He settled down with his paper. The front page news was that the first of Britain's new aircraft carriers, HMS *Courageous,* had been laid down up on the Clyde. There was a long editorial about how this marked the first step for Britain, back to its rightful place on the world stage. Looking around the room, Conrad saw the other guests showing each other the story. It was a shot in the arm, along with proper bread being available at last. Then Conrad caught a little note from the Ministry of Supply. From next month, the old "fruit jam," made from whatever happened to be available, was going to be discontinued and proper flavored jam would be available.

"Crab apple jelly."

"I'm sorry, Father?" Allie was unloading his breakfast.

"In the paper, it says 'fruit jam' is going away and the old proper preserves are coming back. My favorite was always crab apple jelly."

"I don't remember that, Father; honest. It's always been rationing for me; can't remember when it was otherwise. I do remember once my dad got a little pot of blackberry jam; bought it from some folks in the countryside. We all had a little; my mum and dad pretended they didn't like it so us nippers could have more. Then, just before The Big One, things got a lot harder and we didn't even see that."

"It looks like things are getting better now though. Thank you for bringing this over, Allie."

"My pleasure, Father; enjoy your breakfast."

Solihull Police Station. Birmingham.

"Welcome back, Father. After I heard Skelton had given you a ride on his death machine, I'd given you up for lost. You know what we say here about people who ride on his motorcycle? 'Many are called, few are chosen and fewer still survive.' I believe the Good Lord will forgive a strong drink after a narrow escape from an untimely end?"

"Indeed so, Inspector. The Good Book also says 'take a little wine for thy stomach's sake.' Beer and wine are God's gift to us and proof that he wants us to be happy. That makes the sin of abusing them all the greater."

"Amen, Father."

Malcombe eyed Conrad affectionately. Despite his resentment at the interference from London, he valued the help; all the more so, because it came from a man he had come to both like and respect.

"What did you think of Jennifer Durham's book?"

"A remarkable document; all that we were told and more. She truly was a great loss to us all. But, for all I studied it, I cannot see anything there that could have got her killed. I thought perhaps she named names that should not be named, or exposed guilt that the guilty would prefer remained hidden, but I cannot see any of that. What did you see in the pictures?"

"The same, Father. Many of them are pictures of the City before and after; there are those of the Castle Bromwich Aircraft Factory in its prime and after the B-36s finished with it. It's sad. In one of those shots, we can see the building where she was murdered. When she put it in she never knew, of course."

"Any of people?"

"Some. There's one of the leader of the Resistance, but that's no secret. He's the mayor now. Another of somebody who supported That Man; it took courage for him to give her that, but perhaps he wanted to put it all behind him."

"That could easily be so. After years of hiding a bad mistake, it's a relief when it all comes into the open. That's the reason for the confessional, you know. Any others?"

"A few. One of our friend Cross in uniform. Another of his unit when it arrived in Britain. Standard sort of thing; the three half-tracks lined up, with the eight men assigned to each sitting in front of them. Nice shots, too; looks to me they were taken with a really good camera. I don't think they lead us anywhere, though. Where do we go next?"

"I think we should talk with Cross again."

Interview Room, Solihull Police Station, Birmingham

"Mister Cross, I have to warn you that you are not obliged to say anything, but anything you do say will be taken down and may be introduced in evidence.

Do you understand this caution as I have given it to you?" Detective-Constable Skelton read the words off a card, then looked at Matthew Cross.

"Yes, sir. I understand them."

"Constable, do I understand that my client is now being charged with an offense?"

"No, sir; at the moment, the only thing we could charge your client with is possession of a firearm without a permit. If we did that, we'd have to jail three quarters of the city. But, if a charge does become appropriate, this interview will be entered as evidence."

The lawyer nodded, knowing that this interview was unlikely to go anywhere good for his client. Across the table, Conrad took up the slack.

"Mister Cross, that gun is a good place to start. I understand artillery Lugers are rare. How does an infantry private end up owning one?"

"Our officer, Lieutenant Ackermann, loaned it to me. I was going on leave and he said I should have it in case of trouble with the resistance in Britain or France. He had his issue P.38, but he also had the artillery Luger. It had been his father's in the first war. I kept it concealed in my kit until I was sent to live here. I have always hoped, if I met the lieutenant again, I could return it to him."

"I would like to talk to you a little more about Jennifer Durham. What did you tell her about when she spoke to you for her book?"

"A little about our experience on the Russian Front. How barely one man in 30 of the original unit lived through it. I did not tell her the worst things; of how some men died, of what we had to live through. But I tried to give her some of the truth; enough so that she would understand. I told her a little about my family, about Dusseldorf. Not so much about that. Mostly what happened after the day of the bombing; how I came to be here, how I made my life. That was all, really."

"When we spoke before, you said you had never had any contact with any of your old unit. Do you still maintain that is true?"

"Yes. We were dispersed. I do not know where and, if I did, travel is very difficult."

"That is true. You may be interested to know I have met with some of your old unit. They remember you well, Matthias Krause."

"We were together for a long time. And when so few remain, it is hard to forget."

"You will be pleased to know they spoke well of you. They say you were a good comrade, pleasant and never shirked his duty. They also say you were good to go on leave with; that you were good company."

"That is good to know. There were not so many opportunities to be happy in Russia."

"Well, they said you knew how to make the best of what there were. And that you had a talent for finding lady friends, for yourself and your friends."

Cross flushed deep red.

"There were women, yes. Those that hung around the base areas; some German some Russian. The ones who hired themselves out. They were not hard to find. It was harder not to find them, if you know what I mean, Father. I was not proud of going to such women, I was brought up a Lutheran and to do that was a sin. But when I came off the front, having seen so much, having escaped when so many others died, I could not help myself. It was a need more than I could resist. I was ashamed of it but I still could not help myself."

"And was your shame the reason why you were rough with these women? Did you hurt them to punish them for your shame."

"No, Father. I swear to you. I went with them, this is what I admit, and I paid them for their service, this also I admit. But using them was bad enough; I would not make things worse by adding cruelty to the sin. Who told you these things about me?"

"As I said, I found where your unit was dispersed and met with a member of it. The man who I am told would know you better than any other man in the unit. Your sergeant. He is Graham Smith now, but you would know him as Gerhard Schmidt."

To his astonishment, Conrad heard Cross erupt in laughter. The German had to compose himself and wipe his eyes before speaking so great was his mirth.

"Father, you have converted me. I was brought up a strict Lutheran, taught to regard the Catholic Church as heresy; but now I know the truth. Truly yours must be the true Church."

"This is no time to jest, Matthew. This is a very serious time for you."

"You do not understand, Father. You say that you have spoken with Sergeant Gerhard Schmidt in the last two days? Well, in doing so, you have made a miracle that only the true Church could achieve. You see, Sergeant Gerhardt Schmidt was killed in action, in September, 1946."

Conrad's Eye

Conrad stared at Cross in disbelief. He knew the question was going to be stupid before he even spoke, but somehow he couldn't stop himself. "Are you sure of that?"

For the first time, Cross was enjoying himself. At last, he had the initiative. He knew some things the police did not and they had been caught flat-footed.

"I think so. We collected what was left of him after his halftrack was blown up and buried the pieces. His head was quite recognizable; it landed in some soft mud. It was his legs and lower body that were all burned and broken. I am sure he was dead when we buried him. If not, he certainly was a few minutes later."

"But I was speaking with him just a few hours ago?"

"Father, I do not know who you were speaking with. But, I can promise you one thing. I can swear to it on my soul. It was not Gerhard Schmidt."

There was a way of pursuing this further and Conrad had it at hand. He opened his briefcase and took out the stack of identity card copies. Gerhard Schmidt was the one on top of the pile.

"Cross. This is Gerhardt Schmidt."

"No, Father, it is not. I have never seen that man before in my life."

Conrad thought carefully. This is unexpected, yet it seems to make everything else fall into place.

"Cross, I am going to show you more pictures. Please tell me if you recognize them. First, this is Lieutenant Ackermann."

"No, Father, it is not. I have never seen that man before in my life."

"Please wait for a moment. I must get something else."

Conrad left the room and found Inspector Malcombe. "Inspector, I think we have discovered something of great importance. Please come to the interview room and bring the picture of Cross's unit with you."

The Inspector nodded and Conrad hurried back. Cross, his lawyer and Constable Skelton were still sitting, quietly waiting for him. The atmosphere in the room was charged; everybody know that the last few minutes had changed everything. Then Malcombe came in with the picture.

"Please point out Lieutenant Ackermann on this picture."

Cross reached out and put his finger just above one of the crew of a half-track. The man in the picture was crystal clear; a small, dark-haired man with a crooked smile. A likeable smile. The man on Lieutenant Ackermann's ID card was big, fair-haired and looked as if he had never smiled in his life.

"Is Sergeant Schmidt in this picture."

"No Sir, he is not; he was already dead before this was taken. I am here, look." The finger moved to a figure in front of a different half-track. The face was clearly recognizable.

"I don't understand. If Sergeant Schmidt was killed in September 1946, how come his identity card was still in use in June 1947."

Cross flushed with embarrassment. "Father, Gerhard Schmidt was an orphan. He had no family, he never got mail, nobody back home knew about him or cared. So when he died, we never reported it. We continued to draw his rations and his pay and divided them up between us. Not so much extra, but with rations short and pay worthless, a little extra was an important thing. We were going to explain his absence by saying he had gone on leave with me and had gone AWOL. That happened sometimes."

Conrad spoke carefully. "Who else is here with you in this half-track?"

"First there is Paul Inglemann. This is him here, with the machine gun." Conrad sorted through his pile and picked out an ID card. "Yes, that is Paul. A good man who played the piano well. Next to him is Johan Treibitz. Yes that is him; a skillful driver with an inexhaustible supply of dirty jokes."

And so it went on. Cross identifyied each member of the halftrack team that he had served with, then confirmed that each ID card was indeed the man he had just recognized. Then they started on the next halftrack. Cross would identify a man, Conrad would produce his ID card. Every time, the words would be the same.

"No Father, it is not. I have never seen that man before in my life."

The third and last half-track was the same.

"And there we have it." Conrad spoke heavily, even though the mystery was cracked wide open. "Eight ID cards are genuine; 17 are impersonations."

"My unit had only 24 when we got here."

"No, Matthias, you had 25; 24 live men and a ghost. Only those who stole your comrade's identities didn't know that the ghost was a ghost, so they stole his identity as well. Matthias, I must tell you, your comrades who went to Anglesey are dead. Those who stole their identities must have killed them. Otherwise this fraud would have been exposed years ago. The only question is who killed them, and why.

"Now, we also know why Jennifer Durham was killed. This picture was to have been used in her book. It was to have been published and it would have sold all over England, including the places where these seventeen people are living. Sometime, somewhere, somebody would have bought that book, looked at the neighbor next door or down the street and said 'this is not that person.' Then the whole charade would have collapsed. So they had to destroy the photograph and, preferably, the book as well.

"First, they searched the school where they thought the manuscript was kept. Then, when that failed, they tried to take a short cut, kidnapping Jenny and forcing her to tell them where the picture was kept. Only she died before they could get the information from her. So, they searched your flat, planting evidence while they did so, and then her parent's house. But even in death, she defeated them."

"And what you are saying is that I killed her. If I hadn't given her that picture, she would still be alive."

"No, Matthias; you didn't kill her. You are the second person to make that mistake and the first was as wrong as you. Jenny was killed by evil men who had no care for the dignity or sanctity of life. You tried to help a young girl do something that was important to her. In part of what you did for her, her name will live on and her story will be told. I swear that to you, on everything I hold sacred. You cannot blame yourself. You might as well blame the person who took this picture."

Conrad tapped the picture of the three half-tracks and their crews.

"Because he used an excellent camera and good film to produce a shot where the faces of those in it were easily recognizable. Let blame lie where it belongs, Matthias; do not be so quick to take it on yourself."

"Lieutenant Ackermann." Cross's voice was dull, miserable, defeated. "He had a fine camera, a Leica. He was so proud of the pictures he took; some were even published in Signal. The men who killed him must have taken it and used it for those pictures of Jennifer."

"His story will also be told Matthias; again, I promise you this. One question. What did you do between the time you left Russia and the time you came to Britain?"

"We were riding security guard on the railways. It was a common duty for troops fresh off the front line. It was just leave thinly disguised as duty, for nobody harassed the trains when we were out of Russia. We would ride the train between two way points in the morning, back in the afternoon. We were too far east for the Ami *jabos*; too far west for aircraft from the front. After the hell of the Russian Front and the Great Bend of the Volga, riding the trains like that was a happy time. I still remember it as a holiday from the war and everything that happened in it. Looking back, it was clever of our commanders to make sure we had a pleasant time on the railways before we went home and spoke to our families."

"Just out of interest Matthias, did the journey to Britain take long?"

Cross shook his head. "It was quick. Just a train ride, then a ferry to Dover. I think I told you before that the ferries running across the North Sea were beyond the range of the Ami jabos. The only delay was there was too much to go through a limited number of ferries and ports. Why?"

"Because the man claiming to be Gerhard Schmidt said it took a very long time. My guess is that all he knew of the unit was its official record and he made a guess to fill in the time differential. He spoke of his family 'back home,' and that also was a guess on his part. A safe guess, because those records are radioactive ash."

"Now Father, a question for you and this is the flaw in your theory. Whoever did this terrible thing, how did they know of this book?"

"That is an easy one to answer. Gerhardt Smith is a linotype operator at a printers in Oxford. It is my guess that the manuscript was sent to the company where he worked for setting and he saw the picture list. He must have recognized the picture of the 29th. He may have seen a copy when he and his friends killed the men up in Wales and realized the danger it posed. So he probably contacted the others to warn them that danger existed. I will bet they found a way to keep in touch, and set about this course of action.

"If it is of any comfort to you, my suspicions were aroused when Gerhard Schmidt pretended to know nothing of this case. That is impossible; it is still headlines in the London newspapers and all across the country. This placed his honesty immediately in question. He must have known and his denial raised grave suspicions over his integrity. That made his effort to suggest that you liked being rough with your women oddly suspect as well. He went out of his way to point a finger at you and it is hard to imagine an old comrade doing that. Surely, a man with whom you had served for years would have leaped to your defense? Also, what kind of a sergeant would, when asked about one of his soldiers, not comment on what kind of soldier he was? He didn't say a single thing about your performance, duty, or demeanor, only how you behaved on leave. Everything about my interview with Gerhard Schmidt convinced me he was lying and when you told me he was dead, everything fell into place."

Inspector Malcombe cleared his throat. "Matthew Cross, I am obliged to inform you that due to the investigation carried out by Detective Constable Skelton, you are formally cleared of all involvement in the death of Jennifer Durham. If you will stop by my office, I will give you a certificate for that Luger of yours. You don't want to break the law, do you?"

"No, sir. But, Father, I hear you admired Lieutenant Ackermann's Luger. His family has gone; he has gone. I kept it in trust for him but now he will never receive it. May I give it to you? I owe you my life."

Conrad smiled. "I would be honored. If I may, a friend of mine in America collects rare guns; may I pass it to her for safe keeping? I travel a lot and would not be able to look after it properly; and, to be honest, I would not know how to. But it would be secure in the hands of my friend who loves and respects fine weapons.

"Inspector Malcombe, when we first met, I said that I was primarily interested in seeing an innocent man was not convicted of a crime. That task is now done, but there is one thing I must do, I need to make two calls to London so that the people who committed this detestable crime can be brought to justice. May I use your office please?"

"Certainly, Father, and you can collect your new Luger at the same time."

Cross looked at Conrad and the police. It was over; he could go home. He didn't regret the loss of the artillery Luger; after all, he still had an StG-45 tucked away where nobody was likely to find it.

CHAPTER SIX

Office of Sir Humphrey Appleby, Home Office, Whitehall, London

The telephone on Sir Humphrey's desk buzzed. He had a strange presentiment of who it would be, but he picked up the receiver.

"Yes, Alice?"

"A Mister Orrens for you, Sir Humphrey. From Birmingham."

Sir Humphrey raised his eyebrows in mock despair. He really did have better things to do that help Conrad with one of his absurd quests.

"Conrad, my dear fellow, what can I do for you?"

"Humpy, we've wrapped up the Jennifer Durham murder. It links into something a bit bigger. A group of men hiding under the identities of German soldiers."

"SS or partisanjäger?"

"That would be my guess, yes. I cannot think of any reason why anybody else would choose to hide under the identity of a German soldier. There are 17 of them; they killed that many soldiers up at Anglesey. Jennifer Durham stumbled onto them while putting her book together and they killed her for it. What is policy for such people?"

"The Russians have a blanket extradition request out. About every two weeks, the Russian Ambassador comes around with a new list of names or identifies and demands we find them. He goes to the Foreign Office and the FO brings it here. Of course, if they've committed crimes here, we should try them here and punish them here."

There was a silence on the line,

Conrad's Eye

Eventually Conrad spoke quietly, so much so that Sir Humphrey had difficulty hearing him. "I cannot, must not, pass judgment on them. That is for others. Who should be told of this?"

"You've already met him. Brigadier Strachan. In addition to being in charge of records, he also is in charge of hunting down people who have false military records. I have his telephone number here."

Office of Brigadier Strachan, Old War Office Building, Whitehall, London

"Strachan."

"Brigadier, this is Conrad Lorentz speaking."

"Good to hear from you, Conrad; our lunch together is still a pleasant memory. How goes your case?"

"Cracked wide open. Brigadier, seventeen of the twenty-five identity cards issued to veterans of the 29th Panzergrenadier Regiment were given to imposters. We have every reason to believe that the genuine veterans were killed and their places taken by others. Who those others are, we do not yet know; although, I think we can make a shrewd guess. Have you a pad and pen to hand?"

"Wouldn't be caught without them. I did go through Sandhurst, you know. Three times."

Strachan heard Conrad chuckle on the end of the line. "That sort of thing goes with our condition. Here's the imposters we've identified." Strachan wrote quickly as Conrad recited the list of seventeen names. "The other eight, we've confirmed as genuine."

"And the girl, how did she fit into all this?"

"The poor creature was going to put a picture into her book, one that would have identified the imposters. So they killed her to get the photograph and destroy her book. Brigadier, you'll have to move fast on this. I gave Gerhard Schmidt the impression the case against Matthias Krause was all but proved. Let him think that their attempt to frame him had succeeded. That won't last long."

"Don't sweat it, Conrad. We'll pull the addresses and have Redcaps there within the hour. They won't be able to run far anyway. One advantage of a transport system that's still shot to hell."

"One thing, Brigadier. If you can find where the men from the 29th were buried, it would be a good thing to recover their remains. We should give those men a decent burial."

The Academe Printing Company, Oxford

Graham Smith saw the Land Rover with the four British Army military police on board pull up outside the printing works. He didn't need to see the works foreman pointing out his position to know the game was up. He left his machine and tried to make a break for the back door of the works. The military police saw him and gave chase, but he made it to the door first. It didn't do him any good.

There was a second Land Rover out back, with another military police detachment. His attempt to break through them was futile. Smith was knocked down, kicked and handcuffed almost before he could understand what was happening.

"That's him. That's the Birmingham murderer." The young lieutenant in command spoke through a mouth twisted with hatred and disgust.

"I see, sir."

The sergeant 'helped' Schmidt into the Land Rover. At some point, the German got tripped up and his face slammed into the metal tailgate. Helped by a strong hand to the back of his head.

"And that's for Jennifer Durham" said a voice quietly.

"Sergeant! I'll have none of that." The lieutenant spoke angrily. "Don't you dare let me see you doing that sort of thing again."

"Sorry, sir; no excuses, sir. You won't see it happening again, sir."

Cell Block, The Glasshouse, Colchester

Military Corrective Training Establishment was such a dull name, Brigadier Strachan reflected. *The Glasshouse is so much more expressive.*

He could remember a time when this was truly a place to be feared. A place where the strongest, most defiant, most mutinous went and came back cowed and eager to please. Not that he could stomach any of the seventeen men in front of him trying to please him. The Browning Hi-Power on his hip, with its 14 rounds of 7.62 Tokarev ammunition, seemed to want to draw itself somehow. Strachan shook his head. He had come into this room dreading the sensation that would tell him one of these men shared his strange gift. Normally, locating another Daimones was a cause for celebration. Finding one of them here would sully the long life Strachan enjoyed. To his relief, the strange sense in the back of his head was quiet.

Conrad's Eye

The men were in a long line, kept in place by the none-too-gentle prompting of the provost sergeants. All were the worse for wear. Some had put up a fight; others had suffered some improbable accidents on the way down. *In fact, if the accounts are to be believed, this is the most accident-prone bunch of cockroaches ever to infest an Army base. Still, at least they are under control now.*

"Pay attention. We know you are not who you claim to be. At this point, we don't know who you are. To be honest, it doesn't really matter very much. We have a request from the Russian Ambassador to extradite all sixteen of you to Russia, so you can face charges of crimes against the Russian people. Of course, if you can count, there are seventeen of you here. That means we will be keeping one of you to answer charges of the murder of Jennifer Durham and sixteen members of the German Army who were aiding in keeping the King's peace at the request of the British Government.

"Now, let me be honest with you. The one man we keep is very unlikely to escape the noose. There is a slight chance that a really good lawyer might convince a jury only somebody who is utterly insane could do what you did. In which case, that one man will spend the rest of his life in prison. More probably, he will be charged, given a fair trial, found guilty and hanged.

"The rest of you will go to Russia, where you will, in all probability, be sent to work in the uranium mines. So, for one of you it's a nice clean drop on the end of a rope. For the rest, spending the last two years of your lives coughing your lungs out in the radioactive dust of a uranium mine.

"Now, you may ask, how are we going to decide who we put on trial and who gets sent to Russia? After all, you are all equally guilty and, if you didn't do the things we are charging you with, you certainly did many others that are just as bad, or worse. So we really don't care which one of you stays here. We thought about this and we decided to have a little game. You will all stay here in solitary confinement until one of you decides to give us all the information we need about what happened. He will stay here; the rest of you will be on the first plane to Russia. I understand an Aeroflot Constellation is waiting for you at Heathrow Airport while we speak.

"Sergeant, take them away and bring me the first one to decide hanging is better than dying a little bit every day of radiation poisoning."

"Well, Sergeant, how long, do you think?"

"Men are having a pool, sir. Shilling to get in; winner take all. I drew 30 minutes."

"Think you're in with a chance?"

"No, sir. Bit too long. I reckon 15 after the doors close on them."

The provost sergeant was wrong. The prisoner known as Graham Smith caved in after 22 minutes.

Commanding Officer's Office, The Glasshouse, Colchester, UK

Strachan looked at 'Graham Smith' with disgust. The man had a broken nose and mashed lips, which didn't help his speech, but Strachan really didn't care too much. All the men he wanted had been picked up in the swoop, so he had all the time in the world. If that meant waiting until this cockroach recovered, that was fine.

"So, who are you?"

"Scharfuhrer Karl-Heinz Reichling. Polizei-Schützen-Regiment 3, 4th SS Division Polizei."

Strachan nodded. That had been a good possibility; one of the SS divisions stationed in Ireland. He'd pretty well assembled what must have happened; it just needed confirmation.

"You are all from that unit?" Reichling nodded. "Write their real names and ranks on these cards."

Each card had a copy of the fraudulent identity document taped to it. Reichling wrote busily for a few minutes.

"Now, tell me what happened, right from the time you left Ireland."

"It was three months after the bombing. The ANZACs were closing in on us. It was not a fair fight; they were fully equipped soldiers, we were partisan hunters. They were driving us against the coast, breaking us up as they went. If we tried to fight, they would call jabos down on us. Hauptsturmführer Vahl…"

"Hebert-Ernst Vahl, the man we have arrested?"

"That is correct. He led us to the coast. There was a small fishing hamlet there, perhaps four or five cottages and a jetty for a small fishing boat. We moved into the hamlet at dusk. There was no resistance. It was easy. We took all the people out of their homes to the church and killed them with knives. We thought gunfire might attract the ANZACs and, if we put them in the church and burned it, that would certainly do so. Then we took the boat and set out. A few of the men knew how to handle the boat and that made things much easier."

"What was the name of that hamlet?"

"I do not know. It was south of Wicklow, if that is of any help. I do know we landed at a place called Anelog. After that we moved up the coast, looking for a place to hide. After a few days, we came upon a small Heer unit;

181

panzergrenadiers, less than a platoon of them. Hauptsturmführer Vahl came up with a plan to attack them and take their place. We hit them at night, killed their sentries and then the rest; some as they slept, the rest as they tried to fight. They put up little of a fight before we killed them all. Then we took their uniforms and their papers and buried their bodies. "

"Bit of a coincidence there were exactly seventeen of them, less the one on leave, of course."

"That was a problem. There were twenty-three of us. One of us was killed in the fight. That left twenty-two. So Hauptsturmführer Vahl had us draw lots. The seventeen who drew the short straws would stay; the other five would have to move on and find another way to hide. This we did and the men who were unlucky collected their packs and set off down the lane. Then Hauptsturmführer Vahl took an assault rifle and shot them. It was hard, but it had to be done. Then we buried their bodies as well."

"Did Vahl take part in the lottery?"

"Of course not; he was our commander."

"I see." The heavy note of sarcasm went so completely over Reichling's head, it didn't even ruffle his hair as it passed. "And the papers and records?"

"That was easy. The panzergrenadiers were supposed to be setting up a training base. They had spare uniforms, all the documents and files, everything we needed to make our new identities. We kept the original files and paybooks, just made up new identity papers. We went through the files and personal possessions to destroy anything that might identify us. It was easy and we had more than three months to do it in before the British units reached us and we surrendered. By then, we had forgotten almost that we had been anything other than panzergrenadiers."

"And you found copies of the unit picture."

"Of course, and we destroyed them. We thought that was it. Then, a month ago, that stupid child's book arrived for us to set to type and I saw the list of pictures. It showed that there was another photograph of the unit and it was to be published. As soon as that happened, we knew it would all be up. So I contacted Hauptsturmführer Vahl by a system we had and told him what was to happen. He sent two of the men to steal the photograph from the school but it was not there. So he decided to get the information from the girl. We picked her up as she went to school and took her out into the waste ground. Hauptsturmführer Vahl made her take off her dress and he took pictures of her so we could make it look as if Krause had done it. We kept her there a few hours and then we killed her. Hauptsturmführer Vahl thought the fire would make her tell us where the picture was, but suddenly she started to bleed very badly from her wrists and she fainted. By the time we could put the fire out and get to her, she was dead. So, we poured petrol on the body and set it on fire again. Then we went to Krause's rooms and searched them, looking for the pictures. At the same time, we planted the pictures and the girl's dress to incriminate him. Hauptsturmführer Vahl thought it would make a well-contained package and the investigation would end there. Then that damned priest turned up and ruined everything. "

Strachan's hand was twitching by his Browning Hi-Power. More than anything else, he wanted to shoot this man and then the rest of them. It sickened him to even think they regarded themselves as soldiers. He forced his voice to remain even by reminding himself that these men would pay for their crimes.

"I have one more question. She was a young girl, barely more than a child. She'd have told you what you wanted to know if you had just slapped her around a bit, frightened her. Why the hell did you have to burn her like that?"

Reichling shrugged. "Why not?"

South of Llanfaglan, Anglesey, North Wales

"Something down here, sir."

One of the pioneers was probing the ground with a long rod, feeling for an area where the packed earth had been disturbed. It was a strange thing, but it could take decades for the earth to return to its normal state after it had been dug up. Over a large area like a mass grave, the soil would be easier to penetrate for many, many years. This time, the probe had sunk deep.

"Very good, Sergeant. Get the men to dig the area up."

It took a few minutes to work down the two meters to where the bodies were buried. The SS men hadn't been traditionalists in going that deep; two meters was the depth needed to stop animals digging up the bones. There was some grumbling from the pit, but Strachan wasn't worried about that. *I'd be more concerned if there wasn't any. Good natured grousing is never a problem, sullen indifference is.*

"Anything down there?"

"Bones, sir; looks like some bodies thrown in, probably five. Camouflage uniforms, all pretty rotted out. Make that definitely five, sir, unless some of these bastards didn't have any heads."

"These must be the SS men Vahl shot. That confirms part of Reichling's story, anyway. We can tell our Russian friends they can add murdering his own men to the charge list. They'll like that; they love to pile the charges thick and deep. According to the map Reichling drew, the Heer bodies should be 100 meters south of here. I doubt if it's that accurate, so we'll head south and probe the ground as we go. Sergeant, a tot of rum for the men who did the digging."

"What do we do with those bodies, sir?"

Strachan thought for a moment. "I'm tempted to say rebury them, but that's not on. Detail four men to clear the gravesite and we'll incinerate them. Scatter the ashes on the sea."

It took another hour to find the grave of the panzergrenadiers and two more to excavate it and recover the bodies. There were only bones left. They were sorted as best the soldiers could manage into the line of body bags that were waiting. They were under no illusions; the chances of the bodies being perfectly separated were slight. Several of the men clicked their teeth as they removed the skulls; all too many had the distinctive marks of a pistol shot to the back of the head. Once the gravesite was cleared, the earth was filled back in and the body bags placed in the unit's truck.

"Plan for these, sir?"

"We'll take them back to London. The bodies will have to be examined with more care than we can manage; it's possible the coroners can sort the bodies a bit better than we can. The survivors of the 29th will be coming down to try and identify them; go by height, I suppose. Then, each man will be given a death certificate with a cause of death, unlawful killing, of course, and they'll be buried. With military honors."

"Sir?"

"Sergeant, the war ended almost ten years ago. These men were killed three months after The Big One, when they were technically serving His Majesty by keeping order until Free British forces could relieve them. So, we bury them with military honors. Anyway, I promised a friend of mine that they would be properly buried and to me, that means burying them as soldiers."

"We're not putting them under the swastika. Nobody will stand for that." There was a warning note in the sergeant's voice, one that only a foolish officer would ignore.

"Of course not. The matter has already been decided. They'll be buried under their regimental flag. It's an innocuous thing. A light blue flag, with a green diamond in the middle and a sword running top to bottom of the diamond. Nothing anybody could take offense at. But, they'll get the salute and the last post. For *our* honor, as well as theirs."

The sergeant nodded. The silence as the bodies were placed in the truck was broken by a messenger arriving on a motorcycle.

"Sorry to disturb you, sir; urgent message from headquarters."

Strachan broke off for a moment and read the flimsy. "Well, Sergeant, an interesting development. It appears Reichling was charged this afternoon at Birmingham Magistrate's Court and remanded for trial at the Assizes. As he was led from the courtroom, he was shot by a sniper. One round, .303 hollow-point. It hit him in the lower abdomen and shattered inside him. Really tore him up; the local hospital did what they could, but he died within the hour."

"Local citizen doing his nut, sir? Can't say I'd blame him."

"The police found the location of the shot. Sniper's nest; one .303 cartridge case. No fingerprints, of course. Just the letters AU scraped into the concrete, probably with a spike bayonet."

"AU. Auxiliary Unit."

"That's what everybody thinks. The police won't be looking too hard; those guys were damned well trained. Trying to find them on their own ground is pretty futile and the boys in blue know it. And then there's the issue of whether it really was a member of the AUs."

"Sir?"

"The Auxiliary Units are ghosts and legends; specters that hover on the outside of our perceptions of the whole war. We still don't know who was in them or how many. Damn that, we still don't officially admit they ever existed. Then they call attention to themselves like this? Doesn't sit right with me, Sergeant."

"I can't help wondering of there's more of these SS bastards hiding out there, having pulled this sort of trick elsewhere. Might be they were punishing Reichling for opening his mouth, or were they trying to stop him from telling us more? What else did he know that he wasn't telling us? We're going to have to start looking very carefully at the German veterans, and very quietly. We don't want this whole thing getting out of hand. But we'll start when we get back. We'll pull the files on every German unit that surrendered and have a look to see if there are any more likely candidates. We'll also ask the Russians for any clues they come up with when they interrogate this lot."

The Red Lion Inn, Solihull

"There we are, that settles the account."

Conrad counted out the notes and passed them over to the innkeeper, then passed some more over. "Please share this out between the cooks in the kitchen and the others. I've already looked after Allie, Rose, Debbie and the other girls."

"Kind thought, Father; we'll be sorry to see you go."

"I'm sorry to leave, but it's time to move on."

"Father?" Conrad heard John Durham's voice behind him.

"Father, the missus and I wanted to thank you. If it hadn't been for you, we might never have known what happened. Worse, the wrong man might have paid for it and those bastards got free. We, well, we didn't know how to say thank you properly, but we thought you might like this."

'This' was a pot of crab-apple jelly. *It must have taken the Durhams days searching 'down the corner' to find it.*

"We heard you liked it, Father."

"I do, indeed; English crab apple jelly is my favorite. It really is very kind of you. I'll enjoy it.

Conrad shook the man's hand and went outside to where Detective-Constable (confirmed) Skelton was waiting with his motorcycle. "Official business again, Detective?"

"It is, Father, and the petrol allowance to match. Inspector Malcombe said that I was to make sure you caught your train. He also asked to be remembered to you."

"A good man; please tell him I will pray for him."

Then Skelton let in the clutch and he and Conrad departed in a cloud of blue smoke.

CHAPTER SEVEN

The Seer's Home, **Philotas, Saranac, Adirondack National Park, New York, 1957**

"So, did they ever find out who killed Reichling?"

Naamah put her book to one side and looked across the living room. It was still incomplete. The outer walls and interior structure had been finished but the decoration and partitions needed more work. The smell of paint and sawdust were still noticeable; something that caused Nell a delicate sneeze now and then.

Conrad shook his head. "Not when I spoke to Brigadier Strachan last. They're still looking hard, but there's dead ends wherever they go. The primary theories are that it was a member of the Auxiliary Units doing a little freelance revenge, a local citizen doing likewise or a member of another group of SS survivors shutting Reichling's mouth. My guess is that we'll probably never know. Perhaps it's best that way."

"Are the authorities still checking out the Germans for survivors?"

The Seer was only marginally interested in that aspect of things. To him, the whole affair had one or two interesting side effects that were of much greater importance.

"They are. They staged 'reunions' of the old units so that any 'new faces,' as it were, would be recognized. Of course, that didn't pick up any groups where the whole unit had been wiped out and replaced. Trouble is, there are very few records to go on; your bombers made a pretty clean sweep of that sort of thing."

"We aim to please. It's probably better to leave things to simmer down now. If there are SS survivors buried away, the disruption and mistrust caused by a major search would do more harm than anything the survivors could pull off."

"All matching numbers too."

Eyes swung to Achillea who had her artillery Luger dismantled on a table. She'd been cleaning out the long barrel and wiping down all the working parts after firing it all afternoon. She'd put more than two hundred rounds down it and

Conrad's Eye

the local rodent population had thinned dramatically. It was rather fortunate that the house was so isolated.

"The Luger; all the part numbers match. That's rare. Usually service weapons are a mixture of part numbers. Comes from cleaning in the field; all the parts get mixed up. Not with this one. Bore's good as well. This is a nice piece, Conrad, thank you."

"My pleasure. Seer, Do you have any influence with libraries and so on? Try and give Jenny Durham's book a boost?"

"No, that would be a really long stretch. I could make sure the Pentagon library has a dozen or so copies, but that's all. Anyway, its not really necessary."

"Seen the New York Times, Conrad?" Lillith's voice was casual. You'll find this week's best seller's list interesting."

"She's on it?" Conrad was startled.

"The American edition is, right at the top. It was there last week as well. You really should read more that the crime news and obituaries, Conrad."

"I never thought people over here would be that interested in what happened in Britain. You all seem to have forgotten they exist."

"Our eyes look west now, Conrad; across the Pacific. That's where our involvement is. Northern Europe is still poverty-stricken and inconsequential in power terms. Southern Europe is economically well off, but of little geopolitical concern. The Nordic countries are pretty quiet, especially after we emasculated Finland following the war. The whole axis of world events now lies in the Pacific; for the first time in probably three or four hundred years, Europe is not at the center of events any more.

"But, that has its advantages as well. People here have an affection for Britain; the reaction to Halifax's coup and surrender was almost as much a sense of bewilderment as anything else. How could it happen? How could they have done it? That's fading now. It never went that deep, and people are looking for excuses to go back to the old way of thinking. Occupied Birmingham has given them that excuse. They read the stories of how ordinary people dealt with being occupied and empathized with them. They even got a glimpse into what made Halifax and his supporters do what they did. They see it as foolishness and naivety, not as black treason.

"Even what happened in the end, the postscript that described what happened to her, and why, helped in a strange way. It contrasted the SS and their minions with everybody else. And Detective-Constable Skelton is well on his way to being a folk hero. The idea of a traditional British bobby, complete with funny helmet, on his bicycle taking down a group of viciously brutal SS men all by himself really appeals to people this side of the pond."

"He wasn't all by himself. Strachan and his men did the really grim bit. Detective Skelton never rode a bicycle; he has a fearsome motorcycle, though."

"Details, details; don't bother me with technical details."

"Jenny's book has really made that much of a difference?"

"Oh no; not in its own. I think people were looking for an excuse to change their minds and it came at the right time to be that excuse. It is a very good book though; I've got a copy in the library."

"Library?"

Conrad looked around. The house was large, despite looking like a traditional log cabin, but he hadn't seen any trace of a library.

The Seer grinned. "Come with me."

He went over to the fireplace in the corner of the room and opened a door behind it. Conrad had assumed it led outside to where logs for the fire would be stored. Instead, it opened onto a short passage with a heavy door at the other end. The Seer opened it.

"Blast proof. We're a way away from any likely targets here, but better to be safe than sorry."

Behind the door was a series of concrete steps leading downwards. Conrad calculated they must be at least 30 feet below ground. Another blast door marked the end of the first flight. Beyond it, the staircase went down further, while ahead of them was a large circular room, lined with bookshelves.

"My books." The Seer explained.

"And my records." Lillith chipped in. "As safe as we can make them. Our souvenirs are in Washington, but the records and books are here; most of them anyway. The rest are with Eldest, out west."

"There's another floor below this. That's offices, food supplies, etc. I look on this place as a lifeboat in case everything goes wrong. Let me show you something really special."

The Seer took the group out of the library and down the stairs again. The flight ended in two blast doors.

"That one's just to the second floor I mentioned." he explained. "But this one . . . "

He opened the door and flipped a light switch on. Conrad gasped. It was a vertical concrete well, hexagonal in shape and very, very thick-walled.

"What is this thing?"

"Until recently, the Air Force was playing with ballistic missiles. There were several types being developed, along with supersonic, long-range cruise missiles. One of those missiles was called Atlas and this place was to have been an experimental launch shaft for one. Only, about a year ago, the whole Atlas program was cancelled. It wasn't long-ranged enough and, in any case, we need weapons that point west, not east. Also, it was obsolete; it's liquid fuelled and this launcher was a shaft. That means the missile was on an elevator and it would be lifted out of the shaft before being fired. The only missiles we're still working on are solid fuelled and are fired from silos. I don't think they'll survive; I certainly hope not. So, this whole place was surplus before it was even completed. I bought it through a bunch of proxies, ask Lillith for details if you're curious, and we built this house here. I haven't worked out what to do with the shaft yet.

"Amazing."

"I want it as an herb garden." Naamah's voice was emphatic.

"Can be done. The top opens, of course; the Air Force installed the drives that work the slab before they abandoned the program and cancelled this complex. We've got our own airstrip, our own generators, everything." The Seer thought for a second. "I guess a herb garden isn't a bad idea at that. The kind of herbs you grow are best kept under cover. We can do a lot more with it than that though. Perhaps a swimming pool at the bottom?"

He led the way back up to the above ground cabin. It seemed much smaller now that the extent of the underground structures was known. Conrad looked around. He hadn't had a home for many, many years. He'd moved from inn to hotel to boarding house and back again, never staying long enough to become a fixture. In his heart, he knew that would never change; it was a part of the penance that had been laid upon him.

"This is going to be a beautiful home, Parmenio; I envy you."

"Thank you. Do you want to stay for dinner? Lillith and Nell are cooking."

Conrad shook his head. "I've got a plane to catch, there's something pulling me south and I've got to go where the wild geese call. I'm sorry, ladies; I really would like to stay, but I can't."

"That's OK; another time. Gusoyn will drive you to the airport. May the Gods look after you Conrad."

Hours later, Lillith and Naamah found the Seer in the living room of the new house. A giant picture window gave a view of the Adirondacks that was haunting. But, the Seer wasn't looking at the mountains or forest; he was looking at his own reflection in the glass.

"That girl was really brilliant, you know. She had the sort of talent we see one or twice, even in *our* lifetimes. Yet, the SS killed that girl to try and save their secret identities." His voice was quiet.

"They're murderous bastards, we all know that. That's why you destroyed them."

Lillith's voice was comforting; she had an idea where this was going.

"So, how does that make them any different from us? We kill to protect ourselves as well. Remember that guy Richard Soames? We killed him because he could, would, expose us. He wasn't the first and we all know he won't be the last. So how do we differ from the people who killed Jennifer Durham?"

"The fact you ask the question is a good start, Boss. They'd never think to ask it. None of us have ever killed unnecessarily; not even Nammie here."

"Hey, I resent that." Naamah's voice was filled with mock indignation.

"And Achillea killed because she was forced to. Remember what that guy Richard Soames did? He cut up people because he enjoyed it and he would have gone on doing so. We had enough to hang him a dozen times over; only we couldn't, because jailing him would have exposed us. We just did what the law would have done anyway. The choice we faced wasn't whether to kill him, but whether to save him and we chose not to."

"Those SS bastards killed because they enjoyed it. They slaughtered by the thousand. For them, slaughter, massacre, torture were their first resort. If they didn't have an excuse, they did it just for fun." Naamah snorted. "You want to know the difference, Boss? What would you have done if Jennifer Durham had a picture that exposed us. Honestly?"

The Seer thought for a second, still staring at his reflection in the window. "I'd have sent Igrat and Nell in. Nell would have befriended her and found out what was going on and where everything as, Then she'd have either conned the girl into parting with it or Igrat would have broken in and stolen it."

He thought a little more. "No, not stolen it; replaced it with a doctored photograph that didn't expose us."

"There you are, then." Lillith's voice was still quiet and comforting. "Smart as well. The SS gave themselves away with that whole misbegotten plan. You'd have got us out clean without hurting anybody."

The room darkened as the sun set behind the trees. Lillith and Naamah slipped into the shadows, not pressing their presence but there if they were needed. This wasn't the first conversation of this kind and it wouldn't be the last; only they were the only three who knew that.

Eventually the Seer sighed and spoke, more to his reflection that anybody else. "Of course, the best solution would be for us not to have to hide in the shadows anymore."

EYE OF THE IMPOSTER
Elbingerode, Germany, 1961

Conrad's Eye

CHAPTER ONE

Elbingerode, Hartz Mountains, Saxony-Anhalt, Germany, June, 1961

Q uiet. Do not disturb the birds."

Strahlungjäger Michael Ott hissed out the caution to the three men with him. A strahlungjäger needed all the help he could get when facing an enemy that was silent, invisible and almost undetectable. The birds were one ally, a valuable and worthy friend. When the birds were silent, the *kernstrahlung* was out hunting and that endangered the life of every man in the team. Animals were another. If the strahlungjägers could not hear the tiny sounds of rabbits and squirrel in the bushes, then the kernstrahlung was near. To a strahlungjäger, their ears were as important as their eyes and the clicking box that every one of them carried.

This time, the sounds were good. Some birds were singing in the trees and he heard a rustle in the bushes. Ott picked up his Geiger counter and swung the long pole on which it was mounted in an arc around him. Then he shortened his grip by a few centimeters and swung again. The instrument clicked away, its dial showing the readings for the area. Another shortening of the grip, another swing, another series of readings. The process was slow, painstakingly slow, but neither boredom nor the sounds of life around him could make Ott take anything less than the most scrupulous of care. To be a strahlungjäger was a sacred duty, the most important of all the trusts that a community placed in those who defended it. To fail in his duty could result in a child falling victim to an undetected kernstrahlung.

He took a pace forward and started the process again. The Geiger counter clicked away, confirming that the ground around him was clean and the dreaded *kernstrahlung* did not lurk here. Ott took a deep breath. He was sure; he would call it.

"Friends, we are clear to this point. Mark it."

Five paces behind him, two members of his team took yellow-and-black striped poles from their kits and ceremonially hammered them into the ground.

Conrad's Eye

The path was safe to this point. Stretching back towards the town was a string of similar posts, one each side of the path, five paces apart. A final post, hammered into the center of the path, marked the end of the cleared area. They marked the path that had been safely explored and the absence of the kernstrahlung proven. From now on, it would be surveyed regularly but it would be available for people to use. Here, people could walk in the forest safely. Or as safely as anybody could walk in Germany.

"Time for home, I think."

They were about six kilometers from town; two hours leisurely and careful walk. Two hours out, two hours patiently exploring a new area of woodland, two hours back made a full day's work. More than a couple of hours hunting for the *kernstrahlung* and attention would begin to wander. That mean a small one could slip through the net.

"Will we be taking the path further tomorrow, Michael?"

Jans Vierbein was the youngest of the team, the messenger. It was his job to run for help if needed. Every day the team spent pushing this path out meant it would take him longer to get help if disaster struck, but it also brought them closer to the great prize. That was an overland link to the village of Hasselfelde to the south. An overland route would mean trade and contacts, a small addition to the safety margin that kept the populations from disaster. It would also mean fame for the team that cleared the route. Michael Ott had led the *strahlungjäger* team that had proved the road to Huttenrode was safe. He was renowned for that, and his team with him.

Ott thought for a second. "No, we've pushed this one out well. Tomorrow we will start clearing the triangle."

That will be a truly difficult task. The triangle was the area between this cleared path and another one slightly to the west. It will have to be swept very carefully, because the kernstrahlung *were cunning and could hide anywhere.*

Once, Ott had found one up a tree in the fork where the trunk had divided; it was hidden in the split. The kernstrahlung was just a few centimeters across, but a very strong one indeed. It was slowly killing the tree. Ott guessed that, if it had gone unnoticed, one day the tree would have split open as it rotted. Then, the *kernstrahlung* would have been freed to attack those who had gathered underneath. That tree was now surrounded by orange and black markers; ones that meant deadly danger.

The four men started their walk back along the path they had spent almost a month clearing. They had barely gone a hundred meters when Ott stopped suddenly. The sounds were wrong and he raised his hand.

This area was supposed to be clear. Why are the sounds different?

196

"We cleared this area a week ago." Wilhelm Koch sounded aggrieved. "It hasn't been raining."

Rain could sometimes cause a kernstrahlung to move, Ott thought, *but it had been a dry June, a beautiful month. Anyway, the birds and animals aren't silent, they are just . . . different.* He unpacked the Geiger counter and started to swing it over the area beside the path.

"There's nothing here. Readings are as normal as they get. I'll try a little off the path."

He stepped close to the line of stakes and made another cast with his sensor. *Still nothing. What gives here?* He repeated the process the other side and drew another blank. Then, he stood stock still while he used all his experience to listen to the world around him and understand what he was being told by it. *This side*, he thought, *not the other one.*

A deep breath and a small step off the path. Another careful cast with the Geiger counter, one that still recorded no readings that are that unusual. What it did do was move the bushes slightly and that showed him what the problem was. A body was laying the other side of the shrubbery, concealed by it.

A body with blood on its chest.

Swissair Antonov An-2 Romont, *en route to Elbingerode*

Going to Germany meant going in circles. The devastation wrought upon the country by The Big One meant that going directly from England was impossible, since it led directly over the blasted wasteland of Germany's industrial north and coastline. Likewise, going directly from France was ruled out, since it meant crossing the devastated areas of western German and the Ruhr. The passengers on any aircraft that had to force-land in those incinerated wildernesses would not stand much chance of survival. Radiation hotspots and poisoned water would seal their fate.

Getting into the areas of southwestern Germany that were still inhabitable meant going first to either Czechoslovakia or Poland. Then it was a matter of catching one of the small puddle-hoppers that flew to the isolated refuges scattered between the ruined hulks of the cities. Of all those refuges, the largest and most hospitable was the Elbingerode Valley in the Harz Mountains.

Conrad Lorenz was flying in from Geneva, by way of Prague. He had been in Geneva for almost a year, working with Loki to find one person in the chaos of post-nuclear Germany. Dozens of Loki's circle had been in Germany when the bombers had struck. A tiny few had called in; some after a few days, some after weeks, a few after being silent for months. Those that had called in were

Conrad's Eye

stunned, shaken to their souls by the appalling destruction they had seen. But it was the rest, the ones who never made contact, who were the most eloquent. Long life was no defense against a high-flying B-36 with its nuclear cargo. When months turned into years, the missing had to be presumed dead.

Then, suddenly, there was hope for one of the missing. Rumors had reached Geneva that Manannan mac Lir had survived. Conrad had been in the city on his way back to America after four years in Europe. Loki had asked him to stay and follow up on the rumors. It had taken all his detective skills to sift through the mass of information that was available, trying to find the few hints that Manannan was alive and the even fewer that suggested where he was. But Conrad had nothing but time. So he had sorted through the data and, in the end, found him. He was now Manfred von Leer and was in Elbingerode.

Conrad had found him, but he hadn't told Loki. Before he did, he wanted to speak with Manannan and find out why he had remained out of contact for so many years. *It was simple logic, really. If a man had wanted to remain hidden for so many years, he had to have a good reason for doing so.* Conrad would honor that decision, but he would also give Manannan a chance to change it. *Perhaps whatever reason had caused him to remain isolated from the Geneva Orchestra for so long had faded with time and now he missed the people he had known for so many years.*

Looking down from the biplane as it labored on its way to Elbingerode, Germany surprised Conrad. He had expected to see a blackened wasteland; a desert of ash with only a few burned stumps of trees to break the desolation. Instead, the country was rolling green, a mixture of forest and grassland. He found himself leaning forward in his seat, as if getting a few inches closer would help him see something that would prove he was looking at the graveyard of an entire nation. But there was nothing; just the rolling green.

"You are surprised?" The man sitting on his left sounded almost amused at Conrad's action. "That the land is green?"

"I hadn't expected it to look so fertile down there."

"Take a close look my friend, see if you can spot what is wrong." The man smiled at Conrad, the slightly patronizing smile that any veteran gives a novice who is feeling his way. He paused for a few seconds, then gave Conrad a hint.

"Remember what the land the Czech side of the border looked like?"

"There are no fields." Conrad surprised himself by feeling triumph at passing the challenge. "It's all open country down there."

"That is right; it is all wild country. Nobody lives down there; nobody uses the land. See that small village down there? If we were to fly lower, you would see that the trees are growing in the houses and the roads are vanishing as nature

198

takes back its own. In a few years, that village will be gone, as if it had never existed. There is a lesson there for us in our pride. We may have reduced the village to a ruin, but nature will remove it completely. For all the power of our weapons, we cannot compete with the force of nature. But, look ahead and see what man can do when he wishes. The village below us died and just ahead of us is the reason why. See, we are already beginning to turn away from it. Chemnitz."

The position of the city was clearly marked by the cobalt-blue lake that lay in the center of the ruins. *Perfectly circular, it would have been beautiful had it not been for what it represented. A crater lake, formed by the blast and heat of the nuclear initiation that had destroyed the city.*

The ruins were still there, they were blackened by the fires and shattered by the blast, but now they were being slowly swallowed by the countryside. *In fourteen years, woodlands can make remarkable progress.*

Conrad ran the figures in his mind; numbers he wished he did not know and were amongst the many things he prayed that he could forget.

Chemnitz, pre-war population 255,000 people. One B-36 had dropped a single nuclear device on the city, yield 49 kilotons. The best estimates suggested that the day of the event, just over 127,000 people had died; some instantly, others suffering a more lingering death from massive burns and acute radiation poisoning. Then, waves of epidemics and prolonged starvation had swept away the survivors, already weakened by wounds and exposure to radiation. By the time the deaths were over, barely 25,000 were left and they no longer lived in the ruins of Chemnitz.

Nobody would ever live in Germany's cities again.

"It's horrible." Conrad could barely speak. "Nobody lives there?"

"Nobody." The man spoke equally quietly. "The people believe that if they return to the cities, the bombers will come back. I am sorry, my friend. I should introduce myself. I am Albertus de Chesaux. The lady behind us is my wife, Peretta."

Conrad sighed silently; his policy of remaining anonymous as long as possible hadn't survived this flight. "I am honored to meet you. My name is Conrad Lorenz."

The three passengers shook hands awkwardly in the confines of the An-2, where they sat surrounded by two tonnes of cargo. "This is your first visit to Germany, Herr Lorenz?"

Conrad's Eye

You wouldn't believe me if I told you when I had made my first trip here. Conrad thought carefully, but the chances of anybody knowing him were slight in the extreme. "It is, yes."

He was saved from committing further sins by the copilot clearing her throat. She had turned around in her seat and was now facing her three passengers. Beside her, the pilot continued to change course slightly, keeping well away from the ruins of Chemnitz. He quickly looked up at her, nodded, and then returned to flying his aircraft.

"We are now over Germany and there are some things you must be aware of."

The co-pilot doubled as a stewardess; she spoke in exactly the same tones and manner as she had used to give the pre-flight safety instructions.

"First is your radiation badge. You must never take this off. Even in bed, wear it around your neck. If the black mark on the left spreads past the first red line, contact the local administration immediately and an aircraft will make an urgent detour to pick you up and bring you out. If the black mark reaches past the second red line, then there is no urgency about picking you up. It will be too late to save you.

"Secondly, never go outside the area marked with yellow poles that have thin black bands. They mark the boundaries of the area that is cleared and safe. Beyond the yellow and black poles might be safe. In Elbingerode it probably is, but it might not be. If you are unlucky, you could enter an area that will kill you in just a few minutes. If you see an area surrounded with black poles that have thin orange bands, stay well away from it. Those poles mark the position of radiation hot-spots called kernstrahlung."

She took a breath and shuddered slightly. Radiation was invisible, with no smell, no taste. Without proper instruments, it couldn't be detected until it was too late. All the aircrews that flew over Germany feared a forced landing in a radiation-contaminated area, but the bonuses paid for the flights were too good to turn down. A young couple, like the crew of this Antonov, could make enough money to get their life together off to a fine start. And really, the risks weren't that high.

"Thirdly, your accommodation. You'll have to take what you are given and eat what you are offered. Germany is not a hotel; there is no room for personal preferences. Everything is in short supply and much is still donated by charities. The land that is left usable can barely support the people who are left alive. You are an added burden. I am sorry to be so direct, but you must understand. Where you are going, survival is a finely balanced thing and your very presence disturbs the balance. Also, you must remember that a change in the wind or a

200

day's rain can be hazardous. If you are told to stay indoors, do so. The buildings are designed to protect those inside from fallout carried by the wind and rain."

Once again, the co-pilot of the Antonov paused to shudder slightly. "Another thing, you have been issued with coveralls made of a material that does not carry dust. If you do go outside, you must wear those coveralls along with the overboots that go with them. But, when you come back inside, do not bring them in with you. Every building has a small entry hall that is sealed off from the rest. Take off your coveralls in there and leave your shoes there as well."

"I sometimes wonder why I come to this country." de Chesaux sounded almost droll. "It is not the most welcoming place I know. But the services of a notary are always needed. Marriages have to be registered, babies are born, not always in that order, of course, and always there are deaths to be recorded. So many deaths."

"So my husband flies from refuge to refuge in Germany, recording the births, the deaths and the marriages and brings the registrations out so that they will not be lost." Peretta de Chesaux leaned forward and took her husband's hand, squeezing it slightly. The pride in her voice when she spoke of her husband's duties was obvious and touching.

"That is a noble duty to assume." Conrad spoke sincerely. It was an easy thing to undertake some heroic task on behalf of the afflicted, but to go quietly amongst the carnage, making sure that family records were maintained and those in need could find the information they were looking for, that took a self-effacing form of courage that was rare indeed. "I believe I may have used your records in my research."

"You are a historian, Mr. Lorenz?"

"Only in a small way. I am an investigator, working for a charitable foundation that is dedicated to defending the innocent." *The old cover story and still the best.* "But an old friend asked me to find a relative of his. They lost contact in the bombing and my friend assumed his relative was dead. But there were hints he may have survived and he asked me to follow them up."

"It would be wonderful if that were so. So few have found surviving relatives." Peretta de Chesaux squeezed her husband's hand again.

"Do you think your friend's relative really is alive?" Her husband returned the squeeze, then reached backwards to touch his wife's cheek.

"I think there is a good chance, yes. The evidence appears to lead us to Elbingerode."

Conrad's Eye

"Then your friend's relative is most fortunate. For a town so northerly, Elbingerode and its valley have suffered little. A freak of the winds, the protection of the mountains, all conspired to save the town and the valley it lives in. There are few such places left in German and none the equal of the Elbingerode valley. Mostly, they look like Leipzig." de Chesaux indicated downwards.

Conrad followed his wave and saw the ruins of Leipzig off to the east, this ruined city marked by two cobalt-blue lakes. Again, his mind summoned up the numbers he would rather forget.

Leipzig, pre-war population 486,000. Two B-36s had each dropped a single Mark 3 device on the city. By the end of the day, 231,000 people had died. The city had been unlucky; two other targets had been nearby, Halle and Leuna, and both had taken hits from additional weapons. The Leuna one had been bad. There were key factories there, a massive chemical complex that included Germany's source of chemical weapons. That could not be allowed to survive. The B-36 responsible for the laydown on the city had set its weapon to perform a ground-burst. The factories had been destroyed. The atomic bomb had started an inferno in the vast chemical works that had created a vast plume of poisonous toxins mixed with highly-radioactive debris. That plume of poison and fallout had fallen straight across the unbombed section of Leipzig. Nobody had known the danger; nobody had realized the threat. Survivors of the bombing had crowded into the apparently safe area and walked straight into the lethal mixture from the sky. And so barely a tenth of the original population of Leipzig had survived. And so it was, all over Germany.

Conrad thought about the genial and hospitable Americans who had taken him into their homes, looked after him and had helped him with his cases. Yet, at the same time as they had been so friendly and open, they had also planned this devastation, planned it carefully and comprehensively. They had worked out the perfect way to destroy an entire country. They had held their hand, waited for exactly the right moment and then they had put their plan into operation. They had achieved their aim. The bloodiest war in human history had been ended, suddenly, in a single day, with the bloodiest cataclysm in human history. The implications of that thought left Conrad silent, all the way until the little Antonov arrived at Elbingerode.

Elbingerode Airfield

It was hardly an airfield worthy of the name. A single runway, covered with blacktop to keep the dust down when an aircraft landed. The control tower was a simple farmhouse that had been converted into a rudimentary facility. It doubled as an arrivals and departures building, but its use in that role was rare. Few people wanted to come into Germany and even fewer were able to leave. Germans outside the ruin of their country were the subject of hatred and fear. Hatred that they had brought this destruction down on Europe and fear that they might somehow carry the seeds of that destruction to another part of the continent.

"Elbingerode Tower, this is Swissair Flight 837 on final approach. Expect landing in five minutes."

The message from the inbound aircraft echoed across the building. People standing around waiting started scanning the sky to the east, as if spotting the aircraft would make it arrive sooner. In the control tower, Loring Bauer knew where to look and he had the best tool to look with, a pair of German naval binoculars. They actually dated from the First World War, and had been 'salvaged' by his father after Germany's defeat in that war. It was a daunting thought that they were probably the most advanced air traffic control equipment left in Germany. *Other than the NAIADS communication system, of course.*

Bauer looked in the approach pattern and saw the inbound aircraft turning towards the Elbingerode field. The flash of sunlight reflected from the cockpit transparency had given it away. As it made its approach, he got a better look. As he had expected, it was one of the Antonov biplanes. In the early days, the job of contacting the groups of survivors scattered over Germany had fallen to the Australian-built DHA.89 Dragon Rapides. Later, Antonov had taken the theme of the Australian biplanes and produced a bigger and better successor. The An-2 had taken over the work of shifting people and cargo between the isolated pockets of survivors left by the bombing.

Overhead, the Antonov flew past the airfield, then turned through 180 degrees and made its final descent. Bauer heard the pilot throttle the engine back to idle and pull the nose hard back. In any other aircraft, that would have produced a disastrous stall; the An-2 just wallowed downwards. A second or so before impact, the pilot increased the throttle again. The descent slowed enough to allow a surprisingly gentle landing. The An-2 rolled less than 10 meters forward and stopped. It was as close to a vertical landing as any conventional aircraft could manage.

Bauer watched as the propeller slowed down until he could see each blade making its final turns. The doors opened. Three passengers carefully descended from the cabin. Both men paused to help the woman climb down from the rear door. Bauer recognized two of the passengers; one was the registrar, the other his wife who sometimes accompanied him on his rounds and acted as a counselor to the women. Around the aircraft, handling crews closed in to unload the treasures in the back. Medicines, vitamins and mineral supplements for the women who were with child, radiation detection badges, thick sheets of

Conrad's Eye

transparent Perspex to replace glass windows. The list of things that Elbingerode needed from the outside world was endless.

Inside the terminal, what had once been the farm's barn, de Chesaux and his wife were met by a dozen or so couples who wanted to have their unions or a new baby registered. A lesser man might have demanded that he be allowed to rest after a long and uncomfortable flight, but de Chesaux smiled benignly and settled down to distribute forms to the couples and help them fill out the details needed to relate them to any records that existed outside Germany. The country's own records were now just ash blowing in the wind. Sometimes, the records allowed de Chesaux to find relatives of a young couple. More than one pair of newly-weds had found themselves in possession of an unexpected inheritance due to the work of de Chesaux and his wife. In some ways, though, that was a mixed blessing; the windfall came with the knowledge there were no other members of their family left alive to share in the good fortune.

"Good afternoon, you must be Herr Lorentz?" Bauer greeted the third man who was watching the circus around de Chesaux with a fond and indulgent smile. "I am Loring Bauer, I run the airport here. Not an onerous task, of course."

"Conrad Lorentz. It is good of you to greet me yourself." Conrad sighed to himself; he guessed the crew of the Antonov had radioed the names of their passengers ahead.

"Our mayor, Wilhelm Lang, asked me to make you welcome. He would have been here himself, but we have a slight problem that prevented him. One of our *strahlungjäger* teams is late back from its scheduled search and he is readying a rescue team in case they need help. He asked me to assure you that you will be welcome in his office any time tomorrow morning."

Germany had changed, profoundly, and not just in a physical sense. Before the bombing, a request to meet the town mayor from a visitor would have been met by a stone wall of officialdom and days of bureaucratic delays intended to impress the applicant with the status of those he hoped to meet. German officialdom had learned humility. Conrad reflected on the change, noting that there was not a single uniformed person in the airport. As he glanced around, he overheard something from one of the women who was surrounding the de Chesauxes.

"We don't know how to thank you, sir. Now, at least we are married in the eyes of men, if not those of God."

The speaker was a young blonde woman, lean and almost as tall as her husband. What caught Conrad's eye was her hair; a long mane that was swept over her right eye in the peek-a-boo style made popular by the American actress Veronica Lake.

Conrad turned to Bauer. "Herr Bauer, I must thank you again for coming to greet me and please convey my gratitude to Herr Lang for his consideration. I will contact his office and arrange a time for our meeting that will not inconvenience him. Now, if you will excuse me, I fear my calling calls."

He smiled at the airport manager, at least in part in acknowledgment of the weak pun.

"Excuse me, madam."

The woman turned, her one visible eye wary. "Sir?"

"My name is Conrad Lorenz." Any hope of anonymity was long gone, so Conrad gave up the effort. "I am primarily an investigator, but I am also a properly-ordained priest. I could not help but overhear your comment. I would be happy to hold a mass for you and your husband, at which you may renew your vows to each other."

He raised his voice slightly. "And for any other couple who would wish to attend. I am Catholic, but we all worship the same God and all will be welcome."

The woman's one visible eye beamed with pleasure. A radiant smile spread across her face. As it did, her hair moved slightly. Conrad caught a glimpse of the disfigurement it hid. Her other eye was clouded and blind; the right-hand side of her face was cruelly scarred. The spread of the beautiful smile stopped when it met the fixed immobility of the scarring. What had been an elegant curve of well-shaped lips turned into the twisting of a ruined mouth.

Conrad's expression showed no sign of shock at the glimpse. *Bad though it may be, I have seen worse than that. Dear God forgive me, I have done worse than that.*

His train of thought was interrupted by her reply. "Oh, Father, that would be wonderful. But, I don't understand. You said we could renew our vows?"

"I did . . . " Conrad paused. "What is your name?"

"Olinda, Father; Olinda Kruger. This is my husband Wilfred."

"Everybody calls me Willi."

The man stuck his hand out to Conrad, who took it warmly. Willi Kruger had an open friendliness that Conrad found admirable. That he had perceptiveness to overlook his wife's disfigurement and see the deeper qualities that lay within had already made a favorable impression.

"Olinda, Willi, I said renew your vows, for have you not already made them to each other, in your hearts? And does not God see into the hearts of us all and knows what lies within? Since you have already made your vows to each other, and they are already known to God, tomorrow, at Mass, you will indeed be renewing your vows, not taking new ones. There is a building we can use?" Conrad deliberately didn't give her a chance to reply. "Excellent. So, if we hold your Mass at three? Now, would you do me the kindness of spreading the word of our Mass tomorrow so that all who wish will know when to attend?"

Olinda's head bobbed and she took off on her mission. Her husband paused for a moment, and took a breath before speaking. "Thank you, Father. You have no idea what this means to us. Olinda has feared we were living in sin ever since we made our home together. It troubles her greatly."

"And this troubles you because she has suffered enough already?"

Conrad smiled gently as he saw Willi Kruger nod; for more reasons than the obvious one. Today he had met two couples in whom basic decency was manifest. It was such meetings that gave him the strength to carry on with his self-appointed role.

Road from the Airfield To Elbingerode

A horse-drawn cart carried Conrad and the de Chesauxes to Elbingerode. It was the local equivalent of a taxi, for there were no motor vehicles in the valley; or, at least, none that Conrad had seen. Motor vehicles needed fuel and all supplies of that commodity had to come from outside. The road itself had once been smooth and black-topped, but it had long deteriorated past the point where resurfacing would have been considered a priority. Conrad was actually enjoying the ride. The peaceful rural scene and lack of industry or vehicles reminded him of the 18th century. If one forgot what lay outside this valley and the horror that had created it, then this was a garden spot, a German equivalent of Eden. Then the picture was ruined. The cart turned a corner on the dilapidated road. Off to their left was a quarry, shining white in the late afternoon sun.

"The limestone quarry. During the bombing, people sheltered in the tunnels there." The cart driver explained. "There are several quarries here and we can make small quantities of cement. We could make more, but fuel is not available."

He paused for a long second then continued. "And making cement would be an industry. Creating it might bring the bombers back."

For a second, Conrad thought he was making a gallows-humor joke. He caught the man's eyes and there was real fear there. Behind him, de Chesaux spoke quietly.

"It's the same all over, every place we go to. People are creating superstitions about what will bring the bombers back. Don't go to the cities. Don't build industries. Don't carry a weapon. Have you noticed we haven't seen a single gun since we've been here? The bombers aren't seen as man-made aircraft anymore, but as a supernatural force of destruction.

"Anyway, there is little room for industry here and few skills available to build it. Most people are simple farmers, and every square inch of available land is given over to crops. Even so, there is barely enough food to go around."

Conrad dropped his voice to match. "Something confuses me. There are no priests here? I would have thought there would be a few who would do the rounds of these refuges, to marry young couples, baptize their babies and bury the dead. To leave people like this, their spiritual needs unattended, is cruel." *And the grossest violation of their vows I can imagine,* he added to himself.

De Chesaux sighed. "There are a few, mostly in the South. We are far north here. Elbingerode is about the most northerly of the refuges. If it had not been for the mountains that surround this place, it would have died in the bombing. But there are few indeed. Most German priests died when the Americans destroyed this country. They entered the areas hit by the hellburners to succor the wounded and comfort the dying. Nobody knew about radiation then, of course, or how bad it was. As soon as the bombs fell, great numbers of people rushed to the aid of the stricken and the radiation killed them all. Tens, hundreds of thousands, even more, died even as they tried to help.

"Others saw the devastation and lost their faith, unable to understand how their God could countenance such a massive tribulation. Still others believed this was the end of days. More thought that it was their failure to stand for right that had brought the desolation down. They abandoned their cloth and, in some cases, took their own lives in despair. Of course, more have died since; fourteen years takes its toll on all men, regardless of their faith."

Not all men, Conrad thought to himself. *Or, perhaps the toll is there for us all, but we do not see it expressed in the physical burden of years.* His train of thought was interrupted by a group of people on the roadway. They were congregated around a wide path that led south. Conrad could detect the tension in them.

As the cart approached, they started to make way for it. Then those nearest the path started to call out. "Somebody comes! Young Vierbein comes."

Sure enough, a youngster ran out of the woods, panting with exhaustion. Some of the men moved to help him as he looked around for whoever was in charge here. It was a middle-aged man, one whose posture still spoke of being a non-commissioned officer.

"What happened, lad? Are the strahlungjägers safe?" The voice was loaded with concern, for the work of a strahlungjäger was a risky way to make one's life.

"Yes, they follow behind me. But I have bad news. We found a body in the woods. Stralungjäger Ott thinks he was murdered."

Murdered. The whispered word rippled through the crowd, chilling the air. The cart stopped and the driver jumped down to join the crowd. de Chesaux followed him and Conrad, reluctantly, did the same. He had the same sad feeling he always had when he realized yet another case was being dumped into his lap. *Somehow, someway, another innocent would be accused here and I will have to prove their innocence. All too often, that means finding the real criminal.*

"Mayor Lang?"

The middle-aged ex-NCO, turned around. "No. I am Friedensrichter Heim; Werner Heim. May I help you?"

"I am Conrad Lorenz. A priest, but also an investigator of mysteries. If I may offer any assistance to you in this situation?"

"An investigator? An amateur sleuth who has read too many detective novels and now thinks he can solve crimes."

There was a jeering note in the voice, but underneath it some note of hope. Lorenz knew that this man, certainly not a trained police officer, had already realized that he would be well out of his depth if this did turn into an investigation of a murder.

"I do have some experience, yes. I work for a charitable foundation, dedicated to protecting the innocent from false accusation."

"Jennifer Durham!"

de Chesaux's voice cut through the murmuring crowd with the clarity of a trumpet blast. "You are the investigator who solved the Jennifer Durham case in England. I have read her book; the postscript told of her murder and how you saved the man falsely accused, by exposing a group of murderers responsible for her death and those of many more. The book did not name you, but your foundation . . . "

Conrad nodded, not willing to speak more on that particular case. The brutal death of the young girl, who had such remarkable gifts as a historian, had affected him deeply. de Chesaux was speaking quickly to Heim, doubtless giving him the details of the case. Heim listened carefully and then turned apologetically to Conrad.

"I am sorry for my abruptness. I would indeed value your help, if this does indeed turn out to be a murder."

"Let us hope this does turn out to be a false alarm, Friedensrichter." Conrad frowned slightly. "That means 'justice of the peace,' does it not? You are the police here?"

Heim grinned slightly, while watching the path still. "I am. There is an older meaning to the word, one that can be best translated as sheriff. Here, the words for police have been corrupted and have an evil resonance to them. So Mayor Lang and I went through the dictionary and found the old word, one that has not been corrupted by misuse and foul conduct. Ahh, here they come. And they do indeed bring a body with them."

The other four men who formed the strahlungjäger team were moving quickly down the path. Now they were on home ground. They had improvised a stretcher, using long poles and their coats. On that stretcher was a body; one that was so still, there could be no doubt of the fact it was that of the dead. They joined the group waiting for them and laid down their burden. Heim reached out and folded the cloth back.

"It is Doctor Vogel!"

The whisper ran around the crowd again, this time with shock.

"This man was your doctor?" Conrad asked quietly, shocked that somebody in the community could hate this man so much that they would kill him, knowing they were depriving the whole valley of its medical expertise.

"A doctor in name only." Heim was equally shocked; equally determined not to show it.

"Before the bombing, he was a pharmacist; but afterwards, he was all we had. To know a little is better than nothing. Please, what do you think?"

Conrad knelt by the body. "Well, that's what killed him."

He opened the man's shirt to expose the knife wound in his chest. It was wide and deep, a single blow that had sliced Vogel's heart open.

"From his body, I would say he died no more than twenty-four hours ago. And there are no other stab wounds on the body, nor are there defensive wounds on his arms. Somehow, somebody walked up to this man and plunged a heavy-bladed knife into his chest, without him trying to defend himself."

"That is hard to imagine. A heavy-bladed knife; a bayonet perhaps?"

Conrad shook his head. "I think not; something much wider. And sharper; few bayonets I know have sharp edges. This was a hunting knife, something like an American Bowie. See how clean the edges of the wound are? This was a razor sharp knife, not a dull one. It was wielded with some strength, although its sharpness made it cut easily.Friedensrichter, can we get this body to a place where I may study it in more detail. And who found it?"

"I did. Michael Ott, strahlungjäger."

"Can you take me to where the body was found, please? I need to study the scene."

Ott hesitated. "I can, sir, yes. But today? This would not be wise. It would be a two-hour walk to the scene and the sun will have gone down by then. It would be hard to see much and we will be off the cleared path. When the sun is down, it is too easy to fall victim to a kernstrahlung. My team knows these woods better than almost anybody, yet we hesitate long and think hard before going out after dusk."

Conrad glanced at his watch. It was already almost six. *Just three hours to sunset.* "I have a vital appointment at three tomorrow afternoon. Suppose we meet here at six tomorrow morning? That will be enough time to get there and back before three?"

Ott thought carefully and nodded. "Is that agreeable with you, Friedensrichter?"

Heim nodded. "It is. That being so, I suggest we all take great care to get some sleep tonight."

CHAPTER TWO

The Guest House, Elbingerode

"Once, an evil wizard came to the land and stole people's hearts away. Without their hearts, they became cruel and cold. They looked at the world around them and desired all the things that others had. So, because they had no hearts to hold pity, they took the things that belonged to others and made slaves of those who had once owned them. The enslaved people cried out in their misery and begged for rescue. A great silver bird, called SAC, heard their prayers and it looked down on the people without hearts. It saw their greed and cruelty and decided that these people did not deserve to survive. So the great silver bird breathed fire and destruction on them. The ground shook with its anger and everything that the people without hearts owned was burned in the great fires. They were left with nothing but the ashes of their land to remind them of their evil.

"But all was not lost, for the evil wizard had died in the great fires and without his spells, the people's hearts began to grow again. As their hearts slowly grew, so too did the understanding of what they had done and why the great silver bird had destroyed them. They vowed that they would never again let their hearts be stolen away. To help them, the great silver bird left its children hiding in the woods and in the ruins of the cities. These children were called the Kernstrahlung and they watched the people carefully. If they saw somebody who was growing without a heart, they would kill them. So, be very careful what you do and say for if you cheat people or hurt them, the Kernstrahlung will decide you have no heart and they will come in the night and kill you."

Conrad looked around the alehouse and saw some of the women taking their children to bed. The scene was another throwback, to the days when Conrad had walked the forests of Germany by himself; when roads were paths through the forest and communities were small villages where everybody knew everybody else.

A world where people gathered in the alehouses for the evening, and amused themselves by telling stories. Sometimes, the stories were just an adventure; others had morals and were intended to teach. It was a world where

Conrad's Eye

a good storyteller could earn a comfortable living and be sure of a welcome wherever he went. It was also, Conrad reminded himself, a world where each community was a closed-off world. One where a stranger who didn't fit in was regarded with suspicion and the first to be accused when something went wrong.

"Good ale, Father?"

Another throwback to the past, men brewed their own ale and took pride in it. It was served here in small glasses and sipped, not gulped; there was little enough to go around.

"Searching for a kindly word, Fritz?" One of the farmers put a teasing note into his voice. "Here, Father, try my real farmer's ale. Take away the taste of Fritz's pale imitation beer."

Conrad picked up his glass and tasted the beer. "Another fine ale. A stronger flavor, but perhaps a little rougher. I would prefer this one with a meal, but I think Fritz's would make a better after-dinner drink."

"You leave the Father alone." A young woman was standing behind Conrad. "I am sorry, Father, but Fritz and Botho have been ale-rivals for years. They are always trying to score points off each other."

"All in good fellowship, Liese." Fritz laughed at the irritation on the woman's face. "And the Father answered like a true diplomat. For which he deserves another glass."

Conrad couldn't resist the temptation to produce his favorite quotation. "Liese, ale is God's proof that he loves us and wants us to be happy."

Liese raised her eyes upwards in exasperation. Then she shook her head and smiled. "Father, may Ulrich and I attend your wedding mass tomorrow? It would mean much to us."

"Of course; all are welcome." Conrad smiled gently at the women and saw the frown on her forehead vanish.

"Thank you. And, Father, . . . we already have a young child. Will you be holding a baptism as well?"

Conrad mentally kicked himself hard. *How could I have forgotten that?* Then he put on an apologetic smile. "I will now. Thank you for reminding me. I will fix a time with Mayor Lang."

"Father, can you tell us anything about the killing?" One of the farmers had been summoning up the nerve to ask the question everybody wanted to bring up. Conrad glanced at Friedensrichter Heim and got a slight nod in return.

"We know little at the moment. I have examined the body in more detail, but it revealed little more than we already knew. Doctor Vogel was killed by a

212

single thrust from a knife; a large and very sharp knife that penetrated to his heart. He never tried to defend himself or put up any resistance. The killer is right-handed and probably shorter than Vogel was, because the knife-thrust was angled upwards; but we cannot be sure of that. The knife was held sideways, the blade horizontal, rather than vertical."

"Unusual, but all the better to slide between the ribs. And the thrust was probably underhanded, not overhand. Strike at a man's chest overhand and the blade will slide off the ribs." Heim spoke slowly; a man forcing himself to remember things he would rather forget. "I would argue the upward angle indicates that, not a shorter man."

"And you may well be right." Conrad spoke equally slowly, equally seriously. "The first rule of investigating is never to make up one's mind on something early. But Vogel made no effort to defend himself. Even the most peaceful of men is slightly on his guard when approached by somebody larger than him."

"Would this be the sort of knife?"

Michael Ott spun a chair around and sat on it, his arms resting on the back. In one hand was a heavy-bladed knife; double-edged, with the upper cutting edge running about a third of the way down the blade. The rest of that edge was cut in a saw-tooth pattern. It was a wicked-looking weapon.

"Very possibly. It is yours?" To Conrad's eyes, the knife looked like a Bowie, but the upper edge was convex, not concave.

"All the strahlungjägers carry knives like this. It is a good multi-purpose tool; but also, out beyond the cleared areas, it is a needed weapon. Out there, a knifeless man is a lifeless man."

"You mark my words, it was Hans Koertig who killed Dr. Vogel."

The woman's voice was spiteful and petulant, with a streak of vindictive defiance running through it. There was a surge of anger through the crowd, but the woman replied with the defiance more prominent. "It has to be said."

Conrad looked at her carefully. She was short, fat and had small eyes that darted angrily around the room.

"Doctor Vogel proved he was the father, so he killed him. It has to be said," she repeated.

"Along with everything else you have accused him of?"

The voice came from the gathering and was laced with a strange mixture of anger and boredom. "Why don't you just go for a long walk in the woods and meet with a kernstrahlung?" The voice was from the back of the room, but there was a murmur of agreement at that idea.

"That's enough of that." Heim snapped out the order. "Frau Hahn, I have warned you before about these groundless accusations against Strahlungjäger Koertig. Now, if you cannot hold your tongue, leave this room."

"It has to be . . . "

"Leave this room now." Heim's voice was commanding and was not to be contradicted. *Definitely that of an ex-Army NCO.* The woman stood for a second, her face and posture angry and defiant. Then she turned and stamped out of the room, slamming the inner door behind her. Heim paused for a second and then sat down again.

"My apologies, Father, that was not behavior we encourage."

Conrad looked at Heim. "What was all that about?"

Heim sighed and sipped his glass of ale. "Most of the women here who can have babies settle down with their husband and become a normal family. A few, though, say that it is better for them to have their babies by different fathers so the population becomes more diverse. As a community, it makes little difference to us; we all join together in looking after the women and children anyway. Traute Hahn has a daughter, Silke, who is one of those who has chosen to have her babies by different fathers. Or so she says. She has only the one so far, but she will not name the father of that baby. Again, this is no problem; it is a matter between her and the father. Only her mother will not accept this. When she could not bully Silke into naming the father, she took it on herself to decide on his identity. She picked Strahlungjäger Koertig, probably because he was the most prominent man who was without a wife, and accused him. She demanded he be made to marry Silke. When the Mayor refused, she started to accuse the strahlungjäger of committing every offense she could think of. When it snows, it is his fault; if it rains, he is to blame. If somebody slips in the mud, Frau Hahn is there to accuse Koertig of pushing him over."

"Is there any chance Hans Koertig is the father?" Conrad shook his head at the tale. He had run into similar situations all too often.

"No." Michael Ott was emphatic. "Father, please understand. Hans runs his strahlungjäger team very differently from me. My team is very closely knit; on duty or off, we are very close. We work together, play together, break bread together. We are guests in each other's homes.

"Hans's team is entirely different. They assemble for work, but when they have finished, they split apart and have little or no contact with each other. But, for all that, they are a superb team; that is because of the way Hans leads them. He is honorable and dedicated; a man who is careful, meticulous and painstaking. We may be different men with different ways, but I would walk down a path he has cleared without a care in the world.

"So, when I say this, I do not mean any disrespect to him. There is no possibility Hans is the father of Silke's child. He does not like or desire the company of women. He keeps his preference to himself, but we all know. And so we treat Hahn's accusation with the contempt it deserves."

Conrad nodded. Then something Heim had said snapped at his attention. "You said the women who can have babies? Is this so unusual?"

Heim spoke slowly. "Not unusual, but some women, especially those from the ruined cities, have been dangerously exposed to radiation and may not have babies. Sometimes, it is rare, but sometimes, a woman who has previously been safe gets contaminated and she must be excluded from becoming a mother. This is a terrible blow, of course; not just from losing the chance to bear children, but it also means her food ration is downgraded. It is very sad, but a deformed and mutated baby is too great a chance to take."

"And who takes that decision?"

"Well, Doctor Vogel used to. He would collect the radiation badges each month and keep the records of the results. If the cumulative exposure was above a certain level, then he would have to break the news to the poor woman concerned."

"When was the next set of results due?"

"Tomorrow." Heim paused. "Ahh, I see what you mean."

Woods, South of Elbingerode

"The air is chilled, for June."

Conrad looked around him; at the path, marked by the yellow-and-black poles, with mist trails forming in the trees on either side.

"I have known colder." Mayor Wilhelm Lang had his old Wehrmacht greatcoat on nonetheless and wore a spotless white silk scarf wrapped around his neck. "But you are right; the weather is indeed cold for June. It has been so, ever since the bombing."

"Dust very high up in the atmosphere, so the scientists say. It only reduces the average temperature by a fraction of a degree, but it is enough to be felt here. You were on the Russian Front?"

"Kola Front." Lang got the strange, blank, long-distance look of a veteran in his eyes. "I spent most of the war on the General Staff, but I needed some time on the front line to advance further. So, I arranged a posting to the 71st Infantry Division. By the gods, I was a pompous arrogant asshole when I got there. Knew it all and never listened to anybody. I learned though; another officer, Asbach, took me under his wing and taught me the realities of life. And, once I had learned them, I never wanted to go back to the staff."

"What happened to Asbach?" Conrad was fascinated by the insight into the Mayor.

"I tried to find him when I got back to Germany. He'd been killed, in the bombing of Duren. Still, he lives on in a way, though. Whenever I get a problem here, I have a small brandy and imagine I am asking his advice. Sometimes, I can almost believe he answers."

"Perhaps he does." Conrad spoke very seriously.

Lang looked sideways at him. "I am sorry, Father. I mean no offense, but you will find very few veterans of the Kola Front are believers. In anything. Where did you spend the war?"

"In America. There are innocents who have been falsely accused in every country, at every time. Especially when a war is on and suspicious people see enemies in every shadow."

"I thought so. I checked on you using NAIADS last night. When a man claiming to be a priest wants to hold weddings in my community, I make sure he is who he says he is."

Conrad mentally sighed with relief. *Loki's circle includes a friend in Rome. He, amongst many other things, made sure that my official ordination date was plausible. It has, of course, been changed a lot of times over the years.* "You have problems with tricksters even here?"

"Of course. Some are petty confidence men who just go from village to village running fixed card games and offering worthless 'family valuables' for sale. Others are a more repulsive sort; the kind who try and sell machines to 'take the radiation' out of contaminated food and water, or pretend a dowsing rod can point to a kernstrahlung. The tricksters just take money and goods, but the others take people's lives."

"Kernstrahlung. I've heard that word a lot. What is it?"

"Literally, it means nuclear radiation. But for us it means a hot spot. That's a point where the radiation is very intense for some reason. Mostly contamination has faded away by now, but there are still some hot spots around. The worst can give you a lethal dose just by stepping on them. They are rare here, but, in the ruins of the cities, they are still common. Young Ott there has a great talent for finding them before they can harm anybody. So does Koertig.

The one that stupid Hahn woman keeps pestering. How he has the patience to ignore her is beyond me."

"Mayor Lang, while we are walking, may I ask you if you know a person called Manfred von Leer? I undertook to attempt finding him and the trail led to this valley."

"Manfred von Leer. Yes, I know that name. To see him, you will have to go to Huttenrode at the other end of the valley. It is not so far, but, if you wish, you can go there by train. I think you will have to go there anyway."

"Why, Herr Lang?"

"Because that is where Hans Koertig and his team are working from. And you will wish to speak to Koertig about this killing. Even though the accuser is a stupid, vicious, spiteful old woman, you will still wish to speak with him directly."

Conrad nodded. "There is something I do not understand about that. Everybody seems to know that Koertig is a homosexual, yet Frau Hahn picked on him to accuse of being the father. Why him? Was there not a more likely candidate she could accuse?"

Lang looked at him with a half smile. "But, with her daughter married to a man who doesn't want her, she will still be able to dominate and control her child. If she married a man who wanted her, and was a full and proper husband who would stand up for her, Frau Hahn would lose that control. Once, when she was having a fight with Silke, she screamed 'if you marry, who will look after me when I am old?' All the neighbors heard her. That tells us much about her I think. And now, speaking of the strahlungjägers, young Ott is calling us."

Out here, Ott was a very different man from the personable youngster who had drunk ale the night before. Here, he was in charge and made no bones about it.

"Herr Mayor, Father, we are about to step off the cleared path. You will stay behind me. You will not touch anything without me clearing it first. Nobody has ever died under my care and I will be most offended if you break my record. We found the body just a few meters into the woods here. People, now we will start to blaze a trail to that site."

Ott slung his Geiger counter and started to swing it over the grass in a slow, thorough, pattern. After a swing that left every square millimeter of ground covered, he nodded and pointed to one of his assistants. That man stepped forward and hammered one of the ubiquitous yellow-and-black poled into the ground by the left of the cleared area. By the time it was ready, Ott had already cleared a patch of ground to the right of his original patch and a second assistance started driving another pole in.

It took almost an hour to reach the scene where the body had been found and another to clear it and a decent area around it. It was now ten o'clock and the chill had gone from the air.

"I call it. The area is cleared. Mayor Lang, Father, you may enter now. But, I say again, do not touch anything or step outside the cleared area."

Conrad started to look around, but there was little to see. Just the crushed grass where the body had been laying. "Strahlungjäger Ott, how did you get here before?"

"Same route, Father, but I only cleared a path for me and enough to move the body out. It was taking a chance, but it was a small one. And my search now has shown taking the risk was justified. What does the scene tell you?"

"Very little, I fear. There is no blood on the ground, so this is not where he was killed. The knife wound in his heart was massive; the doctor bled profusely while he died. If he had died here, we would know for certain. He was killed somewhere else and carried here. Or, perhaps, thrown from the path.

"Hello, what is this?"

It was a long stick with an odd slot in one end, lying just outside the cleared area. Absent-mindedly, Conrad reached forward, only to have his arm slapped away with force that was painful.

"Father, just what part of 'do not touch anything' did you fail to understand? Out here, the unknown can kill you faster and more silently than any knife. That stick is of interest? Then I will check it."

Ott reached out with his Geiger counter and started to run it along the length of the stick. At first, Conrad thought the young man was being officious, perhaps too keen to assert his authority. The Geiger counter changed his mind. Half way along the two-meter stick, the clicking picked up in frequency. By the time Ott reached the end, the clicks had merged to a steady roar.

"Hot; very hot. Johannes, please hold the stick by the cool end and move it so the hot end is further away from us." Ott paused. "That is correct."

He ran his instrument over the ground where the hot end of the stick had rested. The clicking picked up slightly, but nowhere near the roar before.

"The stick is hot, but not the ground under it. This is not a kernstrahlung. The stick does not belong here. I am sorry I was rude, Father, but, if you had touched the wrong end of that stick, it might have cost you your hand. At least."

"It was that dangerous?" Conrad could hardly believe it.

"Far from the worst I have seen, but dangerous, yes. Some radiation can be detected a long way away; other gets absorbed quickly and cannot be detected until very close. This was one of the latter and was strong enough to do damage." He paused and frowned slightly. "That isn't really a stick. It is a dowel, prepared timber. And there is a slot cut in the hot end. I wonder why."

Mayor Lang had brought a camera and he photographed the stick. As he did so, Conrad looked somber. "Doctor Vogel would have known. But now, he will never tell us."

Dr Vogel's Office, Elbingerode

"So, this is his office."

Conrad looked around the sparse room and surreptitiously hoped he could find a seat to sit down in. The walk to and from the scene of the body dump had worn him out. *I have*, he thought, *spent all too much time in America.* Apart from a desk and office chair in one corner of the room, and another seat in the corner, presumably for patients, there was nowhere for him to rest his aching feet.

"It is little enough, but there was little he could do. We have few medical supplies here and those that we have are reserved for the young women, especially those who are with child." Mayor Lang looked around with something that was close to despair. "Here, in what is left of Germany, those who get sick die or get better according to their luck. If their sickness is radiation poisoning, they just die. There is little even a fully qualified and skilled doctor can do. For a man who is no more than a pharmacist, there is even less."

"Does everybody here understand that?" Conrad could see a motivation there. *A person, driven to despair by the sickness of a loved one or by the death of one, might blame the doctor for not doing enough to save them and seek revenge.* It was an ugly thought, and all too plausible

"They understand. Sickness and death is a familiar enemy here. More died from starvation and the epidemics after the bombing than did from the hellburners themselves. Even today, people still die from them. I do not think that anybody would blame Vogel for not being able to save somebody. That is what you were thinking, was it not?"

"It was." For some strange reason Conrad felt slightly ashamed for having had the thought. In the background, Heim nodded. Conrad knew the friedensrichter had been thinking along the same lines.

"What are these?"

Heim looked at the two sticks in the corner of the office. They were each more than a meter long; each had had a brass attachment at one end. He picked them up and studied them carefully. "They screw together; look. And this one has a long socket at one end."

"A fishing rod, perhaps?"

"It could be, but to eat the fish would be unwise. Some of them fry themselves."

Conrad nodded. "Are these Doctor Vogel's files here? If so, we need to take them away and study them."

Heim opened the metal filing cabinet and took out the records. "They are. These are the readings for the radiation badges. They show the monthly results and the cumulative dosage. Now that is strange."

"That the results would be kept here?"

"No. This is where they belong. But, remember I told you that the next set of results were due to be announced soon? Well, the file for the last quarter has gone completely."

The Church, Elbingerode

During his life, Conrad had visited most of the great cathedrals of Europe. He had been distinctly unimpressed. Allegedly built for the glory of God, they had, in his considered opinion, really been built to display the wealth and power, not to mention the vanity, of the rulers who had commissioned them and the architects who had designed them.

In his eyes, the church he was in now was much more worthy of note than the most extravagant of the recognized cathedrals. This one had been genuinely put together for the glory of God, by people who wanted to honor His Name, and had parted with goods that they could ill-afford for the purpose. Nobody else would see the products of their work. It would remain a hastily converted room from a small building in an isolated refuge. One cut off from the rest of the world by the results of the most destructive war in human history.

He had assembled the Mass carefully, aware that this was northern Germany, an area where Protestantism was dominant. So, he held a service that would be acceptable to all and conducted it in German. Personally, he preferred the Catholic Latin Mass, but it would have been inappropriate to this setting and this congregation. Now, the formal Mass was over and he was ready to move to the real reason why the service had been called.

"I now call upon Willi and Olinda Kruger to come forward and stand here before God and this congregation and renew the vows that you have already made to each other."

Conrad spoke the traditional wedding vows; the couple repeated them clearly and proudly. When they had finished, he looked at them and spoke the final words.

"And so, in the presence of this congregation, I now confirm your status as man and wife. Willi, you may now kiss your bride."

Olinda's head and hand moved. Even though she was standing with the scarred side of her face away from the congregation, she still tried to cover it with her hair. Her husband reached out. He took her right hand in his, moving her hair back. Then he carefully kissed her disfigured cheek.

"Every part of you is precious to me, Olinda."

The words were so quiet that only Olinda and Conrad heard them, but they were enough to leave her with a radiant smile and Conrad with tears half-formed in his eyes. Then Willi took Olinda's arm and escorted her back to their seats. Already, the next couple was coming forward to renew their vows. Conrad smiled at them, before starting the ceremony again.

It is, he reflected, *going to be a long afternoon.*

Twenty-two marriages later, Conrad was seriously considering a few surreptitious gulps of the communion wine. It wasn't real communion wine, of course. One of the local farmers had a few vines and had made some coarse wine from the grapes. He had donated it to the church for these ceremonies. *It has one sterling virtue. It is wet and my throat is parched dry from continuously repeating the marriage vows.* He cleared his throat, thinking longingly of the glasses of ale he had drunk the night before, and began the final stage of his service.

"And so, we have all seen our couples here renew their vows to each other in the eyes of God and this congregation. Let them be honored for making this commitment, just as our Church here honors everybody who contributed in word, deed and thought to its foundation. This time tomorrow, I will hold a baptism ceremony here for all those who wish to take part. I will also be available to hear confession from any who so desire. I thank you all for coming today. May the blessings of Almighty God go with you."

"Father, we have a small gift for you."

One of the farmers at the back stood up. His companions were grinning broadly. He held out an old-fashioned beer stein, one that was filled to the very brim with the local ale.

Conrad's Eye

"After your work here today, we thought you might need this."

It was a princely gift, at least ten times the quantity held by the small glasses that were usually served. Conrad took it and quaffed the contents down with relish.

"Now that was truly a noble gift!"

Conrad's Room, The Guest House, Elbingerode

Conrad had his pack of cards out and was trying to put the events of the last couple of days into some sort of order. He carefully placed the first card out. It was marked with the name of his only suspect so far, Hans Koertig. However poor a suspect he was and however the villagers ridiculed the suggestion, an accusation had been made and it had to be checked. In his own mind, Conrad was convinced that Hans Koertig was the innocent he had been sent here to save.

To remind himself of that fact, he had already written another card out; one with the word 'unknown' on it. He resolutely put that card above Koertig's name. The problem was, he had no idea at all who that 'unknown' person was.

He started to make out another series of cards; these giving possible motives. So far, he had two. One card was labeled 'hiding the results of the radiation tests;' the other was 'hiding the radiation test records.' He sighed and made out a third; 'hiding the father of Silke's baby.' The problem was that linking the card with Koertig's was the only pattern that made sense. Conrad drummed his fingers; hiding the results of the radiation tests made most sense to him, so he put that at the top. He put the card for Silke's baby at the bottom. He wasn't even sure if Vogel had the ability to make such a determination.

The second column still contained just the two cards. Koertig's and unknown. Finally he added the third row, the evidence he already had. One card described the knife that had killed Vogel, the second the strange stick found near his body. It was a stark demonstration of just how little Conrad knew. He drummed his fingers again.

Because of that, he nearly missed hearing the knock on the door.

It was Olinda Kruger. She glanced around her and then spoke softly to him, her voice slightly slurred by her damaged lips.

"Father, you said you would hear confessions?"

Conrad nodded. "I can. But wouldn't it be better to make confession in church?"

"You taught us something today Father, even if you didn't mean to. A church is where our hearts say it is and I would prefer to speak to you here. If you do not mind, that is."

Conrad smiled at her and showed her in, carefully not closing the door behind her. He showed her to a seat and then sat opposite, making sure they could both be seen from outside. She recognized the precautions and smiled knowingly. After all, she was now a married woman, seeing a man alone in his room. As they settled down, the de Chevaux couple passed outside. They gave Conrad a friendly wave.

"Father, forgive me, for I have sinned. I tried to take my own life." Olinda's voice was riddled with shame.

The first condition of absolution is there; sincere repentance.

"When was this, Olinda?" Conrad spoke softly and gently.

"About two or three days after the day the hellburners fell. When I saw my face." She hesitated before continuing. "Father, I was always the beautiful girl at school, you know? The one the boys all wanted to be seen with. I had my choice of boyfriends and chose them for what they would do to be seen with me. Even when they went off to the Russian Front, whether I would see them again when they came home on leave depended on what they could offer me. I wanted to be seen with distinguished officers, not common enlisted men; dashing pilots, not plodding soldiers. You know what I mean."

Conrad smiled comfortingly. "You should, perhaps, confess to the sin of vanity. But no more than any other young woman just starting to feel her way in the world."

"Did I tell you I came from Halle? A city to the west of here; perhaps a hundred or so kilometers. It was a nice city then; all my family lived there. Well, most of them. My uncle and aunt had a farm at Kabelsketal on the outskirts of the city. The day before, they had sent us some turnips and onions. Food was already short in Germany then and they were a welcome gift. That evening, they would have been the center of a feast for us. But, we never had that feast. It was afternoon when the sirens started.

I ignored them, at first. We all did, because they were only ever exercises. We all knew the Luftwaffe would stop any bombers reaching us. So I just stayed there in our kitchen, watching the pot of sliced turnips boil. Then, the flashes started and the sound of the explosions. I saw the great mushroom clouds on the horizon. I knew this was no exercise. I wanted to go to the shelter, but I never got the chance."

Conrad's Eye

Halle, population 237,400 souls. Known survivors less than fourteen thousand. Just numbers but this young woman was one of them. A name and a face to put on to a number.

Conrad thought of the United States Strategic Bombing Commission, the people who had planned Operation Dropshot and the cold, ruthless intellect that lay at their center. *Had the Seer ever imagined what his plans meant in human terms? Did he ever think of his victims as humans?*

"You were burned by the atomic bomb, Olinda?"

She shook her head, her hand moving instinctively so that her hair would still cover her burns.

"No. Before I could run for the shelter, the kitchen was suddenly lit up by a terrible light. I think if the curtains had not been drawn, I would have been blinded. The blackout curtains saved my sight. Then, our building was hit by a great wind, one that tore off the roof and caved in the windows. I was knocked down and heavy timbers from the roof fell on me, on my hips and across my neck, pinning me to the ground. I couldn't move. I tried, but I couldn't. Then an earthquake hit us and everything started to shake and roll. I saw the stove start to topple. I saw our pot full of turnips and boiling water falling and I knew what would happen. It fell to the floor and all the boiling water poured out. I saw it rushing across the floor, felt it scalding my face and my hand. I couldn't move. I had to just lie there and feel it burn me until I passed out.

"When I woke up, the water on the floor had drained away but my face felt it was still on fire. The earthquake must have moved the timbers again, because I managed to struggle free. I think so anyway, I must have done. I remember walking through what was left of the streets. They were all lit up by the fires, flickering red and black. The heat swirling around me. The winds trying to suck me into the flames. I must have wandered until some rescuers found me. They took me to a shelter on the outskirts of Halle. I don't remember too much; everything is confused. Father, I think I was quite insane then, although I am sure there were few who were any better

"Then, one morning, things seemed to be clear again. Then I saw my face reflected in some glass; saw the skin hanging off in sheets and the brilliant red where the flesh was exposed. I remember screaming, begging them to do something. I told them I didn't care how much it hurt or what they did as long as they put it right. But a doctor told me that there was nothing that could be done. The burns were too deep. That was when I decided to kill myself. I tried to steal some pills and take them, but the doctor caught me. He said if I wanted to die, I could go ahead; so many were already dead, one more wouldn't matter. But he wouldn't let me do it using medicines that could help somebody who wanted to live.

"So I decided to starve myself to death. I went to a corner, turned what was left of my face to the wall and waited to die. But it was the people in the shelter who started to sicken and die. Soon, we were told that we had to leave, that we would have to go outside the city, to a place called Teutschenthal. I wanted to stay behind, but there were two old men who would not let me. They dragged me up and out, they shouted at me, insulted me, called me a coward and a sniveling little girl. Those were the polite names. Some of the things they called me were obscene and terrible. They made me so angry that I went with them just to keep them quiet.

"There was a column of us. We left Halle behind and walked to Teutschenthal. I may have had to walk, but they couldn't make me eat and I got weaker all the time. I wasn't the only one though. Many people were very sick by then and the column kept getting shorter as people dropped and died."

Conrad reached out and took Olinda's hands in his. Quietly, he felt her right hand. It was as she had said, burned. Not as badly as her face, but the fingers were clawed and had little strength in them. In his mind, Conrad saw the sight of the destroyed, still burning, city. *The glow from the fires, lighting the way for the columns of sick and desperate people walking out into the countryside. Seeking refuge, even though some of them, perhaps most, must have been already dying from burns, blast injuries or radiation exposure.*

With a flash of insight, he understood why Olinda had survived. *She starved herself, refused to eat food or drink water. Yet without knowing it, the people around her had been eating and drinking food that was heavily contaminated. In a strange irony, it was her desire for death that had saved her life.*

He remembered what The Seer had said to him one evening at his home in the Adirondacks. *Far fewer people could have died, but the Germans did everything wrong. It wasn't their fault; we didn't understand quite what we had done either. By the time we had all learned what to be afraid of, it was too late for them. When we made our laydowns, everybody who could rushed into the stricken areas to rescue the wounded. They dug people out of the wreckage, pulled them from the ruins, but they didn't realize that the area was so heavily contaminated that it was death to go there. They didn't know that debris from the devices was poisoning everything. When they moved the wreckage to get at the people underneath, clouds of contaminated dust rose into the air and they breathed it in. Their first response teams 'saved' people who were already dead in all but name and they died themselves in doing so. Their surviving doctors and nurses hurried in to help the sick and wounded and they only succeeded in bringing about their own deaths. By the time they were able to do something useful, they were already dying. So much so, there were few left with the skills needed to treat the sick and the wounded and that pushed the death rate still higher. Then there were the people who'd got to the shelters. They stayed there in the illusion of safety, instead of getting out as fast as they could. They're still there. Other rescue teams salvaged food and water from the ruins, not knowing they were poisoning the people they gave it to. Twice as many people died in the aftermath of the laydowns as were killed by the attack itself. Most of those deaths could have been avoided. Well, some of them anyway.*

Olinda paused for a moment, her face haunted by the memories.

"When we reached Teutschenthal, the people already there drove us away. They threw stones at us and some even fired shots from rifles. They said we carried the sickness with us; that we were all dead and that shelter was needed for the living. That's how it was all over Germany. We were driven away from place after place, always accused of carrying the sickness, of being the walking dead. We found bodies everywhere; people like us who'd been made to walk from place to place until they died.

"Sometime during that march, I stopped wanting to die and started eating again. I remember stealing food from orchards, fields. I suppose I must have been on my own by then. Perhaps I'd fallen and been left behind; perhaps all the others had died. I don't know. It's all blurred; the days and weeks all mashed up into a stew. All I remember is finding the mountains and then coming here.

"That's when I met Willi. He found me, I think, but it was he who brought me to his farm and nursed me to health. For the first time, I found somebody who loved me for me. To everybody else, I had been the beautiful Olinda; a prize to be won, a decoration for people. A way of proving of their manliness, I suppose. But with my face like this? All of that was gone. But Willi loves me even though I am not the beautiful Olinda anymore."

Conrad sighed softly. Outside, another couple staying in the guest house saw him sitting with her and smiled at the sight of a young wife drawing comfort from the wise counsel of a priest.

"Olinda, you did commit a sin by trying to end your life, but under the circumstances nobody would deny you forgiveness and absolution. As a penance for your sin, I will require you to love and honor the man who you married as much as he loves and honors you. To stand beside him. To help him bear his burdens as he helps you bear yours. If you should be blessed by children, bring them up in the image of you both, that they should be as strong and upright as you."

For a second Conrad almost bit his tongue in anguish. *Suppose Olinda had already been told she had received too heavy a radiation dose to risk carrying children?*

Olinda saw him stop and guessed what had caused him to stop so abruptly.

226

"Bless you, Father. And, do not be concerned. My radiation dosage is higher than it should be, but I am still under the level where I must give up any hope of children. As long as a kernstrahlung doesn't get me, I will bear my Willi sons and daughters."

Conrad relaxed. "Olinda, could you answer a few questions for me? I need help with this murder. What sort of man was Doctor Vogel?"

Olinda tensed noticeably. Her visible eye narrowed. For the first time, her manner was guarded. Also, for the first time, there was real venom in her voice when she spoke.

"Most of the women did not like him. There was something about him that made us uneasy. A few of the women really hated him. They would almost spit when his name was mentioned. But, he was the only source of medical knowledge, so we all held our tongues. Remember, he was the man who could stop us having children; so it was inevitable that we would fear him, I suppose. But, now he is dead. I do not know what we shall do."

Conrad needed little insight to know that she was one of the women who would prefer to spit rather than speak his name. *Just what had Vogel done to incite such dislike? That is too mild a word. Such hatred, from a woman whose gentleness was apparent to all? That might be the most important question that this evening's meeting could raise.*

"And Hans Koertig? What do you think of him?"

"He is very nice and a brave strahlungjäger. I feel very safe around him. All the women do."

Olinda's voice had lost its uncharacteristic viciousness and was droll. Conrad shared her smile. It was just about the most tactful way of describing Koertig's orientation Conrad had ever heard.

"Did Vogel have any enemies in particular?"

"The women I mentioned. Some of the husbands whose wives had been found to have been too exposed to radiation blamed him. He was not a popular man, but I cannot think of anybody who would kill him."

Conrad nodded. It was more or less the impression he had gained.

"Olinda, have there been many murders here?"

She shook her head. "Inside the community, no. In the early days, when people from the cities wandered outside the refuges, sometimes they would break into a house, kill those inside and steal food or other things. But those outside the safe areas all died a long time ago. But, for that, you should ask Michael Ott and Hans Koertig. They know what things are like outside."

"And what do you do here?"

"I work with my husband. We grow vegetables and sugar beet. Everybody grows food, Father, and there is still barely enough. I also am responsible for collecting soil samples that are taken away for analysis. Willi is downstairs. He knows all about farms and what can be grown here."

"Then let me escort you downstairs to join him."

Conrad offered Olinda his arm and they left his room. The only problem was, he still didn't have another name to put on his pile of suspect cards. He did, however, have another motive.

Hatred for Doctor Vogel.

CHAPTER THREE

The Railway Station, Elbingerode

Conrad stopped in his tracks as he rounded the corner. *Glory be, it really was a train.* The 'engine' was a railway handcar with a crew of four men. *Two working the bar from each side of the central pivot,* Conrad thought. Behind it, the consist was three small flat cars. One was clear of goods but had two passengers sitting on it; the other two were loaded with goods. It was hardly an efficient little train, but it served its purpose.

"Jump on Conrad!" Peretta de Chevaux sounded very cheerful. "The train will be leaving in five minutes. We cannot leave our benefactor behind."

That morning, when Conrad had come down to eat breakfast, he had expected to be given a bowl of porridge. Only he had smelt bacon cooking and the gorgeous odor of fresh-baked bread. It had turned out that there had been a procession of women arriving, bearing gifts for him. Fresh-laid eggs, home-cured bacon, bread still warm from the oven. Far too much for a single man to eat, so he had shared his good fortune with the de Chevaux couple.

"There are no seats, Conrad; just hang on to the ropes stretched across the deck." Albertus de Chesaux's voice boomed around the 'railway station.' "If the crew have problems, we may have to help push."

That seemed unlikely. Somebody had brought two horses up and they'd been harnessed to the handcar. The train crew checked out their passengers and cargo, then took their positions either side of the pivot. A deep breath, a rousing cheer from the bystanders and they started to work the handcar. The horses leaned into their harnesses and started to pull as well, putting in the extra effort to overcome the inertia of the train. As soon as it was moving along the rails, they slipped their harnesses and left the little train to its own devices.

That makes sense, Conrad thought. *The track is probably level, so once the train is moving, the effort needed to keep it going is much less than that needed to get it started.* What surprised him was how quiet the handcar was. He was used to the cacophony of noises made by steam trains or the roar of diesels.

Conrad's Eye

Compared with them, the little handcar was almost silent. It didn't even make much noise when it went over a set of points.

Conrad pointed at the track leading away from theirs. "Where do those tracks go?"

de Chesaux looked at them curiously. "South I, think; out of the cleared area. To where Michael Ott and his team are working. Perhaps it might be opened if they are successful in finding a way through the woods and hills. This branch leads us along the southern border of the valley, all the way to Huttenrode. We will pass close to the quarries on the way there. This little railway was originally built to serve them."

"Does anybody still use them?"

"Not as far as I know. There are many of these little handcars on the rails, you probably saw the others parked at the station and there are more at Huttenrode. I suppose, if the strahlungjägers find a way through to the valley south of here, the line will be opened then."

The ride along the rails was curiously enjoyable. He had thought that the men on the handcar would be working furiously to keep the little train moving but Conrad saw they had dropped into a steady, economical rhythm that kept the carriages moving smoothly. They passed the quarries, then ran through an area of trees and bushes, before entering open country again as the train turned north. It took barely half an hour before the Huttenrode station was in sight and the train started to slow down. The crew made it look very easy, but he guessed there was a lot of skill and practice that had allowed them to bring the train to a stop in exactly the right place. Villagers were waiting and they started to unload the cargo as soon as it was safe to do so.

As he got off, Conrad caught the eye of one of the train crewmen. "That was a very pleasant trip. Thank you for your efforts."

"Our pleasure, Father. We do four trips a day; one pair in the morning, one in the afternoon. We'll be ready to take you back at two, if that's all right?"

"That will be perfect. I have an appointment at three. Some baptisms."

"I know, Father; my wife won't let me forget it."

There was a round of laughter from the people gathered at the station, some of it tinged with envy from the women. Most of them had heard about the weddings a little too late to be able to get to Elbingerode to take part. *That can be easily dealt with.*

"We will be holding another wedding mass before I leave for those who wish to attend. All are welcome." *That did it.* The women were smiling again and the day seemed just a little bit brighter.

230

"I need to speak with Hans Koertig. Could anybody tell me where to find him?"

Home of Hans Koertig, Teichstrasse, Huttenrode

It had been a pleasant walk through the town. The villagers had apologized for not offering him a ride, but the carts were needed to take the supplies on the train to their storage area. It was, they had explained, only a couple of hundred meters and they had given very precise directions. So much so, Conrad had known which house to head for as soon as it came into view.

Hans Koertig was working in his garden, carefully hoeing a line of vegetables. *Sugar beet, if I'm not mistaken.* As he heard Conrad approaching, Koertig stood up, brushing his forehead with the back of his wrist.

His appearance slightly surprised Conrad, who had been expecting an obvious outdoorsman like Michael Ott. Koertig was quite different, short and slightly-built in a way that was only partially offset by the carefully-patched turtle-necked sweater he wore.

"You must be the priest investigating the murder of Doctor Vogel?"

His voice was quiet, but had an air of authority to it, that of a man who didn't have to raise his voice to be obeyed.

"Conrad Lorenz. You must be Strahlungjäger Hans Koertig?"

"I am. Let me guess; you have heard the accusations made by Traute Hahn and you think she is a ghastly old woman who failed to get her own way and is now taking a spiteful revenge. But, being a conscientious investigator, you wish to speak with the man she accused, on the slight chance that, this one time, she might be right." There was a twinkle in Koertig's steady blue eyes as he summarized the situation.

"Exactly right. I had to come to Huttenrode anyway, so I fitted both missions into one trip. You will excuse me from taking you away from your garden like this?"

"Of course, Father. I had finished hoeing my sugar beets anyway. I'll be taking my team out later today, trying to find a way through the pass. If there is a way, which is something I am beginning to doubt."

"Strahlungjäger Koertig . . . ."

"Hans, please call me Hans."

"Only if you call me Conrad." The two exchanged smiles.

231

Conrad's Eye

"Hans, I am confused about something. When I heard this place in the Hartz Mountains had survived, I was expecting a deep valley, surrounded by high mountains, Instead, the hills around us are low. I can't understand why this place is so different from the rest of Germany."

"Conrad, what you can see is very deceptive. The hills immediately around the valley are low, yes, but we are at quite an altitude here. Come inside, I will show you the maps."

Koertig's house was almost fastidiously neat inside. A big table in the living room was covered with a large-scale map of Huttenrode and the area to its immediate east. There were charts pinned up; each carefully labeled with its date and location. Conrad guessed the strings of numbers underneath were radiation readings. Other charts mapped weather conditions and wind direction. Koertig saw Conrad looking at them and smiled.

"People think that being a bold strahlungjäger means risking life and limb out in the woods; fearlessly exploring, while knowing all the time that their next step may be their last. In truth, all the real work is done here. Michael and his team spend hours together over charts just such as these, arguing the routes to explore and the best way to clear a specific area until they form consensus. My team, well, we all look at the charts on our own, come to our own conclusions and *then* argue them out; each defending his case until agreement is reached. Same result; different way of working.

"Anyway, this is a larger scale map of the area. Here, at Huttenrode, we are at roughly 450 meters. At Elbingerode, it is almost 460 meters; at Rothehutte, at the western end, it is a mere 420 meters. But the hills around us are 470 to 500 meters. Now, if we go north, or east, or any combination of those, the ground falls away very steeply. Five kilometers east of here, half way to Cattenstadt, it is 300 meters. Cattenstadt is at less than 250 meters and at Blankenburg, barely ten kilometers north east of here, it is at 150 meters. If we go the other way, south and west, the same distances take us to elevations of 500 and 600 meters equally quickly. So, what is named a valley is really a fold in a steep slope upwards."

"So there will be no train from Elbingerode to the valley south of here?"

"Not unless we get a better engine than the handcars. The slope Michael and his team are working on is quite steep; they have already climbed to 520 meters. Even the 10-meter difference between here and Elbingerode tries the strength of the railway crew. Sixty meters in six kilometers; no, this would not be possible. If they get through, it will be a walking trail, or one for pack animals only."

"You say if? The conditions are that dangerous? I thought this area was relatively safe."

232

"The key word is relatively, Conrad. Nothing in Germany is absolutely safe. If you like, I will take you to a kernstrahlung Michael found near Elbingerode. It is a very dangerous one because it is hidden in a tree. The Geiger counter will pick up some small traces, until there is a direct line from it to the spot. Then the readings will rise very quickly. If you know the spot well, you can see how somebody could approach within perhaps two meters very safely, then be poisoned with a small movement further.

"Now, between us and Hasselfelde, are a series of reservoirs. They may be clean; they may not. If they have been contaminated, then they are a barrier that will be hard to cross."

Koertig paused. His face adopted the haunted expression all Germans wore when thinking about the day of The Big One. "The day the hellburners fell, the wind was blowing from the northwest. I have often thought that the Americans waited for just such a day, so that the fallout from the hellburners would cover the parts of the country they did not bomb."

No, they did not. Conrad had been in Blair House the days before The Big One had finally been launched. *The tension grew as The Seer and his team of planners waited for the weather conditions to be right. They had wanted a northwest wind certainly; it had been to give the heavily-loaded B-36s a tailwind to help them cross the Atlantic. The bombers had been so loaded down with fuel, they needed all the help they could get. By the time they had made their attacks, much of that fuel load had gone and the situation hadn't been so critical. The thought of how the wind would spread the fallout from the atomic bombs literally hadn't occurred to anybody.*

"That may be, Hans. But I do not think they understood all of what they were doing."

"Perhaps. But look to the north of us here in the Harz Mountains. We have Magdeburg some 60 kilometers northeast, Braunschweig about 75 kilometers due north of us, Hannover a hundred kilometers northwest. Hannover took two hellburners; Braunschweig and Magdeburg one each. That was enough to destroy them all, and all the filth from their destruction came this way. And then there were the great industrial areas and shipyards of northern Germany. The Americans made very certain they would never be a threat to them again. The destruction was like a great letter C covering the north, the west and the south. And right in the middle of it all, us."

"You must hate the Americans very much."

"Hate them? Conrad, do you know what the Nazis did to people like me?"

"Not precisely. Although every priest who has met the victims of tyranny knows similar stories all too well."

Conrad's Eye

Especially if they are one of the tyrants.

The picture of the small town of Medina del Campo in Castile and an innocent girl, driven mad by injustice, spitting the blood from her broken mouth into his face swept into Conrad's mind. For a brief second, he was there; where the sun beat down, hurting the eyes of the crowd gathered in the square.

Koertig saw Conrad's face whiten with the memory. "I am sorry, Conrad. Sometimes it is hard to remember. I know. So you will understand that I do not hate the Americans for what they did to Germany. They did what they had to do in order to end the war. The people who did what they did to me, and those like me, did it because they enjoyed it. But, all that is in the past. The important thing is that the Harz Mountains formed an island in the middle of the winds. They split them and shepherded them away from us. There are those who say the old gods, the ones who live on the Brocken, stretched out their hands and shielded us. There are more here that believe in the old gods now than will admit that to you, Conrad.

"Anyway, the Harz Mountains are as clean as anywhere in Germany. And so is the water that is collected from within these mountains. But, the same island effect that saved us also caused the winds to interlock and stream around us. In doing so, they deposited much of the poison they carried in the foothills of our mountains. If water comes from outside the heart of the Harz, then it will be too contaminated to drink.

"The work of my team is to find a way though this pass here. It leads down from Huttenrode to Cattenstadt and Wienrode. We even had hopes than there may be a way through to Blankenburg. But each time, we run into increasing background radiation and increasing numbers of kernstrahlung once we reach the 350-meter line. It seems as if the gods that saved us also ringed us in, so that we would never be able to establish land routes to other refuges. It is as if their plan for Germany is that we should always remain a land of small, isolated farming communities."

Conrad looked at him curiously.

"Yes, Conrad. I believe in the old gods as well. Is that so very bad?"

"Not as long as the results of your belief are good, not evil."

"You are a very strange priest, Conrad. I think most of your kind would have held up a cross to protect yourself at the thought of meeting a self-confessed pagan."

"It is not my place to judge." *Dear God help me to never judge again.* "I will pray that your eyes are opened to the true faith, yes; but it is results that count, not the words used to express them. A man who does good serves the good, no matter what words he says in the privacy of his soul. That brings us back to the subject of my visit. You are not the father of Silke Hahn's baby?"

"No, Conrad, I am not. It is not . . . . in my nature. Nor is it in my nature to turn my back on those for whom I am responsible."

"That much is very obvious. Do you have any idea of who might be the father?"

"No, I do not. Although I will tell you something. Before she became pregnant, Silke spoke of marrying and settling down like any other young woman. Only after she found she was with child did she express any desire to have more than one father for her children. And she was not happy to be pregnant. She hid it well, but her pregnancy did not please her. That is strange for a society where mothers are honored, protected and get the best of everything."

Conrad nodded. He had an uneasy feeling that Silke's pregnancy was somehow at the root of this issue, but he simply could not see how or why.

"What do you know of Doctor Vogel?"

"He checked my radiation badge monthly. That was all, Otherwise, I stayed away from him. I do not like doctors."

"I have heard that many of the women disliked him also."

"So I have heard also."

The bluntness of the reply surprised Conrad. Then another matter seized his attention.

"Hans, may I use your restroom here? I fear the little train was a nice way to travel, but the vibration jarred my kidneys."

Koertig laughed. "That also I have heard. But, we are all very proud of our little train. My restroom, as you call it is, just out there. Second door on the left. You know how to use it?"

"If it is the same as the ones in the guesthouse, yes."

"It is."

Conrad stepped into the bathroom. It was as precisely neat and tidy as the rest of the house. *An almost fanatical desire to keep everything in precise order is probably an occupational requirement for a* strahlungjäger. He lifted the seat of the toilet up and eased himself. That, at least, had made his visit here worthwhile.

235

Conrad's Eye

Main Street, Huttenrode

A pleasant morning; warm enough to make walking an enjoyable experience.

Conrad was ambling through the small town almost at random, picking streets because they looked interesting or simply to find out where they went. Exploring the town this way allowed him to think matters through and assemble his thoughts. He had an uneasy impression that there was more to the murder of Vogel than he knew. The sheer paucity of facts that he had to work with showed that. His meeting with Koertig had given him a bit more insight into the situation here and he was actually looking forward to telling The Seer exactly what the situation here in Germany was like now for the ordinary people who had survived The Big One. That train of thought led him to the other reason why he was in Huttenrode.

"Excuse me." He stopped by a house, where a couple was tending their vegetable garden. "Could you tell me where I can find the home of Manfred von Leer?"

The woman straightened her back, her eyes widening as she recognized Conrad.

"Father, you wish to see Mad Manfred? His house is further down this street. Keep going past the turning on the right and go to where the road forks. There is a small house in the fork, You will find Mad Manfred there. Good luck in getting him to answer you."

Home of Manannan mac Lir, Georgenhofstrasse, Huttenrode

"Go away. I don't want to speak to anybody."

The voice from inside the small cottage was weak, wavering. It was but a faint and somehow unwholesome shadow of the rich Irish brogue that Conrad had always associated with Manannan mac Lir.

"Manannan. Manannan mac Lir. It's Conrad Lorentz. I would like to speak with you."

"Go to hell, you bastard."

Well, that was unexpected. Conrad felt his eyebrows lifting. Ever since his marathon wedding mass, he'd been the most popular man in town by a very wide margin. The violent hostility and undiluted hatred in the voice of the person within this cottage brought him back to Earth with a bump.

God works in strange and mysterious ways to save us from the sin of pride.

236

"Very probably, Manannan, but that lies in God's hands and at sometime in the future. But, before then, I would like to speak with you."

"I don't want to speak with you. Now, drop dead."

"Manannan, Loki heard you might still be alive and asked me to find you. I did manage to trace you, to this valley, but I haven't told Loki that yet. Sometimes those who hide have a good reason to wish to do so and I would prefer not to reveal your secret until I have heard yours. But, if you don't wish to speak with me, I will leave and give Loki the information I have when I see him in Geneva."

That caused a long pause. Conrad glanced around the grounds of the little cottage. In contrast to the neat and well-groomed vegetable gardens in the surrounding houses, these were unkempt and overgrown. *At a guess, what little gardening had been done was the work of neighbors whose sensibilities were offended beyond endurance by the mess.* Eventually, the door creaked open.

"Well, get inside. And don't say I didn't warn you."

Conrad's eyes adjusted to the gloom inside the cottage. *It isn't just the voice of Manannan mac Lir that was a pale and unwholesome shadow of its former self; the man himself is the same. He had once been a brawny man, not with the height of Mike Collins, but a well-formed man of strength and endurance. A man whose analytical brain had matched his fine physique.*

What stood before Conrad was a shrunken shell who stepped out of the shadows. Almost tangible malice exuded across the room.

Once his face was lit by light seeping through the window, Conrad could see why he was hiding. *Manannan had once had a shock of unruly black hair, now all that is left were a few strands of sickly gray.* It was his face though that struck Conrad. The skin was bright red; not a healthy glow but a diseased malignant crimson, studded with irregular black ulcerated swellings. Yet that was not the full horror of it, the red and the black surrounded areas where the skin itself had died and peeled back, forced away by the red growths that had burst out on their way to the surface.

Conrad glanced down. *The hands are the same. Twisted and mutilated almost beyond recognition.*

"Cancer. Radiation-induced skin cancer." Manannan mac Lir still spoke with the same thin, malicious tone to his voice. "I would have died years ago, but the gift that we both share has kept me alive beyond my time. Another few weeks and your trip would have been a waste, Conrad. Stuyvesant would have killed me at last." The last seven words were so filled with boiling hatred that Conrad actually felt he was truly in the presence of Satan.

Conrad's Eye

"What happened? What brought you to this sad state?"

"Stuyvesant happened. It was him. He was the one that did this to me." The voice was almost a shriek of fury.

Then, the caricature that had once been Manannan mac Lir took a deep breath. For a moment, Conrad could detect the true voice of Manannan and could believe the man he had known once still existed.

"I knew there was something wrong with the economic information we were getting. All the data we had on Germany was pointing to their economy being so massively mobilized for war, virtually nothing was left for the civilian sector. More than eighty percent, nearly ninety percent, of German productive capacity was being vested in the war effort. Yet, what information we could gather on the United States showed that they had mobilized less than fifty percent, forty four percent to be exact, of their productive capacity. Even so, that was swamping the Germans with sheer production. Two thirds of all the aero engines made in the world came out of American factories. Yet, it was wrong, all of it. The more I studied the American war effort, the more obvious it was to me that I was missing something big. There was a great hole in the middle, something that was consuming resources but giving nothing out.

"This scared me, because it could well mean that I was missing a similar part of the German war economy. Our economic projections were that Germany and its war effort would collapse sometime between 1950 and 1955. If I was missing something as large as the void in the American war effort, that estimate would be pushed back at least five years, perhaps ten. I had to check things. So I went to Germany myself. As a Swiss banker, of course; even in Nazi Germany, a Swiss banker was untouchable. Too many Nazi leaders had too much money in too many Swiss bank accounts. I got the grand tour of the Nazi war effort, designed, of course, to impress me with their inevitable victory.

"On the day of The Big One, I was in Hannover, being shown the NAIADS regional command center. That's when the news of the inbound bomber formation was received. I saw the glee in the Luftwaffe and Heer personnel. At last they would be given a chance to show what they could do. They'd massacred the American B-29s coming in from the East. Now they believed they would do it to the aircraft coming in from the west.

"Then I saw the desperation in their faces when they realized the bombers were flying in too high. They could do nothing. They saw the great wave of American bombers splitting up into small formations, each one aimed at a German city. I remember the confusion as they tried to work out what the Americans were up to. By then, I knew that I was looking at what the great hole I had found in the American war effort had given birth to. The only thing I didn't know was what horrors were still to come.

"Then we got reports of the first great explosion that destroyed a Germany city. Aachen, I think it was, or Dusseldorf, or Duren; I can't remember. There were so many. Everybody in the command center could only watch as, one after another, Germany's cities died. Everybody knew Hannover had to be on the target list. There was a formation of six bombers heading for us. By then we could do the maths. Three bombers meant one bomb; six must mean two. So, we ran for the air-raid bunker. By then, everybody knew what was happening. Panicking people were filling the streets. They could see the ever-increasing number of explosions all around us. Every one meant another city had just died. Our bunker was full. We were trying to push the blast-doors closed, but those still outside were determined to force their way in and we couldn't close them. Then the hellburner blew up right in front of us and Hannover was gone."

Manannan mac Lir stopped speaking. His voice had failed almost completely. Looking at him, Conrad knew that the cancers were not just on his skin. They were deep inside as well and they weren't just physical in nature. There were cancers in his brain, mental cancers and they were as devastating and as ugly as any physical tumor.

"I was lucky, or so I thought. When the blast and the heat from that explosion hit our bunker, they blasted through the still-open doors and swept through the people massed within. The doors were thrown back against the walls. In doing so, they formed tiny pockets in which people could live. Too close to the hinge of the door and the person behind was crushed as it was forced open. To close to the outer edge and they died, blasted and burned. But between the two was a narrow safety zone where our bones were broken but we lived. On our side of the double blast doors, three lived; on the other, two. Other than the five of us, few, if any, in that bunker did. All we could find were charred husks. What had been a place of safety had been turned into a mass graveyard.

"We went outside and we saw that Hannover had died. Hit twice, the whole city was gone; the buildings ruined and burning. The outside walls of our bunker were bleached white from the terrible force of the hellburner. Remember I told you how people outside were trying to force their way in? Well, their silhouettes were still on the bunker wall, where their shadows had stopped the wall from being bleached. I'm told they're still there. If they are, that's all that is left of those people. Their bodies just vanished.

"We stood there, and it seemed like Christmas. There were strange flakes coming down all around us, some white, some gray, some black. They stuck where they hit is and they burned. Oh God, how they burned. We tried to brush them off but we couldn't. They just smeared and spread and the burning spread with them. Cloth rotted where the flakes touched it. Some people ran back to the bunker, preferring to live with the charred corpses that face the rain of flakes. Me, I ran for it. I tried to leave the city.

"You can tell where the flakes hit me, can't you, Conrad. Oh, yes you can. The tumors tell you very clearly. Mine spread more slowly than for most people, but spread they have."

Suddenly, the poisonous hatred was back in his voice. "Stuyvesant killed me. I could have lived forever, but he and his bombers have killed me. He wouldn't even let me die decently, like a man. Instead I've been left rotting alive, inside and out. I'll be dead by the time you see him next. You tell him what I looked like when I died and tell him I died cursing his name. Tell him that I died praying that he would live to see the bitch-slut he calls his daughter looking like me while she dies."

Conrad was horrified, aghast at the thought and the venom behind it.

"Igrat? What has she ever done to you, that you should wish such a fate upon her?"

"She is Stuyvesant's daughter and seeing her die like this will hurt him more than anything else I can imagine. That's enough for me. Now get out and remember to tell him what I told you."

There was such menace in Manannan mac Lir's voice. Conrad stepped backwards out of the house and saw the door slam in his face. He could only think of two things.

I will never, ever tell Igrat that a man she had never met had conceived such a vicious hatred for her. Manannan mac Lir's soul is damned and he is surely going to Hell.

The Church, Elbingerode

Good drives away evil. It was a simple belief and one that Conrad held dear. *Evil could only survive if good made no effort to prevent it getting a foothold. Just as all that was needed to eliminate darkness was to provide light, all that was needed to eliminate evil was to bring good.*

It never occurred to Conrad that he was a force of good whose arrival drove away evil and he would never have believed anybody who suggested the idea to him. His trip from Elbingerode to Huttenrode had been one of simple joy at an unexpected, dreamlike pleasure. His trip back had been almost a nightmare, one filled with the black shadows formed from the memories of the scene with Manannan mac Lir. It was eating at his soul, filling his mind with its own darkness and doubts.

I am a priest; it is my job to bring salvation to those whose souls were in mortal peril. Yet when I met a man, a man like me who shared my gift, or his curse, for Conrad had not made his mind up on that matter, *I had been unable to bring any hint of salvation to him. Is my faith so weak then?*

And yet, when he walked back into the little church in Elbingerode, once again, good had driven out evil. It was filled with fresh-cut flowers and young mothers who took turns complimenting each other on their children while making sure that every detail of the church decoration was just perfect. The sight drove the darkness of Manannan mac Lir from him and replaced it with the light of life affirmed and hope for the future upheld. Across the room, he saw Olinda Kruger helping one mother with a young baby change a sodden diaper. He went over to her. The domestic sight drew the last shadows of night from him.

"Father, I hope this will be all right, but we'd like to start the ceremony half an hour later than planned. If you don't mind, that is. Our train is making an extra trip to bring some families from Huttenrode."

It was a measure of the thoroughness with which the sights around him had driven away the shadows that mentioning Huttenrode did not bring them back. *Far from it.*

"You show much skill with that diaper, Olinda. Do you have children of your own?"

"Not yet, Father. But Willi and I are trying very hard." Olinda flushed slightly as she spoke and looked down at her work.

"Father Conrad, pleased to see you. Did you know every strahlungjäger in the valley has been escorting our ladies to gather flowers for this event?"

Michael Ott was standing behind him; his wife with him and their baby in her arms.

"Have you seen our font?" He took Conrad's arm and led him to where a large bowl and a flower vase had been turned into a wooden-cased font. "One of our carpenters was up all night making this."

"A wonderful effort."

It was indeed; the carving careful and elegant. The woodworking artist hadn't fallen into the trap of assuming complexity and ornateness were equivalent to fine craftsmanship. He'd realized that simplicity was the perfect partner for this church and his skill was displayed by the quality of his carving rather than the quantity.

"It is perfect, I think."

Michael Ott quietly passed his Geiger counter over the water in the bowl.

"So is the holy water; less than background. Will there be enough?"

Conrad's Eye

Conrad glanced around the room. There were a lot of babies and young children waiting for baptism. "I think so."

Ott grinned. "We have a couple of bottles of water tucked away as our reserve. We've checked it and it's clean."

"You always check everything, don't you? I spoke with Hans Koertig this morning. He seems an extraordinary man."

"He is. One of the most careful and meticulous strahlungjägers I have known. When he escorts somebody, when he takes responsibility for them, their safety is his only concern. He takes his responsibilities very seriously."

Ott smiled at Conrad. "You may think I was hard on you yesterday, but Hans would have been stricter. But, yes, we never stop checking. The danger is much slighter than it was five years ago; our charts and maps show that quite clearly. But, the danger is still there."

"Hans told me that the real work of a strahlungjäger is done with maps and charts and I see he spoke wisely. He thinks the pass down to Cattenstadt is too contaminated and so impassible. Do you?"

"He may well be right. The northern slopes of the Harz mountains took the worst of the fallout from the hellburners that hit northern Germany. Where there are pockets in the mountain ranges, like the one around Cattenstadt, the wind eddied and the fallout was concentrated there. We are already speaking of a different approach, following the old railway line north from Huttenrode through the hills. That might take us directly to Blankenburg and bypass the blocked route."

"Albertus de Chesaux told me there is another rail line that leads south to where your team is working. Have you ever used it?"

"No, not yet. It is a steep descent one way and a hard climb back to Elbingerode. But there is another possibility. If we take our existing line, we can go the other way, to the field we use as an airport. That will open very soon. We will have a railway timetable and complaints when the train is late. But, not to the south, the slope is too steep for a handcar pulling weight. Easier to walk."

"Unless one was carrying a heavy load, of course."

"Unless one was carrying a heavy load. Like a man's body. Then, those rail lines would provide a way of moving that load, wouldn't they?"

Ott was suddenly thoughtful. "We will be down there again tomorrow; perhaps we should check for a handcar left by the rails? You know, that southern branch goes very close to where the body was found. Once we open the path a kilometer or so south, we will actually cross it."

Conrad nodded. He was certain he had seen the allegedly disused railway lines shining in the sun as he had gone to Huttenrode. If that was so, then something had been down those lines and rubbed the rust off their surface.

He looked around the room again, where the crowd had already increased. One woman caught his eye. While the other women were wearing what were obviously their Sunday-best dresses, this one was in her work clothes. She was obviously distressed; both by her appearance and the thought that the other woman might consider her disrespectful to the priest who was doing so much for them.

"Another crime to investigate; only a minor one this time."

Friedensrichter Werner Heim was standing beside him, speaking quietly. "Her dress was stolen."

"Her dress? Out of her home, or from a clothesline?"

Oddly, Conrad was interested by this minor piece of theft. *It seems incongruous somehow.*

"Off a clothesline. The women here do the washing in a communal facility, one where the water has been checked. It would not be good to wash clothes in radioactive or poisoned water. Then, they take their wash home to dry." Heim seemed slightly embarrassed by discussing such domestic things.

"Father, you must remember that a dress is a big thing here. We have little local cloth made and that which we do have is coarse. Fine cloth, suitable for the women to make their clothes, must come from outside; flown in on one of the Antonovs. To have a dress, perhaps the only nice one she has, stolen is a great blow to her. And to the other women, because of the fear that the next victim might be them. Last night, my wife took the washing in and hung it to dry indoors."

"That sounds like a wise precaution."

"For her, perhaps. But I got up in the middle of the night to relieve myself and found myself assaulted by a half-wet dress. For a moment, I thought I was back on the Kola Front, fighting Siberians."

There was a general laugh from the men around them, a trifle uneasily from those whom Conrad marked down as veterans. Nevertheless, it gave him a chance to ask about something veterans rarely spoke of.

"It was that bad out there?"

"Yes, Father, especially when fighting Siberians. They would slide through the snow, as silent as ghosts. Then they would just appear, cut down their enemies and vanish into the pine woods. I tell you, Father, the books are all

243

wrong. Hell isn't a place of fire and heat, for heat destroys evil. The people here in this valley, are good people; kind and considerate because the hellburners burned the evil out of them. But on the Kola Front, there was nothing but bitter, unrelenting cold and that allowed evil to grow and flourish."

There was a pause while the group looked at memories the comment had brought back.

The investigator part of Conrad's brain kicked in. "I can't see why somebody would steal a dress. The person who stole it can't wear it in public. It would be recognized and the thief would be in danger of getting torn limb-from-limb. When was this dress stolen?"

"The same night Doctor Vogel was murdered. The victim held off reporting it for a couple of days, thinking it had been a mistake and the dress would be returned. She finally came to me late yesterday evening. And you are right; the way the women feel, limb-from limb is about right. But, once again we are in debt to you, Father. The joy of arranging for the baptism ceremony has driven such thoughts from people's minds."

"Not for everybody."

Conrad indicated with a slight move of his head. Traute Hahn and her daughter Silke had entered the room. The older woman was looking around, obviously hoping she would see Hans Koertig so she could create a scene. Her disappointment at his absence was palpable. Beside her, Silke was disinterested; she barely glanced around to see who was present.

Koertig is right; she is not happy with her pregnancy and obviously found the reminder that soon she would have a baby to care for unpleasant. That time is not too far away, her pregnancy is well-advanced. Conrad quietly said a small prayer that he would be spared having her going into labor during the mass baptism.

CHAPTER FOUR

Conrad's Room, The Guest House, Elbingerode

The problem was that he didn't seem to be getting anywhere. Oh, he was tending to the spiritual needs of the people of this valley, but the strange murder of their doctor was still as mysterious as ever. He took one of his index cards and marked it with "Silke's Baby" and then stared at it. Conrad couldn't shake the feeling that somehow the unwanted baby of Silke Hahn was at the root of this problem. Then, an ugly thought came to his mind, one keyed by the words 'unwanted baby.'

Had Silke Hahn approached Vogel for an abortion, been turned down and had killed him to close his lips? It makes as much sense as anything else. Then, an uglier thought came to his mind. *Had Vogel agreed to perform the abortion and had Traute Hahn killed him to stop it taking place?* The moral dilemma there made Conrad's head ache.

Three more cards. One labeled 'abortion' for a motive; one suspect card each for Traute and Silke Hahn. He took his pack of cards and spread them out. Now, he had a reasonable set of combinations to play with. He added in three more, one for each bit of evidence that he had. A strong knife, a stick with a slot in its radioactive end and a stolen dress. He took a deep breath and added one more, a railway handcar used to carry the body. That was a guess, but he could always remove it when a search had been made. Another question occurred to him as he stared at the motive card with the ugly word 'abortion' written on it. *Why did Silke Hahn resent being pregnant? In a community where pregnancy brought with it social status, better food and an easier life, why did she resent her baby?*

He laid the suspect cards out, thinking carefully over each one. After some thought and shuffling, he put Traute Hahn at the top, followed by her daughter, then the unknown card and finally Hans Koertig at the bottom. Then he searched his soul. *Was that order what I believe? Or is it the product of the fact that I like Hans Koertig and despise Traute Hahn?* He convinced himself that his personal feelings had been left out of this matter and that his opinions were truly based on what he had learned of the case.

Conrad's Eye

Then he laid out the cards for motives. He could feel his eyes begin to prickle as he looked at the card with 'abortion' written on it. *Killing an unborn baby is the worst betrayal of an innocent I can imagine. In this society, where babies are desperately needed, abortion would have the impact and shock that could well bring about murder.* He put that card at the top and then looked at the two covering the radiation records. *There is a subtle difference between "hiding the records" and "hiding the results."* Conrad stared at them both. Another ugly thought came to his mind.

Had Silke Hahn been exposed to radiation? Was she above the limit for a safe pregnancy? Had she or her mother killed the Doctor to hide that and was that why she was uneasy about her pregnancy? Did she fear she was carrying a radiation-mutated monster? Looked at with those eyes, almost any combination of the top two suspect cards and the top three motive cards made sense. *The dress stolen because the killer had been soaked in blood from the gaping knife would in Vogel's chest? She had needed a new dress to get home safely. That points to a woman as the killer.* Suddenly, the Hahn family was looking very good for this murder.

Answers might well be found in the radiation exposure records, Conrad thought. *At least, they might show if Silke had been exposed to radiation.*

He went to the files removed from Doctor Vogel's office and started to read them. *Whatever else he may have been, Vogel was neat and meticulous.* The rows of figures against the name of each person in the village went on for months and years. *There are research institutes in America that would treasure this information. More than a thousand rows of data.* Mostly in neat black numbers; but, every so often, a line would change to red. It took only a moment's inspection to realize that the red numbers represented an excessive dose. In Conrad's eyes, the realization gave those numbers a tragic air; one that spoke of blighted lives and destroyed hopes. *Those too*, he already knew, *could be motives for murder.*

First, to find Silke Hahn. The records were in alphabetical order by surname so the Hahn family was easy to locate. The name, Hahn S followed by an M. *Madchen means a young woman*, Conrad realized, *just as the H indicated a man and F an older woman.* Silke's entry was black all the way through; she had never approached the dreaded level of exposure that would deprive her of the hopes for a family of her own. That, at least, relieved Conrad of one of his theories but it left the main question unanswered.

Why did she so resent her baby?

He leaned back in his seat, stretching his cramped back as he did so. Then, he looked again at the figures for Silke Hahn. There was something in them that worried him, but he couldn't quite put his finger on what. His finger slid down a

246

line to that for Traute Hahn and followed the long line of black numbers. Idly, his mind wandered to her and her irrational hatred of Hans Koertig. It just wasn't reasonable that she should run such a vendetta against the man for such flimsy cause. Still wandering, his mind recollected Manannan mac Lir's violent hatred for Igrat and his wish for her destruction on no firmer grounds than that her death would hurt somebody else. He had found that shocking, not least because it was so far in character from the genial Irishman he had known once. *Did radiation affect the brain and change character? Or did he have tumors deep in his brain that matched the ones that were destroying his skin?*

Conrad carefully remembered Manannan mac Lir as he had once known him, consciously trying to drive out the ghastly memory of today's meeting with those of happier times. In particular, a meeting in 1929 when Stuyvesant had sent warning to as many people as he could reach that the American stock market was about to crash. Loki had wanted to ignore the warning, arguing it was one of Stuyvesant's schemes to get rich off other people's efforts. Manannan mac Lir had simply said that numbers were hard to understand, but graphs were pictures and pictures were easy to comprehend. So, he had graphed out the data and explained how it showed Stuyvesant's warning was right. Loki had finally listened and taken the appropriate action. Ten days later, the bottom had fallen out of the American stock market and the Great Depression had started.

Figures are hard to understand; graphs are pictures and much easier to analyse. Manannan's words rang through Conrad's brain. The problem was, he had no graph paper. He spent the next hour painstakingly drawing up his own. Then, he plotted Silke Hahn's radiation readings on the sheet. As Manannan had claimed, what was hidden when seen as a line of numbers became very obvious when put on a graph. Silke's radiation exposure had been almost static for most of the time the records covered. There was a slight climb upwards in the cumulative totals, but it was lost in the scale of the chart and the inaccuracies of the home-drawn graph paper. Then, 15 months ago, the cumulative exposure had started to climb sharply and had continued to do so for six months. Then, nine months ago, it had resumed the previous almost-static level.

Conrad stared at that chart, trying to understand what it meant. Almost by instinct, he plotted Traute Hahn's figures on the same graph. They were similar, but showed no sharp increase at any time. *I find that curious. From my own, admittedly limited, observations, Traute Hahn never let Silke out of her sight. So, what had happened to cause that surge in exposure?*

Conrad started to plot other graphs, intentionally picking a few where the line of numbers changed from black to red. In most cases, such lines showed a high baseline, probably from exposure during the bombing, and a slow climb to over-the-limit. In a few though, there was the same sudden surge in cumulative exposure. Almost by instinct, Conrad checked those against the identifiers. As far as he could see, all those who had experienced the surge in cumulative exposure had been young women. Some had leveled off short of the cut-off value; others had continued to climb until they had passed that barrier. Conrad bit his lip and turned to the page for Olinda Kruger. Sure enough, her record showed a high initial exposure but a very slow increase that left her well short of the cut-off point. Only the last record showed the same sharp increase that Silke Hahn's record demonstrated.

Conrad put the record books and his homemade graphs away. He had added more pieces to the puzzle, but he really didn't like the shape the case was taking. If this protected valley was a paradise compared with the rest of Germany, one way or another, there was a snake in it.

The Railway Station, Elbingerode

The little station was crowded. It wasn't just the fifteen people gathered around the tracks; it was the fact that there were two trains in the yard. One was the standard train for Huttenrode. The other had obviously been put together for this expedition.

"Come on up, Father Conrad! We are opening a new railway line today." Michael Ott's hearty voice rang across the open yard. "Meet Walter Schubach; he is the strahlungjäger from Mandelholtz come to help us. And you have met Hans Koertig of course. Three strahlungjäger teams working together, Father; this is a rare event indeed."

"I am sorry to have caused so much trouble." Conrad was genuinely repentant. He could imagine how much disruption to the slow, patient clearance effort this gathering was causing.

"No trouble, Father," Schubach's voice was deep and as hearty as Ott's. "We are all pleased to help out with the investigation of this terrible affair."

The two horses were hitched to the handcar. Conrad could swear that they were smirking with the knowledge that this train couldn't work without their help in getting it started. From his trip yesterday, he know that they would be taken down to help the train from Huttenrode climb the slope that led back to Elbingerode. Then, the horses strained and they were off.

It was the same route they had taken yesterday, of course; down the long slope, through the fields and into the trees. The change came at the points. Instead of taking the line they had used before, the train shifted to the other branch. Conrad looked down. His eyes hadn't been playing tricks. The rust from the rails had been scraped clear. Ott noted it as well.

"You were right, Father; something has been down these rails. Quite recently, I would think, or the rust would have come back."

"Where do we go from here?"

"The railway takes us to the quarry. It is the same one you saw when you first came here, just the other side of it. We will go around the south end and then south of that hill you see ahead. That is a 500-meter hill, one we have yet to clear. Father, we are on the edge of the cleared area now, so please, be very careful. The women would never forgive us if we got you killed before you had them safely married."

There was a guffaw of laughter on the train and in the last car, Hans Koertig shook his head. Then he pointed to an array of black-and-yellow striped poles.

"There is the edge, Conrad. Beyond there, it may be safe, but it would be foolish to take the chance."

Conrad looked at them thoughtfully. "Do you mean that every foot of the ground this side of those poles has been checked?"

"Every foot, Father." It was Schubach again. "The first winter after the bombing, my village was cut off, without food. People were starving and so three of the men set out to find some. They did well; they brought back enough fresh meat to feed us all. But within a week, they had died. Their feet rotted and went black. Then they died in great pain. We know now that they had stepped in a kernstrahlung. Michael here found the one we think did it."

Conrad knew he had a priceless opportunity, here on this little train with three expert teams on radiation.

"Could you help me with a problem? What would cause a young woman, who previously had little additional exposure to radiation, to suddenly start accumulating at a much higher rate?"

"Nothing." Koertig was blunt and to-the-point. "That cannot happen without her coming into contact with contamination and we have ensured there is none of that from the areas where people go."

"I agree." Ott was more thoughtful, but he came up with the same answer. "To do so would need exposure in areas where there is a kernstrahlung. In the town and the farmland, they are all known and clearly marked. The woman would have to go deliberately to one and expose herself."

"Or go wandering in the woods outside the cleared area." Schubach had his say as well. "And that is not allowed. Woman are cared for and protected in our community, for they are our future. They are not allowed to wander around."

"And yet, it is so."

Conrad's Eye

Conrad decided to take these men into his confidence. "I went through the radiation records gathered by Vogel last night. There are a small number of young women who have indeed sudden, inexplicable increases in their exposure. In some, the increase ceases while they are still below the limit for childbearing. In other cases, it continues until they exceed that limit and their status is withdrawn."

"Then there is something strange about those records. We are supposed to be alerted if there are anomalous increases recorded, so we can find the cause. But Vogel said nothing of this. The few women who lost their permission to bear children were the result of a slow, steady increase from a high background. Or so Vogel said. You have a mystery here, Father."

"The border is up ahead. Passports ready."

Koertig's voice was droll and the joke brought an appreciative laugh. What was not quite so funny was the line of yellow-and-black poles that crossed the railway line. This was as far as they could go; safely, at any rate.

The crew of the handcar brought the train to a halt and the three strahlungjäger teams dismounted. Conrad remained on the train and watched them as they took their places. Ott went off to the left, Koertig to the right, while Schubach stood on the rails themselves. Then, they started the slow process of ensuring that every inch of ground was checked for radiation.

The process reminded Conrad of some time he had spent at a Hollywood studio. At first, the sights surrounding him were fascinating and he'd lost himself watching the film being put together. Then, once the novelty had worn off, it had become excruciatingly boring. So was it here. After the initial surge of interest had worn away, the meticulous checking of the ground became boring.

At last, Conrad understood why the strahlungjägers were few in number. It was given to only a small minority to maintain concentration during such tedious, painstaking work. After almost an hour, they had cleared barely a hundred meters of the track and its margins. It was enough, though.

"Conrad? Please come up to the front. Remember, you must stay between the marker poles." It was Koertig calling, his voice slightly hoarse.

Conrad followed the call and came up to the discovery. It was a railway handcar, left on the track. Why was obvious; rain or frost had damaged the narrow-gauge railway line and a whole section of rail had been dislodged. Something else was obvious as well.

The front of the handcar was soaked in blood.

"You were right, Father; this is how the body was moved out here. Look at the map. We are only 300 meters or so from where the body was found, although to get there from here without crossing uncleared ground would take about seven kilometers. This area is mostly clean. A brave man, or a foolish one, could walk that short distance with only a very slight chance of finding a kernstrahlung.

"Over here, friends."

Schubach called the team over. He was pointing just off to one side and a little ahead of the cleared area. There was a pile of cloth there; bloodstained cloth.

It took another few minutes to clear the way to it and a few seconds to check it. It was free of contamination and, when recovered, its identity was obvious. It was the stolen dress. Conrad felt sorry for its owner, for there was obviously no way for it to be cleaned or salvaged. The dress, almost certainly the only one she had, was ruined. That made it a cruel and petty theft.

"Since we are all here, why do we not try and clear a path to the place where the body was found?" Hans Koertig was looking around at the area. "It might make your work down here a bit easier, Michael."

"It would." Ott was thoughtful as he studied his map. "If we hit trouble, it would give us a wider base to work from."

"Trouble?" Conrad was interested.

"There are reservoirs south of here and any stretch of open water is hazardous. Some are clean but many are poisoned. Sometimes with radiation; sometimes with other poisons. All too many died because they sought shelter in rivers and lakes when the hellburners fell."

Schubach sounded deeply distressed by the memories.

"And they are poison still. The contamination went to the mud at the bottom of the rivers and has been swept down with them. Whole stretches of country were laid waste, because the poison from the rivers got into the ground water. Some of us think that poisoned ground water rising to the surface is responsible for many kernstrahlung."

Ott looked at his comrades. Koertig was nodding slowly, Schubach shaking his head. "One vote each way. What do you think Conrad?"

Conrad smiled at the question. One that had been obviously been asked to lighten the mood a little. "I think, that if there is a chance that is so, it ought to be checked out with great care."

Conrad's Eye

"Spoken like a true strahlungjäger!" Schubach slapped him on the back. "Now, can we get the Father back to Elbingerode while we work here?"

"Steep trip for a handcar." Koertig looked at the little vehicle. "But, if we detach the flatbeds and it just goes back alone with him and our four strong railwaymen here. . ."

"It can be done. And we need to bring at least one more crew back here to move the other handcar. Perhaps if we then hook them both to the flatbeds, we can give you brave strahlungjägers a ride back to town."

There was much nodding and agreement, which, to Conrad, suggested how much the strahlungjägers would like to get him out of their way. That suited him as well for there was a meeting he very much wanted to have.

The Church, Elbingerode

Conrad hadn't expected anything else. He'd gone straight to the new church after his train ride back to Elbingerode and sent word that he wished to speak with Silke Hahn alone. Privately, he believed that he had about a five percent chance, at best, of actually achieving that right away. So he had taken the precaution of asking Friedensrichter Heim along. As soon as he learned what Conrad wanted him to do, Heim had hastily deputized two strong farmers to help him. It wasn't, as he had quickly pointed out, that Traute Hahn was strong or skilled at fighting. It was just that she was heavy.

Sure enough, Traute Hahn had barged into the church ahead of her daughter and sat down with dogmatic determination. Conrad had sighed audibly.

"Frau Hahn. My business this afternoon is with your daughter. It is in the nature of a confessional and it is strictly between her, myself and God. I would be most grateful if you would leave. Now."

"I have a right to be here. Whatever you say to my daughter, you can say to me." She looked around the room, her beady eyes alight with enjoyment at the trouble she was causing.

"Frau Hahn. I am investigating a homicide. I have duties here, both to God and to the lawful authorities of this community. Both as a priest and an investigator, I have to speak to your daughter in private. Please leave."

"There is no investigation needed. Hans Koertig killed Doctor Vogel because he could prove Koertig was the father of Silke's baby. That is all that needs to be said."

The level of Conrad's voice did not change, but it developed a thunderous quality that echoed off the walls.

"Frau Hahn, there is a reason why bearing false witness against a neighbor is a mortal sin. For false accusation may cost an innocent man his life. By making such accusations, you are in mortal sin and yet you remain unconfessed. Your very soul is in mortal danger, Frau Hahn."

Suddenly Conrad's voice was raised and it had a physical force to it. "This is a House of God, created by and blessed by this community. Leave now. You are not welcome here until you confess your sins, have paid penance for them and are granted absolution."

She rose to her feet, her eyes bulging with sheer fury. "I will not be spoken to in this manner. Silke, come with me, we are finished here."

"Silke, remain where you are. Frau Hahn, obey Father Conrad or we will make you do so." Heim's voice was almost as thunderous as Conrad's.

"You wouldn't . . ." Traute Hahn never got to finish the sentence. Heim and one of his assistants picked her up by her armpits, lifting her so her feet were kicking furiously in the air. The third man grabbed her legs and the three of them carried her from the building. A few seconds later, there was a crash. Obviously they had dropped her somewhere.

There was a long pause, then Conrad looked at Silke. For the first time since he had come to Elbingerode, she was smiling.

"I am sorry, Silke, to treat your mother like that, but the name of justice demands we speak in private. This is a confessional; nothing that you say here will go any further unless you choose to repeat it. Do you understand?"

"Yes Father." There was a long pause, "Is my mother truly in mortal sin?"

"For issuing accusations of such seriousness without good cause, very much so. For doing so with such obvious malice, even more so. Your mother's soul is indeed in peril, Silke, but that is not why we must talk."

"You wish to know about my baby." Her voice was flat again. The smile had gone from her face as if it had never existed.

"Silke, on my word as a priest, the name will never pass my lips without your permission, but I must know. Who is the father of your baby?"

"I will not say. Perhaps, I do not know."

Conrad looked at her with disbelief. "You cannot expect me to believe that. You know, Silke, and it is crucial that I know also. Please, I beg you; take me into your confidence and tell me."

Silke looked at him and started to cry. "It was Doctor Vogel. He did this to me. More than a year ago, he started to tell me that my radiation readings were getting higher. He said he could stop them doing so, but I would have to give myself to him in return. For six months, the readings got higher and higher and I got more and more frightened. Finally, I agreed and gave him what he wanted. Sure enough, the readings stopped increasing but, in return, he had given me this."

She put her hand on her stomach, then she broke down completely. "He told me he was doing me a favor, that I was already plain and soon I would be as fat and ugly as my mother. He told me that nobody would want me, no matter how low my radiation readings were, and I should be thankful that he had condescended to use me. He called me his fat cow and when we were doing it, he made me make noises like a cow."

Conrad had always had a special contempt for people who boasted that 'they spoke their mind' or were in the habit of telling people 'a few home truths.' In his experience, 'speaking their mind' was just an excuse for being deliberately offensive, while the 'few home truths' were rarely anywhere close to true. In his experience, the most vicious and deliberately cruel of behavior always exploited the truth by turning it into a weapon. Silke's story was proof of that, for Vogel's words to her had too much truth to them. Silke wasn't ugly, but her prettiness was that of youth and would quickly fade. She was heavily built, and unless she was very careful indeed, she would become very much like her mother. As to character, only time would tell, but he could sense the need to get her away from the malign influence of her mother as soon as possible.

"Does your mother know this?"

Silke shook her head. "She doesn't really care who is the father. All she wants is for me to look after her."

"Do you have a boyfriend, Silke?"

"I did. But my mother never knew this. We were going to run away to Huttenrode together. But I haven't seen him for months. Not since my . . . since it became obvious."

"He rejected you? Did he know what Vogel did to you?"

"I do not think so. And no, he did not reject me. I could not face him after what Vogel did. Anyway, why would he want me now?"

Conrad smiled gently. "I think you might be surprised by that. To stand by you after such an ordeal would be the mark of a man who is indeed worthy of your love."

He made the mark of a cross with his fingers. "*Ego te absolve.* And as penance for what few sins you might have committed, I charge you to find your young man, tell him the truth in all its details and leave the decision on your possible future together to him. And if he reacts as I think he will, to bring him here so I may marry him to you."

Conrad believed in the confessional; not for any mystical reason, but because he had so often seen the relief and joy in people's faces when they had described their sins to others and been absolved of them. *Sometimes, the sheer relief of telling somebody else was all the absolution they needed. All too often, people punished themselves far more severely than their minor infractions deserved and the confessional was a way of ending that vicious cycle of self-recrimination.* The look on Silke's face was proof of that opinion. She had committed no sin. Rather, she had been grievously sinned against, yet her own conscience and the spite of a selfish and vindictive mother had twisted her mind. Now, those shadows had gone.

He walked to the doors and opened them.

"Friedensrichter Heim, would you escort Silke Hahn to see a young man she will identify. She will speak to him in confidence, and thereafter, I think the two of them will come back here. But, please do not let her mother anywhere close to her and do not let her accompany you."

Silke smiled at him through her tears and started to leave. Just before she left, she turned around.

"Father, what I told you here today. If it helps solve the killing, please use the information. But know that I cannot condemn whoever it was that killed him."

Mayor Lang's Office, Elbingerode

"Well, this puts an entirely different complexion on events. So, 'Doctor' Vogel was abusing his position to take advantage of his female patients." Wilhelm Lang was outraged by the news, but carefully kept his voice under control.

"He was raping them, yes." Conrad was still running the permutations of possibilities over in his mind. "Which gives rise to a whole world of new suspects. One of the women threatened may have spoken to her husband and he then defended her by killing Vogel. Or the woman herself may have killed him in self-defense. We started out by investigating a murder. Now it appears than there may not have been one at all. I assume that killing in self-defense is not considered a crime?"

"I consider it to be an affirmative defense. The defendant would have to prove it was indeed self-defense, but, if that is so, then he would be free to leave the trial without blame. That is in theory only, of course; in reality we have never had such a case here. Oh, we have fights that lead to broken bones, but that is all. Never a killing in such a fight. For myself, I think the hellburners didn't just burn Germany; they burned the desire, the ability, to kill out of the survivors."

Lang paused. "I wonder how many women he abused this way and why none of them ever told their partners."

"I think the first question we can answer by looking through the radiation records. The signature will be a steady level of exposure, then a sharp increase that eventually levels off again. I would suggest that where the radiation total falls short of the cut-off point that prohibits pregnancy, the women succumbed to the blackmail and were raped. Where the increase continues beyond that point, we can assume the women resisted the demands and suffered the consequences.

"As to why they never reported the assaults, shame perhaps? If the account we have to date is representative, Vogel picked his victims with care. He chose those who were already vulnerable, with poor self-image problems, with inadequate and unsupportive family backgrounds. Ones who had already had their self-respect battered out of them. Then he tortured them, psychologically. Imagine what those women must have felt, having to go back to him month after month to be shown their cumulative radiation levels reaching the levels where they would be denied a family of their own. When they succumbed to his demands, he went out of his way to humiliate and degrade them. Mayor Lang, rape is nothing to do with sex. It is about exerting power and control. I believe that if we were able to look into Vogel's history, we would find it had some very unsavory aspects."

"There's a problem with that." Friedensrichter Heim spoke carefully, for he was as nauseated as everybody else in the room by what they had uncovered. "How could Vogel have manipulated the radiation readings like that? It is not as if he can just create the numbers. In theory at least, somebody else could check them and a great discrepancy between the numbers would be seen."

"This, I do not know and it is the question we must answer. How are the radiation readings taken?"

"People went to Vogel and he took the strip from their badges and put it in an envelope with their name. He would put a new strip in and they would go on their way. Next day, they would come back and he would give them the results. It was a very simple test. All he had to do was measure the length of the black strip and subtract from it the control number distributed by NAIADS for that month. Then add the number to the previous month's total from his record. A few seconds for each record."

"So why keep it overnight?" Conrad questioned the practice aloud. "If it is that quick and easy, why not do it right away, so each person does not have that overnight wait?"

"That is a good question." Mayor Lang and Friedensrichter Heim looked at each other and shrugged. "It was always done that way. I suppose we thought it was to speed up the strip collection process, so people would not have to wait. But, thinking about it, it would waste more of their time having to come back."

"We need an expert on radiation." Conrad spoke decisively. "When Michael Ott returns from the field, we should speak with him on how the radiation readings might be tampered with. I know he is already concerned with some other aspects of Vogel's handling of radiation data. In the meantime, the rest of us had better start going through the records and try and identify Vogel's likely victims. Oh, and Mayor? Would it be possible for me to speak with the Vatican on NAIADS?"

Lang did a double-take at that. "I will ask. I know that NAIADS will allow a few lines outside Germany, but whether we can reach the Vatican? Might I know the reason why? You are not planning to have Vogel excommunicated, are you?"

"No, although he merits it more than most I have known. But, this valley needs a priest and a doctor. I can speak with friends of mine in Rome who can, perhaps, find a suitable candidate. If we are fortunate, there may even be one who can fill both roles."

It was a long, boring job but by the end of it, Conrad and Heim had identified more than a dozen women who had been victimized by Vogel. From the look of his data, eight of those women had eventually complied with his demands; six had refused and paid the price. Looking at the list of those six names, Conrad finally knew who the innocents he had been sent here to protect were.

"Friedensrichter Heim."

"Werner. It's Werner, Father. And the Mayor is Wilhelm. Or, if you want to be party to a private joke, Captain Still."

"Thank you, but that sounds like a veteran's story that I should not intrude upon. I am Conrad, as you know. Now, I make it we have eight victims who submitted, six who did not and one who had not yet responded? We must find these woman and tell them that the secret is known. Obviously these records cannot be trusted and I would urge that the limitation placed upon them be withdrawn. We can announce that our investigation has found Vogel's deception and exposed how he used his position to try and victimize the women he selected. I would suggest we phrase it so that it sounds like we only discovered the cases where the women did not submit. That way, those who did can keep their secret if they so wish. I see nothing to be gained by forcing exposure on them."

"Nor do I, Conrad. But I will tell you something that disturbs me greatly. To me, it seems odd that this went on for so many years but Vogel only got killed now. It suggests that something changed with his most recent selection of victim. He picked one who would fight him." Heim reached out and his finger tapped the last name on the list. "Olinda Kruger and her husband."

"Olinda is proud and spirited." Conrad spoke reflectively. "Perhaps Vogel was bored with women who were easy prey. Or perhaps her very pride and free spirit were what made him want to break her. If that was in his mind, he made a bad mistake."

"You think she killed Vogel?"

"She could kill the man who threatened her family. She has that strength in her heart. But it is not in her body. The blow that killed Vogel was delivered with the right hand and was a powerful strike. Olinda's right hand was burned and she has neither the strength nor the grip to handle a knife in the way that this one was used. She did not kill Vogel."

"But her husband may well have done." Heim's mouth twisted. "He loves her more than he loves life itself and if Vogel wished to abuse her, then, yes, Willi Kruger could easily have killed him. And I would not blame him for doing so."

"Nor would I." Conrad put some levity into his voice, trying to reduce the gloom that was suffocating in the small room. "I would have to take his confession, of course. And I would have to give him a penance to perform. Getting me a tankard of ale would seem about right."

"My thoughts exactly, Conrad. You see, there is not such a gulf between secular and religious law after all." The two men burst into laughter. Mayor Lang stopped at the door, slightly shaken by the unexpected merriment.

"I presume we have some great breakthrough in this case? Father, if you would like to come with me now, Potsdam is putting your call through to the Vatican while we speak. And Michael Ott is back. He will be with us as soon as he has changed from his work clothes."

CHAPTER FIVE

At the Kernstrahlung Tree, Elbingerode

"Listen. What do you hear?"

Michael Ott spoke quietly. Something about the sight of the tree ringed by a perimeter of orange-and-black barriers called for silence.

Conrad listened intently, but could hear nothing.

"I'm sorry Michael, I can't hear anything."

"That's exactly it. There are no birds singing. There are no animals rustling in the grass. The wildlife has all sensed there is something terribly wrong here and it has left. If you are ever walking alone in Germany, use your ears as much as your eyes. Stop every few paces and listen. Silence means you are in trouble. Just like living with a woman."

There was a reluctant ripple of laughter at the joke. Ott moved around the perimeter, checking for contamination. Conrad looked at the tree in front of him.

There is something wrong about it. He could see that now. *The leaves are green, but have a sickly tinge to them and there is something malformed about them.* Nothing he could quite describe but they just didn't look right. *Or*, he asked himself, *is it just my imagination? The result of knowing what lay trapped in this tree's trunk?*

The perimeter around the tree was in the shape of a peanut. At its center, of course, was the tree itself. A few feet from the ground, its trunk split into two parts. The kernstrahlung lurked in the fork those branches formed. Where the tree trunk shielded the spot, the perimeter came closer to the tree. Alongside the fork, where there was no shielding, there was a lot more space. Ott had assured them that the perimeter gave them a very comfortable safety margin, but the party was still standing well back.

"Very good. The contamination hasn't spread."

Ott took out a notebook and turned to a page devoted to this kernstrahlung. He entered strings of readings into the table and checked them against previous

259

entries. "In fact, it is slightly weaker. It will fade normally with time, of course, but this is a little more than that."

"Is that strange?" Conrad asked warily. This meticulous, obsessive monitoring of the ground was more than slightly frightening to him.

"I think not. The tree is dying and the radiation is rotting the wood. As it does so, the kernstrahlung sinks deeper into the trunk and that shields us a little better. It makes it more dangerous, of course, because it might not be spotted until we were on top of it. When we first found this one, the tree was still healthy. This is a very dangerous kernstrahlung."

A couple of hours earlier, Conrad, Lang and Heim had explained the problem to Ott. He had mulled it over in his mind and eventually laid the problem out. The only way to tamper with the radiation badges was to expose them to radiation. There was only one source of environmental radiation in Elbingerode and that was a kernstrahlung. The closest kernstrahlung was this one. So, it was time to have a look at it.

"Surely he could not have held the badge over the kernstrahlung?" Lang was visibly nervous at being this close to a dreaded kernstrahlung.

"He might have, but if he had, we would have buried him a long time ago."

Ott looked across the perimeter. Inside the line of poles, the grass was thick and high since it had never been cut. Yet it, like the tree, looked sick.

"And not necessarily from the radiation. We are finding increasing numbers of vipers in the woods and they are becoming more aggressive. If it were not for the kernstrahlung, long grass like that might well contain some. We even found one with two heads once."

The other men exchanged glances, not quite sure whether they were being teased or not. Ott caught the looks and grinned.

"It is true, I promise you. It was an Ursini's viper, but it had two heads, not one. Two heads and two sets of fangs. That meant a double dose of poison for anybody who got bitten. We killed it, of course; pinned it with a stick and cut off its heads with our knives."

Suddenly realization dawned on everybody at once.

"My God, that's how he did it." Heim caught himself. "Sorry, Conrad. That's what the stick was for. He would push the badge in the end of the stick and use that to hold the badge over the kernstrahlung. With the extra lengths we found in his office, he could stand here shielded by the tree but hold the badge right over the contamination. Then, when he had finished, he would throw the bit at the end away and keep the other two. I bet if we raked out that grass we would find more of those split-ended sticks."

Ott nodded. "That would do it. As long as he kept his hands away from the split end, he would be quite safe. He could even drag the card off using one of the safety poles."

As he realized the implications his face was stricken. He and his colleagues had risked their lives to place those poles as a warning and a service to the community, only to see them misused in such a foul way. It hurt him deeply. Conrad reached out and put his arm around the man's shoulders.

"Michael, don't let one man's abuse of your hard work disillusion you. Everywhere, there are people who use good things for bad purposes. We can't prevent that happening; we can only catch them when they do. And your efforts have saved hundreds of good people trying to survive. Think of them, not the one who exploited you."

"Thank you, Father. Logically I know you are right, but I still feel sick about it. Anyway. Let us have a look in this grass, see what we can find."

Ott reached into his backpack and drew out a folded stick. It took only a second to unfold and gave him almost two meters of length, with a fork at one end. "Now let us see."

He stretched out the pole, careful to keep the bulk of the tree between himself and the kernstrahlung it hid. "Yes, I think we have something." It took care to pull out, but it was eventually in clear sight. A pole like the other they had found, with a slot at one end. Ott swept it with his Geiger counter, and grimaced at the rapid clicks from the slotted end.

"I think that confirms it. He exposed the cards of his victims here and threw the stick into the grass afterwards. I think, when we have found the earliest records he has tampered with, they will be shown to have much variability. And, as he grew more skilled, he knew how long to hold out the card for a given exposure. Vogel was guilty of a foul crime and betrayed the trust we placed in him. If that is why he was killed, then, as far as I am concerned, the case ends here." Lang's voice was calm and very decisive.

Mayor Lang's Office, Elbingerode

"During our investigations into the circumstances surrounding the death of Doctor Vogel, we have discovered something quite appalling that we feel may explain his killing."

Conrad watched Willi and Olinda Kruger carefully and saw them both tense up at that point. In a strange way, that pleased him. *It means that, if Olinda had been threatened, she went straight to her husband with news of the threat. That shows a great depth of trust between the two.*

261

Conrad's Eye

"He was threatening women he considered vulnerable, by tampering with their radiation records. If they did not comply with his wishes, he would take away their approval to have children. A disgusting and disgraceful affair."

"Why should this involve us?"

Willi Kruger is putting on a good front, but he simply isn't a very good liar. He knows, or at least suspects, what was going on here.

"Olinda, we know that you were one of the women he threatened. We know that he made his first threat a month ago. I hate to have to ask you this, but did you submit to his demands for sexual favors?"

Between them, Willi was holding his wife's hand tightly. Olinda looked up at Mayor Lang, her one visible eye furious.

"Sexual *favors*? He did not ask me for those. He told me he could have any woman he wanted, so why should he bother with one who only had half a face? He wanted me to do . . . other . . . things for him. I refused."

"And you told your husband?"

"Of course I did." Olinda almost snarled the words out.

Then the implication sank home. She looked at her husband, her sighted eye wide with shock. Then she spoke rapidly, hurriedly, not giving anybody a chance to interrupt.

"Dear God, I know what you are thinking. Well, you are wrong. Willi didn't kill Vogel; I did. When it was time for the second meeting out in the woods, I took a knife and when he reached for me I killed him with it. And I am glad I did."

Conrad took out a strahlungjäger knife he had borrowed from Michael Ott.

"Olinda, could you show me how you stabbed Vogel?"

She took the knife and tried to hold it, but her fingers wouldn't close around the hilt properly. She fumbled the grip and barely managed to avoid dropping the knife on to her leg. Conrad reached out and took it from her before she hurt herself.

"No, Olinda, you didn't kill Vogel."

She looked at him and started to cry. "I am sorry Willi. If I had said nothing . . ."

Her husband reached out and put his arm around her shoulder. Lang looked sympathetically at them.

262

"Willi, if you had killed Vogel to defend Olinda, I would tell you to leave this room now and never worry about the matter again. But you didn't. You see, we know that whoever did kill Vogel was wearing a dress. One for a woman of slightly more than medium size. Between Olinda here and Frau Hahn."

"That covers much ground." Olinda was still sniffling, but her relief at the knowledge her husband hadn't killed Vogel was obvious. With that knowledge, her characteristic wry humor had returned.

"Indeed, and your Willi is not a small man. The only question was whether the two of you did it together and your efforts here today showed us otherwise. What did you do, Willi, when Olinda told you about Vogel's advances?"

He thought carefully. "At first, I was going to go down there and twist his neck until it was tied in a knot. But Olinda said to wait until her next set of results. She would tell him that she had come to me and if he continued with his threat I was going to meet him and give him the worst beating a man had ever suffered. He did make his threats again, but, before I could meet with him, he was found dead. I thought it was another man, whose wife had been threatened, who killed him, so I kept my peace."

"Olinda, did you tell anybody else about what Vogel was doing?"

Conrad was still in the dark about what was going on here. *I have the motive for the killing, but the most likely suspects are clear of any guilt. If there is any guilt, which I doubt.*

"Or, do you have any knowledge of any other women being threatened?"

Olinda had flushed bright red. "No, I could not. And I know of no other women he was blackmailing."

"I must say that I find the trust and love that exists between you two is an inspiration to me and an example for all others." Conrad spoke carefully and deeply. "Willi, how did you meet Olinda?"

"I told you." Olinda was curious.

"I know, but you were very sick and very weak. It is rare to meet people who are as devoted to each other as you two. Knowing you and about you helps me maintain my faith." Willi Kruger stared at Conrad and nodded his head. *He might not be a good liar but he recognizes sincerity when he hears it.*

"There is not so very much to tell, Father. I have always lived here in Elbingerode. The farm I have now is my family farm, only there is not much left of my family. My father and my brothers died in Russia. My mother and sister were in Munich, visiting my cousins, the day the hellburners fell."

Conrad's Eye

Munich, population one million, one hundred and eight five thousand. A city selected for special treatment; a city selected to make a point, just as Berlin had been blasted to make a point. Munich had been hit by eight atomic bombs, a mix of 35 and 49 kiloton yields. Known survivors, less than 400.

The treacherous numbers swept through Conrad's mind. Once again, he wished he had never heard them.

"But, I was in my farm that day. I had an exemption, you see. I was Volksturm only. After the hellburners fell, I waited to die just as everybody else. But, eventually, I realized I was one of the lucky ones. I had survived. Alone, but I had survived.

"Then, one day, I saw two figures coming out of the woods. Well, not out of the woods. One of them was following the narrow-gauge railway track to Blankenburg. He had made a litter out of some branches and two old railway wheels and he was pulling another figure along on that litter. As they came closer, I saw the figure on the litter was a woman, a badly injured and very sick one. He saw me, and he asked if I had clean water he could drink. I started to go over but he waved me back. He said that the woman had typhus and that he probably had it as well.

"Typhus, Father, no man can be asked to risk that. Typhus kills without mercy. But I was already dead, for what is a man who has lost everybody? And what sort of man could turn his back on a sick woman and a man who was struggling so hard to save her? So, I got a tent out from my house and pitched it for them in the yard. Then I got water and food and put it out for them. Every day I did the same, while the man nursed the sick woman through her illness. How she survived, I do not know; for typhus of the most virulent sort was an epidemic then and killed millions. But she lived. When she was past the worst of the disease and no longer infectious, I brought her into my house. The man left. By another miracle, he escaped the typhus fever and I last saw him walking away down the railway line. Or I thought that would be the last time I would ever see him.

"Later, much later, I went to Huttenrode to trade the vegetables I had grown. Father, that man who struggled so hard for Olinda was the Strahlungjäger Hans Koertig. I went to him, I thanked him for what he had done and told him that no matter what happened, there would always be a place for him in our home. He became our friend; not the sort who one sees every day, but one who comes rarely, makes us happy to see him come and sad to see him leave.

"It was our home by then, Father. Olinda had recovered, slowly, very slowly and for a long time she was too weak to do much. But she was so brave, she demanded that she do as much as she could and never complained when

264

food was short. She had so little, yet she took a deep joy in everything that was left to us in a way that made us both feel rich. Later, a long time later, for that was how long it took her to recover from her ordeal, she came to love me and that made my heart glow, for I already loved her. And so we became a couple and later still, the little Antonov brought you and we were married." He looked proudly at his wife sitting beside him. "And she was even prepared to confess to a crime she couldn't commit when she thought doing so would protect me. No man could do better for a wife, Father."

"And Hans didn't resent the fact that Olinda has settled down with you?" Conrad was memorizing the story and the appearance of this couple, so he could recall them on nights when the nightmares were very bad and despair was choking him.

It was Olinda who answered, her voice having regained the bubbling laugh that her injured lips couldn't hide. "No, Father. Sometimes I thought that Hans might be jealous of Willi having me, but then I realized this could not be so. I suppose he must have been just a little jealous of me having Willi instead."

There was a gentle laugh in the room about that.

Eventually, Conrad shook his head, inwardly delighted that this evening's work should have turned out so well. That thought triggered off another in his head. "Which reminds me, I have a suspicion that I need to perform a hasty wedding tonight, one that is pushing the arrival of a stork uncomfortably close."

Heim laughed. "How do you do it, Father? Silke saw her young man and explained everything to him. At first he was very angry; not at her, but at Vogel. Then he was angry with her, for hiding from him and leaving things so close to her due date. They had an argument, shouting at each other. Then they both started crying. In the end, they both decided to come here and get married. I took the liberty of calling Albertus de Chesaux and he is already taking down the details. You need to do another Wedding Mass, Conrad. Quickly, for the hours march by and the midwife is already stirring."

"And where is Traute Hahn?" Conrad asked the question with a certain degree of trepidation.

"She is hunting for her daughter. She hasn't thought to look here yet. She's been back to the church twice, but the doors are closed.

"The doors of a church should never be closed." Conrad said that absently, knowing that all too often they had to be. "But we should get down there fast. Olinda, have you ever felt a strange desire to be a maid of honor?"

"I'm not a maid, Father Conrad."

"Details, details, don't bother me with details." Conrad was uneasily aware that he was quoting a favorite saying of the man who had planned the destruction of the country he was in.

"We need to get Silke married before her mother finds her or her baby decides to enter the world. Or, Heaven forbid, both of those happening at once."

The Church, Elbingerode

"You may now kiss the bride."

Eckart Thyben leaned forward and kissed Silke Thyben carefully. Despite that care, she winced and put her hand on her stomach.

From the back of the church, two women stepped forward and took her hands. "Come, Silke; there is nothing to be afraid of. We'll look after you now."

She went with them, her new husband following along behind. When they had gone, Heim looked around. He had been asked to give the bride away and had done so with aplomb. Now, he felt he deserved a little light relief.

"Well, the only advice I can give Eckie is to keep his wife on a strict diet."

Conrad snorted with laughter then wagged a finger at Heim. "I'll expect to hear you confess to that remark, Werner. A couple of Hail Marys might be in order."

He was stopped from going further by a man running in.

"Excuse me, Father Conrad? I have a message for you from Huttenrode. You knew a man called Manfred von Leer?"

"I do." The humor drained out of Conrad in an instant, when he realized the significance of the past tense.

"I am sorry Father, but I must tell you, he died earlier this evening. It appears that he fell down the stairs in his house during the day and it was some hours before he was found. He was delirious, Father; he didn't know what he was saying, I am sure of that."

"Was what he said so bad then?"

"It made little sense, Father. He spoke some terrible blasphemies and cursed some names. Somebody called Parmenio, and another called Stuyvesant. He cursed them and damned their souls, Father. In a voice that was filled with hate."

"Did he mention any other names? Somebody called Igrat, perhaps?"

"No, Father, just those two. And then he died."

Rest in peace, Manannan mac Lir, and thank you for not cursing Igrat who has done nothing to harm you. I will pray for you; all the more so because your sins are so grievous.

"My friends, I would like to stay here tonight to pray for the soul of Manfred von Leer. Tomorrow, I think we should have a formal interview with the killer of Vogel."

Mayor Lang's Office, Elbingerode

"Perfect, just perfect."

Conrad had an air of bucolic happiness about him. *Once in a while, things work out just right and this is one of those times.* With a little aid from Conrad's advance planning, Traute Hahn had just found out that her daughter was now a happily married woman with a young son to care for. She was absolutely furious about it, and was storming up the path towards the office where he, Mayor Lang and *Friedensrichter* Heim were waiting. *Doubtless she holds us all collectively and individually responsible. As far as that is concerned, it is a responsibility I am pleased to accept, but the other two were blameless.*

"This is going to be noisy." Heim sounded slightly apprehensive.

Conrad looked at him sympathetically. "I don't suppose there is a town museum with a Scold's Bridle here is there?"

Lang burst out laughing. "Oh, how I wish there was. Never was something more suited to a person like Traute Hahn. Where are her daughter, son-in-law and grandchild, by the way?"

"Back in Huttenrode. A special train took them back this morning. It was a very easy birth, so I am told. Silke is well-hipped after all. Sometimes a larger woman has the advantage over her smaller sisters."

Conrad beamed at Heim and wagged his finger at him. "Diet indeed."

"You've solved the death of Vogel, haven't you?" Heim returned the smile.

"I think so; I am fairly certain of it." Conrad hesitated for a second. "If I am right, there was no crime committed here. In Texas, there is a defense called 'he needed killing.' It is an affirmative defense, of course, but what it means is that the killing of a person was performed to protect the community as a whole from somebody who was a deadly threat to that community. I think it might well apply here."

Lang put the bits together quickly. "Please don't tell me it was Koertig. I don't think I could stand that dreadful woman being right after all."

He was interrupted by the outside door crashing open.

"Five . . . . Four .. . . . Three . . . . . Two . . . . . One .. . ... Zero." Conrad timed it to perfection. Exactly on the beat, the inner door nearly flew off its hinges as Traute Hahn stormed through.

"What have you done with my Silke?" The scream of rage nearly bounced off the walls.

"Married her, to her boyfriend. They are very happy with their child, last time I saw them. And, by the way, she is not your Silke anymore."

"Where are they?" Hahn was being driven almost mad by Conrad's unfailingly polite smile. He relished it. *I will have to do penance for my enjoyment of her anger.*

"At their new home. I suppose they will contact you when they are settled in. If they want to, of course. They might not. After all, they have their baby to care for."

For a brief second, Conrad thought he might have pushed her too far. She went bright crimson, her small eyes bulging outwards. To his further delight, in the background, Hans Koertig had just arrived and was looking curiously at the scene. This little show had worked out almost perfectly. Traute Hahn added the final piece when she completely lost control of herself.

"Their baby? It is Hans Koertig's baby. You tricked that poor young man into looking after another man's baby. What sort of priest are you?" She lunged forward in an effort to slap him.

"Frau Hahn. I must ask you to leave right now." Friedensrichter Heim took her arm and half-dragged her out of the room.

In doing so, for a brief second, she faced Koertig. "It was him. It was all him." Then her voice collapsed; in a very tiny whisper, she added "who will look after me now?"

"Step in, Hans. We need to have a formal interview with you." Heim closed the door, so the four were in the office alone together.

"In the names of all the Gods, don't tell me you're taking her accusations seriously." Koertig was furious. "I want to put this to an end right now. End it beyond any doubt. There is no possibility whatsoever that I am the father of her daughter's baby. I'll show you why. This is between us, understand? It must never go beyond this room."

He unfastened his utility belt and dropped the pair of jeans he was wearing.

There was a complete silence in the room. Heim looked at the ceiling and said casually

"Well, that does solve that little problem."

Conrad's eyebrows lifted. *It isn't what I expected but a lot of things now fall into place. And the manner in which this was disclosed is as telling as the fact itself..*

"Your real name is Hannah Koertig I suppose?"

"It is. How did you guess?"

"When people change their identity, they like to stay close to their original name. At the very least, they keep their initials."

"Pull your pants up, for God's sake man . . . I mean ma'am . . . I mean . . . " Lang retreated into flustered silence.

Koertig smiled sadly at him and pulled her jeans up. When they were back in place, she was, once again, Strahlungjäger Hans Koertig. Looking at her, Conrad found a thought crossing his mind *I wonder how many of the women have guessed your secret and keep quiet out of sympathy for you? More than you could possibly suspect I would guess.*

"Why?" Heim was dumbfounded; not just at the deception, but that it had been thought necessary. "Woman are safe and protected here. You could have had an easy life instead of searching the woods for the kernstrahlung."

"Easy life? Protected? Do you realize how much pressure there is on young women to have babies here? To have a partner and produce babies?"

"Is that so bad?" Lang was curious.

"For me, yes. You all thought I was a man who loved other men. Well, you are half right; I love other *women*. To lie with a man and have babies, the very thought is nauseating to me. I wanted to avoid having to explain, to justify myself and this was the easiest way."

"Once you asked me if I knew what the Nazis did to people like you." Conrad stared at Koertig, piece after piece falling into place in his mind. "You do know, don't you?"

"I lived in Magdeburg with my lover. We were very careful. To the outside world, we were just two young women who shared an apartment. Somehow, we made a mistake. Somebody informed on us and, one day, the police came. We were making love and there was no hiding that. They dragged us from our home and took us away. I never saw my lover again. She must be dead now.

"The guards in the prison knew I was a lesbian and they assumed that all I needed was to know what a 'real man' was like to be changed. They of course thought of themselves as 'real men,' so they raped me. Over and over again, for day after day. The terrible thing is, they may even have thought they were being kind. Perhaps they persuaded themselves that they were saving me from what would otherwise happen to me. Father, you know just how devious and deceptive the Devil can be when he takes over men's souls. Eventually, I was put on a small train that headed for Blankenburg. Mayor Lang, you know the narrow-track line through the hills?"

"Of course. You are thinking of opening it up aren't you?"

"I am, and I have good reason to know it is relatively safe. I just have every reason to try alternatives first. Have you ever followed that line? No? Well, into the hills, where the ground folds, there is a junction and a branch line leads away into the trees. After about a kilometer it ends in a blind tunnel. I do not know why; perhaps it was a line to somewhere else that was never finished. That tunnel is full of bodies now. People the Nazis wanted killed, but could not be bothered to take to the extermination camps. I was on a train full of prisoners for that place when the hellburner that destroyed Magdeburg went off. The train was thrown from the tracks and crashed. Many on board were killed, but I was not. I started to run. I ran harder than I had ever run before and I got far away from that train. I do not think anybody else survived.

"Then, I wandered. I found the railway line and followed it, I don't know why. I found clothes that disguised me as a man. I had been badly beaten, my face was bruised and my head had already been shaved, so my appearance was not a problem. I followed the line up into the hills and came across the tunnel I told you about. That's when I realized what the hellburners had saved me from. Then I followed the other line. About halfway through the hills, I found a woman laying on the tracks. She was far gone from starvation and exhaustion but, when I turned her over, I saw her burns and also the rash of typhus fever. I wanted to leave her but I couldn't. I just couldn't. So I found some old railway wheels, made a litter and dragged her out of the woods."

"That was Olinda Kruger." Conrad spoke quietly. "Having saved her life you felt responsible for her. You never desert the people you are responsible for, do you? I think perhaps you are haunted by the thought that you might have done something to save the woman you loved and now you have sworn to yourself that you will never abandon a person close to you to their fate again. So when you heard Vogel blackmailing Olinda, you saw it as your duty to save her again."

"I was walking past Vogel's office and I heard Olinda crying. I recognized it instantly from the time in the woods and at the farm. Vogel was telling her to do things for him, perverted, degrading things, and she was refusing. I heard what he was threatening her with and I knew then that he had to go. The only problem was to get close enough to him. I can act like a man, but I do not have the strength to fight like one. If I had approached him openly, there would have been a fight that would have attracted attention. I had to get close to him. It was easy, really. I took a dress from a line and put it on. It was the first time in many years I had worn one. When Vogel came out of his office, I walked up to him. He never even looked at me until I slammed my knife into his heart.

"The rest was easy. His office was close to the railway yard, a few meters at most. I took the body to the railway and put him on a handcar along with a couple of spare wheels. Then, well, you know the rest. I took him down as far as the line would go and then made another rail-litter for the rest of the trip. I used my Geiger counter to check the way was clear. It was a chance, but only a small one. You'll find the rail litter close to where I dumped his body. Then I changed back into my own clothes and walked back. Just Hans Koertig, strahlungjäger, about his business. I went to Vogel's office and saw he had already corrupted the files. So I took the last month's readings and destroyed them."

"I didn't know it was you until last night." Conrad was quiet, shocked by the way the story had turned out. *Although, thinking about it, all the signs had been there, I just failed to notice them.*

"I thought it was the Krugers working together. But, when we confronted them, it was obvious that the theory was wrong. Then Willi mentioned that it was you who rescued Olinda from the woods. That made so much fall into place. One question, why did you dump his body in the woods where you did? If you had taken him a little deeper, he might never have been found."

"I am a strahlungjäger, Conrad. And those woods can be dangerous. But, most of all, even a man like Vogel deserves decent burial. I thought it would be assumed he was the victim of an outlaw. There are a few such out there still."

"I see. The final clue was when you met Frau Hahn this morning. Implicitly she accused you of being the father and of killing Vogel. You were enraged by the accusations, but you made a great show of offense over the pregnancy one. You even revealed your gender, your most carefully hidden secret, to try and distract attention from the accusation of murder. But it was the murder accusation that would have enraged most people. Only one who was actually guilty and deeply troubled over it would have preferred not to lie his way out of that accusation."

There was a long silence. Eventually, Lang got up and stared out of the window for a while.

"What do you think, Conrad? One way or another, you seem to have become the conscience of this little town."

"I think stealing that dress was a mean thing to do. It was probably the only piece of nice clothing the poor woman had. Whatever else happens, you should make restitution for that. As for the rest, I cannot condemn you for what you did.

Conrad's Eye

Whether Mayor Lang and Friedensrichter Heim agree, or not, is up to them. My concern is only that no innocent person be punished for what happened here."

The Meeting Hall, Elbingerode

The meeting hall was packed tight, with people standing outside to try and hear the news. Word had spread fast that the mystery of Vogel's death had been solved and that a juicy scandal was the result. Eventually, Mayor Lang banged a gavel on the table and stood up.

"My friends, our investigation into the death of Doctor Vogel is complete. The cause of his death was shameful. He abused his position and tampered with radiation records in an effort to force women to provide sexual services to him. When they refused, he forged results, to take away their authorization to have children."

The surge of sheer raw fury that spread through the room was terrifying. Conrad knew that if Vogel had been present, he would literally have been torn apart. Conrad hated mob violence; all too often, he had seen it lead to the slaughter of innocent people, but even he could feel some sympathy for those who were howling for Vogel's blood.

Lang was slamming a hammer down on the table, trying to restore order to the room. It was fairly obvious that he, too, had more than a little sympathy for the people so badly wronged.

"People, friends, please. Dr Vogel is dead. We cannot punish him as he deserves. All we can do is to repair the damage he has done. Starting with his radiation records. Since those records are corrupted and untrustworthy, I have been in contact with Potsdam to ask advice. They counseled me to wipe those records clean. The women he victimized no longer have that prohibition in place."

A gasp of pleasure from several of the women ran around the room. The afflicted couples hugged each other, as the realization that a blight had been lifted from their lives sank in.

Lang held up his hand.

"As to the killer of Vogel, it is obvious that it was somebody protecting one of his victims. Neither I, nor Friedensrichter Heim, have been able to identify the man responsible. Father Conrad, have your investigations revealed his identity?"

Conrad stood up.

"No, Mayor Lang. I can name no man as being responsible for the killing of Vogel."

Lang looked at the assembled villagers and caught the slight smile on Koertig's face. The number of people who had appreciated the subtlety of Conrad's neat evasion would forever be small, but that didn't mean it would be forgotten.

"In this case, I am prepared to rule that Vogel died as a result of his own foul actions. He brought his death down on his own head. As the good Father has shown us, sometimes justice is done without the hand of a man to perform it. If the man who killed Vogel is ever identified, it shall be noted as a case of justifiable homicide in defense of an abused woman. The case is closed."

"If I may, Mayor Lang?"

Conrad looked around the room. "I heard from a friend of mine in Rome this morning. He was shocked to hear that the spiritual needs of this community had been so badly neglected and has sworn to make sure that proper action is taken. The highest priority will be placed on finding suitable priests for the larger communities left in Germany and appointing others to travel between the smaller ones. Soon, Father Edwin Landsmeer, will be arriving here to be your priest. I know this man well. He is from the Netherlands and is well suited to this community, since he has medical training as well as being ordained. This will be his first congregation, so I ask everybody to be gentle with him."

A warm burst of applause swept around the room. Some of the people nearest to Conrad whispered their thanks to him.

"May I ask one other thing? A friend of mine died while I was here. You knew him as Manfred von Leer or Mad Manfred. His experiences during the bombing left him a deeply troubled soul and I doubt that he will rest easily. Please remember him in your prayers since, before the misfortunes of war destroyed him, he was a good man."

After the meeting was over, Conrad walked down to the railway station with Lang and Heim. A small train, just a handcar and a single flatbed, were waiting. The de Chesauxes were already sitting on the bed when they saw him. Peretta waved to him.

"Conrad, this is the inaugural run of the train to the airport. The Antonov is coming in soon."

Conrad waved back and turned to Lang. "Wilhelm, one thing I do not understand. This little train. It is useful, certainly, and great fun to ride on, but surely carts would be more efficient?"

"They would be. But our little train, as you call it, gives the entire valley pride. It's ours, something we built and operate together. By the way, a couple of friends wanted to say goodbye to you before they go back into the woods."

Conrad shook hands with the two strahlungjägers. "Michael, thank you for everything you have taught me about living here. Hans, you too, I have learned much from you both. Might I suggest that one day you write all your experiences down, so that others may learn from them?"

Ott looked slightly surprised. "You think that destruction like this could happen again?"

"I fear that it is all too likely. That was not all I had in mind though. Your calling, your love and care for this community, is surely pleasing to God." Conrad looked at Koertig and smiled. "Or the Gods. You stand as examples of all that is best in humanity. The story of what you do, and why, should be shared with the world. It has been a great honor to meet you and I will pray for your safety as you go about your work."

Conrad and the strahlungjägers shook hands again and Conrad climbed onto the flatbed, aided by a hand stretched out by Albertus de Chesaux.

"Thank you. Are you going back to the world outside now?"

"No, Conrad; we're off to another refuge. There are unions to be recorded, births to be registered and deaths to be listed. Why don't you come with us? Your services will always be needed here in what is left of Germany."

Peretta de Chesaux smiled at him and the day seemed just a little brighter.

"I would like to do that. But, I have to go to Geneva to see an old friend and tell him what I have learned here. From there, I don't know. God will guide my steps. But always know that I will be praying that he watches over you. And over this valley."

CHAPTER SIX

The Seer's Home, Philotas, Saranac, Adirondack National Park, New York

"You are sure of this?"

The Seer's voice was quiet, even, and uninflected, but Conrad couldn't help but notice the deadly menace that lay beneath it. He was suddenly quite sure that the Seer had used the same tones when he decided that Germany had to die.

"Absolutely sure, Phillip. After I left the valley, I went straight to Geneva and told Loki the whole story of Manannan mac Lir. Until then, the thought of a threat to Igrat had not crossed my mind. I had assumed that as he had died, sanity had reclaimed his mind and the thought of harming her vanished. But, Loki saw it straight away. He realized the possibility that Manannan had not cursed her as he was dying, because he had already arranged a worse fate for her than any spoken curse likely to produce. Then he proceeded to show me what a real curse sounded like when he rebuked me for my stupidity in not seeing that possibility and moving quickly. It included bones cracking, various parts of my body rotting and dogs eating what was left. While I was still alive."

The account could have sounded humorous, were not Conrad sweating profusely. He didn't fear death, but the thought that a mistake on his part threatened another innocent with a brutal and horrifying death was worse than any physical agony.

The Seer stared at him coldly. "And what did Loki do? Crack a joke or two?"

"You wrong him, Phillip; you wrong him greatly and I would urge you to pay penance for such unworthy thoughts. You and Loki may dislike each other, but he is very fond of Igrat and would do nothing to expose her to harm. He checked very carefully into the records of Manannan mac Lir and any communications he might have had with the outside world. All messages that went by way of the NAIADS system are logged and they show no messages out from him. Visitors to Elbingerode were few and they were also located and investigated. They were, politely and discretely, interrogated and nothing was

275

found. Loki even investigated and interrogated the de Chesaux couple and made sure they weren't involved. Furthermore, he sounded out all the criminal organizations in Europe and found there was not one who had heard a plot against any member of the NSC or OSS.

"That did not surprise Loki. He was advised that no criminal organization would touch such a contract. Criminals are in the business for profit, not to dice with extermination. They will not tangle with the NSC. Phillip, Loki has contacts and resources all over Europe, at every level and in every walk of life, and he used all of them to try and determine if a threat to Igrat existed.

"If Manannan mac Lir had arranged for Igrat to be killed or mutilated after his death, he did so in a way that defied detection by the most skilled investigators Loki could find. There are possibilities left; that, Loki admits. He cautions you that a radioactive source might have been located either at the home Igrat shares with Michael Collins on Long Island or at her Broadway apartment. He suggests you check those very carefully.

"There is also the possibility of a threat that would not require any great level of organization. A single hireling, not attached to any organization, might take the chance of attacking her. A push on a station to send her under a train, a car running her down in the street or a cup of acid thrown in her face; all of those would take little or no organization. For all our investigations, we cannot prove that such threats do not exist. That might well be Manannan mac Lir's real revenge upon you. This could be a threat that will hang over you for years to come. You dare not drop your guard, even though any reasonable assessment would be that there is no threat to fear."

"The hardest task of all is to prove no threat exists." The Seer sounded thoughtful. "You haven't told Igrat of this?"

"To tell her that a man she has never met has conceived such a virulent hatred for her? I would not wish that on anybody, let alone a young woman."

"Igrat isn't young, Conrad. She's five times older than you are and she's a lot tougher as well. Don't be deceived by the Broadway Baby act; Iggie has seen and done things that would scare you into a catatonic coma. And she's quite used to being hated. Having said that, I don't see any reason why she should be exposed to any more risk than usual. You should have told her immediately, so that she could be on her guard."

Conrad flushed and looked at his feet. Somehow, the mild rebuke cut him far more deeply that Loki's prolonged and luridly obscene tirade had done.

"I was wrong."

"Yes, you were. But we can fix that right now. We'll get her up here and you can tell her the whole story, good and bad."

"She's here? I didn't know that."

"There's a lot you don't know about my family, Conrad. We're a complex bunch. Igrat's probably in the pool, having a swim. I'll get her to come up." The Seer plugged in the telephone on his desk and pressed the paging switch. "Igrat, please come up to my office, right away."

"You really don't like intercoms, do you?" Conrad was amused to see the Seer unplug his telephone again.

"Hate them. A security breach waiting to happen."

"Hi guys, what's the problem?"

Igrat was wearing a white toweling robe over a dark blue swimsuit and was still obviously wet from the pool. She pulled up a seat and sat down, expecting to be briefed on one of her courier runs. Instead, Conrad started to tell her of his trip to Elbingerode and of his meeting with Manannan mac Lir. By the time he had finished, her eyes were moist.

"The poor man. That's terrible."

"You never met him, did you?" Conrad was shocked at her initial reaction. *I expected her to be frightened or furious at the threats against her. Not distressed by his fate.* The unexpected reaction bewildered him.

Igrat shook her head, scattering some drops of water from her hair. "Never, not even when I was doing courier runs to Geneva during the war. The fewer people who met me, the better. Thanks for the warning, Conrad; I'll be careful."

"Iggie, being careful won't cut it. Not this time. I'm pulling you off courier runs for a few years." The Seer's voice was decisive.

Igrat smiled at her adoptive father and raised an eyebrow but her reply was short and succinct. "No."

Conrad expected The Seer to explode at somebody defying his orders but, once again, he was reminded how little he actually knew about the inter-personal dynamics of the Washington Circle. The Seer just grinned. Conrad decided it was up to him to persuade Igrat to change her mind.

"Igrat, you haven't seen the effects of radiation poisoning. mac Lir was horribly mutilated and he wished the same thing on you. You can't take the chance."

"Conrad, every woman lives with that chance. Us, with our gift, more than most. We all deal with it our own chosen ways. Mine was to have a quiet chat with Naamah. If that ever happens to me, she'll make me a nice cup of tea that will ease me out of life. Swiftly, quietly and painlessly."

"Just how many of the girls have a similar arrangement?" The Seer was genuinely curious. It was something he had never thought of.

"None of your business, father. Our lives; our decision. But I will never let anybody stop me doing something by threatening me. So I will not give up my duties because of a threat that is only just slightly this side of not existing."

"You don't get it, Iggie." The Seer was patient. "This threat isn't aimed at you, it's aimed at me. You would just be collateral damage. If we're having to protect the materials you carry against attack all the time, it will limit what we can do and how we can do it. When I take you off your courier duties, it's because it is essential for my work. Your feelings or safety don't come into it."

Igrat looked at him, her eyes narrowed with suspicion. Eventually, she nodded slightly.

"I'll accept that. Just barely. What's the plan?"

"You'll disappear. It's time you did anyway. You've been running messages for a long time now and people know you. Soon, your apparent age will be incompatible with what they know of you. We'll replace you on the runs with one of the short-life girls. A couple of them resemble you very closely. We can be absolutely sure that the people, if any, that mac Lir hired will not know of our secret. So, they probably know your description and courier routes but nothing else. If there is an attack on your stand-in, we'll know the threat is still valid and we can do something. If not, then in a decade or so, you can go back to work."

"You can't put somebody else at risk." The Seer was amused to note that Conrad and Igrat said the same thing almost perfectly together.

"Oh, yes, I can; that's what the OSS couriers are paid for. If one gets hurt, we look after her. That goes without saying."

"You still can't . . . "

"Be quiet, Conrad, or I'll seduce you." Igrat had dropped her voice slightly, both in volume and pitch. "Then you will go to Hell for breaking your vows."

Conrad chuckled at the threat, "I'm going to Hell anyway."

Igrat nodded slightly. She knew Conrad's history and agreed with his prognosis. "What do I do, Father?"

"I'll contact Bill Shaych over in California. You can go out there for a while as his Executive Assistant. Take Nell with you; she needs a break out of the limelight as well. You can both vanish easily enough; you know the drill. Bill has a whole clutch of projects in hand, both in his own scriptwriter's identity and for us. The jobs he'll be doing for us are actually very important and he'll need your help. You haven't been in California for a long time, so nobody knows you, and, in Hollywood, you'll be just one more beautiful girl amidst a whole host of them."

"Thank you, Father. I think."

"Think nothing of it. But, I want you out there immediately. This is a genuine job, Iggie, not makework. You really are badly needed out there. So is Nell, come to think of it. Bill's a great guy and a great scriptwriter, but his organizational skills are next to nonexistent. What he will be doing for us is absolutely essential for our long-term survival. He really does need the pair of you."

Igrat nodded and started to leave. When she was half way to the door, The Seer looked up from his paperwork again.

"And leave the pen from my desk behind, please."

Igrat smiled and took a pen out of the bottom part of her bikini. "When did you spot it?"

"When you threatened to seduce Conrad. I guessed that was misdirection and watched your hands, not Conrad's outraged expression."

After the door closed behind her, The Seer leaned back. "Well, that solves that. Iggie will be safe out with Bill and doing useful work as well. If there is a plot, the girl that replaces her will act as a lightning rod. She'll be safe, Conrad; she'll have Henry and Achillea with her. But, to be honest, I sincerely doubt if anything will come of this.

"Now, tell me everything you learned about Germany."

Conrad's Eye

EYE OF THE PRETENDER
Hollywood, California, 1966

Conrad's Eye

CHAPTER ONE

Head Office, Paramount Studios, Hollywood, California, May 1966

T ell me, have you decided whether you want your audience to hang you in the car park *before* or *after* they burn the studio down?" Bill Shaych sounded slightly curious but distinctly helpful.

"I told you this was a bad idea; a mad idea. Science fiction is for children." The studio chief programmer was belligerent, even though Shatch had essentially just agreed with him.

"It's not actually a bad idea," Shaych was shaking his head. "In fact, it's a very good idea. It's just that the execution is terrible. Science fiction is a limited market niche, certainly, but it is far from being restricted to children. That doesn't matter so much, though. It doesn't really matter what the setting of stories is. As long as they are good stories, set in an environment that will interest the audience, then they'll watch it. Take the best episode of the best western series and play it on a space ship and it will still succeed.

"The same applies in reverse. Take the proposed scripts we have here, take them off the space ship and put them into the best western series you have and they'll still be failures. It's the script and characterization that's wrong here, not the setting. You have to produce what the audience wants to buy, not expect them to buy what you want to produce. Asses on seats, buddy. That's what counts."

"A breath of fresh air at last. Gentlemen, please take note of that very succinct description of our business." The vice-president in charge of production looked severely at his team. "It worries me we had to hire Mr. Shaych here to remind us of that. Bill, you said this proposal was poorly executed. I know the first pilot we did was a flop, but what exactly do you see as being wrong?"

"Mike, as far as I can see, there isn't one group of your prospective audience you are not offending. Take the crew list. We have a German officer on the bridge; the helmsman, I believe. There's a million American families out there who hung gold stars in their windows because of the Germans. Every one of them is going to switch off as soon as he appears. And then there are the Russians. They are our blood-brothers. We stuck by each other, through the worst seven years either of our countries has ever suffered. Nine million Americans served in Russia in one capacity or the other and the Russian-American Friendship League has over 20 million members. The loud noise you just heard was them all switching off when they realized the 'multi-national crew' doesn't contain a Russian. Damn it, we have Russian pilots flying our bombers on exchange missions right now; and ours flying theirs, come to that. The Raffle and veterans will see that as an insult to our allies. And it is."

"I want to show that horror is behind us. That we don't need wars to form a peaceful, progressive union that puts people before profit and politics." Gene Rockerferry was grimly determined to preserve the integrity of his creation.

He's remarkably aggressive for somebody who claims to believe in peace and universal brotherhood, Shaych thought.

"That's another point that's going to turn off whole sections of the potential audience. All the attitudes and beliefs expressed in these texts are straight out of the 1940s. You make a big play of a multi-racial crew. Got news for you, Gene, nobody cares about race any more. We had that stupidity burned out of us on the Russian Front. It didn't matter whether the man beside you was black, white, Hispanic or blue with green spots, as long as he covered your ass when you needed him. That's carried over into civilian life here. Nobody cares anymore and that's a real problem for your whole concept of the show."

"Prejudice still exists and . . . "

"Sure it does; it always will. There'll always be a few people who have their heads screwed up. But, most people don't care and will resent being lectured on something they already take for granted. The few that do care won't like being reminded that they represent the remnant of a discarded way of thought. Both will switch off. By the way, you claim to dislike prejudice, but I note there isn't a single obvious homosexual in the crew, male or female. That's another prejudice that got burned out of us on the Russian Front and another sector of the audience that will take offense and switch off. And all that before we deal with the biggest sub-section of the audience of all. Women. Fifty-two percent of the population, in case you hadn't remembered."

"I went out of my way to include women in prominent positions in the crew." Rockerferry was beginning to get seriously angry with Shaych's ruthless demolition of his pet project.

"You mean that communications officer? Lieutenant Uhura, if I remember rightly? She has 18 lines in the second pilot. Well, that's not true. She had one line, 18 times. 'Hailing Frequencies Open, Captain.' " Shaych inserted a degree of irony into his voice when he quoted the line that suggested he was a pretty good actor himself.

"Michelle Michaels is a damned fine actress and she's being utterly wasted in that role. Then we have a nurse, whose sole function is to make eyes at the Science Officer, and a Yeoman, whose sole function is to do the same at the Captain. This is your idea of women in prominent positions? A telephone answering service and a pair of love-struck groupies? I've got news for you. Women entered the workforce during the war. They've stayed there and are working their way up the corporate ladder right now. Again, the attitudes of this show are stuck in the 1940s. Then, we have those uniforms. Miniskirts? Ridiculous. The actresses are spending all their time making sure they don't give the camera a view of the promised land."

"To be fair, the costume department are responsible for that. They thought it would attract the male demographic. Anyway, mini-skirts are in fashion."

Bill Theiss looked pointedly at Shaych's assistant who was wearing a miniskirt easily as short as the ones in the show.

"The street is the street. This is supposed to be a warship."

"No, it isn't. We say it right at the beginning; the *Enterprise* is built for exploration. Starfleet is not a military organization."

"And yet you have an organization that is armed to the teeth. How many nukes does that ship carry? Three hundred plus? If that doesn't make her a warship I don't know what does. That's something else that will put people off. They'll think you're trying to make fools of them You know the distinguishing mark of the last person who claimed that all he wanted was peace, yet started a war that killed a million American boys? A little toothbrush moustache."

"And we killed sixty million Germans. I know. I flew one of those bombers."

"And you are claiming that a spaceship that carries twice as many atomic bombs than we dropped on Germany isn't a warship? Can't you see how dumb that is?"

"Gentlemen, please." The vice-president in charge of production sounded weary. Shaych guessed this argument had played out many times before.

"Bill, you've summarized what's wrong with this show. Can we put it right, or do we simply write it off?"

"We put it right. There's not anything fundamentally wrong with it; it just needs some tidying up and substituting good story-telling for the obsolete moralizing." Shaych thought for a few seconds. "First thing, there's no executive officer. Every commander has an executive officer who looks after running the routine stuff, while he gets on with commanding. Mine's Irene here."

"We had a first officer in the original pilot, but he was dropped in favor of the science officer."

Shaych grunted. "Good and bad news there. That science officer with the pointy ears is one of the few really good ideas we've had so far. You know we can combine few things here. We need to give women a more responsible and prominent role, yet that'll create problems in other areas. There's already a lot of nausea about women serving in the military. Pro and con. But, everybody knows that the Russians used women as fighter pilots, tank crews and snipers. No problem there. So we make the Executive Officer a Russian woman. We'll call her . . . " Shaych thought for a second. "Irina Antonova Chekhov. Cold, hard as nails, but goes to mush when dealing with children.

"Now, one of the scripts was about a planet where the adults had all died and the children were on their own. That was a very weak filler story. But, with Irina in it, it sets up a massive tension between her typically Russian protectiveness of children and the very real fact that children are the enemy. Also, while we're on the subject of women, we can make Uhura the electronics warfare officer as well as the communications officer and that gives her a lot of room for growth. By the way, Bill, SAC crews wear coveralls. Can you design a uniform that's based on coveralls but still looks sexy? Air Force light blue for the overalls, but colored T-shirts underneath for branch of service?"

Bill Theiss looked thoughtful. "You know, tailor the coveralls right and it could be done. Use the right fabrics . . ."

Shaych grinned while Theiss got to work sketching on his pad. In his eyes, that was the mark of a real expert. *Faced with a challenge, he or she got right down to it.*

"Now, the ship herself. The basic design is OK. We'll just put a SAC band on her somewhere. That'll make people feel comfortable with her. Change the internal sets so wiring and ducting is exposed. Also, throw that damned silly transporter idea away. That thing has the seeds of plot hell in it and it's morally very dubious. People will think about its implications and get uneasy. *Enterprise* can use shuttles instead."

"We can't afford the set of a shuttle or the optics needed to show the launch of one." Rockerferry was almost pouting as his creation was redesigned in front of him.

"Don't need either. The sets for 'Mission To Myitkyina' will be taken down next week. Just ask Films Division to send over the set showing the center-section of a B-60. We can redress it. Some lights flashing past the window will do for launch. We can get the B-60 cockpit set sent over as well. They'll do for the shuttle cockpit."

"Right, anything else?" The studio chief programmer was ecstatic. He could see the show turning into something he could use.

"Yeah, I'll arrange for the writing crew to spend a few days on a Navy ship and a SAC base. That'll give them a better idea of how things work. Things like night watches, crew rosters, striking for promotion and so on. By the way, you have too many officers. We need a lot of enlisted personnel, and we can use them for enlisted-orientated stories that will show our officer stars from their perspective."

The vice-president in charge of production made some notes on a pad. "Bill, can I offer you a contract as Executive Producer on this show? For the next pilot, at least? It's obvious we need a real producer on this show, one who knows how things should look."

Shaych nodded. "Provided we can agree on terms. Get your people to speak to my executive assistant, Irene Shapiro here. She'll sort things out with them."

Gene Rockerferry looked furious. Shaych decided to twist his tail a little. Then he changed his mind and decided to twist it a lot.

"Another thing we can change, the opening narration. Starship doesn't mean anything to most people. Everybody knows its strategic recon birds that do the exploration thing. So let's run it as "Space, the final frontier. These are the flights of the strategic recon ship *Enterprise*. Her five-year mission: to explore strange new planets, to seek out new life and new civilizations and nuke them from orbit. It's the only way to be sure."

Everybody in the room kept a perfectly straight face as they nodded thoughtfully. The studio chief programmer seemed genuinely taken with the idea. "That makes a lot more sense. Let's go with that."

It seemed to push Rockerferry over the brink. He went brilliant purple before storming out of the room. As soon as the door had slammed behind him, the entire meeting erupted into laughter. The studio chief programmer wiped his eyes as he tried to get his breath back.

"Bill, you're an evil, evil man. I see we're all going to get along together real well. Our people will be in touch with your people this afternoon. Meanwhile, let's do lunch. Bill can show us his new costume sketches while we eat. There's a pretty good Kenyan restaurant a few blocks away. One of the Nyarai chain. First one to open up on the West Coast."

"Sounds good."

287

The party left the conference room and split up. The vice-president in charge of production took Bill Shaych and Irene Shapiro down to the area where the executive limousines were parked. Several were pulling out with various dignitaries on board, as the work of the studio transferred from the offices to a variety of local restaurants. A few tens of yards away, one figure in particular was being treated with almost nauseating deference.

"Clyde Grainger. Up and coming. He wants a big series to get him properly launched and isn't above trying to kick a star off the existing cast to get it. Thing is, he pulls in big numbers, so he tends to get what he wants."

Their own limousine pulled up next to them. What happened next pretty much destroyed any chance of a peaceful business lunch.

In the split second between their limousine stopping and its door opening, the one carrying Clyde Grainger exploded, sending a fireball skywards. Irene Shapiro took Bill Shaych down with a dive that put both of them in the blast shadow formed by their vehicle. The vice-president in charge of production wasn't so fast. He was still standing when the blast wave from the explosion struck him. It had been diluted by distance, but it still left his ears ringing and his skin feeling as if it has been sand-blasted.

"What happened?"

He knew it was a stupid question but his brain pummeled by blast couldn't put together anything more logical.

"Somebody just blew up your actor."

Irene Shapiro was looking at the pyre of smoke and flame rising from the shattered remains of the car. The vice-president in charge of production realized it was a very calm and professional interest.

"Looks like somebody didn't want to be replaced."

Hotel California, San Francisco

"Alexander was an idiot."

Conrad Lorenz sighed gently as he heard the words. He'd had a presentiment of trouble when the telephone had rung. Anne Bonney's voice had confirmed it.

"What is the matter, Anne?"

"There's been a bombing at the Paramount television studio in Hollywood. Three people killed."

Conrad didn't need more than a second to put it together. *Paramount is the studio Bill Shaych worked for most often. Igrat, using the identity of Irene Shapiro, is working for him as his executive assistant. She moved to California in order to get out of a highly unlikely but still worrying death threat and now a bomb had gone off in her orbit. Does that mean the death threat wasn't so unlikely after all?* Then another thought occurred to him. *Had the death threat become an ugly reality?*

"Was anybody we know hurt?"

Conrad could hear Anne working desperately to stop herself laughing. He knew that his fear had come through. *I made a bad misjudgment over the whole death threat business, one that could have got Igrat maimed or killed. The Seer had been remarkably mild about it, but I sincerely believe that, if anything had happened to Igrat as a result, I would be remarkably maimed, or mildly killed, as well.*

"No, Conrad. She was on the scene, but wasn't hurt. But, she's being held as a material witness. The Seer asked me to find out if you could nose around a little and make sure she wasn't the target."

Interrogation Room Two, Hollywood Police Station, 1358 North Wilcox Avenue, Hollywood

"What interests us, Miss Shapiro, is that according to witnesses, you actually appear to have started to dive for cover a fraction of a second before the bomb went off."

"What can I say? I have very fast reactions. If you check the surveillance camera footage, I'm sure you'll find I actually started to go down a tiny fraction of a second after the blast. And, before you ask, yes, my reactions are that fast."

Irene Shapiro looked slightly indignant. *If these police saw Achillea in action, they'd get an entirely new definition of fast reactions.*

The detective talking to her reached out for a cigarette from his pack and realized it had gone. Irene smiled, raised an eyebrow and then returned the pack.

"See what I mean?"

Detective Sergeant Ben Romero took the pack angrily and shook it. "That sort of trick won't get you any favors here."

"I don't want favors. I can always get those. I just want to see you trying to find out who blew that poor man up instead of giving me a hard time."

"That's what we are doing. Until you can explain how you knew that bomb was going to go off before it did, we're fairly sure we do know who blew him up."

"Ben, you had better come and see this."

Detective Sergeant Ed Jacobs had opened the door quietly. Romero followed him out of the door.

"We got the 8mm tape from the security cameras and processed it. She's right. The blast came first and then she dived for cover. Taking her boss down with her, by the way. The witnesses were wrong. I guess they heard the blast and saw her diving and assumed she had dived first."

The two detectives sat down in front of the television set. "Look, there's Clyde Grainger. His limousine stops and the door opens. Then the bomb goes off. Run it back and look in the background. You can see Shaych, Shapiro and a network bigwig by another car. The bomb goes off and *then* Shapiro dives. We got the lab to time it by counting the frame rate and her reaction was fast, but not that fast. High end of average."

Romero twisted his lips. "What do we know about her?"

"Not much. She came out to California about four years ago as Bill Shaych's executive assistant. We haven't had a response yet from the East Coast, so we have no track of her beyond that. She had a gun in her handbag, a Czech Model 50 chambered for Tokarev Magnums, and a valid Federal concealed carry permit. According to her driving license, she's forty years old."

"She doesn't look it."

"Come on, Ben, this is California. Land of cosmetic surgery. The pretty young thing you pick up in a bar tonight could be a grandmother. Admit it, she might be mouthy, but she seems like a good guy on this one."

Public Anteroom, Hollywood Police Station, 1358 North Wilcox Avenue, Hollywood

"You didn't take long getting down here."

Bill Shaych was surprised to see Conrad arriving so quickly. The call from Anne Bonney telling him Conrad was on his way down had only arrived an hour before.

"I took one of the new Mohawk Airlines rotodynes. A five-minute taxi-ride from my hotel to the inner city airport, one hour flight down and a five-minute taxi-ride to here. Just walked on and off the rotodyne at each end. Paid for the seat as I got on."

"I heard the rotodynes are noisy."

Shaych was always interested in gathering impressions and opinions. Usually they found their way into his screenplays sooner or later.

"Inside? Not at all. Quieter than a propeller aircraft. Outside? Well, the noise is *different*. It's a higher-pitched whistle than people are used to. I think that's why people are complaining. And Boeing is stirring it up, of course. They've tooled up for short-haul, jet-engined puddle-hoppers and Lillith thinks that rotodynes operating from heliports on top of multi-story parking lots will take away their market. Now, what's going on here?"

"Bombing; killed an actor, his agent and a limo driver. Irene and I were not too far away from the blast, but neither of us were hurt."

"Where's Ig . . . . Irene?"

"In there." Shaych pointed at the interrogation rooms. "Officially, she's being interviewed as a material witness. The truth is that she's being held on 'contempt of cop' charges. You know, Irene; she was her own charming self and talked her way into trouble."

Conrad nodded sadly. Before he could say anything, the doors to the non-public area opened. Irene walked out. She looked out across the reception area, saw Shaych and Conrad, and waved to them.

"Hi, guys. They're done with me at last. Conrad, good to see you again. You here to save me?"

"From yourself, according to Bill. Please, will you tell me what is going on here and whether your father has cause for concern?"

Irene dropped her Broadway Baby act almost instantly and thought carefully.

"I don't think so. The bulls let a lot more drop than they intended when they were trying to shake me up. There are two groups of limousines at the studios. Some, like the one coming to pick us up, are just pool vehicles. Whoever asks for one gets the next one off the line. There's no way anybody could have known that the one coming for us had the job until we walked out the door. The other group is assigned to specific people and wait for them alone. Clyde Grainger had one of those. Everybody knew it was his limousine and his driver in it. So, the bulls have pretty much ruled out the bomb being aimed at anybody but him."

Conrad nodded slowly. "Of course, it could have been aimed at his driver or agent. That's the problem with cases like this; everybody assumes the prominent victim was the intended one. They forget he may have just been in the wrong place at the wrong time."

"An agent I could understand, Conrad." Shaych was also nodding. "They must be the least popular people in Hollywood. But the driver?"

"Conrad, we can be certain this bomb wasn't aimed at me, but there is something else you should know. Everybody, and I mean everybody, is putting pressure on the bulls here to make an arrest. The one who was trying to interrogate me must have been called five or six times, demanding progress, and he got angrier after every call. They're going to bust the first person who they think they have a case against. For a while, they thought that was me. If they bring somebody in with more than a whisper of evidence against them, the railroad will be running full-time."

Conrad kept nodding. Inwardly, relief swept through him. It was a fundamental part of his belief system that God guided his footsteps from one innocent person to the next, so that he could earn redemption by relieving them of false accusation. One day, someday, he would have saved enough innocent people to earn redemption from the guilt he had earned by impeaching the innocent in his days as an inquisitor. He had regarded this trip as a distraction from that mission. A necessary distraction, resulting from his own negligence and thoughtlessness, but a distraction none the less. Now, he knew that his footsteps had been guided here after all. Soon, there would be a falsely-accused innocent and he would once again have to protect them.

"Why don't you two go home?" Conrad saw little point in the two staying in a police station. It was an environment he was more than familiar with but there was nothing to be gained by them staying here. "I'm going to stay here for a while."

"Irene? You want out of here? What did the cops say?"

"They told me not to leave town and the one interrogating me said I would be called back for further investigation. I won't be, though. They're under too much pressure for that."

Conrad watched them leave and settled back in his chair. He'd barely made himself comfortable when a pair of detectives came in with a well-dressed man held between them.

"Whose got the Paramount bomb case?" Their voices echoed around the police station.

"Romero and Jacobs." The reply was shouted out from another room.

"Call them, we've got a hot one."

For the first time, Conrad noticed that the man between the detectives was handcuffed. There was a stir around the room, the atmosphere studded by flashbulbs going off. *This is how its starts. The journalists want a story. The detectives have a case. Suddenly, whomever they bring in is guilty.*

"Is he the one?" "Why did he do it?" The questions were shouted, the tone almost matching that of baying wolves.

The detectives didn't answer. They just hustled the man through to the interrogation room vacated by Irene Shapiro a few minutes before. Conrad moved quietly, positioning himself so he could keep an eye on what was going on. He watched two more senior detectives move in. The door of the interrogation room slammed shut.

The journalists were already on the station phones, calling in their "suspect detained in Paramount Studio bombing" stories.

"You'll have to move out of here . . . sir."

The desk sergeant shook Conrad by the shoulder. Conrad looked up and the sergeant saw the collar.

"I'm sorry, Father; we're just trying to get the press under control. Stay where you are; we need a little faith here sometimes. If you'd like some coffee, just give the desk a wave. It's pretty foul here, but it's going to be a long night."

Conrad smiled his thanks at the sergeant and settled back in his seat. "Thank you, Sergeant . . ."

"Grantham, Father. Adam Grantham. Ten years I've been in this precinct and we've never had anything like this here. The studios keep everything quiet. Worst we've ever had is drugs and loan-sharking, with the odd domestic between a couple of names. Now, three dead in a bombing."

Sergeant Grantham hesitated for a second. "Father, say a word for us with the big boss, will you? Whatever happens, I've a feeling this isn't going to end well."

"Of course, Sergeant."

Conrad got his rosary and started a short prayer that the cops working this case would get a speedy and above all just solution to its complexities. That it would have complexities was something he little doubted.

Then he saw the sun beat down, hurting the eyes of the crowd gathered in the square of a small Spanish town. Standing in the mob, Conrad Antonio de Llorente felt its emotions swirl around him. He realized it was wrong and wrenched himself awake before the familiar nightmare could cause him to wake with a scream.

Conrad's Eye

He looked at the clock and realized he had been asleep for almost five hours before the nightmare had started. That was a luxury he had not experienced for many years. The fact filled him with foreboding.

The innocents here are in such danger, I need to be rested before I can look after them properly.

"He's lawyered up."

The voice came from the door to the back rooms of the police station. One of the detectives had entered the room and was addressing the waiting journalists.

"I guess that confirms it, right? Innocent man doesn't need to lawyer up." The journalist who had spoken was shabby and stained with cigarette ash.

I'd love to hear my friend William Garrow discuss that issue with you. Conrad thought. *But a German shell and* Queen Mary*'s magazines dictated otherwise.*

"Now, hold on. Every man has a right to a lawyer. He'd be a damned fool if he didn't take advantage of his constitutional rights." The detective thought for a second. "I will say the man we are interviewing has important information of relevance to this case and is a person of interest. At the moment, that's all."

"And that's enough, Detective. I wish to consult with my client."

The lawyer was as shabby as the journalist who had spoken out of turn earlier. In a room where even the detectives were wearing expensive suits, the two stuck out. He was with a young woman. She would have been attractive, had not weeping puffed up her face and caused her make-up to run.

I have seen her somewhere before, but I can't quite place where. The trouble is that applies to everybody in Hollywood. Every waitress and cashier is either an aspiring performer, or a disappointed one.

"Can I be of any help to you?" Conrad moved beside her.

The woman's look was angry and suspicious, but dissolved as soon as she saw Conrad's collar.

"Father, he couldn't have done it. He's the gentlest man. He couldn't have blown people up."

"Why did they bring him in?"

That simple question brought a renewed flood of tears. "Merlin has the major lead in a new series coming out next season, *The Moonlighters*, about a group of stuntmen who do private investigation work. But that horrible Grainger man wants the role and he was spreading terrible stories about Merlin and threatening to walk to another studio if he didn't get the role."

"Excuse me, Merlin?" Conrad reflected that his knowledge of the latest pop culture was sadly outdated.

"Merlin Salerno, my fiancé. He was big in *The Hunters* last year." The woman's face brightened. "I'm Crystal Feathers. I was the nurse in some of the episodes of *The Hunters*. You must remember me?"

So that was where I had seen her. Conrad had seen a couple of the episodes of *The Hunters* before it had been cancelled mid-season. *From what I remember, the Shooting Stars out-acted the cast.*

"Yes indeed. I miss that show. But, there must be more to this than that?"

"Oh, Merlin and Grainger had a terrible row a couple of days ago. Ended up with Merlin telling him that if he carried on lying about him, it would be the last thing he ever did. And the police found things they claim were the materials of a pipe bomb in Merlin's apartment."

"Miss Feathers?"

The lawyer had come out from the interrogation rooms and his face was grim. "It's very bad, I'm afraid. Three people killed in a bombing. It's the gas chamber for sure if this goes to trial. The district attorney is offering to take the death penalty off the table if Mister Salerno confesses. I recommended he accept that offer but he's adamant he didn't do it."

Accept an offer? With no real evidence in hand? Either this man is the worst lawyer in the world or the fix is in.

"Miss Feathers, before we go further, may I introduce myself? I work for the Clarkson Foundation. It's a charitable group dedicated to defending people who have been wrongly accused of a crime. Our founder was a very wealthy man who was wrongly accused of murdering his wife. He would have been executed for doing so, only two days before the execution she was arrested for speeding in another state.

"Our representatives have a lot of discretion in the cases we take on and this sounds like one where we may want to offer our help. If your lawyer here would appoint me as an investigator for the defense, I can dig into this. I can't promise anything and my investigation may well convict your fiancé, but at least I'll be investigating with an open mind."

"Oh, please, Father? Mister Beltz, *please?*"

"I see no need for . . . oh, very well."

Conrad's Eye

"Thank you. I'll see the detectives and then your fiancé."

The Bull Pen, Hollywood Police Station, 1358 North Wilcox Avenue, Hollywood

"So you're the famous priest-investigator?" Sergeant Ben Romero sounded amused.

Conrad did a double take. "You knew why I'm here?"

"Of course. You didn't think you could sit in a police station for six hours without us taking the time to find out who you were did you? Oddly, there aren't too many priests who sit in police stations for a living and only one whose presence attracts direct personal interest from Chief Carmady. He telephoned the Captain himself and said if we didn't accept your help, we'd be considered too incompetent to keep our jobs. Then he told us why.

"We like our jobs and, frankly, we'd value your assistance. We're getting a lot of pressure to arrest somebody, anybody. A cooler head will see things better. And having an outsider involved gives us an excuse to do our jobs right."

Conrad relaxed. *I hadn't expected the police to check up on me or for Deke Carmady to put the word in on my behalf. Having the Deputy Chief vouch for me makes things a lot easier.*

"Thank you. To be honest, this is the bit I always dread. Sometimes it's hard to convince people I'm not here to make them look foolish. The foundation I work for doesn't operate like that. We want to do right by everybody involved. How good is the case against that man out there, Merlin Salerno, I believe?"

"On screen, yeah. Real name is Edward Funkhauser. Really. We thought that was a bit rich, so we checked that name out as well. It's real and he's clean. A couple of speeding tickets and a misdemeanor assault, that's all. His bimbo out there, by the way, is really June Rundell. Crystal Feathers is just a stage name. She's got a record that's a little shadier. She was pulled in for doing a couple of porn movies when she was far too young to be involved in anything like that. There's nothing violent, though. Even Funkhauser's assault charge wasn't his fault.

"In this case, how strong our case is depends on who you talk to. The District Attorney thinks it's a slam-dunk and wants to go to trial. Ed and I aren't quite so certain. We're still waiting for the report from the bomb squad. But, it's bad for Mister Funkhauser. Even if he didn't do this, he's still got some explaining to do."

"About the bomb-making equipment in his apartment?"

"If it is bomb-making equipment. It could be; some stuff that could be explosive materials, pipe components, stuff that could be an electrical detonator, some wires and so on. But, it's too early to be sure of that. Could be he liked to look after his plants properly and wanted to fix up the internal plumbing.

"That's the trouble we're having with this case already. The studios want it closed fast and don't care how we do it. They're grabbing at everything in sight and want us to do the same."

"Chief Carmady also said to ask you if you had any of your friends with you." Ed Jacobs had arrived with some cups of coffee and handed them around to the group.

Conrad tried it. *Sergeant Grantham is right, it is dreadful. Why do police stations produce such awful coffee?*

Jacobs took a sip of his and winced. Then, he turned to Conrad again.

"Deputy Chief Carmady wanted you to know, the tailing tricks your friends used are still taught by our Academy here. Chief Parker would like to meet you sometime."

Conrad laughed at that. *I don't know who would be more flattered. Loki, who worked out the theory, Gusoyn, who turned theory into a reality, or Henry who put it to practical use in Geneva,.*

"That was a long time ago. The NSC aren't involved in this; not yet, anyway. If anybody else gets involved, it'll be the FBI. If it turns out there are national security implications, the NSC might send an OSS agent in to assist you, but that's really unlikely."

Especially since, unbeknownst to you, you spent a couple of hours talking to one. You can absolutely be sure that every detail of that conversation has been reported.

"Yeah, a long time ago and San Francisco PD still won't let us forget it was them that nailed the Black Dahlia Killer." Romero sounded distinctly defensive about that. "Look, we'd work together on this, even if Chief Carmady hadn't ordered it. But your part of the deal is, you tell us the inside scoop on that case over a few beers sometime."

"Ben, you can't ask the Father to have a drink!" Jacobs sounded appalled at the idea. Why that was, Conrad wasn't quite sure.

"Of course he can." Conrad put mock indignation into his voice as he came out with one of his favorite quotations. "Beer is God's way of telling us he loves us and wants us to be happy."

Romero laughed, feeling the cleansing power of a good belly laugh surging through him. "You know, Father, I think we're going to get along just fine.

CHAPTER TWO

Renaissance Hollywood Hotel, 1755 North Highland Avenue, Hollywood

Conrad looked at the meal room service had provided and sighed gently. *California is changing and not for the better. Parmesan and garlic-flavored French fries? An angus sirloin burger, served on a brioche with arugula and an aioli of thinly sliced cherry tomatoes and caramelized onions in rosemary-scented olive oil, dressed with Roquefort cheese and crumbled pancetta? It sounds like something Naamah would serve to somebody she really didn't like. Worse, it is pretentious and vulgar. For all its ostentation, it's vulgar. A simple bacon cheeseburger and fries would be much more appropriate for room service to a hungry traveler in need of a good, basic meal.*

He took a bite out of the cheeseburger and sighed again. *Incredibly, it* is tasteless. *All those flavors cancel each other out.*

Conrad took out a pack of six by four index cards and got to work. His first task was to write the names of the three victims on cards and put them into a row. *First, the actor Clyde Grainger. The man everybody presumes was the target. Then there is his agent, Roman Leadingham, one of the men everybody in Hollywood hated. I somehow doubt that is his real name either.*

Finally, the driver, Marvin MacCray. Conrad put him at the bottom of the list. *There is no reason I know of why anybody would be prepared to kill two bystanders to get the driver of a limousine, but that doesn't mean nobody did. But surely, there would be easier ways to kill such a man than to blow him up along with two prominent bystanders?*

There are only two suspects, Merlin Salerno and Crystal Feathers. Conrad made out their cards with both their stage names and real names on each. *Either has a motive for killing Clyde Grainger; Salerno to protect his starring role, Feathers to protect her boyfriend.* Conrad wasn't actually certain which one was the better bet. *Men bluster a lot, but women tended to be deadlier and more ruthless when it came to protecting their loved ones. And they tended not to give any warnings before they acted.*

That brought him to the subject of motive. *Grainger's effort to have Salerno ousted from his TV series is an obvious one. As Grainger's agent, Leadingham was probably deeply involved in that campaign and that made him a possible victim of the same motivation. Viewed in that light, the same bomb probably removed two plausible targets, not one. The problem is, that is it. There isn't any more information.*

Conrad stared at the pattern and moodily ate some of the fries. *They are a good metaphor for the hotel; ostentatious, glitzy and trying hard to impress, but actually not doing their job very well. A hotel without a laundry service for its guests isn't top class, no matter what pretentions it might have.* It further struck him that he was describing Hollywood fairly well. *Style as a substitute for substance.* He was prevented from pursuing that point any further when the telephone rang.

"Mister Lorenz. Mary in reception here. There are some visitors for you. A Mister Romero and a Mister Jacobs."

There was an odd note to the receptionist's voice, as if she knew she wasn't using the right form of address and was making a point by doing so.

"Thank you, madam. Send them up please."

Conrad could play that game as well. Normally he didn't bother, but the pretentious hamburger had him feeling cranky.There was a knock on the door a minute or two later. Conrad let the detectives in.

"Hi Father. The initial forensic reports on the bomb have come in and we thought you'd like to read them before you turned in. Interesting set-up. There were two bombs in the car. One was under the front seats and the other on the gas tank. The forensic guys think they were wired to the car's courtesy light circuit. They were armed by somebody turning on the car's engine. Then, as soon as somebody opened the car door, wham. First blast killed the driver and probably both passengers. Second one, a fraction of a second later, caused a fireball that burned everything up. That's probably why the Shapiro woman went down so fast; she was reacting to the first blast, not the second."

"That sounds elaborate. Professional hit, you think?"

"Could be." Romero looked at Conrad's half-eaten dinner. "What the hell is that?"

Comrad explained and Romero shuddered. "Typical. Look, Father, if you don't mind eating in a room full of cops, we'll take you to a local diner tomorrow. There are a few left and the food there is a hell of a sight better than *that*."

Jacobs nodded emphatically. "One Ben's thinking of is a cop place. We all eat there when we're on the job. We let Salerno go, by the way. With a 'don't leave town' warning of course. He doesn't smell right for this. If Grainger had been shot or beaten down with a bat, yeah, could be Salerno. But not a bomb."

"Any contact between Salerno and Grainger other than the current dispute? Something that could have been boiling in the background?"

Romero shook his head. "They were both on *The Hunters* last year. Grainger was the guest star in one episode; Salerno was a bit player."

"I heard he was big in that show?"

Jacobs laughed so hard he coughed. "Father, this is Hollywood. Every bit player will say he was big in a show, as long as he actually got a line. Five lines and he'll claim to be a star. Salerno played one of the Shooting Star pilots, mostly in the background. He must have said 'break left, the Krauts are on your tail' a few times, that's all. Grainger played an Australian Dragon Rapide pilot in an episode where the squadron had to rescue a girl partisan leader from behind the lines."

"Review said his accent started in New Delhi and ended up in New York by way of New Zealand and New Orleans." Romero recited the newspaper review with relish. "True too."

"Saw a couple of episodes of that show. The jet fighters out-acted the actors. Didn't think it was all that bad, though." Conrad thought for a second. "Salerno's girlfriend claimed to have played a nurse on the show. That an exaggeration as well?"

"Yeah, Angie played the nurse. Only one of the cast who could really act. She's a nice lady. Feathers was a nurse, in the background; may have had a line or two. There was something odd about that show going down so quickly." Jacobs shook his head. "Something went wrong with it. Maybe the cast didn't gel or something. It happens."

Conrad thought about that. "If I've got this right, Grainger was up and coming, right? But hadn't actually made it yet. Suppose, this wasn't aimed at him individually, but at the studio? The studio gets a message; 'that one wasn't a big star, the next one might be. Pay up or your money-makers start having accidents.' That would explain a lot, including the double bomb. First one is the killer; the second one makes the message very public."

"You know Father, that's the one thing everybody has been trying not to think. A decade ago, the Mob was really strong here. They were into all the studios, skimming the take and playing the unions. Meant nobody would dare do what you just said. But now, top Mob talent is going to Cuba and the Feds took down a couple of the big families that were left here. Now, it just might be somebody decided to try it."

Merlin Salerno's Apartment, 1619 North La Brea Avenue, Hollywood

It was a one-room apartment. The entry door lead directly into the kitchen area. The living room doubled as a bedroom, with a folding Murphy bed up against one wall. The bathroom was just an alcove off the living room and had a bath, sink and toilet. No shower.

Conrad had a feeling it was typical of the apartments in the area. *Close enough to Hollywood Hills to sound impressive, far enough away to be cheap. If the relationship between Merlin Salerno and Crystal Feathers is going to be anything more than casual, he'll have to find something better than this for them to live in. He'll have to spend some more on furniture as well.* The apartment was nearly bare. The only fittings being the ones that had been built into it by the developer.

"So, Merlin, tell me about the threat you made against Clyde Grainger?"

Conrad was sitting on a box, with a cup of coffee balanced on one knee. Crystal Feathers was sitting a bit behind Salerno; she caught Conrad's eye, grinned apologetically and rolled her eyes eloquently.

Yes, Salerno is going to have to find a new apartment.

"It was after *The Hunters* was cancelled. I got a good role, a really good one, in a private eye show called *The Moonlighters*. It's the sort of role that can really make a star. Only, Grainger wanted in on it and he wanted me out to make room for him. So he started spreading stories that I was being 'difficult' and that was why *The Hunters* got cancelled. So I told him that if he opened his mouth again, I'd bust his jaw into fragments and end his career that way. Then I gut-punched him to make the point. As far as I know, he shut up after that; or, at least, tried it on somebody else."

"Difficult?" Conrad couldn't understand why that would require a physical altercation.

"It's just about the worst thing you can accuse an actor of." Crystal answered. Her voice was a well of bitterness and anger. "An actor can rape a little girl in front of a room full of film crew and nobody gives a damn. Sorry, Father. But if he gets a reputation for being 'difficult' and delaying production or pushing the studio's costs up, then his career is finished."

"I see, so that was why you threatened to kill him."

Conrad noticed that, while Crystal had been speaking, Salerno had reached back and touched her hand, a comforting gesture. Now, she had pulled her hand away.

"I didn't threaten to kill him." Salerno was indignant. "I told him I'd bust him up."

"And then hit him. What about the assault charge?"

"Misdemeanor assault." Salerno was very firm on that.

In justice to him, Conrad had to admit he had a point. *There is a vast difference between misdemeanor assault and a more serious act of violence.*

"Guy in a bar started to paw Crystal. I smacked his hand away and then clocked him. He went away and a few minutes later came back with the cops. Judge told me if I'd just smacked his hand away and left it there, he'd have thrown the case out and hit the schmuck with costs for wasting court time. Since I'd hit him again, he wouldn't do that and gave me an hour's community service. I swept the courtroom floor after the session was over and he discharged me."

Conrad nodded. *An hour's community service sweeping the courtroom floor is the judge's way of saying "well done and don't ever do it again."* "So you went a step too far. Just like you did with Grainger. Warned him off and then hit him."

Merlin smiled ruefully. "You got me there, Father. Yeah, you're right. But I didn't kill him."

"What about the bomb-making stuff the police found here?"

"I was doing research for the new series. The basic set-up is there's a group of six stuntmen, with different specialties. The catch is they don't kill the bad guys; they use their skills to trick them into convicting themselves. One's a shooter, one's a driver, one's a jumper and so on. My guy is the pyrotechnics expert. Sets up dummy blasts and fires that look bad, but are really harmless. So, I talked one of the real explosives guys into showing me how it was done. Not real bombs; the fake ones used on set. He left some safe bits for me to play with. One thing, he also brought some pictures of what happens when people fool around with the live stuff without knowing what they were doing. Hands blown off, that sort of thing. Scared the daylights out of me."

"What was the name of the stuntman?"

"Patrick Fraser. He's on the Paramount sets all the time."

"Thank you. Now you, Crystal. You've got a record too?"

Crystal shifted uncomfortably before speaking. "Would you like some more coffee, Father?"

Conrad nodded and watched Crystal go to the kitchen area. She rooted around for a couple of minutes before finding the coffee and making the cup. Then she brought it back and settled down on her box, taking a few deep breaths before she spoke.

"Father, I made a couple of really bad decisions when I was younger. Before that, somebody else made some worse ones for me. I was too young to make the decisions I made and far too young for the ones that were made for me."

"I'm sorry, Crystal, but I have to ask this. Did Grainger approach you and try to blackmail you? Threaten to release the details of your mistakes if you didn't persuade Merlin to back out?"

"No, Father, he didn't. Anyway, it wouldn't work. I've already decided to leave the acting business. I'm no good at it and I want to leave while I'm young enough to start another career. Anyway, my mom died a year or so ago and she was the one who really wanted me to be an actress. Now she's gone, I'd rather be a secretary."

"Crystal must be the only girl in the world who wants to run away from the stage and join a firm of accountants." Merlin was teasing her, but there was a wealth of affection in his voice. "Father, Crystal isn't unique. You would be surprised how many actresses made some pretty questionable films early in their careers. Now that they're stars, the studios bury those films and any mention of them.

"If somebody started to use their existence as blackmail, there's no telling what would come out. There would be careers ruined all over the place. I don't just mean in television. I mean in the big cinema studios as well. So, the studios would jump real hard on anybody who tried it. It would be professional suicide and everybody knows it."

Conrad thought about that. "Suppose somebody called them on it and went ahead with the blackmail anyway? Would a studio management kill them to make the point?"

Salerno thought for a second. "You know, Father, given the amount of money involved, I really think they might. So might any of a dozen really big stars that I know of."

Special Effects Area, Paramount Studios, Hollywood

"Excuse me, are you Patrick Fraser?"

"Who wants to know?" The man looked up and then saw Conrad's collar. "I'm sorry, Father. Yup, I'm Fraser."

"Do you have a few minutes to talk sometime? I'm a consultant working with a charitable foundation that looks after the interests of people who may have been wrongly accused of a crime. We're concerned about the Grainger killing."

"If it was a *Grainger* killing. There were two other people there. Still, how can I help?"

"I understand you gave Merlin Salerno some lessons in how to rig explosive devices."

"No. I showed him how to rig something that would *look* like an explosive device but be harmless. That's what he wanted; that's what he got. I showed him how to make a Hollywood bomb with a timing device; a load of jumbled wires and some sausages to simulate the explosives. Also, a pipe bomb that couldn't do much more than whistle Dixie. I left some bits so he could practice making dummies but nothing that would go bang. Anyway, the kid couldn't do it. He's polite, shows respect to people. When he wanted the lessons, he called me first and asked me for an appointment."

Fraser glanced around "Now, if it was Grainger who planted the bomb, that I could believe. Nasty piece of work. Sort of guy who never saw a back he didn't want to stab."

"What's your opinion on that bombing?"

The explosives man straightened his back and thought carefully. "Lot of hate there. Lot of hate. Look, if I wanted to take Grainger out, I could have set it up so he got blown away and the driver and agent just got a busted eardrum each. Even a semi-skilled demo man could have taken him out and at least given the other two a chance. That bomb was intended to kill all three of them. And burn them up, so their folks didn't even get something to bury. Whoever killed them didn't care who else got it. Let me show you something. See that car over there, the green one?"

Conrad nodded. The car was sitting in a deserted area, well separated from anything of value.

"What you are about to see is a Hollywood explosion. We're actually filming this, but what you're about to see will be cut with other footage so that it looks like there are people around it and so on. Now, excuse me. Safety first."

Fraser picked up a bullhorn and started shouting. "Fire in the hole. Fire in the hole. Detonating in three, two, one, GO."

The car exploded into a rolling orange ball of flame. A split second later, a dull, rolling whump echoed across the area. Conrad was confused by the sound.

"That didn't sound like the explosions I've heard before."

"That's because it isn't. That's basically a gasoline explosion. A couple of containers of gas, with just enough plastique to set them off. Impressive, but there's actually very little damage there. We could respray the car, replace the glass and blow it up again for a tenth of the cost of blowing up a second vehicle. What the sound technicians will do is take the sound of a real explosion and blend its blast with the noise you just heard to give a Hollywood boom.

"By the way, Father, something else. There's very little fragmentation from a Hollywood explosion. You could be standing right next to that and your chances of survival would be pretty good. As long as you didn't get burned as well."

2312 West Olive Avenue, Burbank

"They're wonderful people in there you know. I don't know how they do it."

The cabbie had pulled up outside 2312 West Olive and turned to collect his fare.

"I'm sorry?" Conrad counted out the money plus tip and didn't really hear what the man had said.

"The staff at the Silverado Hospice. It must be bad enough working in a regular hospital, but, at least there, the staff can believe that the patients will get better. In there, nobody ever gets better. They must be true saints to work with people they know are going to die soon, yet look after them as if they were their own.

"One of my mates, his kid was near-killed in a motorbike wreck. Was in a coma for three months before he finally passed away. The nurses and doctors in there, they worked real hard to make his last few days comfortable even though they knew he's never know it. Like I said, real saints."

Conrad nodded. "I know what you mean. There are saints in this world and all the rest of us can do is try to live up to their standards. Thank you for telling me about your friend's child. I'll pray for him."

So Mrs. Eunice MacCray is a patient in a hospice.

Conrad walked into the reception area and introduced himself to the nurse behind the counter. She checked a list and nodded.

"We've been expecting you, Father Conrad. We're mostly Baptist here, and we have a Baptist minister on site, but Eunice is Catholic and we had to send out. A policeman was asking about her and he recommended you."

Cop humor. Conrad thought drily to himself. "Has Eunice got long?"

The nurse shook her head sadly. "A few hours, perhaps a day. Lung cancer. We're medicating to keep the pain in check; the doctors are giving her anything she needs to keep her comfortable. It really doesn't matter anymore. Father, we haven't told her about her husband being blown up. She thinks he's there with her. The poor, poor man. First his daughter runs away and vanishes, then his wife becomes terminal and then he gets blown up. I'm sorry, Father, but sometimes it shakes my faith."

"Faith is all the stronger for being shaken sometimes. It tells us that the roots are strong and we can rely on them when we need something to cling to. Could I see Eunice now?"

"Of course. Come with me, Father." The nurse led the way down the corridor and into a room. It was bright and cheery, a large bay window looking out over a grass lawn. Outside, some of the patients were sitting in chairs. Inside, a wasted figure lay on a bed, surrounded by instruments. She was barely conscious and her mind was obviously wandering.

"Eunice, the Father is here to stay with you for a while."

"Father? My father? My baby, where is my baby?"

The woman's voice was incredibly thin and weak. *If it was visible, I would be able to see right through it.* Then she looked at Conrad and saw his cloth.

"Father, you came. Help me please."

This was the part that Conrad for all his years still hated. *When somebody asks for help and there is none left to give.* All he could do was place his Rosary in her hands and help her fingers over the beads while his lips formed the words of the last rites.

Suddenly her voice and her mind were very clear. Conrad knew what that meant. *Her time has come.*

"Father, please, forgive me. I was an evil wife and a terrible mother. My baby, my little girl, please come back. When Marvin was in Russia, I stayed here in California and I wasn't faithful to him. When he came back, I tried to forget that. I tried to make amends, but it was too late. I was ruined. Faithless, loose. Marvin never knew it but I did.

"My baby, how could I have done that. I betrayed them both and it's eaten my soul away. Forgive me, Father please. Marvin, forgive me, Terri, forgive me. I'm evil, evil."

Her voice faded away again.

"Eunice, all that is needed for forgiveness is true remorse and repentance and here, today, you have shown both, with such true sincerity as I have rarely witnessed. Forgiveness will be yours."

Conrad finished the last rites and watched her face relax. Then a dark shadow spread over it. She hissed four last words, the last expelled with her dying breath.

"Marvin, Terri, you came."

"It was fortunate you came, Father. Another priest might have come too late and she would have died with her soul in torment." The nurse was crying for the woman who had just died.

"Her soul was truly in torment over sins that were almost twenty years old. Sins she had done her best to atone for. She had so little to feel such guilt over." Conrad reached out and crossed the woman's hands in front of her. She looked terribly old for her years.

"Still, she is at peace now."

The Code Seven Diner, North Hollywood, California

Conrad didn't care that the juice was running down his chin and on to the napkin protecting his shirt front. The half-pound hamburger was exquisite. A simple bacon cheeseburger and all the better for that. The fries were straight potatoes, with just the right touch of salt. After the grandiose mess that he'd had the night before, the traditional bacon-cheeseburger was a joy.

Across the table, Ben Romero was laughing at the sight of Conrad wolfing down his meal. The diner was a sea of dark blue uniforms. Patrol crews in on Code Seven, mixed in with a few detectives in plain clothes. Ed Jacobs was nursing a cup of coffee and listening to the chatter of the patrol crews. He still missed his time on the street. Somehow, he felt there was an element of real policing to it that being a detective lacked.

Eventually, Conrad finished his burger with a happy sigh and settled back.

"It was lucky you sent me over to the Silverado. If you hadn't, the poor lady would have passed away before a priest got there."

Conrad broke off for a second. A patrol car crew was leaving and they stopped by Conrad for a moment. There was a brief whispered exchange. Conrad made the sign of the cross while very quietly saying a prayer for them. That made it three crews for whom he'd performed the same simple service. Across the room, another civilian was watching with sad, worldly eyes. Every so often, he'd make a note on a pad and then show it to the officer he'd been speaking with. The officer would nod, presumably confirming that the notes were accurate. Romero saw Conrad looking at the man.

"That's Jack Webb; he produces cop shows on television. He comes here all the time to make sure he gets things right. He's good people." Ben Romero spoke quietly. "How did you get on with our acting couple?"

Conrad thought about the young actor and actress. "They're not a couple, not yet anyway. She doesn't know her way around his apartment and it's too small for a couple. And, she's edgy about being touched.

"They don't seem likely to me. He's headstrong, impulsive. Quick to get angry and equally quick to calm down. As you said, if Grainger had been beaten down with a bat or shot, he'd be a good candidate. But, a bomb is like poison. It takes cold-blooded planning and that lad couldn't do it. The girl? Perhaps. I spoke with the special effects man and he confirmed Salerno's story."

"So did we." Ed Jacobs had his pad open. "He gave us an inventory of all the stuff he had given Salerno and it checked out. It looks suspicious, but it's all fake. The wires aren't wires. They're just strips of plastic with the ends painted copper-color. Rest is all the same."

"While you were at the nursing home, we spent our time checking files. Marvin MacCray, wife Eunice and daughter Theresa. Wife now deceased, daughter missing for five years."

"She's dead as well. Just as Mrs MacCray died, she saw her husband and daughter come for her. They could only do that if they were already dead." Conrad spoke with a voice aged by tragedy.

"I know what you mean, Father, but we can't use that as evidence. Theresa is alive until we find her or her body." Jacobs opened his pad to a different page. "She was a runaway. When she was fourteen, she had a blazing row with her mother over something. When we get called to a domestic, it's usually a husband beating his wife. Occasionally, wife beating her husband, or a son and father having it out. A mother and daughter seriously into it is really rare. Daughter ran away before the cruiser got there. We might have suspected murder by the mother, but the girl was seen a few hours later in the Hollywood Hills."

Conrad's Eye

"That might explain the mother's anguish." Conrad was thinking over those last few minutes. "She was really eaten up with guilt and her daughter figured there somehow. She blamed herself for her daughter running away."

"Could be. By the way, we now have a few more details on the bombs. There were two of them. Big pipe bomb under the driver's seat; shaped charge on the fuel tank."

"Shaped charge?" Conrad noted that one. "That's complex, isn't it?"

"Not so much." Romero had done a demolition course once. "But enough to lift it out from the average. We need to talk to that special effects guy again. Father, feel like a milkshake? They do a good peach one here."

Conrad struggled with temptation for a second and then gave in gracefully.

"Thank you Ben, I'd enjoy that. You bring your kids here?"

"Not married yet, Father. But Ed and his partner bring their daughters here once or twice a week."

"Not for milkshakes though. Milk and meat is a no-no. Anyway, they're just getting to the age when they're starting to worry about being fat. Here, look."

Jacobs produced a picture from his wallet.

Two teenage girls, Conrad guessed one was fourteen, the other two or three years older. "Fine looking family, Ed; you must be a proud man."

"Sometimes things just work out right. Kelly's marriage busted up pretty badly. Legal suits flying around in all directions. Relatives stirring trouble for all they were worth. By the time the courts had got around to granting final custody, Kelly and I had set up home together and the Judge gave his daughters to us."

"I suppose they both want to be actresses?"

"In this town? You have got to be kidding, Father. Girls who want to be actresses come from outside. Ones that are brought up here, especially cop kids, know too much about what's involved. Our eldest, Rebecca, wants to be a doctor. She'll probably make it too; she's as a sharp as they come. Miriam's even sharper, if anything, but she hasn't made her mind up yet. She's half-serious about trying to be a cop. She says if the squad room is good enough for her fathers, it's good enough for her."

Jacobs had a tear in the corner of his eye when he said that. Conrad knew why. He'd seen enough bad relationships between young women and their stepfathers to recognize a good one when he saw it.

There was a pause while Jacobs put the pictures of his family away and Conrad blessed another patrol crew on their way out. Then his milkshake arrived and that took up a few more minutes. Eventually he resumed his account of the day.

"One other thing that came up was blackmail. You said the Feathers girl was involved in adult films when she was far too young?"

Romero's face screwed slightly in distaste.

"Yeah, really nasty ones. Illegal ones. Rules in California are that films of acts between consenting adults are protected by the First Amendment, unless they promote the commission of a felony. Only, the same law says that kids less than 16 years old cannot be considered to have given a legally supported consent. Well, guess what the bastards like to film. Under-age girls and felonies. Crystal was underage and what was happening to her was a felony."

"Well, I asked her if anybody had tried to blackmail her over those films. The suggestion came up that anybody who tried it for real would be hammered by the studios and by quite a few top-flight actors and actresses. If they didn't get the message, they could easily be killed."

There was an uneasy silence.

Eventually, Jacobs broke it. "If a big studio is involved, or A-list actresses, we might as well give up now. The studios run this town. If the investigation leads to them, we'll get shut down. Sorry, Father, but that's the way it is here."

Something that Jacobs had said bothered Conrad. It wasn't the fact that the studios would cause their investigation to be ended if it led to them or their stars. Eventually, he put his finger on it.

"Ed, you said A-list actresses; not actors. Why?"

"Because unless the actor in those films specializes in them and does nothing else, he is always is shown with his face shaded or masked. On the other hand, the producers make a point of showing the actress's face. Oh, they may give her a bad wig to wear, but the girl's face is always clearly visible. So, it's the women who have a lot to hide. The men are very rarely identifiable and the ones that are don't care."

"There's one other thing." Ben Romero was thoughtful. "Have you noticed how that series from last year, *The Hunters*, keeps cropping up? It never seems to be at the center of things but, somehow, it's always there in the wings. If you'll forgive the horrible pun."

Jacobs and Conrad looked at each other and chorused, "NO."

All three started laughing. Eventually Conrad dabbed his eyes. "I needed that. You're right Ben; that show does show up a lot. Why don't we talk to Bill Shaych first thing tomorrow? He might know a bit more about it."

Conrad's Eye

Renaissance Hollywood Hotel, 1755 North Highland Avenue, Hollywood

Conrad took off his jacket and hat and hung them carefully in the closet. Then, he got out his display boards and packs of index cards. There was more that he had to add to the puzzle now. He had extra motives with blackmail being at the top of the list.

He thought about it carefully, then placed a card labeled 'blackmail' under each of the three victim's names. He stared at that card thoughtfully, trying to place it into proper context.

Clyde Grainger could have been trying to get parts by blackmail. His agent could have been trying to get him parts by blackmail. Marvin MacCray might have overheard something and tried to use it to get the money to pay his wife's medical bills. For the first time, I have a motive that could be applied to any one or all of the victims.

He took out another handful of cards, for the additional motive had opened up a range of other suspects. One set of three cards he labeled "unknown actress." Another set of three he labeled "studio executives". He thought about that for a second and then added another suspect card, "unknown actresses agent". He couldn't help think that his board was beginning to look a lot more hopeful.

He transferred his attention to the 'blackmail' motive card for Marvin MacCray. *I can not imagine a studio killing one of its up-and-coming stars to get rid of a driver who had heard too much. A knife or pistol shot in a back-alley was far more likely. I can't see the unknown actress herself using a bomb to rid herself of him. She'd would speak it over with her agent and he would handle it.*

Conrad guessed that the agents knew people in the mob who would deal with the problem and they might well use a bomb. So, for Marvin MacCray, that meant agent at the top, actress second, studio third.

That led Conrad to consider Roman Leadingham. *Surely, much the same thoughts the studio would have about killing a star as a byproduct of punishing the driver applied also to the agent. There were simpler, better ways of killing him.* Conrad put the studio at the bottom of his list and then decided the rest of the logic applied as well. *So, actresses's agent first, actress second, studio third.*

That left only Clyde Grainger. *The logic that virtually excluded the studio from consideration in the first two cases puts them at the top of the list for the third. And, to them, a driver and an agent would be entirely acceptable collateral damage.* So, the studio went to the top, with the actresses's agent second and the unknown actress herself third.

Conrad stepped back and looked at his table.

Whichever way I cut it, Roman Leadingham is a much more likely suspect than any of the others. The traditional trifecta of means, motive and opportunity all apply to him.

There was something else he had to add, but he didn't know its significance, if indeed it had any. *Romero is right; it is odd the way the cancelled television series about American jet fighters on the Russian Front kept recurring in this case.*

He wrote out a card for the show and added it to the board. It didn't really fit anywhere. That was the trouble. Conrad couldn't see any logical place to put it. He'd had this sensation before, knowing that something had a place but being unable to see what that place was.

There was an another card as well that needed to go up. It was one that made Conrad profoundly uncomfortable. He wrote 'pornography' on a card and added it to the board. Like the one for the TV show, it didn't really seem to fit anywhere. He stared at it, his mind churning over.

While neither of the two out-of-place cards had any apparent connection with the rest, they do have a connection with each other. Crystal Feathers had appeared in both the television series and adult movies.

The problem was that she, painfully obviously, did not have the expertise needed to go around making bombs; especially the semi-sophisticated shaped charge. But, her connection with the pornography industry meant she had to know figures in organized crime and, as he had already noted, a bomb in a car was a very standard form of attack for them.

Is she still connected with organized crime? Did she make friends with real criminals while making her films and have those friendships survived?

Conrad was well-aware of just how seductive organized crime could be. *The romance of evil.* The quotation ran through his mind and he was familiar with the lesson it held. Wiseguys could be amusing and generous friends and they had the contacts and ability to be very good friends indeed when the need arose. But, that friendship always had a price and the cost could sometimes be very high.

Did Crystal make friends with such people. She needn't have asked for help explicitly. She might have mentioned the problem, perhaps simply discussed it with one of her friends who decided to help her out. Perhaps her behavior is the resulting of dawning horror at the realization of what her casual conversation has caused.

Conrad's Eye

Conrad went to the section of the board that he had prepared the previous evening. Now, he moved Crystal Feathers up to prime suspect, if the motive for the bombing had been Clyde Grainger's efforts to steal her friend's role.

CHAPTER THREE

Bill Shaych Productions Office Suite, 8335 Sunset Boulevard, West Hollywood

"Good morning, Ellen. Could you tell Bill that we're here, please. ? This is Detective Sergeant Romero and Detective Sergeant Jacobs."

"Good morning, I'll tell him you're all here. Please take seats in our waiting room, Bill will be finished in a couple of minutes."

Ellen Wynn thumbed a button on the office intercom and spoke quietly. In the background, Romero glanced at Jacobs; they'd both noticed the subtle but unmistakable antagonism between Ellen Wynn and Conrad.

A few minutes later, Irene Shapiro left Shatch's office with a glamorous-looking Indian actress. Ellen Wynn looked up briefly at the two detectives.

"That's Sha Cuva; one of the Bollywood actresses looking for a break over here. She wants in on a new project we've just got started. Mr. Shaych will see you now."

Bill Shaych's office was breathtaking. A landscape window at one end gave a view of the Hollywood Hills, dominated by the white sign that told the world this was the home of cinema. To Conrad's amusement, the offices were only a few hundred feet from the headquarters of the Directors Guild of America. The furniture was opulent and expensive, without the vulgarity that scarred the rest of the city.

Romero and Jacobs sat down very carefully, well aware that if they had to pay for any damage themselves, they would be in debt for years. They settled into the soft leather seats and allowed themselves a small sigh of happiness. Comfort was its own reward.

"Thank you for seeing us, Mister Shaych. Firstly, I can now officially confirm that you and your staff have been eliminated as suspects from our inquiries. From what we have determined, you were just in the wrong place at the wrong time." Romero went through the officially-worded statement of regret for inconvenience, as he had done many times before. "We would, though, like to ask your help as an insider in the film and television industry. We would like to know, first of all, what information you have on the young actor we pulled in."

"Merlin Salerno? Young actor, D-list at the moment, but probably destined for higher things. He's got passion, he's painstaking and does background research to make sure he's performing his role properly. A professional, never been known to turn up on stage drunk, always knows his lines and what to do. Directors like him because of that. Until now, hasn't had many serious roles but has done a lot of work as a supporter."

Shaych put the file down on his desk. "I've got an eye on him myself for a role in an idea I'm playing with. His agent is Jerry Mikkelson, one of the better sort around here, by which I mean he's only one stage worse than a rattlesnake."

"I'm sorry, Bill." Conrad had waited until Shaych had finished. "I keep hearing these terms; A-list, B-list and so on. What do they mean?"

"Easy enough. A-list are the really big cinema stars, Sinatra, Martin, McQueen, Curtis, Lemmon, Andrews, Dickinson, Taylor, Loren and so on. They do only film work, mostly. Although, Angie likes doing television work now and then. But then, if she wasn't a part of Sinatra's rat-pack, she wouldn't be A-list.

"B-list are the top-grade television stars and top supporting stars for cinema. C-list are the average performers for cinema and top supporting stars for television. And so it goes down. D-list are the youngsters; cast fillers and easy-to-remember but hard-to-name character actors. E-list are persons whose celebrity is so obscure, they are generally only known for appearances as so-called celebrities on game shows. They basically do advertisements and voice-overs. F-list; well, F means failed. You get that message."

"There were rumors that Salerno was being difficult. Anybody take those seriously?" Romero was curious to see what Shaych would say about that and, more importantly, how he would say it.

"Not a chance. As I said, Salerno had a pretty good rep for being a professional. I guess you've already asked around and everybody told you how much they love him?"

"Sure. Not very helpful."

"That's why we call actors 'luvvies.' They 'love' everybody. Clyde Grainger tried that rumor-spreading bit, but he only managed to hurt himself. Grainger was D-list as well. But, unlike Salerno, he was going down, not up. As in, heading for the F-list."

"Wait a minute, we heard he was up-and-coming?" Jacobs was confused.

Shaych thought for a second. "No, not unless he cleans up his act. Look, it's really hard to make it in this town. We get kids coming in from all over . . . I was going to say from all over the States, but that wouldn't be true. We get kids from all over the world.

"The girls were used to being the high school prom queen; the boys were really successful with those girls. Then they come here and find that a high school prom queen from a farm town in Whiscosasee is only just slightly better than homely here. Women here want a handful of aces and all the boys have to offer is a pair of twos. The studios literally have the pick of the world to choose from and they want the best.

"You saw Sha Cuva as she was leaving? She's the biggest star in Bollywood. She's a damned good actress in her own right. Her English is perfect and her accent is just marked enough to be exotic. Her looks are perfect. All that means is that she has a *chance*, nothing more. For reasons of my own, I'm going to give her some help."

Conrad raised an eyebrow. Shaych nodded slightly. The detectives missed it completely.

"So that brings us to Clyde Grainger. He could act, he had the looks and was loved by people who didn't know him. But, he had two problems. One was that he seemed to think he had the divinely-bestowed right to harass the people he worked with. He could get away with that on the A-list. Bogart would do the same. Bogie only had time for people who harassed right back. Grainger didn't have that privilege; he's D-list.

"The other thing was that he had foul breath. I mean really bad. His breath stank however much he tried to hide it by sucking violet-flavored tablets."

"That's true." Irene Shapiro had brought in a tray of coffee and some plates of snacks. "I kissed him once and my mouth tasted foul afterwards. Thank the Gods for Listerine. It was really bad and those violet candies made it worse. Why he didn't try with mints is beyond me."

Romero took his coffee cup and, to his surprise, found it was already the way he liked it. "Miss Shapiro, I've got to ask. How did you know how I like my coffee?"

"We were in a room for six hours. You had coffee then. You didn't offer me any, so I sneaked some of yours." Irene was grinning broadly. "Truce?"

Romero returned the grin and nodded.

"Truce. Mister Shaych, so you're saying that Grainger was on his way down and out. Obviously, he didn't realize that. The studio don't seem to think that either."

"The studio will keep telling you that you're on the way to the top even as they write your pink slip. They'll treat you as if you're their one and only hope right up to the time their heavies pick you up and throw you into the gutter. As for Grainger, I think his ego was such that he would assume he was going up, even while he slept in his car and his only acting was when he sounded interested as he asked 'you want fries with that'. And that is not uncommon, by the way. The corollary to that is that he will justify his lack of success by telling everybody who will listen that everybody has it in for him and that he's the victim of a conspiracy. If he wasn't one of the victims, that could have made him a suspect, I suppose."

"So the studios wouldn't pay up to keep him alive or in the acting business?"

"Not a chance. At most, he would be a useful example to show that whoever made the threats had the ability to strike inside the studio grounds. That isn't as easy as it sounds. Security there is the best money can buy."

Romero looked at his notes. "That brings us to Crystal Feathers. Know much about her?"

Shaych was dismissive. "F-list. On her way out. A bit sad, really; she's a nice girl, a reasonable actress and good-looking but she's got a problem. She can't do love scenes. A couple of times she tried, she froze rigid and in one case she actually started crying. The studio did everything up to and including getting her drunk, but she just can't do it. The time she started crying, she ran off the set and the director worked around it using a body double. She's done."

"Bill, she told me she's given up acting and is leaving. Wanted to do something else while she was young enough to make a new start." Conrad had finished his coffee and put the cup to one side.

"Good for her. That's the smart move. The tragedy of this town is so few people do the smart thing. Mostly they hang on long after the bus has left and keep going down." Shaych looked at the two detectives and saw them nodding. They usually ended up catching the mess when the hopefuls hit rock bottom.

"An odd question, Bill." *For all its glitter, Hollywood is a sad, lonely town.* "Last year, there was a television series, called *The Hunters*. It seems to figure here somewhere, but we can't work out how."

"*The Hunters*." Shaych thought for a second. "I remember that one. That was really strange. The network put a lot of money into it. The trade term is that it had 'very high production values.' They got an old airstrip and rebuilt it as a Russian Front airfield for use as a location setting. Don't ask how they made California look like the Russian Front. The pilots were supposed to be flying F-80Es, but they couldn't get any; so they bought a half-dozen surplus Navy FV-

5s and repainted them. Would you believe some of the viewers noticed and wrote in to complain?

"Hired a good cast, Angie from the A-List, several upper part of the B-List actors for the stars. Usual collection of characters. Sexy romantic nurse, that was Angie, of course. Hard-bitten squadron commander, tough because he's trying to keep his men alive. Young hot-shot pilot who breaks all the rules but scores the kills and is competing with the squadron leader for Angie. Then there was Harry Morgan as the crusty but lovable master sergeant who looks after the aircraft and gives wise advice to everybody. That show had everything running for it and its ratings were pretty good. Then it got axed literally overnight. The studio management actually called the production company and told them to stop where they were and let everybody go. Halfway through making an episode."

"Have you any idea what happened?"

"Not one and it is not healthy to ask. Couple of people tried and their phones stopped ringing. I have heard that the top stars on the show demanded a meeting with the studio. The meeting lasted twenty minutes and the show was cancelled as soon as the management left the conference room. That's rumor, and I'm not going to ask around getting it confirmed. If you guys find out, let me know, will you?"

"A quick question, Bill. Who was Crystal Feather's agent?" Conrad was trying to fill in the blanks of relationships.

"Until recently, she was with Jerry Mikkelson. I suppose Salerno introduced them. Wait a moment."

Shaych thumbed his intercom box and spoke quietly. A few seconds later, Ellen Wynn entered with a file. Shaych opened it and read quickly.

"No, that won't work. Other way around, if anything. She's been with Mikkelson for five years. Before that she was with, wait for it, Roman Leadingham."

"Five years ago. That was when we busted her for. . . ."

"La-la-la-la-la-la-la." Shaych had stuffed his fingers in his ears and was singing loudly. "There are things that are not mentioned and I do not wish to hear them."

"How old is Crystal Feathers?" Conrad asked a question, but he wasn't sure he wanted to hear the answer.

"Twenty. Leadingham was her agent from when she was twelve onwards." Shaych was desperately trying not to make the obvious conclusions from what he was hearing.

"Fourteen and you didn't get her from the earlier ones." Conrad was putting information together now and his earlier impressions had been right. He didn't like the conclusions he was coming to.

"Bill, quite apart from any earlier conversations we might have had and on an entirely different subject. How does the pornography industry in Hollywood work?"

"Legal or otherwise? If you mean legal, there's a water-tight divide between legitimate film and television and the adult industry. No point of contact at all. The crews are different, casts are different, direction and production are different. If a cameraman or a sound man works in adult films, he won't get a job in the studios. Ever. Now, a lot of people find the money attractive despite that. Working in adult films can earn a successful actress much more money than in the studios. The catch is the average professional life of an actress in those movies is three or four years, tops. Then a younger fresher actress will take her place. So, the smart girls in adult films squirrel away all their earnings and then go home. The dumb ones blow the lot and end up selling their ass on the strip. The illegal side of things, I know nothing about."

Romero and Jacobs couldn't help looking doubtful at that.

Shaych hesitated for a second and then decided they needed to know the facts of life his side of the screen. "Look, the Supreme Court ruled that if adults want to make films of their sex lives, that's up to them. Pretty much anything that doesn't involve a felony is protected by the First Amendment and that makes it legitimate adult entertainment. The illegal stuff, by definition, involves children and felonies.

"Now, the legitimate studios, by which I mean those not making adult films, have very strict codes of conduct when making films where children are part of the cast. They can only work a limited number of hours a day. The studio has to pay the State to send tutors to the set so the kids don't miss their schoolwork. They encourage parents to come to the sets and supervise their kids at work. Anything that might cause the child distress or be exploitive is done by body doubles. Most of the adult actors take the kids under their wing and look after them. There are some pretty big guys in the studios, I mean physically big, and they tell the kids, 'anybody gives you a hard time over anything, tell us.' None of that is because the studio management are nice people; it's because they know that a child labor scandal is the one thing that will ruin them all. So, when I say I know nothing about the adult film sector, legal or illegal, that's exactly true. I don't know and I don't want to know. Because, if I did, that knowledge could ruin me. All I know is that the industry exists. Where and how, don't ask me."

"Very well. Let's look at Roman Leadingham. What can you tell us about him?" Romero was slightly set aback by the vehemence with which Shaych had disowned any knowledge of illegal filming activities.

"If the world has an asshole, he'd be the little hairs around it. Something else about this town. The number of children who are absolutely determined to go on the stage is almost exactly equal to the number of parents, mostly mothers, who are absolutely determined that to push their kids on to the stage. Unfortunately, they aren't always paired up. But enough are for grifters to make a living.

"Leadingham was an expert in 'finding young talent and helping it develop.' What that meant was that he latched on to a stage-struck parent and child who had just arrived in town, offered them a lucrative-sounding contract and took them on. Only, then he started to suggest their 'development.' The girl needed dancing lessons; the boy needed speech training. Whatever it is, they get; when they've had it, they need more. All tuition from expensive experts and Leadingham got a big cut from every one of them. Then, when the family has been sucked dry, he dropped them. After all, actors who actually make money on the stage are literally one in a thousand and he did his best, didn't he?"

"We needed to speak with Mr. Leadingham." Romero sounded regretful.

"You can speak to his partners. Not all of them have rabies." Shaych wrote a couple of names on a pad. "Try these two. They walked out on him. They might talk."

"Thank you Mister Shaych."

Jacobs hesitated for a second. "Look, while we're here, I had this idea for a television series. Why don't you do one on our forensic people, the way they piece a crime scene together? You should have seen them at work on this bombing. Took just a few handfuls of fragments and reconstructed everything."

Romero expected his partner to be ridiculed but Shaych leaned back in his chair and stared at the ceiling for a minute or two.

"It might work, but you're in the wrong country. What you are describing is an English detective story. A set-piece logic puzzle that exists independently of the world outside. It depends on coincidence, a contorted plot and an elaborate scheme. You two of all people know that the easiest crimes to solve are the ones where people tried to get clever like that. Those elaborate schemes fall apart under their own weight. The hardest murders to solve are the ones where there is

321

no planning or conspiracy; the ones where somebody gets his head pounded to pulp by a passing stranger in a back alley for the five bucks in his pocket.

"Here in America, our crime stories run like that. They don't follow the British model. The crimes are those that we run into every day and affect all of us and the characters are us. The story is the story of the detective who solves those crimes, not how he does it. The detective is the quintessential American hero; a man who goes down mean streets to solve a crime, but is not himself mean. He is a common man, for he deals with common people and must share common ground with them, but he is a man of honor who will not breech his own code of ethics. He treats women, whether princess or prostitute, with courtesy, even as he charges them with the crimes he has found they committed. He will take no money dishonestly and no mans insolence without due and dispassionate revenge. He is a proud man and the centerpiece of his pride is that you will treat him as such or be very sorry you ever saw him. He searches after the truth because to do so is an adventure and he is a man of adventure.

"That detective, whether private or a police officer, is our hero and we hope that when we are in desperate trouble, one such man is there to aid us. We can plot the development of our society and its acceptance of minorities by the appearance of detectives drawn from the ranks of those groups. In years past, when stories appeared about Italian, Irish or Jewish detectives, we knew that group had made it across the barrier and been accepted by our community. In the late 1950s, we had the first black detectives on television; by the turn of the decade, nobody thought twice when the hero of a TV series was a homosexual detective. Note, there are no detectives with German-sounding names on our TV schedules.

"Your idea of a forensic show will suit the British well, but not us. Anyway, the demands of scriptwriting means that every episode will have to be that bit more of a complex and unusual puzzle and the scientific gadgetry will have to be that more strange and fabulous. Eventually, it will descend to a search for one minute trace of evidence that will be detected by some strange machine and will prove that only one person could have done it."

"Wow," Romero sounded slightly shocked. "I think I feel flattered. That was very Chandleresque, Mister Shaych. Did you know Raymond Chandler?"

"Sadly, no. He died a few months before I arrived here."

Once again, Shaych and Conrad exchanged knowing glances that the two detectives missed completely.

"I liked Chandler. I have all his books." Jacobs spoke sadly. "There was something very Shakespearean about him. Beneath the apparent setting, he and Shakespeare told stories about the same things; the basic problems that people face and how they deal with them. As you said, they told stories about real people one could imagine meeting. Take Macbeth, for example; we could take that play and transpose it to any town hall or union local in the country. Its truths are eternal and universal. I never met either man of course, but I would love to have done so. I think they both had a wonderful insight into the human condition. One day, I think they'll be seen as contemporaries that were only four hundred years apart."

Oh boy, if only you knew. Conrad stared at Jacobs, but it was Shaych who answered.

"Coming from a detective, that's high praise. Now, gentlemen, I have to persuade Paramount that including an Indian actress on a spaceship is a good idea. So, if you will excuse me, I must ask you to leave. We can resume at another time if you so wish."

The Code Seven Diner, North Hollywood

"Anyway, so that was it really. At the 14th Section of the Superior Court of San Francisco, Amos Kincaid was found guilty of the charge of murder in the first degree of Delia Jane Graham and guilty of the charge of murder in the first degree of Elizabeth Short. He was sentenced to the gas chamber but he never made it. A week before his execution date, he was found in the prison shower room. He'd been sliced to pieces, very literally. Nobody ever got charged with that."

"What happened to the girl who got beaten into a coma?" Romero was fascinated, hearing the inside details of the Black Dahlia case finale.

Conrad looked sad. "Sandy? She never recovered. She hung on for a couple of weeks but then got pneumonia and she was just too weak and battered to fight it off. I don't know what happened to Sal. She stuck around until Sandy died and then just vanished into the underworld. May have left the game and made a new life, might have moved somewhere else and kept working, might have picked the wrong client up once too often. Now she could be a respectable housewife, a wino living on the street or in an unmarked grave. We'll probably never know."

"Good detective work, all the same." Jacobs sounded very sad. "You really think it was a generational thing?"

Conrad nodded. "I think Amos Kinkaid learned it from his father and his father learned it from his. We can only guess how many generations it went back or how many women died at their hands. Again, we'll probably never know for sure. Anyway, how are we doing with the current case?"

Romero shook off the sadness that had gone with the tragedy of the Black Dahlia aftermath. "I'm glad you called it that. We still haven't got a legally competent identification of the bodies and, until we get that, no coroner is going to call the case before a jury. A coroner can and sometimes will hold an inquest on a body that cannot be identified, if there is an issue of value to be decided, but he will not assign an identity to that body without affirmative proof. Even in death, every person has a right to his identity. The coroner will do everything in his power to enforce that right. So, it's the 'current case,' not the 'Grainger Case'. Having said that, he's made a few discoveries. One of the two men outside the car was alive when he burned. Enough to get at least one breath full of soot into his lungs."

"Have we any idea which one?"

"The witnesses say that Grainger was standing a little further back from the car while Leadingham was getting in. The problem is they were some distance away from the blast and we have to treat their evidence and identification as mere presumption; only valid if nothing contradicts it. If they are correct and, between us here, they almost certainly are, then Grainger was the one that lived to take a last breath. We may get some confirmation in a few hours; the coroner has sent for those two's dental records."

"Not for the driver?" Conrad guessed what the answer to that was.

"Not enough left. He was so thoroughly blown up that we're working with fragments. We know that Marvin MacCray signed that car out as the driver, so we're presuming it was him in the car five minutes later. There's a chance it wasn't, of course. Again, between us here, it's pretty certain it was him, but we still haven't got that legally competent identification."

"We're just spinning our wheels." Conrad was frustrated. There was so much information available and all of it it pointed in different directions. "Without a clear-cut motive, you can't really point to anybody and I can't exonerate anybody either."

"You know something?" Jacobs sounded pensive. "After our friend Mr. Shaych gave us his little speech about detectives, I went home and read my copy of Chandler's <u>The Simple Art of Murder</u>. Turns out, he lifted the whole thing from that essay."

Conrad felt his stomach tighten slightly at that. *This is what The Seer is afraid of. As people learn more and more about everything and aren't confined to the few miles around their birthplace, it gets easier and easier for them to start making connections. One day, somebody will make a connection that blows our whole secret wide open. All it needs is Jacobs, who is a very fine detective, to look closely at pictures and suddenly realize Raymond Chandler and Bill Shaych are the same man and it's all over.*

"Anyway, I thought, well, that's what scriptwriters do. But, it's a hypnotic essay; once I start reading it, I can't stop. In it, Chandler says something that struck a chord with me. 'He gave murder back to the people who commit it.' I suddenly thought we need to do that. We've taken this murder away from the people who commit murders and got mixed up with studios, big-wigs, A-list actors and actresses and so on. I guess it goes with this being the kind of town it is. Let's give this case back to the man who committed the crime.

"Murderers are not afraid of the seamy side of life, because they already live there. Violence doesn't disturb them, because it's an essential part of the life they live. Murderers don't commit murder because they want to create a few bodies and provide us with a profession. They do it for a reason. In this case, because three people are dead, we can assume that it's because somebody wanted them dead. There isn't one targeted victim here with two innocent bystanders. A murderer would go the simple route and kill the one he wanted. There are three victims because three people were targeted."

"I'm not sure I agree with the logic you used to get there, but I see what you're driving at." Romero was thoughtful. "We've been treating these three victims as if they were individuals, instead of looking for a link between them. The sort of link that causes murders to happen."

"That's a criminal reason. And there's two crimes that link to this case, blackmail and/or the illegal pornography industry." Conrad thought about it. "I honestly can't imagine another crime that could immediately involve all three."

"I took the liberty of pulling the file on the MacCray girl's disappearance. It has a brief physical description that could apply to any early-teenage girl in California. Blonde, blue eyes, five foot two, only distinguishing mark was a large birthmark on her right breast. Very large, apparently; covered most of the tissue. A few more details on the night she disappeared. There was one he . . . . one blazes of a row at their house. Words like 'whore,' 'slut,' 'bitch' being tossed around in large numbers at very high volume."

Jacobs read the police account of the domestic disturbance call and shook his head as he tried to imagine the events that could lead up to that kind of row. He was fairly certain his adopted daughters would have stormed out of the house to cool off before an argument got to that point.

"Mothers sometimes over-react when they find their daughters have had their first lover." Conrad had seen that happen far too often. "They like to pretend it's moral outrage, but I think it's because they realize that they are going to lose their child to somebody else very soon."

"Wasn't the mother doing the swearing. It was the daughter." Jacobs was still reading the case file.

Conrad's Eye

Conrad looked up sharply. "That's betrayal. Daughters look on their mothers as their guardians; when the mother fails disastrously, the daughter will use those insults to convey that breach of faith. A son looks on his father as a source of strength and when he falls disastrously short will call him a weakling or a coward. Here, the daughter felt enormously betrayed. I wonder why?"

Conrad ran over the dying words of Eunice MacCray again. 'How could I have done that?' *What had the woman done that had betrayed her daughter so enormously? Somehow, she had failed to protect her daughter.* Then he stopped himself. *No, her words were transitive, active not passive. She didn't just fail to protect her daughter, she actively exposed her daughter to harm.* That was when Bill Shaych's comments about mothers who pushed their daughters on to the stage came back into his mind.

"Ed, does that file say whether the MacCray women, mother and daughter, were trying to get into acting?"

Jacobs flipped through the file again. "No, it doesn't. But, the MacCray family came down from Fresno when Theresa MacCray was about twelve. That's when family hopefuls start to arrive in this town. So, it's plausible. I wonder if our friend Mister Shaych will know?"

"Worth asking." Conrad got up and went over to the telephone on the wall. It was a measure of how much this diner catered to its clientele that the phone booth had a lot of privacy. He dialed Bill Shaych's number and waited until the phone was picked up.

"Shaych Productions."

"Ellen, it's Conrad here. Is Bill available?"

"In a meeting, ducks. Won't be out for hours. What do you need to know?"

"I just wondered if your marvelous filing system had an entry for a young girl who wanted to enter acting about five years ago. Name of Theresa MacCray."

"If she's not an active actress, we won't have a file on her. What's she done?"

"Disappeared about five years ago after a massive row with her mother. She's the daughter of the limo driver who got blown up."

Conrad heard Ellen Wynn sucking her teeth. "This is a bad town for runaways, ducks. If she hasn't surfaced in five years, she won't now. Especially if she had a terminal break-up with her parents. Your only hope would be to ask her agent about her. Good luck with that, this town is thick with them. Finding one who had her as a client five years ago and even remembers she existed? Not a chance."

326

"Couple of other questions. The girl was a blonde with blue eyes. Is that still a bad thing? And she had a very large birthmark on her right breast. Would that finish her as an actress?"

"No ducks, I wouldn't say blondes are back in, but they aren't poison the way they were a decade ago. The birthmark is different. That's a career-killer for an actress."

Conrad thanked her and hung up. Then he went back to his table. "Sorry, Bill's people won't have anything unless she's an active actress. Ellen says our only hope would be to find her agent. She did say that being a blonde isn't an insoluble problem anymore, but that birthmark would kill her chances in legitimate studios. "

"You and Ellen don't like each other do you?" Romero was slightly amused.

"We're just different people with different outlooks on life. We annoy each other." Conrad gave a sheepish grin. "Sometimes I have to ask forgiveness for thinking uncharitable thoughts about her. You know, if Theresa MacCray was trying to get into acting, we've got a link there that joins all three of the victims up. Suppose her father, Leadingham and Grainger each had a third of a story and they put it all together somehow. And whoever that story would hurt, got rid of them all. That would fit our criteria, wouldn't it?"

Leadingham, Steinsdottir & Partners, 8908 Cynthia Street, West Hollywood

Something about Kristín Steinsdottir Conrad found intensely disturbing. Despite what Ellen Wynn had said, the long, blonde hair was unusual enough to jar. Even so, it was the face that was framed by the hair that concerned him.

There was an immobility to it that suggested too many bouts of age-denying surgery, yet there were mazes of fine lines underneath each eye. The eyebrows were unusually large and excessively shaped, yet they seemed to match the deep folds that ran from the nose down past the corners of her mouth. Her mouth was small and seemed to be set in a sneer by the immobilizing tightness of the rest of her face. Conrad was a firm believer that the lives people lived showed in their faces; he didn't like to think what sort of life could have left an imprint like that.

"What do you want? And do not waste my time. I have many important things to do today."

Steinsdottir's accent was very pronounced, but it was not American. *That is probably the dumbest way to start a conversation with a police officer I have ever heard.* His instinctive dislike for the woman deepened. *Kristin Steinsdottir is either the most arrogant or the most stupid woman I have ever met.*

"Detective Sergeant Romero, Detective Sergeant Jacobs and a consultant working on our case, Conrad Lorenz."

Romero spoke in his most pleasant, cooperative voice; Conrad already knew him well enough to guess that meant trouble for Miss Steinsdottir. He didn't need to look at her fingers to know she wasn't married.

"We are conducting inquiries into the death of your partner, Roman Leadingham."

"That is why I have such little time. I am now the senior partner in this company and I have to decide which of the junior partners to promote. Now, hurry up."

"Miss Steinsdottir, we can either conduct this interview here or we can conduct it at the police station downtown. If you would like to go the latter route, then we will have to get a search warrant and bring this company to a halt while we search for the materials we are seeking. That could take days, or even a week, or more. Inevitably, word would leak out to the press who might well speculate on what we are looking for."

Ed Jacobs had slipped neatly into the 'bad cop' role. Conrad could only marvel how the genial detective, friendly companion and loving father had shifted gears so smoothly.

"Now, are you going to stop behaving like a German and answer our questions, or do I ruin your business?"

"I am Icelandic, not German." Steinsdottir's voice was a snarl of barely-suppressed anger. "Very well. We will speak in the conference room. Alice, hold all my calls until these people have left."

The conference room was a strange opposite of Bill Shaych's. Both were equally opulent and expensive, but Shaych's was both tasteful and comforting. This one was neither. It was garish and there was a vague air of menace about it. Steinsdottir took the seat at the head of the table and drummed her fingers impatiently on the glass-covered surface.

Conrad looked carefully at her. The expensive white silk blouse she wore had too many buttons unfastened just to be for her comfort. The necklace she wore was heavy, made up of large semi-precious stones. Conrad knew his jewelry, from the point of view of cost, anyway. *The necklace is probably much less expensive than the blouse. That is an odd combination.*

"Miss Steinsdottir, are you aware that your partner's real name was Jonathan Parris, AKA Johnny Parris, AKA Johnny "Frenchy" Parris? There are quite a few more aliases listed, if that would help jog your memory." Romero was still speaking in his mild, polite tones.

"He only ever used the name Roman Leadingham to me. I have never heard the names you have just used."

"Ben, let's get this downtown. You cuff her and put her in the cruiser, I'll call for the search warrant." Jacobs sounded angry and impatient.

"Ed, cool down. Miss Steinsdottir is an American citizen. She has her rights."

"Yes, I am an American citizen. By the votes of 180,000 American soldiers, who were alleged to live there, and against the wishes of 120,000 Icelandic citizens."

The venom locked up in the words was palpable. Conrad actually sympathized with her for the first time. *The American take-over of Iceland had been high-handed, The Supreme Court had expressed its dismay at the way it had been done, even if it had found no Constitutional reason why it wasn't valid. Iceland was just too strategically important as a base to be allowed to go its own way. Steinsdottir is wrong on two points, though; about a third of Icelanders had voted for U.S. statehood and not all the Americans living there had been soldiers. The troops' families had joined them, part of a conscious decision to create an American majority who would vote for statehood.*

"I knew that Roman had a past he wished to leave behind him. Many people do. Is this not supposed to be the land of the second chance?"

"According to his record, he was involved in the rackets on the East Coast. Trod on a few toes too many and was left behind when all the smart mob started the move to Cuba."

"That is a lie. Roman was a businessman who was too successful for the big companies to tolerate. So they ganged up on him and forced him out of business. They used their friends in the police to frame him. He came out here to make a new start and changed his name so his enemies would not follow him and ruin him here as well. But they found him and killed him."

"So you did know he was operating under an assumed name. Still, that's an interesting theory, Miss Steinsdottir. We'll look into that. Why didn't you advise us of your suspicions?"

"What good would that do? You would speak with your friends on the East Coast and they would deny everything. And you will go along with that, because you always side with the big companies. The truth is that Roman had a good business here, so his enemies killed him. Nothing you can say will change that."

"Tell me, Miss Steinsdottir, have you ever heard of a girl called Theresa MacCray? Her mother may have come with her about five years ago."

Conrad tossed the question in on an off chance.

Steinsdottir reached over and picked up the intercom phone. "Alice, did we ever have contact with a girl called Theresa MacCray? Do that immediately." There was a pause as a search was carried out. Then Steinsdottir continued, "Ah yes, I remember her now."

She put the telephone down. "About five years ago, they came to see if we would take them on. The girl looked like a horse. She was ugly and stupid and I told her so. She was very upset and her mother was very angry, so they left."

"Are you usually so abrupt with your clients?" Conrad looked at the woman again and thought he detected a flicker of pleasure at the memory.

"Always. It does no good to hide the truth from them. If there is no hope for success, then we tell them. That way they do not waste their money or our time."

"Thank you, Miss Steinsdottir. That's all we need to know right now. Don't leave town without telling us." Romero led the way out.

On the way, they passed a couple, obviously mother and daughter, waiting for an appointment. The mother looked quite normal. The daughter was dressed, made up and her hair styled in a manner suited to a woman in her mid twenties. Conrad guessed her actual age was twelve or so.

"We need to take a closer look at this place." Jacobs whispered quietly as soon as the doors closed behind them.

Romero and Conrad both nodded grimly.

Interrogation Room Two, Hollywood Police Station, 1358 North Wilcox Avenue, Hollywood

It wasn't often one heard people laughing in the interrogation room. Inside, Conrad saw a young girl sharing a joke with Romero and Jacobs. She had a mass of curling black hair, olive skin, heavy arched eyebrows and a pair of lively brown eyes. Looking at her, Conrad realized what Lillith must have looked like at the same age. Jacobs saw Conrad entering the room and straightened up.

"Conrad, I'd like you to meet my daughter Miriam. We thought she could help us. We would have talked at home, but Miriam wants to be a police officer so we thought we'd do it in an interrogation room. Show her the ropes, so to speak."

Miriam was eyeing Conrad's collar with calculation, mixed with a curiosity that caused her to frown slightly. "I thought I was going to get the rubber hose treatment, but I never expected the Spanish Inquisition."

"Nobody expects the Spanish Inquisition." Conrad replied gravely. "It's a pleasure to meet you, Miriam."

Again, Conrad caught the look of curiosity on Miriam's face before Romero set up the tape recorder in the room.

"We tape record every interview in this station. It's not just for the protection of the suspects, but also the officers involved. The mirror behind you is one-way. If this was a suspect interview, there would probably be another officer behind there watching. This is a witness interview, so the room is empty. Now, for the record, please tell us your name."

"I am Miriam Margolis-Jacobs. I am fourteen years old and I attend Hollywood Senior High, tenth grade."

"Miriam, have you ever been approached by an agent suggesting you might consider an acting career?"

"Yes, I turned them down. I want to be a police officer."

"Do you know any other girls, of your age or younger, who have accepted such offers?"

"I do. Three or four girls in my class did. All out-of-towners. Mostly, they started off expecting to be stars overnight and nothing happened, Eventually, they gave up and they moved away. One or two started getting parts and the school sent teachers to the set so they wouldn't miss lessons. None of them really made it, though."

"Did any of the girls who signed on with an agent seem upset or distressed?"

Miriam thought for a second. "All of them. As I said, I think they were expecting to be stars immediately and live that way. They didn't realize how much hard work is involved or how much they would have to give up. Or how long it would take them to get established. Us in-towners know that; that's why agents try to avoid us."

"We meant a bit more serious than just disappointment. As if they were in over their heads."

Miriam looked at her father sharply. "You mean like the girls who got in trouble with the police? Or whose boyfriends got them involved with things that were illegal? I don't think so. Wait a minute, you're asking me if any of the girls who signed up with agents were making illegal films, aren't you?"

Conrad's Eye

"That's my girl. I told you she was as sharp as they come."

Jacobs was almost beaming with pride.

"Well, I don't think any of the girls in my year are. But, the girls whisper about it to each other. You know, like campfire scary tales. Girl gets a job from her agent, but when she turns up it's for a porno film where she gets raped and killed. Or gets kidnapped and sold. I've never heard of any reality being behind the stories, though. Just scary stories. Anyway, everybody knows that when we get parts, our parents are on set with us. The school often sends one of their rentacops as well."

"Miriam, do you recognize this woman?" Conrad had a picture of Kristín Steinsdottir and laid it on the table.

"Oh yes. She was at the school jobs fair a few weeks ago. One of the agents trying to recruit us. She had a man with her; Roman, he was called. I remember that. She pointed at me and said 'don't bother with that one, Roman; she's much too fat.' I just ignored her. I wasn't interested in an agency anyway."

"We are really going to have to investigate Kristín Steinsdottir." Romero was looking at the ceiling.

Half an hour and a dozen more questions about school life and acting agencies later, Jacobs turned off the tape recorder.

"That's it, Miriam. Interview over. That's how it's done; no rubber hoses. But, if you were a suspect, we'd interview you again in a few hours and compare the statements. If they are identical, we'd be suspicious because it would sound rehearsed and suggest you were hiding things. If there was a major discrepancy, we'd pick up on that. Sooner or later, we'd get to the truth. Still want to be a police officer?"

Miriam nodded. "But first, I've got to get to the library. Father Conrad, would you show me to the elevator please?"

While they were waiting for the elevator to arrive, Miriam took a deep breath and obviously made a decision that came hard for a fourteen-year-old.

"Father Conrad, you did something bad to one of my people once, didn't you?"

Conrad was shocked both by the question and the perceptiveness behind it. That perceptiveness and the courage it took to ask the question made him give something close to an honest answer.

"A long time ago, I could have stopped something very bad happening and I didn't. How did you know?"

332

"Father, my sister and I are both very much the way Jewish girls are supposed to look. The first time I went to Schul, the Rabbi looked at me and said 'who's that Jewish-looking girl?' The first time you saw me, I could see guilt spreading all over your face. I'm an expert on guilt trips; my mother used them on me when I was young and I'll use them on my daughters in due course." Miriam thought carefully. "I think you were in Europe when the Nazis came weren't you? I think you could have helped a child escape but, for some reason, you didn't. And when you saw me, that memory came back."

Conrad looked down at the floor. Miriam's theory was only a faint shadow of the truth that burdened his soul, but it was close enough to shame him. Then he felt her take his hand.

"Father, that child wasn't me. It wasn't anybody I know and it wasn't here. Those were terrible times, and terrible things happened to *everybody*. Everybody did things they normally wouldn't. Don't let what happened then spoil now."

Then the elevator doors opened and she skipped inside, a schoolgirl again, making a bye-bye wave with her fingers as the doors closed. Conrad sighed slowly and went back to the interrogation room, wondering how a few words from a young schoolgirl could have helped lighten the burden of guilt he carried, when so much else and so many others had failed.

Bill Shaych Productions Office Suite, 8335 Sunset Boulevard, West Hollywood

"Irene, could I speak to you in private, please?"

Irene Shapiro turned around. Conrad was standing in reception.

"Sure, there's a conference room free." She led the way in and closed the door behind her. "What can I do?"

"Irene, are you still in the OSS?"

Officially, the Office of Strategic Services was the intelligence arm of the National Security Council, tasked with providing the council with customized investigative and administrative services. These included identifying threats to national security before they became critical. Unofficially, they also investigated things that were too odd or tenuous to involve conventional law enforcement agencies. It helped that the OSS had extremely warm relationships with the FBI.

"Of course. I'm just on leave of absence at the moment."

Irene didn't need to explain why. It was Conrad's fault and he knew it.

"Could you contact them and ask them about this person."

Conrad produced Kristín Steinsdottir's picture. Irene looked at it with an eyebrow raised.

"You started dating, Conrad?"

"She's a suspect in your bombing case. Partner of Roman Leadingham, the agent who was killed. She seems a nasty piece of work. My guess is she has a record somewhere, but the Hollywood PD don't have the juice to get to the right people. There's another thing. I need to have your advice on women's clothes."

Irene's eyebrows lifted again. "If you're going undercover, you'll have to shave your legs, you know."

Conrad stopped for a second and drew a breath. Irene had the art of throwing him off track down to a fine art. "There was something about the way Steinsdottir dressed that puzzled me. She wore very expensive clothes but cheap jewelry. And she walked around with her blouse open to her waist."

Irene blinked. "You're joking? Like this?"

Irene's fingers waved at her blouse just above her belt.

"Doesn't happen. Quite apart from anything else, it's ugly. Bra strap visible across the gap."

Conrad swallowed and thought he caught Irene smirking. "Like that, but no bra strap. And a very large, heavy but inexpensive necklace."

"That's weird. Businesswomen just don't dress like that. It's not just asking for trouble; it's unprofessional. Believe it or not, Conrad, there is an unofficial, unwritten, but universally accepted, dress code for women in management positions and by the time a woman gets there, she knows it, understands why it exists and follows it.

"One part is, neckline covers any soft flesh. It's pretty much international; an Australian or Thai businesswoman will go by the same code. And you say her clothes are more expensive than mine?"

Irene tapped her fingers on the table. "You're right, Conrad that is odd. She doesn't belong where she is. I'll see what Washington and Quantico have on her."

1715 Carla Ridge, Beverly Hills.

"If we'd come here in a black-and-white, the lawyers would have beaten us to it." Romero sounded vaguely amused.

The three men got out of Jacobs' car and walked up to the door. It opened before they got there. A Hispanic maid stood politely, but firmly, in the entrance.

"We've come to see the lady of the house. We're detectives from the Hollywood PD and a consultant who is helping us."

Jacobs spoke politely and the party was ushered into a reception room.

"Please sit down. Maria, organize some coffee and sandwiches."

"That's very kind of you, Mrs . . . "

"Please, just call me Angie. Everybody does. I'm researching a possible role as a policewoman and the first thing I found out was that detectives never get a chance to eat properly on duty. How can I help you?"

The voice was soft and had an undercurrent of kindness. Conrad almost instantly liked her. He had to remind himself he was dealing with people whose livelihood depended on them projecting false images of who they were. *But, everybody spoke well of Angie.*

"We're investigating the bombing that killed Marvin MacCray, Roman Leadingham and Clyde Grainger. We've discovered some aspects of that case that take us back to a TV series that was cancelled last year, *The Hunters*. We're trying to find out why that series was cancelled so abruptly."

The coffee and sandwiches arrived and were served by the maid.

"Unfortunately, I can't really help you there. Confidentiality agreements, you understand."

"Angie, we came to you because you are A-list and have power where the studios are concerned. You might be able to tell us things voluntarily that people in less influential positions cannot. There are some very ugly aspects to this case and it's likely to involve subpoenas at some time in the near future. We want to spare you that." Romero had genuine sincerity in his voice. Conrad realized he would probably have made a good actor himself.

Angie's mouth twisted slightly. "I'm only A-List because Frank says I am. If we fell out, I'd be off the A-List next morning. I'll call the studio management."

She went away and only came back after several minutes. "I've been authorized to tell you this. While we were shooting *The Hunters*, we were using two primary sites, a studio sound stage for internals and an old airfield out of town for externals. We'd spend about three days up there and the rest of the time on the sound stages. To save going backwards and forwards, we had some internal sets built inside the hangars we weren't using as hangar sets. Mostly

Conrad's Eye

living quarters and the officer's club. One of the people on set, it doesn't matter who, went to the stag party held for a friend who was getting married. Stag parties being stag parties, the night included some adult movies. Our man recognized the sets as the ones we had up at the airfield. He managed to snag the film.

"He told one of the stars and the four of us who were top billing watched it. It was pretty bad. Let's just say the woman in it was being made to do things I would never agree to. We went the studio management with it and told them that this was completely unacceptable. If it got out, it would wreck the careers of everybody involved in the show; actors, management, technical. They agreed and they shut down production on the spot. Fired everybody, including us by the way, investigated thoroughly and made sure that everybody involved in doing the films would never work in this town again.

"Being fair to the management, the innocent bystanders were found parts in other shows. There were some administrative changes made to make sure this never happened again. I believe that similar locations are now guarded and inspected regularly to make sure the facilities are not being misused."

Conrad got the picture of Kristín Steinsdottir out. "Angie, do you recognize this woman?"

The actress took one look at it. "Kristín Steinsdottir. She's the remaining senior partner of Roman Leadingham."

"One of my friends says that she dressed very expensively. Would you agree with that?" Conrad didn't doubt Irene's assessment, but he was interested in whether the answer would be the same.

Angie smiled at him and the room seemed to light up somehow. "Let me put this in perspective. This family earns 55,000 dollars a week. Of that, my husband contributes 20,000 and the rest is mine. Averaged out, of course. That isn't unfair; his job has no upper age limit and mine has. 55,000 dollars a week, and *I* would think twice about spending as much as she did on the blouse she is wearing in that picture. And I would certainly make it look better. That necklace is dreadful.

"Yes, she dresses expensively, but she doesn't know how to dress or accessorize. Before you ask, we get lessons from the studio, all the time. Makes sure we stay in fashion."

"One more thing, Angie. Have you heard of a young actress called Crystal Feathers?"

"Of course; she was a bit-player in *The Hunters*. She had a love-scene with Clyde Grainger but couldn't do it. She burst into tears and ran off the stage. Some young actresses are like that; love scenes upset them. I think Crystal had only done soap and cosmetics advertisements before and having to do an intimate scene was more than she was ready for. She was unlucky it had to be Grainger. He's got disgustingly bad breath. I kissed him in the same episode and it nearly made me retch."

"My friend has kissed him as well; she recommended Listerine."

Angie laughed. The sound reminded Conrad of wind-chime bells. "Thank your friend and tell her that if I'd ever had to kiss Grainger again, I'd have bought her dinner in gratitude for that advice."

Conrad felt an acute desire to do *something* for Angie, even if it was a minor service. Her charm and good nature had simply won him over and he could see why everybody spoke kindly of her. "I'll do that."

To his great delight, she flashed a quick smile at him. Conrad felt quite pleased with himself but then caught a knowing glance from Jacobs and realized that everybody who met her reacted the same way.

After they'd been shown to the door, Romero settled into their car and looked around at his partners.

"Well, that settles it, doesn't it? The bombing was tied up with the pornography industry. We can pretty much discard anything else. Now, all we have to do is to fit the people into that framework and we're most of the way to solving things. I wonder if Kristín Steinsdottir blew her partner up to take over the business. Everything we've found about her says she has expensive habits. Perhaps she was helping herself to money from the corporate accounts and Leadingham found out. We know he was mobbed up back East; it's quite possible she had to get him before he got her. And she didn't strike me as the sort of person who would care about killing two bystanders to get her target."

"The only thing against that is that we don't know of her having any knowledge of explosives. Of course that wouldn't matter too much. She could easily hire somebody who did. It's not as if the ability to make a pipe bomb is a close-guarded secret."

Jacobs obviously liked the theory his partner had put forward, but any additional comment he might have made was cut off by the radio. Romero picked it up.

"One William Five here."

"One William Five, watch commander would like to see you immediately. Return to the station."

Conrad's Eye

The Bull Pen, Hollywood Police Station, 1358 North Wilcox Avenue, Hollywood

Romero returned to the office from his meeting with the watch commander and threw his jacket on to the desk.

"That's it, I told you it would happen. The brass says that the case is solved. Leadingham was making porno films using studio facilities to cut costs and selling them cheap. When the studios shut his operation down, he couldn't deliver and his customer killed him. End of story. We've been shut down."

CHAPTER FOUR

Renaissance Hollywood Hotel, 1755 North Highland Avenue, Hollywood

His display board was a lot simpler than it had been. Conrad had discarded all the information on it that related to anything other than the pornography business. He now had that as his prime entry and had arranged the cards for the three victims beside it.

The question now is, since the motivation for the killings was the illegal film industry, who would have reason for those killings in that context? He had Crystal Feather's card beside Clyde Grainger's and a new card for Kristín Steinsdottir beside that of Roman Leadingham. *One problem is that I still can't really fit Marvin MacCray into the picture. The other problem is, with the official police investigation shut down, I am on my own.*

There was a quiet knock on the door. Conrad was expecting it. He opened immediately, taking in the sight of an apparently elderly man with a white moustache and piercing eyes.

"Henry! I wasn't expecting you to bring this over yourself. You didn't waste any time. Come on in; come in."

"A VC-144 was coming this way and the package of information was important enough to get a SecDef minion bumped from the flight."

Henry McCarty gratefully took one of the armchairs. He was a tall man, and sitting in the cramped cabin of a VC-144 for two hours had been a painful experience. He'd noticed on boarding that the Air Force stewardess was wearing pants rather than a skirt. Once she had started scrambling over the wingspars that ran across the cabin to look after her passengers, he'd realized why.

"Conrad, you may have stumbled across something with major national security implications."

That caused Conrad to blink.

"Henry, there's a problem. The police here have shut down the investigation. It led to a pornography operation that affected one of the big studios and they run this town. The studio shut the pornographic operation down, fired everybody involved and ran them out of town. All credit to them there; when they learned of the operation they moved fast and decisively against everybody involved. But they don't want the police nosing around in their business."

"Well, the police can open it up again. The studios may own this town but, as of your message via Igrat, sorry, Irene, this is a Federal matter. There's two FBI agents arriving in the morning and Dido will be joining me to represent the OSS."

Henry winced and rubbed his aching back. "She should have flown on the VC-144; it's more her size. Anyway, what do you know about the Icelandic National Freedom Army? Or, the Íslensku þjóðarinnar Frjáls Framan, to give it its proper name."

"Aren't they a group demanding Iceland secede from the Union? I thought they were a fringe party of no real importance."

"That depends on how you define 'of no real importance.' Do they have any significant support? Not really. Although a lot of older Icelanders are pretty nostalgic for their full independence, they're far too decent a people for any meaningful number of them to support a terrorist movement. Do they have enough to be a threat to national security? Not a real threat, but enough to be a concern.

"About ten years ago, a group of them broke into the airbase at Keflavik and tried to attack the aircraft on the hard stand. The Air Force Police saw them, called on them to stop and, when they refused the order, shot all four of them dead. To put that into context, they were about thirty feet from a B-36 loaded with nuclear weapons when they were killed.

"Their leader was Pétur Kristján Steinsson, Kristín Steinsdottir's brother."

Conrad put one of the hotel minibar bottles of bourbon whiskey beside Henry who swallowed the contents in a single gulp. "Thanks, Conrad. You know, Old Number Seven has never quite recovered from prohibition. Anyway, Kristín Steinsdottir spent the first half of the last decade agitating against American control of Iceland. Nobody ever tied her to an incident, but she is believed to have been involved in a couple of bombings at the American bases there. She left Iceland after a scandal concerning her relationship with a teenage girl who wanted to join the INFA. She vanished and was thought to be in Europe somewhere. Instead she's turned up here. Ironically, Iceland being the 51st State now has allowed her to get in easily. Technically, she's an American citizen, although she won't thank you for reminding her of that. Once she was in, there was no reason to take note of her or keep track of her. Until now."

"You think she's planning terrorist attacks here in the U.S.?"

"Worse. We think she's funding the operation of a terrorist group. When the teleprinter message from Irene came in, Lillith pulled the financial and tax statements of Leadingham, Steinsdottir & Partners and compared them with her known lifestyle and expenses. The two don't add up. In fact, the firm accounts don't really add up either.

"You know Lillith; she can read a set of accounts at a glance. If she worked for the IRS, every company in America would be in trouble. Anyway, she believes Leadingham, Steinsdottir & Partners has a much greater income than they are admitting and there's no trace of where it is coming from or where it is going to. Coupled with a senior partner who has known connections with a terrorist group, that was worrying. We took it to the FBI and they agreed to take the case over."

Conrad knew that one of the reasons why the FBI and OSS worked well together was that the FBI was given the credit for every successful operation that resulted from an OSS finding. That brought something to mind.

"Henry, could you suggest something to the FBI agents?"

He spoke quickly for a couple of minutes, after which McCarty shrugged.

"Sure, the final decision is theirs, of course. Any thoughts on the terrorist angle?"

"Suppose, the extra money is being made from illegal pornographic films and funneled back to the INFA. Leadingham didn't know about it and found out. Steinsdottir blew him up to keep him quiet. Did it in the studio as a prelude to shaking them down as an additional source of funding. Did it with a bomb as an overt declaration."

"Could be; mob racketeers are usually oddly patriotic. Look how they kept the docks clean in the war. If one found out his partner was using his racket to fund our enemies, he might well be pissed enough to want to get her, so she got him first. Or, here's another. You said Steinsdottir lives far above her means."

"Even an A-list actress was surprised by how much she was spending on clothes. And how badly she wore them."

"Suppose she was milking the money she was diverting to the terrorist groups to support that lifestyle? And they blew up her partner as a warning to cut it out. That implies she's part of a bigger operation. And that, Conrad, is a very real worry."

341

Conrad's Eye

The Bull Pen, Hollywood Police Station, 1358 North Wilcox Avenue, Hollywood

Miriam was waiting for the elevator when she saw Conrad enter the building. That made her nervous. She'd spent the time since their last meeting worrying that she'd been offensively presumptuous. That made his smile of obvious pleasure on seeing her something of a relief. His first words after they'd stepped into the elevator were a real pleasure.

"Miriam, I wanted you to know something. What you said when we last met, it was a real comfort to me. Back in 1942, just after the Germans had invaded Vichy France, a group of us were heading for Spain. Mixed in with us Jesuits were some Jewish men. We'd chosen them carefully; picking ones that not only looked right, but acted right. You see, the collar is a passport all of its own, but it's a very brittle armor. Its defense is invincible, as long as it's unchallenged. If somebody spots something wrong, and the Gestapo were very perceptive, the defense it provides is gone.

"Just before we left, a mother begged us to take her daughter with us. We couldn't. It would have given the Gestapo the clue and the excuse they needed and all the others we were hiding would have been lost. The face of that young girl as we left her still haunts me. I know she died because we left her behind that day. Your words lifted that shadow a little from my soul."

And the story is true, although it is not at the heart of my darkness. Long, long ago, I watched while a young conversos girl, barely older than you, was being slowly drowned to make her confess that her family was secretly practicing Judaism and engaging in unspeakable rites. Then I believed I was doing God's work and for that, my soul is forever damned.

"I read about that case in Schul, along with other examples of gentiles helping my people escape the Nazis. You must have been very young then. And very brave."

"And still innocent of the evil in the world. Why are you back? Applying for the police?"

Miriam giggled. "Not for another four years. Daddy asked me to come back after he got a call late last night. Something about the statement I made last time I was here."

The lift doors opened to reveal Jacobs standing in front of them. "Good news, Conrad; we're back in business. Between you and me, somebody has thrown a scare into our watch Captain like I've never seen before. We've got a meeting in ten minutes. Miriam, thank you for coming in again. I've called your school principle and explained you're helping us with our inquiries."

342

"Oh, daddy. Everybody will think I've been busted for something." Miriam gave a good imitation of wailing in distress. Jacobs laughed and hugged her quickly.

"Conrad, we're on again." Romero had come around the corner. "The FBI are here and, wait for it, the OSS. Something about the Grainger case has caused a panic. By the way, it is the Grainger case; dental identification came through for both Leadingham and Grainger. Everybody is waiting for us in the main conference room upstairs. We'd better move. Miriam, please come along with us. The agents from the FBI made a point of asking for you to be available. You'll have to wait outside at first, though."

By the time they got up to the conference room, everybody else had arrived. They took their seats at the end of the table. Jacobs noted Captain Hammond wouldn't meet his or Romero's eyes. He also recognized the vice-president in charge of production from the studio responsible for *The Hunters* and who had presumably shut down the original investigation. When Hammond spoke, he was obviously shaky. Jacobs guessed that he had not experienced an enjoyable morning so far.

"Gentlemen, Detective Sergeants Romero and Jacobs and a consultant, Father Conrad Lorentz. I'm Captain Mike Hammond. This is Henry McCarty and Dido Carthagina, from the Office of Strategic Services, and Agents Michael Delgado and William Bussard, from the Federal Bureau of Investigation. We've also been joined by Mark Devers, who is the vice-president in charge of production at the studio in question. Miss Carthagina?"

"The OSS received notification of this case via media coverage of the bombings. We look at every bombing in the USA as a matter of routine, in case it is something more than criminal. When we looked into some of the details and the people involved, we found there were connections with issues related to national security. These included an abortive attack on a nuclear-armed bomber. That caused us to examine the case from a different aspect. When we did so, we determined that it could indeed result in an imminent and serious threat to national security. Accordingly, we handed our findings over to the FBI who have agreed with our assessment and assumed the lead in the investigation." Dido sat down, yielding the floor to Agent Delgado.

Watching her, Conrad got the feeling she was uncertain of herself and desperate for approval. From his brief acquaintanceship with her, that was an attitude that affected all of her work. He whispered quietly to Romero, but loudly enough for her to hear.

"Nice to see somebody getting right to the point."

"Thank you, Miss Carthagina."

Delgado himself was a little uncertain of his ground. He was newly out of the FBI Academy and he was aware that his performance was being scrutinized.

"Without going into excessive details of the financial records involved, it appears that the money being made from the pornographic films produced on the sets used by *The Hunters* may, I repeat may, have been diverted into the financing of a terrorist group that intends operations here in the United States. The link is tenuous at best, but we feel that closing down the investigation at this point is premature. At the very least, we need to establish where the money earned from these films was stashed and who the films were sold to."

"May I point out that the fact that the films in question being made on our property were legal, if highly distasteful, and against company policy and rules of conduct. Despite the cost to our company, we have moved against those involved with the greatest severity. I can promise you that nobody involved in those productions will ever work in this town again." Mark Devers sounded indignant.

"Mr. Devers, nobody is criticizing the actions taken by your studio. We believe they were prompt, effective and a salutary caution to other people who may have similar ideas. The problem is that the investigation did not go far enough and the possible ramifications leading to the bombing at Paramount were not fully explored before the investigation was called off. This is the fault of the Watch Commander at this station and does not reflect on you or the detectives involved."

Delgado looked across at Hammond with severe disapproval. He knew very well that Hammond had given in to pressure from Devers, and the rebuke really was aimed at the studio executive. It was bad luck for Hammond that somebody had to take a hit for the team, but the cozy relationship between the Hollywood PD and the studios had gone on far too long.

"So, now that this investigation is under way again, we come back to the original problem. There is no record in the accounts of Leadingham, Steinsdottir & Partners that they had any income other than that legitimately earned by their commissions from the clients of their agency and those to whom they referred those clients for professional services. So, there is no reason to believe that there is a link between the bombing that led to Leadingham's death and the films made on your property, Mr. Devers. However, an examination by a forensic accountant has shown that the known expenditures of the partnership cannot be accounted for by their legitimate income. So, obviously, there are additional sources of income. We have no reason to believe that their known excess expenditure is all there is. The invariable rule in this sort of case is that where there is some, there is more."

"Will you be taking over the case?" Romero was reluctant to ask, because he had a bad feeling over what the answer would be.

"No. At the moment, this is a Hollywood problem and it doesn't extend beyond state lines. So, please look on us as a resource you may call on, but the case remains in your hands. If, however, there is an extension beyond the boundaries of California, then we will take the lead over.

"Sergeant Jacobs, could you ask your daughter to step in please?"

Jacobs went outside and came back with Miriam. She settled down in a chair and answered patiently as the questions from her earlier interview were repeated. At one point, she gave her father a discrete wink; obviously remembering the lesson she had on interrogation procedure. Eventually, Agent Bussard came to the point where she had been insulted by Kristín Steinsdottir.

"So, after she said you were too fat, you said nothing more to her?"

"I said nothing, no."

Bussard noted the double denial and thought for a second. "What did you do?"

Miriam looked around sheepishly.

"I did this." She lifted her right hand, fist clenched but the middle finger extended straight up. An approving ripple of laughter went around the room.

Suddenly something clicked in Conrad's mind. "That's it. On the way up this morning, Miriam and I were talking about Jews escaping from France in 1942. I told her how it was important that the refugees reacted the right way when they were addressed by the Gestapo. They had to remember their collar protected them and answer back. If they were deferential or submissive, the Gestapo would smell a rat. That's what the Steinsdottir woman does. She insults the kids and ignores the ones that fight back, like Miriam did. But the ones that fold up, she realizes she can bully and exploit. That brings them into the racket."

"We still have to establish links between Leadingham, Steinsdottir & Partners, the films being made on the location set of *The Hunters* and the illegal pornography we believe is also being produced." Romero was reluctant to mention problems, since the morning had gone so well and he didn't want to break the run of luck.

"There's a way we can establish that link." Conrad was thoughtful. "Crystal Feathers. With her background, she may know a lot more than she's let on. Or, more than she realizes. I'm particularly interested in why she just froze up when doing love scenes, but burst into tears and ran off the set when she was expected to do one with Clyde Grainger."

"That's up to you, Romero; you and Jacobs're in charge." Bussard dismissed the issue.

"Now, Miriam, I understand you're interested in a career in law enforcement? I've been looking at your statements, both today and before, and I'm impressed. My primary job in the FBI is scouting for new prospective recruits and bringing them along. Are you interested in joining the FBI after leaving university?"

"I thought you only took Irish Roman Catholics? That's why FBI stands for Fully Born Irish."

Ed Jacobs mumbled "Federation of Bungling Idiots" under his breath, which got him a wagged finger of disapproval from Delgado.

"We take anybody who qualifies and has skills we need. Do you speak foreign languages?"

"English and Hebrew fluently. I can get along in Yiddish. I'm taking Spanish at school; the only languages they do are French and Spanish."

"If you wish, I can advise you on courses to take that will qualify you for the Academy. There's a good languages school in LA; I would urge you to consider learning Arabic and possibly Farsi there. The Bureau will give you grants for your college education, conditional on you applying for the Academy when you graduate. I suggest you talk this over with your fathers and call me if you want to go that route. I think that's all our business concluded for the moment.

"Now, Captain Hammond, Deputy Chief Carmady would like to speak with you."

Home of Marlon Scalisi, 8130 West Kirkwood Drive, Hollywood

"Were Kristín Steinsdottir and Roman Leadingham close?"

Marlon Scalisi thought very carefully about the answer he had to give.

"I suppose it really depended on what they were fighting with. If it was just his fists against her nails, yes, they were pretty close. The time she went for him with a broken bottle and he fought back with a baseball bat, not so much. Of course, if they were shooting at each other, they could be thirty or forty feet apart. As for the normal screaming matches, well, eighty or a hundred feet would be normal. We actually had complaints from the office block across the street once."

"Are you being serious?" Romero wasn't sure whether his leg was being pulled or not. "We are investigating a triple homicide here."

"I'll swear it on a Bible if you wish. Or the Father here can loan me his rosary and I'll swear on that. Those two fought all the time and none of it was pretty. One time, Roman punched her so hard I thought he'd break her neck. Or her jaw. They'd have a screaming match over business decisions that would quickly descend to obscenities and abuse; then they'd lash out at each other. Eventually, he'd storm off to his office and she'd take it out on the first young girl who walked through the door. I'm glad to be out of that madhouse, I can tell you."

Conrad decided to call his bluff. He took out his rosary and laid it on the coffee table in front of Scalisi.

"Do you swear, on your immortal soul, that the information you have given us about the relationship between Roman Leadingham and Kristín Steinsdottir is the truth and only the truth?"

Scalisi reached out and put his hand on the rosary.

"Father, as you have said, I do so swear. I have spoken nothing but the truth." He kissed the rosary and respectfully returned it to Conrad.

"What do you do now?" Conrad was curious about the dynamics that were being so vividly revealed.

"Oh, something nice and safe, I juggle live rattlesnakes. Sorry, Father, that isn't true. I got a job in an agency writing advertising copy. It's wonderful. Quiet as the grave in there."

"If the working relationship was so terrible, why did they continue in partnership?" *Leadingham, Steinsdottir & Partners sounds a pretty fair incarnation of hell.*

"Perhaps they didn't want to make two other people unhappy? Or they didn't want the other one to think they'd won. Who knows? None of us could understand it. We always believed it would end up with one of them killing the other."

"So, you weren't surprised when Roman Leadingham was blown up?" Romero was furiously taking notes. He had a suspicion Jack Webb would want to know about this when the time was right.

Scalisi thought for a second. "Actually I was. Kristín isn't the type to put a bomb in somebody's car. She is all instant screaming and incoherent fury. If she lost her temper with you, she'd lean over you with her face about an inch from yours and scream at the top of her voice. She could go on for half an hour or more like that. Our turnover in secretaries and so on was phenomenal. When she was leaving after ten days, one of the girls told us she thought Kristín was a sadist, a real one. Roman was different. If he was angry with you, he'd say nothing but come up with some really nasty trick, like sending flowers to your wife on her birthday with a card saying they were from you, but with another woman's name on it. If Roman had been beaten to death or shot, Kristín would be at the top of my suspect list. If Kristín had been blown up, Roman would be the prime suspect. Not this way 'round though."

"Did they actually shoot at each other?" Jacobs was having a hard time getting his mind around the situation.

"She shot at him, yes. He'd thrown a glass decanter full of brandy at her. She had a Colt .32 automatic and she fired a couple of shots at him. They both missed every time, of course. More I think about it, those two couldn't have survived anywhere but here. In any other town, they'd have both been in jail by the end of the week."

Conrad watched Romero shuddering at the picture of life in Leadingham, Steinsdottir & Partners. He had already decided that Hollywood was a sad and lonely town, now he was coming to the conclusion it was an ugly one as well. Looking back on the investigation, it seemed to have been a steady descent from superficial gloss downwards into ever more degraded levels of existence. The descent was so steady, Conrad found himself wondering just where the bottom was.

If there is one.

Crystal Feathers' Apartment, 1619 North La Brea Avenue, Hollywood

Although they were in the same building, Crystal Feathers' apartment was a bit larger than Merlin Salerno's and had doors separating it into individual rooms. Also, she had furniture. *Cheap and probably second-hand, but furniture.*

"Miss Feathers, we need to ask you about the films you made when you were much younger. We believe that the industry behind those films was responsible for the bombing that killed Marvin MacCray, Roman Leadingham and Clyde Grainger. If this theory of the crime is correct, it exonerates Merlin Salerno from suspicion." Romero spoke formally; Jacobs nodded.

"First of all, when did you sign up with Roman Leadingham as your agent?"

"Are you sure this will help Merlin?"

Romero nodded; Crystal gathered a shaky breath before starting.

"When I was twelve. My mother took me in and said I could dance and sing. I had to give a demonstration and then she gave me a big talking-up. Eventually, Leadingham said he would take me on. He said I wasn't really very good, but I had a lot of promise and just needed lessons. So, I got sent to singing and dancing lessons, then to acting classes. After about six months, my mother started running out of money. Fortunately, I was getting small parts by then. Mostly in television advertisements, but real acting. My mother was already acting as if I was a big star and telling everybody that's what I was.

"Then the money ran out. Leadingham offered me a part in a movie. Well, he made my mother an offer that would put me in a movie. To be honest, I don't remember what that first film was. I was too young to understand the significance of what I was doing.

"The second film, I remember." Crystal was shuddering; tears streamed down her face.

"The details don't really matter. There was a masked man and a masked woman in it and they raped me. Right there, in front of the cameras. I can't stand anybody touching me now. Even if they are trying to be kind. If somebody does, all I remember is that horrible man in a mask with his foul breath in my face."

Only his experience and quick reactions allowed Conrad to get the question out first. Even so, it was a matter of a split second only. The voices of the two detectives almost formed a chorus with his.

"The man had foul breath?"

"You know how when you get a piece of meat stuck in your teeth and you can't shift it? And soon it tastes like its rotting; a sweet, sickly rot? Well his breath was like that, only far worse, and it was overloaded with even more sweetness and the taste of violets."

"Clyde Grainger." This time the three men did manage a perfect chorus.

Crystal had broken down completely and was weeping helplessly. Conrad looked around the room and saw some stuffed animals on the couch. One, an elephant, looked more worn than the rest. He went over and picked it up. When he gave it to Crystal, she seized it and clutched it to her, rocking backwards and forwards. Through her tears, she was nodding as strongly as she could.

One of the detectives tried to ask her something but Conrad waved him to silence. *The girl needs to speak, she needs to get this load off her soul, but she needs to do it in her time and on her own terms.*

Instead, Jacobs whispered very quietly. "You know, every so often somebody tells me all about 'victimless crimes.' I'd like to have those people here, now. Then I'd like to take them out into a back alley and do some rubber hose work on them. There's always victims, even if they aren't stretched out on the floor at the scene."

Eventually, Crystal's sobbing slowed and she was able to continue.

"Clyde Grainger. I never knew until I had to kiss him on the set of *The Hunters* and I smelled that foul breath again. I couldn't stand it. I broke down and ran off the set. The director retook the shot using one of the other girls who had the same color hair as me and shot it from behind."

"After you were raped, what happened? Why didn't your mother go to the police?"

"Leadingham gave her lots of money, enough money to keep my mother quiet. Said it had all been a mistake, the actors had gone too far, that none of it was supposed to happen, it would never happen again. All of that. And it worked. She made me promise not to tell anybody or I would be taken away and sent to a juvenile hall where it would happen every night. So I kept quiet. I kept on doing advertisements and small parts and kept getting classes. Until the money ran out again.

"By then I was older and street-wise. When Leadingham said there were film parts available, my mother wanted me to take them, but I made certain I wasn't going to get abused again. I told him that I would go to the police if anybody touched me. That limited me to supporting roles, of course. Leadingham said because I'd been out of films for so long, I would have to make three films and I'd only be paid when I finished all three. Earnest performances, he called them."

Crystal managed to laugh through her tears. "Earnest, perhaps, but disaster would be better. Everything went wrong with those films. I think it was his past catching up with him."

"What happened?" Jacobs asked, his voice soft and gentle.

"Towards the end of the first day, there was a terrible panic. Something really bad happened on the set of another part of the film. We were all credited with having completed our contracts for that film and all given a bonus in cash. One of the other girls whispered that an actress had died on the set next door. I think her name was Tobiana. Nobody ever talked about it again. A month or so later, I was called in for the second film and that's when the police turned up. The rest you know."

"Crystal, did you tell anybody about Grainger being the man who raped you?" Conrad asked the question as gently as he could.

"Only Merlin." She clapped her hand to her mouth and started to cry again. "Oh my God; I've put him in the gas chamber."

"No." Romero was very firm about that. "We have a different suspect in our sights."

"Crystal, where did you tell Merlin about this?"

Conrad had an awful sinking feeling that, whatever Romero believed, Crystal had just hanged her boyfriend.

"In the limousine going back from the old airfield to the studio. Merlin and I shared one. He'd heard all about the problem on stage and we talked about it. I told him all of the story, including the rumor about Tobiana. He said it wouldn't matter, that the studio would understand. I knew they wouldn't. I knew I was finished right then."

The Bull Pen, Hollywood Police Station, 1358 North Wilcox Avenue, Hollywood

"Hi, Ed. Is it true the Feds are trying to steal your daughter away from us?" The policewoman had a dazzling smile and had turned it on full force.

"It is, Glennie. They're offering tuition bribes, counseling, a rabbi to help her and early academy admission. Somebody pushed buttons for her. Conrad, please meet Sergeant Glenda Schleicher from Vice. Glennie, Father Conrad is a consultant helping us."

"Good afternoon, Father. Aren't you the priest who helped the SFPD on the Black Dahlia case? I'm not sure if I should talk to you. We're still trying to live that down."

"I was much younger then and youth overcame discretion." Conrad spoke slowly, as if stricken with guilt. "But Ed and Ben are trying to help me make amends. Ed, did you say the FBI are offering Miriam a rabbi?"

There was an eruption of laughter around the bull pen.

"A police rabbi, Father, not a religious one. It's something new in the police force. A rabbi is a veteran police officer who takes a new recruit under his wing and guides them. Gives them career advice, steers them clear of trouble, advises them on ethical problems and so on. It's reduced our internal problems a lot. We've found when police officers go bad, it usually starts early in their careers with minor things. The rabbis pick up on it and straighten the youngsters out before it gets to the point where they're in too deep."

"Well, Ed, we're trusting you to make sure Miriam sees the light and stays local. We were all counting on her joining us. Anyway, how can Vice help Homicide? Or did you just want to see a pretty face up here?"

Schleicher looked around the Bull Pen and sighed noisily.

Conrad's Eye

"Glennie, we are on the Grainger-Leadingham case and it's taken us right into Vice territory. We believe that the motive for the murders was connected with the illegal pornographic film industry and we're developing linkages between the victims and that industry. We've noted, for example, that a lot of the persons of interest in this case were linked to the Leadingham, Steinsdottir & Partners agency. We're working on the theory that at least one of the partners, and possibly both of them, were recruiting under-age children to appear in illegal movies. We believe that there is a lot of money in that agency that is vanishing and there is a chance it is being used to fund a terrorist group."

Schleicher's eyes opened wide. "You're kidding? No, of course, you're not. We've suspected much the same thing, about the films, at least, for some years but we can't prove it. Leadingham's methodology appears to be to recruit young, impressionable mothers and daughters, bankrupt them with expensive 'coaching,' then offer the children movie roles of steadily-increasing squalor. But, we never managed to catch him.

"The Steinsdottir woman kept getting in the way. She drove away far more clients than she ever brought in with her attitude. In the process, she threw out every undercover policewoman we sent in."

"Have you ever heard of a girl being killed on one of these films?" Romero had an undercurrent of affection in his voice that made Conrad guess that these two officers had a relationship off-duty.

"Doesn't happen. It's an urban legend. No vice squad in this country has ever found a film with a woman being deliberately killed in it. Nor have the Federal authorities. We know where the story comes from though. Have you ever heard of positional asphyxia?"

Schleicher barely paused for an answer. "It's where the victim is in a position where she can't breathe, usually due to the weight on her chest. It's an occupational hazard for prostitutes and women in adult films. The problem is that's she's gasping for breath but the man using her mistakes the sound for real or simulated passion and doesn't realize she's dying. That's one reason why prostitutes try to be on top. The younger the woman, the more vulnerable she is. A woman, even a fully mature adult, can die of positional asphyxia in less than a minute as the pressure on her chest interferes with her vital functions.

"We know of several cases where women have died of positional asphyxia while making films. In one case, the crew gave her CPR and called for an ambulance, knowing full well that they were ensuring their own arrest. They put the woman's life first and we made sure they got a little credit for that. They were the exception, though; mostly, the body was abandoned or dumped. Sometimes we found them; mostly, they just vanished."

352

"Did you find any bodies about five years ago?" Conrad was barely hopeful of a helpful answer.

Schleicher snorted with laughter.

"Are you kidding? We found a dozen or so about that time. Mostly natural causes; drink or drugs. I'd have to pull the case files from that time, but I can't remember any adolescent girls being found around that time."

"One thing we can add. We've got a positive ID on one of the men involved in these films about six or seven years ago. Clyde Grainger." Romero added the information in a faint hope it might help.

"Now that's interesting. Identifying the men has always been a problem for us. The studios won't like you finding that out. They don't like the murky secrets of their established casts coming out. Expect to be shut down."

"It's been tried. The FBI and OSS made a point of unshutting us. You may notice we're short a watch commander. It's whispered he's directing traffic somewhere very cold and lonely."

Schleicher nodded, realizing for the first time that the implications of this case were running far beyond the usual boundaries. Jacobs filled the silence. "We have reason to believe the girl might have been called Tobiana. Does that ring a bell?"

"Sorry, boys. Give me a moment and I'll call downstairs."

Schleicher picked up the telephone and dialed an extension. "Central Records? Hi, Jim. Do we have any record of a adult films actress called Tobiana? She would have been in the films about five years ago. It doesn't ring a bell with me, either, but if you could check? Thanks, Jim. I owe you."

"No record of an actress on the open file, meaning she's not still in business. Of course, if she died five years ago, she wouldn't be. Jim's checking the closed files now. If we don't see an actress for a year or two, its assumed she's left the business one way or another."

Schleicher frowned. "Tobiana is an odd name for an actress to choose, though."

"Why, Sergeant Schleicher?" Conrad had a sudden sensation that a frustrating case was breaking open.

"I ride horses when I want a break. Got a cute little pinto mare up at a ranch just outside the city. She's the kind that has a white coat with large red markings. The stallions with those markings are called Tobianos; the mares, Tobianas. This actress was naming herself after a horse."

Conrad's Eye

Leadingham, Steinsdottir & Partners, 8908 Cynthia Street, West Hollywood

"Here we go. Ed, you got the papers?"

Romero didn't wait for an answer. Instead he threw the doors of the offices open and strode in.

"Everybody, stop what you are doing right now. We have a search warrant for these premises and an Impoundment Order for all your records and documentation."

The room froze in mid-beat. The clattering sound of typewriters stopped before Romero had finished the announcement. Secretaries froze in place, their fingers poised motionless over the keyboards. In the background, a couple of junior management figures tried to head, unobtrusively, towards the fire escapes. They were cut off by uniformed officers, who had accompanied the detectives. Other officers were fanning out through the other rooms, making sure that all work had stopped and, much more importantly, nothing was being destroyed. Preserving evidence was the name of the game at this point.

"What is the meaning of this?" Kristín Steinsdottir stormed out from the offices in the back of the suite. "Leave here immediately."

"Kristín Steinsdottir, you are under arrest on charges of pandering, assault, abuse of minors, production and sale of films whose content is in violation of California Statutes, and mopery with intent to gawp." Sergeant Schleicher was enjoying herself. Taking down a major agent was an achievement.

"You have the right to remain silent. If you give up the right to remain silent, anything you say can be used against you in a court of law. You have the right to be represented by a lawyer of your choosing. If you cannot afford a lawyer, the court will appoint a public defender who will represent you at no cost to yourself. Do you understand these rights as I have read them to you?"

"Yes, but . . . " Steinsdottir's arrogance and aggression had been punctured by the cold words of the Miranda warning.

"Kristín Steinsdottir, you are also being held on suspicion of one count of murder in the first degree with aggravating circumstances and three counts of murder in the first degree. You have already been read your rights and have acknowledged that you understand them. Officer Reed, hook her up and take her to Central Booking."

"Here, use these." Schleicher tossed a pair of pink handcuffs over to the uniformed officer. "They'll go with her outfit better."

"Pink handcuffs?" Romero sounded amazed but Conrad caught the note of affection again.

"Use them all the time in Vice. We get them from the Chicago Handcuff Factory. Pimps depend on their tough-guy reputation. Nothing puts them out of business faster than being perp-walked, wearing pink cuffs."

Romero chuckled at the picture, then got back to business. "The rest of you. Remain motionless at your desks and do not touch anything until an officer escorts you to a holding area. If you attempt to interfere with anything on your desk, you will be arrested and charged with obstruction. Does everybody understand these instructions?"

"Sir," One of the secretaries was distressed. "I have an asthma inhaler on my desk. May I pick it up please? I think I'm going to . . ."

Jacobs went over to her desk and looked at the slim tube the secretary pointed at. "That's fine, miss. You can pick that up and use it if you need it."

"Thank you."

She grabbed the tube and breathed deeply from it. Her sigh of relief was profound. Jacobs looked at her more closely; she was very young. So much so, she obviously hadn't been working long enough to buy her own clothes. She was still wearing a school blouse, but she had sewn a little lace around the collar to try and hide its humble origins. She had probably left school only a few weeks earlier and gone to work rather than try for college.

"Have you really arrested Miss Steinsdottir?"

"We have. She's on her way to Central Booking right now."

The girl seemed to relax. "Everything changed here when Mister Leadingham died. He was such a nice man. He said I had the talent to become an actress myself. I'd just need some lessons, that's all. But Miss Steinsdottir just shouted at everybody."

The girl seemed far too innocent to be working in a place like this. That made Jacobs try something. Perhaps she was also too innocent to keep quiet.

"What's your name? Have you ever seen this man around here?" He produced a picture of Marvin MacCray.

"Gloria Foreman, sir. Isn't that the poor man who was blown up at Paramount as well?"

She looked carefully at the picture. "He was here, about three days before he was killed. He was having a meeting with Mister Leadingham."

The sudden flash of interest around the room was apparent. Jacobs had warm appreciation in his voice when he continued.

"Thank you, Gloria, that's really helpful. Did you notice if the meeting was friendly or whether they were about to have a fight?"

"I don't know. They seemed friendly, but I got the feeling that Mister Leadingham wasn't pleased to be seeing him and that the man in the picture was very angry about something. They were too friendly; you know, as if they were keeping their tempers under control."

"That's very interesting, Gloria. This is Sergeant Glenda Schleicher. She'll go to a private room with you, just tell her as much as you can remember about that meeting." Although Gloria Foreman couldn't see it, Jacobs had signaled Schleicher to play this very soft and gentle.

Romero had finished organizing the sweep of the offices. Each member of staff present had been quickly interviewed by a police officer and then led away to the conference room, where they were being watched to make sure they didn't start discussing the situation. After he was happy with those arrangements, he turned back to Conrad.

"Oh-kay, Father, time to search the Big Man's office. You know the rules; stand in the middle of the room and don't touch anything. If you handle any evidence, it could get thrown out. If you want us to search something, point to it and ask. Understand?"

Conrad nodded. He stood in the middle of Leadingham's office as he had been told. Around him, Romero and Jacobs were quickly and methodically going through the room. Conrad more or less ignored what they were doing. *They are highly competent and, if anything was to be found by a thorough search, they'd find it. I am more interested in what they won't search.*

Roman Leadingham had been a racketeer and he was familiar with police search methods. If something is hidden, it wouldn't be where a police search would look. Conrad thought about the kind of man Leadingham had been and looked around the room for something that didn't fit that character. He found his eyes fixing on the windows.

"Ed, Ben, the curtains. Curtains don't seem right somehow. A man like Leadingham would have blinds, wouldn't he?"

The two detectives looked at the windows thoughtfully. Romero fingered the fabric carefully.

"Now, why would he have curtains, instead of blinds?"

"Because curtains go backwards and forwards, while blinds go up and down?" Jacobs offered that tentatively.

"Or because blinds jam, and when they do, somebody stands on the window ledge to free them and he doesn't want anybody doing that?" Romero's offering was equally tentative.

"Perhaps because curtains reach down to the window ledge and cover it. Along with any marks that might be made as it was moved." Conrad was picking up confidence as the oddity of the curtains in a modern office grew on him.

"I wonder what is under that ledge?"

It took a few minutes struggling, but eventually the trick of how to lift the window ledge clear was discovered. Underneath it was a safe. That also took time to open, and it needed the services of a professional safecracker who owed Romero a favor. Once they had it open and the safecracker had departed, the two detectives were able to root through the contents. Mixed in with papers and photographs were six reels of film. Each had a name on it.

The fifth reel removed from the safe bore the name of Clyde Grainger.

Apartment of Kristín Steinsdottir, 6520 Hollywood Boulevard, Hollywood

It was only when Conrad looked out of the window that he realized how small the area they were moving in was. The view was almost identical to that from his hotel window. The Renaissance Hollywood had to be only a few hundred yards away and directly behind him. The apartments owned by Merlin Salerno and Crystal Feathers were barely further away on his left, while the same distance to his right would take him to Bill Shaych's offices. The same distance further along would put him in the offices of Leadingham, Steinsdottir & Partners.

"I never realized how small Hollywood is."

"That's why we call it a town. It is; a small town that happens to be located in Los Angeles. It acts like a small town too, with all the good and bad that goes with that. You'd be surprised how little it has to do with the rest of the city. The whole of Los Angeles is like this. It isn't really a city at all. It's a group of small towns that happen to be very close to each other."

Ben Romero looked around the apartment. "OK, where do we start? Conrad, you know the rules."

"Stand in the middle of the room and don't touch anything." Conrad repeated the instructions he'd had earlier by way of acknowledgment.

He looked around. *The room seems soulless, somehow. The furniture is modern, chrome and leather, but shows remarkably few signs of use. There are no coffee cups left to be cleared up later or magazines put to one side to be read that evening. Kristín Steinsdottir doesn't live here, she just happens to be here a lot. She never put her stamp of ownership on to the place.*

Across the room, Jacobs opened a door leading to a side-room.

"Guys, come and look at this." The room was a perfect cinema in miniature, with eight seats in two rows. A small projection booth contained a one cinema-standard projector for 35mm film and two smaller ones for 16mm and 8mm. The screen was cinema proportions, but scaled down for the smaller room. A quick glance around showed that there were speakers in each corner of the room.

"I've heard of people having these, but I've never seen one."

"Angie's got one in her house. There were pictures of it in a magazine. But hers is cinema only. I think quite a few of the A-list have them, so they can stage private previews of their films. Never seen one in the flesh before though. Your girls would love this, Ed."

"Their boyfriends wouldn't. They'd know Kelly and I were outside watching them, shotguns at the ready."

Jacobs thought for a second. "I'd guess the 35mm projector is used for cinema films. The 16mm and 8mm projectors, for the illegal ones, I suppose. I'd guess there will be some of those films around here, somewhere."

Romero picked up a canister of 35mm film. "*Mission to Myitkyina.* This hasn't even been released yet. Do you think we need to preview it? Purely for the evidential value, of course."

"And, of course, we'd be paying our last respects to *Marisol.*" Jacob's remark caused a moment of silence. Despite the months that had passed since the RB-58C had been shot down, there was still a level of shock that a nation had dared to shoot at one of SAC's bombers. The destruction of Yaffo that had followed hadn't changed that reaction.

"Later, perhaps. Search the place first."

As Romero and Jacobs moved methodically through the rooms, the impression of emptiness that Conrad had gained slowly became stronger. The apartment was being methodically searched by two efficient and capable detectives, yet it was turning up nothing that suggested an identifiable person lived here. There was no alcohol in the living room bar. The refrigerator in the kitchen was empty. Conrad asked for the electric toaster to be shaken out. As he had suspected, there wasn't a crumb in it. He was getting an eerie feeling that Kristín Steinsdottir was a ghost, with no physical presence to leave a mark.

Her bedroom had just a tiny touch of character in it. A bed not quite made properly, clothes in a hamper awaiting washing. Nothing more than that. Romero noted that as well.

"She doesn't even have a naughty drawer. First time I've been in a woman's room and she doesn't have a naughty drawer tucked away. I've been in hotel rooms that have more character than this place."

Conrad looked around and frowned. "According to the floor plan, there's a walk-in wardrobe the other side of the bathroom, yet she has her clothes in free-standing wardrobes here. Now, why would she do that? Every woman I know would kill for a walk-in wardrobe."

"Some of them have." Romero sounded as if he wasn't joking. "Let's try the bathroom."

There was no apparent door to a walk-in wardrobe. Instead, there was a large, full-length mirror where the door should have been. Romero and Jacobs searched around the frame for a latch, but it seemed as if the mirror was solidly-mounted. Eventually, Conrad had an inspiration. "Steinsdottir hid herself in open sight. She probably does the same with everything. Try the light switches on the wall by the dresser."

Romero flipped both of them on and there was a click inside the wall. The mirror moved slightly. The gap it revealed was enough to allow Jacobs to open it. One switch had released an electronic catch; the other turned on the lights in the hidden room. Romero stepped in. When he spoke, his voice was very quiet. "Conrad, you'd better see this."

Conrad stepped in. His eyes took in a scene that was sickeningly familiar to him from his days as an inquisitor. The hidden room was a fully-equipped dungeon, with all the accessories that implied. There was even a water tub in the middle of the room, an old fashioned one made from a half-barrel.

When he pulled her head out of the water, the foul, dirty liquid was streaming from her nose and mouth. I knew she was already in extremis and she would not survive having her head held under again. But I said nothing as he thrust her head into the water and when he pulled it out, she was dead. I killed that poor girl just as surely as if I had drowned her myself.

"So, now we know what her little hobbies were." Romero sounded bitter. There was frustrated hatred in his voice.

"I don't think so, Ben." Jacobs had picked up some photographs taken in the hidden room and was looking through them.

"Marlon Scalisi was wrong. Kristín Steinsdottir isn't a sadist."

Conrad's Eye

The Bull Pen, Hollywood Police Station, 1358 North Wilcox Avenue, Hollywood

"Well, Vice rescues Homicide once again." Glenda Schleicher should have been looking triumphant, but there was an air of tragedy about her that drained any glory from the moment. "We've been through those six films and we can be pretty sure they are potential blackmail material. Well, three of them are. The other three are borderline."

"I thought the response from the studios would be devastating if anybody tried to blackmail an actor over past participation in questionable films?" Conrad was confused. "Surely Leadingham would know that?"

"The studios will respond very badly to attempts to blackmail actors over questionable films." Schleicher spoke in a monotone that suggested she was controlling herself carefully. "These are different; they show the actor committing felonies. My guess is that Leadingham was holding these films until the subjects in them get to be A- or B-list. Then he'd try blackmailing the actors. These are offcuts, material that was filmed but not used in the final product.

"In two of the films, the actress is pleading not to have something done to her, almost certainly anal sex. The actor went ahead and did it anyway, eliminating the First Amendment protection for consensual acts. The actor could be charged with rape. Look, guys, this is a brutal, exploitative industry and we all know that sort of thing happens all the time. Only, this is one of those rare occasions we have evidence of it happening. It's a rare break-through for us and one that means we could put the crew away for a good, long time. The actor could go down for life. I can see he'd pay almost anything to avoid that.

"The remaining film is much more serious. It shows an actress dying while being filmed in a sex act. Our old friend positional asphyxia again. The film shows her fighting for breath and suffocating, while the actor and film crew ignore her distress. At the very least, that's manslaughter and, if it can be argued the actor deliberately ignored evidence of her impending death, that could be enough to go for him on a murder charge. Take a look at the stills."

She handed them around. They showed the actress on her back, her face already swelling and showing every sign of extreme distress. Her hands were on the actor's chest, trying to push him up so she could breath. One still had been taken after she had died. It showed the actor unmasked and it was very clearly Clyde Grainger. That wasn't what caught Conrad's eye, though. The actress, he assumed it was the mysterious Tobiana, was still laying on her back in the foreground of the picture. The heavy purple-red stain of a birthmark was clearly seen to be covering one of her breasts.

The actress who had died was Theresa MacCray.

CHAPTER FIVE

Renaissance Hollywood Hotel, 1755 North Highland Avenue, Hollywood

Conrad raised his cross and lead the way out of the church. The sound of Psalms being sung drifted out across the square. His eyes scanned the crowd, seeking out those who were too enthusiastic in their condemnation of the accused. He looked especially for those who showed too much delight in them being taken to their fate. For every Inquisitor knew how devious and crafty were the ways of the Devil and that a mere appearance of piety was no guarantee that even the greatest show was sincere.

The ringing of the telephone snapped him out of his nightmares. He picked it up to hear the voice of the receptionist.

"Long-distance call for you, Mister Lorenz."

Then there were a few clicks and Lillith's voice came on the line.

"Morning, Conrad. Did I wake you? We've finished going through the accounts of Leadingham and Steinsdottir and very interesting they were. The short picture is that the company was systematically looted by both partners right from the start. The initial working capital came 50:50 from both partners. Steinsdottir brought hers in with her, but Leadingham appears to have borrowed his share from his mob associates. He was repaying them by stealing money from the company accounts.

"Now, Steinsdottir was doing the same, but a little more skillfully. She was bleeding money from the accounts in huge quantities. A lot she was spending on herself and most investigations would stop there. In fact, her personal expenditure was only a part of the amount she had helped herself to. We had a job finding the rest, but eventually we managed to locate where it was going to."

"The Icelandic terrorists?" Conrad had a dreadful feeling about this.

"Oddly, no. As far as we can make out, Steinsdottir has had no contact with them since she left Iceland ten years ago. The group she was in contact with was cleaned up very shortly after she left. Very shortly. In fact, suspiciously shortly. According to the file, when she left, she took the group's treasury with her."

"That's the money she used to buy her share of Leadingham's business." Conrad was getting the picture.

"If the statement from the terrorists as to the amount she took is correct, some of it went for that purpose. They're all doing life without possibility of parole, by the way. They staged a bombing in the center of Reykjavík that killed one person and wounded sixteen more. The rest was used to found a medical unit in Reykjavík, the Pétur Kristján Steinsson Memorial Center. It specializes in the treatment and rehabilitation of blinded people. It's world-famous for its innovative approaches to helping those who have lost their sight. A substantial proportion of its funding comes from the money Kristín Steinsdottir is stealing from Leadingham, Steinsdottir & Partners. When I said she was bleeding that company, Conrad, I wasn't joking. The company would have been better off with a vampire sinking its teeth into its collective neck."

Interrogation Room Two, Hollywood Police Station, 1358 North Wilcox Avenue, Hollywood

"Chief Carmady says that if Conrad interviews anybody, we are to sit quietly, watch and take notes as to how it was done. He promises it will be a post-graduate exercise in how to get a criminal to convict themselves."

Romero was settling in to the observation booth with a cup of fresh coffee, a pad and a supply of pencils. Beside him, Glenda Schleicher was doing the same, except that her drink of choice was lemon tea.

Inside, Jacobs finished repeating Steinsdottir's Miranda warning. That wasn't strictly necessary, but nobody was taking any chances. Although Conrad was conducting the interrogation, a detective had to be present. As usual, the whole interview was being tape-recorded.

"Miss Steinsdottir, do you waive the right to have a lawyer present?"

"I do. And I wish to complain about being placed in solitary confinement all night."

"That was for your protection. The women in the prison system have very strong opinions about people who assault children and express those opinions very forcefully. They had already heard you were being brought in. The Head Warden's opinion was that, if he had let you be placed in the general population, you would have been in intensive care very shortly afterwards." Jacobs couldn't help sounding pleased at that thought.

If you knew what I know now, your opinion might be different. It is not our prerogative to judge people.

Conrad settled down and started to ask his questions. The gentle net started to form around Kristín Steinsdottir. For all her determination not to co-operate, she found herself filling in the details in the picture that Conrad had sketched for himself.

"And so, you blame yourself for the death of your brother and that is why you seek to be punished?"

"It was not my fault. Your Air Force Police killed him. They shot him twelve times. Twelve times! He was just a boy, too full of idealism to be careful. My mother wept when she saw his body torn by the bullets. She never smiled again, not until the day she too died."

"Yet you hold yourself responsible for his death. And always seek to be punished for it?"

"What foolishness you talk. Why should I seek to be punished?" As she spoke, she blinked. Her eyes looked away from him.

Conrad quietly took one of the pictures from the hidden room in her apartment and put it in front of her.

"Why indeed. Kristín? Do you know why the Holy Church no longer recommends chastisement in penance for sins? It is because, taken to excess, penance becomes pleasure and the penitent seeks out his – or her – penance not to show repentance but for the pleasure it brings. And then, the penitent starts to commit the sin so that he can demand that he receive the due penance. So, it is that the Devil gains another soul. Would your brother find peace, Kristín, if he was to see you like this?"

Conrad's finger tapped one of the pictures.

"My brother is nothing to do with this." Her voice was shaking with a combination of rage and grief. "Nothing, you hear me?"

"Then why do you have yourself treated like this? What is it that so fills you with guilt that you hate yourself and the world around you?"

"I was not responsible for my brother's death. You were. You put your bombers and their atomic bombs in our country. You took us and forced us into your union. And then you killed him because he got too close to one of your precious bombers."

She was weeping now, her whole body shaking with grief.

363

"So we decided to strike back at you the only way you understand. With bombs. We planted some outside your bases, but nobody heard of them and your Air Force never mentioned them.

"So we decided to make a bombing in the center of Reykjavík, where it could not be hidden or denied. One of our group drove a bus for the Air Force and he would be picking up some of your personnel. He knew the schedule and he helped us plant a bomb in that bus. Only everything went wrong that day. The bomb went off an hour early. We thought the driver did not set the timer properly, but we did not know.

"The other side of the road, a teacher was taking her class on a field trip. The Air Force bus had a bright painting of an aircraft on the side and she pointed it out to her children. They were looking right at the bus when it exploded. And there was a truck between loaded with old bottles between them and the explosion. The blast smashed those bottles into thousands of tiny fragments and the cloud of glass hit the teacher and her class full in the face. They were well wrapped up against the cold, but their eyes were unprotected. Every one of them was blinded. Every one."

By now, Kristín Steinsdottir was lost in her grief, guilt and misery. The confession was pouring out of her.

"That's what we achieved by trying to avenge my brother. The only person who was killed was one of us, but none of those children would ever see again. I knew then that what had happened to them was my fault. I had done that to them. It had to end, so I informed on the rest of the group to the police. Then I took all the money we had collected and ran away. It was easy to come here; after all, I am an American, am I not? I gave most of the money to an eye doctor so he could start a clinic named for my brother. The rest of the money I used to buy into the partnership with Leadingham. I robbed the company of every penny I could and sent it to the clinic where the victims of the bombing were treated."

"Why do we have to listen to this perverted bitch?"

Jacobs couldn't control himself any longer and the anger poured out of him.

"She says she feels so sorry for the poor little children, but lures them into making pornographic films where they get the life crushed out of them by a oafish thug who cannot even be bothered to clean his teeth now and then. She makes me sick. Just toss her into General Population and let the women there have at her. She'll get all the punishment she wants then."

"Ed, you know the reason why wrath is a mortal sin? It isn't because of what it makes you do to other people; it's because of what it makes you do to *yourself*. Kristín here fell victim to wrath and now look what she has done to herself. It turned her into a murderer and a pornographer. It has turned her whole life into a twisted caricature of what it could have been. Her wrath has cost her everything, even herself."

"I didn't know!" Steinsdottir's voice was anguished. "I never knew about the films until after I'd been in the company for months. I found he was making the films, but not declaring the income, so I started to steal that as well. Then I found out about the young girls he was recruiting. I tried to scare them away, I treated them like dirt, so their mothers would take them to another agent. If I'd told them what was really going on, they wouldn't have believed me. So I drove them away. It was all I could do."

"Do you remember this one?" Conrad laid the picture of Theresa MacCray laying dead on the set in front of her.

Steinsdottir looked at it and broke down again. "I thought I had succeeded with that one. She and her mother walked out. Her mother spat at me after I said her daughter looked like a horse. Leadingham got his hooks into them, after all."

"I didn't know."

The Bull Pen, Hollywood Police Station, 1358 North Wilcox Avenue, Hollywood

Ed Jacobs is more than embarrassed. He looks completely humiliated. Conrad quietly shook his head to himself, then noisily punched the door to the Bull Pen open.

"Ed, there you are. Thank you for helping out in there. You timed that outburst perfectly. We couldn't have done that better if we'd rehearsed it. Your hostility put Steinsdottir and I on the same side at the point where she was closing down and that's why she started to confide in me."

Jacobs looked at him suspiciously, "Father, I hope you're not making fun of me. I know damned well I nearly ruined everything for you. I just couldn't help it. All I could see was Miriam or Rebecca choking to death like that and I just couldn't stand hearing her voice for another moment."

"Ed, do you seriously think I'd make fun of you, in the face of the tragedy in that room? Do you know what the really tragic side of this is? Leadingham borrowed the money to start that business from a load-shark. He had to pay the points, and at least some of the capital, every week. That's why he was stealing money from the business. Then, Steinsdottir came along and started to cream off nearly all the profits. That left him without the money for his loan shark. So, he got into the adult films business to make the money he needed to pay off his debts. Then Steinsdottir found that money and started to cream that off as well.

"Leadingham couldn't understand why he wasn't making money. He was so used to brutalizing and exploiting women, that he never realized a woman could deceive and exploit him. So he went into illegal pornographic films and started to make the money he needed there. Then Steinsdottir put a cramp in that by scaring the younger girls away. Ed, she drove Leadingham into the illegal films business. She didn't mean to, but she did. She's clever and it will only take her a few days to put it all together. Where will that leave her?"

"The road to hell is paved with good intentions." Jacobs repeated the old saying with a new and gloomy understanding of all that it implied. "You think it was the loan shark who killed him?"

Conrad shook his head. "They don't kill people who owe them money, especially not the amount here. If they'd broken his legs and/or taken the business from him, yes, that would be the Mob. If they felt they had to kill him, we'd never have found the body. If they wanted to kill Steinsdottir, she'd have gone into that private room of hers and never come out alive. When her body was found in there, everybody would assume it was one of her games that went wrong. No, Ed, we've solved one crime here; one we didn't know about when we started. We've put a nasty pornography ring out of business, but we still haven't found out who killed Leadingham, Grainger and MacCray."

"Glennie came up with something. You know those other tapes we found? Well, one of them showed Mark Devers taking a kickback from Leadingham, in exchange for a list of outside set locations and when they would be vacant. He's been taking money for years, so it seems. For all his protestations of innocence, he was hip deep in the pornography business. Oh, he never took a frame of film, but he made the sets available.

"And, guess who was the deliveryman for the money? Our friend Marvin MacCray."

"That makes sense. Nobody ever looks at the limousine drivers and MacCray must have been really hurting for money with his wife's medical bills to pay."

Conrad thought quickly of Gusoyn and how his network of limousine drivers unknowingly kept the Seer informed of everything that was happening in Washington. *To the world outside, Gusoyn is just a humble driver, barely more than a servant, yet the Seer regards him as his right-hand man. It is Gusoyn to whom the Seer turns whenever he needed a responsible man who would get something done quietly and tactfully.*

"Steinsdottir is telling the truth; she didn't know everything that was going on, She knew more than she's admitting, but she was far from being an accomplice. I'm not even sure she did anything illegal."

"What? She was stealing a fortune from that company."

"Yes, but it was her company. I have a suspicion if she now declares all of that money to the IRS as charitable donations, she might even get a tax break on it." Conrad had a brief mental picture of Lillith nodding approvingly at that touch.

Jacobs looked at him and sighed. "That's outrageous and I still think you're doing a snow job on me about that outburst. Anyway, why don't you come over to dinner with Kelly and I this evening? Ben and Glennie will be coming as well."

Ed Jacobs' House, 9378 Flicker Way, Hollywood Hills

Once again, Conrad was startled to find out how close the Jacobs household was to his hotel. Barely half a mile separated the two. Looking out at the spectacular view, Conrad believed he could see every one of the locations that had defined his life for the past few days.

"Mister Margolis, your house is truly marvelous."

Kelly Margolis laughed easily.

"Kelly, please. After all the help you've given Ben and Ed over the last few days, I can't stand on ceremony. We really got lucky here though. The land belonged to Ed; he bought it when he got back from Russia and things around here were pretty cheap. Nobody thought the land up here would ever be worth much. After I got divorced, I put up the money to build this place and we put the result into our joint names. One good thing about being Jewish. We can get a family doctor, psychiatrist, lawyer, accountant and architect, all without going outside the ranks of first cousins. No contractors in the family, unfortunately; we had to go to the Irish for them."

"Daddy, when should we have dinner ready?" An older version of Miriam had come in from the kitchen and spoken before she realized company had arrived. "Oh, good evening, Father. Are you hungry?"

"With anticipation, yes." Conrad gave Rebecca a genial smile as he took in the apron tied over an elegant dress. "Are you doing the cooking tonight?"

"All four of us are. Well, sort of. I'm looking after the first course, honey-ginger grilled salmon fingers. Kelly is doing his courgette, tomato and portabello mushroom salad. Miriam's looking after the beef short ribs, while Ed went down to the bakery and got an orange cake with plain chocolate icing."

Conrad noted that she was referring to her fathers by their first names. *A household with two fathers has a problem when addressing its members. It will be a long time before the language caught up with social changes.*

Conrad's Eye

"That sounds wonderful, Rebecca. I hope we can do justice to it all." Conrad hesitated for a second. "We're not making you break any of your dietary laws, are we?"

Rebecca shook her head. "It's all Kosher. Miriam and I keep the kitchen that way. We're a bit more serious than Kelly and Ed. They're reform, we're conservative. Anyway, if you'll excuse me, Father, I must get back to the kitchen and take over from Sis; she needs to get away and get dressed properly."

"Don't let Rebecca lure you into a religious discussion, Conrad. She learned from some of the most devious rabbis around." Kelly paused for a second. "Of course, a theological debate with a member of the Society of Jesus might be a chastening experience for her. Hold that thought, will you? I think that's Ben and Glennie."

Margolis opened the door and let the couple in. As Glenda Schleicher entered the room, she held her left hand so that the new ring on her fourth finger was prominent. That brought her a burst of cheering and a series of hugs from Rebecca and Miriam.

Two and a half hours later, Conrad was so full of food that he could barely move. He was nursing a glass of sherry and listening happily to the sound of conversation about the daily trivia of living in Hollywood. Miriam was passing on her own piece of news. She had decided to take the FBI up on their offer of sponsorship. Glenda had thrown her arm over her eyes in a theatrical display of grief and wailed 'betrayed, betrayed'. But, as Miriam had pointed out, with her college education paid for by the FBI, Rebecca would be clear to go to the best medical school around. From there, the conversation drifted to television shows, and to *The Hunters* in particular.

"I don't think any of them would have lasted very long in a real war." Ben Romero showed an unexpected level of expertise in fighter combat.

"Were you a pilot, Ben?" Conrad was intrigued by this sudden revelation.

"Still am. I flew fighters for NORAD for five years. Started on F-94Cs and transitioned to F-101As. Now, one weekend a month and two full weeks a year, I fly an F-104E for the California Air National Guard. We always reckoned that the ones who were out to make a reputation for themselves ended up by spinning in."

"But the story is really about the people on the ground and how the war affected them."

Miriam was sitting beside Kelly. She'd taken a lot of care to look her best. Reflecting on the party, Conrad realized both of the girls had spent a lot of time and effort on making sure it went well. *They realize their fathers see too much of the ugly side of life in their jobs so they try to make their home as pleasant and happy as possible for them.*

"Remember the episode where the Germans bombed the base destroying the communications and the pilots were coming home, not knowing who had survived and who had been killed?" Rebecca had obviously found that a favorite scene.

"Yeah, and the airbase couldn't tell them the runway was blocked by a delayed action bomb. The fighters were running low on fuel and the ground crews had to make the bomb safe and clear the runway. So the bomb disposal sergeant was sitting on the bomb trying to defuse it before the fighters reached home. He told everybody he sat on the bomb to make sure that, if it went off, he would be killed instantly and not left to die by inches."

Suddenly there was a stunned silence.

Conrad, Romero and Jacobs looked at each other. In almost perfect chorus, they said "Marvin MacCray."

The Bull Pen, Hollywood Police Station, 1358 North Wilcox Avenue, Hollywood

"I know it all fits together." Ben Romero was looking at the card display Conrad had brought in with him. "Leadingham first ruined MacCray's family financially, by exploiting Eunice MacCray's fixation with getting her daughter into acting. Then he destroyed it physically, by luring Theresa MacCray into making pornographic films. I guess that the first time he suggested that, Eunice MacCray tried to push Theresa into doing the films and that led to the row between her and her daughter She might not even have told her daughter it was Leadingham's idea she make them.

"Theresa ran away, and either went back to Leadingham, or Leadingham found her. Perhaps she thought she could trust him; he seems to have had a talent for manipulating women. Either way, he lured her into making those films. In one of them, Clyde Grainger killed her. Almost certainly an accident, but she still died.

"Five years later, Grainger was recognized by Crystal Feathers and she made the link. She told Merlin Salerno in the back of a limousine. Either Marvin MacCray was the driver or another driver told him about it when they were swapping stories about the day's work. MacCray was already working as Leadingham's gofer and he confronted Leadingham about it. Leadingham probably offered to cut him in for a share, not realizing that he was Theresa's father. That's when MacCray decided to blow them both up. His wife and daughter were dead, he was financially ruined and in a menial job with no future. He had nothing left to live for. He put a pipe bomb under his own seat to make sure he was killed outright and a shaped charge on the fuel tank to make sure Leadingham and Grainger were burned even if the blast didn't get them. He drove the car right up to them, waited until they were getting in and then set off the bombs. He may even have passed on a couple of opportunities because there were other people too close. We'll never know that."

"There's a couple of holes still." Conrad sounded greatly saddened by the whole affair. "How did he know the actress who died was his daughter? And where did he get the expertise to make those bombs?"

"I can answer some of that." Ed Jacobs had an Army file in his hand. "Marvin MacCray served in Russia with the 56th Cavalry Brigade, Texas National Guard. It was a horse cavalry outfit before it converted to a mechanized formation in 1943 for deployment to the Russian Front. He was a pre-war Guardsman, so he would have known the horses well. He would probably have known that a Tobiana was a white mare with large red patches and could easily have made the time and description connection. He made sergeant and was honorably discharged in 1949. His specialty was combat engineering. So, he certainly knew how to make a pipe bomb and a shaped charge. Combined with a working knowledge of horses, I think he knew enough."

Conrad thought about it. In the end, he came to a conclusion he didn't like, but The Seer's words echoed in his mind. *See the world as it is, not as you would like it to be. Life won't be as comfortable but you'll save yourself a world of hurt.*

"I'm sorry Ed, but it's not good enough. We're still missing a piece. The row with Leadingham and making the link between Tobiana and his daughter doesn't quite fit. It's like a jigsaw, where the one part left doesn't really fit and has to be forced into place. We have to look at the whole picture again to find where we went wrong."

Several hours passed in almost absolute silence as Conrad, Romero and Jacobs re-read all of the case documentation. Halfway through, Schleicher joined them with the files from Vice. Eventually, Conrad pushed the file he was reading away and sighed.

"As far as I can see, there's only one other part of the puzzle that doesn't fit properly and that's the closing down of *The Hunters*. It seems to me that closing down what seemed to have every prospect of being a profitable and successful show was a very expensive way of making a point. Doesn't it smell to you as if they were trying to choke off an investigation?"

"Could be." Romero was thoughtful. "Although the connection, or rather the absence of any connection, between the legitimate studios and the adult film industry is something that the legitimate industry is very keen on preserving. I wonder if Bill Shaych would be willing to give a little more advice?"

Conrad dialed the number. There was a single ring before the phone was picked up.

"Shaych Productions here."

"Good morning, Ellen. Conrad here; you're on speaker. Could I talk to Bill please?"

"He's available, ducks. Hold on." There were a few clicks on the line. "Bill here, Conrad. What can we so for you?"

"Bill, you must have heard by now of what happened when *The Hunters* went down. Doesn't that seem a little excessive to you?"

There was a few moments thought.

"Depends. Television series are made two ways. One is that the studio itself can make them using its own resources and so on. If *The Hunters* was made that way, then closing the show down would be the only way they could get clear. However, a growing number of shows are made by independent production companies, like ours, and sold to the network. If *The Hunters* was made that way, then a barrier between the show and the company would exist. The network would do something horrible to the production company, including firing them and replacing them with a rival, but they would be unlikely to shut the show down completely. Hold on a minute."

Conrad heard the muffled and indecipherable noise of somebody speaking with their hand over the receiver. After an unintelligible conversation, Bill Shaych's voice cleared again.

"Right, *The Hunters* was made by an independent production company working under contract to the network. Shooting Star Productions. That's undoubtedly a subsidiary created specifically for that show. If you can find who their parent is, you have who actually made the show."

"Thanks, Bill. That is very helpful."

By the time Conrad had put the receiver down, Schleicher was already on the phone.

"Hi, Jack. Who owned Shooting Star Productions? . . .

"OK, and who owns them? . . .

"All right! Thank you."

"Now guys, we have something interesting. Shooting Star Productions was liquidated when *The Hunters* was cancelled but, before that, it was a subsidiary of Mountain View Productions. And majority ownership of Mountain View Productions is held by, wait for it, Mark Devers. Now who amongst us find that interesting?"

"More interesting is who shall obtain the warrants." Ed Jacobs sounded enthused. "Homicide or Vice?"

"Both!"

Interrogation Room Two, Hollywood Police Station, 1358 North Wilcox Avenue, Hollywood

"He really is very good, isn't he?"

Schleicher was impressed by what she was seeing. Devers was proving to be a perfect example of why people in police interrogation rooms shouldn't say anything. He was talking himself into a prison sentence and his lawyer couldn't save him. He had just finished a long exposition on how he had shut down production of *The Hunters*, at considerable loss to himself and his company, the moment he had found out that the facilities his company had provided were being misused. It had sounded like an excellent defense, until Conrad had asked a single, deadly question.

"If that is the case, Mister Devers, could you explain why we have found that nearly all the television shows produced by Mountain View Productions subsidiaries over the last decade have shared sets with adult films produced during the same period?

"One would be unfortunate. Two, a coincidence. Twelve seems to be something more than that. There may be more. The Vice Division is still investigating the phenomena, and the total may well be many more than the dozen we have found so far."

Dever's lawyer restrained himself from breaking his pencil in half and throwing the pieces in the air.

"I think that merely goes to show the extent to which my client was deluded by the people he had trusted. When he found out, he moved against them with all the power at his disposal. He is the victim here."

"Well, this gives us another problem. You see, we have film and photographs of your client accepting payments from the pornographer in question, four years before he shut down production of *The Hunters*. So, since he was aware then of the misuse of the facilities in question, why didn't he move at that time?"

"I was being blackmailed. Can't you see that? I am the victim here."

"The only victim here is the girl who died on your set. Your lawyer will tell you that, if anybody dies as a result of a criminal act, all those associated with the criminal act in question are equally liable for the death of that person. So, depending on whether the forensic analysis of the film supports a charge of murder in the second degree or manslaughter in the first degree, you can and will be charged with that murder."

"But I knew nothing about the death of Theresa MacCray until . . . . ."

"How did you know her name, Mister Devers?" Conrad's voice was its normal, quiet self. Yet the question seemed to crash through the room and bounce around the walls. "I never mentioned it and the film clip gives her name as Tobiana."

This time Dever's lawyer did break his pencil in half and throw it into the air. He had just watched his client convict himself and been unable to stop him.

"Is there a deal on offer here?"

"What do you mean, a deal?" Devers was furious and also a very frightened man. He had suddenly realized that he might have been a big man in the studio world, but those days had ended abruptly the moment his secret business had been exposed. He was on his own.

"A deal over what?"

"The Father here is right. As a participant in the crime of making illegal films with underage persons, you are also guilty of the deaths of any of those persons. That poor girl died of positional asphyxia. If the film shows that the crew were aware that she was dying and did nothing to help her, then they showed depraved indifference to her death. That is a textbook definition of murder in the second degree. If they were not aware that she was dying, they caused her death by gross negligence. That is a textbook definition of manslaughter in the first degree. By using the girl's name, you showed you knew she was employed making that film and were thus party to her death. With those two words, you convicted yourself. So, I ask again, is there a deal on offer here?"

Jacobs had sworn to himself that he wouldn't say a word this time. Anyway, Romero had to make the call, so he waved his partner in. Romero and Schleicher entered the room, taking the two remaining chairs.

Romero sighed slightly. "At the moment, the forensic analysis of the film is not complete. Until it is, we'll offer first-degree manslaughter. That will carry three to eleven years. In California, even a killing that wasn't intentional may be treated as a first-degree murder if it happened during an inherently dangerous felony, which can include rape, carjacking, robbery, arson, kidnapping, burglary or mayhem. This is called the felony-murder rule. If we have to wait until the Vice Division make their determination, we will go for first-degree murder, not second degree. The penalty is death or life imprisonment. To be honest, probably the latter.

So, Mister Devers, you have the choice of three to eleven or life. All you have to do is make a full confession now. Take your pick."

Dever's lawyer balked. "I understand that there was a similar case where the film crew were charged with involuntary manslaughter and got two to four. I want that for my client."

"You're not going to get it." Schleicher cut in and her voice was grim. "I was on that case. The film crew realized the girl was in trouble. They called an ambulance for her. When the police cruisers and emergency medical services arrived, they were still giving her CPR and they stayed with her until she was in hospital. She still died, but they tried their best to save her and went down because of it. So, they got a break. Your client and his team threw Theresa MacCray's body out like a piece of trash. First degree voluntary manslaughter; three to eleven and that's being really nice."

A long sigh from Dever's lawyer filled the room. "Take it, Mark. It's the best you'll get. They'll make that murder charge stick."

"All right, all right. About eight, nine years ago, I set the production company up. It was simple. We'd do TV shows for the networks and the fees would pay for the sets. Then, we'd use the sets for adult films, while Leadingham's agency provided the actors and actresses from young hopefuls. It cut our production costs way down and the money just rolled in. Well, it did to me. Leadingham was already complaining that he was having a job making his payments to the people who had bankrolled him. He was beginning to fall behind and you know what that means. Unpaid points get added to the capital and the payment soars. In the end, we went to using underage actresses so we could make even more money. Leadingham insisted; he threatened to blow the whole thing public if we didn't. By this time, he was so far in the hole that he was capable of anything. We covered up the death of Theresa MacCray."

"We want to know where the body is." Conrad's voice was ice cold. "That poor girl deserves a Christian burial."

"I'll show you. Anyway, when Angie and the others discovered the film we had made on the set of *The Hunters*, in my capacity as programmer I closed the whole show down. It was the only way to stop a major investigation. I made a big thing of how we had to close down every point of contamination and, because I made such a fuss about the ones people knew about, they never asked if there were any more. I think they were afraid of the answer anyway. We carried on with our other locations.

"It was quite easy, I just used our adult film crews as security guards. But, Leadingham was sliding deeper and deeper into the hole. Even the illegal films we were making weren't enough anymore. He wanted to go into blackmail and he started with the Theresa MacCray death. He sent his gofer over with pictures and the message. Pictures that showed me taking my share of the loot. I think he also tried his blackmail on other people, probably Grainger and even his gofer. Anyway, Leadingham and Grainger were blown up and that ended things."

Conrad knew now what had happened. "The photographs of Theresa MacCray's body were in the package, weren't they?"

Devers nodded and Conrad continued. "And you showed them to that driver, knowing that he was Marvin MacCray. Theresa's father. MacCray went to see Leadingham and confirmed that his daughter was dead. He probably got told some story that put Leadingham in the clear and he didn't believe a word of it. He held Grainger and Leadingham responsible for killing his daughter. He killed them both. With nothing left to live for, he didn't care he was taking himself out in the process."

"Just as you knew he would when you showed him that picture." Romero finished the sentence.

"Mark Devers, in accordance with the agreement made with your attorney, we are charging you with the first degree voluntary manslaughter of Theresa MacCray. In addition, we are charging you with the murder in the second degree of Roman Leadingham and Clyde Grainger. We said nothing about charges from the Paramount bombing.

"Get him out of my sight before I throw up."

The Code Seven Diner, North Hollywood

"If certain special circumstances are proven, the prosecution can ask for the death penalty. These circumstances include murder during the commission of another felony, the murder of a law enforcement officer or judge or murder by a destructive device like a bomb. The DA is working out now if we can get him on first-degree murder charges. There's case history that suggests we might."

"Any word on the Steinsdottir woman?"

"You were right, Father. The DA is having a job finding a meaty charge to hold her on. Plenty of misdemeanors, but no felonies. Tax evasion is the most serious and she could easily negotiate a deal on that. My guess is she'll do probation."

Conrad's Eye

Romero looked awkward.

"Look, Ed, I'm sorry to tell you this, but we won't be working together any more. Frankly, Glennie and I are sick of this cesspit of a town and we want out. We're going to Sacramento; the Governor is forming a state-wide investigation unit to deal with crimes that cross county and category boundaries. We applied and we've both been accepted. So, we'll be moving out in a month or two."

Ed Jacobs nodded. "Actually, with Miriam going to college on FBI money and Rebecca going to medical school, Kelly and I have nothing to hold us here. And this case has nauseated both of us. We're moving out as well. To Sacramento, as it happens. You see, the Governor is forming a state-wide investigation unit to deal with crimes that cross county and category boundaries. We applied and we've both been accepted. So, we'll be moving out in a month or two. Oddly enough, just about the same time you and Glennie do. Conrad, you be joining us in Sacramento as well?"

Conrad laughed at the way Jacobs had exactly duplicated the words his partner had used, but shook his head.

"I go where God directs me. And, there are too many innocents who are being wrongly accused to stay here. But, I'll pray for all of you."

After the party broke up, Conrad took a taxi to the inner-city airport. The cab took him to the eighth floor of the multi-story parking lot and dropped him off. From there, it was a one-floor elevator ride to the passenger terminal on the top. The rotodyne was due to land in ten minutes and it was a simple matter to buy a ticket and wait.

Purely by chance, Conrad had a window seat. After stowing his bag in the cargo section, he sat down to wait for takeoff. In the row in front, a man was lecturing his companions on the subject of victimless crimes and how any crime he deemed to be victimless should be struck from the books. From the sound of it, he was a tutor of some kind and his companions were his students. Conrad shook his head and ignored him.

A few minutes before take-off, a woman with a very excited pre-teenage daughter in tow arrived to sit in the same row as Conrad. The rotodyne had five-abreast seating, with the aisle between the third and fourth seats. Conrad took a quick look at the woman and her child. It was obviously their first trip on a Rotodyne and the girl was squealing with delight.

"Excuse me ma'am, would you like to swap seats with me so your daughter can look out of the window?"

The woman flashed a smile of relief, but shook her head.

"I couldn't ask you to do that."

"Ma'am, you'll be doing me a favor. I'm getting on a bit and . . . " Conrad looked pointedly at the rest room at the front of the cabin.

The woman suddenly looked understanding. "Oh, of course. Denise, the nice Father says you can have his window seat. Say thank you."

The girl slid into the window seat just as the Kuznetsov turboprops spooled up for take-off. She bounced up and down in her seat with excitement. Her feet kicked backwards and forwards with the sheer joy of a new experience. And so it was that the tutor who had been pontificating about victimless crimes spent the hour and a quarter of his flight with a constant barrage of excited kicks in the back of his seat.

God, thought Conrad as he left the rotodyne in San Francisco, *works in mysterious ways.*

Conrad's Eye

EYE OF THE SEDUCER
Havana, Cuba, 1975

Conrad's Eye

CHAPTER ONE

24th Floor, Imperial Forum Hotel-Casino, Havana, Cuba, 1975

These were the floors for the high-rollers; those who gambled more on a single hand than most tourists in Cuba bet during their entire stay. A mark of their exclusivity was that they could only be accessed by turning a special key in the elevator control panel. Once up here, the high-rollers were in a different world. They had their own casino, they had their own restaurant, even their own shops, where luxury design houses either sold their wares at discounted prices or simply gave them away, knowing that having a suit, evening gown or jewelry seen on the people who stayed on this floor would guarantee a level of good publicity and sales that far outweighed the cost of the deals.

Hubert Trumpeter was a high-roller. Not just in gambling, but in life as a whole. He'd made his money in real estate speculation, anticipating the suburban housing boom of the 1950s as the veterans from the Russian Front came back and wanted a peaceful home for themselves and their families. A home somewhere warm, for these were men who had seen real snow and never wanted to see it again. Trumpeter had bought old farms and estates at rock-bottom prices, subdivided them and built cookie-cutter houses on the pieces. His niche was that he sold the houses complete, appliances, furniture, everything needed so a family could move right in. Mostly, it never occurred to the purchasers that they were buying overpriced consumer goods with a five or ten-year life and paying for them on a thirty-year mortgage.

Those houses had made Trumpeter's fortune for him; the slogan 'A Trumpeter Home' had come to be a by-word in real estate. By the time the by-word lost its luster and become synonymous with overpriced, shoddy construction, he had sold out and the company was far removed from his interests. The people who had bought his houses and found that their investments were worth far less than they had been lead to believe were somebody else's problem, not his. He'd already invested the money he had made from them in commercial property, just in time to catch the building boom of the early 1960s. The same principle had held good; build property, build lots of it, build it cheap and shoddy, get out before people find out what they'd bought.

He'd bailed again, just before the growth of building codes and safety regulations had shut down his commercial building operations and stuck his customers with huge bills to bring their property up to the new codes. Now he was on the hunt for a new business venture that would make him quick money. That brought him to Cuba. Here, if anywhere, there was money to be made. The glow of lights from Havana's Golden Boulevard proved that. The casinos were opening up to investment from legitimate business interests, Pan American and TWA had already gone into partnership with the people who ran this country to build their own casino-hotels. Others were following; not just casinos but leisure resorts, theme parks, everything. For all the growing diversity, it was still the casinos that made the money. That is where Hubert Trumpeter wanted in.

He stopped outside his hotel room, fumbling for the key in his pocket. He'd been to visit the Cadillac dealer on this floor. They didn't have the cars up here, but they had everything else. All the information; specifications, film shows, pictures, and financing arrangements. The cars were down in the basement garage. All he had to do was to say what he wanted and he could have one for a day, or more, to drive around and get the feel of it. Trumpeter didn't actually want a Cadillac, but he needed to let everybody know he was a man of wealth, of consequence. So he had to be seen to be at least interested in useless accessories.

Speaking of useless accessories, Trumpeter thought quickly about his wife. He'd divorced his first wife soon after his first real estate business had taken off and acquired a much younger model to take her place. With a prenuptial agreement that made sure she wouldn't get a penny of his money, of course. *Not that she is bright enough to take me to the financial cleaners; her IQ is less than her bust measurement.* Which, in his eyes, was a qualification.

The only thing she's been able to talk about since the news of their trip to Cuba had been which designer evening gowns she'd wear for her first appearance in the casino. The cost of her final selection came pretty close to that of a Cadillac come to think of it. At least part of the reason why Trumpeter had gone to look at the Caddies was to get away from her eternal prattle.

He found the key at last and opened up the door. He'd expected to see his wife ready to go down to the casino, but the room was quiet and empty.

"Darling?"

There was still no sound. *That is odd. I would have expected some sort of reply, even if only a grunt or whine.*

"Darling, are you ready to go out?"

Still no reply. He frowned again and went into the bedroom of their suite only to stop dead at the door.

His wife was lying on the bed. Duct tape over her eyes and mouth, her hands taped behind her back. The dress she had finally chosen had been halter-necked. Now the top was torn and pulled down around her waist. The skirt of her gown had been hauled up, leaving her exposed legs spread. Trumpeter didn't need to get closer to fill the rest of the details in.

He was in an agony of doubt. His first instinct was to move her, to cover her, to get the tape off her. But a voice in his head kept reminding him that he had to preserve the evidence. He could hear her breathing; labored, but she was breathing. He made his decision. He picked up the telephone, dialing 0 for the switchboard.

"Operator, get some help up to Suite 2415. My wife has been attacked."

High Stakes Poker Room, Imperial Forum Hotel-Casino, Havana, Cuba, 1975

The exposed cards were the two of spades, four of diamonds, five of clubs and the seven of hearts. Igrat's hole cards were a jack and a ten of clubs. That left her with no possibility of getting more than a pair. But, on the other hand, it would be a good pair. If she got it. The table was down to three; as the seven had been flopped, one of her opponents had thrown his hand in. That left just her and the man opposite.

"Raise you ninety thousand."

The man pushed the chips forward, then grinned at her. He'd counted her chips; there was no way she could call the bet. Despite her winning streak, she'd only fifty thousand, give or take a little. In her eyes, going all-in was a measure of weakness and failure.

"You take payment in kind?" Igrat's voice was dead steady and virtually emotionless.

"Got no use for your jewels, babe."

"Not my jewels. Me. For three days. No restrictions, no limits."

There was a gasp around the table. She heard a man's voice, pitched low. "Now *that's* what I call poker."

The man looked at the bet and the balance of chips. "Seven days."

"Five."

Conrad's Eye

"Done."

The pit boss appeared by magic, bending down to whisper in the man's ear.

"Sir, if the lady reneges on the terms of your bet, the casino can only stand surety for the cash equivalent. Forty thou." The pit boss could count chips as well.

"Sure, I understand. Look at her; don't you think it's a chance worth taking?"

The pit boss grinned in agreement, then went over to Igrat.

"Lady, you understand, if you welsh on this bet, the casino will collect the cash equivalent off you, one way or another."

It was Igrat's turn to grin. "I've never welshed on a bet in my life."

"Glad to hear it, lady." The pit boss raised his voice. "Very well, play."

The croupier burned the top card on the deck; discarded in case the players had it marked or otherwise recognized it. Then he dealt the next one.

The jack of spades.

The man opposite Igrat exposed his hole cards, the king of diamonds and the queen of hearts. He grinned at Igrat, with a level of anticipation.

"Gentleman has king-high."

There was a stir around the table; in a low-value hand, that was good. Igrat exposed her two hole cards and the stir became a gasp.

"And the lady has a pair of jacks. The lady wins."

Igrat reached out and scooped up the pool of chips. She'd paid her five thousand to the casino to join this game and managed to build her ten thousand stake up to $140,000. *It is time to stop.* She glanced around the table, noting the disappointment in the eyes of the women. *They'd wanted to see me lose.*

"I'll cash out now, thank you."

"Very well, ma'am. One of the boys will escort you over to the cashier's station."

Igrat smiled her thanks and flipped a chip to the croupier. "Thank you for an interesting game."

As she turned to leave, the man she had been playing spoke up for the first time after the hand had been played out.

"Babe, if you ever want a replay on that bet, just call me."

Igrat half turned, looking over her shoulder. One of her carefully-shaped eyebrows arched. The skirt of her evening gown swirled around her legs.

"I might take you up on that." Then she and her escort were gone.

A few minutes later, she was stowing her money in her bag, having tipped the man who had escorted her to the cashier's cage. It wasn't really necessary, but the escort by a mob gunman was all part of the image of high-stakes gambling here in Cuba. A couple of seconds later, Igrat wished the man was still with her. Inanna was standing by the hotel elevator, her face tight with rage.

"Igrat, are you insane, making a bet like that? If you'd lost, he could have done *anything* to you. Just what in hell were you thinking?"

"The doing anything bit was the point. And I didn't lose. As to what I was thinking, I wanted to win and the odds were pretty good."

"You always did have the morals of an alley-cat." Inanna's voice was sour and bitter; spiteful, even. "It would have served you right if you had lost."

"I fight like an alley-cat as well. Just remember that before you start with the insults. Not that I'd have fought him. I said no limits. That would have given him rights you don't have."

"Rights? We're supposed to be working here."

"Not now. I've delivered the package of data to Meyer's boys and he's making up our return parcel now. It'll be ready in seven days. Until then, we're on vacation. If I'd lost, I'd have had plenty of time to clear the bet, hide the bruises and do my job. So get off my back."

Igrat looked at Inanna again and decided it was time to let it drop. "Look, this is Cuba, right? The tourists, and that includes us, never really get hurt here. At worst, I'd have spent a few days doing the horizontal tango and got my rump paddled. OK? Anything more and the boys would be breaking the door down. I knew it; he knew it. So no real risk."

Igrat comfortingly patted Inanna on the arm while her other hand slipped Inanna's room key out of her bag.

Having to call room service to get back into her room is justifiable revenge for the alley-cat remark.

The elevator doors opened onto a floor reception area filled with men in gray suits. One of them, obviously the man in charge, reacted to the doors opening, his hand sliding under his jacket.

"You staying on this floor ladies?"

Igrat nodded, her eyes taking in the scene.

Conrad's Eye

"Best you go straight to your rooms; we gotta problem here."

Senate Bar, Imperial Forum Hotel-Casino, Havana, Cuba

"I'll have a pale sherry, please. The best one you have."

Conrad Lorentz settled on his stool and smiled politely at the woman behind the bar. She checked the bottles and lifted a distinguished-looking example off the shelf. Conrad looked quickly at the label; it was indeed a very good sherry.

"That will be perfect; thank you, Samuela."

The bartender poured out his glass, put a glass coaster and paper doily on the bar and then served the drink.

"Here you are, sir. Room tab?"

"Yes please." Conrad produced his room pass. Samuela looked at it, then gave him the chit to sign.

Conrad sipped his sherry, looking around the room with an eye long-practiced at insight into the human condition. A surprising number of the couples in the Senate Bar were married; a slightly smaller number were actually married to each other. *Well*, thought Conrad, *Cuba is America's playground.*

He was well aware that, by his calling, he should condemn the sin of adultery, but long, long ago he had made a vow not to judge until he knew all the facts. Even then, he would take the greatest care, because making judgment lay with others. In the final analysis, it lay with God and him alone. The same God who had judged Conrad guilty and sentenced him to life eternal. A couple of the other women were paid escorts. Again, Conrad refrained from criticizing them, even to himself. That was a lesson he had learned from Nell Gwynne.

"Excuse me, I'm sorry to trouble you, sir, but isn't it . . . "

The polite touch on Conrad's shoulder turned him around. At once, he was glad he'd taken care to age his appearance. Nothing dramatic, just shaved off most of his hair, cropped the rest close to his skull so that its color wasn't obvious and let himself sag a little rather than hold himself erect. Added up to a man who looked twenty years older than Conrad's normal appearance. Which was about right.

"Joe! Joe Catalina. How are you?"

Joe "Pants" Catalina settled down on the stool next to Conrad, his face grinning delightedly.

"Doing very well; very well, indeed. Yourself?"

"A bit older; a bit wiser." Conrad looked at his companion. The young hoodlum he'd known a quarter of a century earlier had matured and put on a lot more weight. "You're looking pretty prosperous. How's Frankie?"

Catalina rubbed his stomach. "Occupational hazard. Every time we hit the mattresses, the boys spend their time cooking spaghetti and meatballs. Get towards middle age and it all catches up. Frankie, he's running the family business back in San Francisco these days. Me, I'm running them out here. Are Nell, Achillea and Nammie with you?"

Conrad shook his head. "I'm afraid not. They all still work for the NSC though. I just came out here on a whim."

That isn't a lie, not quite. I did come to Cuba on a whim, but my whims never come by accident. "Can I get you a drink? Samuela here really knows her business; best bar tender I've seen in years."

The woman overheard and smiled broadly. A customer praising her skills to the boss was never a bad thing. She'd instinctively liked the man who'd bought her best sherry and now her judgment had been confirmed. She also knew what her boss drank and had it ready for him instantly. Conrad nodded slightly and she put it on his bar tab before Catalina could argue about it.

"OK, next round's on me. Anyway, what are you doing with yourself these days? Still investigating . . . "

Catalina was interrupted by a buzz in his pocket. "I'm sorry, I'll have to take this. Bar phone, please, Sam."

Samuela produced a telephone from under the bar and handed it over. Catalina punched a three digit extension number in and introduced himself. Then he listened and went white. He put the phone down as gingerly as an unexploded bomb.

"I do hope you are, because I need your help. Badly. Lady's been attacked on the 24th floor. A tourist."

Catalina scowled for a second, his cheerful good humor dropping away. "Damn it, nobody *ever* attacks a tourist here. It's about the only law we enforce. Just what the hell is going on?"

Suite 2415, 24th Floor, Imperial Forum Hotel-Casino

"Don't do that." The gunman's voice was sharp and insistent.

The doctor stopped. He had been about to pull the tape off the woman's mouth, but he paused at the command. It was always best to do that when one of Cuba's made men gave an order.

"She's starting to choke. We've got to clear her air way."

"That's industrial-strength duct tape. You rip it off, the skin around her mouth will go with it. Leave her face scarred for life and she won't thank you for that. She's OK for a few minutes more."

The doctor looked uncertain.

"Look, Doc, my line of business we know duct tape and skin right? Domestic stuff bought down the local store, that's one thing. The stuff there is another. You got surgical spirit?"

"Whole bottle of it."

"Right, use that to soak the tape. It'll dissolve the glue. Then the stuff will peel off, no harm done. We'll worry about her eyes later."

Doctor Franklin soaked a cotton wool ball in the surgical spirit and started wiping the strip of tape where a corner had got lifted. The woman's breathing was getting steadily more labored as he worked. When the glue had started to dissolve, the tape lifted off. There were a couple of sore spots around her lips, but the Franklin didn't worry about those. Instead, he opened the woman's mouth and pulled out a wad of fine fabric. Her breathing immediately eased and became steady and regular.

"She'll be fine now. Emergency over."

He fingered the tape. Now he looked at it, the gangster had been right. It was thicker and heavier than the type he was familiar with. He looked over at another gangster, who had been using a switchblade to cut the tape on Mrs. Trumpeter's hands.

"You were right; how did you know?"

"As I said, Doc, we know duct tape in our line of business. You know either the guy who did this didn't know there were different kinds of tape, or he had a really nasty mind."

"What happened?" The voice was sharp, insistent, commanding. Doctor Franklin looked up with some shock. Out of simple decency, he'd ordered that people be kept out of this room until the crew from the local hospital got here to move Mrs. Trumpeter. In the mean time, he'd put a sheet over her legs to cover her. As a doctor, he wasn't used to his instructions concerning patients to be blandly ignored. *Once again*, he had to remind himself, *Cuba is different*.

"Tourist came back to his room. Found his wife in here. Been attacked, raped. She's alive, doesn't seem too badly hurt. Crew from Alphonse Capone Memorial are on their way here."

The made man spoke quickly, efficiently. Joe Catalina headed the Cuban Crew of the Bay Area Family; that made him a man of respect.

"May I see her hands?"

Catalina's companion asked politely. The made man glanced at Catalina and got an almost imperceptible nod. Conrad took her right hand and looked carefully under the nails. Then he repeated the process, frowning.

"Doctor, were there any defensive wounds on her arms? Bruising around her forearms, or up by her shoulders?"

"I don't think so; we'll know more when I get her to hospital. Alphonse Capone Memorial you said?" The Doctor's voice was slightly incredulous when he repeated the name. Obviously, he hadn't been in Cuba long enough to fully realize just how different the place was.

"That's odd." Conrad spoke thoughtfully. "I'd have expected her to put up some sort of a fight."

"Perhaps he had a gun or a knife on her?"

"I don't think so; the way she's out of it, I'd say she was drugged and pretty heavily. Again, we'll know more when we get her to hospital." Franklin was interrupted by the banging of a trolley. A medical team came in, pushing a gurney, scattering the suite's inhabitants before them.

"This her?"

"This is Mrs. Trumpeter. Be careful; the tape on her eyes is industrial strength stuff. We used surgical spirit to get it off her mouth, but we didn't want to chance any getting into her eyes."

"Thanks for the warning. Good thing you spotted it, Doctor . . . "

"Franklin, Jim Franklin. My wife and I were staying in the hotel and we got an emergency call."

"Tyler, Andrew Tyler. I'll take over now if you wish. Or, if you prefer, you can ride with us back to the hospital. Trauma?"

"Rape. No knife or gunshot wounds I could see. She doesn't appear to have been beaten, so there shouldn't be anything internal we can't see. The thing that worries me is this coma. I'd like to stay on the case, if I may."

"Glad to have you on board. AC Memorial it is."

As Franklin was leaving, Catalina stopped him for a second. "Thanks for the help, Doc. You and your wife are comped for the rest of your stay with us. On everything. And my Capo will be offended if you don't live high."

Conrad's Eye

The doctor nodded. That was an invitation he hadn't sought but, since one had been made, he would take full advantage of it.

Next order of business, Catalina sighed.

"Mr. Hubert Trumpeter? Your wife's on her way to the hospital right now. We've got two of the best doctors we can find looking after her and she's going to the best hospital in Havana. Now she's in safe hands, we can find out who did this and make him wish he'd never been born. Could you come into the bedroom, please? We need to know if anything is missing."

Trumpeter walked into the room, looking around and visibly flinching when he saw the bed.

"So that's where he did it."

It wasn't a question, but Conrad answered it anyway. "We think so; nothing's certain at this time, Mr. Trumpeter."

There was something in the way Conrad said the words that made Catalina look at him sharply. Whatever it was, Trumpeter hadn't noticed it. He went to one of the cupboards and opened it, revealing the small safe inside. The door was open and it was empty.

"My wife's jewelry. It's all gone. Every piece of it."

"Can you describe what's missing?"

"I can do better. Contact my insurance company; they have photographs and assay reports of everything. I guess your insurance company is going to want those as well."

Joe Catalina's Office, Imperial Forum Hotel-Casino

"You know, there's a lot that doesn't quite add up about this." Conrad spoke mildly, but his words drew nods of agreement from the others in Catalina's office.

"Ya think?"

'Dapper John' Gotti eased himself onto the corner of Catalina's desk. "I'd say there's a few things that do add up, and they ain't in a majority. Just who are you, anyway?"

The question was addressed to Conrad, but Gotti expected the answer from Catalina. The news that a tourist had been attacked had gone right to the top of the Mob in Cuba. Meyer Lansky himself had been woken to hear the message and he'd alerted the members of the Commission. They'd called in Gotti, whose

390

security group was the nearest thing Cuba had to a police force. He answered directly to the Commission and to nobody else.

"We worked together a long time ago. Remember the Black Dahlia case? Our friend here was the key investigator for that." Catalina spoke with respect. Although a much younger man, Gotti outranked him and, in any case, had an air about him that inspired respect.

"A bull?" Gotti's voice was a mixture of contempt and dislike.

"I'm an investigator, not a policeman. I work for a charitable foundation that investigates cases where an innocent person might be, or have been, wrongly accused. I'm not interested in solving crimes, only in ensuring an innocent person doesn't get punished."

Conrad wanted to get that point established early. He didn't think it mattered much; the way these people were going about the investigation showed they hadn't got a clue about proper investigation procedure. They hadn't even taken the most obvious steps in getting started.

"And most times, that means catching the guilty party, right?" Gotti looked at Conrad curiously.

"It might."

"Hm. So, Mister Investigator, what's the first thing that doesn't add up here?"

Conrad thought carefully. There were so many things that fluttered around on the edge of his consciousness.

"It's the top floor, the most secure place in the hotel. Key access only using the elevator. Yet the person who did this got in and out without being seen. The safe was opened up. I'd guess the room safes are as burglar-proof as they get." Conrad decided to permit himself a little joke. "After all, if anybody knows which safes are tough to crack, you guys must."

"So you think it's an inside job?"

"How can it be? Who here has the skills to do something like this? I'd say there are several cracksmen on the mainland who could, but why would they commit suicide by coming here to stage a robbery? Its not as if Trumpeter was so wealthy it made the price of a life running worth paying. Rich, yes; but not that rich. Then we have Mrs. Trumpeter. We are guessing she was drugged, so heavily that she still hasn't woken up, and may not, by the way. So why tie her up like that?"

"I can answer that." Gotti's voice was larded with contempt; not directed at Conrad, but at the unknown person who had started all this. "It's a passive hit.

The bastard hasn't got the guts to kill her, so he just puts her in a position where her death is pretty much inevitable. Way I hear it, her mouth was so stuffed up, she would have choked in a few more minutes. That way, if he gets caught, he can try to get away with manslaughter."

There was a round of laughter at the idea of somebody trying to get away with a legal technicality in Cuba. Nobody ever made a living practicing law in Cuba.

"That suggests an outsider as well then, doesn't it? In fact, everybody on the mainland knows that as well. That means we're talking about a real outsider. Or somebody very stupid."

Conrad thought for a second. "Anything else odd happen this evening up there?"

Catalina picked up the phone on his desk and called Guest Services. "Just a lady left the key to her suite inside, had to ask for help to get in. Wait a minute." Catalina suddenly chuckled. "Well, wadya know. Lady is from our old friends the National Security Council. So's her companion. Names are Inanna Porco and Igrat Shafrid. Know them?"

"I do, yes. I believe Igrat, Miss Shafrid, is mostly a courier. Its NSC practice to send couriers in pairs, or even trios, depending in the risk."

"That's right." Gotti confirmed the information. "They're over here bringing a package of information relating to our security here; we're sending back a pack of stuff we've picked up from our associates."

There was a quiet, unspoken agreement between the U.S. Government and the Commission in Cuba, one that dated from the Biowar two years earlier. The U.S. advised the Commission of anything they picked up that might be a threat to the island. A significant proportion of Cuba's fabulous profits were shared out with other organized crime groups around the world. They kept Cuba advised of any dangers to its security also. Any of that information relevant to U.S. interests went back to Washington, in exchange for their help and discrete protection. It was a way the United States had adopted to work around its weakness in human intelligence on the rest of the world. The events of the Biowar had shown that reconnaissance aircraft and satellites were great for seeing what people were doing, but rarely showed why they were doing it.

"If they're anything like Nammie, Nell and Achillea, they're something really special." Catalina's voice was heavy with fond reminiscence. "When Achillea kicked a door open, it didn't just open, it shattered. Dapper John, you ain't never seen anything like it. What do you know about these two?"

The last remark was obviously directed at Conrad.

"Only a little. They're from OSS. Office of Strategic Security, the security arm of NSC. Mostly, they carry material too sensitive to trust to any communications system. They also do investigations now and then, where something falls in the gap between DCI and the FBI. If you want to have a run-down on how easy it would be to steal from a suite up on the 24th, ask Igrat. She's an accomplished thief."

"I see. So we have an 'accomplished thief' on the 24th floor, and that floor has a tourist attacked and robbed." Gotti's voice was thoughtful.

"I think we had better have a word with Miss Shafrid."

Suite 2415, 24th Floor, Imperial Forum Hotel-Casino

"Been in here before Doll?"

Igrat looked around. "Same layout as my suite. Bedroom through there?"

"That's right, but you didn't answer the question. Try again. You been in here before?"

"Why do you want to know?"

Gotti looked at her. "Still not answering. We could try hurting you until you do." It was a mildly-voiced suggestion, and none the less serious for that.

"It's been tried. It doesn't work. Try telling me why you want to know and we may move a bit faster." She looked at Gotti calmly, mentally wondering how far she could needle him.

"OK, Miss Shafrid. We'll try it your way. Lady here tonight was attacked, raped and robbed. Our friend here tells us you are a first-class thief. So we wondered if you did the heist."

Igrat looked at Conrad with one of her eyebrows arched. "Why, thank you Conrad. So kind of you to think of me. I'll do the same for you, one of these days."

"Well?" Gotti was getting impatient. Igrat decided that it was time to end the game.

"One, I couldn't do the rape. I don't have the equipment."

Gotti laughed. One of his men spoke up from a corner.

"It's true, boss. She was in the bath when we got her. She's got the best equipment I've ever seen on a lady, but not one of them."

Igrat smiled contentedly and blew the gangster a kiss. He made a play of catching it and carefully stowing it away. Gotti wasn't amused.

"You can buy an imitation, any store here. Be a good way of diverting suspicion."

"True, but I was playing Texas Hold'em in your high-stakes casino, from eight to ten-thirty. Your staff will confirm that; I can promise it. When was this attack carried out?"

"Between ten and ten-thirty."

Gotti picked up the telephone and called down to the casino. A minute later, he put the phone down.

"So you're the dame who staked herself to cover a bet. Should have guessed. I heard about that on the way to deal with this affair. OK, you're off the hook; no way you can be in two places at once. Staff confirm about sixty people were looking at you when Mrs. Trumpeter was being attacked. So why didn't you just say so straight away. Instead of mouthing off?"

"Girl's just got to have fun, Dapper John. Now, what else do you want to know?"

"How a place up here with a secure safe can get robbed."

"Secure safe?" Igrat was scornful. "Is it locked now?"

Gotti nodded.

Igrat went into the bedroom and looked at the safe. "Same as the one in my suite. Watch this."

She took a nail file out from the pocket of her bathrobe and ran it across the fingertips of her right hand. Then, she delicately touched the dial lock on the front of the safe and started to rotate it. Thirty seconds later, the door swung open.

"That's a good-quality vault, but no small safe like that is secure. It's only good for protecting things from sneak thieves and light-fingered staff. Opening the safe wasn't hard; getting in here was. That's where you should be looking. Now, can I go back to my suite and get dressed?"

CHAPTER TWO

Joe Catalina's Office, Imperial Forum Hotel-Casino

"Hadn't you better decide what the primary crime was first?"

Conrad had already decided to provide some help to this investigation. *Beside my friendship with Joe Catalina, there is a very reasonable probability that the people here will so foul up the investigation that the perpetrator will get clean away. Then, the gangsters will pick up somebody at random, probably one of the hotel staff, and kill them, just to give the illusion that somebody had been caught and punished. In fairness to them, that is an impression they have to give. The whole Cuban economy depends on tourists being safe here.*

"We know what the crime was." Gotti spoke petulantly, then paused and thought. "Don't we?"

"We've got two crimes here; rape and robbery. Now, which is the primary crime? Did the man who did this intend to rob the suite, find Mrs. Trumpeter there and take the opportunity? Or did he come with rape as his intention, find the safe open and decide to help himself to its contents? The answer to that question defines the kind of man we're looking for. That's our first step."

Conrad was interrupted by the telephone ringing. Joe Catalina picked it up. After a few seconds, he stopped the person on the other end.

"Hang on a moment, Doc. I'll put this on speaker."

"This is Doctor Tyler here. You'll be pleased to know there are no signs of any serious injury to Mrs. Trumpeter, other than her coma, which is indeed drug-induced. Depending on the level of overdose, she should be out of danger in about five to ten hours and we'll be keeping her in the intensive care unit until then. We've got blood tests running on her now and we've pumped out her stomach. A lot of champagne in there; very little food. The contents are down in the lab but my initial diagnosis is chloral hydrate."

Tyler remembered whom he was speaking to. "The traditional Mickey Finn. Her blood pressure and respiration are depressed; she's had convulsions and she's vomited. If she hadn't been found, those would have killed her. I'm going to run a panel for liver damage, but my guess is that she's pretty much OK."

Conrad leaned towards the speaker. "Doctor, the assault on her. Did that cause any injuries?"

"Minor bruising to her thighs, trivial tearing internally. Nothing terribly unusual; certainly none of the injuries one might expect from resistance. More like those from vigorous sexual activity; perhaps a bit of rough play. I don't think the sex wasn't consensual, but I'd say she was already unconscious when she was attacked. By emergency room standards, the rapist was actually quite gentle with her. I've seen much, much worse back on the mainland."

"Thank you, Doctor." Catalina put the telephone down. "You look surprised, Conrad?"

"I wasn't expecting Cuba to have first class doctors and hospitals; that medical exam and analysis was pretty slick. Solves some of our questions too."

"Hospitals are good here, Conrad. Good doctors can make a fortune and the medical profession knows it. So they come here; perhaps not all year round but they come. The incompetents know, if they screw a patient over by malpractice, they get dropped in the bay wearing concrete boots. So they don't come. We make a lot of dough on medical things here; plastic surgery, treatment of rich tourists, you name it. We ain't going to take risks with that income. Anyway, you were saying?"

"We have to identify the primary crime here. The doctor has just told us we're not looking for a psycho. Thank God for that, Joe; one of those is enough for a lifetime." *Your lifetime*, thought Conrad, *I've seen all too many of them.*

"You are going to help us, then?" Gotti sounded relieved; he was out of his depth here and knew it.

"Certainly." Conrad made his final decision. *There were innocents to be protected here, even if I don't know who they are yet.* His innocently dropping Igrat into the center of the case had shaken him more than he'd let on.

"Thank you, God." Catalina's voice was sincere and reverent.

"So, we get back to our question. What was the crime here? Let's walk through it. Mister Gotti..."

"John. Or, if you want to be one of the boys, Dapper John."

Conrad smiled to himself. *In Cuba, an outsider being invited to use Mafia language and nicknames is a mark of esteem. Vanity was a sin, and I knew it better than most, but once in a while it also means knowledge of a job well done.* "Dapper John. You're the rapist who makes an opportunist theft. Joe, you're the thief who gets overcome with desire. John, you start by walking us through the events, like you were doing it. Everybody else, ask questions."

Gotti thought for a second. "Got a question to ask before we start. Did this man pick Mrs. Trumpeter as his victim, or was it a random select?"

"Your choice. What do you think?"

Gotti thought himself into character. "I think I saw her around, got fascinated with her. Thought she was infatuated with me."

"Why?" One of the gunmen in the room asked, then flushed at interrupting John Gotti.

"Good question. Dapper John, why do you say that?" Conrad flashed a supportive grin at the embarrassed wiseguy.

"Because everybody looks for justification. Perhaps Mrs. Trumpeter smiled at me, or walked past me showing a lot of leg, whatever. Could be as simple as seeing me every day. But I say, I thought I saw her encourage me. So I went to her room." Gotti stopped. "Real problem here. How do I get in? Way I see it, either I forced my way in or talked my way in."

"There was no sign of a forced entry." Conrad thought carefully. "And a woman on her own in a hotel won't open a door to a stranger, not even in Cuba."

"Agreed, so I talked my way in. How is a good question. I get in, then I make her go to the bedroom and strip." Gotti paused again. "No, that doesn't work. She'd run or fight or something. There'd be bruises on her. And how does that explain the Mickey Finn? No, I produce a gun or a knife and make her take the drug. Chemical handcuffs. Then take her to the bedroom, hike her dress and rape her. In doing so, see the safe door is open and the jewelry is out, so I take it. Then I tape her up and leave her to choke."

Conrad nodded. He'd seen the problem with that already. "Joe?"

"OK, I've seen Mrs. Trumpeter around. She wears expensive clothes, a lot of jewelry. She's a trophy wife; there to display how rich and important her husband is. I think, that jewelry could be in better hands. So I follow her back, find which suite she's in."

"How? The 24th floor is key access only." Another wiseguy cut in.

Conrad smiled again. *These people are getting into the spirit of the thing.*

Catalina stopped for a second. "Then, I have to have legitimate access to the 24th, don't I? Anyway, I watch the suite, see her husband leave and think the place is empty. Go over, slip the lock get in and – she's there. Sudden change in plan. I pull a gun or a knife, make her take a Mickey. Then I open the safe, empty it. See her lying there, probably exposed when she passed out, and decide what the hell? Why not? Do her, then realize she can recognize me. So I do like Dapper John says. I ain't got the balls to kill her, so I tape her mouth up and leave her to choke."

"Why did you bring the chloral hydrate then? Its not the sort of thing one can get anywhere." Conrad thought for a second. "Is it?" *In Cuba one can buy almost anything.*

"Good question; we'll have to check down in the shops, see what they have. Yeah, but why bring it? It ain't the sort of thing I'd bring to a lift."

"Hmm. I'll ask downstairs." Conrad was trying to put his thoughts in order. "Another question; I wonder how hard these doors are to slip? Joe, can you call Igrat's room and ask her to come down? We need some more advice here."

Suite 2434, 24th Floor, Imperial Forum Hotel-Casino

Igrat closed the door of her suite behind her and tested the handle to make sure it was secure. The door of 2436, next to hers, opened. Inanna stepped out.

"You been summoned to the presence too?"

Inanna flushed slightly.

"No, Iggie. I was coming to see you. I wanted to apologize for what I said to you earlier tonight. I had no cause to say that to you; it was just you scared me so much. All I could think of is what you might be letting yourself in for."

"Don't worry about it. Do you want your room key back?" Igrat smiled to take the sting out of it.

"You took it? Ohhh." Inanna's mouth twisted slightly. "I guess I deserved it, kind of. Look, just be careful; please, Iggie? We've been together a long time."

Igrat smiled again and took the elevator down to the second floor where Catalina had his office. It didn't take much effort to find it. There were wiseguys hanging around, trying to find out what was going on. As she got to the door, enjoying the attention she was getting, Conrad opened it for her. Given the skin-to-fabric ratio on display, Conrad couldn't help but wonder why she'd bothered to get dressed.

Igrat looked around the room. "Hello guys. We've done cops and robbers; what we going to play this time? Teachers and naughty pupil?"

"Miss Shafrid . . . " Gotti spoke a little wearily. He wasn't used to having women goading him for the sheer enjoyment of it. Also, he was beginning to like this woman. That worried him. He was used to people being frightened of him and this woman obviously wasn't. He didn't know quite what to make of it.

"Igrat. Or Iggie, if you prefer."

"Igrat. How easy is it to get into one of the 24th Floor suites?"

"Force the door? Very hard. They're good solid doors. If I had to talk my way in, it would take me 30 seconds to get a man to open up. If you tried it, much, much longer; probably not at all. I keep the door on the chain and nobody I don't know gets past. Slipping the lock, which I guess is what you mean? Don't know. Let me try. Is the lock on the door here the same as the ones up there?"

Catalina nodded. Igrat looked at the door, took a hairpin and a needle and knelt down by the door. It was more than four minutes before the lock clicked open.

"You've got good locks on the doors. That was a hard one to crack. Normally in a hotel, I can bounce the lock open; it takes just a few seconds. At the NSC Building we have the new card access locks; they're really hard to break. Yours are good though. A thief's going to have a hard time getting in and the risk of getting caught is high. My opinion? He didn't slip the lock. And even if he's a hell of a lot better than I am, that still won't get him past the chain."

"So he talked his way in."

Igrat shook her head. "You didn't listen. Mrs. Trumpeter was alone in the suite; her husband was away. She is not going to let a man into that room. Not unless he had a right to come in."

Conrad nodded in agreement. "Room service. It has to be room service. They have access to the floor; they go in and out of rooms all the time. Could be a counterfeit room service person, of course, turns up with flowers or a bottle, but my guess it's the real thing."

"With a bottle." Gotti repeated the words. "And Mrs. Trumpeter had a lot of champagne in her stomach. What's the odds he turned up with a bottle on a cart, saying her husband had ordered it. Champagne already dosed. She's got no reason to see any problem. She lets him in, he pretends to open the bottle and pours her a glass. She drinks it, goes down and it's on."

"We need a list of every room service person who has been up to the 24th in the last couple of hours."

Conrad's Eye

"Make it the last couple of days, Joe; don't cast the net too close. Look, I want to go down, look at the stores in the lobby and see just what stuff they do sell down there. Igrat, could you come with me? You might be able to ask questions I can't. Joe, John, we'll be back in a few minutes."

As the doors on the elevator closed, Conrad couldn't stop himself asking. "Igrat, is it true that you staked yourself in a poker game?"

She flashed a grin over her shoulder. "Sure is; I won, though."

"How could you do that? Sell yourself to cover a bet . . . "

The wall of the elevator shook as Igrat's hand smacked the stop button, bringing the elevator to a juddering halt. It was the only sign of anger in her though. For, when she spoke, her voice was calm and level.

"Just for the record, Conrad, I didn't sell myself; not that I have any particular objection to doing that. I staked myself to cover a bet, one where the odds were pretty good that I'd win. That's point one.

"Point two, *how old are you?*"

"Five hundred and three. You know that, you were at my five hundredth."

"Right. That makes you a quarter of my age. Less that a quarter; a lot less. You have hardly had time to get bored yet. You're going to, you know. You're going to find you've done everything and seen everything and the world has nothing more to show you. So how are you going to cope with that, Conrad? Blow out your brains? Some of us do; we all know that. Not so many now we have stable groups to support us, but still some do. The Seer keeps himself amused playing strategic games with other people's armies and things keep changing just enough to keep him interested. When he doesn't stay interested, he plays businessman and gets his kicks winning battles there. Lillith finds new ways to perfect fraudulent bookkeeping and plays games keeping ahead of the revenooers. Since governments are always inventing new taxes, that keeps her happy. We've all found our hobbies and they keep us sane.

"Me? I like things around me to be dangerous. I like to live on the edge. Why do you think I do high-stakes gambling? I like taking risks with myself, and if I get hurt, that's my business, nobody else's. So if I'd lost that bet, right about now I'd be in a strange man's bed without the slightest idea of what he wanted to do to me. You get it? I wouldn't know. It would be new, unexpected, strange. Of course, it wouldn't really be new; he'd just do the same old things everybody's done before, but I wouldn't know what same old things until he's started doing them."

"He could kill you, horribly. You weren't on the Black Dahlia case; you didn't see what he did to his victims."

400

"Conrad, do you know how I met The Seer? In Babylon? I was a sneak thief and a part-time prostitute. The sort of woman a man picks up in a bar and he wakes up in the morning with her and his wallet both long gone. One day I got caught stealing from a worshiper in the Esagila. That was the blackest blasphemy and I was sentenced to public execution. A very slow, painful, messy public execution.

"The Seer, he wasn't called that then, of course, bought me. Gave a huge donation to the temple and told them I'd be a plaything for the workers on his estate. I believed him too, but I went along because it was the better option and I reckoned I could escape later. But he and the rest told me what I was and invited me to stay as part of their community, so I stayed. Don't tell what could happen. I know."

Igrat took her hand off the button and the elevator started to descend again. "Now, enough reminiscence and get back to work. What do you want to know?"

"What can be bought from the concessions down here?"

"That's easy. More or less, anything you can buy in a mainstreet drugstore, plus everything one might by from a backstreet drug dealer. You realize everybody is going to think I'm a hooker and you're my client, don't you. The apparent age difference, you see."

Conrad flushed deep red as the elevator doors opened and he caught the looks from the people waiting to get in. At that point, he realized that Igrat had timed her remark with just that effect in mind.

"Well, I suppose if I was to break my vows, you'd be a good place to start."

She flashed one of her over-the-shoulder smiles at him in response and set off across the mall. Conrad following in her wake.

The drug store in the hotel shopping precinct was much like those in the States, unless one looked closely at the packages on sale. Conrad ran his eyes along the brand names, Excedrin, Tylenol, Bayer Aspirin, Alka-Selzer, all the usual over-the counter remedies. The next shelf up started with a small package labeled "Happydaze." Conrad stared at it thoughtfully.

"Cocaine." Igrat whispered. "Heroin is a bit further down the shelf.. This is a casino-hotel; you won't see those in the family hotels further down the Boulevard. Not openly displayed, anyway."

"Can I help you?" The concession manager was attentive, no doubt expecting a substantial sale. "We have all sorts of party favors here. Some new ones as well."

"Do you stock chloral hydrate here?" Igrat eyed the "new" products, making up her mind to get some so Naamah could have a look at them.

The manager looked slightly shocked. "He doesn't want a gorgeous thing like you to go sleepytime, does he? That just ain't right."

"Nah, he's just fascinated by everything on sale here. Never seen anything like it back home." Igrat wrinkled her nose slightly and dropped her voice to a confidential pitch. "He's from Kansas."

"Ahh, I see. Sure we've got Mickey Finns here. Don't get much call for them, though. Stock's pretty old; can't remember when I last sold some. Anything else I can get you?"

Igrat looked severely at Conrad. "I need a wooden paddle. He's been a very bad, bad boy."

The manager chuckled and pointed to a display at the back of the store. Igrat took her time selecting one, covertly watching Conrad going deeper red with embarrassment by the minute.

"What's sleepytime?" They'd left the store, but Conrad still had to swallow a couple of times; he was beginning to learn that people patronized Igrat at their peril.

"Woman takes a sleeping draft. Puts her under, so her partner can do whatever he wants with her. Before you ask, no, I haven't. I like taking risks, not being stupid. You heard what the shop guy said? Hasn't sold chloral hydrate for a long time."

"Just means the attacker could have bought it somewhere else. Plenty of other concessions; we'll have to try them all."

Conrad thought for a second. "I wonder if Mr. and Mrs. Trumpeter played sleepytime."

Joe Catalina's Office, Imperial Forum Hotel-Casino

"We thought we'd play shepherdess and the bandits this time." The wiseguy leered at Igrat as she and Conrad re-entered Catalina's office.

"And you want to 'do' the sheep, I suppose." Igrat returned the comment with a deadpan seriousness that made the other three gangsters howl with laughter. The discomfited wiseguy returned to the seats in the corner of the office, knowing it would take weeks to live that little exchange down.

"Did you two have any luck downstairs?" Catalina tried to get back in charge of the situation.

"Not really. All three outlets down there stock chloral hydrate; none have sold any for months."

"Not surprised at that. Playing sleepytime was a tiny niche thing until one of the television networks did a thing on it. Then it got real popular for a few months. After some people got sick and a couple died, not here thank God, it faded away again. Now its back to just a few weirdoes."

That was something Catalina was genuinely pleased about. Having some of his hotel guests voluntarily comatose instead of gambling didn't help his bottom line.

"Of course, the person responsible for the attack on Mrs. Trumpeter may not have got the stuff here." Conrad was thoughtful, running possibilities through his mind. "Could have got it from another hotel; in fact, an intelligent crook would. Iggie, want to take a trip around the other hotels?"

"Not in an evening gown and wearing five-inch heels, no. Anyway, now's a bad time. It's too late and the main shift staff are all tucked up in bed. Which is where I want to be. Tomorrow, Conrad, we'll do a swing around the hotels tomorrow. Give me a chance to buy some more toys."

Igrat gave him a wicked grin; Conrad flushed deep red.

"Why don't I send a few of the boys around to ask? We can split the hotels up, send a dozen or so out to ask the question, get the answer much faster."

"You'll get an answer much faster, Joe. Not necessarily the right one. It must be all over the Boulevard by now that a guest was drugged and raped. Then your guys turn up asking about Mickey Finn? Nobody's going to admit they might be the supplier. But, if Iggie and I turn up at the same place tomorrow morning, we're just a couple of thrill seekers."

"Here." Gotti scrawled a note on a piece of paper. "Show this at reception in each hotel; they'll phone here. If there's any news, they'll get it right to you. And take my limo for the longer hops. I'm not using it."

"That's kind, Thanks, John."

"What, no smart mouth, Igrat?"

"Not when you're being nice, no. And you're being very nice."

Conrad coughed. "I think we'll get a night's sleep and then make an early start."

"That's a good idea, Conrad. We're all bushed. Any more thoughts before we jack it in for the night and get some sleep?"

Conrad's Eye

"There's a lot of donkey work that's got to be done, Joe. Somebody has got to go through all the requests to room service and reconcile them against the floor captain's reports. Try and find a discrepancy. It's going to be a tedious job for somebody. But, remember what Malone and Carmady back in 'Frisco used to say, 'detective work is 90 percent perspiration and 10 percent inspiration?' "

Conrad thought about it for a few seconds. *Each hotel-casino has a captain for every floor of rooms. His main purpose is to help the guests get anything they needed, advise on good restaurants and shows, book tables for them. Put simply, make their lives as easy as possible. It was the first rung up for a would-be wiseguy and a successful floor captain would soon find himself on the way to better things. But, in addition to their other responsibilities, the floor captains sat by the lifts and keep a log of every non-resident who entered their floor. And that includes room service.*

Suddenly, Conrad realized the floor captains had another function as part of their 'keep the guests happy' role. *They have lists; well, they were catalogues really, of commercially available 'escorts' who had proven they were reliable, trustworthy and healthy. Each entry had the escort's name, a picture and the appropriate set of details. A couple who wanted a partner for a threesome, or a guest on their own who wanted company, would just speak to the floor captain and look through the file to pick a suitable man or woman.*

"And Joe, we need to check escorts who went up on to the 24th over the last few nights. See if there's one more than got ordered, or if one was ordered for Suite 2415."

"Now that's a thought. There aren't that many male escorts; I'd say more than 80 percent of the ones ordered are women. We shouldn't have too many candidates to hunt down there."

Conrad's mind was up and running, making connections and hypothesizing from them. "There's one more possibility we have to allow for. Mrs. Trumpeter let the man in."

"No way, didn't you listen?" Igrat was tired and irritable. It showed in her voice.

"Yes. Igrat. She let him in because he was her lover. Her husband was away; she had a quickie assignation."

"With the Caddy dealer a few dozen yards away? Excuse me, Conrad, a girl doesn't take that sort of chance. She'd be begging to get caught."

"I know, but we'll have to keep it as a possibility."

Igrat yawned. "You can if you want; you've never committed adultery, I have and I'll tell you it's not going to happen. Not with him that close. Now, I'm off to bed. Anybody want to tuck me in?"

All four of the wiseguys in the corner got up at once. Gotti snarled a 'Siddown' from his corner of the room. Igrat shrugged.

"Sorry, guys; the word of the boss is law. Some other time."

Then she left the room, Conrad following closely behind her.

"Igrat, you've got to stop goading Dapper John like that. He's dangerous."

"Conrad, we're going to end up sleeping together. He knows it; I know it. At the moment, we're just negotiating terms. That little exchange was him telling everybody he was putting in a claim on me and me acknowledging receipt of said claim. So don't sweat it."

"And what will Mike say about that?"

"Mike Collins is a good Irish Catholic. When we met, he had the idea he'd sleep around and I'd stay home and cook for him. That didn't last too long. Conrad, I've never been faithful to a man in my life and I don't intend to start now. So Mike had to get used to it or find another partner. After some hesitation, he chose the former. This is my suite, so, good night, Conrad. Pleasant dreams."

Igrat slipped through the door and closed it behind her.

Conrad went off to his room, where he also went to bed. There, he quickly fell asleep, where *the sun beat down, hurting the eyes of the crowd gathered in the square of a small Spanish town of Medina del Campo.*

Intensive Care Unit, Alphonse Capone Memorial Hospital

"Irene, just relax, all right. You're safe here and you're not badly hurt. We're all here to help you."

Inanna spoke quietly and comfortingly. Joe Catalina had brought her in. Conrad and Igrat had been contacted at the Steppes Hotel-Casino and told that Mrs. Trumpeter had regained consciousness. She would need careful handling; Igrat's hard edginess wouldn't be suitable for that role. So Inanna would be doing the comforting.

"Mrs. Trumpeter, please. Try to remember everything you can. Every detail, no matter how slight." Conrad also spoke quietly. The woman was still badly shocked and the effects of the drug were still hitting her.

Irene Trumpeter shuddered for a second. "I was in the bedroom, putting my dress on. I had a problem; it was a halter-top with a big bow behind the neck.

Conrad's Eye

The hairdresser had put my hair up and I couldn't get the top over it. So I went to ask Hubert for help but, as I did, the man from room service came in. I stepped back fast, but he saw me. I know he did, I saw him stare."

Conrad frowned slightly.

Inanna sighed and explained. "It was a halter top; Irene wasn't wearing a bra with it. I guess that front of her dress was hanging down and she was topless. Right?"

Mrs. Trumpeter was crying quietly. "You're right, and I saw him stare at me. He left. He'd gone by the time I got back. Hubert had ordered us a bottle of champagne and he poured it out for us. We sat there, got a little tipsy, and talked for a bit. Husband and wife stuff."

She flushed slightly. "Dirty talk; you know. Then the phone rang. It was the Cadillac dealership on the top floor. They said they had a Fancy Free in, but another couple were interested as well. So Hubert went off to see about it and I drank the rest of the champagne while I was waiting for him."

"Fancy Free?" Conrad was confused.

Inanna giggled. "It's a version of the Cadillac Corvette intended for women. It's got white leather upholstery, a driving seat, which is adjustable in more ways than the standard one, and hidden lockable bins for handbags and other girl-things. Holster built into the side of the seat, so a girl doesn't have to fumble for a gun if she needs one. They're very expensive and really popular. Igrat drives one; you'd probably guess that. I'd like one as well, but it's a long waiting list."

Conrad shrugged slightly. Cars didn't really interest him. "And then what happened, Mrs. Trumpeter?"

"I don't know. I must have passed out, because I woke up here. The room service man; he must have seen my husband leave and come back for me."

She was crying again.

"Look, you'll be all right." Joe Catalina was trying to be comforting. "We'll look after you and, as soon as we've got the louse that did this, you can go home."

"Go where?" Crying turned to weeping. "I won't have a home. I'll bet Hubert is drawing up the divorce papers now. I'm a trophy wife, I always knew that. He won't want a trophy somebody has pissed on."

The vulgarity was all the more shocking for the weeping that surrounded it. "Hubert will divorce me, I know it. He made me sign a pre-nuptial before we got married. I get my clothes, my jewelry, a car and five thousand dollars. That's all. What am I going to do? I can't get married again. Who wants a trophy somebody else threw in the garbage?"

"Mrs. Trumpeter, right off the bat, a pre-nup ain't worth nuttin here. This is Cuba, remember? The law here is what *we* say it is." Catalina was genuinely quite angry. In his eyes, men did not treat their wives that way. A Mafia wife didn't expect her man to be faithful, but she did expect to be treated with respect. On the rare occasions a marriage split, the ex-wife was treated very generously. It was simply a matter of common sense; that way they had no incentive to go to the cops.

"When a couple splits here, they sort it out between them. If they can't agree on what's fair, they go to their Capo and have a sit-down over a bottle of wine and a bowl of spaghetti. Husband has his say; wife has hers. Then the Capo says to them, 'this is how it's gonna be, see' and he makes the decision. And its final. Man chucks his wife over something like this, instead of standing by her, well, that's gonna cost him dear. And the other thing. No beautiful woman ever starved on our watch in Cuba, so you ain't got nuttin to worry about. Capisce?"

Quietly, Conrad smiled to himself at the way Joe Catalina was laboring at the 'wiseguy' language. He didn't normally speak like that, but the fact he was doing so now was slowly driving home to Mrs. Trumpeter that she had powerful, and very dangerous, people on her side. Her sobbing slowed down and became less overwhelming.

"Irene, just relax. This will all work out; I promise you that. Just trust us, Conrad is one of the best inquisitors around; he'll get to the bottom of this."

"The Spanish Inquisition couldn't get to the bottom of this." Mrs. Trumpeter was on the verge of crying again.

"Oh, I don't know," Conrad spoke earnestly. "Nobody expects the Spanish Inquisition."

Joe Catalina's Office, Imperial Forum Hotel-Casino

"So, Annabelle, you were visiting a room on the 24th Floor?"

"2480. The floor captain called our manager and said he had a booking for me. I went over to the hotel, called him from reception. He signed me up and authorized me to come to the floor. When I got off the elevator, he signed me in and I went to 2480. Hour later, he signed me out again and I left."

"And you were in 2480 for the whole hour? Doing what?"

"I was with the couple there for the whole hour. For the rest, I'm sorry Mister Catalina, but that's confidential; between me and my clients. If you want to call them to confirm I was there, fine, and, if they want to tell you what we did, that's fine too. But I won't say anything."

Catalina nodded and picked up his telephone, dialing 2480.

"Good evening. This is Joe Catalina here, representing the owners and investigating the unfortunate affair day last night. I understand a young lady was visiting you? . . .

"No, she wasn't the woman who was attacked; we're just eliminating from our investigations everybody who was on the floor last night. . . .

"The whole hour? Thank you very much, sorry for the disturbance."

"Right, Annabelle. They confirm you were there for the whole hour. And, your discretion is noted; the Commission smiles upon people who know how to keep their mouths shut."

The woman left. Catalina spun in his seat and sighed.

"Well, that eliminates the escorts. Two were hired last night; one by the couple in 2480, the other by a single man in 2464. Both checked out; their times were logged in and out by the floor captain. How are the girls doing?"

"Inanna and Igrat? They're on their own. Inanna's shopping; Igrat's back in the high-stakes casino. They said they needed a break."

"So we can talk without any back chat. And Dapper John is reporting to the Commission, so we've got some quiet from that quarter as well. What do you make of this?"

"I think its time to play cards. Do you have any index cards?"

"Got them today; five by threes. I hoped you'd say you need them. How do we start?"

"Same way as we did before, with motive."

Conrad took two of the cards and wrote 'rape' on one and 'robbery' on the other.

"Now, which one goes at the top?"

Catalina sighed. This 'card game' gave him a comforting sense of nostalgia.

"I think its rape at the top, with robbery underneath it. That sound good to you?"

"Why don't you run it through? Like we did before."

"OK, so I'm the room service guy. Come in with the champagne, see Mrs. Trumpeter with her rack hanging out and get full with desire. So I drug the champagne, think I'll wait until they're both out and do it. Only I see Mr. Trumpeter leaving and, this is pathetic, isn't it? No way this can happen."

"So, let's try robbery."

Conrad thought quickly. "The room service guy. He's seen the Trumpeters around and knows they're rich. he put the Mickey Finn in some champagne and takes it up; either Trumpeter ordered it, or he's going to say that it's a comp from the hotel or from Chevrolet or something. His plan is let them drink it, wait until they're out cold, then come in and rob the place. Only firstly he sees Mrs. Trumpeter exposed and that heats him up. Then he sees Mr. Trumpeter leaving; well, that isn't part of his plan but it means he can take advantage of Mrs. Trumpeter. Once Trumpeter has gone, he lets himself in, sees Mrs. Trumpeter is out cold and rapes her. Then, he ties her up, robs the safe and goes."

"That makes more sense. Problem though. We're talking about a thief here who's got everything planned out in advance. Very carefully planned. Then he throws the whole plan over because he sees a rack? In Havana? You can see those, and a lot more, in any nightclub. Hell, we've got them on every street-corner and shop window.

"Listen, this is my world right? I know guys like we're talking about. They get their rocks off stealing things. Compared with that, Mrs. Trumpeter, cutie though she is, ain't nuttin. Another thing; a professional thief isn't a killer. They don't kill. They spend all their time planning so they don't have to. They also know that gagged people can choke and they don't want that either. If we'd found Mrs. Trumpeter face down, with her head turned to one side so she wouldn't choke, then I'd say thief."

Conrad frowned. "Are you sure of that, Joe? I mean, that thieves don't kill."

"Sure I'm sure. Look, we're friends right? But, remember, I made my bones a long time ago. Have you? Professional thieves don't kill. Believe me on that. Why turn three years for robbery into Death Row?"

"So, robbery doesn't fit either. That puts us in a bad place."

Conrad thought again. He took out a third card and wrote 'murder' on it.

"So let's try that one."

"Somebody wanted to murder Mrs. Trumpeter? Why?" Catalina's voice was incredulous.

"Not Mrs. Trumpeter. Her husband. What do you know about him?"

"Not much. Came over here with a pack of money, wanting to buy into a casino or three." Catalina laughed. "Few years ago, he might have made it; not now. Then, a man might have enough to make a go of it. Today hotels cost so much to build, its all consortiums. Families together. But, more and more, families and legit business. Trumpeter missed the boat."

"Well, Joe, he's not a nice man. He got his start building shoddy houses, which he sold to Russian Front veterans at way over the fair price. By the time they found out the houses were built with pine not red fir, the workmanship was bad and the appliances were third-rate junk, he'd sold out and gone. Then he did the same thing with commercial property. Suppose one of his victims saw him and decided it was time for payback? Drugs the couple, perhaps expecting to kill them both or just Trumpeter himself. Only Trumpeter leaves, so he decides to punish him by raping and killing Mrs. Trumpeter."

"You know, that makes more sense than anything we've had to date. This could be a professional hit. Could be his plan was to drug them, tie them both down, then make Trumpeter watch while he raped and killed his wife, then kill him. Only Trumpeter went for his walk and the killer ended up with just the wife."

"I didn't think the Mob went in for killing wives, Joe?"

"We don't. In LCN, we keep families out of business disagreements. But, south of the border, they don't think that way. They do what I said. If there are kids, they rape and kill them as well. Perhaps Trumpeter ripped somebody from down there off and this was their way of getting back at him?"

Conrad and Catalina exchanged nods and re-arranged the three cards so 'murder' was at the top. Then Conrad wrote another card that simply said 'room service.' It was the only card in the second column.

Conrad and Catalina looked at the four cards on the table; the single card for a suspect looked lonely at the side. Their contemplation was interrupted by a knock on the door. A few seconds later, two wiseguys came in, their arms full of packages. Their first action was to look around for Igrat. Their disappointment when they found she wasn't present was almost comical.

"Mister Catalina, some packages have arrived. Big one from Mr. Trumpeter's insurance company; one from the National Security Council. And we were going through the log last night and we saw somethin' we think you should know."

"An extra delivery from room service?"

"No, Mister Catalina. Chips here tried that, went through all the deliveries and compared them with the orders recorded at room service. No extra deliveries. But when we did it the other way, compared the room service record with the floor log, we found something weird all right. There was one delivery short. Room 2415 ordered a bottle of champagne on ice. The bar logged it goin' out, but the floor captain never logged it into the 24th."

"And yet 2415 got its bottle of champagne." Conrad spoke thoughtfully. "So the room service delivery got up there."

"Find out who the waiter was; bring him in for questioning."

"We've already done that, Mister Catalina. He's Ricardo Gomez, a Cube; been with us for about 18 months. No trouble to speak of. A couple of beefs with other staff over tips, but nothing unusual."

"Beef over tips? He short of cash?"

"Nah, not that we know about. Problem was he does too well; guests like him and couple of the others thought he should share out the extra. Led to bad feeling, like we said. Associate who runs room service had a sit-down, ruled in favor of Gomez, told the others if they want better tips they should be more like him. Anyways, we sent Boots and Big Pony to bring him in. Gently."

Catalina nodded. "You boys done good. Earned yourselves some bonus." He scribbled quickly on a pad. "Take this to the cashier, she'll give you the chips."

The wiseguys looked at the note and their eyebrows lifted. "*Thank you,* Mister Catalina."

"Well, we now have a name." Conrad took the card marked 'room service' and replaced it with one titled 'Ricardo Gomez'. "That tends to rule out a professional, I think. Been here too long and wouldn't attract attention the way this one did."

"Yeah, thieves and shooters like to fade into the background. Of course, there's another guy who should be on your cards."

"Whose that Joe?"

"The guy that whacked Ricardo Gomez. If the boys don't bring Gomez in and can't find him, we start looking for his body. Good hit man might think the best way to start is to take out a room service guy, get his access key and load and then take it up. He'd avoid the main elevator and the floor captain, probably come up in the service elevator. Or it might be one of the other waiters; there's tension there."

"Over tips?" Conrad was incredulous. Then he reflected. *In my life, I've known people killed for a few small coins or for the shoes they wore.*

"Bit more than that." Catalina bit his lip slightly, hesitated, then continued. "Look, this stays between us, right? There's a problem in the ranks here. There's kind of two groups. Those what came over from the mainland, we're Sicilian, or Italian anyway and mostly we're LCN. Brought up in The Life. Then there's the Cubans. A whole lot of them, and more every year. They're new to all this; they

411

see us as being just another employer. They don't have the traditions or the commitment to LCN. To them, we're a one more bunch of foreign rulers running their island. That's not so far from true, of course. Our people see them as being a bunch of upstarts lacking in respect and that ain't so far from true either. So, down in the street, there's a lot of dislike building up. The Cubans see themselves as being held down by mainlanders. Our people see themselves as being swamped by the sheer number of Cubans

"Now, that Associate who held a sit-down, he shouldn't have done that. Should have kicked it upstairs to somebody who has been Made. Somebody will talk to him about that. Associates ain't supposed to have sit-downs. Now, if he's Cuban, and a lot of Associates are these days, the mainlanders will think he ruled the way he did because Gomez is Cuban. If he's from the mainland, they'll think in ruling for the Cuban he's let his people down. So somebody could have thought he'd even the score by sticking a knife in Gomez's back.

"And there's another problem with all this. It ain't gone unnoticed that all the people The Little Man is training to take over from him are Cubans. Now, we know why; I mean us Caporegimes and the Commission. The Cubans, they're not Sicilian so they can't be made in LCN and they'll never be part of a family. That means they can make decisions without considering family. Just like The Little Man, everybody will know it's fair.

"But the guys on the street, they don't get that. And if it turns out a Cuban did this, we're in a world of hurt. Could start a street war between LCN and the Cubans. And that's about the worst thing that could happen; for us, for them, for Cuba. This might surprise you, but a lot of us care about this place. Sure it's the biggest money-earner in creation, but it's something a bit more to a lot of us. We've done something pretty good here, taken a rat-hole and built it up to somewhere pretty decent. None of us want to see it going back to a rat-hole again."

"So, if Gomez walks through that door, you're going to be pretty relieved. You won't have a possible civil war on your hands, just a couple of murders or attempted murder."

"Murder's not a problem. Killin's not even illegal here; attempted or otherwise. Upsetting a tourist is the crime we're worried about. And even if Gomez is still alive, there's still a problem. Even if he did do it, a lot of Cubans will believe we hung the rap on him to protect our own. Can't blame them. If I was in their position, I'd think the same. That's why the Commission is so interested in this. You can bet The Little Man had this all figured out within ten seconds of getting the news. Anyway you work this out, it's bad news."

Conrad shuddered slightly. He avoided getting into politics as much as he could, but he could still see the powder keg that was building up under this particular case. He also realized why his steps had been directed to Cuba. *No matter how this case worked out, there are innocents to be protected. The gangsters who run the island had no idea of how to run a criminal investigation, but they are very sensitive to the likely implications of whom they accused of the crime. Left to themselves, they would have picked up the person who they fought least likely to disrupt the smooth running of the Cuban money machine and made a show of whacking that person. And if they got it wrong, the whole island could blow up in their faces.*

"Have you seen these rocks?"

Joe Catalina was looking at the insurance company pictures of the stolen jewelry. Conrad picked one up. *The collection is spectacular, there was no doubt about that, but there is something tasteless and vulgar about the assortment.* It took Conrad a while to put his finger on it, but eventually he realized the problem was that the jewelry was unbalanced. *It consists of spectacular stones, there is no doubt about that, but the settings are inexpensive.* His mind flirted with the word 'junk'. *The sort of things that can be bought at a discount jewelry store.* He looked a bit closer. The chains on the necklaces were thin and their catches were frail. *At a guess, they* had *been bought at a discount jewelry store.*

"Joe, is there an appraisal of these pieces in the package?"

"Sure." Catalina rooted through the pictures and produced a sheaf of typescript, stapled together at one corner. "Catch."

Despite the word, he handed the documents to Conrad. *As I suspected, the stones were fabulously expensive but cheaply mounted; some even using 10 karat gold.* The appraiser had remarked on that in several cases, indicating that compared with the value of the stones, the settings were essentially worthless. Even allowing for that, the jewelry was valued at well over a million dollars.

"You know, Joe, we've got a real problem here. If the thief is a professional, he'll strip the stones out of the settings, throw the metalwork away and just sell the stones. They'll be unidentifiable." Conrad thought for a second. "How does one get rid of stolen jewelry here anyway?"

"You know, that's a good question. Mostly, the jewelry worth stealing belongs to the tourists and anybody getting light-fingered earns themselves a trip out to the bay wearing concrete boots. On the mainland, we'd fence the stuff. But the kind of theft that goes on around here ain't big enough for a fence to make a living. So, I'd guess pawnshops would be the way out. But dumping something like this in a pawnshop? Jeez, that'll attract attention. Them places think a crucifix on a necklace is a big deal. This stuff? It's out their league. So high above their heads it might as well be a SAC bomber."

413

Conrad's Eye

"We'd better circulate the pictures anyway; around the pawnshops and anywhere else we can think of. Somebody might spot something. Is there any way we can check on stuff going out of the country?"

Catalina laughed. "Not a one. We're just not set up for that. Hell, we don't check anything going either way. We don't even keep records of who goes in and out. Only way we can stop the stuff leaving the island is to stop the suspects leaving. If they haven't done so already."

The chain of thought was stopped by a knock on the door. A second later, a Cuban entered the room; not quite pushed by the two men with him, but certainly assisted in his entrance. Catalina waved him to a seat in front of his desk and watched the man slumped down. He was obviously badly frightened, looking from side to side with a hunted, almost desperate, look about him. Conrad watched him and could sense that this man had something he wanted to hide. What that was, of course, was another matter. An unspoken message passed from Catalina to Conrad; the gangster deferring from conducting the questioning in favor of the inquisitor.

Catalina had heard Malone and Carmady speaking with awe about Conrad's interrogation technique. The two detectives had never forgotten his display of expertise in the Black Dahlia case and they'd spent the rest of their careers trying to emulate it. Even now, far into their careers and in high-ranking positions, they openly stated that they felt themselves to be novices compared with the display they'd seen that night.

Now, it was Catalina's turn to watch.

Conrad started to weave his web of questions around Ricardo Gomez. Questions that were innocuous at first, but ones that grew progressively harder to answer and which left Gomez with fewer and fewer ways out. As the net closed, Gomez's desperation became more obvious. He tried not to answer the quiet, polite queries that were thrown at him, but even that proved impossible. The stream flowed through and around him, so that failing to answer was in itself an answer that was more damning than any reply could have been.

"So, you brought the champagne up to the Trumpeter's suite and were opening it for them when Mrs. Trumpeter showed herself off to you, isn't that right?" Conrad had his verbal harpoon ready for the kill, at last. "She stood where you could see her but her husband could not, stood there naked and invited you back later. Did she pose for you Ricardo? Display herself lewdly?"

Ricardo Gomez looked frantically around for a way to escape but there was none. He was trapped and he knew it. He shook his head, dumbly, trying to put off the inevitable.

414

"You weren't there at all were you, Ricardo? You don't know what happened, do you? To you, Mrs. Trumpeter is a nice woman, probably spoke kindly to you but that's all. You can't see her behaving like that can you?"

Gomez shook his head again. "I was away last night. Another waiter took my shift."

"Tell us all about it. And tell the truth, this time; you know by now you cannot lie to me."

Gomez gulped and started to explain. His wife was a showgirl in another hotel. They were starting a baby, so the show manager had taken her off the more strenuous part of the routines and put her on a less active act. For all his care, two nights ago, she had tripped and fallen badly. Enough to be taken to hospital. Last night, she had had a relapse. It looked as if she would lose the baby. So, Gomez had arranged to swap shifts with another worker.

"And is the baby safe?" Conrad asked gently.

"Thank the good Lord, yes. The doctors say it was a close thing for her but the baby is safe."

"Why in hell didn't you just tell us?" Catalina was annoyed. "We would have given you time off for a situation like that. Family's an important thing for us."

"I know, sir. But my wife works for the Golden Palm. And they arranged for her to be taken to the Bonnie Parker Hospital for Women."

Conrad looked confused. "Why should that make any difference?"

"I think I know, although I can't quite believe it. We're West Coast Mob; the Golden Palms is run by the Kansas City Family. Back on the mainland, there's a lot of bad blood between us. That's what's behind this, right?"

"That is right, sir. I thought, if you knew my wife was employed by your enemies and we were indebted to them, you would not trust me anymore and my wife needs her husband now."

"Jackass." Catalina spoke contemptuously. "First rule out here is what goes on in the mainland, stays in the mainland. Remember the rule? 'He who rocks the boat sleeps with the fishes.' If The Little Man found out that somebody had brought over a grudge from the mainland, they'd be in the Bay so fast it would make their head swim. Even if the rest of them couldn't, with all the concrete around their ankles. Especially anybody who started trouble over something as insignificant as a waiter and his wife. This is Cuba, not the mainland. Most we'd do is talk to the Golden Palms and buy some of the hospital debt from them, so they're not carrying the whole load but that's it.

"Big Pony? Take Gomez down to the basement. Don't hurt him; just keep him on ice down there. Feed him from one of the buffets. If he wants to go see his wife, he can, but you take him there and bring him back. Capische?"

"One quick question, Joe." Conrad cut in before the waiter could be taken away. "Who was it who did your shift for you last night?"

"Antonio Cardinal, sir. He is a most reliable man, I would not hand my shift and guests over to just anybody."

"You shouldn't have handed them over at all." Catalina growled, but there was an amused note in his voice. "Next time just tell us, capische? Save a lot of trouble all around."

Once they had the room back to themselves, the two men sighed with a certain element of relief.

"Well, he's still alive." Conrad was writing out a new card with the name 'Antonio Cardinal' on it. He put it at the top of the column for suspects, leaving the other two cards underneath.

"We know that Gomez didn't get whacked." Catalina objected.

"I know, but Cardinal might have been. It may be that Gomez was luckier than he knows. Or, he may have gone back after Cardinal took his shift, and went after Mrs Trumpeter, hoping to frame the man."

Conrad thought that over for a few seconds. "It's a pretty low possibility. He was all at sea when I told him Mrs. Trumpeter was giving a blatant 'come-on' signal. I don't think he was lying."

Once again he ran the situation through his mind. "We need to find out from her husband who the waiter who served them actually was. I'd guess that he doesn't know his name, but she does. Have we got pictures of these two men?"

"Sure, personnel will have them. I'll get them sent up. We get Trumpeter down here to look at them?"

"No, we send Inanna over to the hospital to show them to Mrs. Trumpeter." Conrad smiled slightly, "I've got a better idea for who should show Mr. Trumpeter those pictures. Something that will tell us a lot about the relationship between him and his wife."

At that point the door burst open. Igrat swung in, her face flushed and gleeful. Catalina took one look at her.

"I'm almost afraid to ask."

"Another 30K up. Doing well here; your cards like me."

"Igrat, you'll be driving our hosts bankrupt." Conrad tried to sound severe.

"Not a chance." Catalina was amused at the concept and decided to give his guests a lesson in casino management,

"Let me tell you why we just love big winners here. Firstly, we didn't lose the money; the other gamblers did. All we lost was the table fee when they thumbed a lift out of town. You know the old saying. 'Arrive in Cuba on a private jet, leave working on a fishing boat.

"But, much more importantly, the word of Iggie's win was all over the Golden Boulevard by this morning. Since her little display last night, we've had three women imitating her gambling style, although none of them actually staked themselves. Not yet, anyway.

"Our security people are watching out for one who tries it and then realizes what she's done when she loses. The real secret of running a place like this is to anticipate trouble before it starts."

"When I did my bet, the Pit Boss made it very clear that I'd have to go through with it if I lost or answer to him. Fair enough." Igrat smiled slightly; the memory of her excitement at just making the bet was its own reward.

"Good for him. Apart from that issue, between them they dropped nearly a quarter of a mil. That's just here. By the time we count in all the other casinos, I would say we made back the money we lost inside twenty minutes.

"Iggie's win has made us millions. First lesson for you, straight from The Little Man. The house always wins in the end. There's no need for the games to be crooked and the house does better in the long run if they aren't. Cuba runs on that philosophy."

"Do I get commission on those winnings?"

Igrat gave Catalina a beaming smile and sat on his desk, crossing her legs as she did so. Catalina gulped slightly and reminded himself that Dapper John Gotti had staked his claim there.

"No. One thing you can do. We need to have somebody take some pictures up to Mr. Trumpeter. See if he can identify the waiter who served him and his wife yesterday evening. You mind doing that?"

"No problem. Let me guess; you want to see if he'll make a play for me?" Igrat twitched her eyebrows slightly.

"Got it in one, doll. Although he'd probably make a play for you even if he was dead."

Igrat chuckled at that. "Why Joe, you say the nicest things. Give me the pictures and I'll try him out."

CHAPTER THREE

Joe Catalina's Office, Imperial Forum Hotel-Casino.

"What's the word from the Commission, Dapper John? They pissed?"

"Of course. One good thing; the word from the boys on the street is that the tourists aren't as unhappy as we thought they'd be. Oh, they were pretty worried when the news got out yesterday morning, but, by evening, word was that it was the sort of thing that could happen anywhere and didn't prove anything. A few even saying it proved Cuba really is safe and that it didn't just seem that way because we hid things like this. And having the boys all over the place with Tommy guns out in the open helps as well. Quite a few old ladies like being escorted around by a wiseguy, with her on one arm and a Tommy gun on the other. The Little Man told us that there's more of the boys arriving today and tomorrow from the mainland to help keep things under control.

"As for finding out the guy what done this, they're happy with you. Two days and you've got it pinned down to one possible. Didn't tell them that none of us is happy about that schmo. You got lucky, having that friend of yours here. Wouldn't have got past first base without him."

"Conrad." Joe Catalina said the name with immense satisfaction. "He's good; better than any cop I've ever known. He's out with Igrat, finishing off the rest of the hotels to see if we can find where the Mickey Finn came from."

"I know; she told me this morning." Something in the way Gotti said that made Catalina smile to himself. "They've got my limo again. By the way, she asked me to tell you, Trumpeter couldn't recognize either of the pictures he was shown. And he didn't make a play for her. Speaking of people being pissed, that upset her. I guess she ain't used to that."

"Now that is odd." Cataline spoke reflectively.

"Odd? Freaking unnatural I'd call it. That doll's the reason the riot started."

"Not that. The NSC sent a file on Trumpeter over yesterday. Read it last night. Really slimy customer, but don't seem interested in women much. Mrs.

Trumpeter was right; she's a trophy to him, nothing more. But the Revenooers and the Fully Born Irish are closing in on him; fraud, misrepresentation, you name it. He really screwed up; he built a bunch of his jerry-built office blocks for the Air Force and that made his business a national security matter. But what's odd is that Inanna went to see Mrs. Trumpeter with the same pictures this morning. She picked out Antonio Cardinal right away."

"So Mrs. Trumpeter sees him for a fleeting moment and recognizes him, Trumpeter talks to him and doesn't. Might be he's the kind of high and mighty stiff who doesn't recognize servants. Treats them as part of the scenery."

"Could be, Dapper John."

There was a knock on the door and a couple of wiseguys came in. "Sorry Joey, got bad news. Antonio Cardinal's done a flit. His rooms are empty. His landlady said he went out yesterday, didn't come back. Thought he was spending the night with his frail, but he didn't show up for his shift this morning. We've put the word out. If he's seen on the street, the boys will pull him in."

"OK, keep looking." Gotti looked a bit happier as the two wiseguys left. "That makes Cardinal look a lot more plausible. If he ain't guilty, why did he run?"

Catalina laughed. "Now, you're sounding like a cop, Dapper John. Cardinal isn't even an associate; he's just hired help. He don't have to come when we call him in. And if we were him, would we?"

One of the Mob rules was that when a Made Man or an Associate was called in, he had to come. No excuses. Failure to come in when called could be a death sentence. That didn't apply to the hired help though; by failing to come in when called, they just lost their chance at sharing in Cuba's financial wonderland.

"That's what your friend would ask, isn't it? If we were him, what would we do?"

Catalina looked thoughtful. "Don't know about you Dapper John, but I'd run for home."

"New York dockside for me, but yeah, I guess that is home. Where did Cardinal come from?"

"Small village in the countryside somewhere. I'll get Personnel to look it up. Find out who it belongs to, then we ask permission to go pick him up."

Gotti nodded in agreement. He knew it was an odds-on bet that the village in question was another family's territory. Custom demanded a meeting and a polite request for permission before doing something there. Technically, Gotti's investigation crew reported directly to the Commission and could go where it wanted and when, but he was street-wise enough to know that going through the formalities first was more productive and caused fewer long-term problems.

There was another knock on the door. Inanna made an entrance.

"I thought you'd like to know, Conrad and Igrat are on their way back. They struck out. Three hotel concessions sold chloral hydrate in the last week; in each case, the purchaser was a known guest at the hotel. Oh, Irene had a good night, slept well and her room is full of flowers and candy. Husband is conspicuous by his absence. I guess she was right about him. Divorce on the way."

"Infamita." Gotti spat the word out while looking at the ceiling.

"If he serves the papers here, it'll be the second mistake he's made." Catalina was amused. "The first being getting the NSC involved. Believe me Dapper John, those are people you do not want to mess with. The second would be divorcing Mrs. Trumpeter over this mess here, where we can write the divorce settlement. Inanna, would you and Conrad like to join a couple of the boys for a trip to the country?"

"Will we be coming back?"

Catalina looked shocked for a second then snorted with laughter.

"You heard me, we don't ever mess with you people. Yeah, you'll be coming back, with the guy who served the champagne last night. We send the boys, he'll think just the way you did and he'll run again. You and Conrad, you can bring him in."

"Making us the Judas goats?"

Inanna was suspicious and, for the first time since Catalina had met her, hostile.

"We ain't going to whack him; unless he done it, which we don't think is likely."

Catalina broke off as Conrad and Igrat returned. Both were hot and tired from their morning going between hotels. There was a brief break while Conrad poured out glasses of iced water and gave one to Igrat. She kicked off her shoes and sat down next to Gotti.

"Conrad, do you think Cardinal did it? He's done a runner."

"So would I, in his place." Conrad thought carefully. "I doubt it."

"Why do you say that?" Gotti agreed, but he was curious as to how this strange man had come to the same conclusion.

"Look at our three motivations. Rape; well he wasn't around enough to get a fascination with Mrs. Trumpeter. He was an unofficial stand-in. So why would he bring drugged champagne? Just on the off-chance? Doesn't sound likely, does it?

"Robbery, same argument. A hit? Just look at this set up; changing service personnel, drugged champagne, victim left to choke. It just doesn't add up. You guys know as well as I do that the simplest cases to solve are the ones where the murderer tried to get clever. He ties himself in knots and trips himself up. The ones that really scare investigators is where a body is just dumped in a ditch. Nothing to work with. Which is, of course, why you guys do it that way."

Conrad smiled to take the sting out of his words.

"Got it. No hit man is going to go to all this trouble. He might impersonate a room service waiter but, as soon as he got in, it would be wham, wham with a silenced Nagant and that's it. Shot in the head for each."

"Unless he's South American, of course." Catalina was fond of that theory; it put the murderer out of Cuba's circle.

"There's always that. But the drugging still doesn't fit. If he was from the cartels south of the border, he would still be pro enough to keep it simple. Still go with the gun, but he'd use it to walk the couple into their bedroom. May even make Trumpeter tie his own wife down, then whack them both, cartel style."

"Why a Nagant?" Conrad was curious. He guessed Henry McCarty or Achillea could have given him an answer on the spot, but they weren't here.

"Because they're the only revolver that can be silenced. Most revolvers have a gap between the cylinder and the barrel; that lets the gas out and makes a silencer useless. The Nagant is an odd design; when it's cocked, the cylinder slides forward and seals against the barrel. No gap. Also, being a revolver, it doesn't eject the spent cases. Finally, they're as cheap as dirt; there are millions of them out there."

"I'll remember that." Conrad was impressed and all information was useful.

"Why, who are you planning to whack?" The mafia men present burst out laughing at the idea.

"So, when are we leaving?" Igrat looked around expectantly. She'd never been outside Havana on her trips over to Cuba.

"You, probably not." Gotti had his own motives for that, of course, but there was a real one as well. "Outside Havana, Cuba's pretty conservative Catholic. Your style would rub people the wrong way. Conrad and Inanna better go on this one, with a driver."

"Oh good, I can go shopping again. You got great stores here, Dapper John."

"Haven't you done enough?" Conrad still had the mental scars from Igrat's 'shopping.'

"We had to get things, Conrad, to make the cover stick. Anyway, look what I got, guys. Fur-lined handcuffs for my naughty drawer and genuine leopard skin bra and panties, just like Canadian submariners wear. Look."

Igrat fished around in her shopping bag and pulled out a leopard skin bra. She held it up against herself. "Hey, what do you think guys?"

"I think I'm going to go outside for a minute." One of the gangsters got up and headed for the rest room amid general laughter.

"OK, settle down." Catalina tried to get back in control. "Dapper John, I'm going along as well; may need somebody with weight on this trip. We'll take a Landrover Discovery. Roads out there aren't so good once we're off the turnpikes."

Frank Nitti Turnpike, Approaching Tapaste Exit

"Completed 'bout three years ago, ma'am."

The driver had one eye on the road, another on his passengers. The Marcello Family had insisted that they provide the driver as part of the deal to allow the Bay Area Family to pick up somebody from their turf. Of all the Mob families, the Marcellos were the most determined to prevent other Mob members entering their territory without permission; the branch operating in Cuba was no exception. It had taken two hours of negotiation, in a sit-down, for Joe Catalina to get this arrangement.

"Keep going southeast and next exit takes ya to the Disneyworld place at La Casualidad. Ya like boating, ma'am? They gotta marina on the lake down there."

"It's a good road. From what Joe Catalina was saying, I was expecting something much rougher." Inanna was sitting in the front seat, watching the scenery roll past.

"Twenty years ago, wasn't a road worth calling that in the whole country. Few dirt tracks, couple of paved roads around Havana; that was it. Ya'd think the place was something out of the last century. We built the first proper roads here, 'round the earliest casinos. Now, with the whole country growin', we gotta build more. Tourists want to get from Havana to Disney or the other resorts; they wanna be comfortable. Turnpikes do the job and nobody minds payin' a bit.

The tour busses got a deal. Disney pay a lump sum to the Commission per bus, they don' have to stop for the tolls."

The driver swung off the turnpike using a right-hand exit and slowed down for the toll booth. He handed a ticket and a five-dollar bill to the attendant with the assurance of long practice and got the change back. He stuffed it into a pocket without bothering to count it.

"Are all the roads around here toll roads?" Inanna was fascinated by the sights; she'd never been outside Havana before.

"Sure, ma'am. This one's owned by the Detroit family. They built the stretch of road from Havana to here. They gotta big country club for big shots not far from here; golf course, tennis, pools, riding stables, the works. Even gotta airstrip a Superstream can land on. Then we built the next section. Eventually highway is gonna run all the way to Gitmo."

Sitting in the back, Conrad noted the pride in the gunman's voice. *What Catalina said is true; a lot of the wiseguys who live here do take pride in the way Cuba is developing. The social set-up here might defy common sense but it works; so far at least. But then, the country had been so hammered flat, first by rapacious foreign overlords and then by a government that was corrupt and incompetent beyond belief that having the place run by gangsters is an improvement. In fact, anything is an improvement over the first half of Cuba's 20th century.*

Their driver stopped at the top of the exit ramp and then turned left. The road they were on now was noticeably worse than the tollway below them. Inanna could feel the thumps as they hit dips in the surface. Ahead of them was a crossroads, with four curved filter lanes joining the arms. It looked incongruously complex for what was barely more than a black-topped track. The driver went straight on, crossing the centerpiece and continued along the road. Inanna kept peering through the trees that lined the sides, trying to see the farms that were marked by turnings off the main highway.

"Is this road named after one of your, um, colleagues?"

"No, ma'am. This is just the Tapaste Road. Ya like our farms here?"

"They're neat. I didn't know what to expect out here. What grows?"

"This patch? Tobacco, mostly. Some fruit. Lot of cattle. Tapaste's pretty much self sufficient. It's the way all the patches are. We like it like that. Small independent places where everybody knows everybody and the Man in charge lives right there with them, Each patch looks after itself and sells the surplus to the tourist resorts. Keeps life simple and that makes everybody happy. Meanin' no disrespect, ma'am, you got a man back on the mainland? One who likes cigars?"

"Sure have. Guy called Tommy Lynch. And he loves a good cigar."

"Well, take a tip and buy him a box while we're out here. Cost you quarter what you'll pay on the Golden Boulevard and they'll be better. Family keeps the real good ones for themselves."

"Thank's, I'll do that. Hey, look, Conrad! What cute little houses."

Inanna pointed to the small cluster at the side of the road. There were five of them, with two large buildings on the other side of the road. They shone brilliant white in the sunshine of mid-afternoon; their red roofs a welcome splash of color against the green of the trees and fields.

"Big one's the school, ma'am. Ya know somethun' As a kid back in N'Awlins, I skipped class every chance I got. Was hustling the streets before I hit thirteen. But these kids here, they complain about the school not bein' open enough. They wanna learn so bad. And their parents come in the evenin' to learn as well. Tell ya this, ma'am; it's a cryin shame what was done to these people before we came."

"Who teaches in the school?" Conrad leaned forward slightly.

"Village priest does the religious bit, nat'rally. Local button man teaches them how Cuba runs now. And history, way we sees it. Rest, we hire from the mainland or the other islands. School ain't free; there a charge for each kid and for evening classes for adults. Families'll go short of almost anything to pay for schoolin', but charges ain't so high to need that. Some people back on mainland on our backs to do schools for free, but people don' 'preciate wat they don' pay for. Anyways, ain't nothing on Cuba is free."

The car was running into the outskirts of the town. To Inanna's surprise, the road inside the built-up area was a lot better than the stretch outside. It was fringed by houses; mostly single-story places, with a few trees to provide shade. What struck her most was just how clean the place was. It looked like the road got swept every morning and the houses shone as if they had been freshly scrubbed. A couple of blocks in, their driver turned left and went down what was obviously the main street. Finally he pulled up outside a large, two-story building that had tables and chairs outside. Obviously a local café.

"Right, we're here. Ya let me do the introductions, right? Joe, ya know the drill, but our friends here don'. So I'll introduce. Then it's up ta ya."

Myplace Coffee House, Tapaste

"Señor, there are wild dogs down there and the women are frightened. They think the dogs will attack the children or take a baby from the crib. And they also fear the dogs might have the madness."

"Rabies? That is a serious thing to fear. You are sure these are wild dogs?"

"Yes, Señor. Nobody claims to own them."

"They wouldn't. Very well. We will have a dog hunt; not tonight, but the night after tomorrow night. We will pass word around that everybody who has a dog must keep it inside between dusk and dawn that night. We will use Landrovers with spotlights in the back and I will bring my Tommy gun in case a dog does not wish to die when it is shot. Each man who wants to take part will bring his shotgun and will pay a one-dollar entrance fee. But, each man who kills a wild dog will get five dollars for every dog he kills. In the morning, we will have a breakfast fiesta and tell brave tales of how we have cleaned out the problem."

A murmur of satisfaction went around the men who had gathered at the table; a night's sport, the opportunity to make some money and the promise of a fiesta to cap it off. An excellent solution to a problem that had the women so upset. The men bowed slightly to their patron and returned to their homes to spread the news.

"Hi, Vinnie. Good to see you. I'd like you to meet an old friend of ours, Joe Catalina from Havana and San Francisco. Joe, I'd like you to meet a friend of ours, Vinnie Solano, from here in Tapaste and New Orleans." The driver made the introductions. It was a founding rule of LCN that no member introduced himself to another directly; they were always introduced by a third party who knew both.

"Pleased to meet you, Joe."

Solano waved a hand. A few seconds later four cups of coffee and four slices of tres leches cake appeared. There was a momentary silence while the coffee and cake were tasted; one broken only by an appreciative 'mmmm' from Inanna that brought a grin of pride to Solano's face.

"Home made. The lady what owns this place makes it herself; family recipe. Better than anything on the Golden Boulevard."

"It's gorgeous. Thanks, Mister Solano."

"It's Vinnie." The gangster turned his attention to Catalina and Conrad. "Now, what can I do for you?"

"Good to be here, Vinnie. Thank's for your hospitality. Before we start, I'd like to introduce two friends of mine, Conrad Lorenz and Inanna Porco. They're helping us investigate the rape of a tourist in the Imperial a couple of days back."

"Heard about that. Bad news. I can send a couple of associates if you need'em. Help provide some security."

"Kind offer, Vinnie, but we've got a planeload of boys coming in from the mainland. Problem we got is Conrad here's an investigator. Private, not a cop, and he's been helping out with the investigation. Inanna is a Fed, by the way; National Security Council. We've found a guy we need to speak to real bad about the thing, but he's one of your people here. So we need your permission to take him in to Havana."

Solano tensed slightly. Most people wouldn't have noticed, but Catalina and Conrad both did.

"Who you wanna see?"

"Man called Antonio Cardinal. Our records say this is his home town."

"Sure is. Know the family; his uncle was one of the men here when you came in. Why you wanna see him?"

"The scheduled room service man, Ricardo Gomez, had to go out; personal emergency. Dumb cluck didn't tell us, tried to fix a substitute on his own. That substitute was Antonio Cardinal and he was there just minutes before the victim got raped. So we need to talk to him real bad."

Solano thought carefully. His eyes narrowed slightly as he considered the implications.

"Sorry guys; can't do it. These are my people here."

"We just want to get his story." Catalina spoke quietly, without menace.

"Sure, you say that now, but we both know how this goes down. You drive him out, he never comes back. You hang this on him, saves you embarrassment. Sorry, can't allow that; not with my people."

"May I?"

Conrad got a brief nod from Solano and Catalina.

"Mr. Solano, many years ago, there was a rich man living in a small town. Not a well-liked man, but one whose wife was popular with the local people. Then she vanished and he was suspected of her murder. No real evidence, but he was arrested, tried and sentenced to death. A few weeks later, with the noose already waiting for him, a police officer in a nearby town stopped a couple for speeding. He happened to recognize the woman; she was the allegedly murdered wife. The rich man was released immediately, of course. But, from that time on, he was a changed person. He took all his money and put it into a trust fund that was devoted to proving the innocence of people who had been falsely accused. I work for that trust. Mr. Catalina here may be interested in finding who is guilty, I am not. My sole interest is ensuring that an innocent person doesn't get accused of this crime."

Conrad's Eye

"No disrespect, Conrad, but that's what you say. Once Cardinal's gone from here, he's on his own and it fits too many people's agenda's to have this case hung on him."

"Vinnie, Connie herself says it's OK for them to take him. We got approval to come here directly from her." Their driver, Ray "Sunbeam" Patriarcha, made that point firmly. He was a Made Man also; one who outranked Solano.

"Ray, Connie's in Havana and so is Carlos. I'm here; these are my people. I'm not about to let you take one of them for a ride. I'll answer to either Marcello for that myself; sorry, but that's the way it is."

The Cubans in the room noted that comment. During the evening to come, the word would spread out over the town. Their patron had stood up for them, against even the big shots in Havana and put his own life on the line to do so. It was a far call from the days when they'd been 'ruled' by absentee landlords who took the best of everything and did nothing for those who produced them. These Mafioso might be foreigners and gangsters but they were *here* and at least went through the motions of looking after their people.

The men gathered around the table looked at each other. The meeting was deadlocked. The silence was broken by Conrad.

"Suppose we spoke with Cardinal here? We can find out what he knows, make our decisions and compare it with the other things we have discovered. If he remains a suspect, we can leave him here, in your custody, until we come to a decision. If he does not, he can go where he wills, provided he lets you know where that is. Will that satisfy you?"

Solano nodded. "I can live with that. The man stays here. If he's clean, no problem. If he's not, then he gets held here. If it turns out he's guilty, you show me why and if you make the case, we do him here. Agreed?"

"Agreed."

Solano turned and gestured to a small boy who was standing by the counter and rapped out a series of orders in Cuban Spanish. The boy grinned and ran out, pleased with being entrusted with an errand that would earn him a dollar or two.

A few minutes later, the boy returned and spoke to Solano, who reached into a pocket and gave him a few coins. There was another delay of a few minutes. Then Antonio Cardinal and his uncle turned up, both obviously nervous. Conrad guessed that Catalina had been right. *If a car full of wiseguys had come for him, Cardinal would have run.*

Once again, Conrad took over the inquisition, settling Cardinal down and slowly extracting from him a picture of what had happened that evening. How

428

Gomez had asked him to stand in for him on his shift. How it had been OK'd by the room service manager, who knew Cardinal and had been pleased to get a chance to try him out in a more responsible position. How Cardinal had gone up to the 24th floor in the service elevator because the floor Captain would know he wasn't the authorized room service waiter and that would cause problems.

"You had Gomez's access key for the 24th Floor?"

"Yes Sir." Conrad nodded at Catalina, that let Gomez off the hook. It was possible that they key had been duplicated but it would take a foolish locksmith to duplicate a key from a secure Hotel floor. A foolish locksmith who was also tired of life.

"Then, when you went in?"

"I had a trolly with the champagne bottle on ice. I opened it for the man there. It was no problem. Many make a fuss over opening champagne, but it is easy with a little care."

"And that's when Mrs. Trumpeter showed herself off to you, isn't that right?" Once again, Conrad had his verbal harpoon ready for the kill. "She stood where you could see her, but her husband could not; stood there naked and invited you back later. Did she pose for you, Antonio? Display herself lewdly? Touch herself in front of you?"

"No, sir; that is not true." Cardinal gasped. "She did not know I was there. When I had arrived, her husband had made the silence sign to me so I would not spoil the surprise of the champagne. She stepped around the corner from the bedroom, yes, but she was not naked. She had a dress half-on, with the top hanging down and only her bosom was exposed. When she saw me, she went bright red with shame and embarrassment and held her arms over herself like this." Cardinal crossed his arms over his chest in the classical gesture. "Then she ran back out of sight. I stared at her, may God forgive me, but that was all."

"And then what?"

"Then I left, hurriedly, and went back to room service."

"We checked the times, Cardinal; you took a lot longer on that delivery than you should have done."

"I know, sir. I came up and went down in the service elevator and I had to wait for a long time. The elevator must have been in use on a lower floor."

"We can check that. Did anybody see you waiting?"

"No sir; nobody."

Conrad's Eye

Conrad thought carefully. *Cardinal had escaped the traps I set, but he still has no alibi for the critical time. He doesn't seem like the type to commit a crime like this; but, then, all too few people do. The fact Cuba is run by gangsters tends to highlight the innocence of everybody else.* "Vinnie, we can leave Mister Cardinal with you, but he's not in the clear; not yet anyway. If he runs, well, that'll prove he did it; but, otherwise, we may just need to talk to him again."

Solano looked at Antonio Cardinal and his uncle. "You hear that? You can stay here, but make sure I know where you are, all the time. You don't want us to come looking for you. Capische?"

"Capische." Both Cardinals spoke the acknowledgement together.

"Oh, and Antonio." Conrad spoke quietly and amicably. "Perhaps you ought to go to confession and ask for forgiveness for the lecherous looks you gave to Mrs. Trumpeter. They were only human, I know, but the memory embarrasses her greatly."

Cardinal nodded and the two men left.

"Well that went very well." Conrad was happy. A ticklish affair had been dealt with in a way that pleased everybody. "Back to Havana now?"

"Conrad, can we delay by an hour or so? I need to get my cigars. And I'd like to buy one of these tres leches cakes to take back for Igrat; she'll love it."

"Ray?"

"Sure, we got an hour or so. By the time dusk falls, we'll be back in Havana. Hour and a half will be cutting it fine, though."

Conrad frowned slightly. "Are the roads out here that dangerous? I thought the countryside was pretty safe."

"Not much risk of getting stuck up, if that's what you mean. Problem is that them roads aren't lit well; every so often, some ox or donkey wanders into the road. That can cause all kinds of trouble. Don't sweat it, though; we'll be fine. You like cigars, Conrad?"

"I do, Vinnie, yes; although, I only smoke them on special occasions."

"Good. Why don't I take you to the factory? You can see how they're made and the two of you can buy them there. Inanna's cake will be boxed up by the time we get back."

"Sounds good; that OK with you, Joe?"

"Sure is. Pity we can't stay around for the dog hunt, though; the fiesta afterwards sounds fun."

"Come back down. I'm sure the bosses will allow it." Solano got a quick nod from Patriarcha.

"I'd love to, but too much business."

Solano nodded grimly; being a gangster didn't mean a life of leisure. Every day was an effort to keep money flowing in. That was, after all, the first, foremost and above-all duty of every Mob wiseguy. To collect a percentage of every dollar earned by his subordinates, add to it with the income from his own ventures, rackets and enterprises and then send a percentage of the total up the line to his boss, who would be doing the same for the next boss up the family tree.

Conrad realized that the whole system had now been expanded into financing the running of a country. Then, he understood. *It isn't actually so very different from the way Italian renaissance city-states or feudal empires had been run. The names were changed, the ranks were different and the divine right of kings had been replaced by the ascendancy of a Capo, but the basic principles were the same. Viewed that way, Mob-run Cuba wasn't isn't unusual as it seemed. In fact,* Conrad believed, *Mob-run Cuba was probably more honest than most feudal overlords had ever been.*

Conrad reflected on that as well. "Vinnie, your dog hunt was a generous idea."

"You think? Do the maths, Conrad. Every woman here will want her man to go out and take part on the hunt. Show off his manliness. That's a big thing here. I'm counting on a hundred men turning up; that's a cool century in entrance fees. My guess, there's six perhaps ten wild dogs down there, so I'm out thirty to fifty bucks in rewards. Fiesta won't cost nothing; women will bring the food and the dancing will be for free. I'll clear thirty, forty bucks on the dog hunt, even if I fire a couple of Tommy gun bursts just for show."

"Tommy guns." Conrad spoke idly. "Tommy guns all over the place. Never knew John Thompson made so many of them."

There was a laugh around the table. "He didn't. Most of the boys back in the old days used cut-down BARs stolen from National Guard arsenals. But, when we started to get set up here, the Bruno Family in Philadelphia persuaded Auto-Ordnance to take over the old Cuban National Armory in Havana. They started making Tommy guns there. Cost's a lot less than on the mainland and the tourists love them. We use them just for show. We got M14s for business."

"Does Achillea still collect guns?" Catalina's voice was warm with nostalgia. "If she does, why not take her back one of the special editions? They're really special; it isn't just a name. Made with gold-inlaid scrollwork on the receiver and hand-polished rosewood furniture. They're so beautiful, it's a shame to shoot them. Each one comes complete with a copy of 'The Gun that Made The Twenties Roar,' signed by The Little Man himself."

"I'll do that."

For Igrat, the monthly run to Cuba was business, a matter of getting back up to speed on her courier duties after more than fifteen years working with Bill Shaych in California. In contrast, this trip had been Inanna's vacation; or, at least, it had started that way. In Inanna's eyes, a vacation wasn't complete unless she brought back a few gifts for her friends. .

"If you'd like to come along, people." Solano had finished speaking with the café staff. "It's ten minutes to the cigar factory, so we're gonna need to move if you wanna be back in the City by dusk."

CHAPTER FOUR

Shopping Center, 24th Floor, Imperial Forum Hotel-Casino

"How the hell did they manage that?"

Igrat stopped in her tracks outside the Ferrari dealership in the center of the premium shopping area. It wasn't the only dealership up there; Cadillac, Packard and Lincoln also had their showrooms. The Ferrari dealership was the only one that had a car in its display area. A sleek, streamlined, bright red coupe. While Igrat stood and stared at it, her feet dragged her into the show room.

"What is it? And how did you get it up here?"

She'd only been in the room for a split second when a salesman descended upon her.

"This is our new Grand Coupe, madame; the Ferrari 512BB. And if madame wouldn't mind the correction, we didn't really bring it up here. We carried it up as a slung load under a rotodyne, cut a hole in the roof and lowered it in. Is madame interested in our latest masterpiece? What does madame currently drive?"

"A Cadillac Corvette Fancy Free, 1972. A convertible."

"A very fine automobile, if I might say so, madame. Of course, it doesn't compare with a Ferrari, but then, what does? The 512BB has a five-liter flat 12 engine mounted in the middle of the vehicle. We don't do a convertible version, I'm sorry to say. Mr Enzo does not believe in soft tops on cars of this performance. Would madame like to sit inside?"

Igrat slipped inside and moved her hands expertly over the controls. Mentally, the salesman decided to drop his intended purchase line and treat this woman as a serious driver. Looking at her and the way she handled the car's equipment, she was the rare buyer even Enzo Ferrari, whose distaste for his customers was legendary, might approve.

"How much?" Igrat was impressed by the vehicle.

"58,000 Sovereigns, madame."

"In American?"

"That will be 121,800 dollars, madame. With delivery charges and tax, 125,000. I feel I should warn you, there is a rigorous service schedule that must be obeyed. Failure to do so will void the warranty and seriously damage the engine."

"No problem with that. Anywhere I can test drive one?"

"No problem with that."

The salesman and Igrat exchanged grins.

"In exchange for 30,000 dollars in earnest money, we will loan you a demonstration car for up to a week. If for any reason you decide not to go through with the purchase, we will refund your earnest money in full. Will you be needing to finance the balance?"

"You're very sure of yourself."

"Madame, once somebody has driven a Ferrari just once, we have them for life. We'll be drawing up the purchase papers while you're driving the demonstration vehicle."

"We'll see. And no, I don't need to finance this."

She dug in her bag and produced the thirty thousand dollars she'd won earlier.

"That'll cover the earnest money, I'll pay the balance in cash as well."

The salesman left to get the keys of the demonstration car and start the paperwork rolling. In the office, the sales manager was looking at Igrat in the 512BB. The salesman smiled at him.

"Did you see her legs when she got in? Talk about a fast woman in a fast car."

"I wouldn't talk about that at all. She's John Gotti's comare. Or so the whispers have it."

The salesman went white.

Joe Catalina's Office, Imperial Forum Hotel-Casino.

"You're sure?"

"No. He's got no alibi and he was in the right place at the right time. I just don't think so. Certainly, he's got a good explanation for everything; there's no way you can hang this on him without something solid."

"'If we eliminate all other possibilities, what is left, no matter now improbable, must be the truth.' Only we've got nothing left. So this didn't happen." John Gotti had been reading Sherlock Holmes.

I told Arthur Conan Doyle that was wrong, but he just wouldn't listen, Conrad thought to himself.

"Dapper John, that's a logical fallacy. It presumes that we know all the possibilities that exist and that we know that they are all the possibilities that exist. We have neither that presumption, nor that knowledge. On the contrary; what we do know is that we're missing one or more of those possibilities."

"We're stuck then." Catalina sounded even more depressed than he was. The investigation had been running nearly three days and they'd succeeded in eliminating every possible suspect.

The silence was interrupted by the door opening. Igrat bounced in.

"Well, how's it going?"

"It isn't." Conrad sounded unhappy. He could see his greatest fear, that somebody would be killed at random to try and show that nobody got away with harming tourists in Cuba, was becoming reality. He could sense that Gotti, at least, was beginning to think of that option.

"Iggie, I got you a cake, Try it; it's gorgeous."

"Thank you." Igrat helped herself to a slice from the box and forked a portion into her mouth. Her shaped eyebrows did a little dance. "You're right, this is good. Inanna, you want a Fancy Free, right? Want to buy mine? Yours for nine thousand."

"You been losing, at last?" Catalina sounded relieved.

"Nope, just bought myself a Ferrari. Spent my winnings on it."

"The 512 upstairs?"

"That's right. Sweet vehicle."

"So it should be, for what they're charging. Ten times the cost of your 'Vette. And be careful how you drive it; the engine is over the transmission and that makes it twitchy." There was a note of concern in Gotti's voice.

Igrat made a mental note that she had to remind him she didn't need to be protected.

"I'll give it a try tomorrow. I've got a loaner for a week before I make the final decision. What's the speed limits around here?"

"Speed limits?" There was a chuckle around the room. "If you kill yourself, you exceeded them. If you kill somebody else, you'd better make it good with their family. Both kinds of family. They believe in vendetta around here. And Cuban law applies; don't injure a tourist."

Conrad frowned. Something was dancing right at the edge of his mind and he couldn't quite put it all together.

"Look, let's start again, right at the beginning. Revisit every assumption we've ever made. We've got a list of everybody who was up in that suite right?"

The audience nodded. Conrad got to work, writing out a series of cards with the names of every person who had been identified as going near the suite in question. He shuffled them, and dealt out the first one.

"Ricardo Gomez. Any offers?"

"He couldn't be up there. He'd given his access key to Antonio Cardinal. Unless he'd had a duplicate made, he's off the hook." Catalina was emphatic about it.

Gotti agreed. "No locksmith here will make a duplicate key for the high-security area of the hotel. He could have made it himself, but he'd need a lot of good tools for that. He hasn't got them."

"Right, so we have to put him down low. Next card. Mrs. Trumpeter."

There was a ripple of laughter. "So she raped herself, stuffed her panties in her mouth, taped herself up and waited to choke? After drugging herself into a coma?"

"Could be they were playing a game and it went wrong? Too much Mickey Finn?"

"Not with that tape, no." Igrat spoke firmly, although the words came out mixed with a second helping of Tres Leches cake. "Gods, this cake is good. I owe you, Inanna. No, Irene is a trophy wife; her looks are all she has. No way is she going to allow tape like that to be put over her mouth. What happened to her, she didn't agree with it; you can take that to the bank."

"Bottom of the pile then?" There were nods all around the room and Conrad pinned the card for Mrs. Trumpeter under that for Ricardo Gomez.

"Next card." Conrad dealt it. "Hmm. Unknown. Any offers?"

"Right at the top." Joe Catalina spoke firmly and decisively. This was the conclusion he wanted.

"Could be; you said people around here were into vendettas." Conrad was inclined to agree with Catalina. It suited his agenda as well.

"Problem, people." John Gotti did not agree. "We haven't got a shred of evidence there is an unknown involved. There's no evidence he was on the floor. There's no evidence he was in the suite. Or she; some hit men are female. Mostly the really good ones. The way things went down, it don't smell like a professional hit; too many people still breathing for that. So, how did the hitter get up there? floor captain didn't see nothing."

"Up the service elevator?" Catalina sounded hopeful.

"Not a chance." Conrad hated to say it, but it was true. "If Antonio Cardinal is telling the truth, he went straight to the service elevator and waited there until it arrived, then took it straight down. By the time it would have got back up, it's all over. If Cardinal is telling the truth."

"You don't believe him?" Gotti pushed the question hard.

Conrad thought carefully. "About the elevator? Yes, I do. If he was standing there waiting for it, he would have seen somebody. If he was lying about that, he was in the suite raping and robbing Mrs. Trumpeter. Either way, no unknown involved. I'd put the unknown man third up from the bottom, and that's generous."

"And since we're dealing with him, Antonio Cardinal. Likely?" Gotti was still pushing. It was obvious he liked the young Cuban as the killer.

Conrad sighed. "Likely, yes. The most likely so far, I'm sad to say." He pinned the card at the top of the column, shaking his head sadly. "And that just leaves Hubert Trumpeter."

"Now there's a thought." Catalina was suddenly fascinated. "We've been thinking of that guy as a victim for so long, we never thought of him as the killer. Doing what you made us do, Conrad. Walking through it. Call for champagne. Wife is in the bedroom getting dressed. Room service comes up. Opens the champagne. I dose it with Mickey Finn; wife drinks some, passes out. This makes the motive robbery. He's not going to drug and rape his wife."

"Can't do that anyway." Igrat was slightly indignant. "Legally, a man can't rape his wife. Her consent at marriage is final and binding. One reason why I never get married."

"Has to be robbery, then." Gotti agreed.

Conrad nodded. *This is fitting together better than anything that they'd discussed so far.* He rearranged the motive cards so robbery was at the top, then pinned the card for Hubert Trumpeter at the top of the suspects column.

"You know, that makes a hell of a lot of sense." Gotti was thoughtful. "Joe, finish your run through."

Conrad's Eye

"Sure. Wife's passed out. I open the safe, take the jewels. Then I realize it points right at me. So, I tie her up and rape her." Catalina held his hand up. "This is Cuba, Iggie; we make the laws up as we go along here. If we say it's rape, it's rape. I've already arranged for a call from Cadillac about a car, so the phone goes and I head off to see them. That's my alibi and it worked damned well. Had us all forgetting about him. Then he comes back and reports the attack."

There was a long, long silence around the room.

"So Trumpeter stole his own jewels. Why?" Conrad knew that the answer was in his head; he couldn't quite bring it into focus.

"To keep them from Irene. Her pre-nuptial settlement was her clothes, her jewels, five thousand dollars and a car." Igrat sounded sharp and there was a vicious edge to her voice. "What's the odds, he was planning to dump her anyway? She's good, but she's starting to age; he's probably thinking of dumping her for a new model."

Conrad shook his head. "You don't like men very much, do you, Igrat?"

"I love them, Conrad. You know what the Seer calls me, 'the original good time who's been had by all.' I just don't have any illusions about them. Trumpeter wants a trophy wife, nothing more. He wants things he can possess; that's why he wasn't interested in me. He knew he couldn't own me, so I was of no importance to him."

Suddenly she snapped her fingers. "That tape. Wasn't Trumpeter in the construction business? He knew that tape was bad news. He wanted to disfigure Irene. Probably hoped that, if she survived, the medics wouldn't know the difference, tear it off and ruin her face. Then, he'd smack the hotel with a massive claim for shut-up money. You'd pay him off; a tourist who'd been robbed and his wife raped and disfigured? How much would you pay for his silence? Millions? Tens of millions? And you couldn't kill him, because the publicity would get worse.

"This way he gets it all; he gets the jewels, the hush money, he divorces Irene and leaves her so nobody else will want her. She was his *property*. He doesn't want anybody else to have her."

Igrat looked around; her hair had slipped slightly out of place during her outburst and she was panting very gently. Her anger at what she was describing was very obvious.

Conrad smacked his hand on the table. "That pre-nuptial settlement. I knew something was wrong with it; it didn't fit somehow. Look at it. Her clothes, not a great expense and not worth much. Five thousand dollars, an amount so small it's an insult. A car; note it doesn't say what sort of car. A Hindustan

Ambassador probably, knowing how Trumpeter thinks. And a million bucks worth of jewelry. Does that make sense? It's way out of place. That's why he wanted to steal the jewelry; he wanted to make sure he left her with nothing. Not even her looks."

"Couple of problems with that, Conrad." Catalina was revolving the whole matter around in his head. "He was going to buy Mrs. Trumpeter a Corvette Fancy Free; that doesn't sound like dumping her with nothing. And secondly, where are the jewels? We've been through the suite. They're not there. He's not been outside his new suite since this whole thing started. He had a few minutes to stash them. So where are they? And another thing; he's going to have a huge chunk of change, that's going to cause a lot of questions."

"Dapper John, didn't you say he was trying to buy into the Casinos?"

"Sure was. He offered ten million for a share in the new place the Gambino and Lucchese family is buildin', The Speakeasy. They laughed at him. I mean really laughed at him."

"So suppose he asked for a share as his hush-money over this incident?"

Gotti stared at the inquisitor with sudden comprehension. "He'd get it. Not a big share, but there's so much money flowing round here, a small share means a lot of income."

"And he gets a showgirl for his next trophy wife."

"Yeah." Catalina sounded sour. "And hadn't she better watch her back."

Cadillac Dealership, 24th Floor, Imperial Forum Hotel-Casino

"Are you sure about this?" Inanna sounded uncertain.

"Very sure." Igrat was eyeing the literature all around her. The display didn't have the impact of the car sitting on the Ferrari floor just a few yards away. From the expressions on the faces of the staff, they knew it. Igrat guessed that it would be a very good time to own a rotodyne in Havana. Everybody would want to lift a car up here now. Idly, she wondered if the floor would take the weight.

"Is there a particular car we can interest you in, ladies?"

The salesmen had shrugged off their gloom and descended on Igrat and Inanna with commendable speed.

"I drive a Cadillac Corvette Fancy Free . . . "

Igrat started to speak, but the salesman cut her off before she could finish. At that point, she decided his foot was going to get under her stiletto heel at some time in the very near future.

"And you want to replace it with a new model. Well, we have all the information on the latest model and there are demonstration cars in the garage downstairs."

"No, I've just bought a Ferrari 512."

The salesman looked as if he was about to cry.

"But my friend here likes the Fancy Free and we heard that you'd just had a cancelled order. A Mr. Trumpeter ordered it for his wife, but, after the incident . . . So we wondered if we could jump in and snap it up."

"We would certainly be delighted to take an order from you, ma'am, but you're mistaken about the car. Mr. Trumpeter has indeed bought a car from us, but it isn't a Fancy Free. It's a Fleetwood Brougham d'Elegance, with the Continental Package."

Something clicked in Igrat's mind. "And you've given him a demonstration vehicle to use while the paperwork is done, right?"

"That's right, ma'am, it's our standard policy. And *we* don't ask for earnest money as a condition."

"Has he used it at all?"

"Now that you mention it, no. He went down to the garage to look at it, spend about ten minutes there and then came back up. But he hasn't been back since. Perhaps, the terrible affair with his wife?"

"Perhaps. Thank you. Inanna, you want the literature on the Fancy Free?"

"Yes please. How long is the waiting list for a Fancy Free?"

"About ten months at the moment, ma'am. The current model is priced at six thousand sovereigns, baseline Fancy Free."

Inanna twisted her lips slightly at that. The price was easily affordable, but she hated waiting for things.

"It's a pity about the Trumpeters not putting a cancelled one up for grabs. Anyway, I'll think about it and get back to you."

They started to leave. Igrat stepping backwards, causing the salesman to yelp as her heel dug into his instep.

"Oh, sorry about that."

440

By the time the salesman had recovered his composure, Igrat was hurrying back to the residential area and Inanna had to half-run to catch up.

"Iggie, wait, what's the matter?"

"I've got to see Conrad right away, Trumpeter was lying about the car; he never had any intention of buying his wife a Fancy Free. Or anything else, come to that. He had this whole thing planned right from the beginning. And that includes leaving her ruined,"

Joe Catalina's Office, Imperial Forum Hotel-Casino

"Hey, guys. I know where the jewels are. Trumpeter was lying about the car. He wasn't buying a Fancy Free for his wife; he was buying a Fleetwood for himself. He had this whole thing planned."

"So where's the stones?" Catalina was happier than he'd been since he'd got the pager message. The way this whole business was falling out, it was looking like a domestic crime that could have happened anywhere.

"He's buying a car. From a dealer here, right?" Igrat had a smug grin on her face.

"And the car dealers have demo vehicles they loan out to high-rollers." Conrad was fastest on the uptake, but, then, he was the inquisitor.

"That's right. He's got a Fleetwood loaner in the garage, but he hasn't touched it. Just went down to look at it then, came right back. It hasn't even cost him anything, the Caddy dealer doesn't ask for earnest money."

"Because he didn't want to lead anybody to it." Conrad added another touch.

"And the elevator from the plaza doesn't go past the Floor Captain's desk. Trumpeter could go down, stash the jewels, then come up again and the floor captain wouldn't realize he'd been off the floor. We'd better have a look at that car." Catalina was up; bouncing around in a way that reminded Conrad of the young gunman he'd met a quarter century earlier.

Garage, Basement, Imperial Forum Hotel-Casino

"I'd expected a lot more cars down here." Conrad looked along the rows of parked vehicles. They were a mix of demonstration cars belonging to the various dealers and limousines, very few private cars indeed. "Back on the mainland, the garage would be overflowing."

"We don't encourage people to drive. Not tourist,s anyway. Too much chance they'll get hurt. Sure you can hire a car and drive yourself if you wanna, but why? We make limos here easy to get, and cheap to hire, so why drive yourself? You can do the luxury tour in the back of one of our limos, sipping on a nice Scotch, while a driver we supply shows you the town. And he knows it better than you ever will, so why mess with the map and finding the rental car when all you have to do is ask the desk clerk to bring the car around? Most of the people what come here ain't the real rich. They're the Mister and Mizz Average, sometimes with 2.6 Little Averages. They ain't never had the experience of being driven around in a limo by a chauffeur, especially one they can make themselves believe stuck up a bank on the mainland last week. And sometimes he did. Riding in limos, driven by gun-carrying wiseguys, is part of the Cuba Experience; be like the really rich, laze around just like the rich folks and if ya want to get drunk or stoned, why not? Ya don't have to drive home."

"The old flim-flam." Conrad was quite struck with admiration. "Take any card you want, but you always take the one the magician wants you to."

"Sure, and the cost of providing a limo dirt cheap is nothing compared with the profit we make on people getting plastered. Just present your room key to the limo guy, and he takes you back to your hotel when you're done having fun. Now, which car was assigned to Trumpeter?"

The last remark was tossed at the salesman who was fidgeting nervously.

"The Galloway Green Firemist Fleetwood, sir."

"Open it up." The salesman hesitated slightly.

"I've gotta search warrant." Catalina's hand moved slightly; the Colt M1911 in his shoulder holster was just slightly visible. "You ain't been long in Cuba, have you kid?"

Conrad was struck by how quickly his friend had shifted from his normal amiable good nature to the appearance of a hardened killer. The car salesman gulped and unlocked the doors. Conrad climbed into the passenger seat and started going through the glove compartment while Catalina searched the back seats. Nothing. Going through the contents of the trunk was equally futile.

The car was empty.

"Damn, it sounded too good. Sorry, Conrad." Catalina stared at the car. His instincts told him that the stolen jewels had to be there.

His thoughts were interrupted by a roar behind him. The sleek shape of a Ferrari 512BB pulled up alongside, with Igrat at the wheel. She turned the engine off and swung out, her skirt riding up as she did so. Catalina couldn't help reflect that she had legs that seemed to go on forever.

"Hi, guys. Did you find them?"

"No. Car is clean."

Igrat frowned, stared at the Fleetwood and got into the driver's seat. "They've got to be here; it's the only thing that fits."

She played with the controls for a moment, then looked at the salesman. "My Fancy Free has a hidden locker behind the seats. This one got anything like that?"

"No, ma'am; nothing behind the seats."

Catalina picked up on the intonation right away.

"So where is it?" The menace in his bearing was very apparent.

The salesman gulped again and realized for the first time just how close to an unmarked line he was treading. He'd come to Cuba because he'd heard it was a place to get rich quickly. Now, he suddenly understood that the men who ran the place did not take kindly to gratuitous insolence from somebody at the bottom of the pecking order.

"There's a safe built into the floor. Passenger side, under the carpets. Lift them up while the engine is running, turn the headlights on full beam and press button six on the radio. It'll open."

Igrat turned the key, starting the engine. "The 500 cubic inch V8. I like that. Size *does* matter, you know. Now, turn on the headlights on full beam and press six . . . "

Over on the passenger side, a hatch in the floor popped open, revealing a shallow but wide safe. It was stuffed with jewelry.

"Now that looks about right, doesn't it?"

"It certainly does." Conrad looked at the haul. From an unpromising start, this whole investigation was coming together nicely.

Catalina reached down and picked up the jewelry, running it through his fingers. "D'ya reckon Mr. Trumpeter is going to be pleased we found his stolen jewelry?"

"Doubt it." Conrad looked at the haul. "Mrs. Trumpeter will be, though."

Joe Catalina's Office, Imperial Forum Hotel-Casino

It had been quite a parade up from the garage. Catalina, carrying the bag of jewelry; Conrad beside him. Two gunmen, keeping an urgent watch out for anybody who might get tempted to do a snatch. Igrat following them, trying to work out the best way to make a snatch, purely out of academic interest. Inanna, perfectly well aware of what was running through Igrat's mind, getting ready to talk her out of it. Finally, two tourists who'd been enlisted as independent observers on the promise of free tickets for the late-night erotic show in the hotel club. Meanwhile the car salesman, shaken by his epiphany in the parking lot, had volunteered to run ahead and call the local office of Trumpeter's insurance agency to tell them that the stolen jewelry had been recovered. The representative from the Agency had arrived just as the procession reached Catalina's office.

"These the jewels?" Miguel Alonzo, manager of the agency, had been in the hotel anyway and everything had slotted together well.

"Wait a moment." Catalina was thanking the two tourists for their assistance and giving them their free tickets, along with a voucher for the pre-theater dinner. They shook hands with him and disappeared, clutching their tickets and thinking kindly of those who rewarded so well for a trivial service.

"OK, sure that's the jewels. We got them out of a car in the parking lot a few minutes ago; nobody's taken their eyes off them since."

"That is very wise. I must now call my main office and give them the news. They will be most pleased, but they will want to send an assessor to check these carefully. Who knows what happened between the time they were stolen and you and your men recovered them?"

"We think they just sat in the car, but we may be wrong." *But we aren't* Conrad thought. *We know Trumpeter didn't go down there; so, unless he'd got an accomplice, he's done.*

Catalina produced a safety deposit box and put the jewels inside. "Señor Alonzo, you will sign the seal here please, and I will sign beside you. Conrad, you also."

"And this person is?" Alonzo was friendly, but giving every sign of professional caution.

"I am Conrad Lorentz, a professional investigator. I am also an ordained priest and will swear that my eyes have not been removed from those jewels since they were recovered from the car."

"Thank you, Father Lorenz." The box was sealed and locked and Catalina put it in his safe. As he did so, he caught Igrat's eye and whispered.

"Don't even think it."

"Never crossed my mind." Igrat struck her most virtuous pose.

"Right." Catalina chuckled and shook his head.

Alonzo went off to call his head office, while Catalina sent one of his men to tell Gotti, and by implication the Commission, that the stolen jewelry had been recovered. As the office cleared and people settled down, Catalina opened his drinks cabinet.

"We deserve this. Conrad?"

"Pale sherry, please."

Catalina poured, followed by a shot of 18-year-old The McAllen for Igrat. By the time he had finished handing out the drinks, the six people left had settled down and were congratulating themselves.

"We're sure it was Trumpeter?"

"No doubt about it." Conrad appreciated the sherry; *it isn't quite as good as the one Samuela had in her bar downstairs, but it is excellent.* "The sales manager at Cadillac recognized his picture and they confirmed his ID before taking the order for his car. It was him, and nobody else has been near that car."

"That confirms it then. Fine." Catalina picked up his phone. When the other end answered, his orders were clipped and sharp. "Want two of ya to go to Hubert Trumpeter's suite, the new one, it's 2427, and bring him down to my office. Don't get heavier than needs, just don't take no for an answer."

"What about Mrs. Trumpeter?" Inanna spoke as soon as Catalina had put down the telephone. "She needs to know what's happening. Those jewels are probably her major asset right now."

"Yeah, you tell her, Inanna. Once Trumpeter gets down here, we'll have a proper sit-down in my meeting room. If she's fit to come, it might be good for her to get over here. And we'll have to wait till Dapper John gets here as well, so she's got time." Catalina grinned. "Just tell the desk you want a limo to get you to AC Memorial. The drivers know the way."

"That many accidents?" Conrad was surprised.

"Nah, but people here eat too much, drink too much, go down with the runs. Or they pick the wrong escort and need some real private treatment for Cupid's catarrh. If they're laid up, they can't gamble. One thing that worries me; how come Trumpeter didn't get affected by the Mickey Finn? He laced the wine, sure of that. We'll find where he got it from soon enough."

"That's easy." Igrat sipped her single malt appreciatively. "It's easy to convince people you're drinking when you're not. Just keep sipping but barely wet your lips each time. People with you'll think that you've been refilling, but they just haven't noticed you doing it. It's a good thing for a girl to learn, how to stay sober in a room full of men getting drunk. They all drink far more than normal to impress her and when they're all passing out, she can help herself to their wallets and stash the cash. When they wake up, it's easy to convince each of them that they had ended up paying for the whole party by themselves. Then, once they're all fighting over who paid for everything, she can slip away with the loot."

Igrat stopped and looked at all the men staring at her. "*What?*"

Thirty minutes later, the telephone on Catalina's desk rang. He picked it up and said one word.

"Trumpeter?"

"He's sitting in the room out back. Waiting, with a couple of the boys just staring at him. He started off being aggressive and unhappy; now he's just unhappy."

"He can stay unhappy. Come on in and tell us what happened."

"We went through his stuff. Found this."

Big Pony handed over an envelope full of legal papers. Catalina took one look at it and grunted.

"Divorce papers. All made out, all he had to do was date them and hand them over."

The telephone rang; Catalina picked it up. He listened for a moment and then hung up.

"That was Turtle. He just picked up the insurance assessor from Dillinger and is bringing him in. He'll be here in 30 minutes. Anything else we need to sort out first?"

"Inanna's bringing Mrs. Trumpeter in. She's a bit weak but otherwise seems fine." Conrad was a bit distracted, he was piecing the whole story together in his mind but there were still a few parts missing. Nothing really important; he had the main thread finished.

"And Dapper John's on his way as well. He'll be representing the Commission; they're well pleased with how this has all turned out."

That made Catalina well-pleased also; if something like this had to happen in his hotels, it was best it worked out the way it had. The thought of what might had happened and the effects it could have on the Cuban gambling resorts had been haunting him. He was the man in charge, he was the one who would be held responsible for any losses suffered as a result of the crime that had taken place on his watch. All the prospects he had been dreading were now fading away and already beginning to take on the appearance of a half-remembered nightmare. And so it was that he consumed his drink with more than his usual relish.

A round of drinks later, there was a tap on the door. Inanna brought Mrs. Trumpeter in. She was pale and sloppily-dressed in a cheap T-shirt and jeans. Yet, her arms clutched her clothes to her as if they were treasures or, more likely, if her life depended on them. *In a sense, I suppose she thinks it does*, Conrad thought, *she must be realizing that something is very wrong with the situation and be filled with dread as to what it might be. And, she has more than one idea about how she and her husband are involved. Even if she won't admit them to herself.*

"Mrs. Trumpeter, it's good to see you back on your feet." Catalina paused for a second, while one of the gangsters seated her.

Then, he hesitated a beat before resuming, trying to work out the best way to give her the news. "There's no easy way to tell you this, but your assumption was right; your husband does intend to divorce you. We have the papers here. If it makes it a little easier, what happened to you was not the cause of his decision. He made that before you two came here. Now, the question is, he hasn't served you papers yet; do you want to get in first and divorce him? Do it here in Cuba and we get to write the settlement. Just remember what I said about the pre-nup. Don't mean nothing here."

Mrs. Trumpeter looked around the room and at the men and women gathered there. "Hubert is in a lot of trouble, isn't he? What has he done?"

Conrad took over. "Mrs. Trumpeter, that will become obvious in due course. But, yes, your husband is in very serious trouble indeed and it's getting worse by the hour. You have nothing to concern yourself about; the people here are very well aware of the difference between those who commit crimes and those who are the victims of them."

"You could say our living depends on it." Catalina sounded grim but there was a humorous note to his voice that turned the remark into a gallows joke. Mrs Trumpeter picked up on it and smiled weakly.

Another tap on the door. A large man brought in another, one wearing a dark blue business suit that stood out from the universal light gray of the gangsters.

"Excuse me, gentlemen, I'm Simon Adams, the assigned insurance assessor. I understand you have recovered the stolen merchandise?"

"Welcome to Cuba, Mr. Adams. Pick up and drive back went well?"

"Very well; your man here is most efficient. I have a feeling I may have seen him on the wall of a Miami post office at some time, though?" Adams smiled and was rewarded with a chuckle that raced around the room.

"Quite likely." Catalina opened his safe and took out the box. "Please note that the signatures over the seals are still in place and undamaged. Now, I open the box and we have the jewelry wrapped inside."

Adams took the box and examined the seals carefully. " I confirm that the seals are intact and authorize you to go ahead and break them."

He returned the box to Catalina who ceremoniously cut the seals with his fingernail and opened the box. To his relief, the jewels were still there. Then, he took out the package within and handed it to Adams. The insurance assessor took out the cloth that contained the jewels and placed them on his desk, under the light.

Catalina adjusted it slightly and unnecessarily. "This right for you, Simon?"

"Excellent." The insurance assessor sat down, opened the cloth and looked at the jewelry. Then he screwed a loupe into his eye and started to inspect the pieces.

"They don't look right." Mrs. Trumpeter whispered to Catalina, but was waved into silence by Adams. He methodically inspected each piece, writing notes down on a small pad he had carried in a pocket. The minutes ticked by. The pile of pieces to be inspected grew smaller; the pile of those that had been scanned larger. Eventually Adams sighed, removed his loupe and turned off Catalina's desk light.

"These are the pieces removed from the hiding place used by the thief?"

"They are." Catalina, Conrad and Igrat all could guess what was coming, although their reasons for doing so were different.

"Then I have some bad news for you. There is no doubt that the settings are the original ones insured by our company some years ago. There is no doubt of that at all; my colleague who did the assessment found the combination of valuable stones and worthless settings so unusual that he took great care to ensure that they could be validated in the future.

"But the stones in these pieces are worthless glass. Junk. Not even good quality junk; they are the sort of cheap costume jewelry that a teenage girl might buy. One could buy better quality costume jewelry than this in any shopping plaza.

"I am sorry, Mrs. Trumpeter, but these pieces are literally worthless. I would assess their present value at less than five hundred dollars in total and that is being very generous indeed."

"I said they looked wrong." Mrs. Trumpeter was crying.

"When did you last see them?" Conrad's voice was gentle and supportive as he asked the question.

"Normally they're kept in a bank vault. But Hubert collected them for me to wear here. Said he wanted me to look stunning in them, so he could impress the people he was doing business with."

Conrad and Andrews exchanged glances, each thinking exactly the same thing. *Those stones had been switched before the jewelry had ever reached Cuba.*

For Conrad, it was the last piece of the puzzle. Mrs. Trumpeter had come to the same conclusion. She almost shriveled as the implications sank in.

"He cheated me out of my jewels, didn't he? They were the one valuable thing in the pre-nuptial agreement we signed and he's cheated me out of them."

Conrad watched her carefully, amazed that even faced with this betrayal, she didn't, or couldn't, follow that thought through to its logical conclusion.

Love, even the pale facsimile of it that had existed between the Trumpeters, died hard.

"What am I going to do now?"

"Divorce him."

Catalina's voice was hard as he tossed a pad to her and gave her a pen. "Just write on that pad that you want to divorce the bastard, we'll know who you mean, and sign it. Everybody here's your witness."

At that point, John Gotti had arrived with three men from his security unit.

"The jewels?" were his first words.

"Fakes." Catalina answered as briefly.

"Would have been surprising if they were genuine." Conrad added in the same style.

"Why d'ya think that, Mr. Investigator?" Gotti was curious.

"Can't fence a million dollars worth of stolen stones here; only place they could come from would be tourists. Fencing them is death, but a fence handing the thief over is a good way to get in well with your families. So, they had to be fenced on the mainland."

"Right." Gotti nodded. "Time for a sit-down."

CHAPTER FIVE

Hotel Conference Room, Imperial Forum Hotel-Casino.

The table in the center of the Conference Room filled quickly. Catalina took the position at the head, with Conrad on his right and John Gotti on his left. Igrat slid in next, beside Gotti, while Inanna and Mrs Trumpeter took the seats beside Conrad. There was a brief struggle between the various parties as to who would sit beside Igrat; one that ended when Simon Adams slipped in beside her. Other participants and interested spectators formed up around the walls. Conrad saw Ricardo Gomez being brought in and was relieved to see that, apart from being generally untidy and very frightened, he was unharmed. Ray Patriarcha also arrived and quietly took a seat by the wall. Finally three gangsters brought Trumpeter himself in. He was seated, none too gently, at the end of the table, facing the rest.

"What are you people doing? How dare you . . . "

His voice trailed off as Catalina stared at him. Catalina himself spoke quietly and authoritatively.

"This sit-down is being held to determine the facts of the assault and robbery of Mrs. Irene Trumpeter four nights ago. Conrad, would you tell us what happened please?"

"Certainly. Before we start, I have one question to ask of Mr. Adams. Your company insured the jewelry in question. Was that jewelry re-inspected and revalued at regular intervals?"

"Of course. It was re-appraised once per year."

"That's what I thought. And the next re-appraisal is approaching?"

"It is."

"Thank you." The last pieces dropped into place. "This story goes a way back before the actual incident. It stems from two decisions made by Mr. Hubert Trumpeter. One was that he wished to invest in the casino business here; the other was that he had decided to divorce his wife. I am sorry to put this crudely, Mrs. Trumpeter, but he wished to trade you in for a new model. There is no way to describe his actions other than that."

Irene Trumpeter sniffed and nodded, reluctantly but nodded. Conrad hated himself, more than usual, for the way he had referred to that side of this affair, but she had to understand how little Trumpeter had cared for her. It would make the rest of the story more understandable to her.

"Those two decisions are intimately linked. Mr. Trumpeter tried to buy in to the casinos here but found that he had left the move too late. The price of construction here is soaring; the value of casino-hotels likewise. Individuals cannot buy into the business any more, not unless they are fabulously wealthy, and Trumpeter wasn't that. He tried to maximize the resources available to him; put all his cash reserves, plus everything he could raise, into the pot and it still wasn't enough. He even took the stones from your jewelry, Mrs. Trumpeter; sold them and added the million dollars he got for them to the pool of cash.

"This wasn't a spur of the moment decision, or one taken in desperation. Mrs. Trumpeter, he *always* planned to do that. Your prenuptial agreement specified you could keep your clothes, a car, five thousand dollars and your jewels. Right from the start, he intended to make sure that you took as little as possible from the marriage. The jewels he gave you were expensive stones in cheap, indeed worthless, settings. He always intended to replace those stones with cut glass that matched the worthlessness of the settings.

"Again, to be frank, he didn't think you were smart enough to have the jewelry re-appraised before the divorce; although, if you had hired a competent lawyer, he should have thought of that. And, had you complained after the divorce, it would have been hard to claim that those settings had once held valuable stones. This has been his mode of operation all along; to give people something that appeared to be valuable but which later, after he had gone, turned out to be of little worth. Houses, office blocks, your jewelry, all the same."

There was an explosion from Trumpeter, one quickly stifled by a rapid series of blows and the sight of a .45 Colt carried by one of the wiseguys. Conrad lifted an eyebrow, then carried on.

"This left him with a problem, of course. The jewels were now fakes; a re-appraisal was looming. His attempt to buy into Cuba had been rebuffed. The plan he came up with was intended to solve all his problems with one neat stroke.

"Mr. and Mrs. Trumpeter came to Cuba for a working vacation, or so Mrs. Trumpeter thought. In fact, Trumpeter's attempt to buy into the casino business had already been rejected and he was about to try a different approach. In doing so, he would also get rid of the fake jewelry and collect the insurance money on it. His tool to achieve that end was a faked robbery.

"On the night in question, he had contacted the Cadillac dealership to make the arrangements for purchasing a Fleetwood and having access to a demonstration vehicle. He made his appointment, then he ordered a bottle of champagne from room service and had it brought up. He timed it for the period before going to a show, or whatever he purportedly had planned, so his wife would be in the bedroom getting ready. The champagne arrived. The waiter opened it and left. Trumpeter then dosed the champagne with a large amount of chloral hydrate. He and his wife then gave the appearance of sharing the bottle.

"I say 'gave the appearance,' because Trumpeter actually drank very little. As Igrat rather colorfully explained, it's perfectly possible to give the illusion of drinking a lot without actually doing so. I suspect Trumpeter learned the same trick when entertaining investors. Anyway, Mrs. Trumpeter drank a lot, Mr. Trumpeter very little. Very quickly, she began to feel the effect of the drug, mistaking it for that of the champagne. At that point, Mr. Trumpeter was late for his appointment with Cadillac; they called him, he explained that he was running late but would be down shortly.

"Around this time, the chloral hydrate kicked in. Mrs. Trumpeter passed out. Trumpeter went to the room safe, opened it and removed the jewelry. What happened next, we don't quite know and probably never will. Was he turned on by her comatose helplessness? Or had he already planned the next stage? Whatever the answer, his actions were the same. He roughly stripped his wife and had sex with her."

"Raped her." Gotti's voice was cold and unforgiving.

"He did it to me?" Mrs. Trumpeter's voice was weak with disbelief. "Hubert, you did it to me and let me think that . . . oh Hubert, why? That's just too bad of you."

"Yes, Mrs. Trumpeter, of all the petty cruelty I have seen in my life, allowing you to think you had been raped by a stranger must count as one of the meanest acts I have ever known. If it is any consolation, that act was the first that threw suspicion upon him. Your injuries were so mild, the doctors said that if they hadn't known you'd been raped, they would have attributed them to some rough sex play. However, what comes next was worse, I am afraid. He had already decided to discard you. At some point, his mind went from divorce to murder.

"You see, that was how he planned to get into the casino business here. He would be the victim of a savage crime; one which would strike at the very heart of the whole Cuba set-up. He would negotiate hush-money from the families who run this country, in the form of a substantial share in one or more of the casinos. Just to make sure that he would be paid off, and probably to save himself the cost of divorce fees and the pitiful amount of your settlement, he decided to kill you."

"Life insurance." Simon Adams spoke quietly but authoritatively. "What about life insurance on Mrs. Trumpeter?"

"Did he have any with your company?"

"I do not know. I will check, but I am prepared to wager that there is a substantial policy on Mrs. Trumpeter somewhere."

"Please do so. Anyway, He tied Mrs. Trumpeter up using industrial duct tape, blindfolded her with the same stuff, and then stuffed her underwear into her mouth and gagged her with more tape. Then, he left her laying on her back in the hope she would choke while he was away.

"Having left her to die, he then went to Cadillac, bought his new car, went down to his assigned demo vehicle and hid the fake jewels in the under-floor safe. After that, he simply went back to his room, going through the motions of calling for his wife in case of witnesses or the floor captain seeing him, and went in. Then he found she was still alive.

"That put him in a matter of serious confusion. What to do next? He'd set this up so that it looked like his wife had been raped and left to die. If he just waited until she did, any witnesses might question the length of time between entering his room and calling for help. In that agony of doubt, he made another bad mistake. He had to chose between getting the tape off her and destroying the evidence he had planted, or calling for help.

"Any normal husband, under normal circumstances, would have got that tape off her mouth so she could breathe properly. But these weren't normal circumstances. Trumpeter had allowed for the possibility she might be found before she died; he just hadn't allowed for him being the one to do it. So he had a back-up plan in place. He'd used industrial strength duct tape on her eyes and mouth. If somebody ripped it off, it would take her skin with it, leaving Mrs. Trumpeter with a scarred face. To Trumpeter, that solved two of his self-imposed problems. It increased the severity of the crime committed against him, and thus his pay-off from the families, and it made sure nobody else would want Mrs. Trumpeter now that he'd finished with her.

"It was that tape that decided him. He called for help rather than pull it off himself. It fits the established pattern of him running away from problems and leaving them in the hands of others, but it was not a decision any husband worthy of the name would make; unless he knew the danger that tape represented."

"Oh, Hubert." Mrs. Trumpeter was crying.

"Mrs. Trumpeter, you are very fortunate. Anywhere else in the world, the first responders would have pulled that tape off and injured you. But here, in Cuba, hotel security people are gangsters and they know what effects duct tape have on human skin. They stopped the doctors from pulling the tape off your mouth and foiled your husband's plan. You survived the attack both alive and healthy. For that, you should thank God, who watched over you in your helplessness. And thank the men who came to your aid of course."

Once again, Conrad reminded himself not to pass judgment. *That belongs to powers much greater than me and my own record of such judgments was flawed beyond redemption. But, looking at Trumpeter and his wife, I find it hard to resist the temptation to crunch my fist into the man's mouth.*

He lifted his head and looked around the room, silent as those present thought over Conrad's speech. His eyes caught those of one of the gangsters leaning up against the wall; the man smiled grimly at him. He didn't know the man's name, and never would, but he did know beyond any shadow of a doubt that his own desire to inflict physical damage on Trumpeter was matched by that of the watching wiseguy.

"Well, Sunbeam, it looks like your boy is off the hook. Want us to tell Vinnie that Cardinal's been cleared?"

"Leave it to us, Dapper John; the Marcellos look after their own."

Gotti nodded. "And as for you, Gomez, don't ever switch your shift without telling us again. Now go home to your wife and look after her."

"Excuse me, Mr. Catalina."

Mrs. Trumpeter spoke clearly and steadily although she was still crying.

"Would you please tend to this for me?"

She handed him a crumpled note. It read, quite simply, *I wish to divorce my husband. Signed. Irene Skolnik.*

"That's my maiden name; I don't want to use Trumpeter again. Ever."

"Certainly Mizz Skolnik. Trumpeter won't be allowed to leave Cuba until he has paid the divorce settlement we dictate, in full."

"You can't prove any of this." Trumpeter yelled the words from the end of the table and stared around, his face a mixture of fear and belligerence.

"We can certainly prove insurance fraud, which is all I am interested in." Simon Adams looked positively cheerful. It wasn't often he got to work with the Mob rather than against them. "The stones were genuine at the last reassessment. They were in a safety deposit box and the bank has records of who went to that box. For reasons we've already covered, they had to have been removed by the time you reached Cuba, so you're the only person who had access to them. Open and shut case, Trumpeter. You're going down for fraud."

"Excuse me." Inanna cut in. "The U.S. Government has an issue here as well."

She smiled apologetically.

"I'm working again, now. I'm the Executive Assistant to the Secretary of Defense. I am sure that my principal wants to discuss some areas of defense procurement fraud with Mr. Trumpeter as well. I believe Federal cases take priority over State."

"Cuba's a sovereign state." Catalina was emphatic. "It's up to us to drop the louse into the Bay."

"Why, I didn't do anything wrong in Cuba?" Trumpeter was truly frightened now.

"You raped Mizz Skolnik, which is upsetting a tourist. And you framed one of the boys, which is rocking the boat. Both capital offenses here."

Quietly, John Gotti took the piece of paper from Catalina and vanished from the room. In a couple of minutes, he returned.

"I've spoken with The Little Man. He wants to handle this himself. Tomorrow morning, Presidential Suite, nine AM. Mizz Skolnik, Meyer will determine your divorce settlement then, and that will take priority over everything else. Inanna, please call your boss. Meyer wants a U.S. federal prosecutor, with power to make agreements, over here by that time. Joe, make sure Trumpeter doesn't go anywhere. Break his legs if you have to. The Little Man is firm about making sure he doesn't leave us before we get this straightened out."

Meyer Lansky's Conference Suite, Presidential Suite, Tropicana Hotel, Havana

"Do you have a Cabinet?"

United States Attorney Jeffrey A Morris was fascinated by his surroundings. Since his Gulfstream had landed at Dillinger International, he'd had the interesting experience of meeting people he'd previously only known as faces on wanted posters. Now, he was speaking with the man his office had spent years trying to build a case against. A man who, diplomatic customs ensured, was now untouchable. Or uncatchable, depending on which television program one preferred. Watching *The Uncatchables* was one of the guilty secret pleasures of Attorney Morris's life.

"Sure, want a drink?" Ever the hospitable host, Meyer Lansky opened the drinks cabinet and surveyed the array of bottles within.

"Um, no thank you. Bit early for me. I meant do you have a Government Cabinet? I assume this is your Cabinet Office."

Lansky looked at his guest, his eyes twinkling and Morris realized his tail was being gently twisted.

"No, we don't. Cuba more or less runs itself, done right. Things we need experts for, we hire them. Like air traffic control; the Colombo Family runs the airport, so they hire outside talent to run the flight control side of it. Other times, we need somebody with a title, we just grab one of the boys that's got nothing better to do and give it to him until the job's done."

"What about qualifications?"

"What about them? Any of the guys you work for actually qualified to do their job?"

Morris thought for a second. "No, but they've got their staff to keep them straight."

"Right." Meyer's eyes twinkled again. "Mind you, one of the boys had a legal degree, so we made him Attorney General; but he lost the title in a poker game."

Morris snorted, trying to stop himself laughing. He knew he was supposed to be horrified at what he was seeing, but he was finding it increasingly hard. So, he tried to bring the conversation back to serious ground.

"President Lansky . . . "

"Meyer, call me Meyer."

"Meyer, that's where the problem is. Mr. Trumpeter is an American citizen and we cannot leave him in the hands of a society that has no laws or judiciary. We must demand that he be returned to us for trial."

"We got laws. May not be written down, but we got'em. The Honored Society goes back a long, long way. They got customs and all the boys know them. Some of our laws are written down as well. As for judiciary, we got that too. Couple of wiseguys, a limo and a block of cement."

Morris couldn't help asking. "Is it true your Constitution is written on a paper napkin?"

"Nah. On the back of a beer mat. Attorney Morris, the boys are coming in, We'd better get formal."

A procession trooped into the conference room, taking their seats around the table. Lansky looked at them; some of them he knew well, others were strange to them. He exchanged greetings with Joe Catalina and John Gotti, and politely welcomed the three women. He seated Igrat himself; he knew her well from her previous trips over to Cuba and liked her. She hid it beneath her brashness, but she was warm-hearted as well as being a very highly competent courier. He also noted that Morris knew both her and Inanna. Finally, there was a mild disturbance as Trumpeter was brought in. He was a mess; unshaven, unwashed, his hair unbrushed, his clothes dirty and crumpled.

"Right, I want this kept brief. Somebody tell me what happened here?"

Lansky was now 'The Little Man,' the one person in the world whom every organized crime boss listened to and obeyed. A position he'd earned through skill and his unyielding honesty, not won by force. His eyes swept around the table, noting how the people present deferred to one man for the details of what happened.

"Mr. President. My name is Conrad Lorenz, I am an investigator for a charitable trust. With your permission, I will relate the events as they unfolded."

Conrad stood and started to explain what had happened over the last few months. His pitch was virtually the same as he had given at the sit-down the previous afternoon, slightly modified to include the added information that had emerged at that meeting and a little better organized. He'd been up all night going over the case in his head and smoothing out his presentation. That had meant he'd got no sleep; but it also meant he'd avoided his nightmare for one night at least. Eventually he finished and sat down.

"Has anybody anything to add?" Lansky's voice was mild.

"Mister President." Simon Adams stood up, fastening the jacket of his suit as he did so. "I have some extra information that arrived by courier just a few minutes ago. I have the written records of the Maryland Trustee Savings Bank; they show that Hubert Trumpeter, and only Hubert Trumpeter, accessed the safety deposit box that contained his wife's jewelry. He removed the jewelry from the box the morning he and his wife left for Cuba. Also, I have here a policy from the Guardsman Life Assurance that was made out six months ago. It provides for an insurance settlement of one million dollars in the event of the death of Mrs. Irene Trumpeter. "

"And I have the logs from the floor captain of the Imperial and room service. One shows that no strangers entered the 24th floor during the time bracket in question, the other shows that the service elevator only made two trips to the 24th floor during that time. One coincides with the time Antonio Cardinal went up to that floor, the other with him coming back." Joe Catalina sat down again.

"So," Conrad picked up the thread. "When the jewels were switched for fakes, only Trumpeter had access to them. When Irene Skolnik was attacked, only Trumpeter had access to her. When the jewels were in the car, only Trumpeter had access to them."

"Bada-Bing." John Gotti looked at the ceiling.

"I can go to trial with that." Morris spoke slowly and carefully. "On insurance fraud, it's a slam-dunk. The attempted murder of Ms. Skolnik is harder, but, if you are prepared to testify . . . "

"I am."

Irene Skolnik looked fiercely at the room. She'd cried herself to sleep the night before. In doing so, she had purged herself of the shock at what her husband had tried to do. Early that morning, Inanna had taken her down to the clothes stores and bought her a new outfit for the meeting. Actually, Igrat had paid for them, but that was a detail.

"A wife can't testify against her husband." Trumpeter snarled the response from the end of the room.

"I'm not your wife anymore." Irene snarled the reply in return.

"Actually the law says a wife cannot be *made* to testify against her husband." Morris spoke carefully, as was his way.

"Which brings us to another point." Lansky stared at Trumpeter, his eyes hard and unyielding; the New York racketeer clearly evident. "You wished to divorce Mizz Skolnik; she has asked us to divorce her from you. Attorney Morris, Cuba does have laws; they're our customs. In a matter like this, if the couple divorcing can't come to an agreement, they make their pitches to a capo and he makes a ruling. A final ruling. Now I'm going to do that. Mr. Adams, you got the insurance details?"

Adams handed the file over.

Lansky read it and his eyebrows twitched. "Mizz Skolnik, you're that now. Your marriage is history. Just dissolved under Cuban law. Your jewels are gone, stolen. The fact your ex-husband stole them doesn't matter. The fact is, they were yours in the pre-nuptial agreement. Means they were yours when they were stolen. So that gives you the million bucks insurance settlement. And there are the cars, the house, all the other assets Trumpeter had insured with Mr. Adams' company. And bank accounts totaling three million dollars. This is how its gonna be, see. You get all of this, free and clear. I'm ruling that payment of any debts on these properties has to be paid for out of Trumpeter's other funds as soon as they are recovered. That's down to Mr. Morris here. I guess you'll sell the house and the rest. If you wanna move to Cuba, that's up to you. Beautiful woman is always welcome here. Now, on the other matters . . . "

"Mister President, I am sorry to interrupt, but I must insist that Trumpeter be tried in the United States. You may have your customs, but we need to have a proper trial. We cannot allow these informal proceedings to indict an American citizen; not on charges these serious."

Lansky thought. It ran through his mind that other Americans would think the same way; that, if Trumpeter was tried here in Cuba, there would be accusations of a cover-up. That wouldn't be the case if he was tried in America. Lansky had made his start as a professional gambler and the principle of carefully measuring the odds was deeply ingrained in him. In this case, the odds all pointed to one course of action.

That didn't mean that he couldn't try and get the best deal possible.

"Cuba is a sovereign country. He committed crimes here."

"I know. And there is the expense of a trial to consider. Mr. Trumpeter, I'll offer you a plea deal. You plead guilty to the crimes as described here today, give a full allocution to the court and accept whatever sentence the judge gives you, I will demand you are tried in an American court. Even if that means sending the SEALs in to get you. Otherwise, I will make no effort to have you extradited and the Cuban authorities can deal with you as they see fit. Tic-toc, tic-toc, Mr Trumpeter. President Lansky is a busy man."

Trumpeter looked around in panic. Gotti and Catalina both had their hands inside their jackets, Trumpeter guessing they had their hands on their guns. In fact, he was wrong. There was only one gun in the room and that was in Lansky's holster. He didn't know that though, and he assumed the worst, based on watching too many gangster movies.

"OK, OK, it's what they said."

"You will make a full statement for the record before we leave Cuba?"

"I will."

"Very well. Mister President, once again I must insist that Mr. Trumpeter is handed over to the United States for his trial and sentence."

Lansky looked at him and gave every appearance of reluctantly being forced to a decision.

"This is Cuba, Attorney Morris; we don't take well to being pushed around here. But we do make deals. I'll offer you one. You take personal responsibility for making sure that Mizz Skolnik gets the settlement we dictated here and you can have Trumpeter."

"I see no problem with that. Consider it agreed."

Morris gathered up his papers. "Right, Trumpeter. We'll take your statement outside. No need to waste these people's valuable time. We'll be on my aircraft back to the mainland by evening."

Church of Saint Thomas, Tapaste, Cuba.

Igrat walked quietly down the aisle of the church, looking at the figures kneeling in prayer at the altar or sitting quietly in the pews. She spotted the man she was looking for right over in a corner, secluded from the rest. She went over to join him and quietly sat by his side.

Conrad opened his eyes and blinked in surprise. Igrat was wearing a high-necked white blouse and a full skirt, topped off with a black lace mantilla that covered her hair. It was a remarkably modest outfit and quite unlike her normal dress.

"Igrat, you're errr . . . "

"Appropriately dressed? Of course, Conrad. I'm a tramp, not a fool. And when I want to, I can fit in most places."

Conrad nodded. He should have realized that a professional courier would have that ability. "You drive down?"

"Sure did. Brought the Ferrari. It handles like a dream. Didn't like the Tapaste road too much though. I'm leaving this afternoon, so I've got to get it back to the dealers. My new one's already waiting for me on the mainland. Now, why are you here?"

"I wanted to make sure that Antonio Cardinal was all right. And that everything was settled. He was innocent; all he did was help out a friend. He shouldn't have to suffer for doing that. Nobody should."

"Right. Now what's really the matter?"

"That was all."

"What's really the matter, Conrad?" Igrat managed to combine patience and irritation in a single question.

He sighed, gently but still a sigh. "Iggie, I messed this one up so badly. Joe trusted me and I still messed up."

461

Conrad's Eye

"How? You solved the case in four days flat. That's good going by my reckoning."

Conrad sighed. *How an I explain this?*

"Iggie, I should have solved it almost on the spot. It was almost a 'murder in a locked room' type case. The suspects are those who have access to the room and there were precious few of those. I should have nailed Trumpeter right from the beginning as a prime suspect and if I'd done that, we'd have had him the next morning. But I never even thought of him until almost the end of the case.

"You know why? Because Cuba is run by gangsters, criminals, and I assumed the crime had to be committed by one of them. I ignored the obvious suspect because I was convinced others were guilty. I assumed that a simple case was complex and that the obvious suspect wasn't a suspect because I thought it had to be complex. I talked about hit men and professional robbery when I should have been concentrating on the one man we knew was there. My mind was telling me all along that I was doing it wrong. Remember that night we went shopping and I wondered if the Trumpeters played sleepytime? That was my mind telling me I should be looking at him, but I ignored it. Igrat, God is punishing me for my sins, for the innocent people I tortured and executed in his name. For five hundred years, I've been trying to earn redemption. Now I've just learned I'm as far from it as I was when I started."

"You really believe that you're being punished for your sins, Conrad? That the gift you and I and the others share is punishment?"

"For me? Yes, it is."

"And for me?"

Igrat looked around quickly. There was nobody within earshot.

"Conrad, I'm two thousand three hundred and twenty five years old, even though I only admit to the last twenty five of them. Are my sins so much worse than yours?"

Conrad couldn't help laughing quietly. "What sins have you committed? Other than lusting after your neighbor's husband and coveting his goods? I've killed, Igrat; killed people horribly, people who had done nothing worse than crossing the local priest or saying the wrong thing at the wrong time."

"You know your parents don't you, Conrad? I don't. You can be very certain my mother didn't have any idea who my father was and she threw me in the trash outside a brothel as soon as I was born. I was lucky; one of the girls who worked there found me before I bled to death. I was brought up by the madam and the girls. They taught me how to steal and seduce and, until I met The Seer, that was all I knew how to do. Then he rescued me, adopted me as his daughter and everything changed. I told you once I've never been faithful to a man? Well, that isn't true. I've been faithful to him, in my way, ever since I met him. All that because of my mother; so what do you think she deserves? How many other babies did she kill? How many years should she live for killing defenseless babies?

"You did a lot of very bad things, Conrad; nobody argues that, me least of all. Because if I'd met you back then, I'd have been one of your victims. But how many people have you saved since then? Ten times as many, a hundred times? So just let up on yourself. You might be right. You might be expiating your sins; we might all be. But did you ever think that you might also be here to do good? That your life is a reward for the people you've saved, not punishment for the people you've killed?

"Give yourself a break. You solved the case; you got there. Sure, you could have done better. Once I got picked up by some bad guys and beaten into a pulp because I let my guard drop. Took me quite a time to recover and that's allowing for our gift. If I hadn't been who we are, I might not have made it. But, I learned and I never made that mistake again. So you do the same, huh? As I said, give yourself a break."

Conrad sighed softly and started praying, Igrat sitting quietly beside him. When he straightened up, he smiled ruefully. "I think you're wrong, but I'll admit you could be right. Fair enough?"

"That's fair. Now, do you want a ride back to Havana?"

Joe Catalina's Office, Imperial Forum Hotel-Casino

"They've gone, haven't they?"

Catalina looked up from the book he was reading and waved Gotti to a seat.

"Yeah. And the place seems pretty dull without them."

"It was like that last time. Took six months for things to liven up again. You say goodbye to Igrat?"

"Yeah, I wanted to give her a present but she wouldn't take it. Guess working for the Feds, she couldn't take a present from one of us. But, she says she'll be back when she's next on the rota for Cuba and I can try again then. What's the book?"

"Collection of old photographs from Storyville, early years of this century. We're going into a new Casino-Hotel with the Marcellos, The Speakeasy. Themed after the prohibition era. Carlos has this from the old days and sent it over for us to look at. Ideas for décor."

Catalina flipped some of the photographs over and grinned at the sight of a long-passed era. Then he turned another page over and stopped.

"Well, look here, Dapper John."

Gotti took the book and looked at the picture Catalina had spotted. It was a shot of a Storyville nightclub with Bessie Smith in the background, on the stage singing. There was a group of people in the foreground. Most had their backs to the camera but one had turned around, perhaps because she'd seen the photographer, and had been caught half way between full-face and profile. To Gotti's eyes, the woman looked very much like Igrat.

"Damned if that doesn't look like Iggie."

"Sure does, doesn't it?" Catalina looked at the date. "1915. Can't be of course."

"Course not." Gotti looked closely. "Anyway, nose is different and this one's got more meat on her. Could be her grandmother, I guess. She told me she was an orphan, didn't know her real parents. Next time she's here, I'll show it to her. Could you make me a copy, Joe?"

"Sure can. See to it tomorrow. You wanna drink?"

Gotti shook his head.

"Nah, not tonight. Another time, Joe. Oh, and by the way, the Little Man was real pleased with everything and the way it worked out. You done good, Joe."

"I didn't, Conrad did. We'd have been lost without him. I just hope he's around next time we need him."

THE END

But Conrad Will Return

www.ingramcontent.com/pod-product-compliance
Lightning Source LLC
Chambersburg PA
CBHW020248030726
47499CB00001B/103